MW01365031

GOTAMA
SON OF EARTH

A. H. Salunkhe

Translation by
Dhananjay Chavan

EBD
EMBASSY BOOKS
www.embassybooks.in

Gotama the Buddha: Son of Earth by A. H. Salunkhe
English Translation © Dhananjay Chavan

First Edition 2017

Published in India by:
Embassy Book Distributors
120, Great Western Building,
Maharashtra Chamber of Commerce Lane,
Fort, Mumbai 400 023, India
Tel: (+9122) -30967415, 22819546
Email: info@embassybooks.in
www.embassybooks.in

ISBN: 978-81-933415-5-1

All rights reserved. No part of this publication may be reproduced, distributed, or transmitted in any form or by any means, including photocopying, recording, or other electronic or mechanical methods, without the prior written permission of the publisher. The use of brief quotations embodied in reviews is permitted.

Layout and typesetting by PSV Kumarasamy

Printed & Bound in India by Repro India Ltd., Navi Mumbai

Contents

	Translator's Note	5
	Preface to First Edition	9
	Preface to Second Edition	15
1	Introduction	17
2	Buddhaṃ Saraṇaṃ Gacchāmi	67
3	To Gain Wisdom Your Own Experience Shows the Way; Not the Tradition	101
4	Be the Inheritors of Dhamma, Not of Material Possessions	143
5	Answer Only If Beneficial In Life	211
6	Right Speech for Happiness	253
7	Respect for Householder's Life, Concern for National Character	269
8	Not by Birth, Not by Caste: Man is Great by Morality and Wisdom	319
9	I Don't Burn Wood: I Light the Flame Inside	385
10	The Buddha on Women	431
11	Bhikkhus, Wander for the Welfare and Happiness of Many	461
12	Gratitude for Past Traditions	513
13	Whether Known or Unknown The Buddha Dwells in Our Heart	531
14	Farewell	571
	Appendix – Tipiṭaka	585
	Notes	586

Translator's Note

I was introduced to the Buddha in 1988 through Vipassanā meditation which I learned from Acharya S. N. Goenka. I continued to take small steps on the Middle Path through the years.

Around 2002, I came across an old Marathi booklet on the Buddha's meditation practices titled 'Samadhi Marg'. It is a small book, written almost a hundred years back by Dharmananda Kosambi. It is brief yet comprehensive. Its exclusive focus is on various meditation practices taught by the Buddha and continued in the early Buddhist tradition. I have not come across another such technically precise, comprehensive and yet succinct text on this subject. I started editing and translating it, and though the Marathi edited version is now published, the translation has dragged on for too long.

It was while reading Kosambi's book that I had contacted Professor A. H. Salunkhe for the first time. I had learned that he was planning to write on the Buddha and wanted to know more. I met him a few months later. He is a renowned Sanskrit scholar and philosopher. Little did I imagine that one day I would translate the book that he was planning to write. His book puts the Buddha's teaching in a psychological, social as well as overall historical context.

When I read Professor Salunkhe's manuscript I found that it gave a further rational and historical context to the Buddhist practice by looking at it through a modern Indian's perspective and not necessarily following the traditional interpretations. This is especially true in the Indian context where most Indians have forgotten the Buddha's origin in this soil and don't grasp that his entire discourse, though universal, was rooted in this land.

Later Prof Salunkhe and I spent five days going over the entire manuscript. He is a senior scholar and a famous author but it was clear to me that he looked upon this book unlike any other that he had written earlier. It was also inspiring to see his openness to my myriad comments and suggestions. Rather, it was his openness that encouraged me to be free with my comments.

Translating this book has been as educational as it has been joyous. I was able to revisit many concepts and had to go the Pali sources often to get clarification and better understanding.

In the English translation a few short passages specific to the Marathi reader have been omitted. Some parts have been expanded and some added with the author's permission.

The original author used several Marathi or Sanskrit forms of the words because they have become common in India now. In translation, I used more Pali forms than the original as the English reader may not be familiar with the Marathi forms. Indeed, a student of Buddhism may find the Pali forms more useful.

I have italicized most Pali, Hindi, Marathi and Sanskrit words. I have not italicized some: Buddha, bhikkhu, bhikkhuṇi, Tathāgata, Samaṇa, brāhmaṇa, arahata, sanyasi, Dhamma, Saṅgha, Tipiṭaka etc. I have used brāhmaṇa in the phrase samaṇa and brāhmaṇa but otherwise I have kept the common English usage of Brahmin while referring to a caste or a person belonging to that caste.

There is no satisfactory translation of the word *khattiya* (Kshatriya). Pali literature says *khattiya* is one who owns *khetta* (field). The word 'farmer' would have been appropriate etymologically, but it is not a common practice to use it as a translation for *khattiya*. Warrior, as is used by many to denote *khattiya*, is unsatisfactory and wrong even. Some translators use 'noble' but that too was unsatisfactory as 'noble' is used for *ariya* as in Noble Eightfold Path, Noble Truths etc. Therefore, in many places I have left *khattiya* untranslated. It is one of the four varṇas (castes) in India.

I have avoided capitalization of a few words that are traditionally capitalized in English translations of Pali. I have used secular forms of English words whenever possible.

This book is not final. This translation too is not final. As Dr. Ambedkar says in the preface to his book, The Buddha and His Dhamma,

> "… If I may say so, the pages of the journal of the Mahabodhi Society make, to me at any rate, dull reading. This is not because the material presented is not interesting and instructive. The dullness is due to the fact that it seems to fall upon a passive set of readers. After reading an article, one likes to know what the reader of the journal has to say about it. But the reader never gives out his reaction. This silence on the part of the reader is a great discouragement to the writer. I hope my questions will excite the readers to come and make their contribution to their solution."

If a great scholar like Dr. Ambedkar wants the readers to respond, I too must humbly beg the reader to write if they have any comments, whether critical ones about analysis or about factual information. We will make effort to correct any errors or inaccuracies in future editions.

— Dhananjay Chavan
gotama.son.of.earth@gmail.com

Preface to First Edition

Today, my joy knows no bound as I present this book 'Gotama the Buddha, Son of Earth.' Actually, I should have finished this book many years back. But the scope of the work, collecting references for the work, journeys undertaken for it, etc. took time. Even then I feel great satisfaction in completing this work. Because of this book, I spent several years in the happy company of Gotama the Buddha. This has been the happiest time in my life.

I had read a little about the Buddha in school. For my graduation, my principal subject was Sanskrit. Philosophy was my allied (additional) subject. Therefore, I studied Buddhism at that time. Later as I tried to understand the great reformers Sant Tukaram, Mahatma Phule, Rajashri Shahu and Dr. Ambedkar, I came closer to the Buddha. After a few years, I had the good fortune to translate the English text 'Nāgārjuna' by K. Sacchidand Murty into Marathi. It was published by National Book Trust of India in its series of biographies. This translation acquainted me further with Buddhist philosophy. My efforts to understand myself and others using the illuminating light of the Buddha's teaching continued. This process gathered momentum in the last ten years.

For the publication of this book, countless people have helped me. It is impossible to mention the names of all of them. It goes without saying that whether I have mentioned them or not, I have immense gratitude for them. I must mention a few of them who helped me in procuring books and in travel for this book. My personal gratitude is one aspect of it. But equally important is my duty to let people know that when one undertakes a good work, many people spontaneously come forward to help by spending their time, energy, money, etc.

For a book of this kind, procuring reference books is an important and serious issue. Many people helped me with it. The biggest help came from the Vipassana Centre at Igatpuri. Dr. Dhananjay Chavan of the Vipassana Centre was of immense help. He sent 140 volumes of the entire Pali Tipiṭaka along with commentarial literature to me. My present book is mostly based on the Pali Tipiṭaka. This is a vast literature and I have been able to incorporate only the gist of it in this book. I have put aside all discussion on Abhidhamma Piṭaka for fear of increasing the scope of the book. Dr. Dhananjay also gave me many other rare books. Discussions with him have also been very useful for me.

I also received books from the libraries of Lal Bahadur Shastri College and Arts & Commerce College of Satara. I am sincerely grateful to the principals, librarians, and other staff of these colleges for their help. The library of Dapodi Mahavihara in Pune was also very helpful. I also received many books from the library of the Vihāra at Bhaja. I got the opportunity to converse with Anagarika Subhuti and Suvraja.

My friend, Vijay Latkar, gave me many texts from his own library to help me understand HH Dalai Lama's views. My friend Bhagwan Avaghade and Vilas Kharat also gave me some texts in their possession. Arjun Desai, Dr. Shriram Gundekar, Madhav Bagawe, Abhijit Patil, Prof. Arjun Jadhav, Sayaji Shinde, Dr. Mohan Kamble, Buddhaputra Gaikwad, Dilip Sonkamble, G. S. Bhosale, Prof. Mahesh Gaikwad, Prof. Sunil Shinde, Prof. Sanjay Kamble, Vaidya Santosh Suryavanshi, Dr. Vinod Pawar, and Dr. Dipankar gave me various books. Ven. Sanghasena of Ladakh also gave me several books.

I also travelled extensively to understand the Buddha's teaching and the Buddhist tradition. I travelled with different people. Himachal Pradesh has numerous Buddhists even today.

There are several Buddhist monasteries in the Lahaul-Spiti valley. Kibber which is among the highest towns in the world has many Buddhists. To travel there, I had the company of my senior friend Baba Mulik, Dr. Subhash Desai, and many from Orissa who I became friendly with through Dr. Desai.

Some years back, I had the opportunity to visit Bodh Gaya, Rajgir and Nalanda with my young friend Dharmesh Gajabhiye and his family. Pravin Gaikwad and Gangadhar Banbare were with me when I went to Vesāli. I visited the Sanchi stupa with my friend from Vardha, Dr. Ashok Chopade.

When my friend from Nagpur, Vijay Babhulkar, arranged my lectures at Pavani I got the opportunity to visit several Buddhist places in that region. Vijay Latkar was with me when I visited Shakya College in Deharadun. His tips were very useful.

I visited the Buddhist caves of Lenyadri with Baba Mulik and Dr. Subhash Desai and the Buddhist caves in Nashik with my friends there. My friend from Mumbai, Ashok Ankush and his family accompanied me when I visited caves at Kanheri, Mahakali and the stupa at Nalasopara. I visited countless small Buddhist caves in the vicinity of Shivneri in the company of Ashok's wife Vasanti, his brothers Dr. Avinash and Nitin and his uncle Ravindra Kharat. I went to see the place known as Kapat on a slope on the mountain near Dehu with Dhammacari Varaprabh and other friends.

I also saw the stupa next to the place where Sant Tukaram used to meditate. I visited caves at Karla and Bedase with Varaprabh. I undertook the journey of Sarnath, Bodh Gaya, Saket, Sāvatthi, Kapilavatthu, Lumbini and Kusinārā with Varaprabh and Santosh Salave. Friends of Chandrashekhar Shikare accompanied me when I visited Ajanta for the third time.

When I decided to go to Sri Lanka, I got the company of my friend, Dr. Dhananjay Chavan. Vipassana teachers, Roy Menezes and Suleka Puswella, made arrangements for us to visit all the Buddhist places there. Devapriya Henry and his brother Anura took great care of our comfort during our journey in Sri Lanka to various places such as Kandy, Aluvihara, Nalanda Gedige, Dambulla, Anuradhapura, Keliyana Mahavihara. We stayed at their place in Anuradhapura. In our journey to Colombo, we experienced excellent hospitality by Suleka's father on his estate. So we didn't have to stay in a hotel even for a single day in Sri Lanka.

In Andhra Pradesh, Baba Mulik, his wife, and Dr. Subhash Desai were with me when I visited Amaravati, Nagarjunakonda and stupas found in excavations at Jaggayyapet, Ghantashala, etc. I went to Sikkim with Varaprabh, Dr. Jeevak and his son Amit. Suvraja arranged meetings with some of the Tibetan Buddhist scholars there. Suvraja couldn't accompany me to Darjeeling and Bhutan but the others did. I had the company of Dr. Jeevak, his wife Dr. Asmita and their sons Onkar and Amit when I visited Lahaul, Spiti valley for the second time and then went to Ladakh from there. I visited Dr. Babasaheb Ambedkar's birthplace Mahu before embarking on my northward journey. In Ladakh, Kunsang, a dentist, helped me to visit many places. Ashok Ankush and I went to visit the Global Vipassana Pagoda in Mumbai. In an effort to further understand the teaching of the Buddha, I joined a ten day course of Vipassana at Igatpuri.

I conversed with countless scholars and students of Buddhism during the writing of this book. However, all the opinions expressed in this book are my sole responsibility. There may be errors in these opinions. I say this because I don't want any of those who have helped me to be blamed for my errors. If readers point out shortcomings in my views, I will certainly rectify them. At times, I have expressed a difference of opinion with some people whom I hold in the highest esteem. I humbly submit that it is done as an inevitable part of the discussion.

I feel that those who helped me did so due to their faith in the Buddha arising from their own independent thinking, from their own wisdom. Still, I feel honored to have been the recipient of the showers of their affection originating from that faith.

In the last twenty five centuries, great scholars all over the world have written so much about the Buddha. Naturally, it is not my effort to say something new. I look at this book and my study as a manifestation of my effort to understand him and to imbibe in my life at least a small part of what he taught.

Discussion and analysis of complicated theories about the teaching of the Buddha and subtle differences in various Buddhist sects is beyond the scope of this book. I have also not dealt with all the objections to the Buddha's teaching other than a few incidental issues. There is a lot more to say. The Buddha's teaching is like a great ocean. If I am able to write more on some of the topics that I like, I intend to do so under the title "While Walking the Buddha's Way."

Let me say a few things about the presentation of this book. While quoting Pali passages from the Tipiṭaka, I have avoided the repetitions that are seen in the original text. To make clear the separation between original text and my comments, I have put my comments under the title "Discussion". Though this may give an artificial formality to the presentation, I found it necessary to do so in the interest of clarity. I have used at least some of the original Pali forms such as Gotama, Dhamma, Tipiṭaka, Sāriputta, nibbāna, etc. At the end of the book, I have given references from Pali literature. This is done to give readers a simple and lucid description along with the source in Pali Tipiṭaka. I also wish to incline the reader to Pali.

I have to follow the Buddha for a thousand miles and I have just taken the first step. But I feel satisfied. It is not important whether I have reached the destination or not. I feel that it is important that I am walking in the right direction. I don't envy those ahead of me and don't look down on those behind me. What else can I wish for? If I help a few to turn their gaze away from the feet of their exploiters and instead look at the heart of the Buddha, my life would be worthwhile. If this writing helps even an inch in that direction, I would be happy.

I often felt that I should give up writing and immerse myself in the delightful teaching of the Buddha. However, I decided to include the reader in my joy and therefore completed this book.

The blessings and goodwill of Dr. Adv. Eknath Salve and Mrs Shalinitai Salve have been my lifelong treasure. Dr. Vivek Bhosale, Dr. Suhas, Dr. Geeta Pol, and artist Sagar Gaikwad took care of my health during this period. Also, my family members didn't put any burden of responsibility on me and lovingly looked after me. And most important is the constant encouragement of my readers!

I am confident that readers will welcome this book.

A. H. Salunkhe

Full Moon Day
of Attainment of Bodhi
May 2, 2007.

'Lokayat', 13 Yashwant Nagar,
Gendamal, Satara 415 002
Phone: 02162-250725, 252788

Preface to Second Edition

I have added a supplement in the second edition. I hope the readers will welcome it.

I am grateful to Vijayrao Madhavrao Shinde for giving me the re-edited copy of Rajashri Shahu's *"Vijayi Maratha"* published in 1923.

I am grateful to Dr. Rafique Sayyad and *Weekly Shodhan's* editor Sayyad Iftikar Ahmed for drawing my attention to references to the Buddha in Islamic scriptures and providing all the details.

I am grateful to all readers who have sent their comments. I hope that in future too, readers will send their comments about shortcomings, mistakes, differences of opinion, and expectations freely. Your feedback makes the presentation of the book more error-free.

A. H. Salunkhe

1

Introduction

As naturally as a small child is attracted to its mother, billions of people have been attracted to Gotama the Buddha for the last two and half millennia. That I am one among them fills my mind with peace and joy. He presented a flawless ideal through his impeccable character and showed what magnificent height a human can attain. No matter what test is applied, it cannot be denied that the Buddha was the brightest lamp from the land of India that lit the world. This book is a token of gratitude for that great man. I am honored to be able to do it.

Brief Introduction

Let us begin by some preliminary information about the great man whose life and work we will be discussing in this book.

One tradition believes that Gotama the Buddha (Siddhārtha) was born in 623 BCE and attained *parinibbāna* in 543 BCE. In other words, he passed away in 543 BCE. This puts his life at eighty years. The Buddhist calendar starts from this year.

Several Western scholars bring his life sixty years forward. They believe that he was born in 563 BCE and attained *parinibbāna* in 483 BCE. Renowned Buddhist scholar Rahul Sankrityayan also agrees with these scholars.

At the time of Siddhārtha's birth, his father was the chief of the Sākyan clan. His wives, Mahāmāyādevi and Mahāpajāpati, were daughters of Añjana of the Koliya clan. Siddhārtha was born to Mahāmāyādevi. While travelling to her parental town of Devadaha for her confinement she gave birth under a Sāla tree in a grove in Lumbini.

Siddhārtha was born under the open sky. All his life too remained open—the same inside and outside! Māyādevi passed away a mere seven days after his birth. But Mahāpajāpati nursed him with all care and affection.

To start with, I wish to clarify the title and my thoughts about the Buddha in the context of the title and then turn to the main subject.

Gotama is a Family Name

Gotama is the family name or what is called surname today. Siddhārtha is the given name. Buddha indicates attainment of enlightenment (Bodhi). It is also possible that the name Siddhārtha gained currency later in retrospect. Let us assume for the time being that it was the name given by his family.

The use of Gotama is basic. In Marathi and Sanskrit, the form Gautama is used. Majority of the Indians use this form. I too used it since childhood. Even then I decided to use Gotama in this book for a specific reason.

Gotama the Buddha taught in Pali. He insisted on using Pali instead of Sanskrit. This insistence was right, as we will see later in the book. (We need not go into details about the relation between Magadhi of his time and Pali.) It suffices to say that the form used in Pali is Gotama, not Gautama. In the Tipiṭaka too, Gotama is used everywhere.

Using the Pali forms of words seems correct as it makes sense to stick to the original forms in using proper names.

Since Gotama was the family name, it is obvious that he got it automatically at birth. Thus Gotama was his first identity. The journey of his life began as a man born to the Gotama family. This man then is neither Siddhārtha nor Buddha by birth. His father, cousin Ānanda, etc. were also Gotamas.

"Go" means cow and bull. The suffix "tama" indicates plentiful. The natural assumption is that due to ownership of large herds of cattle the family got the name Gotama. This tradition of owning cattle had continued in the family upto his father Suddhodana's time. We will see later, how during the annual ploughing ceremony Suddhodana would use bullocks to plough his fields. Therefore, among the people in ancient India who opposed cow slaughter, Siddhārtha Gotama was the foremost.

Siddhārtha- the Link that Joins Gotama and Buddha

Before turning to the word Buddha, I would like to discuss Siddhārtha, a word that is missing from the title of the book. This word is an important link that joins the two states, Gotama and Buddha.

Siddhārtha is one who has achieved the aim of one's life, one who has accomplished the goal of one's life. When Siddhārtha's parents named their child they must have hoped that he would truly become *Siddhārtha* (literally one who has achieved the goal).

As long as he had not attained enlightenment (Bodhi), he was merely Siddhārtha, Siddhārtha Gotama. But when he attained enlightenment, he literally became Siddhārtha, became Siddhārtha Buddha. The word Siddhārtha became truly meaningful. Therefore, Siddhārtha is the link between Gotama and Buddha.

No one is born a Siddhārtha Buddha. Everyone starts their life's journey from a state similar to Siddhārtha Gotama. Everyone has the capacity to become a Buddha. How much of a Buddha one becomes depends on how much effort one makes to attain enlightenment. Siddhārtha Gotama journeyed to the very end possible in those times and thus became Siddhārtha Buddha.

When I use the words Gotama the Buddha in the title, I have in mind his journey from being a Gotama to a Buddha. Gotama is the starting point and Buddha is the point of ultimate accomplishment.

Buddhahood is the ultimate accomplishment of Gotama. It is also the annihilation of Gotama. When he attained enlightenment, he ceased to belong to a mere family or clan. He now belonged not only to the entire humanity, but to all living beings.

Buddhahood is the Pinnacle of Human Progress

Let us touch upon the word Buddha in the context of the title of this book.

Buddhahood is the full development of Gotama. It is the ripe fruit. Buddhahood includes proper and complete understanding of oneself, the entire humanity and the entire living world. This understanding is unlike the understanding that we get from, say, the science of physics gives us.

This understanding does presuppose a process of creating a completely harmonious relationship between the inner world and the outer world, both living and non-living. In such a relationship, a Buddha today would be concerned about violence and terrorism *as well as* pollution and global warming.

This understanding includes the combination of ethics, wisdom, and compassion that takes a human being to the pinnacle of humanness. Without wisdom, ethics and compassion become blind. Without ethics, wisdom won't be true wisdom, turning into destructive intellect instead, and compassion would cease. Without compassion, morality and wisdom would become selfish. Therefore, these three qualities must coexist. Gotama's attainment of Buddhahood meant the ultimate maturity of these three qualities. It was humanness at its best.

Buddha and Sammā Sambuddha

Let us also look at some other adjectives used for Gotama the Buddha. Let us start with *Sambuddha* and *Sammā Sambuddha*.

Sambuddha means *Sammā Buddha* (literally a "proper" Buddha). *Bodhi* is the highest noble wisdom. Even if one assumes for argument's sake that *bodhi* is proper and improper (*sammā* and *asamma*), the reality is that *bodhi* generally denotes *Sammā Bodhi*. It follows naturally then that it suffices to call him Buddha. *Sambuddha* is implicit in Buddha. *Sammā* means proper. *Sammā* means right. *Sambuddha* is enough to denote *Sammā Sambuddha*. Thus *Sammā Sammbuddha* is a tautology.

People often indulge in such reiteration out of respect and devotion. In India, the practice of using 1006 times *Shri* is a classic example. *Shri* is a respectful prefix. To show more respect, people sometimes use *Shri* twice, *Shri Shri*. Sometimes, it is used 1006 times. If an adjective or a superlative is used often, it gives rise to a feeling that it is somehow inadequate. Sometimes, the adjective is used for other people as well. In such a case, there arises a need to add another adjective to single out the original person.

There are several *Pacceka Buddhas* (Silent Buddhas) in Buddhist tradition. There is also the concept of *Sāvaka Buddha* (Disciple Buddha). It is possible that *Sambuddha* and *Sammā Sambuddha* was used to denote Gotama the Buddha separately from these. If we start calling several things "the best", then one starts using "one of the best". "Best" then becomes inadequate to denote the truly best. Be that as it may, *Sambuddha* and *Sammā Sambuddha* couldn't take the place of the word "Buddha" which continues to be used as the primary term everywhere at all times.

Sākyamuni

A word that is used often for Gotama the Buddha is *Sākyamuni*. It is similar to the use of Gotama the Buddha. He was born in the Sākyan clan and became a Buddha, a *muni* which was a word used in the Samaṇa tradition for a perfect sage. It could be originally from the Samaṇa tradition or it could also be a combined heritage of the Samaṇa and Vedic traditions.

Bhagavā

Bhagavā is a word that is used again and again in Pali literature to address the Buddha. *Bhagavā* means one endowed with best qualities. The original form is *bhagavat*. *Bhagavā* is the first person singular declension. The form used in Sanskrit is *"bhagavan."* Pali form is *bhagavā*. Using computer search, we find that this word is used in the Tipiṭaka 8,758 times. In the entire Tipiṭaka along with the commentarial literature, *bhagavā* occurs 17,942 times. This count is only for first person singular declension; the other declensions have not been counted.

There are several repetitions in Tipiṭaka. These are called *Peyyālas*. In printed editions, as also in computer editions, such repetitions are omitted and are indicated by the word *"Peyyāla"* or simply *"pe..."* If we include the occurrence of *bhagavā* in such repetitions, the count will be much higher.

K. P. Kulkarni says that *bhagavā* has its root in the Sanskrit word *bhrigu.*[1] He has not given any explanation about this etymology. It is just his opinion. He has not suggested any alternate etymology either. Thus this etymological suggestion by Kulkarni seems to be artificial and without historical roots. Further discussion will throw light on why I reject any connection between *bhagavā* and *bhrigu*.

That the word *bhagavā* is used so often in Tipiṭaka and that it also denotes a colour suggests a connection. *Bhagavā* (saffron colour) has a cultural and religious connotation in India. How? *Bhagavā* means Buddha and denotes one who is endowed with various qualities. It is also one of the colors of the robes of the Buddhist monks. Over time, the word that was used for Buddha started being used for the colour of the robes and slowly became associated with the colour.

With time, the teaching of Gotama the Buddha became influential in India. If a dominant progressive thought cannot be defeated in a straightforward manner, the Vedics defeat it by appropriating it and changing its context. One of the ways of appropriating Gotama the Buddha was incorporating the word *bhagavā* and making it a prestigious symbol of Vedic culture. The followers of the Buddha who had a natural liking for the saffron color thus came closer to the Vedic tradition and slowly got entangled in it.

Prof. Jagannath Upadhyay says,[2]

> "I would like to put on record that in all the Hindu religious texts, the word *bhagavān* was never used for god. *Bhagavān* is a title for humans and this title came into existence because of the Buddha. (With the advent of *bhagavān*) the gods became lower than humans as they were hedonists. Man is greater because he makes effort to attain his goals and does great sacrifices. He is capable of many a great sacrifice for high ideals. That is why he is *bhagavān*. When *bhagavān* was used for the Buddha, those Hindus who believed in God also did the same. In many religious texts such as *Bhāgavat*, they too started putting the epithet of *bhagavān* to all their deities. In Buddhist thought, *bhagavān* means one who has taken the vow to end the misery of the world and misery of the people of the world; a vow to liberate them. God can never be *bhagavān*… but to promote their deities, to promote their God, they started using this epithet of a man for gods."

If we really want to understand our history, we must understand the upheavals in our cultural history. Today *bhagavā* is used in India for a particular flag. It is connected with a particular sect or persons. Thinking that it is connected to the Vedic tradition, many reformists, many who believe in social equality, and non-Vedics don't feel any closeness to the colour. On the other hand, some even feel aversion. They should come out of this confusion.

Vedics wrote in Sanskrit and they used *bhagavān*, the Sanskrit form, instead of *bhagavā*, the Pali form for their deities. But it was essentially the same word. Prof Upadhyay's assertion that *bhagavān* was an epithet for the Buddha seems historically sound. A different form doesn't it make a different word. The British called Mumbai "Bombay" but in essence it was based on and derived from Mumbai. *Bhagavān* is similarly just a different form of *bhagavā*.

The Bhāgavat Sect is Inspired by the Buddha

Bhāgavat comes from *bhagavat*. One who believes in *bhagavant* is *Bhāgavat*. Given that *bhagavan* was first and originally used for the Buddha, the connection seems undeniable. This is also the reason why Shankaracharya looked upon it as a non-Vedic sect and why the *Bhāgavat* sect promoted principles such as non-violence. However, over a period, the sect was influenced by Vedic tradition.

Dr Babasaheb Ambedkar's Inclincation for Saffron Flag

It is possible that having known the relation of the word *"bhagavā"* with the Buddha, Dr Babasaheb Ambedkar was inclined towards saffron flag as national flag of India. At least he was not against it. In this context, Dhananjay Keer's statement is notable,[3] "He was a member of the flag committee of the Constitution Committee. There was a widespread discussion at that time about the national flag. Some leaders from Maharashtra and Mumbai Prantik Hindu Sabha met him to plead for saffron *(bhagavā)* flag. Dr Ambedkar assured Anantrao Gadre, Prabodhankar Thackeray, and Gavade that if there is a dominant lobby behind it and if a strong public opinion is created, he will plead for the saffron flag. When Dr Ambedkar left for Delhi on July 10 from Santacruz airport, leaders of Mumbai Prantik Hindu Sabha and some other Maratha leaders gifted a saffron flag to him… He assured them that if there is a movement for saffron flag, he will support it…

…It is said that Dr Ambedkar spoke a few words in favor of saffron flag in the Flag Committee; but the related leaders didn't create a movement for the saffron flag and therefore he put his weight behind the tricolor with the Ashoka Wheel."

The Tathāgata

One of the common and important words used for the Buddha is the Tathāgata. To put it simply, "Tathāgata" means one who has acquired reality-based understanding. *"Yatha"* and *"tatha"* are two words commonly used together. They denote "as it is." *"Tatha"* denotes reality, truth, the objective condition. If we split Tathāgata into *tatha* and *gata*, it means "one who has reached truth, reality". If Tathāgata is split into *tatha* and *āgata*, it means "one has come to truth". In essence the meaning is the same in both the instances.

The original form of *"Āgata"* is *"ā + gam"* and one of its meanings is to know, to understand. Therefore, "Tathāgata" also means one who has known or understood reality as it is. Buddhaghosa has given eight different explanations for this word. However, in this book we need not go into any greater detail. It suffices to know that it was an epithet for the Buddha and is related to truth-based. T W Rhys Davids says in the Pali English Dictionary[4] , "…it has not been found in any pre-Buddhist work". I have mostly used "the Tathāgata" in this book for the Buddha.

I was faced with the dilemma whether to use *"bhagavā"* or *"bhagavān"* for Gotama the Buddha. I had difficulty with both the words. My preference was for the Pali word. However, *bhagavā* has acquired other meaning in Marathi and I felt it was beyond the effort of a single person to change a deeply entrenched practice. The same thing applies to *"bhagavān."* I do not disagree with those Buddhist scholars who use *bhagavān* for the Buddha but I felt proper to avoid both the words.

The use of "Tathāgata" has none of these difficulties. It is significant that in the Tipiṭaka, the Buddha himself used "Tathāgata" to refer to himself. It is possible to use the epithet for other arahatas (liberated ones) but for most part it is confined to the Buddha. While translating from Pali, I have used the Tathāgata instead of *bhagavā* or its other declensions. Some may find it incorrect. But I did so for two reasons. One, I am translating the word *bhagavā* (and have the freedom to use a synonym). Two, I had difficulties enumerated above with the words *bhagavā* or *bhagavān*.

Sugata

Just as *Tathāgata* is a commonly used epithet for the Buddha, so is *sugata*. Simply put, one who has journeyed to the ultimate truth in a proper noble manner is *sugata*. Thus it is a word very close in meaning to *Tathāgata*.

Samaṇa

The Buddha is repeatedly addressed as Samaṇa Gotama. The Buddha himself has sometimes referred to himself as Samaṇa Gotama. Samaṇa (*samaṇa*) may be looked at as related to *shrama* (effort, thus one who makes efforts) or as *shamana* (peace giving, cooling). Both the meanings apply properly to the Samaṇa tradition and the saintly people of the Samaṇa tradition.

The first meaning *shrama* connotes concepts such as effort, hard word, striving and endeavor to better the life here and after. It also denies and cuts away the unreal things born of imagination.

The second meaning *shamana* conveys a cooling or cessation of mental impurities, keeping away of undesirable things, uprooting destructive things and overall conveying the impulse to make one's life wholesome.

Samaṇa is applicable to Tathāgata in both these connotations. Samaṇa-brāhmaṇa is used repeatedly in Tipiṭaka to describe the two traditions that are separate from each other. The twin form also shows respect for brāhmaṇas.

Bhūmiputra

Not from Heaven, Hence Son of Soil

In translating *Bhūmiputra* as Son of the Soil, the translator faced similar problems that the author faced when using *bhagavā*. The phrase is associated with sociopolitical movements of the local people all over the world. Without going into the details of the sociopolitical issues involved in those movements, it can be said that this phrase expresses the aspirations of the local citizens and at times genuine concern of being disenfranchised in their own land. But sadly, at times, it also implies an intolerance of outsiders and an intolerance of the very poor who want nothing but to earn a living by the dint of their labor.

Unfortunately, Son of Soil has also acquired a shade of narrow regionalism. Any such intolerance is totally foreign to the Buddha's teaching. Therefore, though "son of the soil" is an elegant translation I have not used that phrase as it would have carried a connotation that is totally antithetical to everything that the Buddha stood for.

Let us discuss the phrase used in the title, originally *Bhūmiputra* and Son of Earth in translation.

The Buddha became enlightened by his own efforts by developing, mastering and reaching the pinnacle of wisdom. Thus it is true that he became different from other human beings. However, he was born a human just as any other human of flesh and blood. His journey to Buddhahood is a journey of his humanness. Therefore, he taught that every human being has a seed of enlightenment in him or her. Thus, the person who becomes a Buddha and any other human being who has not attained enlightenment are both basically human. A Buddha has reached the end of the journey whereas an ordinary human being is on the path.

There is nothing unnaturally miraculous about the Buddha. He is not a son of God or a part of God or a messenger of God. There is no place for God in his entire teaching. Therefore, his entire personality remains untouched by the concept of God. He was a human born to Māyādevi and Suddhodana of Gotama clan. He became the Buddha by attaining enlightenment. There was neither a divine revelation at work here nor a miracle. He was not a manifestation of a divine power that came down to the earth from the high skies. Siddhārtha Gotama was the highest and best manifestation of the humanity. His teaching was the doctrine of work and effort that played in the lap of mother earth. In short, he was not born of high heavens but rooted in earth. He was Son of Earth.

Māyādevi 's dream: Partly a truth, partly a myth.

Let us first discuss a few points from the Buddhist tradition before we turn our attention to the phrase "Son of Earth." A commentary in Pali says that Māyādevi dreamed of a white elephant entering her womb.[5] The dream is looked upon as an indication that a great son was going to be born to her.

We can look at it in two ways. It is possible that Māyādevi did have such a dream. There is no reason to dismiss the dream as unhistorical. Dreams, both pleasant and unpleasant, are an integral part of our life. Therefore, at the time of conception in the joyous state of mind, Māyādevi might have seen such a sweet dream. Looking at the unblemished life of the Tathāgata, his comparison with a white elephant is also meaningful.

This much can be easily accepted. However, it seems that a myth was created out of imagination when it was said that he came down from the heavenly abode of *Tusita loka*. Had this myth helped in spreading the teaching of the Buddha among the masses without sullying his character, it would have been acceptable as a beautiful myth, if not as a historical fact.

But Siddhārtha Gotama's great efforts in developing his humanness and the confidence he gave to others for doing the same are nullified in accepting this myth. It goes against the core of his character. That he was in heaven and he came down to earth from high heaven is absolutely unacceptable at all levels. It goes against the principles of nature. It goes against history. It goes against all that the Buddha stood for. It is unacceptable that he was not born in a natural manner like any other human infant and that he was born from the side of Māyādevi's abdomen. This myth may have its origin in the excessive and distorted feeling of respect and devotion for the Buddha.

It is my feeling that we disrespect Māyādevi 's motherhood and Siddhārtha's son-hood by denying that Siddhārtha was born in a natural manner. To insinuate that there is something wrong in natural birth is to disrespect the deep bond between a mother and her child. Therefore, such myths are unacceptable.

Mythological Story about Prophecy

The Commentary to the Tipiṭaka says that eight brahmins predicted Siddhārtha's future. [6]

When the translator first came in contact with the Buddha's teaching, on one hand he experienced the peace and joy of walking on the Middle Path, and on the other hand, he found several beliefs handed down in the tradition that seemed unacceptable to a rational mind. When traced in texts, these beliefs often seemed to originate in the Commentarial literature rather than the Tipiṭaka. Tipiṭaka remains best source we have about the teachings of the Buddha. But even the Tipiṭaka, as Dr Ambedkar has argued in his book, *The Buddha and His Dhamma,* has been subject to revisions and cannot be taken in its entirety as the Buddha's word.

It is said that these eight astrologers predicted that either he will become a Wheel Turning Monarch or, if he leaves home, he will become a Buddha. It is indeed possible that some brahmins made such a prophecy. We have to look at this prophecy objectively. For an astrologer, it is a means of livelihood. An astrologer would most likely be thrown out if he predicts that "Your child will become a slave," or "Your child will be an ordinary person," or "Your child will be a dullard and a failure."

Of the thousands of children about whom great prophecies are made, only a handful turn out to be of men and women of any distinction. The rest lag way behind the predictions. The astrologers often kindle hope in the hearts of parents about their children by making great but vague predictions. This is not because they have a foreknowledge of future events or because they can see into the future.

Asita Devala's case was different. We will look at it later in the book.

It is said that of the eight astrologers, seven were elderly who said that the child will become either an emperor or a Buddha. The eighth, the young Koṇḍañña, was firm in his prediction that the child would become not an emperor but a Buddha. When Siddhārtha went forth from home, Koṇḍañña went to the sons of all the seven other astrologers and suggested that they also go forth with Siddhārtha. Four agreed and left with him forming "a group of five."

Dharmanand Kosambi's Comment on the Myth

In his book, *Bhagavan Buddha: Jivan aur Darshan,*[7] Dharmanand Kosambi says, "…this information about the group of five seems mythical. If Koṇḍañña was sure that Gotama was going to become a Buddha, why did he leave Gotama at Uruvelā and go to Varanasi? When the future Buddha started taking food for sustenance of the body, why did Koṇḍañña lose his faith completely? …It cannot also be said that they were all Brahmins."

We Can't Cut the Buddha's Connection to Earth

If we cut the Buddha's umbilical cord with the earth and connect it to the heaven and assume that his future was predetermined at the time of his birth, we negate the supreme efforts of this great son of earth. If we accept that he came down from the heavens to help humanity, we lose the essence of his character. How then can he say, "Each of you can become a Buddha like me?"

Only if his own journey had started as a mere human can other humans aspire to follow his example! The other humans are not descended from the heavens and their future is not preordained as is claimed for the Buddha. (In the imagination of masses) the journey to Buddhahood for someone descended from heaven is easy while it is far too arduous for the ordinary humans. How then can they take him as an ideal, take him as their guide and how can they follow him? Even when such a power tells them that they too can become a Buddha, the masses are bound to feel discouraged that they are ordinary men of flesh and blood.

The words of the Buddha "Like me, you too can become a Buddha by your own effort," are meaningful only if the Buddha is a human being like the rest of them. His words are meaningful only when he is rooted in earth, a son of the earth and not a son of the high heavens.

Walpola Rahula says - He was Human

In the beginning of the very first chapter of his classic book, *What the Buddha Taught,*[8] Walpola Rahula writes, "Among the founders of religions, the Buddha (if we are permitted to call him the founder of a religion in the popular sense of the term) was the only teacher who did not claim to be anything other than a human being, pure and simple. Other teachers were either God, or his incarnations in different forms, or inspired by him. The Buddha was not only a human being; he claimed no inspiration from any god or external power either. He attributed all his realization, attainments and achievements to human endeavour and human intelligence. A man and only a man can become a Buddha. Every man has within himself the potentiality of becoming a Buddha, if he so wills it and endeavours. We can call the Buddha a man *par excellence*".

Lal Mani Joshi's Objection to Walpola Rahula is Incorrect

There are people who object to this truthful assertion of Walpola Rahula. Lal Mani Joshi, for example, states,[9] "The humanity or the historicity of the man Siddhārtha Gautama is not denied nor doubted. What we want to stress is the fact that that man, by attaining Buddhood, had transcended human nature, become transhistorical, (*sic*) and was called the Transcendent One (Tathāgata). To say that the Buddha was only a human being is not only clearly wrong but blasphemous too."

Actually, overall, the contents of Joshi's book should be welcome. However, his comment on Walpola Rahula's statement is harsh and extreme. Walpola Rahula didn't say that even after becoming a Buddha, he was just an ordinary man. He states categorically that the Buddha is a man *par excellence*. It is wrong to say that Siddhārtha ceased to be a man after enlightenment. When the Buddha said after enlightenment that he was not a god or a *gandhabba* or a *yakkha* or man, he merely meant that he had become different from other men in many aspects; not that he ceased to be human. When it is said that each human being has the potential to become a Buddha, it means that Buddhahood is the ultimate development of humanness. Even then Joshi is free to have his opinion. He can also criticize Rahula's opinion. However, to accuse Rahula of blasphemy or sacrilege goes against the basic tenets of freedom of thought and tolerance of the Buddha's teaching.

A Human Even After Enlightenment

We cannot say that after attaining enlightenment, Gotama ceased to be human or became something other than human. He uprooted mental defilements and attained a state higher than ordinary humans. But this didn't take away his natural humanness.

It is undeniable that from his birth until his going forth into homelessness, he was a human. It is also undeniable that from the time he went forth until his enlightenment, he was human as is evident from his experiments such as fasting, torturing his body, etc.

From the time he became a Buddha till the time of his *parinibbāna* he lived and travelled in his human body. In the Tipiṭaka, so many persons (such as Prince Bodhi or Queen Mallika) are seen asking him directly or through messengers about his health, whether he has any pains (whether he is enjoying bodily comfort). This is a clear indication that his human body was subject to the same natural processes as others.

To make this clearer, it is essential that we discuss his illnesses here.

He is Son of Earth, Rooted in Earth, Because His Body Has Natural Limitations.

There are several instances where it is said that "the Tathāgata is tired," "he is unwell," "he has become old." It should be noted that all these instances occurred after he became the Buddha. Let us look at some of the examples.

Sometimes He Used to be Tired

Once the Buddha was dwelling in Palāsavana in Naḷakapāna.[10] There, he gave a discourse to the monks till late at night. The Saṅgha was still silent (waiting to hear more from him).

Then he said to Sāriputta, "Sāriputta, the Saṅgha is without sloth and torpor. You should have a dialogue on Dhamma with them. I have a backache. I am going to lie down."

Sāriputta agreed to the Buddha's suggestion and taught Dhamma to the monks.

Once when he was visiting Kapilavatthu, Mahānāma Sākya had made arrangements for his stay at a monastery.[11] Since the Buddha was tired, he didn't wait at night to talk to him. He came the next day to ask him questions and get his doubts resolved.

There is also a reference to his being tired when he went to Kusinārā at the end of his life.[12] When he reached the Sāla grove of the Mallas in Kusinārā, he said to Ānanda, "Ānanda, arrange my bed between the two Sāla trees with the head to the north. I am tired and would lie down."

His Illnesses

The Buddha was once dwelling in Nigrodhārāma of Kapilavatthu. At that time he was recovering from a recent illness.[13] Mahānāma Sākya came to meet him and asked him a question about "wisdom first or Samadhi (concentration) first". Knowing that the Buddha was recovering from a sickness and seeing that Mahānāma was asking him a serious question, Ānanda took his arm, led him aside and answered the question himself. This instance of the Buddha's illness illustrates his humanness. It also shows how much Ānanda cared for him.

Once when the Buddha was in Sāvatthi, he had dyspepsia.[14] Upavana was attending on him at that time. The Buddha asked him to get hot water. Upavana went and stood at the door of Devahita Brahmin.

On being asked "What do you want?" Upavana answered that the Buddha had dyspepsia and needed hot water. The brahmin then gave hot water and some jaggery to Upavana. On returning to the Buddha, Upavana bathed the Buddha in warm water and gave him hot water mixed with jaggery to drink. The Buddha felt better after that. Later the brahmin became his devoted disciple.

Once the Buddha was dwelling in Kalandakanivāpa in Rājagaha.[15] He was very sick at that time. One day Mahācunda came to visit him and sat on one side after paying respects. The Buddha asked him to talk about the factors of enlightenment. Accordingly, Mahācunda gave an exposition on the seven factors of enlightenment. Hearing it, the Tathāgata was satisfied and pleased and recovered from his illness

His Body Was Like That of Any Other Human

Once the Buddha was dwelling in the deer park of Maddakucchi in Rājagaha.[16] At that time, he had suffered a wound from a stone splinter. He was suffering from extremely severe pain. He faced the pain with forbearance and without getting overwhelmed. Some deities came to visit him at that time and sang praises of his courage in facing the pain.

These examples make it clear that like any other ordinary man, he used to get tired, and fall sick. Just as other men get injured, he was injured at times. Just as other men suffer pain caused by injuries, he also had to endure pain caused by injuries. He was born and lived as a man of flesh and blood.

His reaction to the pain ***is*** different than that of most men, who not having cultivated forbearance and wisdom become totally dejected. Though he was born a human, the Buddha had travelled a long distance on the path of self-restraint through immense striving. He had conquered misery and achieved a balanced mind. There is no need to forcefully attach miracles to this issue. Such courage can be achieved by all humanity to some extent. When such courage and forbearance is not cultivated, one may not have the capacity to face adversity. But those who cultivate this wisdom are able to face adversity. It is the nature of the human body that it becomes tired and falls ill.

We need not give undue importance to the praises sang by the deities. It should be looked upon as a poetic or mythical expression of the exalted state achieved by the Buddha.

The last days of the Buddha are described in the Mahāparinibbāna Sutta of the Long Discourses.[17] The Buddha was sojourning with Ānanda in Veḷuvagāmaka. He instructed monks to spend the rains retreat (*vassavāsa*) in Vesāli as per their convenience and told them that he would spend his rains retreat in Veluvagamaka.

He became very sick during the rains retreat and was afflicted with excruciating pain. But he overcame the pains with his wisdom. He thought that it wouldn't be proper to attain *mahāparinibbāna* (final passing away) without informing his followers and without taking proper leave of the Saṅgha. He then used his will power to subdue his illness. At that time, Ānanda went to him and saw that he had recovered. Ānanda was delighted and confessed that he had lost his composure due to the sickness of the Tathāgata.

We should understand these instances of his bodily frailty in the proper context. He taught the Noble Eightfold Path to eradicate misery. It is obvious that for one who walks on the path, his suffering is reduced or eradicated. However, it doesn't mean that one overcomes natural limitations of the human body. It doesn't mean that the wayfarer on his path or the teacher of this path doesn't fall sick. However, some people like Barrister Savarkar who look at the Buddha with a prejudiced eye deliberately distort this reality.

Barrister Savarkar has made fun of the Buddha's illness. In his drama *'Sanyasta Khadag,*[18] Kshārā, wife of Shākambhaṭa, is seen poking fun at the cold afflicting the Buddha. "His disciples used to lie that their Teacher cures the world from the afflictions. And see what has happened. The Teacher Buddha has become sick from common cold. Even the womenfolk are singing songs that make fun of him. One woman even sang a song to me… *how is this man, such is this man… … oh lady, my Teacher… he came to cure the world, and himself died of cold!...* "

The writer thought that he could reduce the greatness of the Buddha by showing that the man who took up the mission to eradicate suffering from the world couldn't cure his own common cold. However, the fact that the Buddha used to fall sick doesn't take anything away from his greatness. All it proves is that his body too was subject to natural laws.

Actually, without all the layers of heavenly divinity and inexplicable miracles, the Buddha is brought closer to us ordinary human beings. His greatness was in his conduct, his thoughts, and his teachings. It remains unsullied by the common cold!

The Mahāparinibbāna Sutta then describes the dialogue between Māra and the Buddha, who tells Māra that he would attain *parinibbāna* at the end of three months. All compound things are subject to decay, he reminds Ānanda and tells him that he is nearing the end of his life. When he left Vesāli for Kusinārā, he turned about and said, "Ānanda, this is the last time the Tathāgata is seeing Vesāli." This behavior of the Buddha is also a sign of his humanness. Though the descriptions of his illnesses show his humanness, the Buddha's restraint in food, constant wandering, and purity of mind, etc. ensured that he was usually in good health.

Even His Old Age Showed How Human He Was

There are references in the Tipiṭaka about how old age affected the Buddha's body. Once he was staying in Pubbārāma of Sāvatthi.[19] In the evening after getting up from his meditation, he sat with his bare back to the sun in the West. Ānanda came to give him a massage and said, "Bhante, the Tathāgata's body is not as handsome and strong as before. It has become lax and full of creases. It is bent now. Eyes, ears, nose, tongue and skin all have become weak."

The Buddha replied to Ānanda that it was the nature of the body to get old and explained it in detail.

He again told Ānanda just before *parinibbāna* how his physical condition had deteriorated.[20] He told Ānanda, "I have become old, weak and frail. I have completed the journey of life. I am old. I am eighty now. Ānanda, just as a rickety vehicle is somehow kept in running condition by constant repairs, my body is continuing to function with much care."

This description of his physical frailty doesn't demean him or lessen him in any way. On the contrary, it inspires people.

Being a Son of India, He is Son of Earth for Indians.

Siddhārtha Gotama was born in Lumbini, which is part of Nepal today. Therefore, the people of Nepal can be rightly proud of the fact that he was born there. Culturally the Lumbini of that time was connected to India. The town of his parents was Kapilavatthu. His town, his farms, his home, his subjects and his clan were all in India. He spent most of his life after becoming a Buddha in the present-day Uttar Pradesh and Bihar states of India. This is where he attained enlightenment, gave his first Discourse on Rotating the Wheel of Dhamma, spent his rainy retreats, and wandered for the welfare of many. In this sense, the Tathāgata is as much a son of India as he is a son of Nepal. People all over the world regard him as a son of India. The Buddhists all over the world look at India with respect and affection as the land of the Buddha.

Once I met a woman working in Anuradhapura in Sri Lanka. When she learned that I was from India, she shared her dream with me. She told me that all her life she has been putting money aside from every month's salary so that when she retires, she can go to India to visit Bodh Gaya and other places associated with the Buddha. It shows how much devotion she had for the Buddha and for India, his land. The affection and respect that people have for India as the land of Buddha is certainly a matter of honor.

Of course, this sense of honor shouldn't turn to undue pride and sense of superiority. It should be one of affection, closeness and kinship.

Bhūmiputra Because He Called Upon Earth as Witness

The Commentary on the Jātaka describes the following event.[21]

Siddhārtha sat down under the Pipal tree with great determination. Māra attacked him in various ways. He approached Siddhārtha and said, "Hey Siddhārtha, get up from this seat. This seat is not suitable for you. It is meant for me."

Siddhārtha responded by saying, "Māra, you have not fulfilled the ten perfections or any other perfection; you have not undertaken the five great renunciations. You have done no service to your society and your people. Your conduct is not logical. On the other hand, I have done all these things. Therefore, this seat is for me and will be useless for you."

Having heard Siddhārtha's reply, Māra became angry. He attacked him even more ferociously. Their exchange continued. When Siddhārtha asked him who is witness to your acts of charity, Māra pointed to his army and said, "These all are my witnesses."

Everyone in the army started shouting, "I am witness, I am witness."

Then Māra asked, "Siddhārtha, who is the witness for your acts of charity?"

Siddhārtha replied, "You have all these living witnesses. I don't have any living witness here. But this great earth is my witness."

He touched the earth with his right hand saying, "You are witness, aren't you?"

Discussion

Siddhārtha didn't call upon heaven to be his witness. He called upon the earth. He didn't prove his ability based on some miracle, worldly or otherworldly. He based his claim on earth. He touched the earth saying "I have the right to sit here and the great earth is witness to my rightful claim".

The gesture showing his right hand touching the earth is famous as *bhūmi-sparsh mudrā*. There are countless statues of the Buddha in this pose. The statue near the famous Ānanda Bodhi Tree in Anuradhpura is also in this pose.

Some may say that this entire narration is a mythical exaggeration. Someone may feel that this is just a poetic license. Of course, it cannot be said that Siddhārtha really had a dialogue with a person called Māra. But it is clear that he fought two kinds of battles.

One was a battle within his own mind. A multitude of urges and impulses rise inside humans. Several defilements rise constantly that distract humans from their goal. Only a man who subjugates these defilements and urges to attain his goal can be said to be a truly courageous man. This battle within oneself can be called the battle with Māra. Siddhārtha won this battle within. He repelled the attacks of desires and cravings that make one weak; and proved his merit with great determination to attain enlightenment. What he showed was that there was no power in the universe that could remove him from his seat, that is, divert him from his resolution to attain his goal.

The commentator has used the question "Who is the witness for your acts of charity?" in their exchange. It would have been more appropriate if the commentator had used the entire ethical behavior for the question. We should understand that charity here is indicative of entire spectrum of morality. Siddhārtha does talk about serving the society and ethical behavior. Of the ten perfections, charity *(dāna)* is the first. Therefore, one may also take *dāna* as *dānādi* meaning "charity etc."

The other battle is with the people of opposing thoughts. Most of the times, Māra comes in the form of a brahmin. For example, in the *Māra Saṃyutta* of the Connected Discourses,[22] Māra comes in the form of a brahmin with long matted hair and wearing animal skin to meet the bhikkhus.

Māra is one who kills. Whether it is the inner Māra or the outer Māra, he kills our dedication to our goal, kills our determination to follow our life principles, kills our enthusiasm for constructive action, humiliates us, makes us mentally weak, diverts us from our goal, and at times, may even kill us physically. In short, Māra is the symbol of all those tendencies and weaknesses that constantly try to stop us from getting to our goal.

The Buddha attained enlightenment while sitting unshakably on earth. He didn't go to the sky or heaven to get to that state. The rays of enlightenment radiated from his human body. Wisdom arose in him while sitting on earth. This light of knowledge did not enter his head from heaven or from some divine power that entered his head. If we consider his becoming a Buddha as his second birth, it occurred on this very earth, nowhere else. In this sense too, he is Son of Earth, rooted in earth.

Son of Earth Because He Was Son of a Farmer

Siddhārtha Gotama was the son of Suddhodana. On one hand, at the time of Siddhārtha's birth, Suddhodana was a king; on the other hand, his livelihood was that of a farmer. In this sense there is an unbreakable connection between Siddhārtha Gotama and the earth.

In this sense too, he is *bhūmiputra*.

Suddhodana's Agriculture

There are several descriptions of the farming of Suddhodana. Dharmanand Kosambi says in his *Buddhalilā*,[23] "The Sākyans were very proud of their clan. Their main livelihood was agriculture. They used to give much importance to this livelihood. Suddhodana was one among the Sākyan royalty. It seems that he was elected chief for some time by the Sākyans."

Dr Babasaheb Ambedkar says in his book *The Buddha and His Dhamma*,[24] "Suddhodana was a wealthy person. The lands he held were very extensive and the retinue under him was very large."

Being a farmer, Suddhodana used to celebrate an annual ploughing festival. In this festival, he used to plough the land himself. At one such ploughing festival, everyone was busy witnessing and enjoying the festivities. Siddhārtha's attendants too became engrossed in the festivities.

When left alone thus under a Jāmun (rose-apple) tree, Siddhārtha sat in meditation. This was the first time he meditated in his life, at least, the first time in known history. Though the commentaries have mentioned servants, it is unlikely that he was just three or four years of age at that time. It is possible that he was at least ten to twelve years of age.

Through this meditation, he turned from agricultural farming to farming of the mind, to the farming of cultivating the minds of people, to the farming of sowing the seeds of morality and wisdom in the minds of people. We will discuss this in some detail later.

The Buddha Remembers His First Meditation

While talking to Prince Bodhi,[25] the Buddha narrated his first experience of removing greed and (other) unwholesome things from the mind and attaining the first absorption (first *jhāna*) while sitting in the cool shadow of the rose apple tree. This absorption born out of wisdom produced a higher happiness. The Buddha said he felt "This could be the path to liberation". We find that he shared with Aggivessana the same memory of his first meditation.[26]

Commentary Describes Suddhodana's Agriculture

While commenting on *Mahāsaccaka* Sutta of the Middle Discourses (*Majjhima Nikāya)*, the commentary gives detailed description of Suddhodana's farming. In the commentary on the Jātaka, there is an even more detailed and picturesque description.[27] Here it is in short.

Once there was a festival named *Vappamaṅgala*. This was an auspicious festival of sowing the seeds. The entire capital city was decorated. All the servants, wearing new clothes and decked with perfumes and flowers, had gathered at the king's palace. A thousand ploughs were yoked. Ministers had the charge of 799 ploughs and the king took one plough. The remaining 200 ploughs were being used by other farmers. The king's main plough was decorated with precious stones and gold. The horns of bullocks, ropes and the whip too were decorated with gold.

The king came to the farm with his entire family including his son. There was a rose apple tree on the farm that cast a dense shadow. The king arranged bed, umbrella and marquee; and handed over his son to female attendants. Then the king himself came to the field along with his ministers. The king's plough was golden, the ministers' ploughs were silver and the farmers had the rest.

They started ploughing the field from one end to the other. The sight of the king ploughing the field was a glorious one. To see this majestic sight, the attendants came out of the marquee. Then Bodhisatta (the future Buddha) looked around and didn't see anyone. He sat up and attained the first absorption by observing his breath.

It is possible that due to devotion to the Buddha, the commentary is guilty of hyperbole here. Still, even in recent times, some farmers were affluent. It is possible that, in ancient times, a few landlord kings had huge tracts of land. There is no need to assume or believe that the plough was indeed made of gold. By placing a small gold object on the plough, the plough was made into a symbolic gold plough. The same could be true about the silver plough of the ministers.

One thing though is curious and can't be explained easily. If this was a festival of "sowing." then a sowing device should have been used rather than a plough. It is possible that the word *naṅgala* in Pali was used for such a sowing device. It is also possible that this was not a sowing festival but ploughing festival. Very rarely, ploughing and sowing can take place at the same time one after the other. But this is quite a stretch to explain things.

In Rhys Davids' Pali-English Dictionary, the meaning of *Vappamaṅgala* is ploughing festival. It is also possible that the commentators were not familiar with agriculture and couldn't differentiate between ploughing and sowing. In all likelihood, it was not sowing but ploughing where usually farmers are more likely to gather together even today. In rural India, *akshaya tritiyā* (*ākhāji*) is the day when farmers start preparing their farmland for the impending monsoon. It is considered one of the most auspicious days by farmers. Whatever it may be, it is clear that Suddhodana owned extensive farmland.

Farmer's Village in Lalitavistara

The eleventh chapter of the famous biography of Buddha, *Lalitavistara,* is titled *Krishigrāmaparivarta*. At the beginning of this chapter,[28] there is description of Prince Siddhārtha going to the field with ministers' sons and other boys.

Again in the same chapter, it is mentioned that young Siddhārtha went to *Krishanagrāma*, that is, *Krishigrāma*. It is described how Siddhārtha thought about the misery in the process of farming. Thus, on one hand, there is description of real agriculture, and on the other hand, farming is used as a simile for life's labors.

Various Depictions of the Meditation During Plough Festival

There are several beautiful pictorial depictions of the above-mentioned scene. Keliyana temple outside of Colombo in Sri Lanka has a lovely wall painting of this scene. Two white bulls are yoked to the plough. There are two birds on the left side of Suddhodana who is ploughing. On the left side of the birds, Siddhārtha is shown meditating peacefully.

This incident is depicted on the famous Sanchi stupa built by Emperor Asoka. "The jambu-tree within a railing at the centre marks Gautama's first meditation under a jambu-tree during the ploughing festival in his childhood."[29]

In Cave no. 16 of Ajanta caves too there is a painting of this event.[30] "The right wall is devoted to the illustration of incidents from the life of Buddha. Though the painting is much darkened and effaced, some of the incidents can be easily made out, e.g. … Gautama's first meditation during ploughing festival …"

Indicating that He was the Son of a Farmer is a Considered Decision

Indicating that the Tathāgata was the son of a farmer is not tantamount to confining him to a group. Though he was born to a farmer, the reality that he transcended all such narrow limitations and boundaries to belong to the entire humanity is far more important. That he was involved in agriculture in his youth is clear from his family background and his understanding of farming. But he is respected, followed, and will continue to be followed for the Farming of Dhamma that he engaged in after attaining enlightenment. This Farming of Dhamma described in *Kasibhāradvāja Sutta* is discussed later.

If the farming of Dhamma that bears the fruit of liberation is of primary importance, then why do I say that he was the son of a farmer? Do I have a constricted view behind it? I feel that if such questions arise in the minds of others, they are not out of place. All I ask is a patient and tolerant hearing of my explanation.

About eighty percent of the people of India are farmers or related closely to agriculture. Due to urbanization, the number has decreased but still the majority of Indians are farmers. Though it is true that this huge section of India was drenched in the cool showers of Buddha's teaching at one time, over the centuries, through many upheavals, things have changed.

The tricks and manipulations by the opponents of the Buddha have succeeded to the extent that this huge section has not only become distant to the Buddha but also developed an active antipathy towards the Buddha. The opponents have succeeded in creating a negative attitude towards the Tathāgata in the mind of the farmers. Thus about a billion people (including farmers of the neighboring countries such as Bangladesh and Pakistan) have gone away from the Buddha. This has harmed them by depriving them of his benevolent teaching.

Social and cultural conditioning of centuries has created strong prejudices. These people are not ready to examine the Buddha's teaching dispassionately. They have closed the doors of their minds so tight that they won't allow even a stray ray of the Buddha's benign teaching to enter their heads. Even a drop of his compassion falling on their thirsty hearts feels sacrilegious to them. Therefore, with goodwill and benevolent intentions, we must find ways and means to get into their heart and mind. This worldly argument that he was the son of a farmer might make them reflect that the Buddha may not be so alien after all; that there is an eternal bond between him and them.

The farmers in India need to understand some historical truths. There was an expectation, an insistence even, by orthodoxy that farmers should just plough the fields, herd the cattle, collect cow-dung and till the land; they should not get into the philosophical or spiritual realms.

The Buddha challenged that insistence. He not only challenged it but proved himself worthy. His teaching gave light to the world and brought the fragrance of happiness to humanity. He who followed his teaching gained freedom of mind. She who had earlier lost that basic human right regained it.

The man, who gave this freedom, is not an alien. He is not an opponent, not an enemy. He has not come to enslave you. He is a kinsman. He is also a son of a farmer. He is a brother, a friend. Let us hear him first. Whether what he says is acceptable or not can be decided later. Let us at least open our eyes. Let us at least lend our ears to him for a while. Let get close to him; to see him, to know him, to examine him.

Let us be ready to remove our eyes from the feet of those who have enslaved us and look at the heart of Tathāgata who liberated us from our bondage. Let us then decide whether to walk on the path that he showed to us.

These historical facts can open the hearts and minds of millions of farmers in the Indian subcontinent to the teaching of the Buddha. Therefore, it is not narrow-mindedness to state them. Rather it is a constructive step to take the Buddha's Dhamma to the masses.

The Tathāgata Started Farming of the Dhamma.

This son of a farmer transcended all material boundaries and cultivated Dhamma for the benefit of the entire humanity. In the *Kasibhbhāradvāja Sutta*[31] we find this simile.

Once the Buddha was dwelling in Ekanāḷā, a village of Brahmins in Magadha. It was planting time. In the farm of Kasi Bhāradvāja (literally the farmer Bhāradvāja), 500 ploughs were yoked. Kasi Bhāradvāja was distributing alms. The Buddha stood to one side. Seeing him waiting for alms, Bhāradvāja said, "O Samaṇa, I plough and sow, and having ploughed and sowed, I eat. O ascetic, you should also plough and sow; and having ploughed and sowed, you should eat."

The Buddha replied, "I too plough and sow. And having ploughed and sowed, I eat."

Bhāradvāja brahmin asked, "But I don't see your plough or bullocks or any other farming tools. How then do you claim to be a farmer?"

The Buddha then explained to him, "*Faith* is my seed. *Effort* is the rain. *Wisdom* is my yoke and plough. *Shame of wrong-doing* is the plough-head. Mind is the rope. *Mindfulness* is the ploughshare and the goad. I am *restrained* in body and speech. I have control over my food, how much I eat. *Truth* is the weeding and *humility* is the threshing. *Perseverance* is the bullock that is yoked and which takes me to liberation having eradicated all suffering. This is how I plough and sow. This cultivation gives me the fruit of immortality. This is how I plough and sow to eradicate all suffering."

Bhāradvāja replied, "Gotama, you are indeed a farmer, since your crops bear the fruit of the deathless. Please accept my alms."

The Buddha declined, saying, "I do not accept food in return for the teaching." Then Kasi Bhāradvāja took refuge in the Buddha, Dhamma and Saṅgha.

Discussion

The Buddha cultivated human values to transcend all differences and divisions. This is what should be followed. He truly belonged to the entire humanity. The Kasi Bhāradvāja Sutta underscores his vast and all-inclusive vision.

The Tathāgata was insistent that the labor on our fields should have a foundation of discretion, ethics and philosophy of right thoughts. The comment by Dharmanand Kosambi[32] on the Buddha's stand in Kasi Bhāradvāja Sutta is instructive, "The Buddha has not criticized farming in this discourse. The moral of his discourse is that if farming is without the foundation of ethics, rather than bringing happiness to society, it will give bring misery. If the crop sowed by one is taken away by another, no one will be willing to till the land and there will be anarchy in society. Therefore, our relation to each other should be based on non-violence.

The Buddha understood that without this mental farming, the physical farming wouldn't be of any use, and therefore, he inspired his Saṅgha to bring about an ethical awakening in the society."

Yours is Royal Lineage, Ours is Buddha Lineage

Though the Buddha was born to a khattiya, a farmer; his greatness has nothing to do with it. Through countless generations, billions of people have been born in so called high castes. Just this did not make any of them into a Buddha. The greatness of the Buddha is to go beyond family, clan, caste, *varṇa* to connect to entire humanity. Here is an incident from his life that stirs the emotion of gratitude in our hearts:

After attaining Bodhi, the Buddha went to Isipatana in Sarnath. After his rains retreat there, he went and stayed at Uruvelā for three months. From there he went to Rājagaha (Rajgir). He stayed there for two months. Kāludāyi, a messenger of Suddhodana came there. Autumn was coming to an end. Spring was about to begin. Kāludāyi suggested that the Buddha should visit his hometown. When the Buddha asked the reason for his request for the journey, he answered, "Lord, your father Suddhodana wants to see you, meet you. You should also meet your clansmen there."

The Buddha consented and travelled with his monks from Rajgir to Kapilavatthu.

At Kapilavatthu, he went out on alms round. He adapted the method of *sapādāna* alms in which one goes from one house to the next without missing any house in between. He started from the houses on the outer side of the town. The news of noble Siddhārtha going on the alms round in Kapilavatthu spread like a wild fire. Wealthy people came out on the terraces and balconies of their two-storied, three-storied houses to watch.

The news reached Suddhodana. He was greatly distressed. He rushed out of his palace hastily gathering his robes in one hand (so as to look presentable) and stood in front of the Buddha. "Why are you shaming me, Lord? Why are you going on alms round? Don't I have the capacity to feed all the monks?"

Tathāgata replied, "O King, this is the tradition of my lineage."

Suddhodana countered, "Lord, our lineage is that of the great Khattiya Mahāsammata. No one in our lineage has ever gone on alms round."

The Buddha responded, "O King, this royal lineage is your lineage. Ours is the Buddha lineage."[33]

Our hearts swell with gratitude when we see how he had uprooted and removed all the prestige of birth, family, clan, wealth and power; as well as the conceit arising from it. With his actions, he showed the way to connect the entire human society through the thread of equality to bring about an inner unity.

The Buddha started his alms round from the outskirts of the city which must have been the poorer part. He showed the courage to stand in the front of the houses of the poor for alms in the very city where he had travelled in majestic chariots. He shunned the houses of prestigious Sākyans. The same thing happened with monks such as the Kassapa brothers who were earlier high-caste brahmins; they too now stood at the door of lower caste people for alms.

The Buddha gave the message of futility of pride in caste to the Sākyans who had extreme conceit about their clan. He made it clear that he didn't belong to the lineage that took pride in its royal lineage but to the Buddha's lineage that treated all humans as equal.

The alms round of Tathāgata and his bhikkhus was not begging. We will discuss this later. But it was natural for the Sākyan king to feel his son was shaming him by begging for food. Well, it is comforting to know that once he talked to the Buddha, Suddhodana's thinking changed.

The Nidānakathā says that Suddhodana became an arahata. It means that he too became free of all defilements including those of pride in one's caste. Inner humanity, not outer appearances, is the true sign of a human. This incident of the Tathāgata and his father is bound to overwhelm us when we see it in our mind's eye.

Being Humane is More Delightful Than Even the Symbols of Dhamma

In the Connected Discourses,[34] we find a touching and eloquent verse that tells us that the Tathāgata gave more importance to being humane than to the symbols of Dhamma.

Once Sakka, the king of gods, came to visit him in Sāvatthi. After saluting him, Sakka sat on one side and asked him, "Venerable sir, what is a delightful place?"

The Buddha answered,

"Cetiyas in parks and woodland shrines,
Well-constructed lotus ponds:
These are not worth a sixteenth part
Of a delightful human being.

"Whether in a village or forest,
In a valley or on the plain—
Whever the arahants dwell
Is truly a delightful place."

Cetiyas were an important symbol of the Samaṇa tradition, and especially of the Buddhist tradition. For about five centuries after the Buddha, there were no statues of the Buddha. During these centuries, *cetiyas* were the venerated symbol of the Buddha. But the Tathāgata said that a perfected human life is far more important than such symbols. The word he used can be translated as "the delight of being human." What a sweet and lovely description!

The Buddha Was Not an Incarnation of Vishnu

According to Agni Purāṇa, the Buddha is Deception Incarnate

The Purāṇas believe that the Buddha was an incarnation of Vishnu. This is untrue and unacceptable. Still, we should look at what is said about the Buddha. The sixteenth chapter of *Agni Purāṇa* is about the *Buddha Avatāra* (incarnation).

Here Agni says, "I will narrate the *Buddha Avatāra* that gives desired things to one who reads and listens. In the past, in a battle of gods and demons, the demons defeated the gods. Then those gods ran to God Vishnu screaming "Save us, save us." Then Vishnu became Deception Incarnate and took birth as Suddhodana's son. He confused the demons and made them give up the Vedic Dharma. Those demons became Buddhists. From them arose other people who rejected Vedas. He became an *arhanta* (arahata) and made others into *arhanta*. Thus apostates who rejected Vedic Dharma came into existence."[35]

Bhāgavat Purāṇa Says the Same

Bhāgavat Purāṇa has described various avatars (incarnations) of Vishnu. According to this Purāṇa, Balaram was the nineteenth and Krishna was the twentieth avatāra of Vishnu. This means that Buddha was the twenty-first avatāra of Vishnu. The Purāṇa says, "After the beginning of *Kaliyuga*, Añjana's son named Buddha will be born in Kīkaṭa country to confuse and hypnotize those who hate the gods." The same Purāṇa goes on to say at another place, "Salutations to the Pure Buddha who deceived the demons and the gods."[36]

Shri Narsinha Purāṇa is Not Clear

Narsinha Purāṇa has described the avatars of Vishnu. In all, eleven avatars are reported: Fish, Turtle, Boar, Half-lion-half-human, Dwarf, Ram-son of Dasharath, Parashuram, Balabhadra Ram, Krishna, Buddha and Kalki.

At the advent of *Kaliyuga*, Prabhu Narayan (Vishnu) will become Buddha. Usually ten avatars are counted. However, since Balram is also counted as an avatāra, the number has increased to eleven. In the fifty-third chapter of the book, Mārkaṇḍeya says, "I will now describe in short the pious twin avataras of Ram (Balram) and Krishna."

In the same chapter in the thirty second verse, Vishnu says, "My two powers White and Black will get incarnated in Devaki through Vasudeva and destroy Kamsa, etc."

At the end of this chapter, Mārkaṇḍeya says that after describing these two avatars, we will now describe Kalki avatāra. Buddha avatāra has not been mentioned here. Thus the writers of Purāṇas, after initially enumerating eleven avatars, succeeded in keeping the total number of avatars to ten, by omitting Buddha avatāra in the later discussion.[37]

Harivansha

The book "Harivansha" after enumerating all the past avatars of Vishnu, indicates Kalki as a future avatāra. In the original text, Buddha avatāra is not mentioned. But the Hindi translation by Pandit Ramnarayandatta Shastri Pandey "Ram" gives Buddha avatāra in parentheses. He is credited as a commentator rather than a translator. He added Buddha in translating a verse that doesn't have Buddha in the original.[38]

Discussion

Avatāra is a Planned Hoax

The Buddha had become very popular among the Indian masses at one time. It is always difficult to oppose popular personalities especially when they are righteous and benevolent. A trick used at such a time is to incorporate the revered popular personality; to show falsely that the opponents too revere that person. Then while showing that person as respectable and revered, his original persona is changed to some extent. He is given a fake face that is suitable for one's own tradition. His thoughts are changed to make them less contrasting to one's own tradition. Thus, the revolutionary thoughts and the uniqueness of that person are shadowed. Thoughts that are alien to his philosophy are attributed to him.

Deception

On one hand, Tathāgata was declared as the ninth incarnation of Vishnu. On the other hand, by making him like Vishnu, his Buddhahood was negated. The falsehood was spread systematically that the Buddha deliberately gave wrong, harmful, false teachings to some people. It was only with such a deceptive propaganda that he was declared as an avatāra of Vishnu. This apparently portrayed the Buddha as great because he was now an avatāra of Vishnu but the message was that his teaching was wrong and harmful. Thus he was superficially praised and revered but his thoughts were rejected.

Some Were Not Sure

There were surely some Vedics who were not willing to make the Buddha an avatāra even for the purpose of destroying his teaching. This conflict went on for a long time. Therefore, some texts have added Balram or some other avatāra and omitted the Buddha from the list of avatars. Sometimes, the same text makes contradictory statements about whether the Buddha was an avatāra or not. This shows the confusion of the authors of those texts.

Describing the Buddha as an Avatāra Removes the Essence of His Personality

The Tathāgata was born a man. He became a Buddha with his own efforts. All thought related to Vishnu promotes *yajñas* (ceremonial fire sacrifices), belief in Vedas and an unequal oppressive caste system. The Buddha had patiently but firmly rejected these things. Thus to make him an *avatāra* of Vishnu was to nullify all his tireless efforts of forty-five years for the welfare of people. It undoes all his work.

By making the Buddha an *avatāra* of Vishnu, Vishnu is portrayed as the original basis, a separate ideal, the greatest power irrespective of everything else and the Buddha as a mere shadow, an image or a follow-up act. Making the Buddha an avatāra is not an honor but an insult. He was not an avatāra or a manifestation. He was an independent, original and self-enlightened son of earth.

Dr. R. C. Dhere writes about this depiction of the Buddha in the Purāṇas,[39] "One feels despondent reading about the Buddha avatāra in the Purāṇas. To call him 'Deception' and to say that his teaching was a falsehood to lead the demons astray is a great injustice to the greatness of that man. In making him an avatāra, the Purāṇas have destroyed the Buddhist thought. They made a show of accepting the Buddha but rejected his teaching."

Why the Greatest?

After describing how the Buddha was 'rooted in earth', let us see why the title has *Sarvottama Bhūmiputra*—the Greatest Son of Earth. When I call the Buddha *Bhūmiputra*, I look at him differently than those who consider their revered ideals to be sons of God, etc. Thus it is clear that I don't want to compare him with those persons. Not that it can not be done. It is just that I don't want to do it. For me 'son of earth' is a human being. Among the humans, I find him the greatest. This assertion has two limitations.

First, I do not state or claim that his contribution to every field of human endeavor was greater than all others. For example, I do not claim that his knowledge of physics was greater than that of scientists like Newton. What I mean is that he was the greatest in imparting the best wisdom to live a happy life as an upright human being. There should be no hesitation to say that he was the greatest son of India.

Second, this is my personal opinion. I state it with humility. I accept the freedom of others to accept or reject my opinion or to have a different opinion. The Buddha himself believed that if one takes such a stand about the truth, it protects the truth. While we will discuss it in much detail later, I can't resist the temptation to venture an opinion at this stage.

In the times after the Buddha, the idea of *sthitaprajña* (literally, one established in wisdom) was much honored and praised. But in the known history of India, the Buddha most certainly is the best *sthitaprajña*.

Swami Vivekanand Honors the Buddha

Swami Vivekanand had often expressed his differences of opinion about the Buddha's teaching. Still, there was an immense respect for the Buddha in Swami Vivekanand's mind as is seen from his statement in his speech that he gave on February 2, 1900 in California.[40]

"See the sanity of the man. No gods, no angels, no demons—nobody. Nothing of the kind. Stern, sane, every brain-cell perfect and complete, even at the moment of death. No delusion…in my opinion—oh, if I had one drop of that strength! The sanest philosopher the world ever saw. Its best and its sanest teacher. And never that man bent before even the power of the tyrannical Brahmins. Never that man bent. Direct and everywhere the same…"

Sharad Patil

Renowned Indologist Sharad Patil says,[41] "There are no two opinions about the Buddha being India's greatest man among Indian and Western scholars."

Acharya Rajneesh

Keeping aside controversies surrounding him, it must be admitted that Acharya Rajneesh (Osho) was a serious scholar of Indian philosophy. He has often praised the Buddha. He said, "He was the greatest Indian ever." At another time, Osho said, "Since Buddha, India has not produced a single man comparable to him."[42]

The Buddha Gave Honor to the Downtrodden

The Tathāgata can be called greatest because he gave dignity and self-respect to the countless men and women who were victims of a cruel and unjust social system that denied them basic human dignity.

Prof. Jagannath Upadhyay says,[43] "In reality, the (Buddha's) Saṅgha was the refuge of the culture of the majority that was opposed to the traditional orthodoxy. In creating a Saṅgha in the field of spirituality and culture, he encouraged democratic process. Thus he presented an ideal of the culture of the welfare of the maximum people (including the so called lower castes/ classes) in front of the entire world.

"We thus see that the Buddha gave an exhortation to the whole world for awakening the enormous power of humans by establishing the central importance of man in the field of religion, society and culture. All bow with devotion in front of this supremacy of man. A great poet of the third century says,

> *Aho sansāramaṇdasya buddhotpādasya dīptatā;*
> *Manuṣyaṃ yatra devānāṃ sprahṇiyatvamāgatam.*
>
> *The Buddha's arising on earth was such a light of*
> *human progress*
> *That even the gods became envious of the humans."*

We will see later in this book how the Tathāgata gave Upāli, Sunīta, etc. the opportunity to rise to the highest state and how they became a subject of envy of the gods because of it. The verse quoted by Prof Upadhyay is by a Buddhist poet named Matriceta.[44]

Let Us Be Aware of the Changes that Occurred in His Teachings After Him

The Buddha lived more than 2500 years ago. In this long period, the teaching was transmitted from one generation to the next, from one country to another. During this transmission, it is inevitable that some changes occurred inadvertently or were made deliberately in his teachings. Therefore, to understand his teaching, we must read about his original teaching.

The Pali Tipiṭaka is the Main Basis

Though I have quoted many scholars in this book, my presentation is based mainly on the Pali Tipiṭaka. This is the most ancient literature of the Buddha's teaching. Therefore, the Pali Tipiṭaka remains the most reliable source to understand the Buddha directly and properly. Even then we must also be aware of the distance that has crept in between the original teaching of the Buddha and its arrangement of words in the Tipiṭaka. We will argue why this is necessary.

Discourses Should Not Disappear

Aṇi Sutta, a discourse by the Buddha in the Connected Discourses is thought provoking.[45] The gist of what he said while dwelling in Sāvatthi is:

"In the times past, the Dasāraha people had a kettle drum. When it became cracked, the Dasāraha people inserted another peg. Eventually the time came when the original drumhead had disappeared and only a collection of pegs remained. Similar thing will happen with the bhikkhus of the future. When the Tathāgata's teaching, which is supra-mundane and deep in meaning, is being recited, they will not be eager to hear it, will not pay attention to it. On the other hand, they will listen to those discourses, which are mere poetry, beautiful in words and phrases, created by outsiders. Thus the teaching of the Tathāgata will disappear. To avoid it, you should train yourself to pay attention, to listen, and to apply your minds to understand the teaching."

The discourse is applicable to us today as well. In more than 2500 years, several extraneous, spurious things have entered the Buddha's teaching. It is our duty to use our discretion to remove such spurious additions when we imbibe his original teaching.

Words and Meanings, the Messengers of Language, Are Turned into Traitors

Sometimes, a man gains a new perspective on things and tries to convey it to people for their benefit. He uses language to communicate. Words and meanings are the two components of language. These are two faithful messengers that convey the thoughts of one man to another. But if they are turned into traitors, the true message is not conveyed.

When words are distorted, changed, omitted or added, the meaning of the original message is lost or becomes distorted. The profound thoughts of a great man thus become distorted or get lost. Therefore, the Tathāgata warned again and again that one must be careful about the meaning of word and its meaning.

Entry of Heretics in Saṅgha

To preserve the original teaching of the Buddha was no easy task. It can't be denied that there was some change in the teachings over the time. Mahāvaṃsa text from Sri Lanka gives an important evidence about this.[46]

Due to the patronage of Emperor Asoka, the Saṅgha started getting many gifts. People too were happy with the Saṅgha and supported it with gifts. As the members of the other sects lost both royal patronage and people's support, they started wearing saffron robes and started living with the bhikkhus.

They started to spread their own philosophy as that of the Buddha and started conducting themselves in any way they pleased.

The Elder Moggaliputta saw the danger in this and found that he couldn't help it in the near future. He spent seven years in solitary meditation on a mountain. The heretics who had entered Saṅgha were vile in speech and far outnumbered the bhikkhus who couldn't counter them. Even *uposatha* (the fortnightly assembly of bhikkhus) and *pavāraṇā* (which is held at the end of rains retreat) couldn't be held.

When Asoka heard this, he sent one of his ministers to mediate in the Saṅgha and to encourage them to start *uposatha* again. The minister conveyed the royal order to the bhikkhus who refused to do so saying they wouldn't have *uposatha* with outsiders. Then the minister started beheading the bhikkhus who wouldn't listen. Seeing this barbaric act, Asoka's brother Tissa who was also a bhikkhu went and sat next to the bhikkhus. Seeing Tissa, the minister stopped.

The king was distraught as he felt that he was indirectly responsible for the heinous act. He sent emissaries to invite Elder Moggaliputta Tissa. The Elder came and gave proper advice to the king. The king called all the bhikkhus (true as well as heretics) in the entire region to capital in that very week. He and the Elder sat behind a curtain while they were interviewed. They were asked about what their beliefs were. Alien entrants in the Saṅgha were found to hold beliefs such as eternalism, etc. whereas the real bhikkhus said that they believed in *Vibhajjavāda* (doctrine of analysis).

The Elder Mogggalliputta Tissa confirmed the veracity of their beliefs. Then the king then drove out about sixty thousand fake bhikkhus from the Saṅgha. The real bhikkhus resumed *uposatha*.

Distortion of the Teaching of the Buddha

Even during his own life time, the teaching of the Tathāgata was sometimes distorted and he repeatedly cautioned the bhikkhus about it. The Dutiyapamādādi Vagga of the Numerical Discourses[47] narrates: "Even though the Tathāgata has not said or stated something, some people said that the Tathāgata said it or stated it. Even though the Tathāgata has said or stated something, some people said that the Tathāgata has not said it or stated it. Even though the Tathāgata has not acted in a particular manner, some people said that the Tathāgata acted in that particular manner. They said that the Tathāgata has laid down this rule whereas in reality he has not laid it down; and that the Tathāgata has not laid down this rule whereas in reality he has laid down the rule. Such bhikkhus cause harm to many, misery to many, loss to many… they destroy the noble Dhamma."

The Tathāgata had told bhikkhus to make a careful effort to know his teaching if they felt that it was distorted. Once he was dwelling at Ānanda Cetiya in Bhoganagar.[48]

He called the monks one day and said, "O bhikkhus, a bhikkhu might say—this is Dhamma, this is Vinaya (Discipline), this is the Dispensation of the Lord, I have heard this from the Tathāgata himself. Bhikkhus, when you hear him don't agree or disagree immediately. Rather, understand how the words have been arranged, compare it with the Suttas and the Vinaya. If it is not in keeping with the Suttas and the Discipline, understand that it is not said by the Buddha; that it is a tainted understanding of the bhikkhu and you should reject it."

If a bhikkhu's statement is in keeping with the Suttas and the Vinaya, then it should be accepted as the Tathāgata's teaching and that the bhikkhu has understood it correctly. Similarly, whatever is heard from the Saṅgha, from one or more elders who memorize the discourses, from a bhikkhu, it should be compared with the known Suttas and Discipine of the Buddha.

Discussion

The Buddha was aware that the teaching can be distorted. It had happened in his own lifetime and he had to rectify it often. He earnestly wished that the principles that he espoused and spread for the benefit of society should reach the society without any alteration. If they got distorted then instead of benefitting people, they would harm people. The care he took to keep the original teaching from getting distorted tells us about his discerning, restrained, and civilized persona. Not only did he warn against blindly accepting anything being said in his name but also cautioned against outright rejection without proper examination; certainly against rudeness. He encouraged a balanced examination about the truthfulness of the content.

He once told the bhikkhus,[49] "Two types of people falsely blame the Tathāgata. Which two? One, who explains that which is going to be inferred as that which has been inferred. Two, who explains that which has been understood as that which is going to be understood."

That which is going to be inferred or understood *(neyya)* is about future. That which has been inferred or understood *(nīta)* is about past. Epistemologically, *nīta* is more important than *neyya*. *Nīta* is what is known, what has been already discovered. There is a certainty about it. *Neyya* is uncertain, confusing even. It needs speculation.

Whatever has been proclaimed by the Tathāgata as uncertain or speculative must be conveyed as uncertain and speculative; and whatever has proclaimed as certainly known should be conveyed as certainly known. The Tathāgata understood that just discovering the truth and proclaiming it wasn't enough it was vital to be vigilant in ensuring that it was conveyed exactly as proclaimed without distortions.

Dharmanand Kosambi

In his book on the Buddha, Dharmanand Kosambi writes, "…it is impossible to state how many of the utterances were actually extant at the time of Asoka. There is no doubt that there were additions to them." …

"In this way, many incongruous things entered in the biography of the Buddha."…

"Many parts of Aṅguttara Nikāya (the Numerical Discourses) are later additions."[50]

Rahul Sankrityayan

Renowned Buddhist scholar Rahul Sankrityayan also feels that changes have occurred over time in the original discourse of the Buddha. In the preface to his Hindi translation of Vinaya Piṭaka he writes,[51] "Even Teachers of the past have accepted that some verses in the Tipiṭaka are later additions. Except for *mātikās* (matrices), the entire Abhidhamma is a later creation…

"Then the question arises whether the entire Sutta Piṭaka (Discourses) and Vinaya Piṭaka (Discipline) are authentic words of the Buddha. Many such as Ghoṭamukha Sutta of the Middle Length Discourses are clearly from the time after the Buddha. …All the verses of the Sutta Piṭaka seem to be later additions except those that can be considered spontaneous utterances of the Buddha. It is also safe to assume that all the descriptions of miraculous abilities of the Buddha and his disciples, of heaven and hell, of gods and demons have all been added later on."

In the preface to his classic text *Buddhacaryyā,*[52] Pandit Rahula says, "Some chapters, like some elders in the Saṅgha, stopped considering the Buddha as human and portrayed him as superhuman. They believed in great miraculous powers of the Buddha. For some the Buddha's birth and passing away was merely a show. Thus various beliefs started creating differences in the Discourses and Discipline. To defend the unnatural acts of the Buddha, new suttas were written and added."

Once we understand and keep in mind the view put forth by Pandit Rahula about heaven, hell, gods, miracles, etc.; we will not be shocked when various translations given in this book mention concepts such as heaven, etc. If we accept Pandit Rahula's view, we need not give explanations at every juncture when these concepts are mentioned.

Mrs. Rhys Davids's Opinion

One of the foremost and pioneering Buddhist scholars in the modern era, Mrs. Rhys Davids says, "Yours it is to follow our archaeologists and to dig for the original Troy beneath more than one superimposed city. For that which was Sākya is not that which you find displayed in category and formula, in sermon and reiterated refrain in the Piṭakas. I would go so far as to say in utmost seriousness, that could you now put into the hands of, say, Sāriputta any portion of Vinaya or Sutta, he would tell you it was hard for him to recognize in it anything that he taught as the right-hand man of Gotama! Yet you have no reason therefore to despair of getting at something of original purport beneath these many palimpsests. Nay, your position as serious student becomes so much more interesting. Yours it is, not to follow in newly made 'bypass road', but to aid in the road-making. You are coming to this study just when the labours of a generation and more of pioneers have cut a clearing for the Road of the True through the jungle of our ignorance about Sākya and its birth. The Road has now to be made."[53]

Perhaps, she is exaggerating but there is certainly some truth in what Mrs Rhys Davids says.

Vital for Us to Understand Original View of the Buddha

Our interest should lie in the true nature of the Dhamma that the Buddha propounded. For this we must appreciate the transmission of his teaching over time all over the world, the changes wrought in it, its expansion, the changes in its appearance and essence. It is essential to be aware of the difference between the original and the additional or the distorted. We cannot equally revere and accept both of these. Their merit is not the same. We cannot fathom it if we take a biased view.

There is a possibility that the real nature of the Buddha's teaching may not be apparent to us if we look at it through the eyes of a votary of a particular sect or tradition among the numerous sects and philosophies that go in his name. This is not to belittle his followers. We can't put followers and opponents on equal footing. When his opponents tried to destroy his teaching, his followers tried to preserve it to the best of their ability.

The Buddha's Dhamma was not a rigid set of principles. It was not a closed tradition bound by rituals. It was a journey beyond all boundaries. It was a journey that truly set a wayfarer free. When we embark on this journey we must make an effort to discern as much as possible the unadulterated teaching.

The Process of Give and Take

The Dhamma kept expanding with time. It reached people of various traditions, different regions with differing geographical and cultural characteristics. This lead to a two-way exchange. Various people welcomed Dhamma, accepted Dhamma and their life changed for the better due to inculcation of Dhamma in their life. There were also local influences on Dhamma due to different social customs and cultural thinking based on local background.

In India, the Tathāgata had both dialogue and conflict with the Vedic tradition. During his time and later on, many from the Vedic tradition accepted Dhamma. In later years, some returned to the Vedic tradition. Due to this, many tenets of Dhamma were absorbed into Vedic tradition.

On the other hand, those Vedics who had accepted Dhamma couldn't totally let go of their old baggage. Naturally, their influx changed the appearance of Dhamma. For example, deities such as Brahmā, Sakka, etc., though in a subordinate form as devoted disciples of the Buddha, were accepted by the Buddhist tradition. This also happened outside of India. Sri Lanka and Tibet are two examples.

One more thing should be noted here. Sometimes this reciprocal exchange occurred when very influential persons came in contact with the Dhamma. Nāgārjuna, Padmasambhava and Dr. Ambedkar are some of the examples. The life of these great personalities took a different turn due to contact with Dhamma. Huge changes occurred in the lives of their followers. The presentation of Dhamma also changed due to their influence. We should know these processes when we try to understand Dhamma.

We Should Understand Changes in Language

Over twenty five centuries, huge changes have possibly occurred in both the words and their meanings. Sometimes, a word gets lost. Sometimes, a word becomes ugly. Sometimes it acquires grandeur. Sometimes, it loses its essence. It is like a hero in one drama becoming a villain in another one. Therefore, we should not be surprised about a particular word that we may hear coming from Buddha but try to understand its true meaning.

Know the Boundary Between Poetry and Truth

Sometimes the Tathāgata taught in verse, sometimes through parables, sometimes allegorically. We need not always think of an action expressed in his speech as a miracle or representative of actual historical fact. Sometimes, the line between the truth and poetry is gray and we should learn to recognize it.

Gratitude for Those Who Preserved the Seeds During Famine

Various people, groups, institutes, sects and countries have done something for Dhamma over the centuries. There may be a dispute between some of these groups. If we are associated with one group, we should develop rigid attachment for that group. The Buddha himself never allowed the Dhamma to be tainted by the slightest intolerance. Thus those who follow Dhamma cannot be intolerant. While evaluating other groups, understand their limitations; to reject outright all their contributions is wrong.

For example, we may not like or understand or accept a thing or two in the Dhamma in Tibet or Sri Lanka; but we should not for that reason alone turn our back on that tradition. They have preserved the seeds of Dhamma when there was famine in India. To point out their flaws or blame them without any constructive reason is not proper. This is also applicable to smaller local groups.

No Fundamentalism, Still the Essence of Teaching is Intact

It is not my view that today we should accept whatever the Buddha taught as it is. It is undeniable that humanity has evolved with time. There is no place for fundamentalism in the Tathāgata's teaching. New questions crop up with time and new answers are needed. We will see later how the Tathāgata showed flexibility in sometimes changing rules that he himself laid down earlier. I don't think this view takes anything away from the faith in the Tathāgata.

The human mind is the same as it was at the time of the Buddha. Naturally, the essence of what he taught is still beneficial for humanity. Moreover, its need is even greater for humanity that sometimes seems to be perched on the cliff of self-destruction. Let us then try to reach that essence.

The Reader is the Final Arbitrator

It is said that everyone's universe is as big as his or her head. This is true because whatever knowledge we acquire of inner and outer subjects and its objectivity depends on several things— the capacity of our perception (perceiving intellect) and sense organs, factors that aid or obstruct perception, our view that may be enriched by past experiences or prejudiced by them, our outlook, sources of our information and interests of these sources, etc.

Keeping aside the discussion of the entire universe to one side, two aspects among the several aspects of human understanding are very important.

First, man has the capacity to acquire knowledge of a particular field and to make efforts in that direction.

Second, the knowledge of a particular subject thus acquired is limited, even tainted, by his or her own personality factors.

Therefore, how a person uses her capabilities and how she overcomes her limitations decide the quality of her comprehension. Keeping this in mind, the reader certainly has the freedom to evaluate my present writing.

2

Buddhaṃ Saraṇaṃ Gacchāmi

In this chapter we will look at the journey of Siddhārtha from a Gotama to Buddhahood—the journey that is implicit in the name 'Gotama the Buddha'.

Let us start this discussion with his renunciation, his leaving home. Actually, his journey to Buddhahood started even before that. From childhood, he had a tendency to observe, gather experiences, ask questions and seek answers.. Even so, his going forth into homelessness was the first clear visible step in the journey. If his meditation in the field as a child is considered the first major step, then the renunciation would be considered the second major step.

Traditional View about Going Forth

It is said that some astrologers predicted Siddhārtha's going forth into homelessness. Suddhodana and Pajāpati didn't want their child to leave home and take robes as a Samaṇa. It is said that to prevent his going forth, they took great care to keep him away from all suffering and to provide him with all possible material comfort. In spite of their efforts, one day Siddhārtha saw a sick person, an old man and a dead body and he saw the suffering. Then he saw a Samaṇa and decided to leave home. This is traditional belief.

The episode of Siddhārtha Gotama seeing four sights and leaving home is actually said to have occurred in the life of a previous Buddha Vipassi in Mahāpadāna Sutta in the Long Discourses.[54]

There is no mention in the Tipiṭaka of such an event occurring in the life of Siddhārtha Gotama. The opinion expressed by Dharmanand Kosambi looks fair,[55] "Then how did all these wonderful stories came to be associated with the life of the Bodhisatta? They came from Mahāpadāna Sutta." Kosambi bases his inference on commentarial evidence. The commentary of Mahāpadāna Sutta gives details of the dialogue that have now come to be associated with the charioteer and Siddhārtha. According to the Sutta, however, this episode is from the life of Vipassi Kumāra.

If this entire episode of four sights has been added to the life of Siddhārtha from the life of Vipassi Kumāra, then even according to the Tipiṭaka, these sights cannot be said to be the immediate reason for Siddhārtha's going forth. Even the historicity of the existence of Vipassi Kumāra and the episode associated with his life is doubtful.

There is one more thing about this episode that doesn't seem logical. Even a child would find it difficult to believe that Siddhārtha did not see any such sights until the age of twenty-nine. Didn't he notice his own parents getting old through the years as he grew to the age of twenty-nine? If we assume this to be true, then it is tantamount to accepting that he was lacking completely in observation and comprehension. If we look at his discourses after becoming a Buddha, we see that his experiences were rich, varied and vast; many of the experiences that he details were from the time before his enlightenment. So indefensible is the proposal that he didn't see any of the sights before, that there is no need to discuss this further. Eminent scholars such as Kosambi and Dr. Ambedkar also refused to accept these sights as the reason behind his renunciation.

Still, this episode of four sights can be explained to have figurative meaning as we will see later.

Reasons for Renunciation According to Tipiṭaka

Rejecting the traditional reason of the story of the four sights behind his renunciation doesn't solve the problem. It becomes our responsibility to find other suitable and possible reasons. Two references are important in this context. The first is the discussion on renunciation in Pali texts. The second is the comments by Kosambi on Pali sources.

Let us first look at the information given in the Discourse to Prince Bodhi[56] and other suttas.

Renunciation Because He Felt Undergoing Physical Suffering Will Give Happiness

Once the Tathāgata accepted an invitation by Prince Bodhi for a meal. After the meal, he said to Tathāgata, "Revered sir, I feel that happiness cannot be achieved through happiness; happiness can be achieved through suffering." He meant that only austerities involving torture of the body can lead to spiritual upliftment.

Then the Tathāgata shared with him some of the memories of his life before attaining Bodhi. "I held a similar view. I was very young, my hair was black, at the time when I left home against the wishes of my parents. I shaved off mustache and beard, shaved my head and took saffron robes to go forth into homelessness."

Renunciation After Seeing Subjects Suffering Like Fish Without Water

Another detail is found in Attadaṇḍa Sutta of Suttanipāta.[57] Dharmanand Kosambi developed his theory of the reasons behind Siddhārtha's renunciation based on details from this sutta. Kosambi quotes three and a half verses at the beginning of this sutta.[58]

Fear comes from arming oneself, look how these people fight;
I'll tell you how the urge (to renounce) overcame my being:

Seeing people thrashing around like fish in shallow water;
All hostile to one another; when I saw this, I became fearful.

The world all around seemed without essence, all directions trembling;
I sought refuge to keep myself safe, but I could find no such place.

Seeing people all around in hostile conflict, I became distraught.

Renunciation is Open Sky

The Middle Discourses[59] gives yet another possible reason behind his going forth. Once when he was dwelling in Vesāli, Saccaka Nigganṭhaputta came to him. Ven. Ānanda saw him coming from a distance. Saccaka was a charlatan and used to think of himself as a scholar. He was critical of the Buddha, Dhamma and Saṅgha. After approaching the Buddha and exchanging pleasantries he started a discussion with the Buddha. During the discussion, the Buddha said to him, "Aggivessana, before becoming a Buddha, while I was still a Bodhisatta, the thought came to my mind—living a householder's life is problematic; it is a muddy path. Homelessness, on the other hand, is like the open sky. While living a householder's life, it is not possible to live a complete and pure righteous untainted life. Then why shouldn't I shave my head, remove moustache and beard, take saffron robes and leave home?" He then told Saccaka how he went forth against his parents' wishes leaving them tearful.

A similar explanation is given in Pabbajjā Sutta of Suttanipāta.[60] He says, "I will explain why I renounced, which serious analysis inclined me towards renunciation and then give description of my renunciation. The householder's life is full of troubles. It is full of faults. Homelessness is like the open sky. Seeing this, I went forth."

Renunciation for Noble Search

One more reason is mentioned in the Middle Discourses.[61] The Buddha was dwelling in Jetavana at Sāvatthi. When the bhikkhus expressed a wish to hear a sermon from the Buddha, Ven. Ānanda arranged a talk at the monastery of Rammaka brahmin. Tathāgata explained to the bhikkhus, "There are two kinds of search—noble and ordinary. While being subject to birth, old age, sickness, death, grief, lamentation; to search for things that are also subject to these same qualities is ordinary search. To get attached to son, wife, servants, goats, sheep, hens, pigs, elephants, cows, horses, gold and silver; to become heedless; to become attached to them and try to get these things is ordinary search. On the contrary, to search for peerless nibbāna is noble search."

He said that while he was a bodhisatta he too was engaged in ordinary search but once the thought "why shouldn't I undertake noble search?" entered his head, he went forth into homelessness against the wishes of his parents.

Dharmanand Kosambi's Inferences

In reference to the above-mentioned reasons, the opinion of Kosambi is very important. Based on various details available in Pali literature, Kosambi gives three reasons for the renunciation of Siddhārtha Gotama,[62] "Three reasons have been given for his going forth—

1) He was anguished by his clansmen taking up arms to fight each other;

2) He thought that householder's life is full of troubles and faults; and

3) He felt that while being subject to birth, old age, sickness and death, one should not become attached to the things with the same characteristics. These three reasons can be linked together. … The principal among these three was the constant fights between Sākyans and Koliyas."

Kosambi Rejects Explanation in Commentary

The commentaries contain descriptions of conflicts between Sākyans and Koliyas. According to the commentary, the sermon in Attadaṇḍa Sutta was given by the Buddha to avert battle between their armies on the issue of water. Kosambi says,[63] "The Sākyans and the Koliyas used to fight over the water of Rohini river. Once when they had reached the bank of Rohini river with their respective armies, the Tathāgata stood between the two armies and gave this sermon. We see this description at many places in the Commentary on Jātaka. But it doesn't look right. It is possible that the Buddha gave sermons to Sākyans and Koliyas. He may also have mediated in their conflicts. But there is no reason to give this discourse on those occasions. The Buddha is explaining in this sutta how he developed an urge for renunciation and why he left home. Due to dispute over water of Rohini or some such mundane issue, there used to be fights between Sākyans and Koliyas. The Bodhisatta had to decide whether to take up arms or not. But it was not possible to end these conflicts with weapons. Even if they were resolved using force, it would have not ended there. Then the victor would be fighting with the neighboring king… and again with another neighboring king. Thus weapons would be essential for each battle and each victory. But peace would still elude them even after victory. The sons of King Pasenadi and King Bimbisāra betrayed and dethroned their fathers. What is the use of these weapons? To fight till the end? The Bodhisatta spurned the path of violence and accepted the non-violent path sans weapons."

In short, Kosambi feels that Siddhārtha Gotama may have mediated in the conflicts between the Sākyans and the Koliyas. But it is unlikely that he taught the Attadaṇḍa Sutta on such an occasion.

There used to be hostilities between the Sākyans and the Koliyas even before Siddhārtha's going forth. It was during one such conflict that he shunned the path of violence and left home. This was the background of this homelessness.

Reason for Renunciation Kosambi Offered in His Play

Kosambi dealt with Siddhārtha's renunciation in detail in the play 'Bodhisatta' that he wrote in 1945.[64] In this play Kosambi put into a fictional play what he thought was the real reason for renunciation, because he clearly found the traditional view unacceptable.

In the preface of the play, Kosambi says that he created the fictitious character of Subhadra Koliya in this play. Here Kosambi has proposed that after Siddhārtha refused to take up arms against Koliyas, the general of the Sākyan army threatened him with boycott of his family as well as confiscation of his property.

Let us look at the dialogue as penned by Kosambi. When Siddhārtha refused to go to war, the general threatened him, "… Remember, we may boycott your family and confiscate your lands." Siddhārtha requested, "Please don't boycott my family and confiscate our lands. Don't make all the family destitute. If you wish to punish, please punish me alone." To save his family, he said, "I am willing to be banished from our state. I will become an ascetic and leave on my own." When he later briefed his father about what happened in the assembly, he said, "This is why I thought I wanted to be an ascetic. Our family would have been ruined if the Sākyan Assembly had confiscated our lands, wouldn't it?"

In the publisher's note of the Hindi translation of this play published by the Central Institute of Higher Tibetan Study, Sarnath, the director writes that Kosambi found inadequate, illogical and improper the traditional view that the four sights were responsible for Gotama's going forth. He put forth the Siddhārtha's reluctance to take up arms in the bloodshed due to quarrel over water and consequently when he was censured by the assembly, he left home. The director adds that scholars should think about this view. In the preface of this play, D. B. Kalelkar[65] writes, "I find the theory put forth by Kosambi logical and rational. Further I want to add that only after reading this, do we get a better grasp of the Buddha's teaching."

On the Basis of Commentary, Kosambi's View is not Historical but a Constructive Allegory

Based on what commentaries say, there are certain difficulties in accepting Kosambi's view. We will then see what Bhadant Anand Kausalyayan proposes and leave it to the reader to decide what could have led to Siddhārtha's going forth.

Attadaṇḍa Sutta Doesn't Mention Conflict with Clansmen

Kosambi's theory is based on Attadaṇḍa Sutta but it doesn't mention clansmen. Even Kosambi's translations use the words 'people' and 'subjects'. But when he gives the list of three reasons, he uses the word *āpta*, meaning 'clansmen'. Thus the argument becomes somewhat tenuous.

Difficult to Accept Kosambi's Objections to Commentary

The setting for Attadaṇḍa Sutta given by the Commentary—Tathāgata stood between the two armies when the hostilities escalated into impending war and gave this sermon—looks unreasonable to Kosambi. If one examines the essence of the Sutta, we will find that the sermon not only seems acceptable in that setting but also appropriate. He wanted to explain to both the armies not to fight, not to quarrel. It was proper that he would tell them on this occasion that such conflicts led to his renunciation and he had found that the solution is to "remove ill-will and live in amity."

It is noteworthy that this conflict occurred after Siddhārtha's enlightenment. By the time of this incident, Gotama the Buddha had come to be revered by general society. There is no basis in Pali literature to say that the conflict had occurred before his renunciation and had led to his decision. The whole theory is Kosambi's imagination. Kosambi's description of how taking up arms would lead to a series of violent battles and was futile is certainly in keeping with the non-violent teaching of the Buddha. But this teaching of peace by Tathāgata is applicable to every conflict between humans. He might have seen fights among people and these probably also included his clansmen; but it doesn't mean that he only had conflicts of his clansmen in front of him.

Thus it seems proper that he left home to address the suffering of people who were distressed like fish in shallow water and after he became a Buddha, he came back to mediate between the two armies and shared his memories with them.

Kosambi mentions the sons of Pasenadi and Bimbisāra turning against their parents as an additional factor for renunciation. However, these events occurred a long time after the attainment of Bodhi. Bimbisāra continued to rule for a long time after the enlightenment of Siddhārtha. It is true that Pasenadi was dethroned by his son, Viḍūḍabha and this resulted in Pasenadi's death. However, Viḍūḍabha's birth, even his mother's marriage to Pasenadi, happened after the enlightenment. Therefore, these sons' turning against their fathers could not contribute to the reasons for renunciation. There is one more difficulty. According to the commentary, the Tathāgata mediated successfully in the conflict between Sākyans and Koliyas; whereas according to Kosambi's hypothesis, Siddhārtha left the region without settling the dispute.

The Tathāgata Never Said that He Went Forth Due to Conflict with Clansmen

We see in the Tipiṭaka that the Tathāgata often reminisced about his renunciation. He often described how he left his parents in tears. However, he never said that he took robes because of the conflict between the Sākyans and the Koliyas. He said that he left home to find an end to all suffering. In Mahāparinibbāna Sutta we see that at the end of his life while giving a sermon to Subhadda, he said that he had left home fifty-one years ago with the same aim of finding a way out of all suffering.

Though Siddhārtha was indeed against war, the converse of Kosambi's hypothesis is that had he not been threatened with social boycott and confiscation of the land of his family, he would not have gone forth; and would have led a householder's life of a Sākyan. There is little evidence to support this hypothesis.

Kosambi's hypothesis can be looked upon as a creative license of a poet or a writer. But the Buddha is a historical figure and hence we have certain obligations when we use that creative license. The Commentary too often uses fiction and when it doesn't pass the test of rational scrutiny we have to reject it. Had the Commentary not mentioned the dispute over water, we would have been left with little to find our way to the true history of this important conflict.

Therefore, I feel that we should look at Kosambi's hypothesis as allegory. It is a vivid, persuasive and handsome allegory that depicts Siddhārtha's opposition to violence, bloodshed and destruction.

Questions and Answers in the Connected Discourses

Māra tried to distract Siddhārtha while he was meditating to attain enlightenment. At that time, Taṇhā (*trishṇā*, craving), a daughter of Māra asks him,[66] "You are meditating in the jungle in grief. Have you lost your wealth? Is that why you are worried? Are you on the run from the law? Why don't you meet people?"

Siddhārtha responded, "I am meditating in solitude to achieve my goal, to attain peace of mind, to defeat the army of all that appears dear and enticing. Since this gives me happiness, I don't meet people."

When asked whether he was on the run from the law, he didn't affirm it. This too goes against Kosambi's hypothesis. Kosambi might say that such a question itself is an indication that some such thing had happened. Counter argument to it would be that for a solitary person in the jungle such a question is raised naturally.

Ananda Kausalyayan's Opinion

For the time being we can leave this question open for readers and scholars after noting Kausalyayan's opinion, "… whatever small indicators we find in Tipiṭaka are more in keeping with 'seeing people wilting around him, all hostile to one another' than the story of 'the aged, the sick, the dead and the ascetic'."

Contemplative from Childhood

In his childhood, Siddhārtha had sat in meditation during festivities. This indicates that his nature was contemplative from childhood. Suddhodana, like any other father, would have been worried by it and might have tried to change his mindset.

Wanted a Solution to the Universal Problem

What was this child absorbed in? He had the sensitivity to look beyond superficial appearances. He had the rare sharp intellect to analyze and comprehend events around him; and the organizing capacity to marshal his experiences meaningfully. To say that he once saw a sick person seems a childlike explanation. He saw suffering all around. He saw mistakes of men and their lamentations. He was disturbed by what he saw and also felt compassion. His very existence was consumed by the questions:

Why are people miserable and is it possible to eradicate their misery? It is possible that one or two sad events stirred and heightened his sensitivity or brought urgency to it. The suffering he saw in the people around him must have included suffering of sickness, old age and death making him even more compassionate. Though he may not have seen these three sights of suffering one after the other, we can look upon these three sights as symbolic of all kinds of suffering. His own suffering or that of his near and dear ones surely was part of his contemplation but he set out to find the solution to a universal problem; and through tireless efforts he found it. He went forth due to the inner yearning of a sensitive mind. All his experiments to find a way out of suffering were congruent with that yearning.

Five Dreams

The description in the Numerical Discourses[68] that the Bodhisatta had seen five great dreams and these were fulfilled when he attained Bodhi is noteworthy.

In the first dream he saw that the earth was his bed and Himalayas were his pillow. His left hand was being washed by the eastern sea, the right hand by the western sea and both his feet by the southern sea.

In the second dream, a blade of grass had sprouted from his navel and was touching the sky.

Creatures with black heads and white bodies were climbing from his soles to his knees in this third dream.

In the fourth dream, he saw that four birds of various colors had flown to his feet from four directions and had all turned white.

In his fifth dream, he was walking without touching a mound of filth.

Tathāgata himself clarified the meaning of these dreams.

The first dream meant that he had attained peerless enlightenment.

The second dream meant that he had discovered and proclaimed the noble eight-fold path.

The third dream meant that householders in white clothes became his disciples.

The fourth dream meant that all four varṇas (classes) become one and get liberated in the Dhamma.

The fifth dream meant that he would use various material gifts such as robes and alms food without attachment; that he would not get attached to worldly things.

Discussion

Even though this description is shown as coming from the Buddha, it is possible that these dreams were described in detail later on by someone. Still, we can say that the seeds of these dreams were present in the mind of Siddhārtha when he left home. If we say that he had already seen in his dreams all the significant events that happened after his enlightenment, then all his efforts for enlightenment would be meaningless. It would mean that everything is preordained, predetermined.

We should also remember that all these were subjects of contemplation for Siddhārtha not only after he went forth but also before his renunciation when he was facing storms of questions in his mind. Being dissatisfied with what was happening in society, the quest to give it a new positive direction had formed in his mind.

Siddhārtha had renounced householder's life to attain Bodhi and discover the Dhamma. Bhadant Anand Kausalyayan is balanced in his comment,[69] "Just as in a chain one link is joined to the next, the goal of his renunciation and its fulfillment were the pious poem which is 'the Buddha's Dhamma'. It is understood that he had left home to go to the root of suffering of people, to find out the way to eradicate suffering and to show this path to the people to remove all suffering."

Siddhārtha Gotama Saw a Samaṇa, not a Sanyasi

Of the four sights that Siddhārtha saw, the fourth was a sanyasi. Though we can't take this story literally, we can look at it in another way. We will see later how Siddhārtha had got the legacy of the Samaṇa tradition. Kosambi feels that the visit of Asita Kāladevala to Suddhodana's house after Siddhārtha's birth was probably true. He says,[70] "The story of Rishi Asita predicting Siddhārtha's future seems to be ancient one. We find it in the beginning of Nālaka Sutta of Suttanipāta." It seems that Siddhārtha had the opportunity to spend time in the company of various scholars and Samaṇas (ascetics). When the story says that he saw an ascetic, all it means is that he received the heritage of prior Samaṇa tradition and that gave a particular direction to his thoughts.

Sanyasi is often equated with a Vedic sanyasi. This is not true. The person that Vipassi Kumāra saw (and is popularly also associated with Siddhārtha) was not a Vedic sanyasi. He was a Samaṇa. The Long Discourses describe him as a shaven-headed ascetic with saffron robes. The Vipassi Kumāra's charioteer tells him that the ascetic had taken robes to live a righteous life, to live a life of equality, to perform wholesome actions, for non-violence and to be compassionate to all beings. When Vipassi Kumāra asked the charioteer the reason why the ascetic had shaved his head, the charioteer gave the same reply—to live a righteous life, etc.

It is unlikely that Siddhārtha made up his mind by merely 'seeing' an ascetic. It merely shows how he became favorable to the Samaṇa tradition.

This effort to decide a sanyasi or a Samaṇa is not a mere useless academic exercise. If we find out whose tradition was his heritage—the sanyasi that seeks moksha or the Samaṇa that strives to live a righteous life—we will know better what his inspiration was. He didn't consider the Vedic *sanyāsa* as way to attain Bodhi but thought that he could reach his goal by becoming a Samaṇa.

He says that his hair was black when he left home. This means that he left home in the prime of his youth. He left behind a life of great affluence to walk an arduous path. He did this not under any duress or due to any enticement but with a mind possessed to seek the end of suffering.

He Had Talked to His Family When He Went Forth

The Buddha said that he left home against the wishes of his parents, that they wept when he left home. Clearly, the description that he left home surreptitiously without informing his family is a flight of poetic imagination. He had discussed his renunciation with this family and had told them about his goal and his decision. The inference of Dharmanand Kosambi[71] looks proper, "... ... it seems that the story that Bodhisatta rode on his horse Kanthaka with Channa and ran away is totally wrong. ... these statements (of crying) make it clear that Suddhodana and Gotamī knew that Bodhisatta was going to become an ascetic and that he did so in front of them against their wishes."

Birth of His Son

The Commentary says that on receiving the news of the birth of his son, Siddhārtha said 'a *rāhu* is born, a fetter has arisen'. *Rāhu* means obstacle, fetter. Thinking this fetter will make Siddhārtha give up the thought of renunciation, Suddhodana named the child Rāhula.[72]

Some people spice up historical events with such quotable puns. Unfortunately, those who do so don't realize that by creating the fable for a pun, they are depicting the hero as irresponsible. This legend suggests that Siddhārtha had developed a dislike, an aversion for wife and son. Actually, Siddhārtha didn't leave home due to aversion towards his family but for the lofty goal of finding a way out of suffering for all people. He didn't leave home because he thought that it was desirable for the goal but because it was necessary for the search he was going to undertake.

Now about the name Rāhula: The town of Sākyans was named after Kapila Muni who was an *asura*. He was the son of Pralhāda and the uncle of an asura named Bāli, who is famous as Vairocana Buddha. This means that the people of Kapilavatthu followed the asura culture.

Rāhu was a great asura in this culture. Vishnu had cut Rāhu's head off while distributing *amruta* (the mythical drink that is supposed to make a man live forever) that had surfaced after churning of the sea. It is possible that like Kapila, Rāhu was also remembered by the people there. Just as 'la' is added to various words affectionately in Indian languages (*prema-la, sneha-la, mridu-la, shyama-la,* etc.) 'la' may have been added to Rāhu and thus Rāhula came about. This suggests that the name came not because he was looked upon as a fetter but from tender affection.

Let Us Seek Forgiveness from Yasodharā

Various stories say that Siddhārtha left home while Yasodharā was sleeping. We have seen above that Siddhārtha didn't leave home surreptitiously but after discussion with family. He said that his parents were crying when he left. It is not possible that Yasodharā didn't know about it when her in-laws were crying. It is not possible that the servants in the house wouldn't tell her. It is true that while recounting his going forth, he talks about his parents but not about his wife. Whether or not he had obtained her permission for leaving home, it is unlikely that he didn't discuss renunciation with Yasodharā. What is then the reason behind her omission in his narration? One explanation is that customarily the elders in the family are approached for permission. Anyway, in spite of Siddhārtha's assertions, stories are told about him sneaking out of the house. All great persons in the world often neglect the wellbeing of their families for the greater good of the society. When King Shivaji went to meet Afzal Khan, he gave priority to society over his family. Various leaders such as Mahatma Gandhi and Nelson Mandela, were either married or had the responsibility of their family on their shoulders when they joined the freedom struggle. But they neglected their families for a greater goal. The same is true for Siddhārtha Gotama in a different field.

Even then we must seek a million pardons from Yasodharā. Her sacrifice, whether made voluntarily or forced on her, is the price paid for the sweet and delicious fruit that humanity has enjoyed for the past more than twenty-five centuries and which innumerable people will continue to enjoy in future. Let us thank her for that. Since she took robes and joined the Saṅgha, we can say that she supported his decision even if belatedly.

K. Shri Dharmanand quotes Dwight Goddard,[73]

'Twas not through hatred of children sweet,
'Twas not through hatred of His lovely wife,
Thriller of hearts – not that He loved them less,
But Buddhahood more, that He renounced them all.

He Did Not Use His Father's Affluence

Siddhārtha left behind royal affluence, luxuries and vast fields. He exchanged his rich clothes for the robes of an ascetic. Who told him to do so? Why did he do so? What was the need? An inner obsession motivated him. He didn't seek the affluence of power, wealth and resources. He wanted the affluence of spiritual knowledge and wisdom. To reach that path, he had to renounce royal luxuries.

Siddhārtha didn't use an iota of his father's abundant wealth to go higher. He attained a high state through his own tireless and unremitting efforts; through his creative genius; and through his compassion for suffering humanity.

After Leaving Home

After recounting his renunciation, the Buddha told Prince Bodhi, "I who was seeking the welfare and state of peerless peace went to Āḷāra Kālāma. When I expressed the wish to train under his guidance, he happily consented. Soon I perfected his teaching. To what level do you teach Dhamma based on your own experience, I asked him. He said, to the sate of *akiñcanyāyatana*—state of ownership over none, sphere of nothingness.

"Seeing that I too had faith, effort, awareness, concentration and wisdom, I attained what he had attained and told him about it. To this he replied, 'Friend, it is a gain for me that I have a co-practitioner like you. I have gained a good thing… Whatever I know, you know as well. We are both equal. Come, let us both look after this congregation.'

"Thus though he was a teacher, he offered me, his student, equal status and honored me. But I left him because I realized that I could not attain the highest goal with his teaching.

"Then I went to Uddaka Rāmaputta. There too I attained what he taught {commentary says that Uddaka Rāmaputta himself only knew theory and attained it after Siddhārtha} and told him about it.. He too then requested me to be a teacher alongside him. He used to teach absorptions till the state of *neva-saññā-na-asaññā*—state of neither perception nor non-perception. Finding it inadequate to reach the highest goal, I left.

"Seeking supreme welfare, I wandered in Magadha and reached Senānīgāma in Uruvelā. The land, the woods, the flowing river were delightful. The town was well-established and with pleasing surroundings. Finding it suitable for meditation, I sat there. These three similes that I had not heard before came to my mind."

The gist of what he told Prince Bodhi is:

Suppose there were a wet piece of wood lying in water and someone with a dry piece of wood came and tried to rub the two create fire, would he be successful.

Prince Bodhi replied, "No." The piece of wood is wet and lying in water, so it's not possible to kindle fire with it. It will be a tiring and frustrating task. This is what happens with Samaṇas and Brāhmaṇas. If they indulge in sensual pleasures and have not extinguished lust within, they will be tired and distressed but will not attain enlightenment. This was the first simile.

If the wet wood is lying on land, it still cannot generate fire. Similarly, those who have given up sensual pleasures but have not extinguished craving within will not attain enlightenment. This was the second simile.

If a dry piece of wood is lying on dry land, then it certainly can produce fire. Similarly, those who do not indulge in sensual pleasures and have extinguished the craving within can attain enlightenment if they make proper efforts. This was the third simile.

Then the Buddha said, "I started making efforts. With teeth clenched, tongue pressed against the roof of mouth, crushing mind with mind, I exerted such great effort that sweat ran from my armpits. My efforts were similar to a strong man seizing a weaker man by the head and beating him down, constraining him and crushing him. I tried breathing-less meditation by stopping all in-breaths and out-breaths through my mouth and nose.

A time came when deities said, "Samaṇa Gotama has died." Some other deities responded by saying, "Samaṇa Gotama is not dead. He cannot die. This is how arahats (liberated ones) dwell."

Then I thought of giving up all food. Some deities advised me, "Don't give up food. If you do give up food, we will infuse heavenly food into the pores of your skin." I thought that if I claim to be fasting and if these deities infuse food into the pores of my skin, then it will amount to lying. Therefore, I requested them not to do so.

Then I decided to take a little food. I started taking a handful of bean soup or lentil soup or vetch soup or pea soup. Because of lack of nutrition, my body became extremely weak. My limbs became like jointed segments of a slender vine. My backside became like a camel's hoof. My spine stood out like corded beads. My ribs jutted out as gaunt as the cracked rafters of old buildings. My eyes sank down in their sockets and looked like a gleam of water sunk deep in a well. My scalp withered like a black gourd shrivels and withers in the wind and sun. When I touched the skin on my abdomen, I felt my backbone. Such became my state.

If I went to answer the call of nature, I would faint and fall. When my body was touched, hair would fall off. Some who saw me said, "Samaṇa Gotama is black." Some would call me dark and some would say I was the color of fish. My clear, bright complexion had vanished due to eating so little. But in spite of putting up with such pains, I didn't attain the highest goal.

Then I thought, could there be another path to enlightenment?

While thinking thus, I remembered that while sitting in the cool shadow of the rose-apple tree on my father's field, secluded from sensual pleasures and unwholesome states, I had experienced the first absorption. I thought that this could be the path to enlightenment.

I started taking food again because I felt that it was not possible to continue my efforts with so frail a physique. At that time five ascetics were staying with me because they thought that once I attained enlightenment, I would teach them the Dhamma. When I started partaking food, they left me thinking that I had strayed from my path and had become a materialist. With nourishment, I regained my strength and started dwelling in the- first, second, third and fourth absorptions *(jhānas)*.

After this, the Tathāgata told him how he had attained enlightenment and set the wheel of Dhamma in motion. We will discuss it later.

In the Discourse on the Great Roar of Lion[74] of the Middle Discourses, the Tathāgata shares with Sāriputta the memories of his severe austerities.

Discussion

The Tathāgata said that when he was not enlightened, he too felt that happiness could not be attained through happiness but only through suffering. This was a belief of many people at that time that one could not attain truth without enduring severe physical pain. They believed that enduring harsh austerities took one to lofty spiritual heights. Prince Bodhi felt this way and Siddhārtha too was under the sway of this thought for some time.

Kiṃkusalagavesī

Kusala is wholesome. *Kiṃkusala* is "what is wholesome". *Gavesī* is one who searches. This describes Siddhārtha's journey. He also described it as the journey undertaken with the aim to achieve the highest peace. He wasn't influenced by the mere desire to reject something or rebel against something. He had set out to achieve something that was beneficial and joyous. His

pair of wheels for it?" The chariot-maker answered that he will. Then he completed one wheel six days before six months were over and informed the king about it. The king then said, "There will be a war in six days, is the pair of new wheels ready?" He assured the king that he would make it ready in time. He made the second wheel in the next six days and went to the king with the pair of new wheels. The king looked at the two wheels and asked him, "O Chariot-maker, is there a difference in the two wheels for I see none?" Chariot-maker replied, "Your Majesty, indeed they are different. Let Your Majesty observe for himself."

First, he pushed the wheel he had made in six days rolling on the ground. After going some distance, the wheel lost speed, lost balance and fell down. Then he set in motion the wheel that had taken almost six months to make. After going some distance, this wheel also lost speed but remained upright. The king asked him why it was so. He explained that the motion of the first wheel was crooked, faulty and irregular. Its spokes and axle too were faulty. On the other hand, the motion of thesecond wheel that took much longer to make, was straight, flawless and smooth. Its spokes and axle were faultless.

At the end of the story, the Tathāgata told the bhikkhus that he himself was the chariot-maker. Just as the chariot-maker was skilled in removing crooks, flaws and weaknesses from wood, the Perfectly Enlightened One was skilled in removing crooks, flaws and weaknesses in action, speech and mind. The bhikkhus whose faults are not yet rectified are like the wheel made in six days and those whose faults are all removed are like the perfect wheel that took almost six months to make. Therefore, they should make their actions, speech and mind flawless.

Discussion

The moral of the story is that to make oneself perfect and flawless, one has to make careful efforts for a long time. It also means that one has to follow the guidance of a teacher like the Tathāgata for a long time.

We perform many mental, verbal and bodily actions. If you want good results from these actions, you have to guard your actions, speech and mind.

It is not necessary to take the words, "I was the chariot-maker" as a historical truth. What is important is that the chariot-maker had the skills to remove flaws from wood. The Tathāgata showing oneness with the chariot-maker does help in one sense. Chariot-makers are what is now called a blue-collar members of the society. The Tathāgata thus implied that the chariot-maker was his equal in prestige.

Just like the care showed by the chariot-maker in making the first wheel, Siddhārtha also took great care in his efforts to attain liberation.

His Experiments in Torturing the Body

After thinking about the three similes, Siddhārtha tortured his body in many ways. He also thought of giving up food completely. Ultimately, rather than giving it up completely, he reduced it to such small quantities that he became frail and his body lost all its strength. In one sense, it was good that he did all this and found it useless. He could then claim to know from his own experience that torturing oneself did not take one any closer to his goal of enlightenment. Realizing that all his austerities were in vain, he started taking proper diet. These and other experiments lasted for about six years.

Body Needs Nutrition

The Buddha told the bhikkhus about the need for proper diet even after attaining enlightenment[76]. He was once dwelling in Sāvatthi in Jetavana. Once he gave a sermon on the four kinds of nutrition needed for every being. The first of these is food, solid or liquid. Thus he didn't believe in fasting because the body needs food to survive.

His Companions Felt That He Had Gone Astray

It was not an easy decision for him to eat proper food. When a man undertakes a journey towards a high ideal, he is watched by many. People analyze his behavior. If he changes course, they doubt him and make allegations against him. They feel that he has betrayed his ideal. Siddhārtha's companions turned out to be no exceptions and acted in this way. They left him thinking that he had strayed from his path.

It Takes Courage to Walk Alone

These are life's testing moments. It is not easy to stick to one's new decision when companions abandon you. It takes courage to walk alone. An inner conviction is necessary to walk on the new path without hesitation. This is what Siddhārtha did. He remembered the meditation from his childhood and gained confidence that it was the proper way to know oneself, to know nature and to discover the truth.

He Was Determined

After attaining enlightenment too, the Buddha's fearless resolve was evident many times. A few examples:

Once the Buddha was staying at the Vulture Peak mountain near Rajgir.[77] Once at night he was sitting in the open sky in dark. There was a soft drizzle. At that time, the evil Māra started pushing big boulders in his direction; to which Tathāgata replied, "Even if you push the entire Vulture's Peak, there will be no trembling in the mind of the Buddha."

Whatever stand he took, whatever view he espoused, came from his own experience. He followed it all his life with great determination. Pressure and intimidation had no effect on him. We see this in Suciloma Sutta[78] of the Connected Discourses.

Once the Tathāgata was dwelling near Gaya. Then one day two ogres, Khara and Sūciloma, decided to test him to see if he was a real Samaṇa or a fake one. Sūciloma came and collided against him. He moved to one side.

Then Sūciloma asked him, "Samaṇa, are you afraid of me?"

He replied, "Friend, I don't fear you. But your touch is not good."

Sūciloma then threatened him, "Samaṇa, I will ask you a question. If you don't answer me, I will make you mad, I will tear your heart out or I will seize you by your feet and throw you across the Ganges."

The Tathāgata replied, "There is none who can make me a lunatic or tear my heart or who can seize my feet and throw me across the Ganges; still, go ahead and ask your questions." And then the Tathāgata answered all the questions put to him.

Ate Sujātā's Milk Pudding

Nidānakathā of Commentary on Jātaka[79] describes an event after Siddhārtha's five companions left him:

At that time, in the village āin Uruvelā, there was a family named Senānī. Sujātā was a daughter of the family. On coming of age, she had prayed to the tree deity (banyan tree), "If I am married into a suitable family and beget a son as first offspring, each year I will spend a hundred thousand in your worship."

When she gave birth to a son after a suitable marriage, she kept her promise. She prepared a milk pudding. It was a full moon day of Vesāka. She decided to make the offering in the morning and asked her slave maid Puṇṇā to clean the premises of the banyan tree.

The Bodhisatta had seen the five dreams on the night before and thinking "I will surely become a Buddha" he came and sat down under the same banyan tree in the early morning. Puṇṇā saw him under the tree. She thought that the tree deity had appeared to receive offering from Sujātā. She rushed back and told Sujātā what she had seen.

Sujātā was thrilled. She told Puṇṇā, "From today, you are my elder daughter." She gave Puṇṇā jewellery befitting her daughter and went to the tree with a golden bowl containing milk pudding. She too thought that the Bodhisatta was a tree deity. She put down the bowl containing the milk pudding. She then went to him with a golden pot with scented water. Bodhisatta didn't have his usual earthen pot so he extended his cupped right hand and accepted the water offered by her. Then she offered the bowl of milk pudding to the great man. When he looked at her, she assured him, "It is offered to you. Please partake it and dwell as you wish." She saluted him and said, "Just as my wish has been fulfilled, may your wish too be fulfilled." Saying this she returned with an indifference towards the bowl worth a hundred thousand as if it was an old leaf.

The Bodhisatta got up and circumambulated the tree. Then he took the bowl and went to the bank of the Nerañjā river. He put down the bowl on the bank and went in the river to bathe. After the bath, he ate the sweet milk pudding in the bowl. Then he took the bowl in his hand and thought, "If I am going to become a Buddha today, this bowl will flow in the opposite direction of the current. But if I am not going to become a Buddha, may it flow with the current." Thinking thus he put the bowl in the river. It reached the centre of the current and, like a speeding horse, started flowing in the opposite direction of the current.

Discussion

There is clearly an exaggeration in the description by the Commentary. It is also influenced by the veneration that the Tathāgata received later due to his teaching. We need not take it literally. Still, it has important allegorical meaning.

Siddhārtha Gotama became enlightened on the night of the full moon of Vesāka after partaking the milk pudding offered by Sujātā. Two offerings are of highest importance in the Buddha's life: one after which he attained Bodhi and the other after which he attained *mahāparinibbāna*. Sujātā thus became immortal in human history. Details such as she was going to spend a hundred thousand, she gave water to Bodhisatta in a golden water pot, the milk pudding was offered in a golden bowl are not important. It is possible that the water pot and bowl were earthen. But the purpose for which Sujātā used them made them far more valuable than gold. It is also possible that Sujātā was from an ordinary poor village family. Anyway, there is no problem accepting the Commentary's version that she was from a rich family. The most important thing is her discerning faith and the goodwill with which she encouraged Siddhārtha "May your wish be fulfilled."

Indeed, there should be no doubt that even great men derive strength from the goodwill of common people.

Liberation of Slave

Puṇṇā brought the news of the tree-deity. Pleased by the news, Sujātā set her free from bondage. Moreover, she anointed Puṇṇā as her elder daughter and adorned her with jewelry. A slave girl became a noble woman, became Sujātā's daughter. It is as if it was the preview of the changes Siddhārtha was going to wrought in society after becoming a Buddha. It is also immaterial whether it really was a full moon night. On that night a full moon of wisdom had arisen helping to complete the lives of incomplete men. It is possible that the slave girl's name was not 'Puṇṇā' (literally, complete). As long as she was a slave, she was 'Apuṇṇā' (literally, incomplete). She became Puṇṇā later. From that day until now, countless people have become Puṇṇā and will continue to become Puṇṇās.

The Bowl Flowing Opposite to the Current is a Metaphor

It is obvious that the bowl floating in the direction opposite to the current of the river is a parable, not a historical fact. However, this doesn't make the metaphor meaningless, false, deceptive or full of blind faith. To consider it thus will amount to taking music out of the human life, taking inspiration out of poetry and rendering all figure of speech in poetry meaningless. We should consider the bowl floating in the opposite direction as a delightful symbol for the Dhamma. The Buddha himself said that his Dhamma goes counter to the current. We will discuss it later. All his life, he endeavored to turn the thinking of the society opposite to the established traditional thinking. All his life was a journey against the flow. In India, even today most of that journey has to be made against the flow.

Fistful of Grass

The Commentary on Jātaka[80] says that when Siddhārtha, after eating Sujātā's milk pudding, was going for meditation, a grass-cutter named Sotthiya (Svastika) gave him eight fistful of grass to use as seat for his meditation. This is an entirely believable story and the grass-cutter thus became a benevolent supporter of human society. However, one detail of the story seems to have been added in retrospect. Tathāgata showed the Noble Eightfold Path to humanity. The eight fistfuls were imagined as a prior indication of the Noble Eightfold Path. To accept this is to agree that the discovery of the Noble Eightfold Path was predetermined, takes credit away from Siddhārtha's efforts. All that should matter is that the grass-cutter gave grass to Siddhārtha for his seat.

It is also noteworthy that Siddhārtha didn't use deerskin or tiger-skin as he was opposed to the killing of animals.

Lotus Bloomed Wherever He stepped

It is said that when Siddhārtha got up from his seat after attaining Bodhi, wherever he stepped, a lotus bloomed. Even today in Bodh Gaya, the figures of those lotuses are shown. Clearly, it is not factual as it is against the laws of nature. Still it is a meaningful metaphor. It means that wherever on earth a compassionate wise man steps, it is as if flowers bloom there, and the earth becomes fragrant with the scent of wisdom and compassion. For the next forty five years, he freely distributed the wisdom acquired at that time. The fragrance of the great Dhamma touched the lives of countless people. It is as if the fragrance proclaims the essence of the reality of the universe and shows the way to make human life bright and wholesome. K Shri Dhammanand says while describing Tathāgata,[81] "…the Buddha, the most fragrant flower of the human race!"

His Face Brightened After Attaining Bodhi

The Buddha set out towards Varanasi to teach the Dhamma to his five former companions. Upaka Ājīvaka saw him between Uruvelā and Gaya; and said[82], "Friend, your bearing looks pleasing. Your complexion is clear and bright."

His newly acquired wisdom was no ordinary thing. Its grandeur can be gauged by the fact that people have been venerating that knowledge for the past twenty-five centuries. It is only natural then that Siddhārtha's face had become radiant, his bearing had become pleasing and his whole persona was sparkling with a magnificent glow. The light of this glow dispelled darkness in the entire world.

The Glow of Buddha is Unsurpassed

Darkness hinders eyesight and doesn't allow proper comprehension of things. Naturally, any light that removes darkness helps one to become better sighted. But not all lights are the same. Connected Discourses[83] lists four things that give light. Sun shines during the day, moon at night, fire lights up at various places during day and night. But the greatest light is the light of the Buddha. His glow is unsurpassed.

The light of the sun is essential and beneficial for life. But the light of knowledge brightens up life to far greater extent. In the light of the Tathāgata's Bodhi, innumerable people started living a bright life. The light of Bodhi was not the glow of the personality of Siddhārtha Gotama before he became enlightened. It was the light of a Buddha, a light of the flame of true knowledge.

Wisdom *(paññā, prajñā)* has been described in poetic terms and yet realistically in the Numerical Discourses.[84] The world has four glows; that of sun, moon, fire and wisdom. Among these, the Buddha told the bhikkhus, the glow of wisdom is superior. To underscore the specialty of the light of wisdom, additional words were used: glow, brightness, light, flame, etc. in the four suttas.

When we see the lofty height of humanness attained by Siddhārtha Gotama after enlightenment, we feel that the glow of Sambuddha is truly brighter than the glow of the sun and the moon. We then understand how someone keen to attain Bodhi should endeavor. A verse by Matriceta[85] is fitting:

Your conduct is that of a saint though none has told you to do so,
You are compassionate and caring without any reason or expectation,
You are a friend to strangers (those who have no friends),
You are a brother to those with whom you have no personal relation.

When we look at the life of Buddha, we find that every word in Matriceta's description is true.

Untainted Human Relations

Matriceta has thrown light on the perfectly balanced attitude of the Buddha in a verse. He states that the Buddha is an ideal of how one man can have untainted relations with so many different people from so many different strata of society. He says,[86] "Without having envy for those who had something more, without humiliating those who have something less and without competing with those who were equal, you became supreme in the world."

To eradicate suffering was a lifelong goal of the Tathāgata. One major cause of human misery is the disharmony among people. Some people envy, hate and malign those who are superior in power, wealth, prestige, beauty, etc. and make a petty attempt to prove themselves superior. They try to crush, intimidate and enslave those who are weaker and thus reaffirm their superiority. They strive to compete with their equals and to surpass them, which creates stress and strain.

One who looks upon all as equal, who doesn't think of others or oneself as superior or inferior—lives a joyful life and this joy makes him a superior person. He lives a happy life and creates joy in the life of others. A human being reaches that height after attaining Buddhahood. This beautiful description by Matriceta shows us how to live a blissful life.

We Recoil From His Touch

We don't have as many dialogues of any other person in Indian history as we have of the Buddha in the Tipiṭaka. And this superiority is not merely numerical. We have in front of us an immeasurable treasure of deep meaning. What a vast heritage! Thrilling and enlightening! Educating and enthusing!

And how do we respond? Except for a few, most Indians have retracted their senses to avoid being touched by that wisdom and compassion; have closed their eyes to avoid seeing him! We have closed the doors of our mind and heart to prevent the entry of even a speck of that Bodhi. We have turned our intelligence into barren sand so that its life flow should get lost before it reaches us!

Refuge in Knowledge

Those who don't thus recoil and say "Buddhaṃ Saraṇaṃ Gacchāmi," don't take refuge in a particular person or in the person named Siddhārtha Gotama. They take refuge in the supreme enlightenment attained by one's own efforts. They wish to seek guidance from that enlightenment and want to make it the foundation of their lives. Prof. Shanti Bhikshu Shastri conveys this succinctly and effectively in his modern Sanskrit epic poem "Budhavijayakavyam",[87] *"Buddham hi sharanam gatva te jnanam sharanam gatah."* They took refuge in the Buddha means they took refuge in that loftier knowledge.

"Buddhaṃ Saraṇaṃ Gacchāmi" means I take Refuge in Myself

If we want to acquire that wisdom, that superior knowledge, we must rid ourselves of our pettiness. Let us not draw back. Let us open our senses. Let us open our eyes and feast them on the Tathāgata. Let us create a little opening in our minds for his teaching. Let our mental landscape become verdant by the flow of his teaching. Let us say *Buddhaṃ Saraṇaṃ Gacchāmi.*

When we say that we don't get sullied or blackened or reduced. When we say that we embrace wisdom, we imbibe knowledge, we respond to the call of prudence, we respond to the call of life itself!

Let us also be mindful that the Tathāgata was not interested the chanting of this phrase like a mantra. He wanted us to commit to logical knowledge by this declaration.

The Buddha is not alien to us by any means. He is not our enemy. In reality, he is an external form of our own inner strengths; he is the essence of our entire being.

He is exactly what we will be if we blossom completely. Rather, we are his undeveloped precursor and he is our developed result! "Buddhaṃ Saraṇaṃ Gacchāmi" means not only "I take refuge in wisdom," it also means "I take refuge in myself." Therefore, this refuge is untainted by undue servility or helplessness. This refuge makes us familiar with ourselves, it creates self-confidence in us.

The Buddha is the compassionate heart of man. It is his discerning head. Refuge in the Buddha also means a proper balance in the cool shadow of compassion and the light of wisdom in our own personality!

Once while watching a seven year old girl saying "Buddhaṃ Saraṇaṃ Gacchāmi", I remembered my childhood and felt that if I had heard and understood this fine expression in childhood, I would have avoided so many potholes and rough patches on the road of my life's journey. When I utter this expression, I do so with a joy that I have crossed all obstacles. I have found my essence and am realizing the meaning of my existence.

3

To Gain Wisdom Your Own Experience Shows the Way; Not the Tradition

The Tathāgata assured us that every person in the world has the capacity to attain Bodhi. He exhorted us to make efforts to use this capacity. He discussed epistemological issues in simple and lucid language instead of using complicated and obtuse terms. But this doesn't mean that his was a lesser philosophy.

On the contrary, it is a historical fact that such original thought, which removed all artificial shackles from human mind and set it free, was very rare in ancient times. It was out of compassion for the common people that he used simple, lucid and understandable language.

We have seen earlier how through various experiments, through immense difficulties, using his sharp intelligence and perfecting his personality, Siddhārtha Gotama attained Bodhi and became a Buddha. In this chapter, we will look at him from an epistemological perspective.

To Say 'Saw' Only For That Which Was Actually Seen

His constant emphasis that one should not form an opinion hurriedly and impatiently without adequate basis placed the process of acquisition of knowledge on a superior ethical and scientific foundation. It also created harmonious communication and was beneficial to all. Here is a gist of the discourse from the Middle Discourses[88] that he gave while he was dwelling in Jetavana of Sāvatthi:

If a bhikkhu claims that he has done what had to be done (achieved the goal) and has become an arahata (a liberated being), don't accept or reject his claim. Ask him about the four aspects and see if he is endowed with the fourfold conduct described by the Tathāgata:

1. To say 'have seen' for what he has actually seen.
2. To say 'have heard' for what he has actually heard.
3. To say 'remembered' for what he has actually remembered.
4. To say 'understood' for what he has actually understood.

If you find this fourfold conduct in the bhikkhu who claims to have achieved his goal, you can assume that he has been liberated from all taints in regard to these conducts and you should accept his attainment.

Discussion

The tests that the Buddha gave to confirm the reality of knowledge are important from a philosophical and epistemological perspective (especially the source of knowledge). These tests can also be used by an ordinary person to avoid arguments and to live a happy life.

Say that you have seen something only if you have really seen it with your own eyes. Don't say "I have seen it," when you have only heard about it; say that you have heard it. If you are saying something based on your memory, say so. Don't say that you say so based on your understanding.

One who knows these boundaries in the field of knowledge becomes more honest and straightforward, more tolerant and humble. More importantly, he disentangles himself from the traps of ignorance and gets closer to real knowledge.

Ignorance is the Root of Downfall

The Buddha told the bhikkhus repeatedly that ignorance is responsible for various painful things; and wisdom is beneficial in various ways. Here is a summary of Discourse on Learning (Vijjā Sutta) in Itivuttaka of the Mixed Discourses (Khuddaka Nikāya).[89]

Ignorance is responsible for unwholesome and distressing things. It makes one shameless. It makes one irresponsible. Here or hereafter, defeats caused due to craving and greed, have their root in ignorance. One who is immoral, shameless and impudent commits immoral acts, which leads to his downfall. Therefore, remove craving, greed and ignorance; gain wisdom and avoid downfall.

In the very next sutta of Itivuttaka, the Buddha tells bhikkhus that lack of wisdom makes one suffer in this world and afterwards too. Those who cultivate wisdom become happy here and hereafter. He taught the Dhamma to the people who believe in life after death and those who didn't.

Gain or Loss of Wisdom is the Biggest Gain and the Biggest Loss

The Tathāgata once said,[90] "To lose near and dear ones is a small loss. But the loss of wisdom is a big loss. To increase the number of near and dear ones is a small gain. To cultivate wisdom is the big gain. Therefore, bhikkhus, you should vow to grow by cultivating wisdom."

He made similar observations about material luxuries and about prestige. Loss of material comforts or prestige is a minor loss. Loss of wisdom is a major loss. Getting more material comforts or fame is a minor gain. Getting more wisdom is a major gain.

To become an arahata, to become liberated wisdom is needed, along with morality and concentration. What is wisdom *(paññā, prajñā)*? It is the highest and best state of fully developed understanding.

The Buddha explained in various ways how to cultivate wisdom, how to gain knowledge, how to use intellect and how to preserve our freedom.

The Tathāgata Was Analytical

The Tathāgata would not make extreme comments based on insufficient information. He thought that casually forming and expressing a definitive opinion without taking into consideration all aspects is not right. He was a *Vibhajjavādin* (literally one who analyzes all aspects of situation) and didn't look at just one aspect. He followed the scientific doctrine of using reason and analysis to develop insight. Here is an instance from the Numerical Discourses:[91]

Once while the Buddha was dwelling at Jetavana in Sāvatthi, Sāriputta was approached by two bhikkhus, Samiddha and Mahākoṭṭhika. Sāriputta told them that there are three kinds of meditators (practitioners): liberated by conduct, liberated by understanding and liberated by faith. The three debated which one of the three is superior. Each one differed and put forth his own point of view. Sāriputta suggested that they seek the Buddha's opinion. Then the three of them went to the Buddha.

When Sāriputta briefed him about their debate, the Buddha commented, "Sāriputta, who among these is superior and who has progressed more cannot be decided by looking at just one aspect." He then explained that depending on how one looks at it, different persons would be seen as having progressed more.

Kālāmas Ask, Who is Right in the Commotion of So Many Philosophies?

The Buddha took a revolutionary stand for his time in the field of knowledge. We find it in Kesamutti Sutta of the Numerical Discourses.[92]

Once while travelling in Kosala, the Tathāgata was dwelling in the Kālāmas' town named Kesamutta along with a large retinue of bhikkhus. When the Kālāmas learned about his visit, they came to meet him. After suitable salutations, they sat to one side and said, "Venerable sir, many ascetics and holy men come to Kesamutta. They expound their teachings, and commend it. Also, they criticize the teachings of others, disrespect it and claim they are inferior. Other ascetics and holy men come and do the same: praising their teaching and condemning those of others. We become skeptical as to who among them speaks the truth and who is lying."

Your Own Experience is Important

The Buddha assured them, "Kālāmas, you are right in being skeptical. Doubt has arisen in your mind about that which should raise doubt.

"Kālāmas, do not accept anything based only on what you have heard.

Do not accept anything based on tradition.

Do not accept anything because someone says so.

Do not accept anything merely because it is in the scriptures.

Do not accept anything simply based on surmise (logic not backed by experience) or axiom *(Nyāya)*.

Do not accept anything based on external appearances.

Do not accept anything based on speculation (because it is in keeping with your beliefs and inclinations).

Do not accept anything because of the personality of the one who is saying it (or because it is a possibility).

Do not accept anything because the one who is proclaiming it is your teacher.

Kālāmas, when (after thorough investigation and reflection) based on your personal experience you find that these things are unwholesome, deficient, censured by wise people and when accepted cause suffering and harm; then Kālāmas, you should reject them."

Then the Buddha asked them whether craving, aversion and ignorance are beneficial or harmful.

The Kālāmas responded by saying, "Harmful, Venerable Sir".

The Buddha instructed them not to accept anything based on what they have heard, etc. He repeated it again the second and the third time.

Then he advised them, "Kālāmas, when (after thorough investigation and reflection, with reason) based on your personal experience you find that these things are wholesome, are blameless, are praised by wise people and when accepted are beneficial and conducive to happiness; then Kālāmas, you should not only accept them but also follow them in your life."

Then the Buddha asked them whether non-craving, non-aversion and non-ignorance are beneficial or harmful.

The Kālāmas responded by saying, "Beneficial, Venerable Sir".

The Buddha told them that he considered all these when he told them not to accept anything based on what they have heard, etc.

(Bhikkhu Bodhi, among the foremost Buddhist scholars of our time, warns us that this discourse is not intended as an endorsement for either radical skepticism or for the creation of unreasonable personal truth. As is clear from the above description the Buddha argued that the three unwholesome roots of craving, aversion and ignorance should be abandoned.)

Whether There Is Life After Death or Not, Ethical Conduct Helps

At the end of his discourse to Kālāmas, the Buddha told them that a noble disciple who abandons defilements such as craving, anger, etc. and cultivates goodwill, compassion, sympathetic joy, etc. is assured of four things:

1. If indeed there is life after death and fruit of sinful and wholesome actions, then he will go to heaven.
2. If there is no life after death and no fruit of sinful and wholesome actions, then in this very world and in this very body, having abandoned enmity, anger and misery, he will live a happy and peaceful life.
3. If the thought of harming others does harm others, then by not having such hateful thoughts, he remains untouched by suffering.
4. If the thought of harming others does not harm others, even then he remains unsullied in both ways (by not having hateful thoughts and seeing that the others are not harmed).

All the doubts of the Kālāmas were dispelled by this discourse and they were fully satisfied.

Discussion

Twenty-five centuries ago, the Buddha explained the importance of one's own experience in the field of knowledge.

By saying that no matter how revered the person or the scripture, one should not accept it merely out of devotion or reverence, he put forth a view that truly liberated human intellect and allowed human creativity to blossom.

The word that he uses to describe scriptures is *Piṭaka*. He didn't say don't believe in the Vedas, etc. of other traditions. He brings his own Dhamma also in the ambit of enquiry by saying don't believe it blindly.

He doesn't point a finger merely at teachers of other traditions and make them an object of investigation. It is noteworthy that he says, "Don't blindly believe the teachers of ascetics (Samaṇa teachers)." So as to leave no doubt whatsoever, he put himself in the ambit of enquiry with these candid words.

Our Misfortune: Accepting Manusmriti That Banned Scrutiny of Religions

On one hand, the Buddha destroyed all the obstacles that came in the way of advancement of human mind to the extent that he took care that even his personality or the Dhamma doesn't become a hindrance in freedom of thought.

On the other hand, Manusmriti, an influential religious scripture written about four hundred years after the Buddha, considered examination of religion sacrilege. Though brahminical, it said that brahmins too should be punished if they decide to scrutinize the scriptures. This rule of Manusmriti is a significant reason for the decline of Indian society. It is the misfortune of Indian society that, in spite of the munificent teaching of the Buddha, many Indians in the later centuries decided to follow the dark path of Manusmriti.

Walpola Rahula says about the Buddha's advice to the Kālāmas,[93] "The freedom of thought allowed by the Buddha is unheard of elsewhere in the history of religions."

Accepted Buddha Dhamma Due to the Influence of This Sutta

Renowned scholar monk Ven. Ananda Kausalyayan wrote in the preface of his translation of the Numerical Discourses (Aṅguttara Nikāya),[94] "Kālāma Sutta which is so momentous that not only in Buddhist literature but also in all literature of the world, it has come to be mankind's charter for freedom of thought."

Later while talking about his life he notes with gratitude, "The author is especially grateful to this (Kālāma) sutta because 35 years ago this was the discourse of the Buddha that played a significant role in my taking refuge in the triple gem (the Buddha, Dhamma, and Saṅgha).

Investigate the Merits-Demerits of the Buddha

He didn't make a just theoretical principle of his exhortation not to believe merely based on what one hears etc. and to evaluate others. He also taught with example the practical application of the principle. He said that even a Buddha's qualities should be confirmed by proper scrutiny. Vimaṃsaka Sutta[95] of the Middle Discourses is a veritable light house in the field of religious epistemology.

Once while he was dwelling in the Anāthapiṇḍika's monastery in Jetavana, he called bhikkhus and addressed them thus, "Bhikkhus, a bhikkhu who has the capacity to know the mind of another should examine whether the Tathāgata is a Sambuddha."

The bhikkhus asked him to clarify what he meant.

Examine in Various Ways

The Buddha clarified his earlier comment, "The bhikkhu responsible for examining the Buddha should do so in two aspects: what can be seen with eyes and what can be heard with ears. He should confirm that such unwholesome qualities that can be seen by eyes and heard by ears are not present in the Buddha."

The bhikkhu should also confirm that mixed states are not present in the Buddha.

Then the bhikkhu should further examine the Buddha and confirm that pure untainted states are present in him; and whether these pure states are present in him always or only for a short time (temporarily).

Then the bhikkhu should investigate whether, on acquiring name and fame, taints have arisen in the Buddha.

Then he should check whether he is fearless and yet restrained or is he restrained on account of fear.

Then the bhikkhu should examine whether the Buddha doesn't indulge in sensual pleasures because he is lust-free on account of having destroyed craving.

Thus having examined the Tathāgata, the bhikkhu would explain these qualities to others. Then others should question that bhikkhu, on what ground did he base his observations and the bhikkhu should explain in detail and should declare, "Whether the Tathāgata is dwelling in the community or dwelling alone; while others are well-behaved or not well-behaved; where some teach congregations; where some are entangled in worldly enticements and some are untainted by worldly things; he does not despise any of them on that account; neither when he is with the Saṅgha nor when he is alone."

Then the Tathāgata advised the bhikkhus, "Then bhikkhus should ask the Tathāgata himself whether such defiled states as can be seen by eyes and heard by ears are present in him or not."

Having confirmed that he has no defiled states and mixed states, he should be asked whether he has pure states. If he confirms that he follows the pure states, experiences the pure states and is endowed with these pure qualities, one should go to learn the Dhamma from him.

On going to such a teacher, as the disciple progresses, the teacher teaches him higher and higher Dhamma, ever more sublime, explaining (differentiation of) dark and bright things. As the disciple experiences those higher and higher more sublime states, through direct knowledge and finding fulfillment, he develops confidence in the teaching. He develops faith in the Tathāgata thus, "The Buddha is fully self-enlightened, his Dhamma is well explained and the Saṅgha walks on the right path."

This bhikkhu when asked by others about the Tathāgata is able to articulate his experiences well.

Faith Developed After Scrutiny Is Steadfast

Having thus given a sermon on how to investigate him, the Tathāgata added, "Bhikkhus, whose faith is certain, well rooted, established, in this manner and with these phrases and words; this is called faith well established, rooted in vision, immovable. It is unshaken by any ascetic or holy man or deity or Māra or

Brahmā or by anyone in the world. This is how, bhikkhus, the Tathāgata is investigated rightly and thus is the Dhamma in him well investigated."

Discussion

The word Tathāgata (literally, Thus Gone) is unbreakably connected to the actual state of things, the reality of objects, to the truth. The discourse above tells us how meaningfully this word is used for Gotama the Buddha. While seeking truth and knowing reality, great men too must annihilate ego and prestige to become humble. Of this, the Tathāgata presented an excellent ideal for the society through his own behavior.

A seeker of truth has to clear the cobwebs of conventional thoughts and undertake a free enquiry. Often, at such times, the prestige of the man in society becomes a defensive cover for him and then it doesn't allow his personality to be touched by any investigation.

The Tathāgata pushed aside this phenomenon deliberately and forcefully. He created an independent mindset in these bhikkhus by asking them to investigate the thoughts and conduct of the Tathāgata. He underscored the principle that no man is greater than truth. Needless to say, in doing so, he encouraged bhikkhus to rationally investigate others as well.

Dr Ambedkar emphasized this in his book *The Buddha and His Dhamma*. He wrote, "Principle must live by itself, and not by the authority of man… If principle needs the authority of man, it is no principle… If every time it becomes necessary to invoke the name of the founder to enforce the authority of Dhamma then it is no Dhamma."

The Buddha instructed the bhikkhus to examine whether the Tathāgata had any defilements. He also told them to check for mixed states as sometimes negative qualities overshadow positive ones and adversely affect character. He didn't stop by instructing them to check for absence of negative qualities but also told them to confirm the presence of positive qualities, pure states in the Tathāgata.

Just a Temporary Façade of Goodness?

The Buddha instructed the bhikkhus to check whether pure states, positive qualities existed for a long time or whether they were temporary. This is important to note in spiritual field.

Sometimes, a clever man puts up a good show in front of people and presents a façade of goodness. However in actual life, it is not a constant quality in him and it is not an integral part of his conduct. This pretense of goodness is done as a convenience, for prestige or to gain something. Therefore the investigator must be able to look beyond mere appearances.

An episode narrated in the Numerical Discourses[96] is particularly noteworthy here.

Once when the Tathāgata was dwelling in the Deer Park at Isipatana, some elders were conferring. A young bhikkhu named Citta kept interfering in the discussion. Then the Elder Mahākoṭṭhita requested him not to interfere and to say whatever he had to say after the discussion was over. Citta's friend didn't agree with the elder's request. He was then given this important advice: Some people are humble, restrained and quiet as long as they are with the Buddha or with somebody they revere. After they go away from the revered person, they do not remain restrained.

We can't say that the bull which is confined to its pen or tied down with a rope doesn't eat crops. Because if it is let loose, it will probably eat the crop. Similarly, some people were very humble in front of the Buddha.

Investigation of the Tathāgata should not be cursory. It should be thoughtful and thorough.

The Tathāgata had experienced human behavior in all its subtle forms as is clear from the sermon above.

Defilements Enter On Acquiring Prestige

Another facet of investigation that the Buddha highlighted is also very important. As long as someone is not famous and has no special prestige in society, one is humble and cooperative, but as soon as one becomes successful and famous, one starts to become rude, careless and arrogant. One's behavior becomes irresponsible and disdainful. This happens with many people and therefore this aspect should also be carefully seen while judging a person. It is necessary to see whether the person has carefully preserved his good qualities even after getting name and fame.

Fear Behind Good Conduct?

If someone behaves properly out of fear, then it cannot be said to be commendable. If someone behaves in a noble manner because of one's principles, because it has become one's nature; when there is no outer pressure, no threat or no enticement of some worldly or sensual pleasure; then one is really endowed with good conduct. This is another aspect that the Buddha highlighted.

Criticizing Others in Private

Criticizing others is a favorite pastime for some. Some say one thing in public and in private life behave contrary to their professed views. Therefore, if someone has good words for others in public and in private too displays no ill-will or antipathy, then that person passes the test laid down by the Tathāgata.

Does He Solemnly Declare It?

There is one more important tip for the investigator. One who claims to be a Tathāgata should solemnly affirm that he has no defiled states. This solemn affirmation is important.

Even in modern times, many things are formalized by taking an oath. An oath works in two ways. On one hand while taking an oath, one realizes again the burden of responsibility. On the other hand, people too keep an eye on him or her in view of the oath.

Thus the investigator, having judged the Teacher in various ways, should go to him for training in Dhamma. He should then follow, step by step, all the guidance of the Teacher for one's own liberation.

Faith is a Flower of Honesty on the Peduncle of Investigation

Towards the end of Vimaṃsaka Sutta, The Tathāgata makes a vital point. Often in his discourses, he emphasizes faith *(saddhā)*. In religious traditions, we can see that faith often makes the intellect blunt, curtails freedom and obstructs man's progress. Therefore, many may ask the question as to how to examine the faith so often praised by the Buddha.

The Tathāgata gives a clear answer about this. Faith praised by the Tathāgata is not blind faith. His faith is the confidence one has in the truth that is confirmed by strict investigation. Thus, faith is the fragrant flower of truthfulness that blossoms on the basis of investigation.

Not Custom or Baseless Faith, but the Path of Self-Experience

In Saṅgārava Sutta[97] of the Middle Discourses, we see some more aspects of the Tathāgata's view on knowledge.

Once the Buddha was dwelling in Kosala. A brahmin woman named Dhanañjāni from the Cañcalikappa town developed faith in the Buddha, Dhamma and Saṅgha. Once she was heard uttering praise of the Buddha, 'Salutations to the Blessed One, Liberated One, Perfectly Enlightened One'.

At that time, in that town lived a brahmin named Saṅgārava who had studied the three Vedas. On hearing Dhanañjāni's utterance, he said, "Woe to Dhanañjāni who is praising the shaven-head Samaṇa instead of brahmins."

Dhanañjāni informed him about the Buddha. She said, "You don't know the Tathāgata's virtues and his wisdom. If you come to know them, you will feel that it is not proper to abuse or censure him."

Then he asked her to let him know when the Tathāgata arrives in town. Later, when the Tathāgata arrived in town, Dhanañjāni informed Saṅgārava who then went to meet the Buddha.

Saṅgārava asked the Buddha, "There are some ascetics and holy men who claim to teach the essence of the righteous life after having reached the consummation and perfection of direct knowledge here and now. Where among them did he stand?"

The Buddha said, "Ascetics and holy men are of three types. Firstly, there are traditionalists who like the brahmins of three Vedas claim to teach on the basis of oral tradition. Secondly, there are some who speculate and investigate (not properly but) in ways that support their own faith. Finally, some eschew tradition and discover Dhamma with their own experience (with their own efforts). I belong to the third category."

Discussion

Among the three categories enumerated by the Buddha, the first takes scriptures as the source of knowledge. This group considers that only the traditional scriptures (such as Vedas) are the pure and ultimate truth.

The second group bases its analysis and inferences only on data that supports their faith.

The third group to which the Tathāgata belongs gives primacy to one's own experience based on sound investigation, objective observation and rational analysis.

Ashvaghosha (Aśvaghoṣa) Underscores the Tathāgata's View

In an episode in his epic "Buddhacarita"[98] Ashvaghosha presents the Tathāgata's view about developing wisdom.

After Siddhārtha left home and took robes, Suddhodana sent a priest and a minister to convince him to return home. The minister argued that there have been others in the past who were successful in high spiritual attainments while staying in the palace instead of staying in the jungle.

Siddhārtha's response is significant in the field of spiritual endeavor. "I do not form an opinion based on what other people say in the matters that confuse the world such as whether —'something exists,' or 'something doesn't exist'. I strive to know the reality and to come to a conclusion. It is not right for me to accept any view that arises out of doubt, which is unclear and contradictory. Which wise man will follow another's experience (*parapratyaya)* without due thought? It is like a blind following a blind in darkness."

One shouldn't accept someone else's views completely unquestioningly and blindly. One should use logic and clarify those with one's own experience. Ashvaghosha has put the Buddha's view properly. The Tathāgata felt that one should not accept something merely based on tradition, merely because it is accepted by one's sect or merely because a famous scholar has proposed it.

Kalidas (Kālidāsa) Mirrors Ashvaghosha

Many scholars have opined that the great poet Kalidas was influenced by Ashvaghosha. The view put forth by him above has been accepted by Kalidas along with the word *parapratyaya* (someone else's experience) and has been put forth in the field of poetry. In his play *Mālavikāgnimitra*[99] he writes in a verse, "All that is old is gold and new poetry is bad; is not true. Discerning people examine both and accept one. An idiot, on the other hand, uses *parapratyaya* (another's experience) to form his opinion."

Saṅgārava's Anger is Not Surprising

It is not surprising that Saṅgārava became angry and started censuring Dhanañjāni because she saluted the Buddha. It was a deep rooted belief in the mind of many that only brahmins, even unwise ones, are worthy of salutations and others, however wise and erudite, are not. Shaven-head and *samaṇaka* (a pejorative form of Samaṇa, ascetic) were used with disdain by Saṅgārava.

He does go to meet the Tathāgata but not out of curiosity and not with humility but with a desire to defeat and revile him.

Truth is Protected by Humility, Not by Obstinacy

Once the Tathāgata was dwelling in the sāla (*shorea robusta*) woods named Gods' Grove to the north of the town Opāsāda.[100] Pasenadi had given the town as gift to a brahmin named Caṅki. When the brahmins in the town came to know about the Buddha staying nearby, they went to meet him. Caṅki also prepared to go with them.

At that time about five hundred brahmins from various other places were visiting Opāsāda. When they heard that Caṅki was going to call on Recluse Gotama, they went to him and requested him not to go to Gotama. They tried to convince him that such a thing would undermine his prestige. But Caṅki didn't listen to them. He told them that it was proper and fitting that he goes to Recluse Gotama.

Caṅki went to the Tathāgata with a big retinue of brahmins. After greeting them he sat to one side. At that time the Buddha was discussing Dhamma with elderly brahmins. A sixteen year old brahmin named Kāpaṭika was also present in the assembly. He had studied three Vedas. He kept interrupting the discussion that the elders were having. The Tathāgata told him not to do so and to wait till they had finished discussion.

Then Caṅki told the Buddha, "Let not Recluse Gotama stop Kāpaṭika brahmin. He is high born, erudite and a scholar. He speaks sage words. He is capable of having an argument with you."

Then the Buddha thought that perhaps Kāpaṭika wants to talk about the three Vedas; and therefore the brahmins are promoting him. Kāpaṭika decided in his mind that he would ask a question when Recluse Gotama turned his attention to me. The Buddha understood what was in Kāpaṭika's mind and turned to him.

Kāpaṭika said, "Sir Gotama, the Vedas are the scriptures of brahmins that have come from ancient times and they have a firm faith that 'This is the only truth, all else is false.'"

To this the Buddha replied, "In this assembly, is there a single brahmin who can say that 'I know this. I understand this. This is the only truth. All else is false?'"

The assembly answered in the negative.

The Buddha's further questioned, "Did even the brahmins of ancient times speak from their own experience?"

Again the assembly answered in the negative. Then the Buddha said that it was like a line of brahmins in which those ahead don't see, those in the middle don't see and those in the back also don't see. Thus the faith of the brahmins in Vedas is without foundation.

Kāpaṭika responded, "They don't say this based on faith but based on tradition."

The Buddha then pointed out the contradiction in his assertion that earlier Kāpaṭika talked about faith and now he talked about tradition.

Then the Buddha explained to him the two consequences of faith. Even if one has high faith in something, that thing can be hollow, low and false. On the other hand, even if one doesn't have faith in something, it can be real, truthful and objective. Similarly, there can be two consequences for inclination, tradition, reasoning and contemplation.

Then he said to Kāpaṭika, "Friend, a wise man who wants to protect truth should not hold extreme views such as 'This is the only truth and all else is false.'"

In response to the question as to how to abide in truth, he explained, "When someone has faith, he should not hold the extreme view that this is the only truth and all else is false." He explained similarly about inclination, tradition, reasoning and contemplation.

The Buddha explained that though this extreme view helps in protecting truth, it doesn't help in understanding the truth. When he was asked as to how to understand the truth, he answered:

When a bhikkhu lives in a town or a city, a layman goes to him and checks him for craving, aversion and ignorance. He checks whether the bhikkhu, out of greed, says that he understands something when he doesn't; whether the bhikkhu, out of greed, says that he has seen something when he hasn't and whether he gives sermons that bring harm and suffering to people. When the layman finds that the bhikkhu does no such thing and that he is without greed in mind, speech and action, he also tests him for aversion and ignorance. When the bhikkhu passes the tests, the layman develops faith in him.

The layman then attends on the bhikkhu; listens to his teaching; and behaves according to his teaching; investigates things that he has put into action; such things then become suitable for meditative absorption; this creates inclination in him; due to inclination he develops one after the other, enthusiasm, advancement, courage and then he experiences the ultimate truth in this very body. With his wisdom he penetrates to the deepest truth. Thus he understands truth.

The Buddha further added that understanding the truth doesn't mean attaining the truth. Then he was asked how to attain the truth.

Then he said: One attains truth when one practices, cultivates and abundantly develops these same qualities as explained above.

When asked what leads to abundant development, the Buddha said, "It was due to effort. Effort increases due to advancement, advancement due to enthusiasm, enthusiasm due to inclination, inclination due to contemplation, contemplation due to investigation, investigation of meaning due to righteous conduct, righteous conduct due to listening to Dhamma, listening to Dhamma due to attentiveness, attentiveness due to attending on the bhikkhu, attending on the bhikkhu due to associating with him and association due to faith.

Kāpaṭika was satisfied after listening to the Buddha's explanation. He said to the Buddha, "Gotama, in the past we used to think 'How can these lowly, dark, created from the feet of Brahmā, shaven-headed ascetics (Samaṇas) have any understanding of Dhamma?'

"But today Gotama, you have inspired in my mind affection, joy and respect for Samaṇas." And he requested the Tathāgata to accept him as a disciple.

Discussion

Other brahmins opposed Caṅki when he decided to call on the Buddha. We see such instances elsewhere too in Tipiṭaka.

This had its root in the belief of superiority of brahmins. For a brahmin to call on a non-brahmin was disgraceful not only for that brahmin but also for the entire caste, it was felt. Therefore, they tried to curtail the individual freedom of a brahmin for the prestige of the caste.

Caṅki's Conduct Questionable

Caṅki must be commended for not giving into the pressure by the other brahmins and for explaining to them why it is he who should go to the Buddha and not the other way round. We should, however, examine his conduct.

When Kāpaṭika was interfering again and again in the conversation that the Buddha was having with elders, Caṅki stood up for him and though the Buddha had politely asked Kāpaṭika not to interfere, he asked the Buddha to let Kāpaṭika speak. His motive doesn't seem entirely pure. One possibility is that he had received a town in gift from King Pasenadi. Thus he was enjoying material comforts due to royal patronage. He knew that the king whose handouts he was enjoying was a devoted disciple of the Buddha. It is possible that this played a part in Caṅki's decision to call on the Buddha.

It is not a pleasant thought that Caṅki had this ulterior motive. But had he allowed Kāpaṭika to wait as per the Buddha's request, his conduct would have been blameless.

Clever Move to Promote Kāpaṭika

When the sixteen year old Kāpaṭika was interfering in the Buddha's discussions, he doesn't seem to be doing so out of his own initiative. The Tathāgata rightly guessed that he was promoted and incited by the brahmins. The move was planned by the elderly brahmins. If Samaṇa Gotama couldn't answer a teenage boy, it would certainly be humiliating for him.

On the other hand, if he does win the argument, it would be against a teenage boy and thus there would be no blot on the superiority of the brahmins or undue gain in prestige of Gotama. This was probably the thinking behind the move.

The scholarship of the brahmins was based on Vedas. They would corner others by asking questions about the Vedas. Kāpaṭika forcefully put forth the faith they had in Vedas. This theory that Vedas are all that is true and all else is false has hindered scientific progress and obstructed the flow of progress. Many scholars from Vedic tradition claim "Vedas is the last word." A pet principle of the Vedics is that the human intellect cannot examine the Vedas. Kāpaṭika was voicing this opinion of the Vedic tradition.

Humble Faith Can Protect

When the Tathāgata asks the assembly if they talk from their own experience, it is clear that he considers experience greater than faith. Once he explains this, Kāpaṭika turns to tradition.

Any neutral reasonable man would agree that the Tathāgata's explanation regarding faith, tradition, etc. was correct. No one can challenge his assertion that something that we have faith in may turn out to be false and something that we don't have faith in may turn out to be true. He also implied that the faith can indeed be true.

One should state "This is my faith." not arrogantly but with humility. This stand doesn't compromise truth but expresses one's understanding of truth. It can be true. It can be false. As long as one doesn't become adamant and inflexible about his faith, one *is* a wayfarer on the path of truth. From protecting the truth to understanding the truth to attaining the truth, the various stages that the Tathāgata explained tell us about the hard work that is needed on the path of acquisition of knowledge and wisdom.

The Tathāgata's stand on Vedas is reasonable. Whether he knew a particular verse in Vedas and whether he knew the meaning of that verse is irrelevant. Attempting to judge him on this question (that can be answered only with a speculation without any foundation) raised by conceited people such as Ketkar who say,[101] *"The Buddha's view on Vedas: The Buddha was ambivalent about the Vedas. There is no evidence to show that he knew what the contents of the Vedas. It is doubtful whether he knew Sanskrit. Lack of scholarship could also be the reason why Gotama didn't oppose the Vedas."*

It is clear from the Tathāgata's interaction with Kāpaṭika that he opposed both the Vedas and the Vedic tradition. One doesn't need knowledge of Vedas or Sanskrit to decide whether one should chart one's own path to the truth using discretion and experience or to depend totally and blindly on the Vedas.

At no point in the Tipiṭaka or any other literature is there any direct or indirect accusation against the Tathāgata that he didn't know either Vedas or Sanskrit. In fact, there are suttas where the Tathāgata talks about the various sages of Vedic tradition and also tells brahmins the good qualities about their own tradition.

The issue here is one of principle. It is not necessary that a person knows a particular language to take a stand on an epistemological issue, on issues related to how to acquire knowledge. One, who takes a stand about scientific approach to knowledge based on experience, doesn't need to know all the languages of the world and doesn't have to read all the literature in the world.

I am not saying that the Tathāgata had no knowledge of Vedas or the Vedic tradition. He had enough knowledge of the Vedas and Vedic tradition to hold his own in discussions with erudite brahmins of the Vedic tradition. It is a tragedy that some scholars (as noted above) of the Vedic tradition have no awareness that there could be higher knowledge outside of Sanskrit literature and Vedas.

Kāpaṭika Threw Away the Yoke of Brahminism

At the end of his discussion, Kāpaṭika liberated himself without any hesitation from the yoke of Brahminism and declared that he was satisfied. He also added openly how earlier he used to look upon Samaṇas with disdain. He rid himself of the false conceit that no one other than brahmins can know Dhamma or have the capacity to understand Dhamma.

But it is regrettable for India that even after twenty-five centuries, people like Ketkar couldn't rid themselves of the bias.

Tevijja Brahmins and the Path to the Brahmā That They Have Not Seen

Tevijja means knowers of three-fold knowledge. *Rigveda, Yajurveda* and *Sāmveda* are called three-fold knowledge *(trividyā)*. Thus *Tevijja* are masters of the three Vedas. Tevijja Sutta[102] of the Long Discourses contains a discussion of the Buddha with Tevijja Brahmins to examine their knowledge.

There was a town named Manasākaṭa in Kosala. Once the Tathāgata was dwelling with many bhikkhus in a mango grove on the bank of the Aciravati river to the north of the town.

At that time, there were many brahmins in Manasākaṭa who were wealthy and had gained name and fame for their erudition. These included Caṅki, Todeyya, Pokkharasāti, Jāṇussoṇi, Tārukkha, etc.

Once two brahmins named Vāseṭṭha and Bhāradvāja started a discussion while they were taking a leisurely walk. They were talking about a path leading to the *brahmā* realm. Vāseṭṭha informed Bhāradvāja that Pokkharasāti had told him that such and such path would take a person directly to the brahmā realm if he were to commit a particular deed. Bhāradvāja said that Tarukkha had made exactly the same claim to him about another path. Both were not able to convince the other.

Then Vāseṭṭha suggested that they go to Recluse Gotama. He enumerated various epithets that were used for the Buddha to tell Bhāradvāja about his superlative reputation. He said he would accept whatever Gotama would say about their argument. Bhāradvāja agreed.

Then both of them went to the Buddha and after proper salutations sat down to one side. Addressing him as "Bho Gotama," Vāseṭṭha told him about their argument. The Buddha repeated what Vāseṭṭha had said to make sure that the argument was clear. He also asked specifically about their differences and about the disparities in their views.

Then Vāseṭṭha put forth his view that, though the opinions of various texts (Aitareya, Taittiriya, Chandoka, Rigved) about what was the way and what was not the way were different, they all lead to the brahmā realm. Just as a town has several approach roads that all lead to the same town, the paths of various brahmins all lead to the brahmā realm, Vāseṭṭha claimed.

Thrice the Buddha asked him, "You say 'lead to brahmā realm'?" and thrice Vāseṭṭha answered in the affirmative. Thus having again confirmed his stand, the Tathāgata asked him, "Is there any one among the Tevijja Brahmins who has seen the brahmā with his own eyes?" Vāseṭṭha answered in the negative.

Then the Tathāgata asked him whether any one of the teachers or the teachers' teachers or anyone of the past seven generations had seen brahmā with his own eyes. Again Vāseṭṭha answered in the negative.

Then he said to Vāseṭṭha, "Ancient sages, composers of the Vedic verses such as Atthaka, Vāmaka, Vāmadeva, Vessāmitta, Yamatagni, Aṅgirasa, Bhāradvāja, Vāseṭṭha, Kassapa, and Bhugu were the ancestors of the Tevijja brahmins. Tevijjas of today repeat the chants that were chanted by these ancestors. They chant what the ancestors chanted. They claim what the ancestors claimed. Vāseṭṭha, do even these ancestors claim to have seen the brahmā, whom he lives with and where he stays?"

Vāseṭṭha again said, "No."

Then the Tathāgata pointed out the disparities in the claims of Vāseṭṭha: None of those associated with the Tevijjas claim to have seen the brahmā or have gone to the brahmā realm and even then they all claim to know the direct path to the brahmā realm. They claim to show the path to that which they have not seen and not known. Indicating the inconsistency, the Tathāgata asked him, "Vāseṭṭha, in this situation don't you agree that the claims of Tevijjas are dishonest?"

Vāseṭṭha accepted that the claims were truly dishonest.

After this discussion, the Buddha gave many examples to point out the discrepancy in Tevijja's claims.

It is like a chain of blind men: those in front didn't see, those in the middle didn't see and those at the back didn't see. Tevijja's claim that they showed the path to the brahmā realm was similarly hollow and base.

The Buddha said, "Tevijja Brahmins worship the sun and the moon, praise and salute them with folded hands and turn around in circle. Do the Tevijjas see the sun and the moon?"

Vāseṭṭha said, "Yes."

Can Tevijjas show the path to the sun and the moon?"

Vāseṭṭha said, "No."

The Buddha responded, "Tevijjas cannot show the path to the sun and the moon that they see with their own eyes. Then isn't it an unfair claim of the Tevijjas that they can show the path to the brahmā realm when none of them or anyone associated with them have seen the brahmā?"

Vāseṭṭha agreed that it was an unfair claim.

The Buddha then turned to another example.

A man claims to seek a beautiful courtesan. When asked whether he knows the identity, the family or the clan of the courtesan, he says, no. When asked whether she is tall or short or of medium height he says, he doesn't know. When asked if she is dark or fair, he says, he doesn't know. When asked where she lives, he says, he doesn't know. To the question "Do you seek and desire the beautiful woman about whom you know nothing?" he answers, yes.

Vāseṭṭha agreed that the claim of the Tevijjas is as baseless as that of the man who seeks the beautiful woman he knows nothing about.

On a highway, a man constructs a great staircase to ascend to a palace. On asking whether he knows where is the palace, how tall is it, he says, he doesn't know. But to the question whether he is constructing a staircase to the palace he says, yes.

Again Vāseṭṭha agreed that just like this man, the claim of the Tevijjas is baseless.

The river Aciravati has a flood and is flowing full to the brim. Even a crow sitting on the bank can easily drink water from it. Then a man who desires to cross over to the other side of the river stands on this side and prays hard, "O yonder shore, please come to this side." He requests, pleads and prays.

The Buddha asked, “Vāseṭṭha, will the yonder shore come to this shore due to such requests, pleadings and prayers?”

Vāseṭṭha said, no.

Then the Buddha said “Just like this man, if the brahmins don’t reject the path of vice and don’t accept the path of virtue, it is not possible that the prayers to Indra, Soma, Varuṇa, Ishāna, Prajāpati, Brahmā, Mahiddhi and Yama will take the Tevijjas to the realm of brahmā after their deaths.”

If the river Aciravati is flooded, flowing full to the brim and a man wished to cross it. Then while he is still on this side of the river, if someone ties his hands behind with a strong chain, will he be able to cross over to the other shore while thus shackled?

Vāseṭṭha answers, no.

Then the Buddha compared this man with the Tevijja Brahmins. In the noble discipline of the Buddha Dhamma, the five sensual pleasures enjoyed through the contact of their subjects with the eye, ear, tongue, nose and skin are called the shackles. The Tathāgata then told Vāseṭṭha that if Tevijja Brahmins are thus enthralled by the sensual pleasures, there is no possibility of them going to the brahmā realm.

The Buddha asked, “Will a man lying with his face covered by a blanket on the bank of the river Aciravati that is flowing full to the brim be able to cross to the other bank?”

Vāseṭṭha replied in the negative.

Then the Buddha compared this man with the Tevijja Brahmins. In the noble discipline of the Buddha Dhamma, the five hindrances are like the blanket covering the face. The five hindrances or blankets are craving for sensual pleasures, aversion, sloth and torpor, agitation and regret, and doubt. If the Tevijjas are covered by these blankets, they will not be able to go to the brahmā realm.

The Buddha asked, “When the Tevijjas describe the brahmā, do they describe him as covetous, vile, hateful, tainted and undisciplined or non-covetous, full of goodwill?”

Vāseṭṭha answered, non-covetous, with goodwill, without hatred, pure and disciplined.

Then the Buddha asked, “Vāseṭṭha whether he thinks that the Tevijjas are covetous or non-covetous.

Vāseṭṭha answered that the Tevijjas are covetous and agreed that they can't be one with the Brahmā who is non-covetous.

The Tathāgata said, "The Tevijjas have lost their way. They have gone astray. They are swimming where there is no water. Therefore, it can be said that their knowledge of the three Vedas is barren."

Then Vāseṭṭha replied, "I have heard that Samaṇa Gotama knows the way to the brahmā realm."

Then the Buddha asked him, "Is Manasākaṭa close by or far away?"

"Close by."

"Will a man born and raised in Manasākaṭa take a long time to show the way to Manasākaṭa?"

"No."

"It is possible, Vāseṭṭha, that that man may take time to show the way to Manasākaṭa but it won't take long for the Tathāgata to show the way to the brahmā realm."

Then Vāseṭṭha requested him to show the way to the brahmā realm for the welfare of the brahmins.

The Buddha asked him to listen attentively and gave a description of the virtues present in the Buddha, especially the four qualities of goodwill, compassion, sympathetic joy and equanimity that lead to a mind free of any enmity.

Then he asked Vāseṭṭha whether a bhikkhu possessed of such qualities was covetous or non-covetous.

Vāseṭṭha answered, "Non-covetous" and agreed to the Buddha's assertion that a non-covetous bhikkhu will go the realm of the brahmā who is non-covetous.

Finally, Vāseṭṭha and Bhāradvāja requested the Buddha to accept them as his disciples.

Discussion

When Vāseṭṭha and Bhāradvāja go to the Buddha to seek his opinion, the Buddha repeats what Vāseṭṭha had asked him. Through repeated questioning he understands the exact nature of their doubt. This is not a minor detail in narration but a very significant aspect of the process of acquisition of knowledge and wisdom.

We often see that some people don't fully listen to what is being said or don't read carefully what is being stated. They start making statements based on partial hearing or reading, which create confusion.

The habit of the Tathāgata to first understand carefully what is being stated makes the discussion disciplined.

Questions of Scientific Enquiry

The Buddha asked Vāseṭṭha several questions that lead to Vāseṭṭha accepting that the Tevijjas had not seen brahmā while they claimed to show the path to his realm. The Tathāgata gave importance to one's own experience. He cautioned against flights of fancy. His questions to Vāseṭṭha followed the rational process of scientific enquiry.

The Tathāgata's Use of Parables

To show the discrepancy in the claim of the Tevijjas, the Tathāgata used several parables. All these parables are very effective. They are different from each other and not mere repetitions of the same parable.

Believing something that has come down from generations without any basis in experience, he likened to a line of blind men.

The parable of the sun and the moon shows how if Tevijjas cannot show the way to something that they can see, they cannot show the way to something of which they have no knowledge.

The courtesan's parable shows how the desire to attain something that one has no knowledge about is useless.

The parable of the staircase to the palace goes a step further and shows that striving for something one has no knowledge about is futile.

The parable of the prayer to the far shore is different from the above. One may have a high aim, a great goal. But if one merely prays to Indra and other gods for the goal to be fulfilled, it is futile. One has to make efforts in the form of an upright conduct to get there.

Another and subtler aspect of the same principle is brought to light in the parable of the man in the bondage of chains. Just as prayers won't be effective, efforts will lead nowhere if one is shackled by sensual pleasures. Similar is the case of one who is obstructed by the five hindrances of mental defilements.

If the brahmā realm is really considered to be the symbol of highest achievement, then it cannot be attained by one who is covetous and hateful. It can be achieved only by one who has removed all enmity from the mind through the practice of goodwill, compassion, etc.

Whether to call that highest goal the brahmā realm or not is not relevant here. What is relevant is that this high goal cannot be achieved with a mind that is defiled but can only be attained by a mind that is free of mental impurities. The Tathāgata explained that the highest goal of human life could not be achieved by Tevijjas through various prayers and rituals unless their mental impurities are eradicated.

We can say that the Tathāgata's stand was based on modern parameters of enquiry. This shows that the criticism by Marathi Dnyanakosh[103] that the Buddha spoke out of spite for brahmins is itself indicative of their prejudice against the Buddha.

The Tathāgata Doesn't Get Upset by Criticism

Brahmajāla Sutta[104] of the Long Discourses throws light on the Buddha's wisdom.

Once the Buddha was travelling with a retinue of five hundred bhikkhus on the road between Rajgir and Nalanda. At that time an ascetic named Suppiya was walking on the same road behind the Saṅgha with his disciple Brahmadatta. Suppiya was criticizing the Buddha, Dhamma and Saṅgha in various ways and Brahmadatta was praising the triple gem in various ways.

The Buddha and his Saṅgha stopped at a grove named Ambalaṭṭhikā to rest for the night. Suppiya and Brahmadatta also stopped there for the night. In the night the argument between them continued in the same vain. When the night was over, the bhikkhus started discussing the conversation they had overheard between the two. Then the Tathāgata asked them what they were talking about. The bhikkhus told him about Suppiya's criticism.

The Tathāgata said, "Bhikkhus, if someone criticizes me or the Dhamma or the Saṅgha, you should not become angry or dejected. Doing this will harm you. Bhikkhus, if someone criticizes me or the Dhamma or the Saṅgha, will be you become angry or dejected? Will you harm yourself thus by becoming angry or dejected? Will you examine whether their criticism has any truth in it or not?"

The bhikkhus said that they will not get angry and harm themselves.

The Buddha said, "Bhikkhus, when someone criticizes you, you should find out if there is any truth in the accusation. The criticism should be examined and one should look inside to see if it is applicable to one. Bhikkhus, if someone praises me or the Dhamma or the Saṅgha, you should not become happy, delighted and joyous. If you do so, you may harm yourself. When someone praises one, one should examine it to see if there is any truth in it. Find out the reality. You should look at yourself to see if the praise is based on reality."

Discussion
Criticism is an Opportunity for Introspection

This incidence shows how the Tathāgata was able to look at himself, objectively and to evaluate himself objectively. He was emphatic that bhikkhus should examine blame and praise without bias. This shows that he was honest about opening himself to examination.

In practice, we often lose balance in the face of criticism. We become angry. If someone criticizes the critic, we feel good. Some people consider as enemies not only those who disparage them but also those who make factual critical comments. They even become violent in response to criticism. This includes not only lay people but also those who claim to be saints and spiritual teachers. They are intolerant and yet preach tolerance.

The Buddha looked at criticism constructively. He considered criticism as an opportunity to look at oneself and to correct oneself if needed. He didn't want his followers to blindly believe him to be perfect. He wanted them to investigate and then accept or reject something on merit.

Matriceta (Mātṛceṭa) describes this aspect of the Buddha thus:[105]

> *You are the benevolent friend of those who wish to harm you.*
> *You try to find good qualities in those who constantly seek to find faults in you.*
> *In response to poisonous and scorching invitations, you go with compassion and cool of the deathless.*

Don't Get Carried Away by Praise

What is true of censure is also true of praise. Rather than getting elated by praise, he wanted us to check whether the praise is based on reality. He himself followed the path of truth. And he taught his followers to get as close to the truth as possible in the journey of life. He showed with his own example that one who wants to investigate truth should not be afraid to apply stringent criteria to oneself. The incident narrated above was not the only one of its kind where the Buddha invites unbiased examination.

Among the incidents that show a humble objectivity of looking at criticism was an integral part of his personality, Sampadāniya Sutta[106] (*sampadāniya* means Faith that Satisfies) in the Long Discourses describes one such episode.

Once the Tathāgata was dwelling in the Pāvārika mango grove near Nalanda. Then Ven Sāriputta came, saluted him and sat to one side. He declared, "Venerable sir, I am happy because there has never been, there is none and there will be no ascetic or holy man who is superior to the Tathāgata in the field of enlightenment."

On listening to Sāriputta, the Buddha commented, "Sāriputta, your words are grand and bold. You have roared a lion's roar.

Sāriputta, have you with your own mind known the morality, wisdom, conduct and liberation of the Sambuddhas of the past?"

Sāriputta answered, no.

Then the Tathāgata asked him the same question about present and future Sambuddhas.

Sāriputta again answered, no.

Then the Buddha said, "Sāriputta, how can you make such a bold statement though you don't know with your own mind the past, the present and the future Buddhas?"

Then Sāriputta enumerated several qualities of the Buddha. He sought and got the Buddha's agreement that his assessment was objective.

Then Udāyī who was present there exclaimed, "Venerable sir, it is a surprise. The Tathāgata's non-greed, contentment and purity of mind are miraculous. He doesn't show himself off though he has so much ability and great experience. If someone else had even one of the qualities, he would have not tired of advertising himself."

Sāriputta seconded Udāyī's assertion. Then the Tathāgata asked Sāriputta to give a Dhamma talk such that if someone has doubts about the Buddha, the same will be removed. Thus Sāriputta expressed his happiness about the Tathāgata. Therefore, it is called the Faith that Satisfies.

Just as the Buddha questioned the bhikkhus who were upset with the criticism from Suppiya, he also quizzed Sāriputta over the praise Sāriputta heaped on him. He was untouched by praise and censure.

If a common man cultivates even a fraction of this quality, he or she would live a far more balanced life. Udāyī's assessment of his character is also significant. In spite of his great erudition, the Buddha didn't advertise it or was conceited about it. On the other hand, he also didn't show false humility and deny his knowledge.

The Buddha successfully maintained that fine balance. He was objective about his great knowledge and distributed wisdom freely and openly for forty-five years. Just as a bud blossoms into a flower ever so imperceptibly, even today his eternal teaching leads to blossoming of the heart of millions of people and become fragrant with the wisdom.

Flexibility of Stance

The Buddha was not adamant or rigid; he was willing to make changes in his stance. If he found that a decision taken under certain circumstances was not applicable in other circumstances he was willing to change it. He had done this on several occasions. This flexibility is seen in Tikanipāta[107] of the Graded Discourses.

Once the Buddha was dwelling on the Vulture Peak near Rajgir. At that time, an ascetic named Sarabha had just left the Saṅgha. In an assembly in Rajgir, he claimed that he had left the Dhamma and Discipline of the Buddha after knowing it well. Some bhikkhus reported this to the Buddha.

At that time Sarabha was staying on the bank of the Sippinikā river. On the request of the bhikkhus, the Tathāgata went to meet Sarabha. He asked Sarabha whether he had indeed said what he had heard. Sarabha kept quiet. Again the Buddha asked him the same question and again Sarabha kept quiet.

Then the Buddha asked him, "Tell me, Sarabha, have you understood the Dhamma of the Sākyan Samaṇas. If there is deficiency in what you say, I will clarify. If what you say is correct and indeed there is lacuna in the teaching, I will accept it."

Thrice the Buddha asked the question and thrice Sarabha kept quiet. Other ascetics also requested Sarabha to speak up, but he sat there quiet with his head hanging.

Discussion

Willing to Clarify

If Sarabha had misunderstood his teaching, the Buddha was willing to clarify the teaching and remove his misunderstanding. On the other hand, if Sarabha had a valid objection to the teaching, the Tathāgata was willing to concede it. This means that the Tathāgata was open to correction if there was a valid suggestion. Sarabha, however, did not open his mouth.

This is what happens often. Some people indulge in backbiting, spread rumors, lie and create wrong impression in the minds of people. But these same people when confronted and asked to give evidence for their statements don't do so. When confronted in person, they keep quiet or run away.

Sarabha was one such person. More important here is the Tathāgata's humility, openness and flexibility. Some people stick to their false opinions out of egotism even though they realize that their position is untenable. When this happens in the field of knowledge, it harms the progress of human society. It is yet another big gift of the Buddha to the field of knowledge that he didn't allow such egotism to develop in his case. An opinion, if it is to be called scientific, should always be open to correction when any authentic contrary evidence comes to light.

Willing to Accept if Satisfactory

The Buddha was skilled in explaining this view to others and to convince them. However, he never misused this skill to encroach on the freedom of others. In this regard, his discussion with Vappa[108] is illuminating. The Tathāgata told Vappa: If you find what I say acceptable, second it; if you find it objectionable, object to it; and if you don't understand what I say, ask me and I will clarify it.

Last Sermon

From the time of his enlightenment, the Buddha travelled incessantly to spread Dhamma for the welfare of the people. He kept this commitment till the end of his life. How steadfast he was in his commitment can be seen in the following incident from his life given in Mahāparinibbāna Sutta in the Long Discourses.[109]

At that time an ascetic named Subhadda was living in Kusinārā. He heard that the Buddha is going to breathe his last that night. He had heard that it was rare for a Buddha to arise. He thought that he would seek guidance from the Buddha in person and met Ānanda to express his wish.

Ānanda told him, "The Tathāgata is tired. Do not trouble him."

Twice Subhadda made the request. Twice Ānanda declined.

Subhadda requested for the third time and again Ānanda refused.

The Tathāgata heard their conversation. He called Ānanda over and instructed him, "Do not stop Subhadda. Whatever he asks, will be for the sake of knowledge and not with the intention to trouble me. He will quickly grasp whatever explanation I give."

So Ānanda allowed Subhadda to meet the Buddha. Subhadda approached the Buddha and sat down to one side after salutations. He then asked the Buddha questions about the knowledge of other teachers of that time—Pūraṇa Kassapa, Makkhali Gosāla, Ajita Kesakambala, Pakudha Kaccāna, Sañjaya Velaṭṭhiputta and Nigaṇṭṭha Nāṭaputta.

But the Buddha advised him to keep the topic aside and told him to be attentive as he was going to teach Dhamma to him. He taught Subhadda the Noble Eightfold Path. Subhadda was satisfied. He requested to be accepted in the Saṅgha. The Buddha told him that ascetics from other traditions had to wait for four months before admission to the Saṅgha. Subhadda replied that he was willing to wait for four years.

Seeing his earnest wish, the Buddha asked Ānanda to prepare for Subhadda's ordination. Subhadda was gratified to receive ordination at the hand of the Buddha. He turned out to be the last disciple to receive teaching from the Buddha himself. Later he became an arahata.

After explaining Dhamma to Subhadda, the Tathāgata called Ānanda and told him, "Ānanda, it is possible that when I am no more, you will feel that now you are without your Teacher. But Ānanda, you should not think thus. I have taught Dhamma and Discipline. In my absence this Dhamma and Discipline will be your Teacher."

Then the Tathāgata gave important advice to Ānanda.

Afterwards, he called the bhikkhus and asked them, "Bhikkhus, if any one of has any doubts or questions about the Buddha, Dhamma or Saṅgha, feel free to ask. You should not later regret that I had some question and I didn't ask the Buddha when I had the opportunity."

The bhikkhus were silent. For the second time, for the third time the Buddha asked the same question and each time the bhikkhus remained silent.

Then the Buddha suggested to them, “If anyone is quiet out of respect to the Teacher, let him tell another bhikkhu and let that bhikkhu then ask the question to me.”

The bhikkhus continued to be quiet. Ānanda expressed satisfaction that they had no doubts. In his last moments, the Saṅgha in front of him didn’t have any doubts. He said that even the most junior among the bhikkhus was a stream enterer and on the way to liberation. Thus he knew that none of them had any doubts.

Lastly, the Tathāgata said to the bhikkhus, “Look, bhikkhus, I am exhorting you. All compound things are impermanent. Don’t be heedless and achieve (the goal).”

These were the Tathāgata’s last words.

Discussion

Even the Last Moments Were Reassuring and Comforting

The last episode of his life shows that just as his life was complete, the end was equally superior. The last moments of his life were reassuring and comforting. Many of us often talk about commitment to do something all through the life, to the end of the life. Often this is just a poetic imagination. Most of it is an exaggeration and only a small fraction is real. Even then such pledges inspire us to work consistently towards a desirable goal.

When we look at the Tathāgata’s last days, we see that he literally followed his declaration of working for the welfare of many, for the happiness of many *(bahujana hitāya, bahujana sukhāya)* till the last breath. He used the last moments of his life for the welfare of people. It may be difficult to fully comprehend the greatness of such men but we can certainly make an effort to walk on the path showed by him to the best of our ability.

Four Elements in the Last Event

The last episode of his life has four elements: Sermon to Subhadda; telling Ānanda that the Dhamma and the Discipline are the guide in his absence; encouraging bhikkhus to speak out if they had any questions or doubts; and his last advice to keep striving.

Of these four elements, we will take up elsewhere the subject of the Dhamma and the Discipline being the guide in his absence. Here we will discuss the other three.

Subhadda had an honest quest for knowledge. He had not met the Tathāgata prior to this. On finding out that the Tathāgata didn't have long to live, he felt that it was an opportunity not to be missed. The urge took him to the Tathāgata. On reaching the spot, he expressed his ardent wish to Ānanda and in spite of Ānanda's refusals kept requesting him repeatedly.

Both were right in their own place. Subhadda had but one opportunity to hear the Dhamma from the Buddha himself. He wanted to quench his thirst for knowledge.

On the other hand, Ānanda too was right. He knew the Tathāgata's physical condition. The Tathāgata was tired. Ānanda had spent several years in his company. He knew that the Tathāgata needed to rest in those final moments after a lifetime of hardships in the service of people. He conveyed this to Subhadda. His intention was not to deprive Subhadda of Dhamma but to only allow the Tathāgata a much needed rest. There was neither arrogance nor the pettiness of misuse of his position in Ānanda. Both Subhadda and Ānanda were right in their own place.

Sermon to Subhadda on Deathbed Was Part of His Lifelong Principle

Even during the last moments the mental faculties of the Buddha were as fresh as ever. We have seen in the foreword, what Swami Vivekanand said about the Buddha's compassion. The Buddha knew that Subhadda was an honest seeker. In his life, he had met many people who had come to him not to seek guidance but to test him, to harass him, to insult him. Even to those people he had not denied a meeting. He wouldn't do so for Subhadda. He was always prompt and energetic in helping those who came to him to seek guidance.

We should understand that it was not to demean Ānanda or to change his decision in a negative way. He trusted Ānanda and Ānanda was happy to comply when the Tathāgata felt otherwise about his decisions. Ānanda was mature enough to understand his dedicated commitment to a lifelong mission.

The Buddha circumvented the questions about other Teachers of those times. It was not because he didn't want to give his opinion with reasons on the teaching of these Teachers. He had surely done so in the past. When one is proclaiming the truth to the world, it is essential to tell the world what is not truth and to point deficiencies in the arguments of those who say otherwise.

This, however, was a different situation. He had very little time left. After talking to Subhadda, he also wanted to address the bhikkhus. Thus he had to have an efficient plan to teach Subhadda in a short time. Generally, any sermon has two parts. One part is to contest falsehoods or harmful misconceptions. The other is the positive aspect in which one gives truthful and beneficial teaching. This aspect conveys the essence of the one's position. When time is short, one often has to forego the first aspect of contesting the falsehood and focus on the essence of one's message.

The Tathāgata did exactly this. He focused on the Noble Eightfold Path and guided Subhadda to the right path.

The sermon to Subhadda offered no material gain or physical comfort to an extremely tired and ailing Tathāgata. It was actually a physically taxing endeavor. The exhaustion, if anything, would perhaps shorten the life by a few moments. This is one way of looking at it. It is quite likely that the joy of helping Subhadda gave him comfort and extended his life by a few moments and he used that time to address the bhikkhus.

His Compassion Never Wavered till He Breathed His Last

After comforting Ānanda that the Dhamma and the Discipline are the guide in his absence, the Buddha addressed the bhikkhus.

This is a touching moment. He was literally moments away from his last breath. He wanted to use these moments to clarify any doubts that the bhikkhus might have. His compassion for people at this moment was equal to the compassion he had felt while tirelessly wandering when he was much younger and physically strong.

We will see later how he had courteously explained to Lohicca brahmin who held the view that one should not share one's knowledge. Tukaram's words of compassion in helping people apply to the Buddha.

People wallowing in misery,
Can't stand that sight;
Compassion wells up within,
That's why I help.

Repeatedly and in various ways, the Buddha encouraged the bhikkhus to ask if they have any doubts. One thing that he did at that time showed his infinite compassion as well as his scientific commitment to knowledge. He was full of love and affection when he told them to seek clarification for their doubts lest they regret later in life.

Many times in one's life, even though there is a doubt in one's mind, one doesn't build courage to ask questions. Lack of confidence, diffidence, belief that asking questions will be disrespectful to the person in whom one has faith, undue humility are some of the reasons why people don't speak up and suppress the questions in their mind.

Some teachers, directly or indirectly, discourage questions as they treat them as threats to their doctrine.

The Tathāgata knew this. Therefore, he showed a way out. A person who is not able to ask questions to the seniors often talks freely to one's colleagues or equals. A bhikkhu who may not have courage to address the Buddha may feel free in talking about the same matter with other bhikkhus. Therefore, the Buddha suggests that anyone who feels diffident about asking should tell someone else to ask the question. This shows his commitment in removing doubts, false beliefs and ignorance.

Faced the Death Calmly with Balanced Mind

On confirming that the bhikkhus had no doubts in their mind, he gave them his last exhortation. All his life he had explained the principle of impermanence. He reiterated it to impress its importance upon their mind.

While stating that 'all compound things (by their very nature) decay' he is on one hand reiterating the fundamental quality of existence and on the other hand also preparing the bhikkhus to face his death with fortitude.

His physical existence was an example of the principle of impermanence that is applicable to all compound things. This is a law of nature that is applicable to one and all: to a helpless pauper as well as to an all-powerful emperor. It is applicable to someone who is enslaved by greed and ignorance as well as to a fully enlightened one. The Tathāgata faced death with total calmness, balanced mind and contentment.

Today, after twenty-five centuries, his last words "strive tirelessly to achieve the goal" resonate with equal freshness and inspiration.

The Tathāgata's Love for Freedom

An episode towards the end of his life in which he gave a guideline to Ānanda shows how much the Buddha loved freedom.[110]

In the first synod held after his great passing away, Ven Ānanda said to Ven. Mahākassapa, "Venerable sir, at the time of his passing away the Tathāgata told me, 'Ānanda, if the Saṅgha feels necessary they may do away with minor rules after my passing away.'"

Mahākassapa asked him whether he had asked the Buddha which rules were to be considered minor. Then various bhikkhus started giving different opinions about which rules were minor and which were not. When Mahākassapa saw that there was no consensus on this, he took a decisive step.

He declared, "Rules of our discipline are known to laypeople. They know what is proper and what is improper for the Buddha's bhikkhus. In this situation if we cancel some rules, they will say, 'Samaṇa Gotama's rules were like a soot of smoke. As long as the Teacher was there, the bhikkhus followed it and now have stopped following them.' To avoid this allegation, let us continue with all the rules."

Ven. Mahākassapa got the assembly to agree to his view. Then he said to Ven Ānanda, "Friend Ānanda, you didn't ask the Tathāgata which were the minor rules. This was wrong. You should seek the Saṅgha's pardon for this breach."

Ānanda responded only as Ānanda would, "I didn't do it deliberately. I don't think that I have made a mistake. But out of respect to you, I will seek pardon."

The bhikkhus also made some other allegations against Ānanda.

Discussion

If we were to look at the history of freedom of thought in history, this permission granting freedom to do away with minor rules was a pinnacle, a high point of that freedom of thought.

I would like to point out here that had the Buddha specified which rules were minor, it would have again become the part of a rigid rulebook. He didn't want to do it. He wanted the Saṅgha to decide whether with changing times, some rules were to be modified or changed.

This will be clear if we look at the constitution of any modern nation. The Indian Constitution (just like many others) gives future generations the right to amend it. If the makers of the Constitution had specified all the amendments that could be made, then it would have not allowed freedom to the future generations to decide independently and freely. And the right to amend the constitution would have become useless.

This simple and yet momentous statement of the Tathāgata has three parts. First part is "if the Saṅgha feels," the second is "minor rules" and the third is "the Saṅgha may cancel them."

Situations change with time. Some things become outdated. Some new needs arise. Then the Saṅgha can initiate the process of change. One has to be careful that the changes are made without affecting the essence, the inner core.

An amendment in the Constitution of India changed the minimum age at which men and women can marry. But we can't remove the democratic principle from the constitution. If one does that, one destroys the very constitution.

Similarly, bhikkhus are free to make decisions about food, medicines etc. but if they do away with the Noble Eightfold Path then it will destroy the whole Teaching. The Buddha himself authorized the Saṅgha to cancel rules of Discipline. It is not easy to bear the responsibility that comes with this freedom. Eric Fromm has explained in his book 'Fear of Freedom', how and how much people fear freedom.[111]

Time, place and situation necessitate changes in lifestyle even for bhikkhus. An upright bhikkhu may feel anguished and distressed if he finds it very difficult or impossible to follow certain rules. If he breaks a rule due to a special situation, he will carry the guilt of having slipped. The Tathāgata's advice to do away with minor rules if the Saṅgha so feels removes such unreasonable pressure and makes the bhikkhu free.

If wisdom can't make a person free, if it doesn't impart confidence and courage to him and if it doesn't end his dependence on others, then what is the use of that knowledge and wisdom? Can such knowledge be called real knowledge?

The knowledge that the Tathāgata proclaimed and taught was different. He felt that one who acquires knowledge should be grateful to the one who imparts it but one should not develop a dependent attitude towards that person. He made countless people aware of their own wings of freedom so that they could fly freely and fearlessly in the sky of peace and happiness. He didn't make them insecure about their own abilities and didn't confine them to their nests!

4

Be the Inheritors of Dhamma, Not of Material Possessions

Dhamma is a lifestyle that maintains proper balance between the subjective and the objective resulting in the highest individual, family and social welfare giving one an untainted happiness. The word 'dhamma' is also used in Tipiṭaka for a thing, an object, quality, specialty etc. Here we will not discuss these meanings of 'dhamma' but will discuss the Dhamma as taught by the Buddha.

The bodhi—the enlightenment that made Siddhārtha Gotama a Buddha— is his Dhamma. One way to look at enlightenment is acquisition of knowledge that was absent earlier. Similarly, one way to look at Dhamma is knowledge that was not taught earlier. Before its proclamation, Dhamma was present in the form of enlightenment (bodhi). After its proclamation, enlightenment was present but in the form of Dhamma. The statements *Buddhaṃ Saraṇaṃ Gacchāmi* and *Dhammaṃ Saraṇaṃ Gacchāmi* have different words, different facets but in essence they are the same. That is why the Tathāgata said, "He who seems me sees the Dhamma and he who sees the Dhamma sees me."

He Who Sees the Dhamma Sees Me

We get a new understanding when we see how the Tathāgata separated himself from his personal life and became one with the Dhamma. In other words, there was no separate personal life for him. Vakkali Sutta[112] in the Connected Discourses sheds light on this. Though it is based on superior reasoning, its gentleness is touching.

Once the Tathāgata was dwelling in the Bamboo Grove of Rajgir. At that time Ven. Vakkali was staying in the house of a potter. He became very sick and afflicted with pain. He sent the bhikkhu who was nursing him to the Buddha. He told the bhikkhu to convey his humblest salutations to the Buddha and to invite the Buddha to visit him because he was very sick. Accordingly, the bhikkhu went to the Buddha and conveyed the message. The Buddha gave consent by remaining silent.

When Vakkali saw the Buddha coming, he started arranging the bed properly.

The Buddha stopped him, "Vakkali, let it be. There are other seats here. I will use them."

Then he sat on one side and asked Vakkali "Are you getting better? Is your affliction decreasing?" Vakkali replied, "Venerable sir, I am getting worse. Pain is becoming unbearable."

Then to the Buddha's question "Do you feel sad and guilty?" Vakkali replied, "Venerable sir, I feel very sad and full of regret."

When the Buddha asked him whether the guilt was because he was not able to live a moral life, Vakkali replied in the negative, meaning he was living a virtuous life.

Then the Buddha asked him the reason for his regret. "Venerable sir, for a long time, I wanted to come and see the Tathāgata but I didn't have the physical strength to do so."

The Buddha comforted him, "Don't say this, Vakkali. What will you gain by seeing this body containing excreta, etc.? Vakkali, he who sees the Dhamma, sees me. And he who sees me, sees the Dhamma."

Discussion

Even at the worldly level, this incident is touching. On the philosophical level, it illuminates the principles of Dhamma.

Vakkali was sick. He was bedridden. He is not able to go to see the Tathāgata. He fervently wishes to see the Tathāgata. Ordinarily, he would have gone to see the Tathāgata. But in the circumstance of his being sick, he thought he could see the Tathāgata by inviting him and he made the request through a bhikkhu. On seeing the Buddha, Vakkali started arranging things for proper seating. Due to Vakkali's sickness, the Buddha brushed aside the formality and sat on one side. He was not one of those who insisted on a "proper" welcome in spite of extenuating circumstances.

When he enquired after Vakkali's health, Vakkali told him the truth. Perhaps, he had realized that he didn't have long to live and it seems that the Buddha also had an inkling of it. Therefore, he asked Vakkali if he felt any sorrow or regret. Vakkali replied it bothered him that he couldn't go to see the Buddha in spite of fervently wanting to. He was caught between physical incapacity and the ardent wish to see the Buddha. The Tathāgata rescued him from his sorrow and regret by explaining to him:

The Tathāgata's body is not important. His Dhamma is important. The body contains many impurities. The Dhamma is free from all impurities. Therefore, the Dhamma has real importance. He who sees Dhamma, sees the Buddha. It doesn't mean that one who follows Dhamma should see the body of Dhamma. There is no need to worship the body of the Tathāgata. The true existence of the Tathāgata is not in his body but is in the Dhamma taught by him. The practice of Dhamma *is* seeing the Buddha. One who sees the Dhamma sees the Buddha. The other side of this statement is that seeing the Buddha is seeing the Dhamma.

This doesn't mean that one who sees the body of the Buddha sees the Dhamma. It means that one who grasps the Buddha's thoughts sees the Dhamma. The duality of the Buddha and the Dhamma vanishes. In the cessation of duality, the importance is not to the Buddha but to the Dhamma. The Dhamma is not submerged in the body of the Buddha. The body of the Buddha has plunged in the Dhamma. To understand how high he placed the Dhamma and how unsullied he kept it, we also have to rise a little. The Tathāgata didn't speak in this way to debase the body but to elevate the Dhamma and to emphasize the centrality of the Dhamma.

Refuge Not in a Person but in the Dhamma

The Buddha's decision to take refuge in the Dhamma and not in a guru was to give importance to the Dhamma. We find this in the Numerical Discourses.[113]

The Buddha was once dwelling in Sāvatthi at Jetavana. On one occasion, he called the bhikkhus and reminisced thus: He had just attained enlightenment. He was meditating alone under the Ajapāla Nyagrodha tree near the river Nerañjā in Uruvelā. While thus meditating, the thought occurred to him, "It is unpleasant to dwell without venerating someone, without honoring someone. Why don't I take refuge in some Samaṇa or brāhmaṇa, venerating and honoring him?"

He thought that such a person might help him in perfecting his morality, concentration, wisdom and liberation. But he didn't find anyone more developed than him in these qualities.

Not finding anyone under whose guidance he could develop further, he thought, "I should respect and honor the Dhamma, and take refuge in the Dhamma that I have attained through enlightenment."

At that time Brahmā Sahampati came down and supported his decision and told him that all the past Buddhas too had dwelt taking refuge in the Dhamma. He then started living by taking refuge in the Dhamma.

Discussion

Refuge in Dhamma

Enlightenment was the highest moment of Gotama's life. It was like reaching the top of the highest peak of the mountain. He stayed in the proximity of the Bodhi tree in Uruvelā for about seven weeks. During this time, he thought long and deep about how to apply his enlightenment in practice. The thought that he had above was part of that process.

Many great people stay in the vicinity of a guru and follow his guidance as they feel that the guidance of the guru will enrich their lives. This thought flashed through the Buddha's mind too. This was a time when he was making practical decisions. Often one gets various contradictory thoughts in the process of coming to a conclusion. One has to evaluate both the positive and negative aspects and use discretionary intelligence to make the correct decision.

He decided to take refuge in the Dhamma rather than a person. When he said that he didn't find anyone with higher virtues, he is making a factual observation. It wasn't due to arrogance or a narrow-minded attempt to demean others to prove his superiority.

We should keep in mind that if one has discovered something totally new and wants to present it to the world, one has to be firm. False or undue humility in the field of knowledge is harmful to society. An individual, however great, has limitations. He or she may have deficiencies. Therefore, in the field of knowledge and conduct, one should not depend on an individual or carry his or her flag. It is much more beneficial to follow life affirming principles scrupulously and encourage others to do the same. Therefore, the Buddha decided not to depend on any another person but to depend on the Dhamma.

To Teach or Not to Teach

For a few weeks after his enlightenment, he lived in Uruvelā. Once while sitting under a banyan tree, he thought,[114] "I have discovered the Dhamma that is profound, difficult to perceive, difficult to penetrate, peaceful and superior, impossible to grasp with mere logic, subtle and understood only by the wise. But the people are drowned in craving. They are lost in and take delight in sensual pleasures. They won't be able to understand Dependent Origination. They will not be able to comprehend cooling of all conditionings, giving up all attachments, cessation of craving, destruction of greed, eradication of suffering and *nibbāna* (the deathless). Even if I teach them the Dhamma, they won't understand it. It will cause me distress and pain."

At that time, some verses that he had not heard before, arose in him spontaneously:

The Dhamma that I have grasped with much effort,
It is not proper for me to teach it;
People afflicted with craving and hatred will not understand it easily,
Ignorant and greedy, they can't know the Dhamma;
That goes against the stream, is profound and difficult to perceive,
Is difficult to penetrate and subtle, understood only by the wise.

This thought made him reluctant to teach Dhamma. When Sahampati Brahmā learned this, he became concerned. He felt that it will be a big loss to people if the Buddha didn't teach Dhamma. He went to the Buddha, and after saluting him, requested him to teach the Dhamma to people, "You will find people who will understand the Dhamma." Twice he made this request and the Buddha repeated the above mentioned verses.

When requested for the third time, the Buddha looked at all beings with compassion. Just as some of the blue, red and white lotuses are totally submerged in water, some are floating on the surface of water and some rise above the water, he found that people are in various stages. He decided to teach the Dhamma and conveyed his decision to the Brahmā.

Discussion

No Impatient Decision

After attaining Bodhi, the Buddha clarified, deepened, precisely arranged and organized his thinking from a practical point of view. He was in two minds: to keep his wisdom to himself and live a solitary life or to use his wisdom to guide others.

He had discovered the principles of Dhamma by strenuous effort and using his extraordinary acumen. But the people to whom these principles were to be taught made him hesitate. They were blinded by various opinions and prejudices. Was their mind not clear enough to comprehend their own welfare? He doubted the extent to which the Dhamma discovered by him would be accepted, liked and understood by them. Therefore, in the beginning, he wasn't eager in teaching the phenomenon of Dependent Origination. He examined his own understanding, his own thoughts. He also seriously considered how people will respond to it.

Once he decided to teach the Dhamma, he did so for forty-five years with unwavering dedication and untiring zeal. But the decision to do so, was taken with due consideration, without any impatience. It was his character to analyze all the aspects carefully, meticulously and without haste. However, once he took the decision, he implemented it diligently and with determination.

A Well-wisher Shares His Wisdom

The decision of the Buddha to share his wisdom was consistent with the aim of his renunciation. He had left home after seeing the suffering of people and with a view to find a way out of suffering. Having found the solution, it was not possible for him to keep it from the people. The thought processes in his mind after enlightenment were not to deny people the Dhamma. They were aimed at polishing it, readying it, judging and anticipating people's response. Once he started his benevolent work he showed unparalleled commitment to it as we see in Lohicca Sutta[115] of the Long Discourses.

Once while he was dwelling in Kosala, the Buddha went to a town called Sālavatikā which was gifted by the king of Kosala to brahmin Lohicca.

Lohicca had developed a false view, "If any ascetic or holy man discovers wholesome knowledge, he should not share it with others. What can one man do for another? It is as if after cutting one bondage, one is bound in another bondage. Sharing one's wisdom with others is a sinful greedy deed. Because what can one person do for another?"

Lohicca learned that Samaṇa Gotama had come to Sālavatikā, and having discovered the Dhamma, was spreading it among people. He heard from people that meeting such an arahata is good. Therefore, he sent a barber named Rosikā to the Buddha to invite him for a meal. Rosikā did likewise and the Buddha accepted the invitation. The next day when the meal was ready, Lohicca again sent Rosikā to the Buddha to escort him to Lohicca's house. On the way, Rosikā told him about the false view that Lohicca held and requested the Buddha to free Lohicca from his false view. The Buddha assured him that he would do so.

After the meal, Lohicca sat next to the Buddha. Then the Buddha asked him whether he thought thus. On his affirming it, the Buddha asked him, "You have received this Sālavatikā town in gift, haven't you?"

"Yes, sir"

"If someone were to say that since Lohicca reigns over Sālavatikā, all the income and the produce of Sālavatikā should be enjoyed only by Lohiccca, won't that person be harming those who are dependent on you?"

"Yes, he will be causing harm."

"Will that person be a creator of obstacles for them or will he be sympathetic to their welfare?"

"Creator of obstacles, sir."

"Will he have goodwill towards those he is hurting or will he have enmity towards them?"

"Enmity, sir."

"Will someone with enmity in mind have the right view or wrong view?"

"Wrong view, sir."

The Buddha then added that one with wrong view would go to the nether world or the animal realm.

Then the Buddha gave the example of Pasenadi. "Pasenadi is the lord of Kosalan kingdom. What will happen if someone were to say that Pasenadi should enjoy all the income and the produce of the kingdom?"

This led to a similar question-and-answer series as given above.

After giving these two examples, the Buddha told Lohicca that his view is similar to that of the person above. He explained that not sharing one's knowledge of wholesome Dhamma with others is a false view.

The Buddha said that there were three types of teachers who were worthy of criticism, "A certain teacher has not attained the goal of the renunciation for which one leaves home. Though he has not attained that goal, he teaches his disciples, 'This is for your welfare. This is for your happiness.' His disciples don't listen to him or pay heed to his words. They don't follow his guidance. It is as if a man were to pursue one who pulls away or to embrace one who turns his back. Saying 'What can one person do for another?' is applicable here. This teacher is worthy of criticism, and such criticism is well-deserved.

"The second type of teacher has not attained the goal of the renunciation for which one leaves home. He teaches his disciples and they listen to him. It is as if a man neglects his own field and imagines that another's field should be weeded. This teacher is worthy of criticism, and such criticism is well-deserved.

"The third type of teacher has attained the goal of the renunciation for which one leaves home. He teaches his disciples but they don't listen to him. It is as if a man breaks one bond and creates another bond (for himself). This teacher is worthy of criticism, and such criticism is well-deserved."

Lohicca then asked him who would be a teacher not worthy of criticism. The Buddha explained in detail that the teacher endowed with morality, concentration and wisdom would not be worthy of criticism and his teaching would be beneficial to his disciples.

Lohicca then told the Budha, "Just as if someone were to grab by the hair a person who is falling into a deep abyss, pull him up and set him on the ground, you have saved me from going to the nether world. Just as if someone were to place upright a container that was overturned, to reveal what was hidden, to show the path to one who had lost his way, or to take a lamp into the dark so that those with eyes could see, in the same way has Venerable Gotama, in various ways, brought the Dhamma to light for me. Please accept me as your disciple."

Discussion

This sermon by the Buddha is an invaluable treasure in the field of learning in India. Rarely has someone made the philosophy of learning so humane in the entire history of India. This sheds light effectively on the difference between two major schools of learning in India—vedic and samaṇa. It is significant that this is not a story from the life of an imaginary person. It is from the life of a historical person who spent his life according to the principles that he espoused.

There was a narrow-minded and arrogant school in India that denied learning to others to enslave them. Lohicca's initial stance was representative of that school.

Wise One Must Teach

The Tathāgata was once dwelling on the Vulture Peak near Rājagaha (Rajgir). Then a yakkha named Sakka came to him and commented, "It is not proper that a liberated Samaṇa like you who has destroyed all fetters is teaching others."

The Buddha responded, "Sakka, people come in contact with each other for some reason. A wise person develops compassion for others at such times. If one gladly advises others, he doesn't develop a new fetter because that compassion has origin in concern for others."

Any Great Discovery Is Profound in the Beginning

We will now discuss some of the adjectives that the Buddha used for the Dhamma. He discovered the law of Dependent Origination which is about cause and effect relationship. The essence of this principle is that if there is a cause, there is an effect; when the cause ceases, the effect ceases.

Ignorance leads through a series of steps to suffering. Thus when there is ignorance, there is suffering. When ignorance ceases, suffering ceases. Cause and effect relationship has a huge role in modern science.

For example, scientists show that a particular bacteria or virus causes a disease, and when we get rid of that bacteria or virus, the disease is cured. Thus they establish the relationship between the disease and the agent. Those of us who have been raised in this atmosphere of scientific temperament may not find much novelty in the cycle of Dependent Origination. We may even wonder why the the Tathāgata called it profound.

A scientist might have spent a lifetime in arduous research to discover a principle. In the flow of time we get so acquainted with that principle that we get as used to it as we are about our breath. Those scientists who discovered that certain illnesses were the result of bacteria and viruses started a new era in science. It took a Newton to discover the law of gravity. The Buddha's discovery was as momentous as these discoveries. It should be noted that these modern discoveries happened in the last four hundred years or so. The Buddha's discovery is more than twenty-five centuries old. It gives an indication of his intellectual brilliance. This doesn't mean that he was familiar with the details of modern discoveries. However, we should note that his theoretical perspective was clearly and emphatically scientific.

The Dhamma Flows Against the Stream

The Buddha said that his Dhamma flows against the stream. There was darkness in both individual and social life at that time. People would draw suffering to themselves because they didn't know how to behave and how to speak. As is true for our times, people were entangled in excessive attachment. They were running blindly after material things.

They would waste time on questions such as whether the world is eternal or not, while neglecting the issue of suffering in this very life. In addition there was an influential Vedic thought. It considered the Vedas to be the truth, the standard. It denied freedom of thought to humanity. It confined people to the rituals of *yajña*s. It divided society through the oppressive and unjust caste system.

It was easy to continue to flow in this internal and external flow of human tendency. To oppose that flow required all one's energies. Unfortunately, even twenty-five centuries later, the Indian mind doesn't feel the need for the rational, benevolent teaching of the Buddha to oppose that harmful flow.

It is not because of a flaw in the Buddha's teaching that Indians look at it as adversarial even after twenty-five centuries. Psychological mean-mindedness and intellectual poverty are the reasons. Even today, his refreshing and lofty teaching is not digested easily by Indians for the lack of an openness to even examine it. It is no wonder then that centuries ago, there was a brief but strong tussle in the mind of the Tathāgata whether to put forth his teaching that went against the flow.

Sahampati Brahmā is but a symbol of that mental tussle. It doesn't mean that some outside deity came and requested him. The parable makes it easy for the people to understand it. The dramatic and poetic expression is therefore welcome. However, we should not forget that it is a mere parable and not a historical event.

It is also possible that some person or group of persons made such a request to the Buddha on learning about his hesitation and that person or group was then represented as a brahmā in the story. It is also possible that by suggesting that a brahmā itself welcomed the Buddha's Dhamma, the opposition of the Vedics to his teaching was blunted to some degree.

Parable to Explain the Dhamma That Flows Against the Stream

The Buddha gave a parable[116] to explain this.

A man is flowing along in the river without resisting the flow anticipating that he will get pleasant and joyous things ahead. Seeing him flowing like this, a discerning man sitting on the shore calls out to him, "Hey good man, you are flowing along in anticipation of pleasant and joyful things. Friend, downstream in the river there is turbulence, gulches, crocodiles and demons. If you go downstream, you will face death or untold pain!"

Heeding the advice of the discerning man, the man in the flow starts energetically using his hands and feet to swim upstream.

Then the Buddha explained the parable. The flow of river is the flow of craving. The man who flows along is the man who runs after sensual pleasures. The discerning man on the bank is the Buddha. To swim upstream against the flow is to give up running after sensual pleasures and live a restrained life.

We have seen earlier the parable in which Siddhārtha Gotama, after eating the milk pudding, places the bowl given by Sujātā on the river and the bowl starts flowing upstream.

It is easy to go along with the flow. Even if one doesn't make much effort, the flow of life drags us along. However, this is dangerous. One may feel it is safe and secure to flow along the existing popular views in society created by ignorant and selfish forces. These views may be harmful blind faith promoted in the name of religion to increase ignorance or consumerism encouraged by sellers to increase greed. One may feel that this is going to lead to pleasant results. The actual results, however, are harmful and self-destructive. One thinks that going along with the flow is easy and we don't have to make much effort. There is also lack of vision to understand where it is going to lead us ultimately. Such a journey is often harmful and self-destructive. A wise person, knowing that this flow is calamitous, advises people to turn back. Turning back is not easy but is not impossible either. One has to be determined and willing to work hard. This effort brings wonderful results.

The Tathāgata's Dhamma is also similar to going against the flow. People fear going against the flow. Generation after generation, they stumble around in the dark and face all kinds of suffering. They are saved the trouble resulting from going against the flow but their true welfare suffers. On the other hand, a bit of effort, a bit of courage and a bit of fortitude goes a long way in avoiding the dangers and changing one's life. They can truly help themselves.

Teaching According to Aptitude and Capacity

The Tathāgata looked at people with compassion and wisdom. The parable, mentioned earlier, of lotuses is appealing as well as meaningful. Red, blue and white colored lotuses indicate people of different mindsets and backgrounds. Lotuses submerged in water, floating on the surface and rising above the surface indicate difference in mental development of people. The Tathāgata understood that people are at different levels of morality and thinking. It is well known that he modified his discourses accordingly.

He had certain broad principles about when and how to teach. In the Discourse on The Simile of the Field[117] of the Connected Discourses, the Tathāgata clarified this.

Once he was dwelling in the mango grove named Pāvārika in Nalanda (Nalandā). At that time, Asibandhakaputta, a village chief came to him and asked, "Venerable sir, the Tathāgata dwells caring for the welfare of all the beings, doesn't he?"

"He does," the Tathāgata answered.

"Then why is it that the Tathāgata teached the Dhamma thoroughly to someone and while not thoroughly to others?"

Then the Tathāgata counter-questioned him, "Let me ask you, you answer as you find proper. Suppose a farmer has three fields. One has superior fertile soil. Second has medium grade soil and the third has low grade, non-fertile and barren soil. Which field should the farmer plough and sow first?"

Asibandhakaputta replied "The farmer should plough and sow the farm that has superior fertile soil first. Then he should attend to the farm with medium grade soil. Finally, he should attend to the barren land where he would be happy even to get grass for his cattle to graze."

The Tathāgata said that his discourses are similar, "The bhikkhus and bhikkhuṇis who have gone forth for the Dhamma are like the superior field. The lay followers are like the medium field. The ascetics of other traditions, brahmins, wandering recluses are like the third field. If the people from the third category understand even a few words of the teaching, it is beneficial to them for long."

The Tathāgata gave one more simile.

Suppose someone has three earthen water pots. The first doesn't have any cracks or seepage. The second has no cracks but has seepage. The third has both cracks and seepage. Just as the owner of the pots will decide which pots to fill first, I decide the sequence of my discourses.

Matriceta (Mātṛceṭa) puts it beautifully in a verse[118] that though the Tathāgata taught differently to different people, he had the same good intentions for the welfare of them all.

Your words delight the learned,
Add to the intellect of the medium,
Remove darkness from a still lesser intellect;
Thus it serves one and all.

Whom to Teach First

Upon deciding that he would teach the Dhamma to people, the Buddha reflected on who to teach first. He had gratitude and affection for Āḷāra Kālāma and Uddaka Rāmaputta. He also had confidence in their ability of comprehension. Had they been alive, he would have certainly shared the Dhamma with them with great joy. Their demise prevented it. Then he remembered his five former companions. When he learned that they were living at the Deer Park, he went there.

When his five former companions saw him coming from a distance, they decided not to honor him except by offering a seat because they thought that he had strayed from the path of austerity and renunciation of all material comforts. However, as the Buddha approached them, their resolve weakened. One came forward to take the alms bowl from him. The second one rolled out a seat for him. The third one offered water to wash his feet. The fourth one placed a footboard for his feet. The fifth one placed a plank as back-support. The Tathāgata sat down and washed his feet.

At that time, they were addressing the Tathāgata by name or as "friend." He told them, "Don't call the Tathāgata by his name or as 'friend'. The Tathāgata has become liberated and fully enlightened. He has attained the deathless. Let me teach you the Dhamma. If you follow my advice, you will soon attain your goal. You will attain and know with your own experience in this very life that great holy life for the sake of which sons of good families go forth into homelessness."

The former companions expressed their doubts, "Friend Gotama, you could not achieve the transcendent superhuman Dhamma, when you were on the correct path and practising severe austerities. And now how can you claim to have attained that after straying from the path?"

Then the Tathāgata explained to them that he had not gone astray from the right path; that he had attained the deathless and was keen to teach them the Dhamma. When for the second and third time this conversation was repeated, the Buddha asked them, "Bhikkhus, did I ever made such a claim in the past?"

They answered, "No, sir."

And they became willing to listen to his teaching.

Discussion

When we discover anything new, we feel like sharing it with our acquaintances, our near and dear ones. We would hesitate to share something, especially something as serious and profound as the Dhamma, with a stranger. After his enlightenment, the Buddha had met some traders and brahmins. He did not teach them the Dhamma. It is also possible that these strangers didn't show interest in what he had to teach.

The case of Āḷāra Kālāma and Rāmaputta was different. Though he had left them, it was not out of disrespect. He had not left them due to any conflict but due to his wish to achieve a higher goal. Naturally, he felt that he could tell them freely about the principles of the Dhamma and they would understand them easily.

After learning about their death, he thought about his former companions. They had abandoned him but he didn't hold any grudge. He carried the positive memories of their company and support during his severe austerities. This purity of mind that didn't allow for any grudges was a special aspect of the the Tathāgata's personality.

The five companions had a negative reaction at first when they saw him from afar. But as he approached them their resolve not to accord him a proper welcome dissolved and soon they were doing the very things that they had decided not to do. We see that during the next forty-five years, people kept coming under the benevolent spell of the allure of his conduct and personality. Not all but many of his opponents also failed to resist the attraction of this allure.

When one presents something new to people, they often have doubts, they oppose it and create obstacles. But the one who presents something new should not get upset at such behavior.

If someone raised doubts, the Tathāgata, rather than getting upset, would answer them calmly and create a favorable field for his thoughts. This graceful conduct of the Tathāgata should guide our behavior even today.

At first, the group of five didn't like the Tathāgata's arrival at the Deer Park. They thought of him as 'gone astray.' They had their own limited concepts about the way to attain the truth. Gotama's partaking of normal nourishing food didn't fit that concept. Therefore, their decision not to show any respect must be considered natural. They were not blind or credulous. Therefore, their decision was a valid one. It was in keeping with the philosophy of learning that the Tathāgata propagated. Therefore, even from the perspective of the Tathāgata, their skepticism was not improper.

They did decide on one thing correctly. They didn't take an extreme decision of not even offering a seat to the Tathāgata. They decided to show minimum courtesy. This gesture allowed light to enter their lives. They kept the door open. Once light comes, darkness can't stay.

We can't say how much of the weakening of the resolve of the group of five was due to the Tathāgata's personality but it is clear that they couldn't resist for long the influence of his enlightenment. Though they welcomed him spontaneously, they still had doubts about him. They were not ready to accept Samaṇa Gotama as the Buddha. They continued to call him by his name. They used the address *"āvusa,"* which was used for either friends or juniors. They were impressed but still had not accepted the Tathāgata.

Seeing the doubt in their minds, the Tathāgata felt that it was essential to state a few things confidently. Sometimes, even light has to give its introduction, prove its existence, and reveal its form. The Tathāgata did exactly that. He told the group of five that he had discovered the truth. They were still skeptical because they firmly believed that truth could be attained only by severe austerities including torturing one's own body.

Then the Tathāgata reminded them of an important facet of his character. He pointed it out to them that even when he was on the brink of death due to extreme austerities, he had not claimed to have discovered the truth. If he had even an ounce of pretentiousness or falseness in him, he would have made some claim or the other during his austerities. He had always been transparent about his experiences. This argument did strike the group as a fair one and they became willing to listen to him. This was an appeal for a hearing. It didn't take away their right of investigation. They had that right at that time and in future too.

Middle Path

Before turning to the core of the Dhamma, the Tathāgata talked about an important foundation for the discovery of the Dhamma. He said,[119] "Bhikkhus, one who has gone forth should stay away from two extremes. Which two? One extreme is a life of indulgence in sensual pleasures and lust, which is degrading, sensual, vulgar, ignoble, and profitless. The other extreme is a life given to self-mortification, which is painful, ignoble, and profitless. Bhikkhus, the Tathāgata avoided both extremes and discovered the Middle Path."

Discussion

Though this discourse was given to bhikkhus, the Middle Path is also applicable to householders. It may appear simple on the face of it but it was a revolutionary idea. People have a tendency to swing to one or the other extreme. Excessive indulgence in sensual pleasures and excessive self-deprivation are both signs of mental imbalance.

Healthy living avoids the greedy and giddy pursuit of material pleasures, as well as self-deprivation that affects one's health and wellbeing; and endangers the very journey of life. This Middle Path is not useful only in the spiritual field, it is beneficial in most things in life. It helps us in all processes such as forming an opinion, giving a comment, making a decision and acting on something.

We never see any instance in the Buddha's life where he has taken an extreme, disruptive, destructive or imbalanced stand. Clearly, he had put in practice the Middle Path that he had discovered. We have already seen as stated in the Graded Discourses[120] that he followed the doctrine of analysis and did not focus on just one aspect of a situation or an issue.

I Teach Both Action and Non-Action

Throughout history, opponents of the Buddha's teaching have consistently adapted a strategy of false propaganda. They distort his teaching and then portray a corrupt form in front of people so as to confuse them and create misunderstanding about his teaching. He countered it by following the Middle Path. In this reference, the Soṇakāyana Sutta[121] of the Graded Discourses is particularly noteworthy.

Once a brahmin named Sikhāmoggalāna went to the Buddha and sat down to one side after proper salutations. He then told him, "Gotama, a few days back a young brahmin named Soṇakāyana told me, "Samaṇa Gotama teaches non-action in respect to all the deeds. Teaching non-doing of actions makes him an annihilationist. In reality, the world survives on action. It remains steady due to action."

The Buddha replied, "Brahmin, surely I have not met Soṇakāyana, then how could we ever discuss this? I describe four types of deeds based on my own experience and understanding. That which brings dark results is a dark deed, a bad deed. That which brings a bright result is bright deed, a good deed. That which brings both good and bad results is a dark-bright deed, a mixed deed. That with neither dark nor bright result leads to cessation of deed."

Then he further clarified: "If a person acts or speaks out of anger or becomes mentally angry, he faces dark fruits of that mental, verbal or physical action. If a person's actions are free of anger, he enjoys happiness as a result. If a person does deed partially with anger and partially without anger, he gets mixed fruit. Someone without anger goes beyond all these deeds. Thus there are four kinds of deeds.

As is the case with anger, so is the case with violence, stealing, sexual misconduct, speaking lies and drinking alcohol.

The Tathāgata taught non-action in deeds of anger, violence, etc. but didn't teach non-action in deeds that were free of anger, etc.

In the Numerical Discourses[122] in another discourse, the Buddha makes it even clearer.

Once a person came to him and sat down to one side. He asked him, "What is your doctrine? What do you teach?"

The Buddha replied, "I teach both action and non-action."

"How so?"

"I teach non-action in wrong mental, vocal and physical actions. There are several bad, sinful and unwholesome deeds where I teach non-action. But I teach action about right mental, vocal and physical actions. There are several good, flawless, wholesome deeds where I teach action. Thus, I teach both action and non-action."

Discussion

The Tathāgata explained this in a way that should leave no doubt in anyone's mind. He shunned the tendency to use complicated and difficult language to give the impression of a high philosophy. He used to teach in simple language that the common man understood. In spite of such lucid and simple language, the quality of his discourse was the highest if tested on any parameter of philosophy. He had the skill of simplifying complicated things and making them easy to understand. There would be no scope for any confusion in the mind of an honest seeker who listened to him.

Those with deceit tried to play a game of words. They sometimes tried to corner a speaker by making a division of doctrine of action and doctrine of non-action. Those who didn't get attached to superficial forms of words had no difficulty grasping his thoughts. How can opposing vile actions be annihilationism? And if it is called so, it is for the welfare of the people.

The Middle Path Gives Vision

The Buddha used to say that the Middle Path that he had revealed was sight-imparting *(cakkhukaraṇī)* and wisdom-imparting *(ñāṇakaraṇī)*. The adjective *sight-imparting* is beautiful from the literary angle as well as beautiful in meaning: as if the blind get sight; as if the Middle Path offers them all that was earlier lost to them in darkness.

Don't go to this extreme. Don't go to that extreme. Live a balanced life. This is the true way to live a happy life. Therefore, *wisdom-imparting* is added to *sight-imparting*. This path leads to extinguishing of fires of defilements. It leads to cessation of all that is undesirable. It leads to nibbāna, a state of no suffering.

Noble Eightfold Path is the Middle Path

This much praised Middle Path is the Noble Eightfold Path. Right view, right thought, right speech, right action, right livelihood, right effort, right awareness and right concentration are the eight parts of the path. Here the word"right" *(sammā)* is repeated. This repetition is apt and necessary. Often such repetition is boring and meaningless. Here it serves an important purpose: it manifests the true effectiveness of eightfold path. This word makes the adjectives *sight-imparting* and *wisdom-imparting* meaningful.

Everyone has a view. If one's view is prejudiced, tainted, petty or unbalanced, such a view is not part of the Eightfold Path. It is also not possible that such vision can create true learning, true wisdom. Therefore, the adjective right *(sammā)* is needed. This word has all the positive shades.

The Noble Eightfold Path is the fourth truth of the Four Noble Truths taught by the Buddha. In his first discourse to his former companions, he declares the fourth truth first to them. We will discuss it when we discuss the Four Noble Truths. We should only note here that though he stated the Eightfold Path first, in reference to the Four Noble Truths, it is at the fourth number.

In the Satipaṭṭhāna Sutta (Discourse on the Establishment of Awareness)[123] of the Long Discourses, various parts of the eightfold oath have been explained. Here is the gist:

Right view is wisdom of Four Noble Truths.

Right thought is thought that is devoid of greed, hatred and violence.

Right speech is speech devoid of lies, backbiting, harshness and frivolous speech. (We will discuss the Buddha's teaching about speech in a separate chapter later in this book.)

Right action is abstaining from killing, stealing and sexual misconduct.

Right livelihood is making a living through wholesome means. (We will discuss the right livelihood for householders in a separate chapter later in this book.)

Right effort has four parts.

To wish, and strive; to control and restrain the mind to prevent un-arisen evil and unwholesome deeds from arising is the first part.

To wish and strive; to control and restrain the mind to remove arisen evil and unwholesome deeds from arising is the second part.

To wish and make effort to generate un-arisen wholesome deeds is the next part.

To wish and strive to protect, preserve, develop, cultivate and increase the arisen wholesome deeds the fourth part.

When one is alert and concentrates one's mind, abandons craving and aversion and dwells mindful about body, feelings (sensations), mind and mental contents; then he is said to have right awareness.

Right concentration can be briefly described thus: Abandoning lust and unwholesome deeds, grasping the object of concentration and bearing it, dwells in the first absorption *(jhāna)* experiencing mental and physical exhilaration.

Then the grasping of object ceases and mind becomes totally focused. It creates an inner delight. This is the second absorption.

In the third absorption, he develops equanimity towards the mental exhilaration, dwells with focused mind experiencing comfort in body *(kāyasukha)*.

Lastly, he transcends feelings of mental and physical pain and pleasure to dwell with equanimity in pure awareness. This is the fourth absorption.

In the Janavasabha Sutta,[124] it is said that to complete and fulfill right concentration, mind must be focused and refined along with all other seven parts of the Eightfold Path. If one has right view, one gets right thoughts. Similarly each preceding part leads to the next part of the Eightfold Path. Thus when one attains right concentration, one has right wisdom and one with right wisdom attains right liberation.

The Tathāgata's Brahmacariya (Brahmacharya)

The word *brahmacariya* (*brahmacharya,* holy life) occurs often in the discourses of the Buddha. This word in India means celibacy. However, abstaining from sexual misconduct is just one part of the meaning of this word. For the Buddha, *brahmacariya* was synonymous with the Dhamma. Thus it was synonymous with the Eightfold Path.

Once while he was dwelling in Sāvatthi, he was asked, "It is said *brahmacariya, brahmacariya*. What does it mean?"

He answered, "Noble Eightfold Path itself is *brahmacariya*."[125]

Once in Sāvatthi, he had said that the Eightfold Path is "to be a samaṇa" *(sāmaññabhāva)*.[126] Thus, following the Noble Eightfold Path and being a Samaṇa (being a true ascetic) were the same thing. If someone is practicing right speech, then even if he or she is a householder, in the sphere of speech, he or she is a Samaṇa who is practising *brahmacariya*, living the holy life. It proves how much importance the Tathāgata gave to the Noble Eightfold Path.

The Noble Eightfold Path is Morality, Concentration and Wisdom

The eight parts of the Eightfold Path are often divided into wisdom, morality and concentration.[127] Right view and right thought are grouped in wisdom. Right speech, right action and right livelihood are grouped in morality. Right effort, right awareness and right concentration are grouped in concentration.

Eightfold Path and Auspicious Eights

In India, there is still a tradition to recite *maṅgalāshṭaka* (literally, auspicious eights) in marriage ceremony. The word *maṅgala* is very common in Tipiṭaka. Not as a blind faith, but as an expression of goodwill, *maṅgala* is a very important concept in Buddhist tradition. *Ashṭaka* is obviously related to the Eightfold Path. Reciting eight auspicious verses was originally a vow to follow each of the eight parts of the path. Even if Buddhism vanished outwardly from India, its imprints have been preserved by the people here in many cultural traditions. In this reference, one must read Maṅgala Sutta[128] in Khuddakapāṭha. The necklace that Indian women often wear in India after marriage is called *maṅgala sutra* (Pali version, *maṅgala* sutta). It is possible that this nomenclature came about due to this important and popular sutta.

Eightfold Path is the Vehicle of Dhamma and the Vehicle of Brahmā

Let us look at some of the examples of the Eightfold Path in Tipiṭaka.

Once when the Buddha was dwelling in Sāvatthi,[129] Ven. Ānanda set out on alms round and saw brahmin Jāṇussoṇi coming out of the city in a white chariot. The horses, the adornments of the horses, the chariot, the brahmin's family, the reins of horses, the handle of the whip, the umbrella, the head-cloth and all other clothes as well as the frills were all white. The people were awestruck and exclaimed, "O vehicle of the brahmin! Vehicle of the Brahmā!"

After returning from the alms round and finishing his meal, Ānanda went to the Tathāgata, narrated the incidence of Jāṇussoṇi and asked, "Bhante, is it possible to show the vehicle of brahmā in this Dhamma?"

The the Tathāgata replied, "Yes, Ānanda, it is possible. This Noble Eightfold Path is also called the vehicle of brahmā *(brahmayāna)*, the vehicle of the Dhamma *(dhammayāna)* and "unsurpassed victory in the battle." Right effort based on right view and right thought lead to destruction of craving, aversion and ignorance. In the end, he recited four verses, the gist of which is:

Faith, wisdom and the Dhamma are yoked to this vehicle.
Diffidence is its stick; mind is its reins.
Mindfulness is its protective charioteer.
Morality is the adornment of this chariot.
Concentration is the spokes, effort its wheel and equanimity the axle.

Understanding of impermanence is the awning.
Non-hatred, non-violence and discretion are the weapons.
Tolerance is the protective armor.
People use this peerless brahmā-vehicle and liberate themselves:
This is its crowning glory.

Features of the Eightfold Path

The eightfold path has several special qualities. It is totally positive and constructive. It is not negative. It tells us that we must base everything on correctness, on discretion. It guides us about how to speak and how to behave.

It doesn't imply even the slightest dependence on any divine or superhuman power or deity or god or their grace. It has no place even for the worship of or prayer to the Buddha himself. Whatever you have to do to come out of suffering, you have to do yourself. If a doctor gives us medicine for our ailment, then the treatment (with medicines etc.) is the way to gain health. If one ignores the treatment and prays to the doctor or worships him, it will not eradicate the disease; rather, it may make the disease worse.

In explaining the Eightfold Path, the Buddha didn't take flights of fancy in the skies of philosophy. He didn't indulge in scholarly exhibition that mesmerized people. If a person is stunned by sudden light, he or she gets confused and loses bearings for some time. Similarly, the flashy display of scholarly oration, instead of helping people, may hinder them. A common word for scholar in India is *paṇḍita*. But in Tipiṭaka, the word *paṇḍita* is used not for a scholar but for a wise person.

The Buddha had no interest in impressing people with his personality and erudition. His interest lay in teaching them how to walk step by step during the journey of life. He gave every detail of how to think, how to form an opinion, how to talk to people, how to carry out one's activities, how to calm down mental storms and how to make the mind focused and balanced.

Four Noble Truths

The Buddha told the group of five that the Eightfold Path is the Middle Path. As if to tell them the reason why he explained the path, he gave them the Four Noble Truths. There is suffering, there is cause of suffering, suffering can be eradicated and there is a path leading to the eradication of suffering. Suffering, arising of suffering, cessation of suffering and the path leading to cessation of suffering is how the Four Noble Truths are described.

He states that he has understood the Four Noble Truths in three ways. "Bhikkhus, about things that I had never heard before, that 'suffering is a noble truth'—vision arose, knowledge arose, wisdom arose, learning arose in me and light arose in me. Then vision that 'suffering should be understood' arose in me. Vision that 'suffering has been understood by me' arose in me. Thus I gained the three-fold wisdom that 'there is suffering,' 'it should be understood' and 'it has been understood.'"

Similarly, he gained the three-fold wisdom for the other three noble truths. He told his former companions that as long as he had not attained this three-fold wisdom of Four Noble Truths, he had not claimed to be a fully enlightened one. It was only after gaining this wisdom that he made the claim.

The five bhikkhus showed wholehearted agreement to this declaration. Of the five, Koṇḍañña was the first to obtain the spotless, pure eye of the Dhamma.

When the Tathāgata thus set in motion the wheel of the Dhamma, the land deities exclaimed, "The Tathāgata has set in motion the wheel of the Dhamma in the Deer Park of Isipatana of Varanasi. None in this world of samaṇas, brāhmaṇas, devas, Māra, brahmā or anyone else can set it back now."

Hearing the exclamation of the land deities various other deities also exclaimed the same. This sound reverberated and reached the brahmā realm and the whole universe of ten thousand world systems quivered and shook. There was light—greater, brighter and more illuminating than the light of all the deities of the world. The Tathāgata uttered spontaneously, "O! Koṇḍañña knows! Koṇḍañña knows!"

Discussion

Dependent Origination

The Four Noble Truths proclaimed by the Buddha, are also alternatively termed Dependent Origination *(paṭicca samuppāda)*.

If the Dhamma and the enlightenment of the Buddha are to be described in a single phrase, it would be Dependent Origination. If they are to be described in three words, it would be "Four Noble Truths." These four truths are: there is suffering, suffering arises due to cause, suffering can be eradicated and there is a way to do so. The word in Pali *ariya* is translated as noble. In Prakrit, there two other forms of this word: *ayya* and *ayira*.

During the time that he spent in Uruvelā after his enlightenment, the Buddha was in a way consolidating and formalizing the wisdom and giving it a stable concrete form.

At one time, during meditation he dwelt on the principle of Dependent Origination. **"If this exists, that exists. If this happens, that happens."** The converse of the principle was, **"If this doesn't exist, that doesn't exist. If this ceases, that also ceases."**

Then he dwelt on the principle both ways.

"If this exists, that exists. If happens, that happens. If this doesn't exist, that doesn't exist. If this ceases, that also ceases."[130]

Discussion

Cause and effect relationship is the core of Dependent Origination *(paṭicca samuppāda)*. The Buddha explained this clearly and unequivocally. The core as well as the foundation of his enlightenment is Dependent Origination. Due to a cause, effect comes and when cause is removed, effect also goes away. The Buddha gave this principle in clear and robust terms. He gave it after refining it and polishing it thoroughly. It shows his objective and penetrating vision of looking at things in nature. He solved the problem of human suffering based on this principle.

Ignorance is the basic cause of suffering. From ignorance starts a cascade of events that leads to suffering. The eightfold path removes the cause, that is, ignorance, and thus eradicates suffering. This is how he developed practical application for his principle.

Ven. Ānanda's Opinion about Dependent Origination

Ven. Ānanda once broached the topic of Dependent Origination in front of the Buddha.[131] The Tathāgata was dwelling at Kammāsadamma in Kuru region. At that time, Ven. Ānanda claimed, "Bhante, it is wonderful! It is surprising, bhante, that Dependent Origination is profound. It appears profound. But to me it seems open and easily understandable."

The Buddha responded, "Don't make such a statement, Ānanda… For lack of understanding of this Dhamma, for lack of grasping this doctrine, people are entangled as if in a tangle of ball of string; as if knotted in a string; tangled like coarse grass. Thus entangled, they are unable to cross the state of woe. This causes their ruin."

Discussion

"The law of Dependent Origination is profound. It is not easy to grasp. On the other hand, its profoundness is only in appearance. It is simple, straightforward and easy to grasp. There is nothing deep about it. I see it as if one sees something kept in a box on opening the box." This was Ānanda's feeling. He meant that while appearing to be profound the principle was not actually difficult to grasp. In this small dialogue, we see a conflict not only about Dependent Origination but also about most of the benevolent principles in life.

The Buddha takes a slightly different stand. This is easy for Ānanda to grasp because he was wise but it was not easy for others. This is how the commentary explains it. This analysis of commentary is reasonable. Those who use wisdom to look at the Dhamma with an unprejudiced eye are able to grasp it easily. However, those who lack wisdom find it difficult.

Often small things can bring big changes in people's life but people lack discretion. They don't understand small things and this ignorance of apparently minor issues then makes a difference of life and death. (The use of oral rehydration solution in children with diarrhea is a life saving measure. But as recent history of developing countries is witness, parents' lack of this simple information leads to loss of thousands of lives.)

Kosambi: Dependent Origination Was Expanded Later

The original principle put forth by the Buddha was simple and easy to understand. However, it seems that it became more and more complicated over time. Dharmanand Kosambi says,[132] "Giving such a long chain of causation behind suffering made it difficult for common people to understand suffering. Dependent origination became a philosophical issue and led to doctrinal debates. Acharya Nāgārjuna based his *Mādhyamikakārikā* on this Dependent Origination. Acharya Buddhaghosa devoted an entire sixth section of *Visudhimagga* (about 100-125 pages) to its analysis. Reading all this analysis leads to confusion even for a scholar. How then can one expect a layman to understand it? … Four Noble Truths are easy to comprehend. It is no surprise that they became acceptable to all people." Kosambi also says,[133] "It seems that Dependent Origination was written about a century or two after the Buddha. It was then included in the Buddha's biography to increase its importance. Slowly, it was highlighted even further in the Buddha's biography. The result was that the simple teaching of the Four Noble Truths was pushed to the background and this complicated doctrine was given undue importance."

I agree with Kosambi's overall argument. The original Dependent Origination taught by the Buddha may have been limited to the Four Noble Truths and perhaps a little more. But later on, many complicated parts were added to it.

Four Noble Truths

It is a fact that there is suffering in the world. Often, one is not even aware of one's suffering. If one lacks this awareness, then one can't find its reasons; can't find its cause; and work towards its eradication.

It is in a way like cancer. Often this disease is present in the body and the person has no idea of its existence. Naturally, the person then doesn't seek treatment.

Awareness of suffering is the first step towards its eradication. The suffering that the Buddha was thinking about was a much bigger, widespread suffering. D. B. Kalelkar, in his preface to Kosambi's play "Bodhisatva," writes,[134] "Finally, we should understand that the suffering that the Buddha wanted to end and discovered a way to end, was not mere personal suffering. It was also social suffering. If the behavior of one man to another becomes pure; and if one's life is not anti-social, then both the individual and the society will become happy."

While describing how he understood suffering, the Buddha said that he developed vision *(cakkhu),* knowledge *(ñāṇa),* wisdom *(paññā),* learning *(Vijjā)* and light *(āloka).* The Buddha was a versatile poet as his verses and spontaneous utterances show. Even while speaking in prose, his poetic genius was obvious. He is not uttering empty words. These words describe the myriad meaningful fountains that surged from his heart spontaneously after his enlightenment. One word wouldn't have conveyed the entire meaning, the importance, all the shades, and all the joy of the enlightenment. Therefore, he wove these five words into a garland.

He developed three-fold wisdom. Wisdom that there is suffering is awareness of existence of suffering. The next step is to know the real nature of suffering. It is only when one becomes curious about something that one starts the journey to find more about it. And only after completing the journey does one gain full knowledge about the object of curiosity. The Tathāgata reached that stage.

Just as with suffering, so with the cause of suffering. Ignorance is the root cause of suffering. Ignorance creates craving in the minds of people. It creates various defilements such as greed, anger, hatred, etc. and causes misery.

The next step, after the truth of suffering and its cause, is the comprehension that suffering can be eradicated. If one believes that suffering is endless, eternal and impossible to eradicate, then that person will never come out of suffering. But if one is confident that suffering can be eradicated, one will look for a solution.

The fourth truth taught by the Buddha about the way out of all suffering is the Noble Eightfold Path. It is important to remember that this path is not only for bhikkhus but also for laypeople. It is not only bhikkhus who need right view. It is not only bhikkhus who taste the sweet fruit of right speech. This is important to know and remember for those who believe and tell others also that the Buddha's teaching is only for bhikkhus.

Those who portray the Buddha as pessimistic and say that he only saw suffering in life have not understood the Four Noble Truths. They act as if the Buddha gave only one truth: the truth of suffering. They ignore the other three noble truths either deliberately or through ignorance.

It is true that the Buddha pointed out the existence of suffering. But he didn't stop there. He discovered the cause of that suffering. If cause and effect is the law of nature, then it is important to understand suffering and go to its root cause. Once we know the reason we can keep it away or prevent it from arising. He didn't stop at the cause of suffering. He gave confidence to humanity that suffering can be destroyed.

People distort his teaching when instead of calling his teaching the fresh bloom of confidence that it was, they call it the soot of pessimism. Not only did he give confidence but also offered a remedy in the form of the effective and decisive eightfold path that gives results here-and-now and that can be experienced by one and all.

When we consider all this, it becomes clear that the Buddha did not look at suffering only from one angle. He had studied the subject in all aspects, completely and in a positive manner. Acharya Goenka's response to the charge that the Buddha was a pessimistic is fully satisfactory.[135]

The Buddha Discussed Happiness

Once while the Tathāgata was dwelling at Jetavana in Sāvatthi, Jāṇussoṇi came to meet him. At the end of his discussion with Jāṇussoṇi,[136] he said that he lived in the forest to experience happiness and comfort here and now; and to set an example for future generations with compassion for them.

At another place he tells bhikkhus to dwell experiencing happiness in this very body.[137]

When he sent out the first batch of bhikkhus to teach the Dhamma to people he asked them to wander "for the happiness of many'.

Once Ven. Mahācunda came to him. To Mahācunda's questions about how various beliefs regarding soul, self, etc. arise.[138]

A bhikkhu abandons mental defilements and with the experience of mental and physical thrill dwells in first, second, third and fourth absorptions *(jhānas)*. In the noble discipline *(ariyavinaya)* it is called "dwelling-in-happiness-here-and-now" *(diṭṭha-dhamma-sukha-vihāra)*.

He used the word happiness again and again in this discussion. He also emphasizes that a bhikkhu dwells in happiness *here and now, in this very life, in this very body*.

Acharya Goenka gives an explanation for *pītisukha* (mental and physical joy) which is apt.[139] "We should keep one historical fact in mind here. In the Buddha's time, the word *ānanda* was not used for joy arising out of absorption meditative practices. It was referred to as *pītisukha*." Acharya Goenka states—with ample evidence—that the Buddha discussed happiness countless times.

After describing the wisdom that he acquired about the Four Noble Truths to his five companions, the Buddha gives one important testimony. He said that as long as he had not developed threefold knowledge of all Four Noble Truths, he had not made the claim to full enlightenment. He didn't make a claim based on hearsay, imagination or speculation not backed by evidence. He made claims only after he tested something thoroughly on the basis of his own experience. Since his argument was flawless, the five companions expressed agreement with him.

Setting the Wheel of Dhamma in Motion

His discourse to the group of five former companions was his first Dhamma discourse. This was the first act in the great movement that subsequently spread far and wide all over the world. Therefore, using a meaningful symbol, it is said that through this discourse he set in motion the Wheel of Dhamma.

A wheel is a material instrument of motion and even figuratively it is a symbol of motion. It is a vital part of vehicles. It is also a symbol that indicates intellectual, psychological and ethical progress of humanity.

In the material progress of human society through history, the invention of the wheel is an important milestone. Similarly, understanding the concepts that set human mental progress in motion can also be said to be an invention of a different kind of wheel. Now the Buddha was confident that the motion of the wheel could not be reversed.

In the Vinaya Piṭaka (the book of monastic discipline) this confidence is expressed as exclamations by various deities. We need not assume that these divine utterances are a historical event. It is a poetic expression showing that the Dhamma taught by the Buddha would benefit countless future generations. It is borne out of a desire to show just how momentous the occasion was for the humanity's welfare.

A *cakkavatti* (wheel turning monarch) is a sovereign king. He wanders to distant places on earth on the wheels (*cakka*) of his chariot. He turns the wheels of the chariot, therefore he is a wheel-turning monarch. The Tathāgata set in motion the wheels of the chariot of the Dhamma. Thus he is also a "wheel-turning" person. *Vatti* is one who sets in motion. *Pavatti* is one who sets in motion properly. The Buddha is not just *Dhamma-cakka-vatti*. He is *Dhamma-cakka-pavatti.*

Sovereign kings usually use force and wealth for their victories. The Buddha wins over the world with his compassion. Therefore, it was not just a *cakka-vattana* but a *cakka-pavattana*. And it is known as the *Dhamma-cakka-pavattana*.

It is said that the soles of his feet had a wheel mark. It is believed to be one of the thirty-two bodily characteristics that he had. Let us keep aside the poetic imagination in this. Perhaps, the Buddha *did* have a wheel symbol on his sole. However, it is irrelevant here. The symbolism is that he had the capacity to set in motion the wheel of Dhamma. He travelled on foot for forty-five years to spread the Dhamma among people. Isn't it the symbol of the wheel that he had the ability and the commitment for such wandering? He gave motion to his feet for the Dhamma and therefore we received this Dhamma. This wheel of Dhamma is important for us—whether or not there was a wheel on his soles!

Eric Fromm

In his book "To Have Or To Be?'[140] Eric Fromm often praises the Buddha. While proposing a framework for suffering, he bases it on the Buddha's teaching. Even the title of the book is influenced by the Buddha.

Fromm writes:

Assuming the premise is right—that only a fundamental change in human character from a preponderance of the having mode to a predominantly being mode of existence can save us from a psychological and economic catastrophe—the question arises: Is large scale characterological change possible, and if so, how can it be brought about?

I suggest that human character can change if these conditions exist:

1. We are suffering and we are aware that we are.
2. We recognize the origin of our ill-being.
3. We recognize that there is a way of overcoming our ill-being.
4. We accept that in order to overcome our ill-being we must follow certain norms for living and change our present practice of life.

These four points correspond to the Four Noble Truths that form the basis of the Buddha's teaching dealing with the general condition of human existence, though not with cases of human ill-being due to specific individual or social circumstances....

Opinion of Orientalist Sharad Patil

Orientalist Sharad Patil[141] says, *"The Buddha as far as his contribution of Dhamma and Saṅgha are concerned was a Marx before Marx and for his contribution to ending caste and promoting democracy was a Marx after Marx!"*

The Dhamma is the Flag of the Sages

The Buddha praised the Dhamma repeatedly and in various ways.

Once he was staying at the Pinnacled Hall at Vesāli. There, Vesākha, son of Pañcāla, was teaching the Dhamma to bhikkhus using flawless, meaningful, relevant and lucid words. In the evening the Buddha got up from his meditation and went to the place where Vesākha had given the discourse. He received information about it and congratulated Vesākha on a sermon well taught. Then he uttered two verses differentiating between good and bad sermons:[142]

A wise man among the ignorant masses remains unrecognized
As long as he doesn't speak. But once he starts speaking
His teaching in ambrosial words makes him known to others.
Teach the Dhamma. Hold aloft the flag of the sages.
Good sermon is a flag of the sages. The Dhamma is the flag of sages.

The Yajña of the Dhamma

The Buddha explained one more thing about the Dhamma in the Numerical Discourses[143]. He said, "Bhikkhus, there are these two gifts. Which two? Material *(āmisa)* gifts and gift of the Dhamma. Bhikkhus, of the two, gift of the Dhamma is greater. There are two *yajñas*. Material *yajña* and Dhamma *yajña*. Of the two, Dhamma *yajña* is greater."

Āmisa originally meant meat. But over the period, its meaning expanded to include material things, objects of enjoyment. *Āmisa dāna* is donation of various material things.

The Buddhist tradition praises donation. It is true that later on, the Buddhist bhikkhus, like the priests of Vedic tradition, started praising donation excessively and improperly.

The Buddha himself praised charity but he didn't exaggerate its importance or created a craze around it. In fact, he showed its limitation and proper place in society. Even properly donated material things can't equal the gift of Dhamma. Material gifts are helpful only for a while. But if someone is taught the Dhamma, one gets a resource for all life, a map for life that has the potential to change one's entire life. Naturally, a material gift can't compare with the gift of the Dhamma.

What is true of the gifts is also true of the *yajñas*. In *yajñas* various offerings are made to fire. The *yajña* of Dhamma is greater than all such *yajñas*.

The Buddha made us aware that the Dhamma that changes our life is far more important than any material gift.

The Joy of Dhamma Excels All Other Joys

A verse in Dhammapada praises the Dhamma thus,[144]

The gift of Dhamma excels all gifts
The flavor of Dhamma excels all flavors
The delight in Dhamma excels all delights
Cessation of craving overcomes all suffering.

Let us understand this verse and what exactly was meant by Dhamma in this verse. The Dhamma here doesn't mean stereotyped rituals of a religious tradition or narrow sectarian principles. The Dhamma that the Buddha had in mind was a refreshing way of life where people are benefitted by proper conduct and coming together harmoniously.

Most material gifts give temporary comfort to the receiver. They may even create a hoarding tendency along with greed and craving. On the other hand, if one is taught how to live a proper life, his whole life changes. After sequentially enumerating the gift of the Dhamma, the flavor of the Dhamma and the delight in the Dhamma; cessation of craving is mentioned as the crowning glory of the Dhamma. Cessation of craving due to following the Dhamma overcomes all suffering.

Greatness Comes from Dhamma; Not from Birth in a Caste or Class

The Buddha put forth the argument very effectively that a man is not great by birth but due to the Dhamma. Many conceited Brahmins found it hard to accept this. We see this in Aggañña Sutta in the Long Discourses.[145]

Once the Tathāgata was staying in the Pubbārāma monastery of Vesākhā. At that time Vāseṭṭha and Bhāradvāja were staying with bhikkhus with the intention of joining the Saṅgha. In the evening, the Buddha came out from his residence and started walking in the shadow of the building.

Vāseṭṭha saw him and suggested to Bhāradvāja, "Let us go and follow the Tathāgata. We will be able to hear Dhamma talk."

They went to the Tathāgata, saluted him and started following him.

Then the Tathāgata asked Vāseṭṭha, "Vāseṭṭha, you are both brahmins. You have renounced and left home. Do the brahmins criticize you? Do they laugh at you?"

Vāseṭṭha replied, "Yes, *bhante*, brahmins denigrate us, they heap a 'flood of insults' on us. They laugh not a little at us but a lot."

The Tathāgata asked him, "In what way do the brahmins criticize you?"

Vāseṭṭha answered, "They say, 'Brahmin caste is the greatest. Others are low. Brahmins are fair. Other castes are dark. Brahmins are pure-bred. Others are not. Brahmins are rightful children of Brahmā. They are born from the mouth of Brahmā. They are created by Brahmā. They are the inheritors of Brahmā. Having gone to the low, black, shaven headed ascetics who are born from the feet of Brahmā, you have left your high caste and fallen to lower status. This is not suitable for you.' Thus, bhante, other brahmins criticize us…"

The Tathāgata then told Vāseṭṭha that brahmins are speaking thus because they have forgotten the past. "Vāseṭṭha, brahmin women have menses, get pregnant, give birth and suckle their babies. Thus brahmins are born the same way as others… they lie about Brahmā."

Then the Tathāgata discussed conduct of all the four castes: *khattiya* (warrior), *brāhmaṇa* (priest), *vessa* (traders) and *sudda* (lower caste). In each of these castes, someone might indulge in unethical conduct such as killing, stealing, sexual misconduct, lying, etc. while someone else might abstain from these. Thus it could not be said that people from one caste were all moral while all people from the other caste were immoral. In all the castes, there were good people and there were bad people. In such a case, how could brahmins claim that only brahmins were superior?

Even though brahmins made such claims, the wise didn't agree with them. Anyone from the four castes, who eradicated his defilements, acquired wisdom and became liberated, became superior. The Buddha clearly stated that one became superior based on the Dhamma, not based on wrong teaching. He explained how, here and hereafter, the Dhamma is the greatest.

To explain the greatness of the Dhamma, he gave the example of King Pasenadi. "Vāseṭṭha, King Pasenadi of Kosala knows that the Tathāgata comes from the Sākyan clan. The Sākyans are vassals of King Pasenadi. They pay obeisance to King Pasenadi. They salute him. They do everything necessary to honor him. Vāseṭṭha, whatever the Sākyans do for King Pasenadi, King Pasenadi does for the Tathāgata. When he does so, he doesn't do so because he thinks that Samaṇa Gotama is well-born, strong, handsome and mighty or because he thinks that he is low-born, weak, ugly or insignificant. He reveres, praises and attends on the Tathāgata to respect Dhamma, revere Dhamma, obey Dhamma, honor Dhamma… Thus, Dhamma is superior in humanity."

Then the Tathāgata said, "Vāseṭṭha, various people from various families, various clans, various castes go forth from home into homelessness and take robes. When they are asked, 'Who are you?' they emphatically say, 'We are Samaṇas, the Sākyan's sons.' One who has complete confidence in the Tathāgata, whose confidence in him is steady, deeply rooted, strong and firm—such a person's confidence in the Tathāgata cannot be shaken by any samaṇa, brāhmaṇa, deva, māra or brahmā. 'We are the rightful sons of the Tathāgata, born from his mouth, born from his Dhamma, created by the Dhamma, inheritors of the Dhamma'—such claims by them is proper and correct. Why, Vāseṭṭha? Because *Dhammakāya* (One with Dhamma), *Brahmakāya* (One with Brahmā), *Dhammabhūta* (Being Dhamma), *Brahmabhūta* (Being Brahmā) are the names of the Buddha himself."

Discussion

Some from the brahmin caste accepted the teaching of the Buddha. They entered the Saṅgha. Other brahmins used to think of this as the downfall of those brahmins. For them, to accept guidance from others in the field of learning was a taint on their greatness. The Tathāgata's comment on the brahmins' claims as narrated by Vāseṭṭha a little harsh. In reality, he was merely stating that all the castes are equal when it comes to good or bad qualities.

The view of those brahmins was derogatory to other castes whereas that of the Tathāgata respects humanness of all castes including that of brahmins. The Tathāgata didn't take the wrong and immoral stand that a brahmin is immoral whether he performs good deeds or bad deeds. He said that irrespective of caste of birth a moral person is a good person. This view stands true when one applies tests of all human values.

The example of Pasenadi is also significant. As a member of a vassal clan, Siddhārtha Gotama was expected to salute Pasenadi. Gotama had become the Tathāgata due to the Dhamma. Now Pasenadi saluted him. This happened due to the Dhamma. Therefore, all credit must go to the Dhamma, not to birth, class or caste.

People from all castes came to the Saṅgha and became one. Saying that they were now born of the Dhamma; that they were the rightful sons of the Tathāgata was not at the same level as the brahmins' claim of being born from the mouth of the Brahmā.

Both are symbolisms. But one is committed to social equality and the other is poisoned by social inequality. One is untainted and acceptable. The other is tainted and unacceptable.

Qualities of the Buddha's Dhamma

In Tipiṭaka, there are countless descriptions of the qualities of the Dhamma taught by the Buddha. Some of the qualities are quoted repeatedly. These adjectives are meaningful. Let us take a look at them.

The Dhamma is Always Benevolent

Tipiṭaka describes the Dhamma as beneficial in the beginning, beneficial in the middle and beneficial in the end.

It is an objective assessment of the Dhamma that it is beneficial at every step of the journey and from all sides. If someone doubts that such a claim is false, exaggerated and is made out of devotional zeal, one should take time to look at the Dhamma that followed the middle path. The sweetness of a piece of jaggery is not restricted to one spot. It pervades and occupies every molecule every moment. Similarly, the benevolence of the Buddha's Dhamma is all pervading.

The qualities of the Dhamma are:

Ehi Passiko (Come and See)

Ehi means come. *Passa* means see. Whosoever wants to know the teaching of the Buddha or whosoever has any doubts or questions about the Dhamma is invited thus, "Come and see." See for yourself. A Dhamma that invites people to come and see is called *ehi passiko*. The Dhamma has this "come and see" quality.

These two words put the Dhamma at the highest level of learning and removes all objections and doubts. Do not believe because I say so or a bhikkhu says so or a scripture says so.

Come and experience yourself. Then if you are convinced, accept it. If you don't find it proper, reject it. This is how all learning, all knowledge is set free. Nothing is forced on the seeker. He or she is humbly requested to give the Dhamma a try. He or she is politely requested, affectionately invited. There is an affinity for the invitee. There is goodwill.

Unless one has the confidence that the Dhamma is objective and truth-based; it is beneficial to one and all; it can stand any investigation in the world; it will pass the most rigorous tests; one can't have the courage to say "come and see." Those who are not sure about their philosophy or religion make a rule that it can't be investigated. The Tathāgata never made any attempt to hide the Dhamma from the analytical eye.

Svākkhāto (Well Explained)

Well explained. Because it was explained by the enlightened person, it was properly explained. He taught in a lucid language so that ordinary people can understand. To make it easy for people to understand, he used to give fitting parables. He didn't teach the Dhamma to impress people about his intelligence. He taught the Dhamma for the welfare of people.

No Closed Fist of Teacher

Once the Tathāgata was seriously ill. After he recovered, Ānanda felt much relieved. He told the Tathāgata that he had become disheartened due to the illness. Ānanda also told him that he drew solace from the belief that the Tathāgata would not pass away without advising the Saṅgha.

Then the Tathāgata asked him,[146] "What does the Bhikkhu-Saṅgha expect from me now? I have taught the Dhamma in its totality without hiding anything; without reservation. Ānanda, in the field of Dhamma, the Tathāgata has kept 'no fist of teacher.' (In some Indian traditions, it is said that the teacher should not pass on the entire knowledge to the pupil so as to maintain his superiority and relevance. This is called 'fist of teacher.') Ānanda, one who feels that 'I own the Saṅgha' or 'The Saṅgha exists for me,' would advise the Saṅgha. But Ānanda, I don't feel that 'I own the Saṅgha' or 'The Saṅgha exists for me.' Therefore, what would I advise the Saṅgha?"

He always taught openly and freely. He didn't reserve anything. He didn't hide anything as someone hides a hidden treasure. He didn't discriminate between those who came to learn from him. He never discriminated based on caste, class, gender, closeness, etc.

He Teaches for Me

He taught without prejudice, without expectation, without malice. Therefore, all those who listened felt as if the sermon was meant for them. What a lofty and refreshing relation between the speaker and the audience! This is a lesson to all the teachers and pupils of the world about how to maintain this relation.

He once narrated this moving experience,[147] "Aggivessana, I remember that I used to give a talk to an assembly of several hundreds. Each one of the assembly used to feel, 'Samaṇa Gotama's sermon is directed at me'. Don't think, Aggivessana, that the Tathāgata teaches the Dhamma for appearances or display."

Had show of scholarship or any other selfish motive driven his sermons, he would not have touched the hearts of his audience so profoundly.

Four Kinds of Preachers

He was very careful and disciplined about the essence of the Dhamma and how he taught it. He insisted that those who taught the Dhamma should be perfect in both.

Once while talking to bhikkhus, he told them about the four types of *dhammakathikas* (preachers of the Dhamma):[148]

The first type of bhikkhu speaks less and whatever little he says is meaningless. But the audience is not discerning and skillful. For them, this bhikkhu is a preacher of the Dhamma.

The second type of bhikkhu speaks less but says what is meaningful. His audience is discerning and skillful. For them this bhikkhu is a preacher of the Dhamma.

The third type of bhikkhu speaks a lot but what he says is meaningless. If his audience is not discerning, he is still a preacher of the Dhamma for them.

The fourth type of bhikkhu speaks a lot and what he says is meaningful. His audience is discerning. For them he is a preacher of the Dhamma.

In these four types described by the Buddha, there are three important aspects: How much does one say, whether it is meaningful and whether the audience is discerning. A short meaningful talk is more beneficial and much better than a long meaningless talk. Meaningfulness of speech is more important than its quantity.

For an audience that is not discerning, both the meaningful speech and meaningless speech is of the same level. Thus, just as one who teaches the Dhamma has a responsibility, one who listens also has the responsibility to apply his mind, to judge properly and to expand his ability to judge.

Only the preacher of the Dhamma who speaks meaningfully is able to take the Dhamma to the people.

Whose Dhamma Discourse is Totally Pure?

Once the Buddha asked the bhikkhus, "Whose Dhamma discourse is totally pure and whose Dhamma discourse is impure."[149]

He explained when the bhikkhus asked him to clarify.

If one gives a discourse with the feeling that people should listen to his Dhamma talk, be impressed by it and praise it, then his Dhamma discourse is impure.

On the other hand, one knows that the Buddha's teaching gives results here and now; feels that people should listen to the

Dhamma and having listened to it they should follow it. Thinking thus about the goodness of Dhamma, with love and compassion in mind, a bhikkhu gives a discourse. Such a discourse is said to be pure.

The first type of preacher is happy with his own sermon. He is conceited. Therefore, he expects those who like his sermon to express their appreciation. He is not concerned about whether the sermon is going to influence the lives of the audience positively; whether they are going to follow the Dhamma in their lives. He is more concerned about his own image.

The second type of preacher is different. He has no ego. He doesn't crave for praise from audience. He feels that his effort is worthwhile if due to his sermon people start following the Dhamma and benefit from it. His sermon is pure because it arises from a mind full of compassion.

Not Even a Sound of a Cough

People would listen to the Buddha's discourse attentively. Once he was staying in the Bamboo Grove of Rājagaha.[150] At that time, some ascetics including Sakula Udāyī were chatting in their living quarters. Since there was still time for the alms round, the Buddha went to their quarters. Udāyī welcomed him and narrated to him a recent incident. People from various sects had gathered. One of them told others about the Tathāgata thus: Once the Tathāgata was giving a discourse in an assembly of hundreds of people. At that time, someone in the audience coughed. Then the person sitting next to him nudged him and requested, "Don't make noise. The Teacher is giving a Dhamma discourse." When the Buddha gives a talk even in a big assembly of several hundred, there is no noise of cough or throat clearing.

All the audience would be eager to listen to his talk. They would take care not to disturb others as well as ensure that they themselves would hear it properly. Even someone who was coughing was told politely with a gentle touch. This person didn't get angry or shout but whispered in the neighbor's ears. There was no coercion or pressure to listen to his discourse. There was discipline but no threat of punishment. The audience would be drawn to him due to his grand personality, his rich experience, the depth of his thinking, the benevolence of his teaching and the immense compassion in his heart for the welfare of the audience.

This incident gives us a twofold lesson. It is wrong if the speaker is giving a dry, useless and meaningless sermon and it is also wrong if the audience is not paying proper attention.

Power Can't Force Audience to be Attentive

The Buddha would attract audience to him not with power but with love and affection. He could do it easily while a ruler would not be able to do. This difference was highlighted by King Pasenadi once.[151]

The Tathāgata was staying at a Sākyan town. At that time King Pasenadi went to visit the Tathāgata.

Observing the interaction between the Tathāgata and the bhikkhus, he commented, "I am an anointed warrior king. I can kill someone if I wish to. I can use my authority to banish someone from my kingdom. Though I have such immense power, I find that when I am speaking, people keep interfering with their comments. Even when I tell them to wait till I finish, they continue to speak in between. And here I see these bhikkhus—When the Tathāgata gives sermon to an audience of several hundreds, there is hardly a noise even of cough or clearing of throat."

Then the king also repeated the incident narrated by Udāyī. The king then expressed his thoughts, "Surprising it is! Miraculous it is! Without a stick, without any weapon, the assembly becomes so polite and quiet! Bhante, I have not seen such a disciplined assembly anywhere else. This is also a reason why I see the Dhamma in the Tathāgata and I think that the Tathāgata is fully enlightened; well-explained is his Dhamma and on the right path is his Saṅgha."

This comparison done by a mighty emperor of that time shows how the Buddha was such a marvelous teacher. It also shows that Pasenadi was a candid person who shared openly how in spite of his sovereign power he was unable to keep his audience quiet.

Sandiṭṭhiko (Here and Now. In This Very Life)

The Dhamma gives results here and now, in this very life. When the Buddha was trying to convince his five former companions to listen to him, he told them that the Dhamma he taught gave fruit in this very life, in this very world. Those who don't believe in life after death also benefit from the Dhamma. They can experience it in real life. It is not based on imagination. It doesn't create confusion.

Akāliko (Immediate. Timeless)

The Dhamma can be experienced in the present time. There is no empty future promise.

Opanayiko (Leading to Goal)

It gives fruits. It leads one to the highest goal of life. Thus it is *opanayika.* It means that the practice of Dhamma is never futile.

Paccataṃ (Pratyakshagamya, Can Be Experienced Directly)

One more quality of the Dhamma is that a perceptive person can experience it directly. He had told the five companions at the beginning of his discourse that they should directly experience it themselves.

While describing the Dhamma to the bhikkhus, Sāriputta said:[152]

It is well taught.
It takes one beyond the suffering.
It gives peace, cools down the fire of defilements.
It is taught by a person who has attained full enlightenment.

Fruits of Teaching and Listening to the Dhamma

Teaching the Dhamma has four fruits: it makes one dear to the Teacher; one experiences more and more the meaning and the emotions behind the discourse; one understands with wisdom the serious meaning of the discourse; and one is honored by associates. Once the Tathāgata said that the fifth fruit of teaching the Dhamma is that those who are still not liberated are inspired to work harder and those who are liberated, dwell happily listening to the Dhamma.[153]

At another time, the Buddha gave five benefits of listening to the Dhamma.[154] One hears what one has not heard before. Whatever one has heard before gets clarified. Doubts are removed. Thinking becomes straightforward. The mind becomes joyful.

Reasons for the Decline and Demise of the Dhamma

The Buddha taught the Dhamma (sometimes referred to as *Saddhamma* to separate it from other Dhammas) for the benefit of many, for the welfare of many. On one side, it finds place in the hearts of the people. On the other side, it declines and even vanishes. This twofold process has been going on for the past twenty-five centuries. This was happening even in the time of the Buddha. Having seen for himself how the Dhamma declines, he had repeatedly warned the bhikkhus about the possible causes of the decline.

Once he gave four reasons for the decline of the Dhamma.[155]

The bhikkhus misunderstand the Dhamma and sometimes use wrong words in its recitation. Due to wrong words being used, the meaning also becomes distorted. This is the first reason for the decline and loss of Dhamma.

The bhikkhus use wrong speech. They are not capable. They don't follow discipline. This is the second reason for the decline of the Dhamma.

The bhikkhus are erudite. They know the *āgamas*. They know the discourses of the Buddha, the rules of the monastic discipline, the matrices. But they don't teach others properly. They don't transmit their knowledge in depth. When such learned bhikkhus pass away, the Dhamma's roots are shaken and it becomes without support. This is the third reason.

The senior bhikkhus start hoarding material possessions. They become lax. They follow the road to downfall. They avoid giving Dhamma discourses. They don't make effort to attain that which they have not attained; to know about the Dhamma that which they don't know; to comprehend that which they have not comprehended. Others follow them. They also run after wealth and other material things. This is the fourth reason for the decline of the Dhamma.

After giving an exposition on the four reasons for the decline of the Dhamma, he said that when the bhikkhus don't behave like in the above four ways, the Dhamma doesn't decline. Indeed, it endures for long time

Discussion

Sometimes external factors are responsible for a philosophy or a spiritual tradition to decline and vanish; often the conduct of those teach that path to the people is also responsible for it. The Tathāgata knew this well. Rather than blaming external factors, he has pointed out the flaws in the conduct of the bhikkhus.

Though the Buddha's Dhamma was perfect, the responsibility of taking it to the people rested with the bhikkhus. The image of the Dhamma in the hearts and minds of people depended on the character of the bhikkhus. If the bhikkhus became lax, it would affect the image of the Dhamma among the people. Therefore, for the spread of Dhamma, the conduct of the bhikkhus was very important.

It is obvious that if the bhikkhus did not understand the Dhamma properly, they would recite it wrongly and use wrong words. This would affect the essence of the Dhamma and corrupt it. The Buddha has emphasized this point elsewhere repeatedly. To avoid corruption of words and meaning, one should be careful with the use of words.

Right speech in one of the parts of the noble eightfold path. Elsewhere in the book, it is discussed in detail. If bhikkhus were not capable and they were ineffective, they would be unable to do the Dhamma work properly. Undisciplined bhikkhus would disturb and disrupt the harmony and coherence of the Dhamma mission.

The third reason given by the Buddha is also very important. This is not applicable only to the *Saddhamma*. It is equally applicable to the entire history, culture, etc. of the masses of India. Someone does great work in one generation but there is no planning or system in place to carry that work to the future generation. This has happened for thousands of years in India. The great work vanishes. Whatever remains becomes corrupt and is misrepresented. The Buddha has indirectly pointed out this situation.

It is not enough for one generation to reach the pinnacle of achievements. It is important to see that the merit is passed onto the next generations without a break. New generations also need to receive with gratitude the heritage from earlier generations. They need to treasure it carefully and to pass it on to the next generation. If this is not done, then the great flow of the life's values may get lost in the sand of indifference.

Those responsible to spread the Dhamma sometimes start running after material luxuries, wealth and fame. Their behavior becomes lax. They start avoiding hard work. They become lazy. They worry only about maximizing their luxury and security. And then this illness starts spreading everywhere like a contagious disease.

Having studied human mind and human society in depth and in subtle details, the Buddha knew that this could happen with the Dhamma. He had warned bhikkhus that if these flaws emerged in them, the benevolent Dhamma would decline. He warned them to stay away from these defects.

How the Dhamma Endures…

He dealt with this again in the Kimila Sutta of the Graded Discourses.[156] He was once staying in the bamboo grove of Kimila region. At that time Ven. Kimila came, saluted him and sat to one side. He asked the Buddha the reasons behind non-enduring of the Dhamma after the Buddha was no more.

The Buddha replied, "After the passing away of the Buddha, bhikkhus, bhikkhuṇis, laymen and laywomen lose respect for the Buddha, the Dhamma, the Saṅgha and the discourses. They become irresponsible. Similarly, they don't respect each other. They don't care for each other. These are the five reasons for the decline of the Dhamma. If the followers didn't behave in this manner, the Dhamma endures for a long time."

Discussion

Just as bhikkhus and bhikkhuṇis have responsibility for the protection and spread of the Dhamma, laymen and laywomen also have responsibility. It is not enough that they honor and respect the Buddha, the Dhamma and the Saṅgha; they must also respect each other. If they lack respect for each other, they can't unite and with one voice take the Dhamma to the people.

Fake Dhamma Causes Saddhamma to Decline

In the Compounded Discourses,[157] we see that the Buddha has explained this effectively.

Once he was dwelling at Jetavana in Sāvatthi. At that time, Ven. Mahākassapa came to him and sat down to one side after saluting him. He then commented, "Bhante, earlier there were fewer monastic rules and yet many bhikkhus attained liberation. These days there are several monastic rules but not many bhikkhus become liberated." The Buddha told him that this happened when there was decay in essence of Dhamma and decline in *Saddhamma*.

Then he added, as long as a fake Dhamma that gives the appearance of the Dhamma doesn't appear in the world, *Saddhamma* doesn't decline. Then he gave a simile to clarify his statement. As long as fake gold is not created in the world, real gold continues to be valued.

Then he added an important point. Earth, water, fire or air—none of these four elements can cause the decline of the Dhamma. But worthless men can cause decline in the Dhamma. A boat when too many people sit in it capsizes. This *doesn't* happen with the Dhamma.

He also narrated the reasons given earlier for the decline of the Dhamma and said that if the bhikkhus etc. respected the Buddha, the Dhamma, etc. the Saddhamma would endure for long.

Discussion

From the question of Mahākassapa, it is clear that even during the lifetime of the Buddha, some bhikkhus were becoming lax. It also becomes clear from the Buddha's saying that the essence gets decayed.

In his discussion with Mahākassapa, the Buddha made two very important points: One of worthless, foolish people and the other of the fake Dhammas.

The Buddha said that the elements such as earth, water, etc. could not cause decline of the Dhamma but worthless, foolish people could. When people who are inspired to attain a goal take a leap in that direction and also inspire others to do so, physical conditions can't stop them or defeat the principles of their life. But if one loses one's commitment for the goal, one strays from the goal and one's feet walk in a different direction, then that goal is certainly destroyed. It is not that the physical conditions are not important. But true test of human character lies in not allowing the physical conditions to overcome us and instead in overcoming the physical conditions.

The Buddha has given the simile of a boat. The Commentary explains the simile thus:[158] Those who wish to cross a river or a lake take a boat. If the boat is overloaded it sinks. This doesn't happen in the case of the Dhamma. Following more and more principles of the Dhamma doesn't burden it, doesn't cause it to sink. But if the ethics decline, conduct declines. If conduct declines, knowledge declines.

On the other hand, cultivating morality perfects conduct and it in turn completes knowledge. The Commentary says that the simile means that progress in ethics will lead to increase in the Dhamma just like the moon in the waxing cycle.

The Buddha described various internal reasons for the decline of the Dhamma. It doesn't mean that he ignored the external reasons. He was mindful of all the threats to the Dhamma. Therefore, his statement about the fake Dhamma is important. He has also aptly explained it with the example of gold.

The principles of the Dhamma explained by the Buddha are beneficial for people. They appeal to the people's intellect. People like them. Therefore, they feel affinity, affection and attraction for the Dhamma. This popularity of the Dhamma is exploited by cunning people in society. They propose principles that are superficially like the Dhamma but which contain lower values. This way they confuse people and attract them to the fake Dhamma.

Be the Inheritor of Dhamma; Not of Material Things

Once the Buddha was dwelling in Jetavana in Sāvatthi.[159] At that time, he exhorted the bhikkhus, "Bhikkhus, be the inheritor of my Dhamma; not of material things. I have this compassionate feeling for you that you should become the inheritor of Dhamma and not of the material things. If you become inheritors of material things, people will censure you and will also censure me. But if you inherit the Dhamma, this won't happen."

Then he clarified his point with one more example.

He said, "Suppose, I have eaten to the capacity of my stomach. And some food is still remaining. At that time, two bhikkhus who are hungry come there. I tell them that there is some food remaining after I have finished my meal and if they wish they can eat it. If you are not going to eat it, then throw it where there is no grass or in water where there are no animals. One thinks that the Buddha has asked us to be the inheritor of the Dhamma, not of the material things. Food is a material thing. Thinking thus, he doesn't eat and spends the day and night hungry. The other bhikkhu eats the food."

Then the Buddha added, "Of these two bhikkhus, for me the first one is praiseworthy and worthy of respect. Because his conduct would lead for a long time to his wanting little, contentment, meditation, ease of completing work and effort."

Discussion

The Buddha wanted bhikkhus to inherit his Dhamma. Therefore, he didn't want them to gain anything material from him or from others to enrich their material life. He said that this was his compassionate wish for them. He supports them with his goodwill. This discourse also arises out of his compassion. What we should take from great men is their teaching, not material benefit. This is applicable not only for bhikkhus but also for laypeople.

When he said that if bhikkhus ran after material possessions, it would bring disrepute to them as well as to him, he wasn't worried about his reputation. He felt that the untoward conduct of the bhikkhus would bring disrepute to the benevolent Dhamma.

The Buddha has placed huge responsibility on his followers. It is essential that while taking the name of the Buddha and claiming to be his followers we don't become irresponsible, wayward or immoral. It was with this context that Dr Babasaheb Ambedkar had asked his followers to take care not to sully the name of the Buddha Dhamma.

To further clarify his point, the Buddha gives the example of the food remaining after his meal and the two hungry bhikkhus. While food is available and the bhikkhus are hungry, the Buddha praises the one who doesn't eat saying he is more worthy of reverence than the other. Prima facie, this doesn't seem reasonable. We do feel that it is not proper to throw away food when one is hungry. On deeper reflection though, we can understand why the Buddha said this. I think we should take a figurative meaning rather than taking it literally. (At several places, the Buddha had demonstrated by his various instructions that he didn't promote fasting.)

Food here is symbolic of material inheritance. Many a time when we associate with a great personality who transforms society through his teachings, our focus should be on his thoughts. We should not be distracted by small or big material things. Once we allow a weakness to enter our mind, all the defilements related to greed get an opportunity to raise their head. Even a small slip in morality can open all roads to our downfall. Therefore, to win control over oneself, it is prudent and beneficial in the long run to face difficulty and suffer deprivation. The first bhikkhu recognized this. Therefore, the Buddha calls him more worthy of reverence. It should be noted that he has not criticized the second bhikkhu.

Usually, the Buddha's parables are easy to understand and clarify the issue. They remove confusion; not increase it. In this one instance though one may think that the parable has increased the confusion; that it would have been better had the Buddha given some other symbol for material possessions instead of food. Here we should note that the parable was meant for bhikkhus. He wanted bhikkhus to be restrained in food. He himself used to have only one meal a day and recommended it. (Though he left the choice to bhikkhus and did not make it a monastic rule.) Therefore, food as a symbol for material things came naturally as being close to monastic life.

Practising Dhamma is the True Worship of the Buddha

We have seen earlier in the Mahāparinibbāna Sutta of the Long Discourses that the Buddha asked Ānanda to arrange a bed for him between two sāla (*shorea robusta*) trees. At that time the Buddha described what was happening in nature around, "Ānanda, these twin sāla trees have blossomed non-seasonally. They are covered with flowers. They are worshipping the Tathāgata by showering flowers on him. Divine flowers are being showered on him from the skies. Divine powder of sandalwood is being poured on his body. Divine music and divine songs can be heard. All this is happening to worship the Buddha. Ānanda, in reality, all this is not proper worship of the Buddha. This is not how the Buddha is revered. When a bhikkhu or a bhikkhuṇi or a layman or a laywoman follows the Dhamma, practices the Dhamma, conducts oneself in accordance with the Dhamma, then one honors the Buddha, worships him, reveres him, venerates him. Therefore, Ānanda, you should honor the Buddha by practising the Dhamma, by following the Dhamma."

Discussion

It is not that the non-seasonal blossom of sāla trees was not a historical happening. It could have happened. Various natural causes can sometimes lead to such things. But what is more important and what touches our hearts is the symbolism of it. It was as if the nature outside was doing all it could to give a proper farewell to the Buddha by showering flowers on him. It indicates that the Tathāgata's compassion was not limited to the animal world, he was kind to the trees as well and therefore it was as if the trees were responding this way to his imminent passing away.

It seems the Buddha had a special connection to the sāla trees. He took birth under a sāla tree. It seems he remembered this special relation with the sāla tree and treasured this relationship even in his last moments. This was not an undue attachment. It is wrong to get entangled in something but to keep a healthy and innocent relationship is a different thing. This great man's birth and death both didn't occur inside four walls. He was born and he passed away under the open sky. Throughout his life, between these two points, no walls (of traditional thinking, fear or insecurity) could confine him, restrict him or curb his quest for total freedom from all suffering.

His stand on what is true worship and honor is a great ideal created by him. Generally, people like to be praised and honored. Therefore, when people want something from others, they use praise, flowers and outward respect. Just as sometimes these things are done with the selfish intention of getting something from the person who is honored, sometimes, it is also done with genuine reverence. Whether it is done with a selfish motive or with selflessness, such honor is of limited importance.

Often people show much veneration but don't follow the teaching or advice of one who is being honored. The Buddha emphasized that this is not true worship. He insisted that living an upright life and following the Dhamma is the true worship. True ethical behavior involves following the teaching of the person who is being honored and not to be entangled in artificial exhibitions. He knew that the human mind often gets trapped in external rituals and forgets the fundamental principles. He didn't want a personality cult, rather he wanted his followers to practice Dhamma.

After Me the Dhamma is Your Guide

In Mahāparinibbāna sutta, we see that he made it clear to Ānanda that after he was no more, the Dhamma and the Discipline was their guide. This is important in various ways. He didn't appoint any single person as his successor. This has to be interpreted carefully.

He wanted to be consistent with whatever he taught all his life and presented to the society through his own conduct. That is why he put this restriction. If he had wanted to create a personality cult around him, he would have asked Ānanda to preserve him as the guide, to remember him and worship him after his death. He gave importance to the principle, law, truth and learning, which means he gave importance to the Dhamma.

This Dhamma was not discovered through someone's whim or fancy or someone's grace or casually or serendipitously. The Buddha had discovered it through immense efforts resisting all enticements on the way and countering all the pressures. He had thrown his very existence into the effort. He had discovered it through his unsullied morality and brilliant wisdom. Therefore, he wanted the Dhamma to be the guide to people.

Barrister Savarkar's objection[160] that the Tathāgata gave more importance to the Buddha than the Dhamma has no basis. The Tathāgata never told anyone to take refuge in Siddhārtha Gotama. To take refuge in the Buddha is to take refuge in a person who has attained enlightenment. Therefore, it is the refuge in enlightenment. Every person has the capacity to attain Bodhi.

Attainment of Buddhahood was in a way cessation of the personality of Gotama. Therefore, refuge in the Buddha is not refuge in any person. He didn't want anyone's personal limitations to limit the Dhamma. He wanted the Dhamma to endure eternally to guide generations upon generations of humanity.

Be an Island of the Dhamma

Once the Buddha was staying at Mātulā in Magadha. While exhorting the bhikkhus to be an island unto themselves, he said,[161] "Be an island of the Dhamma. Take refuge in the Dhamma. Take no other refuge." When he referred to the Dhamma, he didn't mean a sect framed by tradition or ritual. He meant the principles of the Dhamma.

Just as a boat in the sea finds refuge in an island during storm and becomes safe; while facing the storms in life, the Dhamma gives support and makes life secure.

We Take Refuge in Dhamma—Ānanda

A few days after the Buddha passed away, Ven. Ānanda was dwelling in Kalandakanivāpa in Rājagaha. At that time, while Ven. Ānanda was talking to Gopaka Moggallāna, Vassakāra brahmin, the Minister of Magadha came there.

In the course of the conversation, he asked Ānanda,[162] "Ānanda, has Gotama appointed anyone as your guide saying 'He would be your refuge when I am no more' and are you following any such bhikkhu now?"

Ānanda answered in negative. Again Ānanda answered in negative when asked if there was anyone who has been chosen by the Saṅgha and approved by various elderly bhikkhus. Then he was asked, "How can the bhikkhus live together when there is no refuge, no protection for them?" Ānanda answered, "We are not without refuge. We have refuge. We have refuge in the Dhamma."

Ānanda explained to him: The Buddha has laid down rules for bhikkhus. He has asked them to gather regularly. All bhikkhus living near a village or a field gathered together every fortnight and recited the rules of monastic discipline. If there had been a transgression on the part of any bhikkhu, the other bhikkhus ask him to take corrective action in accordance with the Dhamma and the rules. It is not the bhikkhus who made him do it, it was the Dhamma that made him do it.

When asked if there is even a single bhikkhu who all the bhikkhus honor and respect, Ānanda answered, "…The Buddha has described ten qualities that delight. We honor, respect and worship whosoever has those ten qualities. We dwell under his guidance." Then Ānanda explained those qualities such as morality, etc.

The Dhamma is Like a Raft

The simile of the raft was one of the favorite similes of the Buddha. The Buddha said that just as one would escape assassins or poisonous snakes on one bank by making a raft and crossing over to the other side, a meditator used the raft of the Noble Eightfold Path to cross over to the safe shore of nibbāna.[163]

Just as he emphasized the importance of the Dhamma and the raft, he was also aware of the limitations. He cautioned them,[164] "Bhikkhus, you will not get stuck to this view that is flawless and pure from all angles, will you? You will not play with it, will you? You will not think of it as your possession, will you? You will not think of it as your own, will you? You understand that I have given you this Dhamma which is like a raft that is used to cross over to the other shore, don't you?"

The bhikkhus replied that they wouldn't get stuck to the Dhamma. The Buddha again cautioned them not to get unduly attached to the Dhamma.

At another time, the Buddha again gave the simile of the raft.[165] While staying at Jetavana in Sāvatthi he told bhikkhus, "I give you the Dhamma just as a raft: to be used to cross over to the other side, not to hold on to." Then he explained it in detail.

"Suppose a traveler in the course of his journey has come to a lake. Then he finds that this shore is unsafe and dangerous. The other shore is safe and without dangers. But there is no boat to cross over to the safe side. The traveler collects grass, wood, twigs and leaves to build a raft. Then he gets on to the raft and uses his hands to row over to the other side. When he gets to the other side, he feels gratitude towards the raft. Thinking 'This raft has helped me,' he decides to carry it on his head on his onward journey. Now in this case, bhikkhus, is his behavior towards the raft proper?"

The bhikkhus answered in the negative. Then the Buddha said that it would be proper for the traveler to leave the raft on the shore or set it down on the water.

"My teaching too is like the raft. Therefore, once you have achieved your goal, you should leave even the Dhamma behind (meaning, you should not get stuck to the formal presentation of it); what to talk about *adhamma*?"

Discussion

The Dhamma taught by the Buddha is a tool both to regulate and uplift the human life. To take refuge in the Dhamma means to follow the ideal lifestyle presented through the Dhamma. He advised Ānanda that rather than taking refuge in a person after him, one should take refuge in the Dhamma. All this explains the importance of the Dhamma for the Buddha. But there is one more specialty about him.

However important the Dhamma may be, it's presentation is a tool that is used to achieve our goal. He explained this to the bhikkhus, "Don't get entangled and stuck with Dhamma because the Dhamma is so great."

The Buddha's advice about the Dhamma is sensible, objective and beneficial. One is amazed to see someone looking at his own teaching with so much detachment and neutrality. Many great people become very sensitive and touchy not only about the philosophy they propound but also about the presentation. They also want their disciples to stick to it in every way. They don't give their disciples the slightest leeway. They don't give freedom to the disciples to analyze or examine their views.

Here the Buddha not only gave his disciples freedom to examine his teaching but told them that it is their duty to examine it. He was careful to ensure that his teaching didn't shackle future generations. He wanted his disciples to use his presentation as a medium to progress towards their goals. He didn't just give up his royal inheritance, he totally dissolved his ego in case of the Dhamma that he had himself discovered by the dint of his efforts. Such direction liberates humanity psychologically and intellectually.

Purification of Morality is but a Milestone in the Journey

In a sense, Rathavinita Sutta[166] of the Middle Discourses elaborates the simile of the raft.

The Buddha was dwelling in Kalanadakanivāpa of the Sākyans at that time. He asked the bhikkhus which bhikkhu possessed all the good qualities in his homeland. The bhikkhus mentioned Puṇṇa, the son of Mettāni. On hearing this, Ven. Sāriputta developed a wish to see him. They finally met in Sāvatthi in the Blind Forest.

Sāriputta asked him, "Do you follow the holy life under the Buddha for the purification of morality?" Puṇṇa answered in the negative.

Then Sāriputta asked him in series whether Puṇṇa was following the holy life under the Buddha for purification of concentration, wisdom, removal of all doubt, differentiation between path and non-path, knowledge of the path, direct knowledge of wisdom. To all these questions, Puṇṇa answered in the negative. Then Sāriputta asked him why he was living the holy life. Puṇṇa answered, "To attain nibbāna without any attachment, I follow the holy life under the Buddha."

Then he again answered in the negative to the question as to whether nibbāna without attachment was different from purification of morality. Sāriputta then asked him how to reconcile his statements.

Puṇṇa answered that had the Buddha called purification of morality etc. as nibbāna without attachments, then it would have meant that he was calling nibbāna with attachments as nibbāna without attachments. On the other hand, if nibbāna without attachments were to be without purification of morality etc., then even ignorant people who don't have purification of morality would attain nibbāna without attachment.

Then to clarify his statement, he gave a simile. "Suppose, King Pasenadi left for Sāketa from Sāvatthi for some work. On the way, at seven places, he left the earlier chariot behind and took a new chariot to the next stage. Ultimately, he reached Sāketa in the seventh chariot. What would he answer if the people asked him whether he travelled the entire journey in that chariot?"

Sāriputta answered that the king should reply that he changed chariots on the way. Puṇṇa then said that on the journey of the Dhamma too one has do the same.

While travelling on the path of Dhamma, one uplifts oneself more and more. One keeps purifying oneself in various ways. But all the purifications one attains on the way are like the stations on the way. They are not the destination. Nibbāna is the ultimate aim.

The Tathāgata Shows the Way but One Has to Walk Oneself

Gotama perfected morality and wisdom; and attained full enlightenment. He discovered the Dhamma that he distributed freely for forty-five years.

The Buddha gave many discourses on the Dhamma. But he never said that one could get liberated merely by listening to his discourses or by worshiping him. He did give advice about the road and the journey but he didn't undertake the journey for anyone else. The law of nature is such that he couldn't.

One who seeks one's own welfare should seek direction from the Buddha. However, he has to walk on the path himself. He has to avoid the potholes, remove the thorns from the path and take each step on the path. This is put succinctly in a verse in Dhammapada.[167]

You have to make efforts and meditate;
the Tathāgatas merely show the way.

Meditation (*tapa*) here doesn't mean a ritualistic endeavor that gives importance to the outer appearances. It means effort in overcoming and removing defilements within to reach gradually higher and higher stages of purity.

His stand may appear dry and even harsh to some. "Anyone can show the way. True compassion is in liberating others," they might say. We see at every step people falling prey to such grandiose promises, enticements and invitations.

What is the truth then? The truth is that we have to walk ourselves in the journey of life. We can see this even in the material world. One may inherit wealth from parents but one can't inherit morality and wisdom. Let alone the highest wisdom, one has to learn even small things oneself as one grows.

Suppose a person knows a dictionary by heart. He knows the meaning of each word. Such a person's child doesn't automatically inherit that knowledge. It has to be taught word by word for the child to acquire that knowledge. Even if the parent has an ardent desire to pass on his entire knowledge to his child without such an effort, he won't be able to do so. If the parent decides to save the child the trouble of learning, the child would be deprived of the knowledge and subsequent success in life. In a sense, such a parent would prove to be the child's enemy.

If this is the situation with the simple education in life, surely, the highest goal of life must be reached by journeying there oneself. This journey can't be undertaken by someone else on one's behalf, not by mother and father, not by brother and sister, not by friends. Even compassionate great people like the Buddha can't do it.

This is both the mystery of the human life and its reality. None can deny it. None can overcome it. The Buddha understood it in all his wisdom. He explained this to people with all earnestness, with all the compassion and with all the firmness.

A man reaches his destination by recognizing his responsibilities, by fulfilling his duties and by walking on the path himself. This is the one and only way to reach his destination.

Be Your Own Island

Once in Sāvatthi, the Buddha told the bhikkhus,[168] "Be your own island. Be your own refuge. There is no other refuge. Make the Dhamma your island. Make the Dhamma your refuge. There is no other refuge."

"Be your own island" is a thought that gives spine to humanity. It enables us to live life without fear. It teaches us to take responsibility for every action, every breath that we take. It is a message that gives us the courage to face life fearlessly and joyfully.

The Buddha told his followers that his Dhamma was like a raft and they shouldn't get attached to it. Therefore, while saying "Take refuge in the Dhamma," he also says emphatically "Take refuge in yourself."

This exhortation makes us realize our responsibility to walk on the path. The Pali word for "your own island" is *attadīpa*. Some people translate it as "be a lamp unto yourself," or "be your own lamp." Most scholars, however, translate it as "be your own island'.

If a shipman on a boat that is caught in storm while journeying through the sea finds an island where he can moor the boat, he feels safe and secure. Similarly, while one is stumbling through the darkness of life, one finds three shelters, three islands: the Buddha, the Dhamma and the Saṅgha. But one cannot complete the journey only based on these. One has to find one's own refuge, one's own island within oneself.

Inner Security is True Security

Discourse on One's Security[169] in the Connected Discourses tells us how inner security is more important than outer security. It also gives the message to be one's own island.

Once when the Tathāgata was in Sāvatthi, King Pasenadi came to meet him. He told the Buddha that the following thought arose in his mind: People who indulge in unwholesome deeds of body, speech and mind remain unsafe even if they hire horses, elephants, chariots and soldiers for their security. Because this is outer security, not inner security. On the other hand, those who perform wholesome bodily, vocal and mental actions remain secure even though they may not have soldiers, chariots, etc. for their protection.

In Spite of Prayers, Stone and the Evildoer Will Certainly Sink

There is a sutta[170] in the Connected Discourses that is instructive about the need to be one's own island.

Once the Tathāgata was dwelling at the Pāvārika mango grove in Nalanda. At that time, a village chieftain named Asibhandakaputta came to him.

He asked the Tathāgata, "There are brahmins in the west, who carry a ritual pot and garland of flowers. They dive in water. They worship fire. They invite the dead; make the dead appear in front of us and send them to the heaven. You are a Sammā Sambuddha, a fully enlightened person. Can you do something so as to make sure that all the people go to heaven after death?"

Then the Tathāgata put a counter-question, "Chieftain, let me ask you a question. You may answer as you think fit. If someone who kills, steals, lies, indulges in sexual misconduct, etc. passes away and if many people gather together and pray with folded hands for his passage to heaven, do you think that person will go to heaven?"

"No, he will not," answered the chieftain.

Then the Tathāgata asked, "Suppose, someone puts a big stone in the lake. Then many people gather and start praying, 'Come up, come up on the surface.' Do you think that stone will rise to the surface?"

The chieftain answered in the negative.

Then the Tathāgata said, "If an earthen pot of oil or butter is broken in the water, the broken pieces of the pot sink to the bottom but the oil and butter will rise to the surface; no matter how many prayers are offered for the oil and butter to sink below. Similarly, one who abstains from unwholesome actions will not go the nether worlds in spite of all the prayers to send him to hell."

The Dhamma is Stable Like a Pole with Deep Foundation

The Tathāgata was confident that the principles he has understood and taught were benevolent. He said that the Wheel of Dhamma rotated by him could not be turned back by anyone. He again expressed this confidence at another place.[171]

Once he told Cunda that the ascetics of other traditions might claim that the bhikkhus of this tradition were not established in the Dhamma. To refute this charge, he advised Cunda to assert that the bhikkhus would never transgress the Dhamma that the Tathāgata has taught to his disciples after understanding it himself. The Dhamma taught by the Buddha was firm and could not be transgressed, just as a post deeply planted in the earth that stands firm and unshakable.

The Dhamma of the Righteous is Never Outdated

A discussion[172] between King Pasenadi and the Tathāgata about the long enduring Dhamma:

Pasenadi once asked the Buddha, "Is there anyone who doesn't die?"

"No," the Tathāgata answered, "There is none who doesn't die. Wealthy nobles, brahmins, businesspeople, even arahatas who have eradicated all defilements can't avoid death."

Then he uttered a verse:

The best royal chariots become dilapidated,
And this body too falls prey to ravages of age,
But the Dhamma of the righteous never becomes decrepit.

We Indians Turned Upside Down the Vessel of the Deathless

If we take an worldwide overview of the Dhamma, we see that the Wheel of Dhamma rotated by the Buddha has not turned back. It is going forward.

In India, on the other hand, it seems that it is stuck. We must accept with a heavy heart that though it has not completely stopped, it has certainly slowed down. To put it bluntly, we Indians turned upside down the vessel of the nectar of deathless.

The Buddha had given that vessel to us with so much compassion! We enjoyed it for centuries but later we rejected it, repulsed it and began to loath it.

The nectar is still there. It has penetrated this earth. If we open our eyes, we will soon find the stream of that nectar. It will flow again for us with all its purity. If we lack courage to take a handful of nectar to drink from that stream, let us at least taste a drop. If it burns the tongue, spit it out. But if the drop on the tongue creates a joyous thrill all through the body, then let us make our entire existence fragrant, free and bright. Let us fearlessly take a handful from that stream! Let us welcome it. For oneself and for others too! How can one resist sharing it with others! The answer is clear.

5

Answer Only If Beneficial In Life

Philosophy is a basic cultural element of all societies. Some philosophies are simple and straightforward—easy to understand. More often, they are complicated, mystical and usually almost impossible to understand. This doesn't mean that these philosophical theories have no relevance for the common masses. Though the people do not use those philosophical terms and may not argue about reason and evidence, the philosophical views established in the society do percolate to some extent into their lives.

The prevalent philosophical theories directly or indirectly influence innumerable elements in society such as religious beliefs, myths, legends, folklore, routine and festive rituals, rites, religious observances, festivals, beliefs about the life after death, traditions, etc.

Naturally, if one wishes to be familiar with a particular community of people, it is vital that we gather information about the various philosophical beliefs in that community.

In the sixth century BCE, many thinkers were experimenting in the field of philosophy. Among those, the Buddha and Vardhamāna Mahāvīra are the highest. Vardhamāna Mahāvīra is often referred to as Nigaṇṭṭha Nāṭaputta in the Tipiṭaka. It is notable that at several places in the Tipiṭaka, Mahāvīra is used as an address for the Buddha. Though, *jīna* is often used for Vardhamāna Mahāvīra and Jain comes from '*jīna*', we see that often in the Tipiṭaka, *jīna* is used for the Buddha. Though there are both similarities and differences in the views of these two, both are worthy of respect as great philosophers of India.

Other than these two, there were several others; namely, Pūraṇa Kassapa, Makkhali Gosāla, Ajita Kesakambali, Pakudha Kaccāna and Sañjaya Velaṭṭhiputta.[173]

The philosophers of those days used to debate passionately about the issues such as:

Whether the world is eternal or non-eternal.
Whether the world is created by God.
Whether the self or soul is different from body or not.
Whether soul exists after death or not.
What is the nature of karma (*kamma*) and its fruit, etc.

The Buddha too thought deeply about such issues but he examined them from a unique perspective.

One Sided Theory

The Tathāgata would look at all aspects of the issue before forming an opinion. This aspect of the Tathāgata's character is also seen in his philosophical views. In this regard, a parable of an elephant and the blind men given by him to describe the chaos of multitude of opinions jostling for a place in public opinion is apt.

Once he was staying in Sāvatthi.[174] At that time, people of various sects were living in the city. They had different inclinations and different views. Some would say the only truth is that the world is eternal, and all else is false. Some would say that the world is not eternal, and all other views are false. Some would say body and self are same. Some would say self and body are different. Each would say that only their view represented true Dhamma and all else was false. Thus they quarreled and hurt each other by using abusive language.

The bhikkhus told the Buddha about these quarrels. Then to describe the situation of those who give importance to only one dimension or aspect, the Buddha gave a parable.

"In this same Sāvatthi, there lived a king. He asked his servant to gather all the blind men in the city who were blind from birth. When he did so, he asked the servant to show them an elephant. Accordingly, the servant asked each blind man to touch the elephant. They touched various parts of the elephant. The servant informed the king about it. Then the king asked the blind men to describe the elephant.

"The one who touched its head said it was like a pot. The one who touched its ear said it was like a winnowing basket. The one who touched its tusk said it was like a nail. The one who touched its trunk said it was like a plough. The one who touched its stomach declared that it was like a granary. The one who touched the upper part of its tail claimed it was like a pestle. The one who touched the bushy end of its tail claimed it was like a brush. They could not agree with one another and came to blows."

Then the Buddha explained to the bhikkhus that those who didn't understand what was helpful and what was harmful, who didn't understand what was Dhamma and what was not Dhamma quarreled like that. People who looked at just one dimension of the things or issues thus kept quarrelling.

Discussion

All dimensions of reality must be grasped before one forms an opinion. One should not draw conclusions based on half-baked information. One should not be adamant and say, "mine is the only truth," when one's knowledge is incomplete. One should not create conflicts by making extreme statements.

Rejected the Existence of Eternal Soul

The Buddha clearly rejected the theory of soul which has held sway over generations after generations of Indians. The following incident throws light on his view in this matter.

Once he was dwelling in Sāvatthi.[175] While he was giving a sermon to the bhikkhus, he was asked by one bhikkhu, "Venerable sir, does one get troubled by not having a material thing?"

The Buddha explained, "One is troubled by thoughts such as 'I owned that thing, now I don't have it. I should possess it. I am not going to possess it.' Such a thought troubles one, makes one miserable, causes grief. Thus, not having a material thing is upsetting. On the other hand, one who doesn't think thus, doesn't grieve thus, is not troubled by loss of material things."

Then the bhikkhu asked, "Does not having something cause inner suffering?"

The Buddha replied, "Someone believes that there are realms. There is soul. After my death I will become eternal, constant, timeless, unchanging and will stay so forever. Such a man listens to the discourse given by the Buddha to his disciples. The Buddha teaches to eradicate all our shackles of view, sticking points, rituals and latent tendencies; to cool our complexes; to leave behind all our attachments; to destroy craving; for detachment; to uproot all defilements and to attain nibbāna. On listening to such a teaching, a man feels I will become annihilated, I will be destroyed, I will cease to exist. On thinking thus, he is distressed. He grieves. He beats his chest and laments. He loses his bearings. Thus he suffers inward. On the other hand, when one who doesn't have such a view listens to the Buddha's discourse, he doesn't grieve thinking that he would be annihilated."

He said further, "If something is permanent, then surely one should accept it as permanent." Then he asked the bhikkhus, "Do you see anything that is permanent?"

The bhikkhus repled, "No, bhante."

The Buddha said that he too didn't see anything that is permanent. "If accepting a belief in an eternal soul makes you free from grief, lamentation, misery, mental affliction and pain, then you should accept such a belief in soul. Do you see such an effect of accepting the belief in soul?"

The bhikkhus replied, "No, bhante."

"In this situation, unable to attain an everlasting and real soul, isn't thinking that 'After the death I will become eternal, constant, timeless, unchanging and will stay so forever,' a fool's paradise, an ignorant thinking?"

The bhikkhus agreed that it was an ignorant thinking. Then the Buddha explained the impermanence of all things including this body and how it is wrong to think of them as soul.

Discussion

More than anything else in the world, one cherishes "me" and (an expansion of me) "mine" that includes all near and dear ones. Even if one were to lose something that one owns, or if it were to be broken or destroyed, one would feel dismayed, sad and distraught.

Then if someone tells one that one would lose one's existence that is most valuable to one, the shock is unbearable for some. They don't have the courage to face the truth. They like to live in the sweet, even if false, belief that they would continue to live after death. The Buddha's teaching that there is no eternal soul is distressful for them. On the other hand, those, who have the capacity and wisdom to face the truth calmly, don't get affected by it.

The Buddha put forth his views on the existence of soul on numerous occasions.

One he was dwelling in Jetavana at Sāvatthi.[176] Thinking that Rāhula had become mature in the field of liberation and needed to be taken further about eradication of defilements, he said to Rāhula, "Carry a seat with you, Rāhula. Let us go to the Blind Grove."

There the Buddha explained to Rāhula how "this is my soul," is a false belief.

Once Māra said to a bhikkhuṇi named Vajirā,[177] "Who created this 'self'? Who is the creator? How did 'self' arise? How does 'self' cease?"

Vajirā replied, "What you call 'self' is a false belief on your part. There is no self. Just as a chariot is a composition of various parts, the five aggregates together are referred to as self in practice."

Vajirā was repeating the Buddha's teaching to the Māra.

No Place for Soul

We see in the Graded Discourses,[178] the Buddha's following thoughts, "Bhikkhus, it is not possible for one who has attained right view to accept anything as his soul. There is no scope for such a thing. An ignorant person, on the other hand, may accept something as his soul."

We find similar thought in Bahudhātuka Sutta in the Middle Discourses.

Wrong to Believe Non-self as Self

The Buddha reiterated again and again that all things are impermanent. There is no eternal soul. Something that doesn't last and is not me or mine cannot be called soul or "self." We see his assertions in the Numerical Discourses,[179] "Bhikkhus, to believe something that is impermanent as permanent is a distorted thinking, distorted mind and distorted view… Bhikkhus, to believe non-self as self is a distorted thinking, distorted mind and distorted view."

He said that it is right to believe impermanent as impermanent and non-self as non-self. People with false view, scattered mind and no wisdom take something impermanent for something permanent, non-self for self. When an enlightened Buddha arises in the world, then the wise listen to his teaching. Their mind is freed. They consider that which is changing as changing; and take non-self as non-self. They have right view which takes them beyond all suffering.

Baka Brahmā's Claim 'This is Eternal'—An Ignorant Claim

There is a sutta in the Middle Discourses[180]. The Buddha was once dwelling in Jetavana at Sāvatthi and narrated a past incident from his life.

"Bhikkhus, once I was living under a Sāla tree in Subhaga grove. At that time, Baka Brahmā, developed a false view. This is permanent. This is constant. This is eternal. This is ultimate. This is unshakable and immovable. It is not born. It doesn't decay. It doesn't die. It doesn't pass away. It doesn't arise. One can't go beyond this (there is nothing beyond this)."

The Buddha came to know about his thoughts and went to him. Baka Brahmā greeted the Buddha and conveyed his thoughts to him. The Buddha commented, "Baka Brahmā is making an ignorant statement. He has become ignorant."

Hearing this, Māra possessed a member of the Baka Brahmā's retinue and said to the Buddha, "Bhikkhu, bhikkhu! Don't insult him. Bhikkhu, this brahmā is a maha-brahmā. A great brahmā. He is greater than all. He is Undefeated, All-seeing, All-possessing, God, Creator, Greatest and Father to all past and future beings. Bhikkhu, in the past there have been ascetics and holy men who criticized gods, hated gods, criticized brahmā, hated brahmā... After death, they took birth in lower realms. But... those ascetics and holy men who praised brahmā have been born in divine realms. Therefore, bhikkhu, I advise you. Do as the brahmā bids you. If you contradict the words of the brahmā, you will be as someone who pushes away wealth that is coming to him or one who while falling in the abyss of the nether world pushes away land with hands and feet. Therefore, do as the brahmā tells you. Do not transgress his words. Don't you see the assembly of the brahmā?"

Saying this, Māra took the Buddha to the assembly of the brahmā.

The Buddha told him, "I know you are Māra. Don't think, 'He doesn't know I am Māra.' This brahmā, this assembly of brahmā are all under your influence, in your hand, in your control. Evil Māra, you think, 'This one is also in my hand, in my control.' But I will not be in your hand, I will not be in your control."

When the Buddha thus rebuffed Māra, the brahmā got into the discussion.

He stated, "I call permanent and eternal that which is permanent and eternal. There have been ascetics and holy men in the past who meditated for the duration equal to your entire lifespan. Had there been anything beyond this principle, they would have said so. Therefore, you will not be able to see beyond it. If you try to do so, it will bring you nothing but distress and trouble. On the other hand, if you do as I say, you will become close to me like my shadow. You will live at my abode. You will be free to do whatever you wish. You will be respected."

The Buddha replied that though if he heeded the brahmā's words, he would become close to the brahmā, he would not do so because he knew the brahmā's fate. Then the Buddha proved himself superior in knowledge and wisdom to the brahmā.

Discussion

The part of the sutta which shows the Buddha defeating brahmā by display of great miraculous powers is not important and is not likely to be part of the life of the Buddha who opposed all such miracles. What is relevant here is that he totally and summarily rejected any belief in an eternal self or soul. He knew and emphasized that all things were impermanent. This also makes it abundantly clear that he didn't carry forward the tradition of Vedic Upanishads. The scholars, who claim so, distort facts and make false claim. Brahmā also promised him 'respectability' if he followed brahmā.

Wise Man Won't Consider Non-self as Self

Again the same thought is put forth in the Graded Discourses with a slight difference[181] The Tathāgata asserted that one who has developed right view will never consider any conditioning, any compound thing *(saṅkhāra)* as permanent and will never accept anything as soul or self.

At another place in the Numerical Discourses[182] we come across this again The Tathāgata was saying in Jetavana in Sāvatthi. At that time, a bhikkhu named Girimānanda was very ill. He was suffering from great pain due to illness The Tathāgata sent a message through Ānanda to him to give him mental strength. He asked Ānanda to convey ten perceptions *(saññās)* to Girimānanda. Perception of non-self (*anattasaññā*) was one of these ten perceptions.

While describing this perception, he said, "Ānanda, what is perception of non-self. Ānanda, a bhikkhu goes to the forest and sits down under a tree or in a cell for meditation. He thinks thus, 'eye is non-self, form is non-self; ear is non-self, sound is non-self; nose is non-self, smell is non-self; tongue is non-self, taste is non-self; body is non-self, objects that can be felt through touch are non-self. Mind is non-self. Subjects of mind are non-self.' Thus he dwells understanding these six internal sense doors and external objects as non-self. This, Ānanda, is perception of non-self."

Once he was dwelling in Sāvatthi.[183] One day he repeated his discussion with some ascetics and holy men to the recluse Poṭṭhapāda:

These ascetics believed that after death there is a soul that is always in bliss. When asked whether they truly believed so, they said yes.

Then the Buddha asked them, "Do you dwell knowing and seeing a realm that is ever blissful?"

They said no.

Then the Buddha asked them, "Do you know for a day or a night or half a day or half a night a soul that is ever blissful?"

They said no.

Then the Buddha asked them, "Do you know that this is the way leading to direct experience of an eternal blissful realm?"

They said no.

Then the Buddha said, "Have the deities that are born in an eternal blissful realm said, 'Your way is the right way to reach an eternal blissful realm. We are also born here in this way.'?"

They again said no.

He asked Poṭṭhapāda whether in such a scenario did he find the view of those ascetics and holy men without foundation. Poṭṭhapāda said that he found it without foundation.

The Buddha said that it was like coveting a beautiful woman whom they have never seen and about whom they know nothing. It was like building a staircase at crossroads to climb a palace that they have not seen and about which they know nothing. Poṭṭhapāda agreed with the Buddha.

Empty Because Without Self

Once Ānanda said to the Tathāgata, "Bhante, people say, 'world is empty, world is empty'. In what sense do they say 'world is empty'?" The Tathāgata replied, "Ānanda, world is devoid of self or anything related to self. Therefore, it is said 'world is empty'."

Tathāgata was not supporting an annihilationist view that nothing exists in the world. He makes it clear that emptiness is 'devoid of self'.[184]

Better if People Believed Body to be Soul Rather Than Mind

Once the Tathāgata was dwelling in Jetavana at Sāvatthi.[185] He gave a discourse to the bhikkhus about body, mind and self.

The gist of it is: People who have not developed wisdom see the decay of their body that is composed of four elements. Therefore, they may be able to come out of attachment to the body. But it is difficult to be detached from this mind or consciousness. This is because, for long they have been attached to it thinking "this is me, this is mine, this is my soul."

In reality, it would have been better if they had considered their body to be soul. This is because the body lasts one year, two years… even hundred years or more.

But the mind is fickle. It arises and passes away with such rapidity. It is like a monkey in the jungle that grasps one branch and leaves it and jumps on to another. This is how mind is. Therefore, a noble disciple should think carefully only about Dependent Origination.

To explain to those who can't bear the thought of not having a soul, that rather than regarding this extremely fickle mind as soul, it is better to regard a relatively stable body as soul. This does not contradict his view of non-self but points out the danger of thinking of mind as soul.

Rahul Sankrityayan Rebukes Dr. Radhakrishnan

In spite of clear and unequivocal statements by the Buddha, there are scholars like Dr. Radhakrishnan who try to create confusion in the minds of people about this. Rahul Sankrityayan has some choice words for him.[186] Under the heading of Sir Radhakrishnan's White Wash, he discusses his five opinions. Sankrityayan writes, "In spite of there being no place in the Buddhist philosophy for God, Soul, Brahmā—any kind of eternal, constant thing… writers like Sir Radhakrishnan dare to make such irresponsible statements. Then in Dharmakirti's words it has to be called *'dhig vyāpakatamāh'* (down with ignorance!)."

Dr. Radhakrishnan's first statement is, "He (the Buddha) turned to the path of meditation and prayer."

To this Sankrityayan asks, "Whose prayer?"

He rightly objected to prayer but not to meditation which is truthful in case of the Buddha. Since the Buddha didn't believe in any God or divine power and never prayed to such a power nor taught others to do so, it is clear that the use of "prayer" misrepresents the Buddha.

Dr. Radhakrishnan's second statement is, "In the Buddha's opinion, only consciousness *(viññāṇa)* was momentary, other things were not."

Sankrityayan comments, "What a wonderful definition of 'all things arise from a cause!'" The Buddha stated all things to be impermanent, not just consciousness.

In further discussion, Dr. Radhakrishnan says, "That Buddha never said yes or no to the existence of Brahmā, cannot be taken to mean that he rejected the Ultimate Power (Brahmā). It is difficult to understand as to which among the things in the flow of life the Buddha felt were impermanent. In the world sans peace he didn't find any resting place where a man's heart would find peace."

To this Sankrityayan comments, "Sir Radhakrishnan has tried to equate nibbāna in Buddha's teaching with Ultimate Power. In reality, nibbāna can not be described in such terms. It is always described in terms of absence. When the Buddha thought of this soul that is looking for a resting place as utter foolishness, only Radhakrishnan can find a resting place for it! Moreover, he has quoted the following, 'this is a flow in which there is nothing permanent. There (in the world) nothing is permanent, neither consciousness nor body (corporeal structure).'"

Sankrityayan's satire is rather biting but it does remind the reader of the reality.

Sankrityayan then goes on to quote one more opinion of Dr. Radhakrishnan. "There was another reason why the Buddha kept silent on the issue of soul… The Buddha was silent on the soul described in the Upanishad—he neither accepted it nor rejected it."

To this Sankrityayan comments, "Absolutely not sir! The Buddha's philosophy is doctrine of non-self (*anattā*)! The prefix *an* is attached to the Upanishad's *attā* (soul). Your making such statements about one who proclaimed 'impermanent, unsatisfactory and non-self' (*anicca, dukkha, anattā*) makes it clear that you are not fit to write about philosophy."

Sankrityayan goes on to quote Dr. Radhakrishnan further, "Without this implicit principle, we cannot define life. That is why the Buddha always refrained from rejecting the reality of soul."

To this Sankrityayan makes a biting comment, "This is called *mukhamast īti vaktavyam dashahastā harītakī.*" This is an expression in Sanskrit used for blatant falsehoods. It literally means 'since I have a mouth, I will say that myrobalan is ten hands big'. To know what would have happened to Dr. Radhakrishnan, read the *Māluṅkyaputta's* incident.

The last opinion of Dr. Radhakrishnan that Sankrityayan commented on was, "Nāgasena severed Buddhist thought from its parent (Upanishadic) branch and planted it in pure rational field."… "The Buddha's aim was to accept the superior idealism of Upanishad and make it easier for human society according to its day-to-day needs. The meaning of the historical Buddha Dhamma is spread of Upanishadic philosophy among the masses."

To this Sankrityayan responds, "The Buddha himself, his contemporary disciples, Nāgasena (150 BCE), Nāgārjuna (175 CE), Asaṅga (375 CE), Vasubandhu (400 CE), Dignāga (425

CE), Dharmakirti (600 CE), Darmottara, Shāntarakshita (750 CE), Jñānashri, Shākyashrībhadra (1200 CE)—All of these great people could not do what Sir Radhakrishnan has done: proving that the Buddha, who actually taught the doctrine of non-self, spread the Upanishadic belief in soul! What a great misunderstanding has spread for 2500 years and across India, Sri Lanka, Burma, Siam, China, Japan, Korea, Mongolia, Tibet, Middle Asia, Afghanistan and many other countries that the Buddha didn't believe in soul or God! And it was their utter 'ignorance' the way many brahmins; such as Akshapāda, Bādarāyana, Vātsāyana, Udyotakara, Kumārila, Vācaspati, Udayana; had understood the Buddha's philosophy!"

We cannot but agree with Rahul Sankrityayan's satirical comments in face of such great distortion of truth by Dr. Radhakrishnan.

Prof Jagannath Upadhyay

The opinion by Prof Jagannath Upadhyay[187] on Eternilistic View throws new light on the subject. He says, "Brahminism against change: The philosophy of Brahminism is Eternalism, that is, theory of 'no change'. This translates in social terms into belief in 'status quo'. Its orthodoxy is 'let things be as they are traditionally'. Through this view, traditional beliefs and blind faith are promoted in society. In this mission, Brahmanism is not alone. It has a complete family accompanying it. Theism, Belief in Soul, Belief in Rebirth, Belief in Written Word (as final truth), Class and Casteism are its special members. All these have one aim: In society and life, keep status quo of permanence, constancy and non-dynamism. All these lead to social consequences in one direction: to deny religious, cultural and social validity to anything that promotes change and gives life a new vision."

Even if one keeps aside the philosophical view of Eternalism, the poisonous nature of its social aspect has been highlighted by Prof Upadhyay.

Former Birth and Rebirth

Do You Know Whether There was a Former Birth?

Once the Tathāgata was dwelling in Nigrodha monastery in Kapilavatthu.[188] At that time, Mahānāma Sākya came to meet him The Tathāgata told him about his discussions with ascetics who were practising austerities to free themselves of the bad karma (kamma) of past lives The Tathāgata asked them whether they knew that they had past lives. Then the Tathāgata told them that it was false view to believe without knowing what their past life was.

Consciousness from This Life Doesn't Go to the Next Life

The Great Discourse on Destruction of Craving in the Middle Discourses[189] is important to understand the Buddha's philosophical stand on this issue.

Once he was in Sāvatthi at the Anāthapiṇḍika's monastery. At that time a wrong view arose in the mind of Kevaṭṭaputta Sāti. He thought, "I understand that the Buddha's Dhamma tells us that the same consciousness *(viññāṇa)* goes from one body to another and keeps going around in the cycle of birth and death; not another."

Other bhikkhus heard about his opinion. They asked him whether he really believed so. When he said yes, they tried to bring him out of his wrong view. They told him, "Friend Sāti, don't speak thus. Don't misquote the Tathāgata. It is not proper that you misrepresent the Tathāgata. He has not said any such thing. He has explained in various ways that consciousness arises due to Dependent Origination. It doesn't arise without cause." In spite of the bhikkhus' efforts, Sāti stuck to his opinion. Then the bhikkhus went to the Tathāgata and informed him about Sāti's wrong view. He sent a bhikkhu to call Sāti to meet him.

Sāti came to the Tathāgata. He said yes when asked whether he had said such things. He said, "I understand that the same consciousness goes around in the cycle of life and death."

When asked which consciousness, he answered, "Bhante, this one that speaks, experiences, which bears fruits of good and bad kamma (in various lives) is that consciousness."

To this the Tathāgata replied, "Useless fellow *(moghapurisa)*, to whom I have taught the Dhamma in this manner? I have said in various ways that consciousness arises due to cause. Without cause, consciousness can't arise. You are showing me in error by misunderstanding things. You are also harming yourself and earning demerit for yourself. This will cause harm and misery to you for a long time."

Then the Tathāgata asked the bhikkhus whether they felt that Sāti had the slightest grasp of the Dhamma. They replied in the negative. The Tathāgata asked the bhikkhus whether he had taught the Dhamma the way Sāti had reported. They replied that he had not. Then the Tathāgata explained Dependent Origination in detail. It has been discussed separately later in this book.

Discussion

If the Buddha wanted to show his disapproval about anyone's speech or action, he would use the word 'useless' (*moghapurisa)* for him. This word may appear mild but it emphatically conveyed his opinion.

It is clear that the Tathāgata didn't believe that any essence transmigrated from one body to another. He says later in the same discourse that the life force in human beings come from the union of their parents. That is the cause, the *paccaya.* One can write a lot more about this issue but it is better to leave some things unsaid as was his policy sometimes. Let us adopt it here.

Craving Is the Cause of Rebirth

Once a recluse named Vacchagotta came to meet the Buddha.[190]

He told the Buddha: Once recluses from various schools were sitting in the discussion hall (*kutūhalasālā,* literally hall of curiousity). Then they said that when a disciple dies, Pūraṇa

Kassapa and other teachers tell others where he has arisen (taken birth). They said that Samaṇa Gotama also did the same but when his best foremost disciple, one who had achieved the final goal passes away, Gotama doesn't tell where he has arisen after death. On the other hand, he declares that the disciple has destroyed craving, broken fetters, left ego and brought an end to all suffering. Hearing the talk among the recluses, Vacchagotta became curious about 'Gotama's Dhamma.'

The Buddha then explained to him, "I tell arising after death only of one who has attachments. I don't tell arising of one who has severed all attachments, all afflictions. Fire burns as long as there is fuel. If fuel is not there, fire doesn't burn."

To Vaccha asked, "When fire throws off flames, what is its affliction?"

"Air is its affliction," the Buddha replied.

Vaccha asked, "When an animal goes from one body to another, what is its affliction according to Master Gotama?"

"Craving is its affliction," the Buddha replied.

Discussion

Great philosophers of those days used to tell several stories about rebirth. Therefore, common people had firm beliefs about rebirth. They expected their teacher to give answers to this. Vaccha met the Buddha on several occasions for the answer to this question and each time got different answers.

In the present incident the Buddha gave an answer without breaking his faith. He made it clear that for one who had destroyed craving there was no rebirth. He said that craving is the affliction responsible for rebirth. One who fears non-existence, dreams about self being eternal. For one who believes that craving of 'I should get this and that' should be abandoned, there is no question of rebirth—because one doesn't crave for anything and hence it is irrelevant.

The Buddha used to answer questions based on the capacity of the questioner, his mentality, and his faith. It is clear that the meeting between Vaccha and the Buddha happened after the meeting described in Ānanda Sutta that we are going to discuss later. At that time, the Buddha had simply refused to give any answers to Vaccha. Since the Buddha has answered Vaccha here, this meeting is a later incident. In short, one who has craving that I should get rebirth, has rebirth. And one who has no such craving, has no rebirth.

How Does a Being Gets a Body

Indaka Sutta from the Compounded Discourses helps us understand the Buddha's view on soul or self.[191]

Once he was dwelling in Indakūṭa mountain at Rājagaha. At that time, Indaka *yakkha* came to him and asked, "The Buddha says that this form (body) is not self. Then how does one get a body? How does one get skeleton? How does it enter the womb?"

The Buddha answered that the being conceived in the womb of mother grows gradually into an embryo with appendages as well as hair and nails. Whatever water and food the mother takes nourishes the embryo."

It is noteworthy that the Buddha doesn't say that any eternal, constant soul or self enters this body from another body. It seems that even the yakkha who asked question knew that the Buddha didn't believe in soul or self; and therefore he asked such questions. The Buddha's answer gives the biological phenomenon of human birth.

Heaven

Discourse on Divine Realm

This discourse is very important if one wants to understand what kind of human being the Tathāgata wanted to create.[192]

Once he said to bhikkhus, "Bhikkhus if recluses of other traditions asked you whether Samaṇa Gotama followed the holy life for attaining divine realm, would you feel troubled, ashamed and disgusted?"

They said, they would.

Then he told them, “Bhikkhus, you will feel ashamed of, troubled by and disgusted with the divine life with its divine complexion, divine joy, divine fame, divine authority. But bhikkhus, you should feel ashamed of, be troubled by and disgusted with unwholesome bodily actions, unwholesome vocal actions and unwholesome mental actions.”

Discussion

This discourse of the Buddha brings to light his two major views about life. People have huge attraction for heaven and divine world. They feel that they are going to enjoy various pleasures there. People obsessed with the divine world live the holy life to attain the divine realm.

The Buddha makes it clear that he had not the slightest attraction for heaven. The bhikkhus were well conversant with his view. They had no doubt that he didn’t have the slightest attraction for any divine attainment. He wasn’t following the holy life for the sake of heaven. He was following it as an integral, natural and spontaneous part of an ethical lifestyle. Therefore, any insinuation that he was following it for heaven was unacceptable and painful for the bhikkhus. Their emotions were so strong about this as to feel shame and disgust!

His view about heaven shows his highly developed mental state. But the uniqueness of his position doesn’t end here. He accepted that bhikkhus would feel ashamed and disgusted about any such allegation but felt that this was a secondary issue. It was much more important for him that they be ashamed of and disgusted with any immoral, unethical act. He made them aware that it was more important to correct oneself and live an upright life than be distressed by troublesome questions of others.

Said and Unsaid

The Buddha rejected certain theories in established philosophies of that time. He made his rejection clear repeatedly.

Even then often he wouldn't feel it right to waste his time and energy in debating the truthfulness or otherwise of these theories. Some scholars have an urge to debate such theories. They like the intoxication of defeating others in argument.

The Buddha had a different perspective on this. If he felt that discussing something would not benefit people, he would not insist that "this only is true." Therefore, he wouldn't quarrel or debate on issues to which people clung tenaciously.

He divided theories in two groups: 'said' and 'unsaid'. He often left unanswered questions that had no relevance to and no benefit for human life. On the other hand, he taught Noble Eightfold Path in detail as it brought welfare to people. This doesn't mean that he was afraid of philosophical issues or that he lacked the intellectual capacity to deal with deep philosophical issues of life or that he ran away from the battleground of philosophy.

He answered these questions whenever necessary and his answers are beneficial to rescue people from the web of confusing thoughts. However, if someone was obstinately holding onto a view, he avoided argument with him. This was out of compassion for people. Through his actions, he connected philosophy with men of flesh and blood.

Discussion with Maluṅkyaputta

Once the Buddha was dwelling in Sāvatthi.[193] At that time, bhikkhu Maluṅkyaputta thought that the Buddha had left unanswered certain questions:

Whether world is eternal or non-eternal. Whether it is with end or without end. Whether the self is same as body or different.

Whether the Tathāgata exists after death or whether the Tathāgata doesn't exist after death or whether the Tathāgata both exists and doesn't exist after death or whether the Tathāgata does not exist and does not 'not exist' after death.

He went to the Buddha, thinking, "The Tathāgata doesn't give answers to these questions. I don't like it. I don't accept it. Therefore, let me go and ask him these questions. I will continue to live the holy life under his guidance only if he answers these questions, otherwise I will return to the householder's life."

He asked his questions to the Buddha and told him to answer if he knew the answers and to say honestly "I don't know" if he didn't know the answers.

After hearing what Maluṅkyaputta had to say, the Buddha asked him, "Did I ever tell you, 'Maluṅkyaputta, come and practice the Dhamma with me. Then I will answer these questions?'"

Maluṅkyaputta said, no.

"Did you ever say to me, 'I will practice the Dhamma with you and you answer these questions.'"

Maluṅkyaputta said no.

Then the Buddha said, "Useless fellow, if this is the case, then who is leaving whom?"

He further warned him that whosoever decided not to practice the Dhamma unless he got answers to these questions would die before he got answers to these questions. To clarify his meaning, he gave a parable.

Once a man was struck by an arrow with poisonous head. His friend, associates and clansmen brought a surgeon to treat him. But he didn't allow the surgeon to remove the arrow.

He said, "I wouldn't allow you to remove this arrow unless I know the caste, clan and family of the person who shot the arrow. Whether he is tall, medium and short. Whether he is fair or dark. Whether he is from a village, a town or a city. I won't allow the arrow to be removed unless I know the type of bow from which the arrow was shot. What is the string of the bow made from? From what plant is the shaft of arrow made? Whether the feathers on the arrow are that of a vulture, duck, eagle or peacock? What is the tip made of? Unless I know these answers, I won't allow the arrow to be removed from my body."

The Buddha said, "Maluṅkyaputta, that man would die before he got all his answers."

Then the Buddha asked him, "Is it that one can practice the Dhamma only after knowing whether the world is eternal? Is it that one can practice the Dhamma only after knowing that the world is not eternal? Whatever your belief, old age exists, death exists, grief, lamentation, sadness and distress exist. I teach how to remove these afflictions in this very life… Therefore, Maluṅkyaputta, accept whatever I have answered as 'answered', accept whatever I have not answered as 'not answered.'"

Then the Buddha told him why he had left these ten questions unanswered. "Why I have left them unanswered? They don't take us to our goal. They are not helpful to the practice of the Dhamma. They do not lead to disenchantment, detachment, destruction of suffering, peace, wisdom, enlightenment or nibbāna. Therefore, I have left them unanswered… I have described the Four Noble Truths of suffering. They lead to disenchantment, detachment, destruction of suffering, peace, wisdom, enlightenment and nibbāna. Therefore, I have proclaimed them."

In the end the Buddha again urged him, "Therefore, Maluṅkyaputta, accept whatever I have answered as 'answered', accept whatever I have not answered as 'not answered.'"

Maluṅkyaputta was satisfied with the answers and he praised the Buddha's exposition.

Discussion

The questions that Maluṅkyaputta asked the Buddha were considered very important in those times. Even today in Indian society, such questions are important. Often a spiritual guru who answers such questions is considered a real spiritual guru. Maluṅkyaputta is representative of countless such questions.

He put his questions to the Tathāgata frankly. To ask such questions of a teacher with such grand personality required courage and for that Maluṅkyaputta should be given credit.

This incident also shows that due to the Tathāgata's openness to questions, people asked him questions fearlessly, without hesitation, without feeling any pressure. The Tathāgata set an ideal that for progress in the field of knowledge such open debates were important. Maluṅkyaputta could openly tell him that if he didn't know he should say so. This was because his demeanor would remain calm even in the face of oblique questions. Ramdhari Singh Dinkar says,[194] "Even during debates, he was calm, composed, tolerant and generous."

Before the Tathāgata gave the simile of the man struck with an arrow, he got Maluṅkyaputta to agree that neither had the Buddha promised him answers nor had Maluṅkyaputta sought any such assurance from him.

The Buddha would not give any enticements or show any miracles to attract people to his Saṅgha. He wouldn't go around requesting people to accept his Dhamma or to enter his Saṅgha. Whosoever agreed with his teaching accepted it voluntarily. He followed this principle during his entire ministry. He showed to Maluṅkyaputta how if he decided to leave the Saṅgha, it was entirely his responsibility. Maluṅkyaputta couldn't blame the Tathāgata for it.

It was not the Tathāgata's wish to defeat Maluṅkyaputta in argument or make him out to be a liar or to humiliate him. It was the Tathāgata's duty as a teacher to make him aware of reality, to tenderly remove the thorn of doubt that was bothering him. Therefore, he gave a striking simile.

The Buddha was a master in the art of using parables and similes to clarify a point. He made a complicated issue simple, easy and understandable in a convincing manner with this simile.

No man who is pierced by a poisonous arrow would say, "First find out who shot the arrow before taking it out," but it is equally true that for thousands of years people have been neglecting real problems and running after imaginary issues. Therefore, though it seems exaggerated, it is true that people do act like that man stuck with the arrow The Tathāgata wanted to change the direction of their thinking. He wanted to get them out of the trap of false or useless philosophical issues and to bring their attention to the reality of life.

Rather than speculating about whether the world is eternal or not, it is more helpful to practice right speech and make our life joyous.

Rather than debating whether body and self are same or different, it is more helpful to know that eradicating greed, anger, etc. makes our life happy.

Therefore, rather than trying to find useless answers to irrelevant questions, we should pay attention to the questions which when answered make our lives happy and peaceful.

That is why in the end the Buddha again urged him to accept whatever he had said as 'said', accept whatever he had not said as 'not said'.

This was a manifestation of his Middle Path Realism and of its practical application in real life.

Ramdhari Singh Dinkar says,[195] "He was a practical teacher and never got entangled in speculative philosophy that was not understandable by intellect and was not helpful in life."

It is indeed a great fortune to find such a practical religious teacher!

Dinkar's comments too are noteworthy, "After the Budddha, many great scholars and thinkers in Buddhist tradition started walking on the very trail that the Buddha had prohibited."

His 'Unanswered' View Had Penetrated the Saṅgha Too

The Paramamaraṇa Sutta of the Connected Discourses[196] helps us understand further the Buddha's view on soul. This sutta has a conversation between Sāriputta and Mahākassapa.

Once they were dwelling in the Deer Park of Varanasi. At that time, one evening, Sāriputta went to Mahākassapa after his evening meditation. He asked Mahākassapa, "Friend, does the Tathāgata exist after death?"

"The Tathāgata has not clarified these things."

To further questions by Sāriputta as to whether the Tathāgata doesn't exist after death, etc., Mahākassapa answered in the same way.

Then Sāriputta asked why it was that the Tathāgata had not answered these questions.

Mahākassapa replied, "Friend, these answers are not helpful to us. They do not lead to dispassion, detachment, cessation of suffering, cooling of defilements, wisdom, enlightenment and nibbāna."

When Sāriputta asked him as to what the Tathāgata *had* explained, Mahākassapa replied that he had explained the Four Noble Truths of suffering. When asked why, he replied because they are helpful and lead to nibbāna.

Discussion

The Saṅgha had imbibed the Buddha's teaching that one should avoid useless and frivolous discussions on issues that are not helpful. Bhikkhus used to discuss this point of view with each other and made sure that they understood it correctly. Both these bhikkhus were wise. Sāriputta was referred to as the General of Dhamma. It is so refreshing to see him discussing this with his friend without any ego. Again, it emphasizes how the Buddha stopped people from useless speculations and brought their attention to the problems of living.

Middle Path Avoids Both Ends

In Compounded Discourses[197] we find one more incident about how the Middle Path avoids both extremes in philosophy.

Once when the Buddha was dwelling in Sāvatthi, Ven. Kaccānagotta asked him, "What is right view?"

"Kaccāna, usually people think in duality; existence *(atthatta)* or non-existence *(anatthata)*. One who understands the arising of the world objectively doesn't have what the world calls 'view of non-existence'. One who understands the passing away of the world objectively doesn't have what the world calls 'view of existence'. People who are enslaved by craving, greed, and attachment lack right view. But one who has right view is not enslaved by craving and doesn't think in terms of 'this is my soul'… Kaccāna, everything exists is one extreme. Nothing exists is the other extreme. Kaccāna, the Tathāgata avoids both extremes and follows the middle path."

The Tathāgata Remained Silent

As we will see here, the Tathāgata didn't discuss things with Vacchagotta the way he did with Kaccānagotta. This may appear contradictory. But he did so with a purpose. He found that it was not helpful to give the same discourse to people with different backgrounds. His view expressed in Ānanda Sutta of the Connected Discourses[198] clearly reveals his opinion on the issue of soul. It is a subtle key to this huge and hugely complicated issue.

Once a former recluse Vacchagotta came to him and sat down to one side. He asked the Buddha about whether the doctrine of existence was true. The Tathāgata remained silent.

Vacchagotta then asked whether the doctrine of non-existence was true. Again the Tathāgata remained silent. Then Vaccha got up and left.

After Vaccha left, Ānanda asked the Tathāgata, "Bhante, why didn't you answer him?"

This is the gist of the Tathāgata's reply: If I had said yes, it would have seemed like I was agreeing with the ascetics and holy men who promote eternalism. On the other hand, if I had said no, it would have seemed as if I was agreeing with the annihilationists.

Then he asked Ānanda, "If I had said yes, would it have helped me impart the truth of 'all things are non-self'?"

"No, bhante."

"If I had said no to the doctrine of existence, Vaccha would have been further confused and thinking, 'Earlier I had a soul, now I don't have one!' he would have been distraught."

Discussion

This discourse is vital in understanding not only the Buddha's view on soul, self or eternalism but also to understand the foundation and goal of all his teachings.

From the way he referred to 'non-self' (no soul) while talking to Ānanda, it is clear that the doctrine of extistence *(atthatta)* referred to existence of soul and that of non-existence *(natthatta)* to non-existence of soul. The question was whether the Buddha accepted eternal soul or rejected its existence.

He kept quiet and Vaccha left him. What would be the turmoil in the mind of Vaccha when he left? "Gotama didn't know the answers. I shut up Gotama with my questions. He doesn't have knowledge befitting his reputation."

Then why did the Buddha remain silent? Ānanda had the same curiosity.

One thing is clear. The Buddha had clear answers to these questions. He didn't believe in eternal soul. The answer to Vaccha's second question too was unequivocal. Why then did he keep quiet? He was not being adamant or arrogant. There was no haughtiness or intention to humiliate.

Sometimes, his opponents would ask 'yes or no' questions to him to corner him. He didn't bother with such tricks. To counter such things, he used different ways at different times. To remain silent was one such way.

The strategy of his opponents was, "If he says 'yes' then we can say that he shared our view and make him flow in our flow. If he says 'no', then we can say that he taught annihilation of all things and prove him to be an annihilationist."

The Tathāgata wasn't ready to be painted in the soul theory. He didn't believe in it. But to tell Vaccha etc. about his truth of non-self had two difficulties.

First, he wasn't annihilationist about wholesome things such as the Noble Eightfold Path. His opponent wrongly painted him as a total annihilationist though in truth he was *vibhajjavādin* (analysis and reason). Sometimes, it was no use telling these people and at such times, he preferred to remain silent.

The second reason behind his silence, as Walpola Rahula puts it, was his compassion for Vaccha. For those who believe that soul is eternal, the very idea of there being no soul left to live on after death was frightening. Merely imagining such a scenario was shocking for them. They were already possessed by the idea of 'the soul is eternal.' When anyone opposed it, they become confused. The Tathāgata didn't want to frighten them, unsettle them or confuse them further. He was willing to wait and gradually deal with the issue.

The Buddha couldn't lie and he didn't want to upset Vaccha with a truthful statement. Therefore, he decided to remain silent.

Walpola Rahula has said it very well,[199] "The Buddha was not a computing machine giving answers to whatever questions were put to him by anyone at all, without any consideration. He was a practical teacher, full of compassion and wisdom. He didn't answer questions to show his knowledge and intelligence, but to help the questioner on the way to realization. He always spoke to people bearing in mind their standard of development, their tendencies, their mental make-up, their character, their capacity to understand a particular question."

Matriceta has said about his flair:[200]

You knew what was proper time and you knew people's mind;
Thus at times, you kept quiet when asked a question;
Sometimes, you went to people to engage them in discussion;
At times, you first created curiosity and then quenched it;
You understood the thinking and emotions of those you taught;
And used appropriate language and fitting action with them.

Four Ways to Answer Questions

People ask questions for different reasons, with different intentions and in different ways. Naturally, the Buddha told bhikkhus that they should not give stereotypical answers to all questions.[201]

"Some questions are to be answered with 'yes' or 'no'.

"Some questions are to be answered with proper analysis after examining both sides.

"Some questions are to be answered with a counter-question.

"Some questions are best left unanswered."

At another time, the Buddha described the four types of intellect that comprehends and gives answers.[202] Right answer but not immediate. Prompt but incorrect answer. Right and prompt answer. Neither prompt nor correct. It tells us how well he had grasped the inner side of communication between people.

No Undue Insistence

Let us now turn to a sutta in the Middle Discourses.[203] Once the Tathāgata was dwelling in Jetavana in Sāvatthi. Vacchagotta came to him at that time. Again he asked the same useless questions. He asked the Tathāgata, "Do you believe that this world is eternal and that all other views are false?"

"No, I don't believe thus."

Then Vaccha asked him whether he held views that the world being non-eternal; ending; boundless; etc.

The Tathāgata answered 'no' to each question.

Then Vaccha asked him whether self and body are the same or different; does the Tathāgata exist after death or not, etc.

Again, the Tathāgata answered 'no' to each question.

Vaccha then asked him, "What faults do you see in them that make you reject those views?"

The gist of the Tathāgata reply: "All these views are in error, uncertain, fettered, with suffering, injurious, laborious and scorching. These views do not lead to dispassion, detachment, cessation of suffering, cooling of defilements, wisdom, enlightenment and nibbāna. Seeing this fault in these views, I stay away from them."

Vaccha asked him whether the Tathāgata had any views of his own. He answered that the Tathāgata had rid himself of all such views.

The Tathāgata told Vaccha that he had experienced that this is form (body), this is cause of arising of body, this is cause of cessation of form. He also told him that he had experienced the same about feeling (sensation), perception, conditioning and consciousness. Because of his experience, he had rid himself of all wrong views, wrong thinking, ego, attachment to self (to 'me' and 'mine'), conceit and latent tendencies. Such tendencies can't arise in him again. Thus the Tathāgata is free.

Vaccha then asked, "Where does such a bhikkhu whose mind is free arise after death?"

He answered that it was not proper to say 'arise'.

"Is it then proper to say 'doesn't arise'?"

He answered that it was not proper to say 'does not arise'.

Vaccha asked several related questions to all of which the Buddha replied in the negative.

Then Vaccha said to the Buddha that he was answering in the negative no matter how the question was put to him. Therefore, Vaccha was not able to understand him. He was getting confused. Whatever faith had arisen in his mind from earlier conversation had also vanished.

"Vaccha, there is no need for you to fall into ignorance or confusion. This Dhamma is profound and difficult to perceive, hard to penetrate, not to be grasped by logic alone (it needs actual practice), subtle and understood only by the wise. One who has different pre-established views, faiths and inclinations, who comes from a different sect and from other teachers, will find it difficult to understand."

Then the Buddha said, "Let me ask you. Answer as you think fit. If there is fire in front of you, would you understand that there is fire in front of you?"

"Yes, I would."

"What is the affliction of fire?"

"Grass and wood."

"If the fire ceases in front you, would you understand that it has ceased?"

"Yes, I would."

"If you are asked whether the fire has gone in north, south, east or west direction, what would you say?"

"Master Gotama, this is not how things happen. The fire was burning on the basis of grass and wood. When this basis is finished and when no new fuel of grass is added, it is said that fire has cooled down."

"Vaccha, it is the same with the Tathāgata. The form that is used to refer to the Tathāgata has ceased, has been uprooted. It is like the palm tree that has been uprooted. The form ceases to exist. There is no opportunity for it to arise in future. Being free from the perception of form, the Tathāgata is profound and fathomless. Therefore, one cannot use terms such as 'arises', 'doesn't arise' for him. What is applicable to form *(rūpa)* is also applicable to sensation, perception, conditioning and consciousness *(vedanā, saññā, saṅkhāra* and *viññāṇa)*.

On hearing this, Vacchagotta said, "Master Gotama, it is as if there is a huge sala tree. And all its leaves, branches and bark are stripped off and only its essence remains. Such is your discourse. Please accept me as your devoted disciple from now onward."

In the sutta that follows, we find the description of what happened later. Vacchagotta met with the Buddha in Kalandakanivāpa in Rājagaha where the Buddha again taught him and after which he requested the Buddha for admission to the Saṅgha. He was told that those coming from another sect have to wait for four months. Then in proper time, he got admission to Saṅgha and received higher ordination. He worked hard and became liberated.

Discussion

When Vaccha first met him, the Buddha remained silent. This was to avoid further confusion in Vaccha's mind. Later, he was given answers to guide him further on the path. But on empty philosophical questions, the Buddha did not answer though on some of the issues, the Buddha had a clear stand. This was to make Vaccha realize that his questions were irrelevant and hence useless.

The Buddha also sowed a seed in his mind about what is actually beneficial. The Buddha wanted him to spend his energy in what is useful, to avoid running after the mirage of irrelevant questions. The Buddha made it clear to Vaccha that he himself had dispellled all such views; had disengaged himself from such arguments and removed himself from such entanglements.

The Buddha conveyed to Vaccha that in nature there is a cause and an effect. The wisdom of understanding this cause and effect is really important. One who understood this becomes free from the obstinacy of 'mine is the only truth' and eradicates all defilements. He becomes free from all negativity. Having known this directly with experience, the Buddha had no wish to rush into the battle of debates around issues irrelevant to life.

Vaccha again asked him an 'yes or no' question. Again the Buddha abstained from being drawn into it. Vaccha's questions reflect a mentality common among many. They don't want to use their intellect and reason. They want readymade definitive answers from their teachers (and leaders). In reality, often such ready answers cannot be given by one man to another. A true seeker himself embarks on the journey to find answers. This is what the Buddha wanted. People, on the other hand, don't want trouble, travel and toil. They seek answers without efforts. Vaccha was one such person.

Vaccha's description of his own confusion is gripping. It is true that a seeker of truth goes through such psychological states. One develops immense faith in one from whom one wants to learn. Sometimes, the faith is shattered. Sometimes, it grows. Sometimes, it declines. Amid all this churning, a seeker continues his journey on the path. In this both the teacher and the disciple are tested. Sometimes, both become successful. Sometimes, one of them ends up being deficient. At times, both struggle in darkness.

Vacchagotta in the company of the Tathāgata kept progressing on the path and ultimately became an *arahata*. Thus both passed the test successfully.

Many coming from other traditions and other teachers argued with the Buddha. The Tathāgata would first calm and clear their minds and then slowly explain his teachings to them. In Vaccha's case too, he gradually prepared him, counter-questioned him and slowly explained the truth to him.

There is a question about nibbāna that they discussed. Since we are going to talk about nibbāna in detail later, we will refer to the conversation between Vaccha and the Tathāgata about nibbāna at that place.

Wise Disciples Don't Worry About Unsaid Things

The Buddha once told a bhikkhu that a wise disciple didn't have doubts about things that were unanswered by the Buddha because their wrong view was destroyed.[204] Such a disciple, through the knowledge of the Four Noble Truths, has freed himself from all misery. "…A wise disciple doesn't become fearful about unsaid things, doesn't get anxious, doesn't get terrified and has no mental distress because of it."

The Buddha didn't give answers to speculative philosophical questions, instead focused on real problems of life.

Questions Relevant to Life Were Clearly Answered

Once the Tathāgata was staying in Jetavana of Sāvatthi.[205] He told a recluse named Poṭṭhapāda that he had kept unanswered some questions such as those about eternalism. But he said that he had answered those questions relevant to life, such as the Four Noble Truths.

After the discussion was over and the Tathāgata had left, other recluses attacked Poṭṭhapāda and accused him of agreeing to whatever Samaṇa Gotama said. They told him that they didn't think that Gotama's statements were acceptable and coherent.

To this Poṭṭhapāda replied, "Gotama didn't make one-dimensional statements on issues. I also didn't see him giving one-sided answers to questions such as whether the world is eternal. But Samaṇa Gotama while being steadfast in truthful Dhamma proclaims it and guides one how to attain it. Therefore, how can I disagree with him and not say 'He speaks right' when he does speak rightly?"

After two-three days, he went to the Tathāgata with his friend Citta. He repeated to the Buddha his conversations with the other ascetics and holy men. The Buddha then told him that he had given non-categorical teachings as well as categorical teachings. About issues such as whether the world is eternal, I have given non-categorical teachings. Because they are not useful. On the other hand, I have taught in categorical way about the Four Noble Truths etc. because they are useful.

Discussion

Poṭṭhapāda's associates claimed that the Buddha didn't give definitive answers and definitive guidance. Actually, this is the case with many from the time of the Buddha till today who criticize his teaching. Some go further and claim that the Buddha kept quiet on these issues because didn't know the answers.

The absurd part is that speculative issues such as whether or not the soul lives on forever and whether or not the world is eternal are very important for Indians, especially for Indian philosophers—as important as the questions of life and death. In discussing and answering these issues, they take such flights of fancy; make up such a world of dreams; use such flowery philosophical jargon so as to create an impression that they understand all the realities of the world. This impression so paralyses the people that they forget real and principal issues of life. Naturally, those who proclaim such theories and those who listen to them are both pleased with themselves. It is no surprise then that they think of anyone who keeps quiet on those philosophical issues as not a real philosopher and a novice or alien in the field.

Actually, the Buddha had made his view clear about them. He didn't speak adamantly about some of these issues, but not for lack of a clear view. He would not waste his time in discussing and debating those things that are absolutely useless in life.

The opinions and teachings that he proclaimed for the eradication of suffering from human life were clear and confident, explicit and emphatic. They were not mere hearsay. He based them on his own experience.

In short, he didn't evade issues when it came to real life and human happiness. Here he was categorical and clear.

Karma of Past Lives, God and Destiny

If God Is the Reason, No Scope for Human Will and Effort

We find a discourse by the Buddha on past karma, God and related topics in the Numerical Discourses.[206]

Some sectarians believed that whatever a man experiences is because of past karma. The Tathāgata talked to such ascetics and holy men. He would point out to them that their view meant that killing, stealing, sexual misconduct, lying, backbiting, harsh speech, frivolous talk, greed, hatred and wrong view all come to a man because of past karma.

"Once we accept this, it means that we lose our free will that we should act thus or we should not act thus. There is no evidence for this assumption. Those who consider past karma to be responsible for all events, dwell without mindfulness, without restraint. They cannot be said to be all-knowing Samaṇas. I reject their view with reason. I object with reason to the view held by some ascetics and holy men that all man's happiness and misery is dependent on past karma."

Just as he talked about the theory of past karma being the reason for all, he also discussed the theory that God is the reason for everything. He also analyzed at length the view that human happiness and suffering has no reason whatsoever.

Discusssion

In this discourse, the important issues of free will and effort are discussed. For the Buddha, free will was very important. He believed that every human has the freedom to lead his life to achieve his or her goals. In expressing his view, he rejected with reason all three prominent prevalent theories. He refused to blame past karmas for all the ills of human life. He rejected that God creates and has control over all our actions. He also refused to accept the theory that there is no cause at all for human happiness or suffering—that everything is pre-destined.

He declared that man himself is his own creator, he shapes his own future. On one hand, he made humans aware of their abilities and rights; and on the other hand also made them responsible for their actions.

This was a proclamation of the constructive freedom of humanity.

Tathāgata rejected the existence of God. However, he didn't try too hard to deny His existence. The Sāṅkhya philosophers also denied God by not mentioning Him. They enumerated components of existence of universe such as nature but didn't mention God. Similarly, the Tathāgata didn't give any place to God in the Four Noble Truths and the eight-fold noble path. But there were times when the issue needed to be addressed directly and at such times he rejected the existence of God clearly.

It is a surprising that the epithet *(bhagavān, bhagavā)* used to describe the greatness of one who rejected God itself came to be used as synonym for God. His opponents were and are at the forefront of those who use *bhagavān*.

He proved by his own example that a man can reach the supreme height based on morality and wisdom, and doesn't need a separate God.

Swami Vivekanand says,[207] "To many the path becomes easier if they believe in God. But the life of Buddha shows that even a man who does not believe in God, has no metaphysics, belongs to no sect, and does not go to any church, or temple, and is a confessed materialist, even he can attain to the highest. We have no right to judge him. I wish I had one infinitesimal part of Buddha's heart. Buddha may or may not have believed in God; that does not matter to me… Perfection does not come from belief or faith. Talk does not count for anything. Parrots can do that. Perfection comes through the disinterested performance of action."

Nibbāna

The Buddha said repeatedly that attaining nibbāna by eradicating all suffering is the highest goal of human life. Nibbāna literally means extinguishment. When the flame of a lamp extinguishes after the fuel (oil) is over, its extinguishment is called nibbāna in Pali. When a fire is quenched after the supply of wood, grass etc is exhausted, that is its nibbāna.

In India (as also in many other parts of the world) people don't like the concept of extinguishment. It is considered so inauspicious that when a flame is destroyed rather than saying it was extinguished, it is said "it has increased." (Similarly, due to superstitions attached to a broken bangle that women wear on their hand, when a bangle breaks, it is said "bangle has increased.")

Therefore, we are bound to be curious as to why did the Buddha use this word for the highest goal of life. Nibbāna that is attained in this very body, in this very life and nibbāna at the end of life are two shades of the same concept. For convenience, let us use nibbāna for the first and parinibbāna for the second. Let us remember however that the Buddhist tradition has no such differentiation. I am doing it merely to distinguish the two shades of the same concept.

Nibbāna is Within

The Buddha repeatedly asserted that the nibbāna that he referred to can be attained in this very life, in this very world.

Once he was staying in Sāvatthi. He taught the bhikkhus about impermanence. At the end, he said,[208] "… when mind is free of afflictions, it becomes free from defiling impulses; thus freed it becomes steady. A steady mind is contented. Contented mind is untroubled. Once trouble ceases, it attains parinibbāna inside."

Once Ven. Ānanda and Udāyī were dwelling in Ghositārāma at that time.[209]

Udāyī said to Ānanda, "The Tathāgata has often said that this body is impermanent and explained it. Can we similarly say that consciousness is not self, not soul?"

Ānanda replied, yes, we can say that, and explained, "Eye consciousness arises due to eye and form (object of eye). Then, if the reason based on which eye consciousness arises is totally destroyed, ceases totally, will eye consciousness remain?"

He also asked similar questions about all the other senses and mind. He explained to Udāyī how if their basis ceases, the consciousness of these senses would cease.

He gave a parable. ''Suppose a man were to set out in the jungle with an axe. He sees a tender thick stalk of a plantain. Then he cuts the plantain's roots, cuts its top, cuts the stalk and separates out all the layers. That man will not get even the outer part, what to talk about the inner solid core (because plantain has no solid core).

"Similarly, when a bhikkhu removes the six basis of contact, there is nothing that can be referred to as self or related to self. He has no affliction. He has no trouble. He experiences parinibbāna within."

We see in the Tipiṭaka it being said often that nibbāna is to be experienced here and now within oneself. The Buddha said repeatedly that liberated beings *(arahatas)* dwell in ultimate happiness in this very life, in this very world, in this very body. While stating that his Dhamma is *sandiṭṭhika* (here and now) and *akālika* (immediate, timeless), the Buddha expressed the same view. A word in Marathi *"nivānta"* (literal meaning is relaxed, at leisure, at peace) has come from nibbāna. The meaning has changed to some extent, but the core is the same.

The concept of nibbāna is clarified in a sutta in the Connected Discourses[210] in a very lucid and simple manner.

Once Ven. Sāriputta was staying at Nālaka in Magadha. At that time, a wandering recluse named Jambukhādaka came to him and asked, "Friend, 'nibbāna,' 'nibbāna' it is said. What is this nibbāna?"

Sāriputta answered, "Friend, cessation of craving, cessation of aversion and cessation of ignorance is nibbāna."

"Friend, is there a way to achieve nibbāna?"

"Yes, friend, the Noble Eightfold Path is the way to experience nibbāna."

At another time, the same conversation occurred between Sāriputta and the recluse Samandaka at Ukkacelā in Vajjīan country.[211]

Sāriputta, the General of the Dhamma, was explaining the Buddha's view here. The concept of nibbāna has been clarified in such transparent and clear terms that there is no scope for any confusion. Cessation of defilements is the state of nibbāna and the way to achieve it is the Noble Eightfold Path. This is a pure, blameless, happy and bright state. It is not a negative state. The negation is of negative things that are undesirable and harmful. After all the undesirable and harmful qualities are removed whatever remains is full of positive essence. This is a positive state in life. It does not refer to self or soul or any such so called everlasting thing.

Let us see with our own example. If our hatred is eradicated, what is negated? Undesirable element is negated. Thus once whatever is undesirable and harmful is extinguished, whatever remains is not inciting and arousing; rather what remains is a proper, right and balanced life flow.

His Mind Became Free Like the Extinguishment of a Lamp

When one's life ends, that is, when one dies, then from the practical point of view, the nibbāna is different than the nibbāna of life flow.

In this condition, not only are craving, aversion, and ignorance extinguished but all the elements of existence are extinguished. Let us look at some of the descriptions in Tipiṭaka.

We have seen in Aggivacchagotta Sutta that the Tathāgata had explained the nature of nibbāna to Vaccha. As long as the grass and wood afflictions of fire are present, the fire goes on. Once the fuel (affliction) gets exhausted, the fire is extinguished. Then we cannot say whether the fire has gone in north, south, east or west direction.

Same is the case of the human mind. When one dies, we cannot say that the soul or self has left the body and gone in some direction. Just as fire ends without fuel, life is extinguished (nibbāna is attained) when there is no affliction. This is an unequivocal presentation of the concept of nibbāna.

After the Tathāgata's parinibbāna (passing away), Ven. Anuruddha uttered these verses:

His mind was steady, none had his conduct in life;
That one with eyes has attained parinibbāna;
With an untainted mind he has ended suffering;
Like a lamp put out, his mind has become free.

Rahul Sankrityayan writes about the concept of nibbāna,[212] "Nirvana, nibbāna means extinguishment. Lamp or fire burns and gets burned out… Just as after old fuel of a lamp is exhausted and if no new fuel is added that lamp or fire gets quenched, destruction of defilements of mind (wrong views about sensual pleasures, rebirth and self being eternal, etc.) puts an end to the cycle. Nirvana is quenching, extinguishing. This is how the Buddha had chosen it to mean. At the same time, he had refused to say what happens after death to a man who has attained nibbāna. What happens can be easily understood in the doctrine of no-self. But this thought is terrifying to the ignorant people. Therefore, the Buddha didn't say anything clearly."

Not How Many, Who?

Once the recluse Uttiya came to the Tathāgata.[213] He asked the usual questions whether his view was that the world is eternal and other views are false etc.

The Tathāgata told him that he had left these questions unproclaimed.

"Then what have you proclaimed?"

"Having it experienced myself, I teach the Dhamma to people. The Dhamma is for purification of beings, for ending of grief and lamentation, for cessation of suffering, for gaining wisdom and to experience nibbāna."

"How many people, all or one third or two third will attain nibbāna?" Uttiya asked.

The Buddha kept quiet.

At that time, Ānanda who was present, thought that Uttiya might think, "Samaṇa Gotama keeps quiet when asked a higher level question. He doesn't answer because he cannot answer."

If Uttiya had this misunderstanding, it would be harmful to him in the long run and cause him suffering.

Then Ānanda explained, "Uttiya, let me give you an example. Suppose, there is a border town of a king. It has strong fortifications. There is only one gate. On top of the gate, there is a clever and alert doorman. He allows only known people inside. He stops strangers. He goes around the fortifications and finds that there is not the smallest gap, not even a small one so that a cat might enter. He doesn't think how many enter the town and how many exit. But he is sure that only suitable known people are able to get in and others not.

"Similar is the case with the Tathāgata. He doesn't count how many people have attained nibbāna. However, he does assert that whoever has attained or will attain nibbāna, must get rid of the five fetters (craving, hatred, agitation, sloth and torpor, and doubt).

"You asked the question with a different intention. That is why he didn't answer it."

Discussion

There are several important points in this sutta. The Buddha didn't answer irrelevant questions. Ānanda's statement implies that people like Uttiya didn't ask questions out of honest curiosity. Sometimes, these questions were asked to corner him, insult him, defeat him and show him down. He answered with much patience. If he felt that it was not possible to change the intentions of the questioner, he would keep quiet.

Uttiya asked him mockingly how many people are going to get liberated by your discourses. Ānanda gave a fitting reply to Uttiya. There is no need to keep count. Just as to enter a town with only one gate, one had to use that gate; to attain nibbāna, the only way is to eradicate defilements.

I Don't Argue With People; People Argue With Me

Once while living at Jetavana in Sāvatthi, the Buddha said to bhikkhus, "I don't argue with people, people argue with me. Bhikkhus, a Dhamma person doesn't argue with anyone in the world. Thing about which the wise say 'it doesn't exist,' I say the same. Things about which wise say 'it exists', I say the same."

At the end of the discourse,[214] he says, "A lotus arises from water and grows in water but stays detached from water. Similarly, the Tathāgata is born among people, grows among people but still remains detached from people.

He Liked Discussion, Not Argument

The Buddha gave to humanity much that was novel both at the theoretical and practical levels to eradicate suffering and gain happiness. Those who found it difficult to welcome the new teaching would raise objections, make allegations, indulge in false propaganda and spoil his name. They would also behave rudely with him.

The Buddha would always be courteous and soft with these people. He did wander tirelessly and constantly to teach the Dhamma but he never deliberately created controversy. He was never aggressive or offensive. He would respond in different ways with people who were insolent to him. But he never created mischief on his own.

This doesn't mean that he was weak, spineless or yielded in the face of external pressure. He was firm. His determination was strong. He expressed this determination with great restraint and in a constructive way. He rejected the then popular theories of soul and God firmly. But he was never crude or bombastic while doing so. He would enter into people's hearts skillfully and then bring the light of the truth to their heads.

When he said, he didn't argue with people, people argued with him; it was the truth both about his communication style and its elegance.

His practicable solution to live a life free from suffering in real world is his great contribution to not only India but to the entire world.

6

Right Speech for Happiness

The Tathāgata taught the Noble Eightfold Path to remove misery. Right speech *(sammāvaca)* is one part of the Eightfold Path. A man's success or failure depends to a large extent on how he uses language.

We understand from the Buddha's discourses that right speech is an important part of the Eightfold Path.

What exactly is right speech according to the Buddha? There are several ways to get the answer. We can understand it from the discourses of the Buddha as well as from his language and manner of discussing things. He made comments about his own speech. Others talked about his speech. From these, we can understand and follow him. He gave advice to bhikkhus and laypeople about what to say and what not to say.

Let us take a look.

Be Careful With Words and Meaning

Pāsādika Sutta[215] is from Pāthikavagga of the Long Discourses. Here the Buddha says that to protect a thought one has to be careful with language.

Bhikkhu Cunda came to know that after Nigaṇṭṭha Nāṭaputta passed away at Pāvā, there were differences of opinion among his followers. He shared this with Ānanda. Then both of them went to Tathāgata and reported it to him. At that time, the Buddha gave a detailed sermon on the Dhamma to Cunda and at the end explained thoroughly what care should be taken to protect the Dhamma taught by him.

The Buddha said, "Therefore, Cunda, my disciples—to whom I have made known the truths that I have discovered—should come together in harmony and rehearse together those teachings and not quarrel over them. Compare meaning with meaning, and phrase with phrase, in order that this pure Dhamma may endure for a long time; in order that it may continue for the good and happiness of the great multitudes, out of compassion for the world, for the good, the gain and the happiness of gods and men."

Then he explained with examples how they should be careful to avoid any distortion of his teaching in word and meaning.

"Suppose, bhikkhus dwell together in harmony, without quarrel. While one of them is speaking about the Dhamma, the others think, 'This friend has grasped the meaning incorrectly and is also using incorrect words.' At such times, others should not agree with him or criticize him. They should discuss with him. They should ask him whether to convey such and such thing, would the use of such and such words be more suitable. If he remains adamant insisting that what he said was correct, then one should not accept or reject that meaning. They should ensure that the proper meaning is conveyed through the proper use of words and explain this to others.

"Suppose, another bhikkhu is giving a sermon on the Dhamma. He has grasped the meaning incorrectly but is using correct words. At such times, others should not agree with him or criticize him. They should ask him whether such and such meaning would be more appropriate for those words. If he remains adamant insisting that what he said was correct, they should ensure that the proper meaning is conveyed through the proper use of words and explain this to others.

"Similarly, if a bhikkhu is teaching the Dhamma and the meaning is correct but words are incorrect, the other bhikkhus should again deal with it as discussed above.

"Now, if a bhikkhu is giving a sermon on the Dhamma. He is grasping the words properly and is also using the correct words. Then others should commend him saying 'well said; well said, indeed.' They should say that it is their great benefit that they have an associate who uses the proper words to convey the correct meaning."

Discussion

Positive Discussion Even if the Speaker is Wrong

The news about differences of opinion among his followers after Nigaṇṭṭha Nāṭaputta passed away was significant. Often after a great man's death, there is confusion about his exact views. The Tathāgata was keen that this didn't happen to his disciples. He gave important guidelines to bhikkhus about how to pass on his teaching correctly; not out of personal ego but out of compassion for people, for their welfare.

Whether a person is making a mistake in meaning or usage of words or both; the Buddha wanted others to discuss it with him. If both meaning and words were flawless, others should congratulate him, express gratitude to him and encourage him.

Thus this discourse gives subtle tips about how to engage someone positively in discussion, how to understand him and how to respond to him.

He cautioned bhikkhus against immediate criticism if they found someone saying wrong things. If they believed that they were right and the speaker wrong; and out of arrogance humiliated the speaker, it would hurt him. Then it would lead to friction and split in the Saṅgha. This would hamper the Dhamma's transmission to people. He wanted bhikkhus to be aware of this danger. It is another thing if the speaker is making a terrible mistake or destructive distortion that requires immediate correction; otherwise, it is better to wait and have a gentle dialogue. The Buddha didn't want rude or bombastic behavior while trying to maintain suitable coordination between words and their meanings. He taught bhikkhus to do it skillfully and with affection.

Dual Protection of Language Necessary to Protect the Dhamma

We have already seen that the proper use of words and their meanings is vital to prevent distortion of the Dhamma. In the Numerical Discourses,[216] we see that the Buddha gave two important tips for protection of the Dhamma.

He once said to bhikkhus, "Two things are responsible for the destruction and disappearance of the Saddhamma. Which two? Improper change in arrangement of words and wrong meaning. If the words are not arranged properly, the meaning also gets distorted. On the other hand, proper word arrangement and correct meaning cause the Dhamma to endure long without destruction or loss."

Discussion

The Buddha was aware of the distortion in the use of language. Even during his lifetime, there were attempts to distort his teachings. It happened after him too, as many scholars have pointed out.

The following verse of Dhammapada gives us guidance about suitable relation between words and meaning.[217]

Better one utterance full of meaning that calms;
Than a thousand utterances full of meaningless words.

Plough the Field and also the Land of Speech

If we want to understand our history properly, we should embark on a journey in search of the history of words and their meaning in our language. Such a search would lead to finding countless things from our culture.

Let us take the example of Darjeeling. "Ling" in Tibetan language means "place.". Darjee is a variation of the Tibetan word dorje. Vajra of Vajrayana Buddhist tradition is dorje in Tibetan. Thus the word Darjeeling denotes the influence of a Buddhist tradition in that area. I have narrated my own experience in a reference[218] at the end because I felt it was important from social and cultural history.

Four Right and Wrong Speeches

The Buddha enumerated four right and wrong speeches.[219] Wrong speech includes lying, backbiting, harsh words and useless chatter. Right speech includes truthfulness, abstaining from backbiting, gentle words and meaningful speech.

Avoid Misuse of Language

Brahmajāla Sutta, the first sutta of the Long Discourses gives detailed description of what type of language to use and which language to avoid. People would praise the Buddha for such restrained use of language. For him however, it was not a big achievement. He told bhikkhus that it was a minor morality. Minor doesn't mean not important but something that was not difficult. It didn't take efforts.

In this sutta, he said that he avoided four flaws in speech that are narrated above. Falsehood is the first among these flaws. People said, "Samaṇa Gotama speaks the truth. He has commitment to the truth. He is steady in his speech. He doesn't keep on changing his stand. His speech is trustworthy. There is no contradiction between his speech and actions."

People often indulge in backbiting. Tathāgata abstained from it. People praised him, "Samaṇa Gotama doesn't indulge in divisive speech. He keeps confidential what is said to him. On the other hand, he unites those who are divided. He strengthens the unity of those that are united. He likes it when people live together harmoniously without divisiveness. He is delighted where people are united. He finds happiness there. He uses language that causes unity."

Harsh speech is the third flaw in speech. This fault was not found in the Tathāgata. "He speaks flawless speech that is endearing, affectionate, heart-warming, honorable; that pleases and brings happiness to many ."

Frivolous and useless speech is yet another flaw in speech. Tathāgata didn't have that flaw. People said, "Samaṇa Gotama knows the proper time to speak *(kālavādi)*: he speaks at the proper time and his words are suitable for the occasion. He knows truth *(bhūtavādi)*: he speaks as it happened. His speech is meaningful. He doesn't indulge in frivolous speech. He speaks the Dhamma. He speaks the Discipline. He speaks essence at proper time. He speaks with reason. He doesn't speak wildly without looking at cause and effect relationship. His speech is directed at the goal. His speech is true to meaning."

Discussion

This one description describes the lofty heights to which the Buddha took his speech. We get a glimpse of the right speech that he talked about. People were impressed because they couldn't exercise restraint in their speech. They knew that people around them too couldn't be restrained in their speech.

For the Buddha himself this was not a high achievement or worthy of too much praise. For him it was an integral and indivisible part of his morality. For a common man, it may not be as easy but with efforts one can raise the level of one's speech. If one deliberately imbibes even a part of the ethics of the Buddha's speech, one's life would become full of joy.

Tathāgata's Language Doesn't Divide, It Unites

Backbiting was a flaw in speech, the Buddha taught. Backbiting leads to misunderstandings. Minds become polluted. People turn away from people. This division hurts individuals and harms society. Therefore, he emphasized abstaining from backbiting and . He taught to remove misunderstandings. We see an example of this in the Kinti Sutta of the Middle Discourses.[220]

Once the Buddha was staying at Kusinārā in the grove named Baliharaṇa.

At that time, he invited the bhikkhus and said, "Bhikkhus, do you think that Samaṇa Gotama teaches the Dhamma in order to get robes, alms-food, bed and seat or to get a good future birth?"

The bhikkhus said no.

He then asked them, "What do you think of me then?"

The bhikkhus answered, "Bhante, Tathāgata is compassionate. He is our well-wisher. He teaches the Dhamma out of compassion. This is what we think."

After their reply, the Buddha gave a discourse the gist of which is:

"If you feel thus about me then follow what I have taught with a joyous mind and without quarrel. While you are thus dwelling in harmony, it may happen that two groups may disagree about the Dhamma. If you find that the disagreement is about both words and meaning, then go to the wiser bhikkhu in one group. Tell him, 'There is a difference of opinion between you two about words and meaning… even then you two should not quarrel.' Then go to the wiser bhikkhu in the other group. They should explain to both groups, correct things as correct and incorrect as incorrect. Explain the Dhamma and the Discipline. Whether the discrepancy between two groups is in the meaning or the words, wiser and restrained bhikkhus should be approached from both groups. If there is no difference in meaning and no difference in word, then they should be told not to quarrel.

"Do not be eager to admonish a bhikkhu if you find him making a mistake or if he transgresses a rule of discipline. First find out the truth. Test him. Check whether such a discussion would trouble you or hurt him. It is proper to speak to that person if he is not prone to anger, doesn't hold grudges, is not adamant, is flexible; and if it seems possible to remove the unwholesome and establish wholesome factors in him.

"If you find that speaking to him is not going to trouble you but he is going to be troubled; ignore whatever trouble may be caused to him if there is possibility of his understanding the issue properly and getting connected to the right things.

"If you find that speaking to him is going to trouble you but he is not going to troubled; then one should ignore one's trouble and explain things to him.

"Even if the discussion is going to trouble both but there is possibility of him understanding the issue properly, one should go ahead.

"If you find that both are going to be troubled and there is no possibility of his understanding things, his turning away from unwholesome towards wholesome, then one should ignore the issue and not discuss it.

"While all of you are dwelling in harmony, without arguments, there may arise discrepancy in statements and difference in views of two groups of bhikkhus; hurt may be caused, distrust and discontentment may arise. At such a time, go to the more prudent one in one group and discuss with him, 'Wouldn't wise ascetics criticize us for such behavior? Can we experience nibbāna if you go on quarreling?' He will agree that the quarrel will invite censure and they cannot attain nibbāna if they quarrel. Then go to a prudent bhikkhu on the side and do the same.

"When a bhikkhu thus mediates to end the quarrel, people will praise him. At such times, he should remain humble. He should say that I merely explained the Dhamma taught by the Buddha to those bhikkhus and this in turn lead them from unwholesome things to wholesome things. This way, he avoids praising himself. He should avoid criticizing others. Thus, he speaks in accordance with the Dhamma and he is not censured in any debate."

Discussion

With great care and very skillfully, the Buddha had impressed upon bhikkhus to avoid impatient reaction, unthinking interference, harsh criticism and undue publicity so that the situation doesn't get further complicated. Often the differences are superficial. Often when there is no difference of opinion in understanding of principles and in goals, some minor external things lead to quarrel. It is essential to bridge the gap in them and to explain how their differences are superficial. Even when one is sure that the difference of opinion is serious, advise them to avoid quarrel and discuss things amicably to overcome the differences.

Avoid harsh criticism even if someone has made a mistake. Judge whether it is practically possible to correct the other person and bring him or her to the right path. If it is going to be a futile effort, better to avoid it.

Always go to the prudent person first. Going to an adamant person may actually complicate the situation.

One should not be proud of successful mediation in a quarrel. One should derive satisfaction from the fact that one has done good. If one gives credit to the Dhamma, envy and enmity don't arise. Arrogance arising from good work can be dangerous. Saying that one worked in accordance with the guidance of a senior and wise well-wisher helps keep the atmosphere harmonious.

Care in Questions and Answers

In Ayonisa Sutta of the Graded Discourses,[221] the Buddha explains the care to be taken while asking questions and answering them. A person who doesn't ask questions properly, doesn't answer properly, and doesn't commend one who gives proper answers is a fool indeed.

A wise person knows how to ask questions, gives proper answers to questions and seconds the proper answers given by others.

Wrong Speech Can Never Have Good Effect

The Buddha said repeatedly that unwholesome bodily, verbal and mental actions cannot have beneficial consequences. He said about speech,[222] "Bhikkhus, it is not possible that the misuse of speech will lead to desirable, beneficial and pleasant consequences. On the other hand, it may cause undesirable, ugly and unpleasant effects."

Three Kinds of Speech

He told bhikkhus that people have three kind of speech in the world.[223] One is 'tricky tongued' *(gūthabhāṇī)* if one goes to assembly or gathering or among clansmen or traders' meet or king's court and when he is asked to depose as a witness, "Gentleman, tell us what you know." Then he tells what he doesn't know. He tells things he has seen as not seen and vice versa. For his or someone else's gain, he deliberately lies. Such a person is tricky tongued. He uses ugly speech.

One who tells in an assembly truthfully what he knows is 'fair-tongued' *(pupphabhāṇī).*

If one gives up harsh speech and uses only faultless, melodious, affectionate, heart-warming, civilized language that is lovely and dear to many, he is 'honey-tongued' *(madhubhāṇī).*

Like Honey-Ball, The Buddha's Discourse is Sweet From All Sides

The Buddha was both 'fair-tongued' and 'honey-tongued'. We see this in the Discourse on Honey Ball (Madhupiṇḍika Sutta) in the Middle Discourses.[224]

Once he was dwelling in a monastery in Kapilavatthu. He ate his alms food after the alms round and entered the forest. He sat under a bamboo tree. At that time, Daṇḍapāṇi (literally, one with stick in the hand) Sākya came there. After courteous greetings he stood to one side resting on the stick in his hand and asked him, "Samaṇa, what is your doctrine? What philosophy do you teach?"

The Buddha answered, "Friend! Someone lives in the world with its devas, māras, brahmās, ascetics, holy men, humans, etc. without quarrel with anyone. He is truly a sage who dwells detached from all greed and lust; who has no doubt; who has no confusion; who had no craving for being and non-being. Perception doesn't follow him. This is my doctrine. This is my philosophy."

On hearing this, Daṇḍapāṇi shook his head, put out his tongue mockingly, frowned and went away taking his staff with him.

That evening after solitary meditation, the Buddha went to the Nigrodha monastery. There he narrated the incident of the morning to the bhikkhus. Then one bhikkhu expressed desire to know precisely what doctrine the Buddha taught.

He replied, "Bhikkhus, whatever cause makes perception to continue, don't welcome, commend or follow it. This leads to the end of the latent tendencies of craving, anger, view, doubt, conceit, ignorance, craving for being and ignorance. It leads to the end of the use of stick and weapons, quarrels, conflicts, debates, confrontations, backbiting and lying. It leads to the total end of all sinful and unwholesome deeds."

Then the Buddha got up and went away.

After he went away, bhikkhus started talking among each other. They started thinking about who would explain in detail what the Buddha had narrated in short. Mahākaccāna's name came up. They went to him and requested him to explain what the Buddha had said. First, Mahākaccāna said that they should have learned it from the Buddha himself but later he relented and conceded their request.

After listening to Mahākaccāna, the bhikkhus went to the Buddha and told him what Mahākaccāna had explained. The Buddha said, "Mahākaccāna is erudite. He is wise. If you had asked me to explain, I would have explained exactly the same way. Now follow, put in practice what is explained."

Then Ānanda said, "Bhante, if a very hungry man were to get a honey-ball, then from whatever side he would eat it, it would taste very sweet and delicious. Similarly, in whatever way, from whatever side a clever and intelligent bhikkhu would evaluate this discourse, it would make him contented and happy. Bhante, what should we call this discourse?"

"Well then, Ānanda, you may remember it as the Discourse on Honey-ball."

Discussion

It is said that the Sākyan who met him was Daṇḍapāṇi (literally, stick in hand). It doesn't seem right. He was so called because he came with a stick in his hand. The Buddha answered him politely. Still, he went away displeased. Then the Buddha gave a Dhamma talk to bhikkhus. He explained how to destroy unwholesome qualities and live a good life. It was a short discourse that was filled with compassion and sweetness. Therefore, Ānanda compared it with a honey-ball. Actually, this was not the only discourse of the Buddha that was fit for this title. His life tells us that his entire personality and all his teachings throughout his life can be described as a honey-ball—sweet on all sides.

The Tathāgata Walks the Talk

It is important for language to be good. There is one more thing that is important. Sweet language that is not matched by deeds makes the sweetness futile. In fact, it deceives the listener. Therefore, it often becomes harmful. People who speak harshly but truthfully are better than such cunning deceivers. Sweetness of speech is important but far more important is righteous conduct. Therefore, the Buddha's life sets an example for all of us to follow.

Various scholars give different explanations for the word '*Tathāgata*'. One important opinion is given in Itivuttakapāli.[225] The text says that it was given by the Buddha himself, "Bhikkhus, he is '*yathāvādi tathākari, yathākari tathāvadi*' (literally, he does as he says and he says as he does) that is why he is called Tathāgata."

Discussion

The Buddha himself set a yardstick for the epithet 'Tathāgata'.

One aspect of his enlightenment was that there is no discrepancy in speech and action. There was perfect harmony in his actions after his enlightenment.

Often people put forth great theories, declare attractive hypotheses, and make promises that engender much hope. But either they forget their statements or they made these promises with an intent to deceive. Therefore, there arises great discrepancy between their words and actions.

Sometimes, people act in a certain way but don't inform people about its true nature. They use ambiguous language to cover their dishonorable deeds.

In Marathi Tukaram's exhortation is famous, '*bole taisā cāle tyāchī vandāvī pāule*' (literally, salute his feet who acts as he speaks). Saint Tukaram had inherited moneylender's business from his father. He threw into the river the debt-documents of all debtors, thus setting them free. His actions matched his words.

People's Language Rather Than Sanskrit

A small incident in Vinaya Piṭaka (Book of Discipline)[226] is very significant in the history of India and of Buddhism:

Yameḷa and Kekuṭa were two bhikkhus who were brothers. They were brahmins. They spoke sweetly and nicely. Once they went to the Buddha and sat to one side after saluting him.

Then they said, "Bhante, these days different people from different clans, different castes, different families take robes and become bhikkhus. They pollute the words of the Buddha with their language. Therefore, bhante, we will translate the words of the Buddha into Sanskrit (*Chāndas*, Vedic Sanskrit)."

They were admonished by the Buddha, "Useless fellows, how did you say 'we will translate the words of the Buddha into Sanskrit?' Useless fellows, this doesn't incline those to the Dhamma who are disinclined, doesn't increase the inclination of those that are inclined and disinclines some who are be inclined."

Then he called bhikkhus and said, "Bhikkhus, the words of the Buddha should not be translated into Sanskrit. Whoever does so, will be committing a transgression. Bhikkhus, I give permission to translate the words of the Buddha into your respective languages."

Discussion

He didn't allow bhikkhus to translate his words into Sanskrit and specifically laid a rule to prohibit it. Thus he declined to teach in Sanskrit. This was a revolutionary event in the linguistic history of India. This doesn't stem from hatred for Sanskrit. It was based on an objective and mature reasoning of the Buddha.

One is able to express one's emotions, feelings, thoughts and views in his own language properly and effectively. One is also able to comprehend others' emotions, thoughts, etc. if conveyed in one's language. To make communication between humans faultless and meaningful their own language is the best.

In India, Vedics have given huge prestige to Sanskrit as the language of the gods. It was the gods' language, which means it wasn't the language of the people. The Buddha didn't want to teach the Dhamma to a handful few. He wanted to bring about a total transformation in the lives of ordinary people. Only teaching in their own language would reach their hearts and minds. That is why he insisted on teaching in their own language. His opinion that translation into Sanskrit wouldn't bring closeness to the masses gave a desirable direction to the social history of India. He called the bhikkhus who wanted to translate into English as *'moghapurisa'*. *'Mogha'* means useless, futile. Indeed, to leave one's own language and take refuge in Sanskrit was useless for common people of India.

Prof. Jagannath Upadhyay's Opinion

Prof. Jagannath Upadhyay writes,[227] "When history of Indian culture is studied, it is not taken into consideration that Pali, Prakrit are languages of our nation. It is said that the mother of all Indian languages is Sanskrit. This is a blatant lie. Sanskrit is not the mother language of Bengali, Marathi, Hindi, etc. Prakrit and Pali are the mother languages of these languages. The literature of Indian culture is in these languages; not in Sanskrit… It is said that Sanskrit and Indian culture are same thing. This is a total lie. Sanskrit is the language of a class. It is the language of the class that has been oppressing the true people of India and their culture for centuries. Only a part of India's great history is contained in Sanskrit and it is called language of the gods. Words of the gods. And who can read this language of the gods? Only the gods of the earth, brahmins. On one hand the language of gods and on the other hand the brahmin readers: gods of the land, gods of the skies. The implication is simple and straightforward, it is neither the language of Hindustan nor the language of Bharat; and no Indian has expressed the feelings of his heart in this language. It is the language of the attackers, the invaders. And Sanskrit does contain a big history of the webs that were cast and philosophies that were created to invade and attack."

In later period, Buddhist scriptures were translated into Sanskrit. That process had its benefits and drawbacks. But that is a different subject.

Mahanubhav Tradition Took the Buddha's View on People's Language

Later on the Mahanubhav (Mahānubhāva) tradition also took the same stand and insisted on local dialects instead of Sanskrit. Once Keshavadeva asked Swami Cakradhara's disciple Nagadevacarya a question in Sanskrit to which he replied that I won't answer in Sanskrit. Cakradhara has taught me in Marathi (local language in Maharashtra, India). Ask me in Marathi and I will answer.[228]

Kabir on Sanskrit

Dr. Komal Singh Solanki has quoted the great saint Kabir while discussing the relation between Sanskrit and vernacular languages.[229] "The following is attributed to Kabir regarding Sanskrit—'Sanskrit is stagnant water (hence turbid), languages are water that flows (hence clear).' " (*sanskirata hai kūpajala, bhāshā bahatā nīra*)

Right Speech is Great Welfare

The Buddha emphasized again and again the importance of good speech. There is a beautiful quotation in the Suttanipāta.[230]

"Good speech leads to excellent welfare." (*subhāsitā ca yā vācā, etaṃ maṅgalamuttamaṃ.*)

This is a sweet quote on the wonderful benefits one gets in life due to right speech. It also denotes that words— *subhāsita, subhāshita* and *maṅgala*— that are popular in Indian languages today come from the Tathāgata's discourses. If one wishes to enrich one's life with better and greater experiences one has to take care of several things—careful use of language is one such thing. Right speech is of great benefit. Great *maṅgala*! This is such a tender, such a heartwarming and such an objective statement. It is doubtless that on the path of happiness, welfare and wellbeing, good speech is a benevolent friend.

7

Respect for Householder's Life, Concern for National Character

The Buddha had established a Saṅgha of monks (bhikkhus). He is often seen giving discourses to monks. If one looks at the various events in his life, it is clear that in his Dhamma, bhikkhus have an important place. Due to this, some people become confused about his teaching. His opponents try to increase that confusion. They allege that he ignored householders. Let us see how valid is this allegation.

All His Discourses to Laypeople Have Not Been Collected

For 45 years, the Buddha gave several discourses to monks. He also gave thousands of discourses to householders. We cannot be sure that all these discourses would be found in the Tipiṭaka today. It was the bhikkhus who took on the responsibility of preserving his teaching. Therefore, the Tipiṭaka mostly has discourses for bhikkhus. This is apparent also from traditional sequence of texts in Tipiṭaka, where the Book of Discipline

(*Vinaya Piṭaka*) comes first followed by the Discourses (*Sutta Piṭaka*). This is not surprising and we can't blame bhikkhus for it. However, we must consider the possibility of the discourses to the householders being lost over time. The Buddha certainly gave far more discourses to the householders than are contained in the Tipiṭaka today. Even if it is so, the discourses in the Tipiṭaka are enough to give us a clear idea about the form and direction of his advice to householders.

Four Things for Success in Householder's Life

Once he was living in the Kakkarapatta town of the Koliyan republic. At that time, a Koliyan named Dīghajāṇu (literally one with long arms) came to him and sat down to one side after saluting him.[231]

Then Dīghajāṇu told the Buddha, "Bhante, we are laypeople who indulge in sensual pleasures and are entangled in children." He gave details about the various pleasures and luxuries such as use of gold and silver that laypeople indulge in. "Bhante, please give us guidance for our wellbeing and happiness here in this world and yonder."

The Buddha replied, "There are four things that bring a clansman wellbeing and happiness here in this world. Which four? Wealth of effort, wealth of protection, noble friendship and living according to means.

"What is wealth of effort? One derives his livelihood from agriculture, trading, cattle, archery (skills in weapons), employment in the royal court and artisanship. One is vigilant in one's work, doesn't become lax or lazy, knows how to complete the work, knows how to evaluate the work, is capable of finishing the work. Such a person is said to possess *weath of effort*."

"What is wealth of protection? One through efforts and action, by the dint of his own work, with his own sweat, through proper means while following the Dhamma becomes affluent. He takes care that his fortune is not snatched by thieves or by kings, protects it from fire and flood and takes care that his fortune is not inherited by undesirable people. This is *wealth of protection*."

"What is noble friendship? One associates with householders who are his juniors or seniors. He judges their morality, faith, charity and wisdom and learns these things from them. This is *noble friendship*."

"What is living according to means? One knows one's fortune. One spends in proportion to his fortune. One doesn't spend more than one earns or too little. One makes sure that one's income is more than one's expenses and that one's expenses are not more than one's income. Just as one who holds a weighing scale (balance) is aware of the weight in the two pans and their relative position and decides according to this observation how much to spend. If one is throwing money around in spite of having little income, people comment, "This clansman is spending money as if he eats fruits of *udumbara* (a kind of fig tree that gives abundant fruit)." On the other hand, if someone is living a life of penury in spite of a substantial earning, people comment, 'This clansman will die heirless.' Therefore, one spends according to one's income. This is *living according to means*."

He went on to add, "There are four reasons for destruction of the fortune earned through one's efforts: *philandering, alcoholism, gambling and bad friendship*. Suppose, a lake has four inlets and four outlets. If the owner of the lake were to block inlets and leave the outlets open; and if it doesn't rain well, then the lake will become dry. This is what happens to one with these four vices. On the other hand, the situation of one who doesn't fall prey to these four habits is like a lake whose outlets are blocked but inlets are open. When it rains, the level of water in the lake rises."

Then he said to the Koliyan, "These are the four things that affect one's happiness and wellbeing."

Then the Buddha said that beyond this worldly wellbeing, to attain higher happiness and wellbeing, *the wealth of faith, morality, charity and wisdom* helps and explained their nature.

In Gotamī Vagga, this sutta is followed by Ujjaya Sutta. The essence of that sutta too is the same. That discourse was given in response to the questions by Ujjaya who seeks his advice on happiness and wellbeing. These are two different instances but the guidance is similar.

Discussion

Many people have failed to understand the Buddha properly because they have ignored the fact that many householders used to seek and get the Buddha's guidance. He didn't just talk about nibbāna. He also talked in great and accurate detail about how to live a happy family life. He shed light on various facets of various livelihoods. The Noble Eightfold Path that he taught for eradication of suffering also contains right livelihood. His comment on wealth of effort tells us that he emphasized the importance of right efforts for householders. He didn't make laypeople inactive. On the contrary, he inspired them to be zestful and active for a successful householder's life.

He did advise abandoning of defilements such as greed, etc. But he warned them against carelessness about the wealth earned through hard work. He gave practical guidance about how to protect ones' wealth. He showed them the importance of association with those who are elder, more experienced, better qualified, progressive and ethical; who know the nuances of practical world. Those who think that they know all and that there is no need to learn anything from others block with their own hands ways of their own progress.

Living according to means, especially living within means is very important. We see many people around us who have a lifestyle far beyond their means. Many get in trouble by spending on things for which they have no money. We see many irresponsible people of meager means who waste their money due to false prestige, desire for exhibition of wealth and lack of evaluation of their own means. Such people harm themselves and devastate their families. We also see people who have great wealth but do not spend anything even for suitable causes. They don't understand that wealth is a means and a happy life is the aim.

Those who follow the fourfold advice of the Buddha are sure to be successful and to overcome any temporary setbacks to bounce back in life. If these four practical guidelines are supplemented with faith, morality, charity and wisdom then it further enriches one's life.

This shows that the Tathāgata didn't look at human life superficially or from one angle only and that he took into consideration all aspects of life.

Four Fruits of Hard Earned Prosperity

Once the Buddha told Anāthapiṇḍika about the four fruits that accrue to one who has earned wealth through hard work.[232]

In a sutta in the Numerical Discourses, the Buddha has enumerated four types of timely fruit that come to one who is desirous of worldly pleasures:

One who has with effort, with his own hands, through his sweat and by following the Dhamma earned wealth gets *happiness of having*.

One enjoys this wealth and uses it for noble causes, for wholesome purposes, charity, etc. This gives him joy and mental satisfaction. This is *happiness of indulging*.

One doesn't owe anything to anyone; neither a lot nor a little. Such happiness of being free of debt is *happiness of being debt-free*.

A noble disciple's physical, verbal and mental actions are untainted and pure. This is *happiness of being blameless*.

At the end of this discourse to Anāthapiṇḍika, the Buddha says, "A wise one knows that the first three types of happiness are not even one-sixteenth of the happiness of being blameless."

Discussion

This discourse makes it clear that a householder has every right to enjoy worldly pleasures. The Buddha repeatedly stressed that wealth and other material things necessary for such joys must be earned through proper means, through hard work.

The first happiness that comes from wealth is the happiness of possessing it. Often one is not able to enjoy one's wealth immediately and completely but the knowledge that one has means gives one a mental security. It takes away to some extent the anxiety about future. One has confidence that even in adverse circumstances one will be able to tide over the crisis through one's wealth. It is absolutely wrong to be greedy about material enjoyments but it is undeniable that wealth is necessary for contentment and security.

Happiness of using one's material wealth is different. It includes actually enjoying the things one has, sharing them with others, and helping and supporting others.

When one has enough to support himself, one doesn't need to borrow from others. Income and expenditure are nicely balanced. One doesn't face the tensions of debt. This is important for one's pride and self-respect.

Poverty and Debt due to Poverty Are Painful

The Buddha taught that one should not be greedy for wealth, one should not get entangled in its allurement and should not run blindly after wealth. For monks, he felt that the minimum needs for survival should be enough. His own needs were minimal. Still, he had the prudence to understand the necessity of money for laypeople. This prudence lead him to make the statement that poverty is painful. Let us look at Ina sutta (Discourse on Debt) in the Numerical Discourses.[233]

He said once while teaching bhikkhus, "For laypeople who enjoy material pleasures, poverty is painful."

A poor man lacking means takes a loan. Being in debt is painful. He agrees to pay interest on the loan. This is painful. If he is unable to pay interest the creditor insults him. This is painful for him. Even after demands, when principal is not paid, the creditors harass him. This is painful. When he is unable to repay the loan, he is imprisoned. This too is painful.

A bhikkhu who is lacking (poor) in wholesome deeds is just like the layman who is poor and gets in debt.

It is noteworthy that the Buddha did not glorify poverty. He commented in detail about how poverty was painful and how one must have means to look after one's family. He also chastised the bhikkhus who were poor in wholesome deeds.

The Happiness of Being Blameless

The Buddha laid an ethical foundation for *the joys of having wealth, enjoying wealth and being free from debt*. He said that *the joy of being blameless* is many times higher than the other three combined. It is certainly a great happiness to know that one has done nothing wrong, not used wrong speech and has not generated unwholesome thoughts. Happiness for one who leads such a life is lofty and transcendent. The peace and satisfaction of one who keeps his morality intact while earning wealth is incomparable.

The Buddha has given sterling guidance about how to harmonize the practical world and spirituality in a constructive and delightful manner.

Savarkar's Objections

Savarkar has alleged that the Buddha asked farmers to abandon agriculture.[234] In his play, the general of the Sākyan army says to the Buddha, "...if you continue to spread your message like this, these hundreds of people will break their plough, abandon their loom, desert their shops to increase the number of beggars in the bhikkhu-Saṅgha that lives on the labor of others. Because, abandoning agriculture is the second vow of asceticism! Others should toil on farm till death, and it is not evil for monks to eat the produce of their work... "

In reality, the Buddha never advised against agriculture. Savarkar makes it appear as if he was propagating leaving plough, loom, shops to become a bhikkhu. There is no historical truth in it. Not only did the Buddha not advise to abandon agriculture, he gave excellent guidance to householders about how to do farming properly and how to run a shop well.

Savarkar says that if a monk had farmed and eaten his own produce, it would not have been a fraud. Manusmriti says that out of four ashrams of Vedics, three should get alms food *(bhikshā)*. This Manusmriti was created through the inspiration of Pushyamitra Shunga, the same Pushyamitra who Savarkar chooses to include in his six golden pages from the vast history of India. At that time, he doesn't remember his own view on this issue. Savarkar includes Raghoba Dada Peshava in these six pages but excludes King Shivaji. Does this indicate a lack of bias on the part of Savarkar?

Every society has division of labor. Not everyone does business. It is not possible to do so. Principle of proper society means each one should do his job properly. There should be freedom for people to choose. It should be based on merit. Though bhikkhus were not doing farming, they were fulfilling the vital task of ethical education of people. If the Buddha had asked those who were farming and running shops to stop doing so, Savarkar's objections would have been valid. Buddha's advice to farmers about proper methods of farming is well known.

The Buddha's Advice About Agriculture

Suddhodana had vast fields. Gotama knew about farming from childhood. He had thorough knowledge of fertile and infertile soil in a field. He has described the difference in Khetta Sutta (Discourse on Field) in the Graded Discourses.[235]

"There are eight faults in land. If one sows in such a field, the crop is less, the grain not tasty and the yield paltry. The eight faults are: the field has many highs and lows—the land is not flat. It has many stones and pebbles. The soil is poor. The plough can't penetrate deep into the soil. There is no provision of entry of water. The excess water doesn't percolate and flow out. There are no water canals in the land. The land is not fenced properly. If the soil in a field has none of these flaws, it gives superior yield."

He said that this description is also applicable to samaṇas and brāhmaṇas. Any donation given to samaṇas and brāhmaṇas who don't follow the Noble Eightfold Path is wasted. And support to those who follow the Noble Eightfold Path gives wonderful fruit.

Discussion

It is clear that the Buddha knew details about agriculture. The Buddha didn't discriminate between samaṇas and brāhmaṇas when it came to donations. Gift to a samaṇa not following the Eightfold Path is useless and gift to a brāhmaṇas who follows the Eightfold Path is fruitful—this shows lack of prejudice in the Buddha.

Guidance for Good Farming

The Buddha has often given examples of agriculture in his discourses. These show that he had knowledge about farming. Some of the suttas in the Numerical Discourses are noteworthy.

Once he explained to the bhikkhus that a farmer has to do three tasks on time.[236] After taking all precautions for future, a farmer ploughs and prepares his field. Then he sows seeds at the right time. He waters the farm at the right time and ensures that excess water gets out. Similarly, bhikkhus should be careful about morality, wisdom, etc.

In Paviveka Sutta[237] the Buddha has given several specifics about what a farmer should do when the crop is ready.

After the crop ripens, the farmer doesn't delay cutting of the crop. After crop is cut, he immediately bales it. Then he takes the bales to a protected place and stores them. Then he gives further details about what a farmer should do in Paviveka Sutta.

Discussion

The specific information that the Buddha gives about various steps in farming shows his knowledge. Such knowledge is not possible for someone who has never seen it from close. The Buddha knew from experience the long process involved before the food gets to our plate.

He never dissuaded people from farming!

Simile of Successful and Unsuccessful Shopkeepers

Various people adapt various means of livelihood. Business, small or big, is one such mean. Some do it skillfully and some can't manage it well. Just as businessmen are of two types, bhikkhus too are of two types. The Buddha explains this in a sutta in the Numerical Discourses.[238]

Once he said to the bhikkhus, "Bhikkhus, a shopkeeper who has these three things can't get wealth that he doesn't have and can't increase wealth that he does have. These three things are: not doing proper work in the morning, not doing proper work in the afternoon and not doing proper work in the evening. On the other hand, one who works properly at these three times, gets wealth that he doesn't have and increases what he already has. Similarly, a bhikkhu who establishes himself in concentration (absorptions) in the morning, afternoon and evening can attain and increase the wholesome *dhammas*. A bhikkhu who doesn't do so, cannot attain and increase the wholesome *dhammas*.

In the following sutta, he has further explained the comparison. If a shopkeeper is mindful, clever and if he has support of an influential person, then he accumulates wealth in a short time and increases it. A shopkeeper is said to be one with eyes (mindful) if he is aware of buying price, selling price, stock, capital and profit. He or she is said to be clever if is skilled in buying and selling. When a person with great wealth sees that a shopkeeper is mindful, clever and able to support his family, then he gives him capital saying, "Hey, shopkeeper, take this capital, earn money from it, support your family and return my money in time." Thus the shopkeeper gets the support of influential people.

Similarly, if a bhikkhu is mindful, clever and has support of elders, he is able to attain wholesome *dhammas* and increase them. A bhikkhu who knows the Four Noble Truths is mindful, is one with eyes. When a bhikkhu starts putting forth efforts to abandon unwholesome *dhammas*. Such a bhikkhu is said to be clever.

A bhikkhu visits learned, erudite bhikkhus who know the Dhamma, the Discipline and the Matrices and asks them, "Sir, how is this? What does this mean?"

They answer his questions. Such a bhikkhu is said to have support of influential people.

Discussion

Successful Householders as Ideals for Bhikkhus

The principle that the Buddha has enumerated in *wealth of efforts* etc. has found practical application in the simile of shopkeepers. This discourse is not given to a householder but to a bhikkhu. To tell a bhikkhu to keep the ideal of householder is in a way honoring and respecting the householder's life.

The Buddha also underscored the importance of the doctrine of efforts by stating that one who is not lazy, one who works diligently and carefully becomes successful.

Advice to Householder Sigāla

In the Sigāla Sutta from the Long Discoures,[239] the Tathāgata was staying at Kalandakanivāpa bamboo grove at Rājagaha. In this sutta, we see him advising Sigāla. This Sigāla woke up early in the morning and went outside Rājagaha in wet clothes and with wet hair to salute all the four directions as well as the two directions, above and below.

Once the Buddha saw him and asked him why he was doing this in the morning. To which Sigāla replied that it was the advice his father had given to him on his deathbed. Sigāla was following his father's advice literally. Tathāgata explained to him the true meaning of his father's words: to worship directions means to follow certain guidelines in household life.

A householder should avoid four kinds of harmful deeds, four kinds of unwholesome deeds and six things that destroy material luxuries. If one abstains from these fourteen things, one protects all six directions. The gist of these things is:

Killing, stealing, sexual misconduct and wrong speech are the four harmful deeds. A householder should avoid these. If he does these four unwholesome things related to greed, hatred, ignorance and fear, his fame decreases like a waning moon. If doesn't break these rules his success increases like a waxing moon.

Alcoholism, wandering at unusual hours, addiction to song and dance (entertainment), gambling, association with criminals and laziness lead to destruction of material things that one enjoys.

Alcoholism leads to immediate decline in wealth. It leads to quarrels, physical ailments, bad name, shamelessness and decline in intellectual ability.

If one wanders at unusual times, one may put one's life at risk. One puts one's family at risk. One may get robbed. Due to one's presence at wrong places, one is looked at with suspicion. One may be accused of wrongdoing. One may have to face unpleasant consequences.

One who is addicted to song and dance, etc., is distracted by them and neglects his work.

Gambling leads to many adverse outcomes. If one wins, one creates enemies. If one loses, one gets into worries about money. One's wealth is destroyed. One is not trusted in an assembly. Friends and associates dislike him. When the time comes for his engagement or marriage, people say, "This man is a gambler. He won't support his wife and children."

Association with wrong people means association with cunning, greedy, ungrateful, deceptive people; with alcoholics and criminals.

The last undesirable thing is laziness. A lazy person finds excuses for his laziness. The weather is too cold or too hot. It is too early in the morning or too late in the night. One is too hungry or too full. Such a person doesn't acquire any new luxuries and loses the material comforts that he already has.

At the end of this discourse, the Tathāgata uttered several verses. The last one of them exhorts men to gather their inner strength and act energetically: Happiness accompanies a man who doesn't give any importance at all to heat and cold and diligently carries out his duties.

Then the Buddha explained to Sigāla who are enemies in the guise of friends and who are real friends. After giving several tips to Sigāla, he went on to explain which are the six directions that must be worshipped. Mother and father are the east. Teacher is south. Friends and associates are the north. Servants and workers are in the direction towards earth and Samaṇa-brāhmaṇas in the skyward direction. He told Sigāla that fulfilling one's duties towards these six groups is equivalent to worship of the six directions.

Parents prevent children from going on the wrong path. Parents teach them good things, educate them, feed them, support them and pass on the wealth to them in inheritance. Therefore, one should support and serve one's parents. Serving parents is worshipping the east.

Teachers educate pupils. They instill good qualities in students. Therefore, one should welcome them, serve them and learn from them respectfully. This is worshipping the south.

One should respect one's wife, not transgress the relation (by committing adultery) and not insult her. One should give her wealth and ornaments. This is worship of the west. Just as husband is duty-bound in the above mentioned manner, the wife too fulfills her duties, works well, behaves properly with servants and workers, doesn't commit adultery, protects wealth and is not lazy.

Relation Between Employer and Employee

The Buddha has given extremely noble advice about how a person should behave with servants. The fifth direction that he narrated is the direction of the earth. It belongs to servants and workers. To worship this direction means keeping relationship with them scrupulous. He gave five guidelines for behavior with workers.

1. Give work as per his or her capacity.
2. Give proper food and salary.
3. Attend on him when he or she is sick.
4. Give him or her nutritious food.
5. Give enough and timely holidays.

When an employer behaves thus with the workers, they in turn reciprocate by

1. Getting up earlier
2. Going to bed after the employer.
3. Taking only what is given to them (they don't steal).
4. Carrying out their tasks correctly.
5. Spreading the name and fame of the employer.

The Buddha said that the samaṇas and the brāhmaṇas are the sixth direction. Gratitude to them is worship of the sixth direction.

Discussion

Here we find an objective lesson to householders with all the details about a happy and successful household life. It is enumerated in a textbook fashion covering all pertinent points in methodical manner. It gives subtle hints about what a layman should and should not do.

Sigāla was stuck in the outward trappings of a tradition. He had not understood the essential inner core of his father's advice.

We can also say that Sigāla was representative of the established religious system. The tradition that gives more importance to the outward rituals and appearances rather than purity of mind cannot lead to perfection of a man. Therefore, the Tathāgata emphasized inner change. He gave the ethical dimensions of the six directions to Sigāla. His advice is affectionate. It doesn't oppress the listener. It is as natural and informal as a mother holding a child's finger and helping it to learn to walk.

The four hurtful deeds that he has enumerated may appear simple. They are as essential as they are simple in the journey of life. They are needed consistently and seriously. These things often mean the difference between a huge success and a big failure. His guidance about alcoholism etc., points to the pitfalls, dangers and slippery slopes in the journey of life.

The Buddha's advice about laziness is especially important for Indians. Those who wish to avoid work invent several lame excuses and harm themselves. He emphasized that those who stick to their task in spite of all hardships and adversities go on to become great. Sant Tukaram has given a humorous example about how lazy cowards invent laughable excuses and end up in failure. "My hands are tied in holding this sword and shield, how can I fight now? I have been put on horseback, how can I walk and run about now?"

Gratitude to Parents

Wise, positive and mutually beneficial relations between parents and children make family life stainless and scrupulous. The Buddha praised the quality of gratitude and clarified the importance of affection.

In Numerical Discourses[240], we find a sutta describing the importance of gratitude to parents. The Buddha explained to bhikkhus how children should behave with parents. The houses where children worship parents are said to be houses with brahmas, former teachers, former deities and guests. Why? Because the parents do so much for the children raising them from birth till they become ready to face the world. In the verses that the Buddha uttered in the end, we find details about how to care for parents by offering food, drink, clothes, bedding, bathing place, place to wash feet. etc.

Husband and Wife Should Not Transgress Each Other

One of the five basic moralities that the Buddha prescribed deals with this issue. Husband and wife should understand each other properly, care for each other and respect each other. This not only makes married life ethical but also joyous and fulfilling.

We find the Buddha's advice about rapport between husband and wife in a discourse in the Numerical Discourses.[241] It is also repeated in the subsequent sutta, which he gave to bhikkhus. It is curious that the same discourse is given to bhikkhus. Perhaps, it was given to them because they are supposed to teach laymen and should know about it. It is also possible that the discourse was inadvertently repeated while compiling the Tipiṭaka.

Once the Buddha was travelling between Madhurā and Verañjā. At that time some householders were also travelling on that road with their wives. Then the Buddha sat down on one side. The householders came, saluted him and sat on one side. The Buddha gave them advice on relation between husband and wife—

"Companionship of husband and wife is of four types: Companionship of a corpse with a corpse, a corpse with a deity, a deity with a corpse, a deity with a deity.

"A man kills, steals, lies, indulges in sexual misconduct and uses intoxicants. He is full of defilements. He abuses virtuous ascetics and holy men and calls them name. His wife too behaves in the same manner. Their company is that of a corpse with a corpse.

"A man kills, steals, lies, etc but his wife abstains from such unwholesome actions. Their company is that of a corpse with a deity.

"A man abstains from killing, stealing, lying, etc and leads a virtuous life but his wife indulges in unwholesome, sinful actions. Their company is that of a deity with a corpse.

"A man abstains from killing, stealing, lying, etc. and leads a virtuous life. His wife also does the same. Their company is that of a deity with a deity."

Discussion

The words corpse and deity used by the Buddha here are to be taken in the figurative sense. Deity is used to denote a healthy, upright personality. Corpse is used to denote a tainted character. When both husband and wife have upright conduct; they trust each other and complement each other in life; then they become happy and help their partners to be happy. Such restrained couple finds fulfillment in each other's company.

If one of them lives a blameless life and the other doesn't, then they contradict each other. There is conflict, bitterness and lack of closeness. Since one of them is virtuous, it somewhat blunts their conflict and lessens the stress and strain; but they can't live a truly happy life.

When both the partners have the defects enumerated above, they themselves can't be happy and can't make others happy. Rather they destroy the happiness of all and push each other into the abyss of misery. People who don't understand companionship, love, affection, trust and ethical behavior—in other words people who don't understand life—destroy their own life. They miss all zestful spontaneity and joyous fulfillment of an authentic life. Indeed, their life is as a corpse living with a corpse.

Noble Friendship

The Buddha underscored the importance of friendship in the householder's life. He repeatedly praised *mettā-bhāvanā*. It is relevant to quote some of his thoughts in this context.

He also repeatedly clarified the concept of a *kalyānamitta* (benevolent friend).

He said once,[242] "I don't see anything as effective as noble friendship *(kalyānamittatā)* when it comes to arising of wholesome things that had not previously arisen and cessation of unwholesome things that had previously arisen."

Eight Fruits of Goodwill

Once when the Buddha was dwelling in Jetavana at Sāvatthi, he explained the importance of *mettā* to the bhikkhus.[243]

He said, "If one practices, cultivates, multiplies, makes a habit of, experiences, perseveres in and makes himself familiar with goodwill that frees one's mind, such enriched love and affection yields eight types of wholesome fruit. Which eight? One sleeps well; gets up refreshed; doesn't see bad dreams; is loved by humans; is loved by non-humans; gods protect one; one is not affected by fire, poison and weapons and after death, one reaches at least the brahmā realm." Then he uttered some verses about importance of *mettā-bhāvanā* (goodwill, love and affection): All afflictions get eradicated for one who practices infinite goodwill.

He stated, "Even if one befriends one animal without generating the slightest negativity in the mind, one is doing a wholesome deed. That superior human who has love and compassion for all beings accumulates great meritorious deed. After performing useless sacrifices such as horse-sacrifice and human-sacrifice, Vājapeya, kings don't get even one-sixteenth part of the fruit that one gets after generating goodwill for others.

Who Is Friend and Where?

The Compounded Discourses[244] have a short sutta that tells us who is friend and where. The Buddha replied to his own questions, "One who undertakes a journey has weapons as friend. In the house, mother is friend. One who comes forward in times of need becomes friends again and again. One's own good deeds become friend for one's future." Immediately after this Discourse on Friend, comes Discourse on Thing in which he asks the question who is the greatest friend and himself answers that (for a man) one's wife is the greatest friend.

Goodwill Is Greater Than Donation

In the Connected Discourses, we find it stated that goodwill, love and affection are more important than donation.[245] Once the Buddha was dwelling in Sāvatthi. He said to the bhikkhus, "Bhikkhus, someone donates rice cooked in a hundred huge vessels, morning, afternoon and evening. Another practices goodwill equal to one cow's milk, morning, afternoon and evening. Between these two, the one who practices goodwill gets more fruit."

A Benevolent Friend Means a Successful Life

In the Connected Discourses, we find a sutta[246] where the Tathāgata talks about a benevolent friend. Once he was wandering in a Sākyan village. At that time, Ānanda went to Tathāgata and said, "Bhante, I feel that noble friendship is half the holy life. (It is half the fruit of ethical life.)" Tathāgata replied, "No, Ānanda, don't say that. Noble friendship is the whole of the holy life." In the Sāriputta Sutta that follows this one, Sāriputta says, "Noble friendship is the whole of the holy life." Tathāgata upholds his statement.

Taking Care of Servants is Worship of the Direction of Earth

In any social structure, there exists some kind of a master-servant, employee-employer or boss-subordinate relationship. It is natural that if this relationship is based on exploitation and injustice there will be unrest in society. Such a social structure gets decayed from inside. It becomes hollow and hinders progress. Then instead of love and affection in interpersonal relations there is hatred and disgust. Instead of harmony there is conflict. Such a society becomes unstable and fractured.

On the other hand, a society where these relations are affectionate, trusting, mutually respectful and caring leads to inner peace of mind. All roads open for the progress of society.

If one wants to salute the direction of earth in a meaningful manner, then the labor that makes the earth fertile, that sustains society must get justice. In modern times, the industrialized world has made these relations very complicated. It was not so at the time of the Buddha. Even so, the principles behind his guidelines apply in today's progressive (or complicated) times.

The founding principle of the employer-employee relationship is that the master must ensure adequate compensation for the servant's toil. The Buddha vigorously opposed the condition forced on the lower castes in Vedic caste system. Though the affluence of the upper castes was based on the toil of the lower castes, they were denied suitable compensation.

The Buddha laid down five guidelines for the way an employer should treat an employee.

First, he should give work to a servant as per his or her capacity. Often servants are loaded with so much work that they get crushed under the workload. They are made to work just as a cruel person would make a beast to work. The servant is distressed and anguished in such a situation. It affects his or her physical and mental health. An employer should ensure that this doesn't happen.

Second, the servant should get proper salary and food. Don't get free work out of him. Often employers adopt unfair means and deny employees adequate compensation. A person who doesn't think twice when splurging huge amounts on luxuries frowns or even acts as it is a shocking calamity when faced with the prospect of giving a small reward for the labors of the poor servants. The Buddha tried to rein in such selfish behavior.

The third guideline takes the relation to even loftier heights. Usually a servant is supposed to serve the master. We often see that as long as the servant is capable, he serves the master in every way but when the servant becomes sick, he is retrenched, abused, his pay is cut, etc. Thus the servant is left to fend for himself just when he needs support. The Buddha's guidance on this changes it all. The Buddha said that if the servant is sick, the master should serve him and nurse him. The Buddha took the relation out of the master-servant context and put it on a pure humanitarian ground. Rich-poor, master-servant, powerful-weak; all relations become irrelevant here. They all become one human level. One has the capacity to serve and the other need to be cared for.

The fourth guideline is about the quality of things that are provided to employees. Often, unwanted, poor quality, old and decrepit things are given to servants. This offends human dignity. And the pretense is that one is helping them. This taints human relations. Whatever you may give to servants, make it good quality.

However efficient and energetic a person may be, nature has put certain limitations on humans. For proper physical and mental health, adequate rest after certain period of work is essential. Employees should be given a few hours of rest daily as well as holidays after a certain number of days of work. This is their right. This is essential for taking care of various personal things as well as for healthy family life. When this happens, the employee's freedom is protected. This also ensures that he is mentally fresh and physically fit for his work.

In modern times, we see such statutory regulations in most countries. Various guidelines are laid down for work, hours of work, minimum wages, sick leaves, health insurance, other leaves, etc. We must see the Buddha's guidance in the context of his time. This was twenty-five centuries ago. Another thing is that these guidelines had not come by a royal decree but in an ethical and Dhammic form. This makes people's faith in it stronger and creates a voluntary urge to follow these guidelines and to make it a natural and integral part of their life.

If an employer behaves in such an honorable manner with the employees, the employees too reciprocate in a similar manner. They wake up before their employer and go to bed after him. This means that they take care of him. They work to help him get enough rest. While doing this, they have affection for their master. No discontent simmers beneath the surface.

Since their employer gives them enough salary, they don't have the intention to deceive or rob him. They do their work sincerely and to their utmost ability. They don't do a cursory job. They don't shirk work. They don't deliberately sabotage work causing a loss to their employer. Lastly, they speak well about him even behind his back. They do it on their own. The employer doesn't have to spy on their behavior. They spread his fame with joy and gratitude. His image in society improves, his prestige increases and he get more material success.

If the relation between employers and employees is harmonious and professionally successful, it is mutually beneficial. If this relation becomes negative and mutually disadvantageous, it is distressing and harmful for both. Therefore, both are responsibile to create a harmonious relationship.

How Servants Were Treated in Suddhodana's House

Once while narrating the memories of his childhood, the Buddha said to bhikkhus,[247] "Bhikkhus, in other households servants were given inferior food but in my father's house, they were served excellent rice cooked with meat."

This indicates that he had inherited from Suddhodana and Mahāpajāpati the guidelines about how to treat servants. It puts his parents in a positive light. Often kings, aristocrats, and wealthy people are unrestrained in their expenses for their own luxuries but are far from generous when it comes to their servants. Suddhodana and Mahāpajāpati stand out as honorable masters here.

Respecting the Learned

The Tathāgata taught Sigāla that we must have respect and gratitude for those who impart knowledge and give us guidance about an ethical life.

Earn Ethically

Sāriputta once explained how a householder should follow ethics while earning a livelihood.[248] Once the Tathāgata was dwelling in Kalandakanivāpa of Rājagaha. Sāriputta was in Dakshināgiri. At that time one bhikkhu ended his rains retreat in Rājagaha and came to Sāriputta. Sāriputta enquired after the Tathāgata's and the bhikkhu-Saṅgha's wellbeing. Then he asked about Dhanañjāni brahmin.

He is well, the bhikkhu said.

Is he heedful, asked Sāriputta.

Then the bhikkhu replied, "Friend, how can Dhanañjāni be heedful? He robs brahmin householders through the king and robs the king through brahmin householders. His wife was upright and from a noble family. She passed away. Now he has married a faithless woman from a family that lacks faith in Dhamma."

Sāriputta felt bad. He said that he would go to meet Dhanañjāni.

Later, in his wanderings, Sāriputta reached Rājagaha. Then one day he went to Dhanañjāni. He offered Sāriputta milk and asked him to wait for the meal to get ready. Sāriputta told him that he had already eaten and invited him to meet him under a certain tree where he was going to spend the day.

When Dhanañjāni was asked whether he was heedful, he answered, "People like us have to look after parents, wife and children, servants and workers, etc. We have to do our duty towards friends and associates, clansmen, guests, ancestors, gods and king. We have to take care of this body. How then can we be vigilant in being upright and righteous?"

Sāriputta answerd, "When someone commits a sin for the sake of his parents. This conduct of his leads him to nether realms. When he is thus being dragged to the nether worlds by the guards of hell, can he say that he did it for his parents and therefore he should not be taken to hell? Can his parents say that he did it for their sake and hence he should be pardoned?"

"No, he can't say that. Even if he keeps shouting thus, the guards of hell will drag him to hell."

"Who is a better person; one who commits unwholesome, unethical deeds for his parents or one who commits wholesome, ethical deeds for his parents?"

"One who does wholesome, ethical deeds."

Sāriputta told him that serving parents is wholesome but one can't follow unwholesome means to serve them. One must follow ethical means.

Discussion

Dhanañjāni was justifying his behavior saying that he had to take care of so many people. Sāriputta's guidance is useful for all householders. That he did it for parents was a lame excuse. Sāriputta told him that one had to follow ethical means to care for one's dependents. Here going to hell means facing the consequences of one's unwholesome actions. For good ends, the means also have to be good. Sāriputta had summed up the essence of the Buddha's teaching here.

High Level of Morality Expected

The Tipiṭaka often shows the Tathāgata teaching gods in addition to humans. Many ethical views of Tathāgata are often conveyed through the deities. One incident in the Connected Discourses[249] shows how superior morality was implicit in his teaching.

Once a bhikkhu was living in a jungle in Kosala. Once while returning from alms round, he entered a lake and started smelling a lotus. A deity of those woods felt compassion for him. She went to him with the intention of cautioning him.

She uttered a verse that meant: "You are smelling a lotus that has not been given to you. This is theft in a way. You are stealing the fragrance."

The bhikkhu replied, "I am neither stealing nor destroying the lotus flower. I smell it from afar. How then can you call it a theft of fragrance? Why don't you say anything to these men who snatch lotus stems and destroy lotuses?" The deity responded, "One who has greed in his mind is like a dirty cloth. I won't say anything to him. However, even the smallest misdeed of a upright seeker looms large like a huge black cloud."

The bhikkhu said, "You have been very kind to me. You have prevented me from committing a misdeed. Henceforth too, if you see me doing anything wrong, please caution me."

The deity replied, "I am not your servant. I don't take salary from you. O bhikkhu, you yourself should be mindful about the path that will lead to liberation."

The bhikkhu was thus chastened.

Discussion

This extraordinarily touching discourse puts the highest ideal in front of us. It is an example full of the essence of what the Buddha taught. There are two more peculiarities of this sutta. First, even a very upright person might have a blot in his character. Around such an upright, virtuous person, there might be many people full of immoral traits. At such a time, the virtuous person should not justify his faults by saying that others are committing greater faults.

Second, it clarifies that one should not always be dependent on others for correction but that one should correct oneself using one's own wisdom and discretion. Thus, a virtuous person has a greater responsibility.

Layman or Bhikkhu, One with Untainted Conduct Is Praiseworthy

Once the Tathāgata was staying at Jetavana in Sāvatthi. At that time, Subha, the son of Todeyya, was staying at someone's house in Sāvatthi as a guest.[250] He expressed a desire to his host that he wanted to meet an ascetic or a holy man. The host informed him that the Tathāgata was in Sāvatthi.

Subha went to the Buddha and asked him, "Brahmins say that only householders can successfully acquire Dhamma, wholesome things and justice. An ascetic can't do so. What do you say about it?"

The Tathāgata replied to Subha, "I will answer this question from different angles, not from one angle."

The Tathāgata meant that he didn't want to take an extreme stand based on one side only. Rather he would analyze and examine the issue.

He told Subha, "Whether he is a layman or an ascetic, I don't praise him if his conduct is wrong. One whose actions are wrong can't attain Dhamma etc. On the other hand, if one performs wholesome actions, I praise him. Such a person can acquire Dhamma etc."

Subha conveyed to the Buddha the brahmin's view that that the householder's scope of work is large from a material point of view. Therefore, the householder gets bigger fruits. Ascetics have very few material things to manage and hence their fruits are smaller.

The Buddha replied that big works if not done properly can lead to smaller fruits and big works if carried out properly lead to big fruits. Small work if not done properly lead to small fruits and small work if done properly can give big fruits. Then he gave example of agriculture and business. Whether it is a big or small, if not done properly it leads to smaller fruits. Irrespective of whether it is big or small, if it is done properly, it gives big fruit.

He explained that the same thing applies to a householder and one who has left home. Whether they get good fruits depends on how they carry out their work. Just because one is a householder or an ascetic, one wouldn't get a particular kind of fruit. It is the quality of the performance of their duties that matters.

Then the Buddha and Subha discussed things at length. There is one more thing that must be mentioned here. Though it is not proper to judge based on just one thing, as a general principle, it *is* easier for an ascetic to follow the Dhamma.

Discussion

Through Virtuous Conduct a Layman Can Be as Great as a Bhikkhu

We often see the Buddha's skill in gently going to the root of the issue in a complicated issue and unraveling it. People often form extreme opinions without understanding all aspects of the situation. Such opinions can often be wrong and at times harmful.

The Buddha would take into account all positives, all negatives, and all limitations and form an opinion after careful analysis. Therefore, he didn't take one side or the other in the debate of whether a layman is superior or an ascetic. It is not important where one lives and whether he is a householder or an ascetic. What matters is how one discharges one's duties, how one carries out one's tasks. The examples he gave were also apt.

Even today we see that a farmer who owns vast fields ends up losing his fields if he neglects his work. On the other hand, if a small farmer is diligent and efficient, and does his work in a timely manner, he lives a happy and contented life. A big businessman may become irresponsible and end up bankrupt. A small businessman may do his work properly and become successful and satisfied.

The life of a bhikkhu is more suitable for practising the Dhamma. It is a statement of fact and it doesn't mean that bhikkhus are greater than householders.

No Difference Between a Layman Without Craving and a Liberated Bhikkhu

Once the Tathāgata was dwelling in Nigrodhārāma at Kapilavatthu.[251] At that time, many bhikkhus were patching together a robe for the Tathāgata to wear during his wanderings to teach the Dhamma at the end of rains retreat. At that time, Mahānāma Sākya came to the Tathāgata and said that many lay disciples and several sick people had not heard the Tathāgata's discourse. Would he please consider giving a discourse?

At that time, the Tathāgata's discusson with Mahānāma touched upon several important points. He told Mahānāma that he should tell those disciples and sick people to have confidence in the Buddha, the Dhamma and the Saṅgha; and be moral. Similarly, he advised that a disciple should be free from all attachments to all—from parents, wife and children to all deities.

Lastly, he makes a momentous statement, "Mahānāma, I say that there is no difference between a disciple whose mind is thus freed and a bhikkhu who is liberated from all defilements. (Their liberations are the same.)"

Discussion

This discourse gives solid evidence that the Tathāgata never took a view that entering the Saṅgha was the only way to get liberated. He said that a layman could follow moral discipline and by his own effort attain the highest goal of life and such a layman is not inferior in any way to a liberated bhikkhu. Their liberation is equal. Both are equally successful in life. This disproves the allegation that the Tathāgata neglected householders and gave excessive importance to going forth. Take for example the statement by Ramdhari Singh Dinkar,[252] "But the Buddha said that only he would attain nibbāna who would go forth from householder's life to become a bhikkhu."

Sakka Salutes Householders

We must take a look at the Discourse on Worship of Householders.[253] At that time, the Buddha was dwelling in Sāvatthi. At that time, Sakka, the king of gods, asked his charioteer Mātalī to keep his chariot ready. On learning that the chariot was ready, Sakka started descending the steps of his palace. While doing so, he saluted all directions.

Then Mātalī asked him, "O Sakka, you receive salutations from various beings including those learned in three Vedas, all nobles on earth, and protectors of four directions. Then who is it that you are saluting?"

Sakka agreed with Mātalī about how he is saluted by many and then replied, "I salute those who are endowed with morality, who have a balanced mind, who have gone forth into homeless life and who live the holy life. O Mātalī, I salute those householders who righteously support their wives and perform meritorious deeds."

Sakka saluted all directions and climbed into the chariot.

Discussion

Though this is a legend, it conveys how the Buddha felt about the householder's life. Sakka *(Indra)* is an important god in Indian mythology. He salutes both upright bhikkhus and virtuous householders as he comes out of his divine palace. It shows clearly that in the Buddha Dhamma, the householders have not been neglected. Only those bhikkhus whose conduct is blameless are worthy of salutations. The same applies to householders.

Sakka salutes householders who supports their wives, and by extension, their families. The message in this legend is that a man must fulfill his household responsibilities and must follow ethical means while doing so.

A Nation Is Truly Protected by Internal Unity

When we think of a nation, we must address issues of wider society. Even so, society is made of families. It is not independent of families. One cannot imagine a nation without families. Without the support of the nation, families cannot maintain their freedom and can't earn their living. Therefore, families and the nation are not just interdependent but also unified. Therefore, many issues are the same for the family and the wider society.

One can gauge a nation by looking at the family. Guidelines for the success of one are often applicable to the other. Causes of failure in one are often the causes of failure of the other. Therefore, it is right that along with his views on family life, we discuss the Buddha's views on a nation and nationhood.

The Buddha's Advice to Licchavīs

Once the Buddha had given seven tips to remain undefeated. We find it in the Sārandada Sutta of the Numerical Discourses.[254] The Vajjīs of Vesāli were called Licchavīs. Dharmanand Kosambi says,[255] "Vesāli was the capital of the Vajjīs. People living there were called Licchavīs."

Once the Buddha was dwelling in Sārandada shrine of Vesāli. Then many Licchavīs came to him and sat to one side after saluting him. Then the Buddha told them, "Licchavīs, I give you seven guidelines which if followed will keep you undefeated. Listen to them carefully and remember them… "

When the Licchavīs became attentive, he asked them, "Licchavīs, which are the seven things that will make you unconquerable?" He gave the guidelines, and after each one of them, he told them that when followed these guidelines would lead to prosperity of Vajjīs and not decline.

1. As long as Vajjīs assemble regularly, keep unity in large number they will prosper, not decline.
2. As long as they come together in harmony and disperse in harmony and together follow their responsibilities towards their subjects…
3. As long as they follow decrees decided upon earlier and not break such decrees; and follow traditional rules…
4. As long as they respect elders and listen to their counsel…
5. As long as they refrain from abducting women and maidens from good families and detaining them…
6. As long as they respect, honor, worship and venerate shrines in the town and around the town; and carry out their traditional responsibilities towards them…
7. As long as they duly protect and honor arahatas so that those who have not come to the republic might come and those who have come stay on…

Again the Buddha strongly stated that as long as the Vajjīs followed these guidelines, they would grow and not decline.

Discussion

These seven guidelines bring prosperity of both the nation and the family. Though Licchavīs had not asked any questions and had not expected any specific guidance, the Buddha himself advised them to follow these seven guidelines. He might have done this spontaneously. He did sometimes give guidance to the visitors as per his choice.

But here it is possible that there was another reason for the Buddha's advice. Did he hear reports that the Licchavīs had become lax in their discipline? It is possible that the Buddha cautioned them that they should assemble regularly; gather and disperse in harmony; follow decrees of the state; respect elders and listen to their counsel; refrain from abducting women and maidens; respect, honor, worship and venerate shrines; protect and honor *arahatas*. Otherwise it would lead to their destruction. Whatever it may be, the Buddha's discourse was for their long term benefit.

The first guideline was that of concord. If they assembled together in harmony and concord, they would grow. If a society is bound together with a tightly woven fabric of harmony, an external enemy cannot enter. It is not easy to conquer a society where people love each other, care for each other and are prepared to sacrifice for each other.

The second guideline clarifies the first. It is not enough to gather together. Sometimes people gather and quarrel, abuse each other and indulge in violence. In a society where people discuss their differences, overcome them, solve their problems for the common goal and take decisions together, those decisions are executed effectively and harmony is maintained.

Even as we welcome new things, we must follow some traditional rules that have stood the test of time and are related to the identity of the society. To respect elders doesn't mean yielding to their wrong beliefs. We must skillfully reject traditions that are based on ignorance; traditions that are undesirable and harmful. While doing so, we should not be ungrateful and must not show disdain; lest we hinder the wholesome growth of society.

The rule about women is self-explanatory. A society where women face abuse gets destroyed. We know about the great ideals set by King Shivaji and Rana Pratap by their orders of respecting the womenfolk of the enemies.

Respecting shrines and caring for them as well as creating proper atmosphere for arahatas to stay in the region is important for the society's wellbeing. Here the shrines that the Buddha had in mind are not the ones where there is exploitation of the poor and breed discrimination, injustice and immorality. Here shrines are places that are the heritage of generations, centres of humanity and equitable culture. It is clear that *cetiyas* (shrines) existed in

India even before the time of the Buddha. What is true of *cetiyas* was also true of arahatas. There is a difference between people who promote inequality and discrimination; and arahatas who promote equality and humanity. Naturally, if arahatas are given their proper place, they would instill refreshing ethics in society and keep people away from selfishness, narrow-mindedness, hatred and treason.

Description in Commentary

The Commentary on the Mahāparinibbāna Sutta (Discourse of the Great Passing Away) further clarifies the guiding principles that the Buddha gave to the Licchavīs for their prosperity.[256]

Those rulers who don't meet often don't get news from all parts of the country. They don't know where there is unrest in border regions and where the nuisance of thieves is increasing. Once robbers realize that the rulers are lax, they attack and plunder towns. Rulers who come together often can take quick cognizance of such news and send suitable military forces. Then the thieves too run away. In those times, a drum would be beaten to call people together in assembly. At times, some people would avoid going there due to their personal work and neglect the common good of society. On the other hand, if the common good of society takes precedence, people leave whatever they are doing and immediately rush to the assembly.

It is not enough to gather together; the next step is to take decisions and implement them. If volunteers are found quickly to combat the menace of thieves, the town doesn't decline. People of such towns are involved in each other's celebrations and illnesses; standing together in happiness and misery.

For a nation's prosperity it is important that laws are implemented fairly. If someone is unfairly punished, his family, relations and friends become unhappy, turn rebels and may indulge in antisocial acts. Therefore rulers have to be careful in administering justice. To clarify how traditionally justice was administered among Vajjīs, the Commentary gives an example:

If someone were caught for alleged theft, he would not be punished immediately. He would be sent to the investigating minister who would make proper enquiries. If he were found innocent, he would be set free. If he were found guilty, he would be sent to the executive minister, again he would follow the same procedure and the person would be sent to the coordinator, from the coordinator to the higher minister, then to the general, from the general to the viceroy and from the viceroy to the king. If he were found innocent by the king, he would be set free. If he were found guilty, the king would pronounce punishment as per the book of law. Thus it was ensured that no innocent man was ever punished and that the punishment was in proportion to the crime. Hence there would be no injustice. Naturally, when justice prevails there is less discontent among people.

If the rulers trouble and molest women and abduct them, it would lead to great anger among the people and rebellion would be the natural consequence, harming the state. Those rulers who refrain from such immoral acts prevent rebellion from their subjects.

Vassakāra Caused Split to Defeat Vajjīs

Vassakāra Sutta follows immediately after the Sāradanda sutta. Here is the gist of it:

Once the Buddha was dwelling on the Vulture Peak. At that time, the king of Magadha was planning an attack on the Vajjīs. He wanted to defeat the Vajjīs and conquer Vesāli.

He called Vassakāra, the chief minister of Magadha and asked him to go to the Buddha; to make polite enquiries about his health and welfare and then to tell him that the king was going to attack the Vajjīs.

"Listen carefully to what the Buddha says and report back to me."

Accordingly, Vassakāra went to the Buddha and told him about the plan to attack the Vajjīs. At that time, the Buddha asked Ven. Ānanda whether the Vajjīs followed the seven guiding principles enumerated above.

Ānanda answered yes.

Then he told Vassakāra that he had advised the Vajjīs about these seven guidelines while staying at the Sārandada shrine. As long as they were following them they would grow and not decline.

Vassakāra replied, "Master Gotama, even if they follow one of these seven rules, they would prosper. If they are following all seven, they are invincible. Gotama, it would be inadvisable for Ajātasattu, king of Magadha, to attack the Vajjīs now. They would be conquered only through bribery or causing a split among them."

Then the Buddha invited the bhikkhus and gave them advice about seven things to follow to avoid downfall of the Saṅgha. The guidelines for the Saṅgha are similar to those he gave to the Vajjīs: Meet regularly, meet in concord, take decisions unitedly, follow monastic rules (Vinaya), respect seniors, stay away from greed, wish for a dwelling in the jungle and wish that a bhikkhu who has not come should come and dwell peacefully. If bhikkhus followed these things they would prosper, not decline.

The description in the Commentary about how Vassakāra caused a split in the Vajjīs is noteworthy.

Ajātasattu knew that as long as the Vajjīs were united, they were invincible in battle. Since not a single blow of the Vajjīs goes waste in battle, he decided to take refuge in the intellect of Vassakāra. After meeting the Buddha, Vassakāra told Ajātasattu that the only way to defeat the Vajjīs was either through bribery or split. The king said that bribery would be too expensive and decided to cause a split among the Vajjīs. He asked Vassakāra for advice.

Vassakāra said, "The king should bring up the topic of attacking the Vajjīs in the royal court. I will say 'Why attack the Vajjīs? Let them carry out their agriculture and business peacefully,' and leave the court in anger. You should then say that this brahmin is scuttling the discussion on attacking the Vajjīs. Then I will send a gift to the Vajjīs, which will be intercepted by you. Rather than torturing and imprisoning me, you should shave my head and banish me from the kingdom. I will threaten you by saying, 'I have built this city's fortifications and moats. I know your strengths and weaknesses. I will set the account straight.' You should then banish me from your kingdom."

Then everything was done according to plan.

When Ajātasattu banished Vassakāra, the Vajjīs said to each other, "This brahmin is cunning. Don't let him cross the Ganges."

But some of them differed, "He is facing this punishment because he spoke in favor of us."

Then it was decided, "Let him come."

When he reached, they asked him, "Why have you come?"

He said that he was punished for taking their side. The Vajjīs said that it was not proper that he was punished so severely for such a minor offence.

They asked him, "What was your post there?"

"I was an investigating officer."

"You will be given the same position here."

He then started discharging his duties diligently.

The young Licchavī princes went to him for education.

Once Vassakāra established his reputation among the Licchavīs, he took one of them aside and said, "Do your young men work on farms?"

Yes, was the reply.

Then he asked him, "Do they yoke bullocks while farming?"

Again, yes was the reply.

The Licchavī then went away.

When another Licchavī asked him what the conversation was about, he received a truthful answer but the Licchavī didn't believe him.

Distrust arose in his mind, "He is not telling me the truth."

Then Vassakāra took another Licchavī to one side and asked, "What did you have for lunch?"

When this Licchavī was asked by another about the conversation, similar distrust was generated after a truthful answer.

On another day, Vassakāra took yet another Licchavī to one side and asked, "Are you really in much difficutly?"

"Who says so?"

"Such and such Licchavī."

At another time, yet another Licchavī was taken to one side and asked, “Are you afraid?”

“Who says so?”

“Such and such Licchavī.”

Vassakāra did this for three years. This lead to such disharmony among the rulers of the Vajjī Republic that not two of them agreed with each other or trusted each other. When the drum was beaten to call them to assembly ‘Let the chiefs among you gather, let the brave ones gather’, no one came.

Then Vassakāra sent a message to the king. “This is the proper time. Come and attack.’

The king beat the war drums and left his city to attack. Vesāli’s Vajjīs came to know about it. The drum was beaten, “Don’t allow him to cross the Ganges.” But even on hearing it those who spoke thus “Let those who are brave go” didn’t gather to defend the city. The drum was beaten, “Don’t let the king enter the city. Block the gates of the city and stand firm.” No one came.

King Ajātasattu came in through open gates and conquered Vesāli.

More About This Account in Commentary

Superficially, this event seems commonplace. But if one looks at it carefully, one realizes that this is not the history of just the Vajjīs but of the entire Indian society through thousands of years. Distrust for each other and lack of unity nullified all other qualities of society and destroyed all strengths. Misunderstanding led to infighting and surrender to the enemy. All were enslaved.

An extremely distressing aspect is that though people know it is destructive, they allow themselves to get trapped. The Vajjīs were close to the Buddha. He had affection for them. The Vajjīs were brave and skilled warriors. He had advised them on unity and assured them that they would be invincible if they remained united.

On the other hand, Vassakāra was the trusted advisor of the enemy. They knew he was cunning and manipulative. But what did they do? They forgot the Buddha’s advice and started listening to the very person who was intent on destroying them. They offered the fertile land of their hearts to him to sow the seeds of poison. They surrendered their intellect and allowed Vassakāra to weave the net of mistrust and hatred. No wonder then that the fruits were bitter.

How can we hope to be free, to keep our self-respect and protect our prosperity, if we ignore the advice of one who tirelessly works for us and give importance to one who systematically destroys us?

Securing the Border Towns

Once the Buddha told the bhikkhus that if a disciple follows seven things, Māra would not be able to defeat him. To explain further, he said, "Just as a king secures and cares for a town on the border of his kingdom, a disciple should take care."[257]

He said to the bhikkhus, "Bhikkhus, there are seven things that make a border town safe; and gives four types of supplies for the people there as per their wishes, which they can procure without much trouble. When this is done, external enemies are unable to attack the border town." He then enumerated the seven things and said that these should be done for internal security and to repel any external attack.

A pillar is erected in the town. It is firmly and deeply set in earth—steady and unshakable. There is a broad and deep moat around the town. There is a wide and high road that goes all around the town. There is enough supply of weapons in the town. The town has a large army. The army includes elephants, cavalry, charioteers, archers, flag-bearers, military trainers, cooks, princes, swordsmen, slaves and commandos that raid and seize weapons from the enemy. The town should have a smart, sharp, strong and brave doorkeeper who roams around openly. He stops strangers and allows only known people inside. The town has a strong, high and wide protective wall all around.

The four types of 'food' are: Abundant grass, wood and water; abundant rice and barley; enough supply of sesame, pulses, etc; adequate store of things of medicinal value such as butter, clarified butter, oil, honey, sugar and salt. If all these are available in the city in abundant quantity the people living there remain happy, satisfied, and confident. This makes it easy to defend the town from all enemies.

Discussion

The Buddha's guidance to the bhikkhus talks about both internal and external security. He suggests that a person has to take care of himself just as a border town is protected by various means. Though he taught non-violence, he didn't advise abandoning army, weapons and becoming irresponsible about national security.

The pillar in the town is a symbol of unity, freedom and self-respect of the people. A pillar with deep foundation means that our society is strongly united. Attack on the pillar is attack on the unity of society. Uprooting of the pillar means split in the society.

The Buddha's description of moat, roads, army, weapons, gatekeeper, fortified wall, ready supplies, etc. indicates that he found these essential for protection. On the other hand, when he tells the bhikkhus to keep themselves ready in a similar manner doesn't mean that he has abandoned the principle of non-violence. His guidance is for one's own protection. It is not for attacking others. He has always been clear on that issue.

Successful Mediation Between Sākyans and Koliyans on Water Issue

Though he didn't advise the people to disband the army or abandon weapons, the Buddha wanted conflicts to be resolved wisely and with restraint. He insisted on avoiding conflict, violence and war. He pointed out how small misunderstandings take a disproportionate toll. He put the highest value on human life. Therefore, he did everything in his power to stop killing. His message was that this is the highest principle of humanity. Therefore, abstention from killing is the first precept.

An incident from the Commentary on Dhammapada.[258] Kapilavatthu was the capital of the Sākyans while Koliya was the capital of the Koliyans. Between the two cities was the Rohini river. Both the Sākyans and the Koliyans had built a dam together on the river from which they would draw water for their farms. Once at the end of summer, when crops started withering in the heat due to lack of water, workers on both side went to the dam.

The Koliyan workers said, "If we divide this water, it won't be enough for you or for us. Our crop will survive with just one watering. Allow us to draw this water."

The Sākyan workers said, "If we allow this, you will fill your granaries and we will have to beg for grain from you in exchange for gold, jewels, sapphires and coins? No, we won't do it. Our crop also needs just one watering. Give this water to us."

The quarrel escalated. Verbal confrontation turned physical. One worker hit another. More joined the fight. Each side made unflattering references towards the royal clans of the other side. The Koliyans questioned the lineage of the Sākyans. They mocked their elephants, horses, swords and shields. The Sākyan workers retaliated with similar abuse. The workers on each side reported the abusive comments to the ministers who in turn went and reported them to the respective royals. Then the Sākyans got ready for war, "We will teach the Koliyans a lesson." The Koliyans also prepared for war, "We will show the Sākyans our strength."

When the Buddha came to know about it, he went and sat on the river bed. His brethren on both sides saw him and put down their weapons to salute him.

Then the Buddha asked them, "O kings, why are you fighting?" Warriors on both sides said that they didn't know. They then asked the ministers who in turn asked the workers. They found out that the dispute started over sharing water and informed the Buddha, "Bhante, this is a dispute over sharing water."

"Kings, what is the value of this water?"

"Some. Not much."

"Kings, what is the value of the warriors?"

"They are invaluable."

The Buddha then said, "It is not proper than you sacrifice invaluable warriors for the not so valuable water here."

The kings remained silent.

The Buddha then said, "Kings, why do you do such a thing? If I were not present today, a river of blood would have flowed. What you did is improper."

Then the Buddha spoke verses about living without hatred.

Discussion

This conflict shows how people become self-destructive if they don't understand a situation, don't examine the reasons and consequences of their actions and become slave of their anger.

In daily life, we often face such issues. We should sort them out amicably, peacefully and wisely. Often the original issue that sparks the conflict is minor. But just as a small wound festers if left untreated, the situation starts getting out of hand.

Such a conflict can be between two persons, two families, two societies, two communities or two nations. When such a conflict occurs, the decision makers should ask themselves two questions that the Buddha posed. On one side there is some material benefit and on the other side there is our life. We must show discretion in judging their value and in deciding what do we sacrifice for what. Otherwise, behind an ostensible gain, there is a severe loss.

The Buddha was concerned about the suffering of the entire humanity. However, this doesn't mean that he was insensible or irresponsible about his own clansmen. When someone works for the entire humanity, that person's kith and kin are also part of that wider humanity. They too are beneficiaries of his efforts. Thus the mediation between Sākyans and Koliyans is not a narrow-minded focus on his clansmen just as his compassionate effort for the entire humanity is not irresponsibility towards his clansmen.

Story of the Destruction of Sākyans

The Commentary on Dhammapada[259] tells us a heart-rending story of the slaughter of the Sākyans.

Pasenadi, king of Kosala, revered the Buddha. He sent alms food for bhikkhus through servants rather than offering it himself. Therefore, the bhikkhus went out of the palace compound to eat the food. Pasenadi felt sad about this. He wanted the bhikkhus to accept his welcome. He wanted their love and respect. He thought that if he married a woman from the Sākyan clan, he would become a relation of the Buddha and then the bhikkhus might accept him more readily.

Therefore, he sent a message to the Sākyans through messengers "Give the hand of a Sākyan lady in marriage."

When the message was delivered to the Sākyans, they held a meeting. "The king will be upset if we decline his request. But we can't give him a daughter in marriage because his clan is inferior to ours. What should we do?"

Mahānāma said, "Vāsabhakhattiya, the daughter from my slave is beautiful. Let us offer her to the king."

They conveyed their consent to the messengers.

"Whose daughter is she?"

"She is the daughter of Mahānāma Sākya."

The messengers went back and reported to the king. The king was happy and asked them to bring her over.

Still, he had a doubt. "The khattiyas are deceptive. They may give daughter of a slave in marriage. Ask her to eat with her father and then bring her."

The messengers went back and did so. Mahānāma put up a show as if he was eating with her. Then the messengers took her to Sāvatthi. The king became happy and made her the chief queen among his queens. Soon she gave birth to a beautiful boy, Viṭaṭūbha.

As the boy grew up, he saw that the other princes went to visit their maternal grandparents and other maternal relations; and received various toys and other gifts from them.

Viṭaṭūbha started pestering his mother. "Why don't you send me anywhere? Don't you have mother and father?" She told him that his grandfather was the king of the Sākyans but they lived far away and therefore she couldn't send him there.

When he turned sixteen, he insisted that he wanted to go to his mother's hometown. She tried to prevent him but ultimately gave in to his demand. Then he informed his father and set out with a large retinue of servants. Vāsabhakhattiya sent an urgent message to her father, "I am fine here but don't let my son see any difference."

On coming to know that Viṭaṭūbha was visiting, the young Sākyan boys were all sent away so that they wouldn't have to bow to him. When he arrived at Kapilavatthu, all the Sākyans gathered in the assembly hall and extended him a grand welcome. The Sākyans made him pay respect to various Sākyans saying, "Child, this is your grandfather, this is your uncle." When Viṭaṭūbha questioned as to why he was paying respect to many but no one was bowing to him, he was told that all the young Sākyans were away.

Viṭaṭūbha stayed there for a few days and then returned to Sāvatthi. At that time, a soldier from his retinue came back for a weapon he had left behind. He saw a slave woman cleaning the seat where Viṭaṭūbha had sat with milk and water. While cleaning it, she said, "The son of a slave sat here." He went back and told the others.

When Viṭaṭūbha came to know about this, he was enraged and thought to himself, "Let them wash my seat with milk and water. When I get the crown, I will wash the seat with their blood."

On returning to Sāvatthi, the minister gave the news about Vāsabhakhattiya to the King Pasenadi. He was enraged that he was given a slave's daughter in marriage. He took away the royal status of both the mother and son.

After a few days, the Buddha met the king. The King came and saluted him. He justified his actions regarding the mother and son. The Buddha told him, "O king, the Sākyans did a wrong thing. There is no doubt about it. But Vāsabhakhattiya is the daughter of a khattiya (noble) king. She was anointed in a khattiya household. Viṭaṭūbha too is born to a khattiya. In ancient times, wise men had given the status of the Chief Consort to a low-caste woman called Kaṭṭahārikā. Her son became the king of a vast kingdom around Varanasi and became famous as Kaṭṭavāhana."

The King accepted the Buddha's advice and restored Vāsabhakhattiya and her son to their original status.

Later, Viṭaṭūbha usurped his father's kingdom. Pasenadi went to his nephew, Ajātasattu, to seek help. He reached the Magadhan capital at night and couldn't get inside. He died that night outside the city gate.

The newly crowned king Viṭaṭūbha remembered his humiliation and set out with a large army to wipe out the Sākyans. The Buddha came to know about the imminent annihilation of Sākyans. He went and sat under a sparse tree on the Sākyan side of border under strong sun. On the Kosalan side was a banyan tree with dense foliage and cool shadow. Viṭaṭūbha went to the Buddha and saluted him. He requested the Buddha to sit under the banyan tree on his side of the border. The Buddha replied, "King, the shadow of clansmen is cool."

Thinking that the Buddha had come to protect the Sākyans, Viṭaṭūbha saluted him and went back to Sāvatthi, his capital. This happened the second time and the third time, he tried to attack the Sākyans. When Viṭaṭūbha set out to attack for the fourth time, the Buddha considered the Sākyans past actions and didn't intervene. Viṭaṭūbha ordered his army to kill all Sākyans except his grandfather.

After winning the war, he took his grandfather with him and started the journey back to Sāvatthi. On the way, they stopped for meals. Viṭaṭūbha asked his grandfather to have food with him. But the grandfather thought "Khattiyas don't eat with a slave's son even if it costs them their life." He told Viṭaṭūbha that he wanted to bathe first and committed suicide in the lake nearby. Viṭaṭūbha waited for him and then journeyed ahead. On the way, they set camp in a dry river bed at night. During the night, a gigantic flood swept away the army along with Viṭaṭūbha.

Discussion

Pasenadi was unhappy that the bhikkhus were not eating their alms food within the palace. He decided to marry a Sākyan maiden hoping that it would bring the bhikkhus closer to him. His thinking was wrong. The decision of the bhikkhus was based on the fact that king himself wouldn't offer alms to them. The issue would have been solved had he offered the food to bhikkhus with his own hands. By trying to link himself to the Sākyans through marriage, he complicated the issue. The Sākyans were extremely proud of their lineage though they were his vassals. Pasenadi had total control over their republic, so his prestige and power was much more than theirs. However, Pasenadi wanted to move higher up in lineage. People's false concepts of superiority of caste, clan, lineage and race often hurt others and themselves.

The Sākyans invited their own destruction through unreasonable conceit in their lineage. Mahānāma didn't eat a meal with the daughter because she was born to his slave. He wouldn't eat a meal with his own daughter! The deception was successful temporarily. Later on, he preferred to die rather than eat with his own grandson! Mahānāma was the Buddha's cousin. His own brother Anuruddha had entered the Saṅgha. The Buddha was against all such conceit in clan and caste. He persuaded Pasenadi to restore the status of Vāsabhakhattiya and Viṭaṭūbha. It seems Mahānāma had not learned from the Buddha. Having physical relation with a slave woman was not a blot to his pure lineage but eating from the same plate with his own daughter born to a slave woman was an affront to his lineage!

Viṭaṭūbha's rage on knowing that his seat was washed with milk is understandable. This led to his mind getting deranged. This resulted in the destruction of Sākyans and his own destruction. It doesn't seem that he was blindly bloodthirsty. Otherwise, he would not have gone back three times out of respect for the Buddha.

Savarkar's Objection to the Buddha's Non-violence

Savarkar has alleged in his play 'Sanyasta Khadag' that the brave Sākyans were destroyed and countless future generations were defeated due to the Buddha's philosophy of non-violence.[260] Let us look at some of his arguments…

He has written the following dialogue for Vikrama, the Sākyan General. "…even greater harm to the society, to the nation is caused by the third precept of the bhikkhu; that of giving up weapons. Great harm is done and will be done by the extreme and brainless precept of non-violence! Bhagavan, this is not extreme non-violence, it is extreme self-destruction! And the destruction of soul is again violence; therefore, extreme non-violence is again extreme violence!"

While putting the prophecy in Vikrama's mouth that the Buddha's teaching would annihilate the Sākyan state, Savarkar writes, "Those people incined towards retirement who take precepts that they won't touch plough and won't pick up a weapon are bound to become so poor that they would certainly suffer from lack of food, they would certainly become weak and be sure to fall prey to an attacking nation!"

Savarkar's Vikram also calls the Buddha's teaching a perverted aim. "In such a situation, I feel it is a perverted aim for the people of a nation not to take up weapons, to be extreme in ethics and to consider it a holy path to please the Buddha." And, "The allure of non-violence will make them bite the bait of violence! The devastating consequences of the mistake—of giving entry to anyone in the Saṅgha and making hundreds of thousands impotent through the vow to giving up the weapons—will be felt for twenty-five generations of India!"

Savarkar's Kosalan general calls the Sākyan followers of the Buddha, "nincompoop Buddhist Sākyans."

A soldier in his play pokes fun at the Buddha's non-violence, "Understand! I am no stupid (*buddu*) donkey that has two long ears of cruel compassion and harmful non-violence."

Savarkar then attacks the Buddha through his character Shākambhaṭa who alleges that warriors could become bhikkhus and thus avoid war and the possibility of death in battle. "Once one takes the robes of a bhikkhu and gives up householder's clothes, the sword automatically drops down. Then there is no need to go to battle. Whether the Kosalan king attacks or the Magadhan, to enjoy the royal luxuries, the Sākyans had to take initiative in going to war. But once they become bhikkhus, they become free from the possibility of death in battle. Luxuries can be enjoyed in the monastery as well! Thus this is doubly convenient for you khattiyas (warriors)."

Savarkar did admit in his play that the Buddha had given permission to take up arms against aggressors. The dialogue goes like this,[261]

"Buddha: I am not an advocate of extreme non-violence. Not only that to protect the good people, using counter-force and counter-blow is not violence but a meritorious deed that prevents violence. But this is the duty of *grihasthāshrama* (householder's life), not of *sanyāsāshrama* (retired life)."

For the moment, let us keep aside whether the Buddha had really made any such comment about *grihasthāshrama* and *sanyāsāshrama.* Even so, what is objectionable in the Buddha's view that Savarkar himself has put forward? How can Savarkar say on one hand that the Buddha had allowed use of force to protect oneself and say on the other hand that the Buddha's teaching was responsible for the defeat of India by foreign invaders? The Buddha's non-violence is not the kind that makes one weak or makes one a supplicant. Was the objection to the fact that he put the responsibility on the shoulders of householders and freed the bhikkhus from this duty? Then the Vedics are even more guilty. Didn't the Vedics put the onus of battle on khattiyas (*kshatriyas*, warriors)? Did Vedic householders, let alone sanyasis, go to war? Savarkar's allegation that India was defeated because of the Buddha's teaching of non-violence is baseless and false.

To repulse an enemy, society has to be united. How will there be unity if men are not treated on an equal humanitarian footing? Who taught (and put into practice) the ideal that if you want unity, you have to treat all people in society with love and affection? The Buddha or the promoters of the caste system?

In spite of the balanced views of the Buddha, the characters in Savarkar's play attack him in an ugly manner. The argument that in the play one cannot consider the opinions expressed by the characters to be the writer's views, doesn't hold true here because the main aim of the play was to create confusion about the Buddha and to promote false allegations. It was like a newspaper printing malicious false news about a person on the front page and then printing a small item somewhere inside that gives the correct information.

Savarkar calls the Sākyans who follow the Buddha nincompoops. If the Buddha's non-violence were useless, weak and cowardly, it would not have invited the enmity of the poisonous and destructive Vedic system that discriminated between man and man. The great man faced this enmity with calmness and showered his compassion equally on both the discriminators and the discriminated. Certainly, his commitment to his views was consistent and fearless. If that had not been the case, he would have spent his life as a supplicant and trying to hold on to physical comforts. He renounced violence not because of fear or weakness but because he felt that killing is a heinous crime against humanity. His non-violence was a tender blossom borne out of love and compassion for all the beings.

In this same play, we should take a look at the dialogues of Sulochanā[262] who wears a man's garb. Savarkar uses the legend of thirty-two bodily marks on the Buddha's body to deride the Buddha. One of these marks is having long ears. Agni Purāṇa[263] describes him as *"shāntātmā, lambakarṇa, gaurānga... …* Buddha who gives boon and protection." It is not relevant here whether the Buddha had thirty-two bodily marks and whether his ears were really long. Savarkar has used these to poke fun at the Buddha: one ear is of cruel compassion and the second of meaningless non-violence. The words '*buddu* donkey' are distressing.

In India, the donkey is a symbol of foolishness. These days it is referred to as *lambakarṇa* (literally, long ear). It is likely that it has some history behind it. Possibility, it was propagated by the Buddha's opponents who like Savarkar wanted to demean him. *Buddu* in India has likely come from Buddha and was given currency by his opponents with the meaning a fool or an unintelligent person. Actually, originally this word means one who has gained superior knowledge. In some South Asian languages, 'du' or 'hu' are suffixes used to denote respect. For example, we see in Tamil usage such as Virabhadradu, Anjaneyudu, Kuberudu. In Sinhalese, we see respectful usage such as Buduhu, Rajahu. However, in Marathi and other languages *buddu* was propagated to mean fool. Savarkar used the word derisively for the Buddha and also strengthened the tradition of mockery.

What Lead to India's Defeat? The Tathāgata's Non-Violence or the Degeneration of Society Caused by the Caste-System?

The Licchavīs obtained an invaluable lesson from the Tathāgata on how to protect themselves. The principle of unity is the first and foremost. All the other principles are components of this first principle. Where there is no unity, enemy has an easy job at hand. All that the enemy needs is enough cunning to take advantage of the division.

We can see this easily if we see the history of India's political defeats and slavery. Our society has been internally splintered by *varṇa* and caste system. It has succumbed countless times to attacks by enemies. Even when it had the strength to win, it was defeated. When people like Savarkar blamed the Tathāgata's teaching for India's defeats and decline, they ignore the fire created by caste system that scorches men. They forget that this society was fractured from within. Sometimes, those in favor of the caste system blame the Tathāgata to turn our attention away from the real cause— the dastardly caste system. To what extent did the unity that the Tathāgata tried to instill took root in India? If we don't understand that the real reason for our defeats was lack of unity, history will repeat itself in future.

Who encouraged the *khattiyas* by exaggerated praise of their valor, martyrdom, and sacrifice to protect religion and fight in battles? Who emasculated society by propounding scriptures that forbade *vessas* (traders) and *suddas* (lower castes) from taking up arms?

If lower castes were given weapons, it would have been difficult to dominate them consistently. Who forbade the lower castes from accumulating any wealth? The same people adopted the same tactic in the field of knowledge. The same people were more worried about any internal challenge to its superiority than external enemies. Savarkar was well aware of the history of our society where men born in this land were treated worse than the enemies who attacked us.

Dr Ambedkar Questions Savarkar

Savarkar's effort to blame the Tathāgata for the destruction of the Sākyans doesn't stand the test of history. The Sākyans were destroyed because of their pride in their lineage. They made terrible mistakes out of this conceit; and they paid a terrible price for them. The Tathāgata saved them time and again but they didn't learn from the Tathgata. If one decides to answer all allegations in Savarkar's play, it would need a separate book. That is beyond the scope of this book. It is, however, pertinent to note a question asked by Dr Ambedkar to Savarkar.[264] "I want to ask Savarkar, who were the Peshavas? Were they bhikkhus? How then did the English snatch their kingdom from their hands?"

Acharya Satya Narayan Goenka has written in detail about the reasons behind the destruction of Sākyans. Some of this thought-provoking points are quoted here. He writes,[265] "Compared to the powerful neighbouring kingdom of Kosala, both the Sākyan and Koliyan republics were extremely weak. About 500 Sākyans had entered the Buddha's Sangha. Some Sākyans and Kolians young men had entered Sangha earlier too. But we cannot say that this made Sākyan army weaker compared to Kosalan one…

"Similarly, if the ruler of Kosala sent his army to attack the vassal Sākyan state, it would be impossible for the Sākyans to face the mighty Kosalan armed forces with the soldiers who were meant only for domestic security. It is clear that the Sākyan republic could not have resisted the Kosalan army… … the true cause of their downfall was their great pride in belonging to a high caste. The Sākyans did not follow the teaching of the Buddha; they acted contrary to his teaching. That is the reason why they were defeated."

Acharya Goenka writes further, "The Vajjians were ruined because they became a victim of the deceit of the minister Vassakāra and started to neglect the teaching of the Buddha. Similarly, the Sākyans were ruined not because they followed the teaching of the Buddha but because they disregarded his teaching that birth should not be the basis for high or low status. The khattiyas of the Sākyan and the Koliya clans were so haughty about the superiority of their clan that they were not ready to marry their daughters even to other khattiyas. ….

"The real cause of India's decline as a nation has been the destructive caste system, which has divided the people into factions and weakened them. The nation has never been able to unite for its own defence and has been suffering the dire consequences of this disunity."

Acharya Goenka's analysis makes it clear that Savarkar's allegations are without foundation.

Right Thinking About Family Life and Society

It is clear that the Buddha thought in a balanced way about family, society and nation state. The bhikkhu Saṅgha was a part of his Dhamma. But he didn't think of it as the whole society. The vast population outside of the Saṅgha was another part of his Dhamma. The order had bhikkhus and bhikkhuṇis, but outside of the order, there were many times more householders. Just as he took his Bodhi to bhikkhus and bhikkhuṇis, he also took it to countless laymen and laywomen. Since bhikkhus and bhikkhuṇis had dedicated themselves exclusively to the Dhamma, they had more time to learn and practise it. They contributed more to the Dhamma. But the Dhamma was also for the benefit of lay people. The Tathāgata couldn't reach all the population by himself. He trained bhikkhus and bhikkhuṇis to make them proficient in the Dhamma and then sent them in all directions to take the Dhamma to the masses. This teaching was not just for the sake of heaven nor was it just for meditation. It also taught lay people to live their worldly life in a proper way. For example, right speech doesn't just benefit bhikkhus but is useful for all sections of society and reduces their suffering. It is likely that later on, bhikkhus inflated the number of bhikkhus that were in the Saṅgha at the time of the Buddha. In reality, householders far outnumbered bhikkhus. The Buddha had maintained that balance. Just as he gave attention to the family life, he also seriously thought about the wider society and nation.

His intention was: all people should live a pure, happy, and contented life.

8

Not by Birth, Not by Caste: Man is Great by Morality and Wisdom

It won't be an overstatement to say that there is no more efficient system of protecting the narrow interests of a select few than the caste system of India.

We know that the Buddha rejected this system.

Here we will see, with examples, what were his views, the principles he espoused, the arguments he put forth and what actions he took about this issue.

Though caste has its origin in *Varṇa* system, caste and *Varṇa* are not the same thing. There are only four *Varṇas: khattiya* (princely or warrior caste), *brahmin* (priests), *vessa* (trader or business caste) and *sudda* (lower caste). There are innumerable castes in India. The word "Class" cannot be used for Varṇa as Varṇa, unlike class, is a closed class decided strictly on the basis of birth. Therefore, in this chapter, for want of a better alternative the word caste is used for both *jāti* (caste) and *Varṇa*.

It is painful but true that people continue to be discriminated against because of their caste and race even in modern times. The bias continues. Therefore, these issues are as relevant today as during the Buddha's time.

As Rivers in Ocean, Castes Unite in Saṅgha

In Cūḷavagga[266] of Book of Discipline (Vinaya Piṭaka) we find the Buddha addressing bhikkhus thus, "Bhikkhus, when the great rivers Ganges, Yamuna, Aciravati, Sarabhu, Mahi reach the ocean, they discard their old names and acquire one name—that of the ocean. Similarly, when people from the four castes—nobles, brahmins, traders and lower castes—go forth from home in to homelessness and take robes to enter the Dhamma and the Discipline of the Buddha, then they give up their old names & castes and acquire one name—Sākyaputta Samaṇa" . These are such clear thoughts that there is no need to comment on it.

It must be remembered that bringing people of all castes together doesn't mean bringing together immoral and moral people together. The Buddha always emphasized morality. The superiority of a person should be decided by morality and wisdom; not by caste acquired at birth or by rituals. This was a fundamental principle of his Dhamma. Anāthapiṇḍikovāda Sutta[267] of the Middle Discourses says, "People become pure due to deeds, learning, Dhamma, morality and upright life; not due to caste or wealth."

Give to the Virtuous from All Castes

Both Buddhist and Vedic traditions have put forth various views about whom to give donations. The views are vastly different. Sometimes, the Buddha was misrepresented. Let us look at Vacchagotta Sutta[268] to know what the Buddha said about it.

Once the recluse Vacchagotta came to meet the Buddha. He told him, "Gotama, I have heard that Samaṇa Gotama says 'Give donations only to my disciples, don't give to the disciples of others. Only donations given to me are meritorious.'… … Is what I have heard is true?"

The Buddha replied, "Vaccha, those who speak thus speak falsely about me. They make false allegations against me. What I say is this—donation to a moral person is meritorious and donation to an immoral person is not."

Then he gave an example to Vacchagotta to explain his point. There are cows that are while, black, red, yellow, grey or with spots on them. To one cow is born a strong bull that is good at ploughing and doesn't shirk work. Such a bull is put to work. Its color is not considered when putting it to work.

Similarly, among men irrespective of whether one is born a khattiya, a brahmin, a trader, a low caste or a scavenger, it is proper to give donation to one who is restrained, virtuous, truthful and who is ashamed to do wrong…"

In Issatta Sutta[269] of the Connected Discourses, the Buddha has given another example to make the same point. Once while he was in Sāvatthi, King Pasenadi came to meet him and asked him to whom he should give gifts.

The Buddha answered, "One that you find agreeable, one that you like." When King Pasenadi asked the gift to whom is more meritorious, the Buddha answered, "To whom one should give and giving to whom brings more merit are two different things. Giving to the virtuous brings much merit but giving to the immoral doesn't."

Then he asked the king, "Suppose it is a war time. A young khattiya (warrior caste) comes for recruitment in army. He is not skilled in using weapons, he hasn't practised weaponry, he is anxious and fearful, his hands tremble and he is likely to run away from the battle. Would you recruit him? Would you recruit a similar young man who is a brahmin… a trader… a low caste... ?" The king answered that he would would not recruit any of the four men. Then the Buddha asked him whether he would recruit a young man who was trained in using weapons, was adept at it, etc. The king answered that he would employ the young man irrespective of whether he was a khattiya, a brahmin, a merchant or a low caste.

Then the Buddha answered his original question again based on this example. A moral person who refrains from violence, killing, etc. is a suitable recipient of charity.

Then he uttered two verses the gist of which is: A king would recruit in his army a young man skilled in archery, strong and energetic. He wouldn't recruit an unskilled one because of his caste. Similarly, one should worship a person who is tolerant, has fortitude and is upright, a noble and wise person even if he is from lower caste."

Discussion

Vaccha reported a wrong propaganda that the Buddha insisted that charity should be done only for him or his disciples and not for others. This was a selfish, narrow and malicious allegation that had no basis in reality. All that the Buddha said is that one should support the moral, not the immoral. At the same time, as is clear from his initial answer to the king, he said that the donor is free to give to whoever he pleases.

The Buddha's principle on charity was not convenient for immoral people. But they couldn't oppose it in its true form. So they distorted it in a way that would appear biased to the listener. As we see, this happened in his lifetime.

Two fitting similes were used by the Buddha to emphasize the importance of qualities over caste. The value of a bull depends on its qualities, not on its color or the color of the cow it was born to. Varṇa the word used for the four major castes in India also means color. It is possible that the pun was intended when he used the simile of color of the cow and its calf. It disregards color and gives importance to qualities.

War requires valor. Just because someone is born in a particular caste doesn't mean that he is automatically suitable to join the army. One more inspiring aspect of this example is that the Vedic tradition had denied the right to bear arms to the business class and lower castes. In this example, their right to bear arms has been justified.

The Buddha's advice of charity based on qualities and not on birth was not acceptable to the brahminical system. Brahmins insisted that it was more meritorious to give donation to brahmins.

Manusmriti[270] says that if a donation is given to a non-brahmin, one earns merits equivalent to the donation. If donation is given to a brahmin who is not learned, one earns merit double that of one's donation. If one gives donation to a learned brahmin, one gets merit a hundred thousand times that of the donation. If one gives donation to a brahmin learned in Vedas, one gets merit that is incalculable times the donation. This shows the vast abyss in the views of the Buddha and that of the brahminical system.

Purity of Brahminism and Purity of Dhamma

Once the Buddha was staying in the mango grove of Cunda, son of Kammāra, at Pāvā.[271] At that time Cunda came to meet the Buddha.

The Buddha asked, "What virtue, what purity do you like?"

Cunda replied, "Bhante, brahmins stand facing the West, hold a *kamanḍalu* (a pot with a handle), take a garland, worship fire, go into the water for ritual bath. They thus show their purity. I like this purity in them."

When asked how these brahmins express their purity, Cunda detailed their conduct, "They make their disciples touch earth on waking up in the morning. If they can't touch the earth, they are asked to touch wet cow dung. If that too is not possible, then green grass. If not, then to worship fire. If that is not possible, then to worship the sun with folded hands. If that too is not possible, then to take bath thrice. This is how they express their purity."

The Buddha replied that this purity of brahmins and the purity of the Noble Discipline (*ariyavinaya*) was different. When Cunda asked for an explanation, he clarified, "A man manifests impurities in three physical, four verbal and three mental ways.

"Three bodily impurities are killing, stealing and sexual misconduct.

"Four verbal impurities are lying, backbiting, harsh speech and frivolous talk.

"Three mental impurities are coveting the property of others, wishing harm to others and having false view…

"One who has these ten types of impurities will remain impure whether or not he does all the rituals such as touching the earth on waking up, worshipping the sun, etc. On the other hand, one who does not have these ten impurities is indeed pure, whether or not he carries out those rituals."

Why People Subscribe to the Theory of Brahminical Superiority

We find the Buddha's views on the four *varṇas* (major castes), their services and possessions in Esukāri Sutta[272] of the Middle Discourses.

Once he was dwelling in Jetavana of Sāvatthi. Then Esukāri brahmin came to him and asked, "Master Gotama, the brahmins tell four kinds of services. Brahmin, khattiya, traders (business caste) and low caste should serve the brahmins. Khattiya, traders and low caste should serve khattiyas. Traders and lower caste should serve traders. And lower caste should serve lower caste. What do you think about it?"

The Buddha put a counter-question, "But, brahmin, do these four people, four castes give permission to the brahmins to order such service?"

Esukāri said no.

"O brahmin, suppose there is a very poor man who has nothing. Without his asking for it, against his wishes, someone offers him a bowl of meat and says, 'O householder, eat this meat and pay for it.' Similarly, brahmins are making rules without permission of the four castes, of ascetics and holy men…

"O brahmin, I don't say that all people are fit to be served or all people are unfit to be served. I don't say that someone is suitable for service if such a service brings harm and no benefit to the server. On the other hand, if serving someone brings benefit and no harm, I say that such a person is suitable to be served…

"If a khattiya… a brahmin… a trader… a person from low caste is asked whether he would serve someone serving whom brings benefit and no harm or someone who service bring no benefit but brings harm; then that person would say that he would serve one whose service is beneficial and not harmful."

"If a khattiya… a brahmin… a trader… a person from low caste is asked whom he would like to serve: one that results in benefit and no harm or one that results in harm and no benefit. Surely that person would prefer to serve one that results in benefit and no harm."

Lastly , the Buddha puts forth a great point, "Brahmin, I don't say that being a high caste is good and I don't say that being a high caste is bad. Being affluent too is neither good nor bad...

"Someone may be born in a higher caste and may kill, steal and commit adultery. Therefore, I don't say that being born in a higher caste is good. Someone may be born in a higher caste and may abstain from killing, stealing and committing adultery. Therefore, I don't say that being born in a higher caste is bad."

Then Esukāri told him that the brahmins stated four types of wealth: living on alms food for brahmins; archery for khattiyas; farming, raising cattle and other occupations for *vessas* (traders) and cleaning for lower castes.

Again the Buddha asked him whether others give permission to brahmins to make such statements and again he gave the example of a poor man being forcibly sold a bowl of meat.

Then the Buddha told Esukāri, "O brahmin, I say that the noble transcendent Dhamma is the true wealth of a person. One gets specific nomenclature because of birth in a specific family, lineage and caste. It is as if when wood, grass and cow-dung is lit, the resultant fire is called wood fire, grass fire or cow dung fire. But any person who comes to the Dhamma and the Discipline (*dhammavinaya*) from any caste abstains from killing, stealing, etc., acquires right view and gains merit. It is not that only brahmins are capable of non-enmity, non-hatred and loving kindness; others too are capable of these."

Here again the Buddha gave the example given many times by him, that no matter who lights the fire, the fire does its work.

Soṇadaṇḍa Brahmin and Tests of Brahminity

Brahmins claimed that their status was the highest in the caste system. The Buddha asserted that their superiority must be based on morality and wisdom rather than on birth, color or study of Vedas. In Soṇadaṇḍa Sutta[273] of the Long Discourses we see him clarifying his view on brahminity.

Once the Buddha was living at Campā in Aṅga country on the bank of a lake named Gaggarā. Soṇadaṇḍa was then the master of Campā, the city being gifted to him by Bimbisāra, king of Magadha. The brahmins of Campā came to know that the Buddha was staying nearby and set out to meet him. Soṇadaṇḍa had retired to the upper floor of his house in the afternoon. When he saw the brahmins going towards the lake, he asked his servant where they were going. When he learned the reason, he sent a message to them, "I am coming too."

At that time about five hundred brahmins from various places had come to Campā as guests. When they learned about his imminent visit to the Buddha, they went to him and asked him if it were true. He said yes.

On learning this, they objected, "You should not go to meet Samaṇa Gotama. It is not proper that you go there. If you go there, it will hurt your reputation and add to his fame. It is proper that he comes to visit you. From both mother and father, you belong to a superior clan. There is no blot in your lineage in last seven generations. This is also a reason why you shouldn't go to him. You are wealthy. You enjoy many luxuries. You study the scriptures; chant sacred verses; are expert in the three Vedas, with the indices, the ritual, the phonology, the exegesis and the legends. You are learned in the words and in the grammar, versed in *Lokāyata* (one Indian philosophy), and in the theory of the bodily marks of a great man. You are handsome with pleasing personality. You have bright complexion and you are a brahmin endowed with brahminical splendor. You are virtuous and have noble speech. You are the teacher of many. You teach sacred verses to three hundred brahmin youth. Young brahmins come to you from all directions, from various places to learn sacred verses and for study. You are senior and elderly. Samaṇa Gotama is young. He has gone forth at a young age. King Bimbisāra of Magadha and Pukkusāti brahmin have honored you, revered you and worshipped you. All these are reasons why you should not call on him. Rather, he should call on you."

Soṇadaṇḍa then told them to listen to his reasoning as well. He put forth the following arguments, "Gotama's birth is pure both from his father and mother's side. He has left behind a great clan to become a monk. He has given up vast wealth. He has gone forth into homelessness in the prime of his youth. He took saffron robes in spite of his parents' tears (of sadness at his separation). He is handsome and endowed with brahminical splendor. He is virtuous. His speech is noble. He is the teacher of many. His craving has ceased. He teaches action. He has gone forth from a high lineage. People from far off regions and towns come to ask him questions. He is endowed with thirty-two bodily marks of a great man. He is honored and revered by mighty kings like King Bimbisāra of Magadha. He is living near Gaggarā lake. Whoever, Samaṇa or brāhmaṇa, comes to our area is our guest. Guests are to be welcomed and honored. Samaṇa Gotama is our guest. From that angle too it is proper that I visit him and not the other way round."

Convinced by Soṇadaṇḍa, the visiting brahmins too decided to go with him.

As Soṇadaṇḍa reached the bank of the lake with the brahmins, he became overcome with doubts. He started thinking about what will happen if he asked a question to Gotama. May be he would say, "O brahmin, one should not ask a question in this way. This is how one should ask a question.

"If that happens, the assembly would think that I am ignorant and dishonor me. One who is dishonored by the assembly also loses his reputation. If one loses one's reputation, one's comforts (through earnings) decrease because it is our reputation that gives us possessions and comforts…

"If he asks me question and I answer he might say, "Brahmin, this is not how a question is answered.' And again I would lose my reputation and gains.

"However, if I go back now after coming so close, the assembly would feel that I am ignorant or I am an egoist or I am afraid. This too will harm my name and fame."

Finally, Soṇadaṇḍa went to the Buddha and after proper greetings sat down to one side. Some brahmins sat on one side, some sat on the other side. Some gave their name and clan as an introduction, as a courtesy. Some kept quiet. Again Soṇadaṇḍa was overcome with the same doubts. He thought that if Gotama asked him questions about the three Vedas, he would be able to answer properly.

Perhaps the Buddha guessed the mental turmoil in his mind and decided to ask him about the Vedas. He said, "O brahmin, what qualifications does one need to make other brahmins accept one as a brahmin? When he says 'I am a brahmin' what makes his assertion true and what makes it false?" Soṇadaṇḍa was happy that he was asked a question that he wished for.

Then Soṇadaṇḍa gave five tests of brahminity: Purity of blood from both father's and mother's side; expertise in three Vedas; being good looking with fair complexion; morality and wisdom (*paññā, prajñā*).

The Buddha asked, "If someone doesn't fulfill one of these criteria and still wants to be recognized as brahmin, is it possible?"

Soṇadaṇḍa answered ''Yes, it is possible,'' and added that fair complexion was not a mandatory criterion. One could have the other four and still be a brahmin.

Then the Buddha asked if one of the remaining four criteria could be omitted.

Soṇadaṇḍa replied that even without the study of the Vedas, one could be a brahmin if one fulfilled the other three criteria.

The Buddha then asked him if one more criterion could be omitted. Soṇadaṇḍa said yes, caste (birth, lineage) could be done away with. One endowed with the remaining two is called a brahmin.

Then the other brahmins became agitated and said, "Soṇadaṇḍa, you shouldn't speak thus. You are rejecting color. You are rejecting sacred verses. You are rejecting birth! You are actually following the view of Samaṇa Gotama!"

The Buddha then said to them, "If you think that Soṇadaṇḍa has little learning and lacks proper speech; that his intellect is inferior and he is incapable of holding his own in a debate with Samaṇa Gotama, let us stop Soṇadaṇḍa. You talk to me about it. On the other hand, if you think that Soṇadaṇḍa is learned, intelligent, has noble speech and is capable of holding his own in a debate with Samaṇa Gotama, you should stop and let him continue."

Soṇadaṇḍa suggested, "Let Gotama stop. Let Gotama be silent. Let me lawfully answer their questions."

Then he told the other brahmins not to say that he was following the Buddha's view by rejecting color, etc. 'I don't reject color' he told them.

At that time a nephew of Soṇadaṇḍa named Aṅgaka was sitting in the assembly. "Do you see my nephew Aṅgaka?" he asked the assembly. They said yes. "In this assembly there is none other than Gotama who has the complexion as fair and bright as Aṅgaka. He is proficient in three Vedas. He is well born on both father's and mother's side. I teach him sacred verses. I know his parents…

"Now, if this Aṅgaka were to kill, steal, commit adultery, lie and drink, what use would be his color? What use would be his study of the Vedas? What use would be his birth? Those who are moral and wise are called brahmins by brahmins. Such a man when he makes the claim 'I am a brahmin' speaks truth and not falsehood."

Then the Buddha asked Soṇadaṇḍa if it was possible to do away with one of these two criteria and still call someone a brahmin.

Soṇadaṇḍa replied, "No, it is not possible. Wisdom is purified by morality and morality is purified by wisdom. Where there is morality, there is wisdom. Where there is wisdom, there is morality. The moral have wisdom and the wise have morality. Even so, morality is considered foremost—even above wisdom—in the world."

The Buddha replied that it was indeed so. Then at Soṇadaṇḍa's request, he gave a detailed exposition on morality and wisdom; at the end of which Soṇadaṇḍa requested the Buddha to accept him as his devoted disciple. He also invited the Buddha for lunch the next day. The Buddha accepted by remaining silent.

The next day, after the Buddha had finished his meal, Soṇadaṇḍa sat on a small stool to one side and said to him, "Gotama, in the assembly if I were to rise and salute you, they would despise me, my reputation would suffer, and when reputation suffers, income suffers; for it is reputation that gives us income. Therefore, Gotama, if on entering the assembly, I should join my palms in greeting, may you take it as if I had risen from my seat. And if I should take off my head cloth, may you take it as if I had bowed at your feet.

"If when riding in my carriage, I were to alight to salute you, the company would despise me... Therefore, when I raise my goad, may you take it as if I had got down from my carriage, and if I close my umbrella, may you take it as if I had bowed my head at your feet."

Then the Buddha instructed Soṇadaṇḍa with a talk on the Dhamma, and inspired and delighted him. Then he rose from his seat and departed.

Discussion

Soṇadaṇḍa Possibly Had a Gold Stick in His Hand

Soṇadaṇḍa was an influential brahmin in Campā. It is likely that this was not the name given to him by his parents but an epithet. After the initiation ritual, the brahmin children are given special wooden sticks *(daṇḍas)*. Soṇa means gold. One who has a gold stick in his hand is Soṇadaṇḍa. It seems that due to Bimbisāra's patronage Soṇadaṇḍa had ample wealth. This could be the reason why he used a gold stick instead of a wooden stick; and came to be known as Soṇadaṇḍa.

Brahmins Had Different Reasons for Visiting the Buddha

On coming to know that the Buddha had arrived near their city, brahmins set out to meet him. It is possible that some of them had genuine respect for him. Others wanted to test him with their questions.

Opposition by Brahmins Coming from Different Countries

When these brahmins came to know about Soṇadaṇḍa's decision to visit the Buddha, they tried to dissuade him from doing so. They praised Soṇadaṇḍa in various ways and put forth various arguments about how it was improper for him to visit the Buddha.

This shows how brahmins used to protect their privileged status even in small matters. In their mind, Soṇadaṇḍa's visit was not problematic just for him personally, but to them all as a caste. The reputation of brahmins would decrease if they started visiting Samaṇas. Their rites and rituals *(yajñas)* would dwindle. It would be a monetary loss to them. Such may have been their fears.

Soṇadaṇḍa Was Different

Though others were taking a narrow view about the Buddha, Soṇadaṇḍa's stand was refreshingly generous. He praised the Buddha in various ways and accepted his greatness. He expressed humility and hospitality in wanting to go to the Buddha. It is clear that there were some brahmins who looked beyond caste.

Soṇadaṇḍa felt that the Buddha was superior to him. He had respect for the Buddha but he was also under pressure due to the presence of the other brahmins. He feared that his inability to answer Gotama's questions would lower his prestige in their eyes. This made him somewhat confused. He didn't disrespect the Buddha but couldn't build the courage to ignore the adverse reactions of the other brahmins.

Tests of Brahminity

The Buddha could skillfully debate complicated and controversial issues and draw positive conclusions. This is one example of his skill. He didn't reject brahminity totally. He sought to give it a foundation of high morality. It was in this context that he questioned Soṇadaṇḍa about tests of brahminity.

The criteria of brahminity that Soṇadaṇḍa gave included some traditional brahminical beliefs but also included ethical elements. The way the Buddha guided the conversation ensured that the stereotypical brahminical beliefs were taken out and only the ethical foundation remained. Leaving aside color, Vedas and birth as criteria for brahminity was unacceptable for other brahmins. They gave more importance to external appearances than mental state. They felt that Soṇadaṇḍa was repeating the Buddha's views. This was in a way true because the Buddha was adept at discussing issues in a way that even when the opponent gave up his view, it wouldn't seem like a defeat of the opponent!

The Buddha silenced these brahmins by inviting them for discussion. They knew that they were incapable of holding their own in debate with the Buddha. Soṇadaṇḍa also showed skill in preventing such a debate and preventing other brahmins from being humiliated. He successfully told them that he wasn't going over to the Buddha's side and that the three traditional elements were not as important as morality and wisdom. His example of his own nephew was apt and settled the issue. He argued that his nephew's fair complexion, study of Vedas and high birth would not help him if he led an immoral life.

Both Morality and Wisdom Are Important

Soṇadaṇḍa showed sagacity in excluding the first three criteria but insisted on including both morality and wisdom. The Buddha agreed with him. Many times in his life, the Buddha asserted that if one were to accept and revere brahminity, it must be based on morality and wisdom, not on birth or color. His view on brahminity is seen prominently in the Dhammapada.

Pressure of Other Brahmins on Soṇadaṇḍa

After his discussion with the Buddha, after requesting the Buddha to accept him as a disciple, Soṇadaṇḍa respectfully invited the Buddha for a meal. He expressed his compulsions to the Buddha after the meal. It shows a sad part of Indian social history. He couldn't bring himself to acknowledge and express his reverence for the Buddha openly.

The Vedic scriptures had strict directions that a brahmin was not to salute a non-brahmin; not to welcome him with folded hands and not to get down from the carriage to salute him. This was one of the reasons why some of the brahmins who had gone with Soṇadaṇḍa had refused to salute him.

We see more explanation about this in the Commentary of the sutta. Some of the brahmins had joined their hands in the traditional Indian greeting but had not bowed their head. If someone objected to their saluting a Samaṇa, they could say that just joining hands doesn't make a salute. If someone questioned them why they had not saluted the Buddha, they could say that joining hands was a salute, one didn't need to bow one's head. Soṇadaṇḍa knew the brahminical egoistic mindset. He wanted to salute the Buddha but was afraid of the censure of the other brahmins.

Learning and Conduct Makes a Man Great

The Buddha would sometimes encounter arrogant brahmins who would claim superiority based on their birth rather than on learning and conduct. Ambaṭṭha Sutta[274] in the Long Discourses shows us how the Buddha handled such encounters.

Once the Buddha was living in Kosala with a retinue of five hundred bhikkhus. His wanderings took him to Icchānaṅgala, a town of brahmins. At that time brahmin Pokkharasāti was living in a town named Ukkaṭṭha, gifted to him by King Pasenadi. He came to know that the Buddha was residing close by. He had heard the Buddha's fame.

At that time Ambaṭṭha, a brahmin youth, was studying under him. Pokkharasāti told Ambaṭṭha about the Buddha and sent him to the Buddha to find out whether his fame was factual.

Ambaṭṭha went to the Buddha and after greeting him sat to one side. The Buddha was walking at that time. Ambaṭṭha continued to be seated and started asking questions while seated. When the Buddha sat down, he stood up and started asking questions.

Then the Buddha asked him, "Ambaṭṭha, do you speak to elder, senior, brahmin teachers the way you speak to me?"

"No, Gotama. It is proper that one walks while conversing with a brahmin who is walking. One stands while talking to a brahmin who is standing. Similarly, one should be seated while talking to a brahmin who is seated. But, Gotama, while conversing with these shaven-headed ascetics, inferior like servants, dark, born from the feet of Brahmā, one should converse as I am conversing with you."

The Buddha replied, "You have come here to learn something. It is improper that you keep your curiosity in your mind (and not seek clarification). Though you are ill-bred, you have pride about your culture as if you have been properly trained."

Ambaṭṭha got angry and upset on hearing this. He thought 'Samaṇa Gotama is evil' and said to Gotama, "O Gotama, Sākyans are fierce, violent, harsh, inferior and given to big talk. Though they are inferior, they don't revere brahmins, don't respect brahmins, don't worship brahmins. They don't welcome brahmins properly. Gotama, the conduct of Sākyans is wrong."

The Buddha asked to him, "What wrong have the Sākyans done to you?"

He replied that once he had gone to Kapilavatthu as directed by his teacher Pokkharasāti for some work. He reached the community hall of the Sākyans. Many Sākyans and Sākyan children were pointing fingers at each other and laughing. He felt that they were laughing at him. None of them offered him a seat. He felt that though the Sākyans were inferior they didn't welcome and respect him as inferiors should. This was not proper.

The Buddha replied, "Ambaṭṭha, even a small sparrow freely tweets in its own nest. Kapilavatthu is the city of Sākyans. Because of this minor incident, you should not get upset at them."

Ambaṭṭha said, "Gotama, khattiya, brahmin, vessa (traders) and sudda (lower caste) are four varṇas (castes). Of these, the other three castes are servants of brahmins. Therefore, Gotama, it is not proper that Sākyans though being inferior don't honour brahmins."

Since Ambaṭṭha was constantly criticizing Sākyans, the Buddha asked, "Ambaṭṭha, what is your clan?"

"Gotama, I am Kaṇhāyana."

"Then Ambaṭṭha, if you take into consideration your father and mother's lineage, Sākyans are your masters. You are a descendent of the slaves of the Sākyans.

"But Sākyans trace their line back to King Okkāka."

"Long ago, Ambaṭṭha, King Okkāka, wanted the son of his favourite queen to succeed him as king. Therefore, he banished his elder children from the land. They took up their dwelling on the slopes of the Himalaya, on the borders of a lake where a mighty saka (teak) tree stood. Because they lived in the forest of saka tree, they were called Sākyas.

Okkāka had a slave girl called Disā. She gave birth to a baby with dark complexion *(kaṇha)*. He was the ancestor of the Kaṇhāyanas. And that is the origin of the Kaṇhāyanas. And thus it is, Ambaṭṭha, that if one were to follow up your ancient name and lineage, on the father's and on the mother's side, it would appear that the Sākyans were once your masters, and that you are a descendent of one of their slave girls."

Then the other young brahmins said to the Buddha, "Let not the Master Gotama humble Ambaṭṭha with this reproach of being descended from a slave girl. He is well born and from good family. He is erudite, an able reciter and a learned man. And he is able to answer Master Gotama in these matters."

The Buddha said, "Quite so. If you thought otherwise, then it would be for you to discuss this with me further. But as you deem it fit, let Ambaṭṭha himself speak."

They said that they wanted Ambaṭṭha to continue the discussion.

Then the Buddha said to Ambaṭṭha, "Then, Ambaṭṭha, a further question arises about the Dhamma which you should answer, even if unwillingly. If you do not give a clear reply, or change topic, or remain silent, or go away, then your head will split into pieces on the spot. What have you heard, when elderly brahmins, your teachers or their teachers, were talking together about the origin of Kaṇhāyanas and who the ancestor was to whom they trace themselves back?"

Ambaṭṭha remained silent. The second time he remained silent on being asked the question. Then the Buddha cautioned him, "You had better answer now, Ambaṭṭha. This is no time for you to be silent. For one who does not, for the third time, answer a reasonable question put by a Tathāgata, even though he knows the answer, his head splits into pieces on the spot."

At that time, an ogre bearing a thunderbolt hovered above Ambaṭṭha and was visible to both Ambaṭṭha and the Buddha. Ambaṭṭha became terrified and asked the Buddha to repeat the question.

The Buddha asked again. Then Ambaṭṭha said, "Gotama, it is true. That is what I have heard. We are descendents of Kaṇha. Kaṇha is our ancestor."

When he said this, the other young brahmins raised an uproar. They said, "Ambaṭṭha is low born. His family is not of good standing. He is descended from a slave girl. The Sākyans are his masters. We thought that the Samaṇa Gotamawas not to be trusted! But he speaks correctly."

The Buddha thought that the brahmins were going too far in their deprecation of Ambaṭṭha as the offspring of a slave girl. "Let me set him free from their reproach."

He said to them, "Do not disparage Ambaṭṭha on the ground of his descent. That Kaṇha became a great seer. He went to the South where he learnt sacred verses."

Then the Buddha said to Ambaṭṭha, "What think you, Ambaṭṭha? Suppose a young khattiya should have relation with a brahmin maiden and a son should be born. Now would that son receive a seat and water from the brahmins?"

"Yes, he would, Gotama."

"But would the brahmins allow him to partake of the food offered to the dead; of the food boiled in milk; of sacrifices; of food served to guests?"

"Yes, they would, Gotama."

"Would the brahmins teach him their sacred verses?"

"Yes, they would, Gotama."

"Would he get a brahmin maiden as wife?"

"He would."

"But would the khattiyas allow him to get consecration as a khattiya?"

"Certainly not, Gotama."

"Why not?"

"Because he is not of pure descent on the mother's side."

Then the Buddha asked Ambaṭṭha, "What think you,

Ambaṭṭha? Suppose a young brahmin should have relation with a khattiya maiden and a son should be born. Now would that son receive a seat and water from the brahmins?... Would the brahmans allow him to partake of the food offered to the dead; of the food boiled in milk; of sacrifices; of food served to guests?... Would the brahmins teach him their sacred verses?... Would he get a brahmin maiden as wife?"

Ambaṭṭha answered yes to all the questions.

"But would the khattiyas allow him to get consecration as a khattiya?"

"Certainly not, Gotama."

"Why not?"

"Because he is not of pure descent on the father's side."

Then, Ambaṭṭha, whether one compares from the women's side or men's side, the khattiyas are higher and the brahmins are inferior.

"Ambaṭṭha, suppose the brahmins for some offence or other were to outlaw a brahmin by shaving his head, whipping him and banishing him from their town. Would he be offered a seat or water among the brahmins?"

"Certainly not, Gotama."

"Would the brahmins allow him to partake of the food offered to the dead; of the food boiled in milk; of sacrifices; of food served to guests?... Would the brahmins teach him their sacred verses?... Would he get a brahmin maiden as wife?"

Ambaṭṭha said that he would not get any of these.

Then the Buddha asked him, "Ambaṭṭha, suppose the khattiyas for some offence or other were to outlaw a khattiya by shaving his head, whipping him and banishing him from their town. Would he be offered a seat or water among the brahmins?"

"Yes, Gotama."

"Would the brahmins allow him to partake of the food offered to the dead; of the food boiled in milk; of sacrifices; of food served to guests?... Would the brahmins teach him their sacred verses?... Would he get a brahmin maiden as wife?"

Ambaṭṭha said yes.

Then the Buddha said, "Ambaṭṭha, a khattiya whose head is shaved as punishment is considered low by other khattiyas. Even in that stage, khattiyas are proved higher. Ambaṭṭha, Brahmā Sanatkumara has uttered the verse:

The khattiyas are the best among those
Who consider lineage in such matters.
But he who is perfect in wisdom and righteousness,
Is the best among gods and men.

"This verse is correct. Not incorrect. It is well-spoken. Not ill-spoken. It is meaningful, not useless. I agree with it. Ambaṭṭha, I too say,

The khattiyas are the best among those
Who consider lineage in such matters.
But he who is perfect in learning and righteous conduct,
Is the best among gods and men."

Then Ambaṭṭha asked him what (righteous) conduct was and what learning was.

The Buddha answered, "The wealth of superior learning and conduct has no relation to caste, lineage or pride that says 'you are worthy of me or you are not worthy of me'. Where there is marriage, caste is considered. Those who are in bondage to the notions of birth or lineage or the pride of social position or of relation through marriage are far away from this incomparable wisdom and conduct *(vijjācaraṇa)*.

"Ambaṭṭha, only after the bondage of birth, lineage, the pride of social position and of relation through marriage is broken, can one attain this incomparable wisdom and conduct *(vijjācaraṇa)*."

Ambaṭṭha again asked about the nature of conduct and wisdom. Then the Buddha explained morality and concentration, etc. in detail.

Then he explained the four hindrances in the attainment of righteous conduct and wisdom.

"An ascetic or a holy man, without having attained perfection in wisdom and conduct, goes into the forest and eats only fruits and roots or eats only bulbs and roots with a hoe or builds a fire shrine near the boundary of a town or builds an alms house at the cross-roads of a town and welcomes any ascetic or holy man who pass there."

After enumerating the four hindrances, he asked Ambaṭṭha whether he or his teacher had gained wisdom and right conduct.

Ambaṭṭha said no.

Then the Buddha asked whether they had attained at least those things enumerated above that are considered hindrances. Again the answer was no. Then he asked how could Ambaṭṭha say that there was no comparison between samaṇas and brahmins just because he was told so by his teachers that 'there was no comparison between dark, low, inferior etc samaṇas and brahmins proficient in three Vedas'? He added that this was his teacher Pokkharasāti's fault.

Then the Buddha put forth many arguments. "Pokkharasāti survives on gifts by King Pasenadi of Kosala. He can't even see the king. When the king speaks to him, he does so from behind the curtain. Ambaṭṭha, suppose, King Pasenadi holds consultations with his warriors or generals mounted on an elephant or a horse or inside a chariot. Then the king goes to another place. A servant repeats whatever discussions were held by the king. He says whatever the king said. Just because of this, does he become a king or a minister of the king?

"Similarly, would you become a *rishi* (a sage) or a person on the way to sagehood, if you say that you recite the same mantras that were recited by ancient rishis such as Aṭṭhaka etc.?"

Ambaṭṭha said no.

"Did the ancient sages live as you and your teacher live—eating high quality rice, good meat, various sauces and curries; being waited upon by women who wear fine clothes; and going around in chariots drawn by horses?"

"No."

"Did the ancient sages live as you and your teacher do now—guarded in fortified towns, with moats all around, guarded by security men?"

"No."

Then the Buddha asked him if he had any question about the Buddha and assured him that he would answer any question.

Ambaṭṭha checked that the Buddha had all thirty two bodily marks of a great man. On being satisfied on that account, he went back to his teacher Pokkharasāti who was waiting with many other brahmins. He told his teacher that the fame of Gotama is factual. He also told him the details of his discussions with the Buddha. Pokkharasāti was displeased and scoffed at 'our learning, our knowledge and our proficiency of the three Vedas'. He decided to visit the Buddha himself but was stopped by others because it was late in the day.

Accordingly, he went to meet the Buddha next day. They talked about the discussion with Ambaṭṭha. Pokkharasāti asked the Buddha to forgive Ambaṭṭha for he was young and foolish.

The Buddha responded by saying, "May young brahmin Ambaṭṭha be happy."

Pokkharasāti offered the Buddha a meal. Then the Buddha gave a Dhamma discourse to him, after which Pokkharasāti asked the Buddha to accept him as his devoted disciple.

Discussion

Investigating the Fame is Proper

King Pasenadi had given Pokkharasāti a town in gift. Naturally, he was living an affluent life. There was nothing wrong in his desire to find out the truth about the fame of the Tathāgata. It is a principle in the field of learning that one should not accept anything without investigation and enquiry. The Tathāgata himself was emphatic about this principle. Such an enquiry is welcome when it is done out of genuine curiosity, to find out the truth. Ambaṭṭha didn't seem to have such a seeker's attitude. Ambaṭṭha was of the opinion that such a high fame of a non-brahmin's couldn't be factual.

Ambaṭṭha's Arrogance Unbecoming

Let us put aside the fact that the Tathāgata had greater learning than Ambaṭṭha; because this was going to be discovered after investigation. He was older than Ambaṭṭha in age. But in Ambaṭṭha's mind that seniority of age was irrelevant. He valued only being a brahmin. Therefore, he was not courteous in his behavior with the Tathāgata. This was disrespectful to the Tathāgata. Still, he used restrained language in questioning Ambaṭṭha who became agitated and angry when asked questions about his etiquette. He used abusive language for all samaṇas (ascetics and recluses not belonging to the brahminical tradition). This was applicable to the Tathāgata, as he too was a samaṇa. The Tathāgata was forgiving in nature and had eradicated all his mental defilements, so he didn't get angry. Instead, he gently corrected Ambaṭṭha. The Buddha reminded him that he had come to learn something and he should do so. He also told Ambaṭṭha that one who is trained should be polite and courteous.

The Tathāgata Himself Observed Etiquette

There are several incidents in which we see that when the Tathāgata visited other monasteries etc, he observed etiquette. Let us see Pāsarāsi Sutta[275] of the Middle Discourses.

Once while the Tathāgata was in Jetavana of Sāvatthi, some bhikkhus told Ānanda that they wished to listen to the Tathāgata's sermon. Ānanda invited them to Rammaka brahmin's ashram and also requested the Tathāgata to go there. When Tathāgata went there, several bhikkhus were discussing the Dhamma. Then Tathāgata stood outside waiting for their talk to end. Then he coughed to draw their attention and knocked. The bhikkhus opened the door for him.

The Tathāgata was senior, a teacher, the source of the bhikkhu's learning, the head of the Sangha. Still he was so courteous in his behavior. Contrast this with Ambaṭṭha's insolence and lack of etiquette.

Let us look at yet another example.[276]

Once the Buddha was dwelling in Kalandakanivāpa of Rājagaha. At that time, a forest dwelling bhikkhu named Goliyāni had come to the monastery. Sāriputta gave a talk on the Dhamma to bhikkhus and advised them that those who are visiting from the forest should be 'skilled in seating'. For example, they should not sit until the elder bhikkhus have sat. They should not ask new bhikkhus to give up their seats. The guideline about elder bhikkhus is understandable and expected but the guidance about the new bhikkhus takes courteous behavior to a lofty level. Thus even in small matters the teaching of the Buddha was meaningful.

Ambaṭṭha Was Insolent

The Tathāgata asked Ambaṭṭha what wrong the Sākyans had done to him. The incident narrated by Ambaṭṭha was not misbehavior of the Sākyans. Ambaṭṭha expected special treatment for being a brahmin. He wanted the Sākyans to welcome him and honor him.

The Tathāgata tried to calm him down by giving an example of a sparrow that chirps freely in its nest. This is a very touching statement. This small observation is one of the most telling examples of the value of freedom. Even animals and birds like their freedom, what to talk about men? The Sākyans had not come to Ambaṭṭha to ask for anything. They had not directly insulted Ambaṭṭha or used disrespectful language towards him or derided him or harmed him in any way.

On the other hand, Ambaṭṭha had come to meet the Tathāgata and was behaving insolently. He was acting thus because of his belief in the superiority of his caste. Even as the Tathāgata tried to mollify him, he continued to insult the Sākyans and call them inferior.

Tathāgata Reminded Ambaṭṭha of His Lineage

Only after Ambaṭṭha alleged that the Sākyans were 'low' thrice did Tathāgata ask him about his clan. When he told his clan, Tathāgata told him history of his lineage. There was no possibility of his being proud of his lineage. But sometimes people, in their conceit and effort to denigrate others, forget to look at themselves objectively. This is what happened with Ambaṭṭha. He knew that the very Sākyans whom he was saying were of low and inferior lineage were the masters of his ancestors. His companions thought that this was an unfair and unjust accusation by the Tathāgata. Then the Tathāgata invited them for discussion. But they demurred.

The Tathāgata Asked Ambaṭṭha to Speak the Truth

Ambaṭṭha had brought up the subject unnecessarily. Having said uncivil things about the Sākyans, he now had to conclude it. The Tathāgata was not going to let him turn back or remain silent . On the topic that he himself had broached, Ambaṭṭha had to speak under oath, so to say. If you don't answer, your head would split in seven parts, the Tathāgata said. On the face of it, it looks like a threat. One looks askance at this knowing how he was always polite and courteous in his conversations. It seems that he said so to Ambaṭṭha so that he takes the question seriously and speaks only the truth. It is not an actual threat but a figure of speech.

Splitting of Head Was a Colloquial Use

We can look at his statement from one more angle. Words in a language have different meanings in different contexts. Even words used in different branches of Science have different meanings. Whatever Tathāgata had said to Ambaṭṭha was a colloquial use as is clear from Suttanipāta[277] of the Minor Discourses.

Bāvarī, a brahmin from Kosala had gone south and was staying on the bank of Godavari. Once another brahmin came to him and asked him for a loan of 500 coins. Bāvarī politely offered him a seat and told him that since he had given up all his wealth, he didn't have the money.

On hearing this, the brahmin was enraged. He threatened Bāvarī, "If you don't accede to my request, then within seven days, your head will be split in seven."

Bāvarī became very distressed and anxious on hearing this. Seeing Bāvarī's mental condition, a deity felt compassion and came to him. She told Bāvarī that the brahmin was greedy and cruel; that he didn't know the real meaning of head and beheading. Bāvarī asked her what the real meaning was. She said that she too didn't know but that the Tathāgata would know.

Then Bāvarī called his disciples and told them to go to the Tathāgata and ask him the real meaning. They went to the Tathāgata and asked him. He replied, "Here head should be considered ignorance; and wisdom arising from faith, mindfulness, concentration and diligent effort as causing beheading or split head."

It is clear that Tathāgata used the phrase in a different manner. He probably meant that wisdom would destroy ignorance. It is also possible that the Tathāgata wanted to warn and caution Ambaṭṭha.

The way the brahmin who wanted money from Bāvarī used the phrase was different from the way the Tathāgata used it. The brahmin was greedy and wanted money. He wasn't speaking with the intention of destroying ignorance with wisdom.

On another note, there is need for research on the topic 'Bāvarī from Kosala'.

When Ambaṭṭha's Companions Deserted Him, the Tathāgata Took His Side

Ambaṭṭha had prestige in society. His companions respected him. They also benefited from his prestige. But they went into turmoil when they learned that he was the descendent of a slave of the Sākyans. They started humiliating him about it.

The Tathāgata didn't like it and defended Ambaṭṭha. He didn't feel vengeful about Ambaṭṭha's earlier insolence and didn't want Ambaṭṭha to be humiliated further. It was not the Tathāgata's nature to humiliate anyone, least of all because he was the descendent of a slave.

The Tathāgata never gave importance to caste or clan. He always said that qualities make a person superior or inferior.

Therefore, he praised Ambaṭṭha's ancestor Kaṇha for his qualities and declared that it was an honor to be descendent of such a sage. He had earlier mentioned Ambaṭṭha's lineage only to remove his conceit and insolence. He wanted to show him that the way of conceit in caste would not ultimately prove his superiority.

The Tathāgata's View on Equity

If one were to go by lineage, if one were to consider birth, khattiyas were superior. This was the social situation of that time in India. This was not the Tathāgata's opinion. I am not saying this to give a slant to his statement as is clear from the summing up he himself did in a verse. The Tathāgata declared that he who is perfect in wisdom and conduct is the best among gods and men. This was his consistent stand. Birth and caste were not the criteria for superiority. Morality and wisdom were. This was applicable not only to brahmins but also to khattiyas.

The Tathāgata's answers to Ambaṭṭha after uttering this verse further strengthen his stand on this issue. He emphasized that those who gave importance to clan and caste couldn't attain wisdom and righteous conduct. He further added that only after removing the narrow-minded belief in caste, was one able to attain wisdom and conduct.

Dr. Ketkar of Marathi Encyclopedia was angry that the Tathāgata gave prominence to khattiyas over brahmins. But Brihadaranyaka Upanishad[278] says, "...Therefore, brahmin stands below khattiya and worships him..." Though those who believed in the Upanishads didn't remove the original sentence, they added many sentences that made the original secondary.

One Doesn't Become Great Due to Past Traditions

The Tathāgata explained with various examples that mere superficial imitation of ancient sages didn't make one a sage. He also showed Ambaṭṭha that though he was proud of his caste, he didn't have the simplicity and restraint of the ancient sages of his caste. He showed the contradiction between the claims of being inheritors of past sages on one hand and indulgence in sensual pleasures and material luxuries on the other hand.

Ambaṭṭha went back and reported to Pokkharasāti. It seems that Pokkharasāti accepted the Tathāgata's greatness. He went to the Tathāgata and did the honorable thing. He apologized on behalf of Ambaṭṭha. The Tathāgata pardoned him and wished him well. Pokkharasāti requested to be accepted as the Tathāgata's disciple. Earlier Ambaṭṭha was banished by Pokkharasāti. We have no record as to what happened to Ambaṭṭha—whether his conceit decreased or whether his views about the Sākyans and the Tathāgata changed.

Dr. Ketkar's Objections to Tathāgata

Whether or not Ambaṭṭha changed his views in those times, in modern times he has a strong ally in Dr. S. V. Ketkar. He alleged[279] that Tathāgata believed brahmins to be lower than khattiyas, that the Tathāgata was not really against caste structure, that his real goal was to deride brahmins and inflate the ego of the khattiyas. He writes, "We cannot call Gotama opponent of caste and proponent of equality… he didn't launch a campaign against casteism but did agitate against the brahmins… he would often say that brahmins were lower than khattiyas; that brahmins were of inferior birth etc. This means that he was not against caste discrimination but was filled with envy for brahmins."

Dr. Ketkar First Distorts the Tathāgata's View

It is clear that Ketkar has made allegation based on the Ambaṭṭha Sutta because contrary to what Ketkar alleges there are hardly any references to the superiority of khattiyas in the Tipiṭaka.

We have seen the gist of the entire discussions in this sutta. We have also seen the behavior of Ambaṭṭha and the Tathāgata. We know who had conceit of caste and who believed in equality. Though it may look repetitious, let us repeat the verse. "Khattiyas are the best among those who consider lineage in such matters. He who is perfect in wisdom and conduct is the best among gods and men." If this stand of the Tathāgata had a lacuna, it was Dr. Ketkar's right to point it out. But he doesn't do it. He first distorts the Tathāgata's statements and then blames him based on this distortion. The first sentence in the verse refers to those who give importance to caste. The second sentence refers to the importance of wisdom and conduct in deciding real superiority.

The first line was not the Tathāgata's opinion. It was a statement of fact about the social realities of that time predominantly in Kosala and Magadha. At that time Pasenadi was the king of Kosala and Bimbisāra was the king of Magadha. Many prominent brahmins who took pride in their caste were enjoying royal patronage including lavish gifts from these two khattiya kings. And at the same time, they were denigrating all non-brahmins as inferior to brahmins.

Though the Tathāgata stated this social reality to Ambaṭṭha, he didn't consider the caste structure ideal. He didn't support it. He didn't like it. Therefore, it is wrong to say that he suggested that khattiyas were superior.

The Tathāgata stated his view clearly and unambiguously. He stated that a virtuous brahmin was superior to an immoral non-brahmin. However, a virtuous khattiya or a sudda (low caste) was superior to an immoral brahmin. This second aspect was unacceptable to Ambaṭṭha and his companions.

Vedic tradition had repeatedly claimed that even an immoral brahmin is superior to a virtuous non-brahmin. If Dr. Ketkar had distanced himself from this Vedic view even a little, he would have not supported the conceited Ambaṭṭha and criticized the Tathāgata, an advocate of equality.

Dr. Ketkar also forgets that this subject was brought up by Ambaṭṭha who had used abusive language about samaṇas. Ambaṭṭha was disrespectful towards the Tathāgata who was very senior to him. Dr. Ketkar doesn't utter a word about the discourteous and insulting conduct of Ambaṭṭha. Instead, he attacks the Tathāgata who was civil and courteous.

It is noteworthy that the Tathāgata never said that brahmins were low. He even supported Ambaṭṭha to save his face. He explained that though a son of a slave, Ambaṭṭha's ancestor was a mighty sage and it was an honor to be his descendent. It is impossible that the Tathāgata, who was so generous towards Ambaṭṭha, would make a sweeping statement against brahmins.

The Tathāgata Rejected Excessive Rights of Khattiyas

There are several instances showing that the Tathāgata didn't try to prove the superiority of khattiyas. In this context, we should read Metta Sutta[280] of the Numerical Discourses.

The Tathāgata has enumerated the material benefits of *mettā-bhāvanā* (loving kindness, selfless love) taught by him.

One of the benefits is, "Someone may belong to a low caste but with the practice of loving kindness, he acquires vast wealth and many resources. He becomes an able, affluent and successful king. He becomes the master of the rose-apple continent (Indian sub-continent). Who won't rejoice in this?"

Discussion

Just as Tathāgata rejected the notion that learning and philosophy were the exclusive domains of brahmins, he also rejected the unfair assertion that only khattiyas should rule. His critics should take note of this with a calm mind. One who is born in a lower caste may become a king because of his abilities and acquire authority and affluence. The Buddha emphasized that none can take away his right.

Contrast this with the rule in Manusmriti that prohibits a sudda (low caste person) from being appointed as an advisor to the king no matter how wise and capable the sudda is.

The statement about the effect of loving-kindness should not be taken as being a miraculous effect. This is not like claims that performance of fire-worship gave some mystical supernatural powers. It means that the practice of selfless love makes one's relations with others pure and harmonious. One gains many friends. One's enemies decrease in number and their enmity too decreases. This and other material benefits lead to one's success.

Barrister Savarkar's Objections

Savarkar has made a similar allegation through a character, bhikkhu Kāṇā, in his play 'Sanyasta Khadga'. He writes,[281] "Go and advice people to condemn the Vedas, to condemn brahmins, and rather than running after brahmins, follow bhikkhus!"

Discussion

It is clear by now that the Tathāgata never censured all brahmins. He did reject their authority to decide superiority based on caste. He didn't dislike them because they were brahmins. Whether he was talking about virtues or vices, he always used the twin words "samaṇas and brāhmaṇas." He didn't say that an immoral samaṇa was better than a moral brahmin. At the same time, he also refused to acknowledge the superiority of an immoral brahmin over an upright Samaṇa. It was his 'crime' that he rejected such a conceited view.

To Recognize an Upright Person…

While reading the opinions of the Tathāgata's critics, one remembers Vassakāra Sutta[282] of the Graded Discourses.

Once Tathāgata was dwelling in Kalandakanivāpa of Rājagaha. At that time, Vassakāra, the chief minister of Magadha came to him and asked, "Gotama, can a wicked person recognize other wicked person?"

Similarly, he asked three more questions:

Can a wicked person know an upright person?

Can an upright person recognize a wicked person?

Can an upright person recognize another upright one?

The Tathāgata replied that a wicked person won't recognize either a wicked or an upright person but an upright person would recognize both a wicked and an upright person.

Vassakāra praised him and narrated an incident.

Once Todeyya brahmin's disciples were talking about a king and said, "The king is a fool. He is a sheep. He likes Samaṇa Rāmaputta. He is polite to that samaṇa, salutes him, gets up to welcome him, greets him with folded hands, generally honors him." They also said that the king's servants too were fools like him because they too behaved in the same manner.

Then Todeyya brahmin asked some questions about that king and his servants. He skillfully made them say that they were adept at their work. He also convinced them that Samaṇa Rāmaputta was more erudite than the king and therefore the king was treating him with respect. Same was the case with the king's servants.

Discussion

All that needs to be said here is that to understand the utmost upright person such as the Tathāgata, one needs, like Todeyya brahmin, some uprightness in oneself.

All Four Castes, Pure or Impure, Based on Conduct

Assalāyana Sutta[283] of the Middle Discourses has the story of other brahmins who like Ambaṭṭha was denigrating non-brahmins.

Once the Tathāgata was staying in Jetavana of Sāvatthi. At that time five hundred brahmins had come to Sāvatthi from various different places. They thought, "This samaṇa talks about purity of four castes *(vaṇṇas, varṇas)*. Who will debate him?" At that time a young brahmin named Assalāyana was staying in Sāvatthi. They felt that he could argue with the Tathāgata so they requested him to debate with the Buddha.

Assalāyana replied, "The Tathāgata speaks the truth and it is difficult to win an argument with those who speak the truth. I won't be able to argue with him." They requested him a second time; and a third time.

Then they said to him, "Don't be defeated in battle even before the defeat." Assalāyana repeated his earlier statements but said that he would argue with the Buddha for their sake. He went to the Tathāgata with a big company of brahmins.

After exchanging greetings, Assalāyana sat to one side and addressed him thus, "Master Gotama, the brahmins say, 'Brahmins are the superior caste; any other caste is inferior. Only brahmins are fair; other castes are dark. Only brahmins are pure, not non-brahmins. Only brahmins are the sons and offspring of Brahmā: born of his mouth, born of Brahmā, created by Brahmā, heirs of Brahmā.' What do you have to say about it?"

"But, Assalāyana, brahmin-women have their periods; they are seeing becoming pregnant, giving birth, and suckling their babies. And yet the brahmins, being born this way, say, 'Brahmins are the superior caste; any other caste is inferior. Only brahmins are fair; other castes are dark. Only brahmins are pure, not non-brahmins. Only brahmins are the sons and offspring of Brahmā: born of his mouth, born of Brahmā, created by Brahmā, heirs of Brahmā.'"

"Whatever Master Gotama may say, still the brahmins think, 'Brahmins are the superior caste…'

Then the Buddha said to him, "Assalāyana, have you heard that in Yona and Kamboja and other outlying countries there are only two classes — masters and slaves — and that a master can become a slave, and that a slave can become a master?"

He said that he had heard so. Then the Buddha asked him what basis remains for the assertion of the brahmins. Even then Assalāyana said that the brahmins were firm on their stand.

Then the Buddha asked him, "What do you think that if a brahmin were to kill, steal, fornicate, lie, backbite, speak harshly or frivolously; were to be greedy, angry, hold wrong views he would go to the lower realms in the same way that a khattiya or a vessa or a sudda would if he were to do so?" Assalāyana said yes. Still, he stood firm on his assertion about the superiority of the brahmins.

Then the Buddha asked him whether a brahmin refraining from the above evil deeds would get the same wholesome consequences as a person from other castes doing so. Again, Assalāyana said yes but again he stuck to his view.

The Buddha asked him whether only brahmins can spread the message of non-enmity, non-hatred and loving kindness and whether only brahmins can use soaps and scented powders to clean themselves of bodily dirt. Again Assalāyana conceded that all castes could but repeated the claim about the superiority of the brahmins.

Then the Tathāgata gave yet another example. "Suppose, an anointed khattiya king were to invite hundred men of various castes. He told khattiyas and brahmins amongst them to light a fire of teak, deodar, sala, sandalwood, etc. Then he called outcastes and men from lower castes and asked them to burn the wooden bowls containing water for dogs or pigs, the wooden containers of laundrymen or any other wood. Does it happen that the wood lit by khattiyas and brahmins would produce and the other wood wouldn't?" Again Assalāyana gave the same answer.

Then the Tathāgata gave another example, "Suppose, a khattiya man were to have relations with a brahmin maiden, can the son born to them be called a khattiya as well as a brahmin?" Yes, he can be, answered Assalāyana. He asked the same question about a khattiya maiden and a brahmin man. Then he asked whether the offspring of a horse and a donkey could be called both a horse and a donkey.

Assalāyana answered no and added that there is a difference between the offspring and its parents (horse and donkey) but it is not so in case of brahmin and khattiya parents.

The Tathāgata asked, "Suppose there are two brothers. One of them has studied the Vedas and has undergone initiation ritual. The other brother hasn't studed the Vedas and hasn't undergone initiation ritual (*upanayana*). Who will the brahmins serve first on occasion of death, fire sacrifice, ceremonies, etc?"

Assalāyana replied, "One who has studied the Vedas, for what merits would one get by serving one who hasn't studied the Vedas?"

"Suppose, of the two brothers, one has studied the Vedas and has undergone initiation ritual but is immoral and of evil conduct. The other brother hasn't studied the Vedas and hasn't undergone initiation ritual; but he is moral and virtuous. Who among the two will be served the meal first?"

"The one who is moral and virtuous."

Then the Buddha said, "Assalāyana, first you were giving importance to caste, then to the Vedas and mantras, then to austerities and finally to the same purification of the four castes that I advocate."

Then Assalāyana became silent and sat dejected with drooping shoulders.

Seeing him in this condition, the Buddha narrated an incidence from the past.

Once seven brahmin recluses were living in a thatch of leaves. Then the evil thought arose in their mind that brahmins alone are superior, other castes are inferior. This reached the ears of the sage named Asita Devala. He went in front of their thatch and started pacing the ground while saying, "Where have the brahmin sages gone?"

The seven brahmin recluses mistook him for a rustic idiot and cursed him, "You low-caste rascal, may you burn and turn to ashes." The more they cursed him the more handsome and radiant he became.

The brahmin recluses felt that their austerities, their holy life had gone waste. "Earlier if we put a curse on a low-caste person, he would turn to ashes but this one has become more radiant."

Sage Devala told them, "Your austerities and your holy life has not been futile but first you have to get rid of the grudge you hold against me."

Then they discovered who he was and saluted him.

Then Sage Devala questioned about brahminical superiority, "Are you sure that the mother you were born to had relation only with a brahmin, and not with a non-brahmin? Are you sure that this was the case for all mothers up to seven generations in your lineage? Do you know about your father and your father's father up to seven generations?"

They said no.

Then the sage asked them if they knew how a woman conceives. They told him that relation between an ovulating mother and father in the presence of the *gandhabba* (an entity that was thought to be necessary for conception) leads to conception. The sage asked whether they knew if the *gandhabba* was a khattiya, a brahmin, a vessa or a sudda. They said no.

Then Sage Devala asked them, "So do you know who you are?"

Then the Buddha told Assalāyana that when Sage Devala debated with the seven brahmin sages, they couldn't answer him. Compared to them, Assalāyana was not fit to be even a cook to those seven sages, how then could he answer Sage Devala's questions.

Then Assalāyana requested the Buddha to accept him as a disciple.

Same Process of Birth

Brahmins insisted that they were born from the mouth of Brahmā and claimed that they were superior due to their birth. This was their foundation in asserting dominance over other castes. It was therefore necessary to show how hollow their claim was and that was the reason why the Buddha talked about the physical realities of birth.

Instability of Varṇas

By giving the example of two classes of master and slave in other countries, which were interchangeable, the Buddha showed that the same rules must apply to entire humanity. If there were people without the four castes, it cannot have the basis claimed by the brahmins.

The Tathāgata Raised Outcastes to the Level of Khattiyas and Brahmins

When he gave the example of fire in rejecting the discrimination between castes, he gave example of not only of the four castes but also included outcastes or casteless. (Traditional Indian society was divided into four major castes. In addition, there is a class that is considered so low that they don't belong even to the *sudda,* low caste.)

Based on Biology

The Buddha further clarified the issue by using the example of a mare and a donkey. There are different kinds of animals. Khattiya, brahmin, etc. do not belong to different species. They produce the same offspring unlike animals from different species. An offspring of a human remains a human irrespective of caste difference in the parents.

Assalāyana Went Over to the Buddha's Side

The Buddha talked about the study of Vedas and initiation ritual of brahmins that has a significant place in their cultural life. He gave the example of two brothers to underscore the importance of Vedas and initiation ritual of brahmins. Then he asked about morality and Assalāyana had to agree that when compared to ethical conduct, knowledge of the Vedas, initiation rituals, traditional rites, etc. became irrelevant. Assalāyana didn't realize that he had gradually started going over to the Buddha's view while answering his questions. The Buddha then made him aware about what had happened.

The Fault Lies in the Mind

It can be said that the Buddha did to Assalāyana and his companions, what Sage Devala did to the past sages. It is possible that this Kāla Devala and the Kāla Devala who visited Suddhodana's house when Siddhārtha was born were the same persons.

Devala's Question Not Uncivil

It may appear that the question of Sage Devala to the brahmin recluses about their lineage was unfair, uncivil and improper. Here we should remember the background against which he asked the question. He asked the question to bring down to earth those who were intoxicated with the arrogance of caste. It is certainly uncivil if such question is asked to denigrate those who are innocent and are not claiming any superiority. But when it is asked after provocation by arrogant abuse based on caste, it must be seen in that light.

The Tathāgata's Bhikkhus Didn't Discriminate

Inspired by the Tathāgata's views, bhikkhus also opposed discrimination as we see in Madhura Sutta[284] of the Middle Discourses.

Once Ven. Mahākaccāna was living in Madhura. Then King Avantiputta Madhura went to Mahākaccāna and asked, "Brahmins say, 'Brahmins are the superior caste; any other caste is inferior. Only brahmins are fair; other castes are dark. Only brahmins are pure, not non-brahmins. Only brahmins are the sons and offspring of Brahmā: born of his mouth, born of Brahmā, created by Brahmā, heirs of Brahmā.' What do you have to say about it?"

Mahākaccāna said that it was an empty boast and gave several arguments to prove equality between the various castes.

Mahākaccāna said that a king could hire anyone from the four castes in exchange for money and appoint him as servant. He asked if such a servant would get up before the master, go to bed after the master retires, would attend on him, work as instructed, doing what the master wants and have pleasing speech.

Madhura said yes.

Then Mahākaccāna asked whether a brahmin could hire someone from any four castes in exchange for money, whether a vessa… a sudda… could hire someone from any of the four castes in exchange for money.

Madhura said yes.

"Then king, what do you think? Aren't all four castes same in this regard?"

Madhura said yes and added that he doesn't see any difference in this regard.

Then Mahākaccāna said, "Therefore, it is a mere boast that brahmins are superior…"

Then Mahākaccāna argued in a different way. "If a khattiya were to kill, steal, fornicate, lie, backbite, speak harshly and frivolously; if he were to covet others' property, wish harm to others and have false view, would he go to the lower realms as a consequence?"

Madhura said yes.

Then Mahākaccāna asked the same question about a brahmin, a vessa and a sudda and received the same answer. Mahākaccāna asked, If a person from any of the castes abstained from these evil deeds, wouldn't he go to a higher realm as a result of that restraint?

Again Madhura said yes.

Mahākaccāna said that from this too it was clear that it was a mere boast of brahmins that they were superior.

Since Madhura was a king, Mahākaccāna put forth a relevant question, "If a khattiya were to break into a house, rob, ambush or fornicate, and one of king's men were to bring him to you and appeal to you to do as you please, what would you do?"

"I will hang him or banish him or imprison him or give him some other punishment as per his crime."

"Why so?"

"Because he is not a khattiya but a mere thief now."

Then Mahākaccāna asked similar questions about a brahmin, a vessa and a sudda.

Again the king answered in the same way.

Then Mahākaccāna asked the opposite, "If anyone of the four castes were to abstain from such evil deeds and were to live a virtuous life, a holy life, how would you behave with him?"

Madhura replied, "I would salute him; stand up and greet him; offer him a seat; gift him robes, alms food, residence and medicines, etc. and protect him."

"Why so?"

"Because he is not reckoned as a khattiya, brahmin, vessa or sudda any more. He is now reckoned as a samaṇa."

After this discussion, Mahākaccāna asked Madhura whether all the castes were equal or not and he answered that indeed he could see no difference in the castes.

Then Mahākaccāna said that this too proved that it was a mere boast of brahmins that they were superior.

Madhura was pleased with the discussion and accepted that he had now developed clarity on the subject. He expressed the wish to go to Mahākaccāna's refuge, but was told, "O King, don't take refuge in me. Go to the refuge of that Tathāgata to whose refuge I have gone."

When Madhura asked where the Tathāgata was dwelling, Mahākaccāna replied that he had passed away. Then Madhura said that had the Tathāgata been alive he would have gone ten, twenty, thirty… even a hundred yojanas (yojana is about seven miles) to meet him. Even though the Tathāgata had passed into *mahāparinibbāna*, he would still go to the refuge of the Buddha, the Dhamma and the Saṅgha. He requested Mahākaccāna to accept him as a disciple.

One Who is Immoral is the Real Outcast

The Buddha repeatedly stated that one becomes a brahmin or a sudda not by birth but by deeds. We see this in Vasala Sutta[285] of Suttanipāta. This sutta is also called Aggika Bhāradvāja Sutta.

Once the Tathāgata was dwelling at Jetavana in Sāvatthi and set out on alms round. At that time, sacrifices were offered to fire in the house of Aggika Bhāradvāja. The Tathāgata would not miss a house during his alms round; he went from one house to the next and stood before each. In this manner, he went near Bhāradvāja's house.

Seeing him coming from afar Bhāradvāja shouted, "Stop shaven-head, stop there wretched samaṇa, wait there, outcast!"

The Buddha asked him, "O brahmin, do you know who is an outcast? Do you know what things makes one an outcast?"

Bhāradvāja replied no and asked the Buddha to explain.

The Buddha explained in 27 verses, the gist of which is:

One who is angry, has hatred, and is talks badly about others, having distorted views, and deceitful — he is an outcast.

One who kills living beings, who has no compassion for living beings— he is an outcast.

One who robs and destroys villages and towns, and becomes notorious as a tormentor — he is an outcast.

Whether in the village or in the forest, one who takes that which belongs to others and is not given to him — he is an outcast.

One who having borrowed runs away when he is asked to pay, saying, "I owe no debt to you." — he is an outcast.

One who covets anything, kills a traveller and steals whatever that person has — he is an outcast.

One who for his own sake or for the sake of others or for the sake of wealth, utters lies from a witness stand — he is an outcast.

One who, by force or with consent, has relations with the wives of friends and relatives — he is an outcast.

One who though being wealthy doesn't support his mother and father who have grown old — he is an outcast.

One who strikes and uses harsh speech towards mother, father, brother, sister or mother-in-law or father-in-law — he is an outcast.

One who when asked about what is beneficial, says what is detrimental, and talks in an evasive manner — he is an outcast.

One who having committed an evil deed, hides it from others and commits evil in secret — he is an outcast.

One who having enjoyed choice food at another's house is not hospitable to that person when he comes to visit — he is an outcast.

One who deceives a holy man or an ascetic, or any other recluse by uttering lies — he is an outcast.

One who on seeing a holy man or an ascetic during mealtime uses harsh speech for him and does not offer him alms — he is an outcast.

One who speaks harsh words in ignorance or lies out of greed — he is an outcast.

One who is debased by his conceit, praises himself and belittles others — he is an outcast.

One who is given to anger, is miserly, has vile desires, and is selfish, deceitful, has no shame or fear in doing evil — he is an outcast.

Finally the Buddha told Bhāradvāja, "One doesn't become an outcast by birth and one doesn't become a brahmin by birth. One's conduct makes one an outcast or a brahmin."

Then the Buddha gave the example of Sage Mātaṅga who was an outcast's son, born in a caste that ate dog meat. He achieved fame as a great man. Many khattiyas and brahmins served him. Since he had conquered his defilements, he had no difficulty in attaining the brahmā realm.

On the other hand, there were several brahmins who were drowned in evil deeds. They were censured by people. Their caste didn't prevent them from going to lower realm and from being condemned.

The Buddha again stated how birth doesn't decide an outcast. Bhāradvāja was convinced and became his disciple.

Who Is a True Brahmin

The Buddha repeatedly refuted the theory of brahminical supremacy. However, he didn't have any negativity towards brahmins and didn't reject anyone just because he was a brahmin. On the contrary, we often see him showing utmost respect for the brahmins. However, he repeatedly told them that they would be honored not because they were born to brahmin parents. They would only be honored if they lived a righteous life. He insisted that if the word brahmin was to be used respectfully, it must be linked to high ethical qualities. Let us look at some of his utterances in the Brāhmaṇa Vagga[286] of Dhammapada.

Brāhmaṇa Vagga is the last chapter of Dhammapada, which ends with the Buddha's utterances on brahmins. The Dhammapada was not arranged as such by the Buddha. It was part of the editorial process that various chapters were created and arranged. The Buddha explicitly prohibits attacks on brahmins and reprimands those who kill brahmins. He also makes it clear as to who he calls a brahmin,

"One who is fearless and without craving, I call him a brahmin…

"One who does no evil by body, speech and mind, I call him a brahmin…

"Matted locks, lineage or birth doesn't make one a brahmin. One who has truth and righteousness, he is pure, he is a brahmin.

"You of evil mind, what would you gain by growing matted locks? What would you gain by wearing animal skin? You are dirty inside and you are washing the outside…

"He who is born to a brahmin mother, such a one I don't call a brahmin—if he is greedy and covetous, he is a merely *bhovādin* (brahmin in name). One who is not covetous and has no craving, such a one I call a brahmin…

"One who doesn't get angry, follow ethical norms, is virtuous, without pride, restrained and bearing the last body, I called him a brahmin…

"One who doesn't kill or make others kill, he is a brahmin…

"Just a mustard seed drops from the point of the needle, one's craving, hatred, conceit and deceit has dropped, such a one I call a brahmin…

"One who speaks not harshly, speaks lucidly and speaks without hurting others, him I call a brahmin…

"I call that pure person a brahmin who has no grief and craving…

"One who is without impurity, clean, delightful and pure; one whose craving is destroyed, him I call a brahmin…"

True Brahmins and Brahmins in Name Only

The Buddha didn't reject brahmins or brahminity. He tried to link brahminity with the concept of ethical living. Otherwise, according to him, the brahmins were merely brahmins in name or (as they were called in those days) *bhovādin*. *Bhovādi* literally means one who says *'bho.'* While addressing non-brahmins, brahmins used to add *'bho'* before their name. This address is intended for someone of lower social status or at the most for equals. It was how brahmins asserted their superiority.

The Buddha respected ethical and learned brahmins but showed the limitations of *bhovādi* brahmins. T. W. Rhys Davids writes,[287] "Bhovādin— a brāhmaṇa, i.e. one who addresses others with the word 'bho', implying some superiority of the speaker; name given to the brāhmaṇa, as proud of his birth, in contrast to brāhmaṇa, the true brāhmaṇa."$$$$$

What Makes a Man a Brahmin?

After attaining Bodhi while living in Uruvelā, the Buddha uttered some verses. One such *udāna* (spontaneous joyful utterance) is[288] "When a meditating brāhmaṇa gets wisdom of the Dhamma, the army of Māra trembles with fear." After this *udāna* comes the story of a brahmin named Hunhuka in the Book of Discipline. The same story is repeated in Hunhuka Sutta[289] in the Udāna of the Minor Discourses.

Question of Hunhuka Brahmin

Probably after hearing the *udāna*, one Hunhuka brahmin came to the Buddha and asked him, "Bho Gotama, what is a brahmin? What makes a person a brahmin?"

The Buddha replied, "One who has washed away all sins, one who doesn't say 'hun, hun' (hmm, hmm) out of spite, one who is free from all defilements, liberated, restrained, learned, living a holy life and speaks the Dhamma—for such a brahmin there is no equal in the world."

In the Udāna, Hunhuka Sutta is followed immediately by Brāhmaṇa Sutta. The gist of it is: The Tathāgata was once dwelling at Jetavana in Sāvatthi. One day, Sāriputta, Moggallāna, Mahākassapa, Mahākaccāna, Mahākoṭṭhika, Mahākappina, Mahācunda, Anuruddha, Revata and Nanda came to meet him. Seeing them coming from afar, the Buddha said, "The brahmins are coming, the brahmins are coming."

Then one bhikkhu who was brahmin by birth asked him, "Bhante, what makes one a brahmin? Which things make one a brahmin?"

The Buddha uttered this *udāna*, "Having washed their sins, their conduct is based on truth. Their attachments are all uprooted—such Buddhas are the brahmins in this world."

Discussion

The issue of who is brahmin has been discussed from ancient times in India. The Buddha gave it an ethical foundation. However, many brahmins didn't like it. They insisted that to be a brahmin, birth was most important. They also didn't like it that the Buddha was teaching the Dhamma, though he was not born a brahmin.

If one defines brahmin as one who contemplates the Dhamma, then the Buddha was certainly a brahmin. The language of his original utterance might not have been exactly what we have today. Still, it is clear that the Buddha is proclaiming his right and authority about the Dhamma.

The first objection to his right came in Uruvelā itself from a brahmin named Hunhuka. This probably was not his real name but an epithet given in view of the brahminical tendency to reject spiritual thought of non-brahmins by 'hun, hun' (hmm, hmm). He asked questions with a dismissive attitude implying that the Buddha could not have knowledge about brahmins.

The incident from Brāhmaṇa sutta in the Udāna throws more light on this. The Buddha pointed to the bhikkhus and said that the brahmins were coming. Two of them were his cousins, which means they were non-brahmins. If Mahācunda is same as Kammāraputta Cunda, then he was probably an iron-smith or a gold-smith. It is clear that not all of them were brahmin by birth but the Buddha called them all brahmins. This was a deliberate statement of the Buddha to give brahminity a moral dimension.

The Buddha Called Non-brahmins as Brahmins

This Brāhmaṇa sutta is important from another angle. The Buddha called those who were not brahmin by birth as brahmins. He also called an outcast a brahmin. This is an important detail, which some scholars have ignored. They have given brahmin as a caste of some of the bhikkhus who were actually non-brahmin by birth.

Though there is no mention in the Book of Discipline that the first five disciples were brahmins but still it has become a widespread assumption in the Buddhist world. Dharmanand Kosambi has rightly questioned this. Anyway, once someone has entered the Saṅgha, he loses his caste!

Since it was a rule of the Buddha to go serially from door to door, he would sometimes stand in front of a brahmin's house. Once he stood in front of the house of Aggika Bhāradvāja.[290] At that time, a pudding prepared with ghee (clarified butter), a delicacy, was cooked in his house. The brahmin thought that he would put some in the fire as sacrifice and donate the rest. When he saw the Buddha, he said, "One who is well-versed in three Vedas, born in high caste, learned and endowed with wisdom and good conduct should eat this pudding." Then the Buddha explained that one doesn't become a brahmin by birth. After listening to the Buddha's discourse, the brahmin said, "You are a brahmin, you are a brahmin! Please accept my food."

The Buddha explained that he didn't accept food in exchange for teaching Dhamma (that is, after he had taught the Dhamma). "Accepting such a meal is not the Dhamma of the wise."

Not Like Other Animals

In Vāseṭṭha Sutta[291] of the Middle Discourses, we come across an incident that deals with the issue of brahmins.

Once the Buddha was staying in the woods near Icchānaṅgala. Many scholarly brahmins lived in Icchānaṅgala at that time. Vāseṭṭha and Bhāradvāja were two such brahmins. During a stroll, they started discussing what makes a person a brahmin.

Bhāradvāja said that if the man has pure blood for seven generations on both mother and father's side, he is a true brahmin. Vāseṭṭha disagreed and said that a true brahmin was one endowed with morality and wisdom. They couldn't convince each other.

Vāseṭṭha suggested, "Let us go to Samaṇa Gotama." Bhāradvāja agreed. On reaching the Buddha, Vāseṭṭha said that they were both brahmins learned in the three Vedas. Vāseṭṭha said that he was the disciple of Pokkharasāti and Bhāradvāja was the disciple of Tārukkha. They informed the Buddha about their argument and said, "People look at you as 'the Eye that has arisen in the world'. Please resolve our doubt."

Then the Buddha explained the difference between the human and the non-human world. "In grass and trees, there is something that separates them from one another. The same can be said of insects, kites, small and big four-legged animals, serpents, fish, and birds. But in human beings there is no such differentiating characteristic that will separate one caste from another when it comes to hair, head, ears, eyes, mouth, nose, lips, eyebrows, neck, shoulder, stomach, back, buttocks, chest, private parts, hands, legs, fingers, nails, hips, thighs, color or voice.

Some of the nomenclature has come because of profession. Farmer, artisan, trader, employee, thief, warrior, king, *yājaka* (one performs sacrifices), etc. are names given due to professions. Then he put forth the view that one is brahmin due to deeds and not due to birth. He uttered several verses which are similar to the verses from the Dhammapada in meaning. The first verse means, "Just because someone is born to a brahmin mother doesn't make one a brahmin. If he is covetous, then he is a mere 'bhovādin' brahmin in name."

The Tathāgata Stimulated Inner Strength of the Downtrodden

The Tathāgata gave opportunity to many people from downtrodden communities to live a fulfilling life and to stand tall with head held high. Upāli, the barber of the Sākyans, is one such example.

Barber Upāli Goes to the Buddha with the Sākyan Princes

We find Upāli's story in Cūḷavagga[292] of the Book of Discipline (Vinaya Piṭaka).

Six Sākyan princes— Anuruddha, Bhaddiya (who was the king at that time), Ānanda, Bhagu, Kimila and Devadatta—decided to go to the Buddha to seek ordination. They set out with an army as if they were going to the battlefield. Upāli, the barber was with them.

After some distance they sent the army back and crossed the border of the Sākyan republic. Then they removed all their jewelry and tied it in a cloth. They gave the bundle to Upāli and told him that it was sufficient to support him all his life. Upāli started his journey back.

Then a thought entered his mind, "The Sākyans are short-tempered. They might suspect me of murder of the princes and kill me." Then he thought further, "These princes are going to get ordained. Why shouldn't I follow them?"

He then tied the bundle to a tree saying "It is given to one who sees it" and joined the Sākyans. When they saw him, they asked why he had returned. He told them what happened. They too agreed with him.

The six princes went to the Buddha with Upāli. They saluted him and sat to one side. They requested the Buddha, "We Sākyans are very proud. Bhante, this barber Upāli has been our servant for a long time. You should ordain him first so that he becomes our senior in Saṅgha and we will have to salute him, get up and welcome him, greet him with folded hands and do other things suitable for a senior bhikkhu. Doing so will take away our pride in our Sākyan lineage."

Then the Buddha ordained Upāli first and then the Sākyan princes.

In Cūḷavagga of the Book of Discipline[293] we find some other information about Upāli.

A few days after the Buddha's mahāparinibbāna a synod was arranged during the rains retreat to ratify the Dhamma and the Discipline. Five hundred erudite bhikkhus participated in it. This is known as the First Synod or the First Council. At the beginning of the synod, Ven. Mahākassapa said, "Friends, let the Saṅgha listen to me. If the Saṅgha approves, I will ask questions about the Discipline (vinaya) to Upāli."

Then Venerable Upāli said, "Sirs, let the Saṅgha pay attention. If the Saṅgha approves, I will answer questions about the Discipline put to me by Venerable Mahākassapa."

Then Mahākassapa asked him questions and he answered them. Thus the Discipline was ratified.

Discussion

Two reasons are given as to why Upāli didn't return to Kapilavatthu and instead went to the Buddha for ordination. The first one is that he feared for his life if he went to Kapilavatthu with the jewelry as then the Sākyans might suspect him of murder. However, this was the reason only for his not wanting the bundle of jewelry. Going to the Buddha out of fear would not have been in keeping with Dhamma principles. Therefore, the second reason is more important.

Upāli thought that if the Sākyan princes could go forth, surely, he could also do the same. He became curious about the Dhamma and was attracted to the Buddha. He asked himself, "What was it that made the princes give up their royal luxuries?" Surely as one who didn't have those luxuries and whose lot it was to serve others, it was wise to go forth too.

He took the decision not out of fear or helplessness but because he now saw a new possibility, a new goal to aspire to.

This was a momentous decision in his life. The dormant capacity in him to reach the highest goal of human came to life and he made that revolutionary decision.

Upāli Was Ordained Before the Sākyans

The request of the Sākyan princes to the Buddha to ordain Upāli before them was a remarkable event in Indian history. Since the Sākyans had come to the Buddha for ordination, they must have understood the Dhamma taught by him to some extent. They knew that conceit in caste had no place in the Buddha's Saṅgha. Their request shows that they were starting their homeless life on the right note. It shows how even an introduction to the Dhamma can bring about a fundamental change in life.

Apparently Small But Very Significant

Upāli was a servant of the Sākyans for many years. He saluted them, attended on them, got up to greet them with folded hands and served them in various ways. The Sākyans had a very high social status and he was a low caste. He was also much younger in age. If the Sākyans were given ordination before him, their earlier relation would have continued in the Saṅgha. Though they would have been equals in Saṅgha, still their seniority in Saṅgha would have meant that he continued to salute them. Thus, it would have appeared as if the old order was continuing. This would have not helped the Sākyans to remove their conceit in their caste. And Upāli too would have remained servile. This meant that even though they had accepted the Saṅgha that was based on equality, the relation would have been tainted by the past.

Several things happened due to the ordination of Upāli. The Sākyans started saluting him. They started showing their respect in other ways too. The Sākyans lost their pride. Upāli too lost his feeling of being a servant. It is one thing to salute a senior bhikkhu and a totally different thing to salute someone who for a long time was one's servant. And there was no force, no material enticement behind such a salutation. It happened merely because the mind was becoming pure.

This event presented an ideal example in front of Indian society. It is not just about Sākyans and Upāli. It is also about how the qualities dormant in Upāli as a person and as a bhikkhu were developed by the Buddha into a great tree laden with fruit. This is important. This shows how if one is given an opportunity, one's qualities can flourish. Upāli went on to acquire a very high position in the Saṅgha as the master of monastic discipline.

Once a Servant, Master of Discipline When Given an Opportunity

The Dīpavaṃsa is an important Pali text from Sri Lanka. In the fourth paragraph of this text[294] we find detailed information about Upāli.

The gist is as follows: Five hundred bhikkhus had come together in the First Synod. They recited and ratified the entire Tipiṭaka. Among these bhikkhus, Elder Upāli-Paṇḍita (*paṇḍita* means erudite scholar) was the foremost among those who knew the monastic discipline (Vinaya). In the Synod, Venerable Upāli was asked questions about the Vinaya and as per his answers, the Book of Discipline (Vinaya Piṭaka) was created. In the Dīpavaṃsa after giving the above details about Upāli, he is referred to as *'satimā'* literally the mindful one.

The Dīpavaṃsa goes on to give further details: Sixteen years had passed since the Buddha's passing away and Upāli Paṇḍita was sixty. Dāsaka obtained ordination from him. Then Upāli passed on the entire teaching of the Buddha to Dāsaka. He had learned it directly from the Buddha himself.

Therefore, the Buddha had said about Upāli once, "In my Dispensation, Upāli is the foremost among those who know the monastic discipline." Thus Upāli, who was praised by the Buddha himself, taught the Tipiṭaka to the group of one thousand bhikkhus headed by Dāsaka. While he was teaching Dāsaka, five hundred liberated bhikkhus who were good orators also sat next to Upāli to learn. Venerable Upāli taught the Discipline to the bhikkhus continuously for thirty years after the passing away of the Buddha. He taught to Dāsaka the entire teaching of the Buddha consisting of 84000 discourses and endowed with nine aspects. Dāsaka completed the study of all the Piṭakas and he became a teacher in the Saṅgha. Upāli passed away after passing on the entire Vinaya to Dāsaka Paṇḍita.

In the fifth paragraph of the Dīpavaṃsa, the tradition of Vinaya is repeated. Upāli taught Vinaya for thirty years after the Buddha. He was called Mahājuti (greatly resplendent one). He remained the chief of Vinaya till the end of his life. He passed away at the age of 74 after establishing Dāsaka as the chief of Vinaya.

Mahāvaṃsa[295] also gives details about Upāli. When the First Synod was convened, all the senior bhikkhus appointed Upāli as the chief on all matters of monastic discipline. Mahākassapa sought permission to ask questions and Upāli sought authority from the assembly to answer questions put to him. Kassapa sat on the Seat of Elders to ask questions. Upāli sat on the Seat of the Dhamma to answer questions. Thus all the elders recited Vinaya as per the guidance of Upāli.

Discussion

It is thrilling to see the lofty heights attained by Upāli under the Buddha. He grabbed the opportunity with both the hands. Later on he was referred to as Paṇḍita again and again. It was his erudition that brought him this name. This was a bright example in Indian history.

The Rising Graph of a Servant...

Upāli rose to great heights in knowing the Buddha and the Dhamma. He taught to his disciples 84000 discourses and nine aspects (discourses, expositions, inspired utterances, verses etc) of the Dhamma. This shows his erudition and his devotion.

The epithets used for him are all apt: Elder, Paṇḍita, Māhagaṇī, Mahājuti, etc. The Buddha had said that after him the Dhamma will be the teacher of the Saṅgha. He didn't appoint anyone as his successor. Still, by declaring Upāli as the foremost[296] he had stated his position in the Dispensation. That is why he answered the questions on Vinaya in the First Synod.

The rising graph of a servant inspires us.

Vinaya Piṭaka is the book of monastic discipline. It is the Constitution of the Saṅgha. On one hand, in Vedic tradition the suddas were not allowed even to listen to the Vedas or to utter Vedas and they were given harsh punishments if they did so. On the other hand, we see Upāli being given the respect and authority to ratify and formalize the all important scripture, Vinaya Piṭaka. This did two things. It proved that even a person coming from the lowest social strata has immense talent. It also showed that the ideal that the Tathāgata envisaged could be put into practice.

It is also significant that for thirty years after the Buddha, Upāli was the Chief of Vinaya. This shows that it was not mere pressure or authority of the Buddha that gave this position to Upāli. Had it been the case, it would have been a defeat of his teaching of equality. Had the Saṅgha not accepted the teaching of equality, it would have pushed Upāli aside. But this didn't happen. This is such a joyous thing. It shows that the Buddha's teaching of equality triumphed.

Dāsaka became the chief of Vinaya after Upāli. This too is noteworthy. The name Dāsaka denotes low caste. If Dāsaka was born a sudda (low caste), his becoming the head of Vinaya after Upāli is significant from a sociological point of view.

Mahāvaṃsa calls Dāsaka '*sotthiyo.*'[297] *Sotthiyo* (*Shtrotriya* in Sanskrit) denotes brahminity. The Mahāvaṃsa also says that Dāsaka had studied Vedas for twelve years. Though it is impossible to draw a clear conclusion from this, some observations are pertinent here. It is clear that Upāli was a barber and a servant before becoming a bhikkhu. Even so, Dāsaka who had studied the Vedas for twelve years asked Upāli about certain knotty issues in Vedas which Upāli answered. Dāsaka accepted Upāli's discipleship only after this.

This means that Upāli knew the Vedas. It is not possible that he acquired it from Vedic brahmins since it was against their religion to teach a low caste. Also, he went directly from being a servant of the Sākyas to being a bhikkhu in the Saṅgha. It is possible that Upāli acquired that knowledge in the Saṅgha or from the Buddha.

Similarly, it is possible that Dāsaka didn't acquire his knowledge of Vedas in a brahminical tradition. According to the definition of brahminity in the Dhammapada, even someone born a non-brahmin was called a brahmin and knower of the Vedas under certain circumstances. If Dāsaka was from a lower caste, then we can say that after Upāli again a person from humble background was appointed as the chief of Vinaya. *Sotthiyo* might be related to *svastika* which means benevolent.

Even if Dāsaka was a brahmin it shows the triumph of the Dhamma as it shows that a brahmin by birth became the disciple of a teacher who was barber by birth.

Upāli received respect and fame during his lifetime. After his death too he became famous forever as the First Teacher of Vinaya after the Buddha.

People feel gratitude for him. In countries like Sri Lanka he is remembered with respect. His name is seen used commonly on boards. I saw this and felt deep joy. It shows how the Tathāgata's teaching has the potential to bring a constructive change in society that brings to blossom all latent potential in a man; indeed it brings to blossom the very humanness of a man.

Why Mention Upāli's Caste?

Actually, Upāli's caste had ceased the moment he joined the Saṅgha. Why should one bring it up? Is it wrong to do so? Does it negate the principle of equality of the Buddha? If the revolution of the Buddha was not followed by the counter-revolution of Manusmriti and if that counter-revolution had lost its influence completely in our times, it would have been improper to take up this discussion. However, we still live in an unequal and caste-ridden society. At such a time, it is necessary to look at history and see how the downtrodden were brought to an equal platform. To this end, it is not only proper but also essential to look at the life of Upāli.

Gods Salute a Scavenger

The story of Sunīta, the scavenger, is poignant as well as inspiring. We find Sunīta telling his story in the Theragāthā.[298]

Sunīta says, "I was born in a low caste. I lived in penury. I would hardly get anything to eat. My work was low. I was a scavenger. People used to be disgusted with me. They would insult me. I used to feel inferior and would salute all people. Then one day I saw the Mahāvīra Buddha entering the Magadhan city with his bhikkhu Saṅgha. I put aside my broom and approached him to pay respect. That best of the men stopped out of compassion. I stood to one side after saluting him and requested ordination from him who was the best of all beings. Then the most compassionate teacher said to me, 'Come, bhikkhu' That was my ordination!

"Then I started living alone in forest heedfully, without laziness. I put into practice what the victorious lord had taught me. Then one day, I remembered past lives in the first part of night. I developed the clear and divine eye in the middle part of night. And I destroyed all darkness of defilements within me in the third part of night.

Then when the night was over and the sun had arisen, Sakka and Brahmā saluted me with folded hands. They said to me, "We salute you, the wise one, the best of men, one who has destroyed defilements. You are worthy of worship."

Then seeing me being worshipped by the gods thus, the Buddha smiled and said, "Meditation, following the principles of Dhamma, restraint and subjugation (of defilements) makes one a brahmin. This brahmin is the best."

Discussion

Life's Journey

Sunīta has described his life's journey in an agreeable and straightforward manner. His narration is authentic and lively. There is no exaggeration. He describes his earlier painful condition but he doesn't become melodramatic. There is no self-pity. He also describes attainment of the highest goal of human life. That too is a factual description untainted by self-aggrandizement. In a few words, he tells us the story of a journey that is accomplished, mature and balanced.

Asked for Going Forth, Received Ordination

The seeds of reaching the highest state are inside a human being. The deprivations endured by large sections of society don't let these seeds to germinate, to blossom, to fructify. A scavenger is at the very bottom of this social order. He lives a disadvantaged and lowly life.

In two words 'Come bhikkhu' the Buddha destroyed all the degradation and desecration. No rites. No rituals. No formalities. No complications. Just two words from a pure and compassionate heart. Two words broke down all the boundaries of generations that surrounded the personality of Sunīta. All forces that suppressed him were nullified, and the seed in him burst forth with all the power and all his qualities. He wanted the going forth (the stage before one is admitted to the Saṅgha). Instead he received higher ordination. He became a bhikkhu.

Two Extremes of Indian Social Structure

We should look at the figurative meaning when it is said that Sakka and Brahmā worshipped him. In his earlier deprived state, even humans had disgust for him. Now, even the gods were bowing to him. These are two extremes in Indian society. There is a huge distance between these two.

The Tathāgata removed the distance. He did not uplift Sunīta. It was Sunīta himself who attained the highest goal. But the Tathāgata removed the hindrances in the way.

The Buddha Smiles: An Epic Smile in Indian Cultural History

Sunīta says that when the Buddha saw the gods saluting him with folded hands, the Buddha smiled. This was a singular smile in India's cultural history. It is impossible to describe its meaning in words. This pure and innocent smile denotes a social structure that is equally pure and innocent. The verse that the Buddha uttered at that time gives meaning to his smile. If the word brahmin were to be used for the wise and moral, for lofty and high principles, then people like Sunīta were true brahmins. Commentary on this verse says,[299] "Birth, clan, region, lineage and wealth don't make a person noble (ariya). Morality and wisdom make a person noble."

Ordination of an Outcast

We find in Theragāthā[300] a narration by an Elder (thera) hailing from an outcast community named Sopāka.

Let us first see what the Commentary[301] says about Sopāka before turning our attention to his own narration: Sopāka lost his father when he was four months old. His younger uncle raised him. Soon, he turned seven. Then one day, his uncle became angry because "he fights with my son." He took the seven year old child to a cemetery. There he tied the child's hands with a rope and then tied the child to a dead body. He thought that the wild beasts would eat the child along with the corpse. The uncle didn't kill him. The wild beasts too didn't attack him immediately. The child started lamenting, "Futureless me! What will happen to me? Brotherless me! Who will be my brother? Tied down in cemetery! Who will protect me?" When the Buddha learned about it, he said, "Sopāka, come. Don't be afraid. Look at the Tathāgata."

Sopāka freed from cemetery answered some questions by the Buddha. That was his ordination.

In the Theragāthā, Sopāka says, "Seeing the best amongst men walking in the shadow of his dwelling, I went to him and saluted him. He asked me questions. I answered them fearlessly. He indicated that my answers were correct. Then looking at the bhikkhus, he said, 'Whose gifts of the robes, alms, medicines and residence are used by Sopāka, such people of Aṅga and Magadha are fortunate. O Sopāka, come and meet me daily. Sopāka, consider this as your ordination.' Thus I received ordination at the age of seven. This is my last life. Look at the greatness of the Dhamma!"

Discussion

The Greatness of the Dhamma

The Buddha changed the life of a pariah. People of Aṅga and Magadha started saluting him. This big change is not difficult to perceive. It was important that the Buddha saved his life but it was not as important as the removal of the stain of caste. Saving a life helps one person and the benefit may extend to the family. The Buddha showed the society a new path by making a pariah worthy of worship by higher castes. The Commentary says that the Buddha suggested to him: Don't be shy that you are born in a low caste or that you are young in age. The Buddha gave ordination to Sopāka without any formality. Indeed, this is the greatness of the Dhamma!

In the Theragāthā, we see the story of another Sopāka Thera. We also see stories of Anāthapiṇḍika's servant Dāsaka, Supriya, charioteer Channa, fisherman Yasoja. The Buddha's effort to bring all castes together was becoming successful at least to some extent.

Samaṇas Are Forever Freed from Bondage

We find a question and answer in the Connected Discourses.[302] "Who is freed from slavery forever?"

"Samaṇas are freed from slavery forever."

The same sutta states that khattiyas salute an outcast samaṇa. A pariah when he becomes a samaṇa, is saluted not only by khattiyas but also by gods.

Dr. Ketkar Rejects the Buddha's Work

It was not a significant or praiseworthy thing that the Buddha gave entry to barber Upāli and scavenger Sopāka. Dr. Ketkar says,[303] "**The Buddha's work on casteism**: We cannot say that Gotama was an opponent of caste discrimination or proponent of equality. Bringing proof that he gave entry to a barber or an outcast in his Saṅgha doesn't clarify his position on caste. Anyone's entry in the bachelor Saṅgha doesn't make any difference to social structure… He didn't launch movement against caste but did agitate against brahmins."

If Ketkar had given credit for what the Buddha did and then criticized his shortcomings, his criticism would have been balanced. An objective review of the Buddha's work and pointing its limitations shouldn't upset anyone. But to say that whatever he did was to oppose brahmins, means that Ketkar wanted the birth-rights of the brahmins to be protected.

The Buddha Doesn't Respect Elderly Brahmins?

In the fourth chapter of the Numerical Discourses[304] the Buddha explains who is elderly.

He tells bhikkhus an incident that happened in Uruvelā soon after his enlightenment. He was sitting under a tree in Uruvelā on the bank of Nerañjā river. Then many old, elderly brahmins came to visit him.

They said to him, "Bho Gotama, we have heard that Samaṇa Gotama doesn't salute, doesn't get up to greet and doesn't offer a seat to old, elderly brahmins." The Buddha replied that the allegation is false.

After narrating the event to bhikkhus, the Buddha said, "Bhikkhus, at that time it occurred to me that these people don't know who should be called elderly. Bhikkhus, one may be eighty, ninety or even hundred year old. But if he talks at improper time, talks falsehoods, says meaningless things, talks against the Dhamma and talks against discipline; if he talks without paying heed to time and place, if he talks irrational, aimless and meaningless drivel, then he certainly earns the name 'Childish Elder.'

"On the other hand, if someone with black hair (indicating his youth) speaks at proper time, speaks truth, speaks meaningfully, speaks Dhamma and discipline, he earns the name 'Wise Elder'."

The Buddha gave a detailed explanation of the four things that decide an elder. These are: morality, knowledge, four absorptions (concentrations) and destruction of defilements.

Irrational Expectation

Some brahmins were complaining against the Buddha though he was particular about following etiquette and was always civil. He was polite even with those much younger to him. He was never uncivil when talking to those who opposed him. Why did then these brahmins complain against him? Because they had irrational expectations.

The Tathāgata gave more importance to morality than to age. Manusmriti[305] that was written about four centuries after the Buddha took a similar view.

Once a learned young man was teaching to ignorant elderly people. In the flow of his talk, he addressed them as 'children.' They became upset and complained to the gods. The verdict of the gods was, "Age in years, white hair, wealth and relations are not important. Whoever is learned is great in our view… this is the *dharma* of sages… just because someone has white hair doesn't mean he is an elderly. One who is learned though young, is called an elderly by the gods."

Even so, there is a great difference between the views of the Buddha and that of Manusmriti. The Buddha's principle was applicable to all castes. It allowed a virtuous *sudda* or *vessa* (lower castes) to be elder to an immoral khattiya or brahmin. When Manusmriti considers erudition as a criterion, it applies only within brahmins.

Kumārila Bhaṭṭa's Insensitive Shamelessness

Kumārila Bhaṭṭa shamelessly represented this mentality of some brahmins in his text Tantravartika[306] while writing on Mimāṃsasutra of Jaimini:

"One past view has come up in front of us that would make it suitable to dwell, live and draw boundary *(Vihāra, ārāma* and *maṇḍala)*; as also will be in keeping with the Buddha's guidance on seclusion, meditative absorptions, study, non-violence, truthful speech, restrain, charity and compassion."

In other words, the opinion that has come to Kumārila Bhaṭṭa is that the Buddha's guidance should be taken as reliable and trustworthy. Kumārila Bhaṭṭa rejected this opinion with one word 'no'. According to him (and his tradition), only certain texts are approved as religious scriptures (Shāstrās) and in these texts the books of the Buddha and arahatas are not included. Therefore, the Buddha's words cannot be taken as evidence. They cannot be relied on.

Kumārila writes, "Fourteen or eighteen sources of learning have been decided that are acceptable as standards of Dharma by the gentry. The Vedas, Upavedas, Aṅgas, Upa-aṅgas, etc. are such sources. Books by the Buddhas or arahatas are not included in the standards of Dharma which are Purāṇas, Shāstrās, Shikshā, Daṇḍanītī, etc."

Then he adds, "Therefore, the Dharma one learns from those Shāstrās that do not transgress the source of Vedas is the only beneficial Dharma... That which is understood by a low caste, such a learning is not acceptable. Similarly even logical words of those that that transgress the Vedas are not acceptable. The Purāṇas say that in Kaliyuga, the Sākyans are the cause of decay of Dharma. Who then would listen to the Sākyans. Even if the origin of the principle of non-violence is good, but it comes from the Sākyans and appears to be Dharma. Therefore, it is as useless and unacceptable (unreliable) as the milk put in the bag made of dog's skin. It is found only in their texts. Therefore, as long as it is not found in the texts that are considered standards of Dharma, it is not acceptable. When one scripture decides a meaning and since it is proved by that scripture, other texts are useless. Therefore, anything not found in the standard texts such as Vedas etc. should be rejected."

While describing the *pramāṇa* (standard) of self-satisfaction *(ātma-tushṭi)*, Kumārila again attacks the Buddha. He writes, "The Sākyan speaks with malice while censuring Vedas and brahmins. He feels satisfied in doing so. A person who indulges in unwholesome deeds gets the same satisfaction as this. Similarly, brahmins feel satisfied in sacrifices *(yajñas)* involving killing of animals. But the Sākyans become pained and distressed; and get angry with the sacrifices *(yajñas)*."

Discussion

The words *vihāra, ārāma* and *maṇḍala* are associated with Buddhist culture. To say that their creation is good is to accept Buddhism to some extent in a way.

To say that the principles of meditation, non-violence and truth (promoted by the Buddha) were not against the standards or proofs (that lead to knowledge of truth) was an acknowledgement of the Buddha's teaching. Therefore, he rejects it with a 'no'.

Won't Accept Even if it is Logical!

Kumārila Bhaṭṭa rejected the Buddha's teaching summarily. Why? Was it wrong? Was it based on falsehood? Was it illogical? Was it unethical? No, he didn't reject it because of these reasons. He rejected it because Buddhist scriptures are not included in the scriptures considered standard by Vedics. It is clear that in his opinion, it didn't matter if the view was truthful and ethical; and if it was beneficial for humanity.

It was an adamant stand that no matter how good the views of a text or a person may be, if our tradition doesn't accept it, we will reject them. On the other hand, even if our scriptures tell us falsehood, unethical and harmful things, we honor those views.

Any reasonable man can decide whether Kumārila's stand promotes proper learning or destroys it. By rejecting even logical knowledge of low caste persons, he showed that he was speaking out of an arrogance that abhorred true knowledge.

Fear Due to Feelings of Inferiority

Kumārila felt that accepting the Buddha's teaching would lead to loss of their Dharma. Loss of their Dharma meant loss of caste system. He felt that to protect the Vedic system that gave him dominance and superiority based on caste, he had to reject equality and humanity. He was frightened of the consequences if the Buddha's thoughts were allowed to spread freely.

Transgressing Civility

One can understand his desperate attempts to preserve the system but his argument later on goes beyond common courtesy and crosses the boundaries of civil behavior. He says that even though the principles of non-violence etc. are good, they have become corrupt because they have come from the mouth of someone who is not allowed to teach the Dharma!

The simile given by him is clear. The principles of truth, non-violence, etc. are acceptable and enjoyable like milk. But if the same milk is offered in a bag made of dog's skin, it won't be acceptable. Thus the Tathāgata is like a bag of dog-skin. Those who say that Tathāgata was against brahmins should look at this offspring of Vedic culture and pause to give it a thought. While describing the mentality of caste bias, Uruvelā Dhammaratana Thera says,[307] "Kumārila Bhaṭṭa's story can be taken as an example of this mentality. The Tathāgata is against caste. Therefore, Kumārila pours vitriol on him."

The Thera's comment is mild and it is a tribute to the Buddha's teaching that he didn't stoop to Kumārila's level.

Swami Vivekanand on Kumārila Bhaṭṭa

While talking about Kumārila Bhaṭṭa, Swami Vivekanand's speech on 31 March, 1901 throws light on his views on Buddhists,[308] *"And to the Brahmins I say, 'Vain is your pride of birth and ancestry. Shake it off. Brahminhood, according to your Shāstrās, you have no more now, because you have for so long lived under Mlechchha kings. If you at all believe in the words of your own ancestors, then go this very moment and make expiation by entering into the slow fire kindled by Tusha (husks), like that old Kumārila Bhaṭṭa, who with the purpose of ousting the Buddhists first became a disciple of Buddhists and then defeating them in argument became the cause of death to many, and subsequently entered the Tushanala (a fire of husk) to expiate his sins. If you are not bold enough to do that, then admit your weakness and stretch forth a helping hand, and open the gates of knowledge to one and all, and give the downtrodden masses once more their just and legitimate rights and privileges."*

Even if You Have Gone Forth from High Caste…

The Buddha used to take care that there should be no discrimination based on caste, wealth, etc. We see this in the Middle Discourses.[309]

Once he was dwelling at Jetavana in Sāvatthi. He called the bhikkhus one day and addressed them, "Bhikkhus, I will tell you about an honorable and a dishonorable man's personality characteristics. Listen carefully."

The gist of his discourse is: Someone who has gone forth from a high caste thinks. "I have gone forth from a high caste. These other bhikkhus are from low caste." Thus he is conceited and disparages others. This is a quality of dishonorable man.

On the other hand, an honorable man who has gone forth from a high caste thinks thus, "I was born in high caste. This alone doesn't make me free from craving, aversion and ignorance. If someone has gone forth from a low caste and he follows the

Dhamma and the Discipline; follows the right path; then he is worthy of respect and praise." He does not have conceit about his caste and does not disparage others. This is a quality of an honorable man.

What is true of one from high caste is also true from one who comes from a wealthy family. The same applies to one who is famous and successful.

One who feels pride in robes, alms food, etc. is a dishonorable man while one who doesn't feel pride when he gets robes etc. is an honorable man.

The same applies to one who is erudite… learned in Discipline… orator of the Dhamma… forest dweller… wearer of patched robe… eating only food obtained from going on alms rounds (not accepting invitations to meals)… living only under a tree (not living in a building)… living in a cemetery.

One whose perception *(saññā)* has ceased, views everything with wisdom *(paññā)*. The Buddha described him, "Bhikkhus, such a bhikkhu has no conceit, has no arrogance anywhere and is not haughty in his conduct towards anyone."

Discussion

Equality

The Buddha insisted that there should be equality in the Saṅgha. There was certainly some difference due to morality and period since going forth (seniority), etc. However, this didn't create undesirable feelings of superiority or inferiority. The original family of the bhikkhu was not important. What was important was whether one was eradicating his defilements.

Lack of conceit was important not only in matters of clan but also about desirable things that one strives for and follows on the path of the Dhamma. There is a detailed discussion in this sutta about how one's mind can get polluted with pride. It also tells how joyous it is to make oneself pure-hearted.

Pride in Caste Is Cause of Defeat

More than twenty five centuries ago, the Buddha told the world in all earnestness that pride in caste leads to defeat. He also made every effort to take people beyond caste. We see his burning message in Parābhava Sutta (Discourse on Defeat) in the Suttanipāta.[310]

Once while he was dwelling at Jetavana in Sāvatthi, a deity asked him the reasons for the defeat of a man. The Buddha gave several reasons. One of the verses says, "Someone is vain due to caste, vain due to wealth, vain due to lineage. One considers oneself higher than one's brethren. This vanity is the cause of his defeat."

It seems that even after twenty-five centuries, Indian society is not willing to pay attention to this warning. It's as if the taste of defeat is inebriating! One fears coming out of defeat!! Even then it is certain that one day the Buddha's words will touch the heart and mind of our society and it will come out of all these things; it will come out of all defeats!!

9

I Don't Burn Wood: I Light the Flame Inside

Just as the Buddha rejected the authority of Vedas and the caste system, he also set aside the system of sacrifices *(*yajñas*)* which was a major pillar of the establishment. There were several reasons for his opposition to *yajñas*.

First and foremost, he didn't approve of the killing of animals in *yajñas*. Of the five precepts prescribed by him, abstaining from killing was the first. This was in accordance with his principles of non-violence and compassion to animals but there were also other factors.

People were told that yajñas (sacrifices) lead to heaven. This cause and effect relation between sacrifices and heaven was deceptive. The ritual of yajñas was not useful for purification of mind. The Buddha also opposed other irrational and deceptive things such as rituals involving torturing oneself, miracles, good and bad omens and astrology.

The Buddha Opposed Killing in Yajñas (Sacrifices)

Killing Cows Harmed Agriculture

Often, the animals were taken forcefully and this hurt the owners of the animals. This forced sacrifice was unfair. The large scale slaughter of cattle had an adverse effect on agriculture. Thus in addition to the basic principle of non-violence there was also a practical or economical reason. The Suttanipāta[311] tells us more about it.

Once the Buddha was dwelling in Sāvatthi. One day many elderly and well-known brahmins came to meet him. They asked him whether the qualities of the brahmins of the past were seen in the brahmins at that time. The Buddha said no.

Then they asked him what the qualities of the brahmins of the past were. The Buddha narrated qualities such as selflessness, erudition, etc. and added, "In yajñas (sacrifices) of the past they didn't kill cows. Like our parents, siblings and other relations, cows are our great friends. They give us medicines. They give us food, strength, complexion and happiness. Considering these things, they didn't kill cows."

Discussion

The Buddha made it clear that the cattle were an integral part of the life of the majority of people. Cattle were required for agricultural work, for milk and for manure (cow dung is an excellent manure). Many people depended on cows even as many continue to do today. Such animals are dear to them. They are like family to them. Seeing such an animal being killed gave immense pain to people. The Buddha understood their pain and opposed violence in fire sacrifices. The ancient brahmins that the Buddha referred to could have been non-Vedic priests of the Indus civilization.

Large Scale Killing in Yaññas (Yajñas)

Yañña Sutta[312] in the Connected Discourses is important to understand the Buddha's view on killing in yaññas (sacrificial rituals). It describes an event in Sāvatthi.

King Pasenadi of Kosala decided to conduct a huge sacrifice . Five hundred bulls, five hundred calves, five hundred milking cows, five hundred goats and five hundred sheep were tied to sacrificial pillars. The slaves, workers, and servants had been threatened. They were all going about their work with tears in their eyes. That morning, some bhikkhus came to Sāvatthi for alms round. After returning from their alms round, they went to the Buddha and narrated the scene of the sacrifice.

The Buddha uttered four verses, which have been translated by Bhikkhu Bodhi in his Connected Discourses of the Buddha:

The horse sacrifice, human sacrifice,
Sammpasa, vājapeya, nirggala:
These big sacrifices, fraught with violence,
Do not bring great fruit.

The great seers of right conduct
Do not attend that sacrifice
Where goats, sheep and cattle
Of various kinds are slain.

But when yajñas free from violence
Are always offered by family custom,
Where no goats, sheep, or cattle
Of various kinds are slain:
The great seers of right conduct
Attend a sacrifice like this.

The wise person should offer this,
A sacrifice bringing great fruit.
For one who makes such sacrifice
It is indeed better, never worse.
Such a sacrifice is truly vast
And the gods too are pleased.

Discussion

A large number of animals were slaughtered in the sacrificial ritual *(yaññas, yajñas)*. There is no reason to believe that the numbers given here are wildly inflated because the descriptions of animal slaughter in Vedic tradition confirm the numbers.

The condition of servants and workers when they were tying the animals to sacrificial posts and going about their work is heartrending. Their hearts bled at the thought of the imminent wanton slaughter. We don't see many such descriptions of the mental state of the servants in other descriptions of sacrifices. It is possible that the servants were not willing to help in killing and wanted to leave. Hence they were threatened with violence.

When the wealthy and powerful were showing how their minds had become cold and numb, the ordinary workers were showing great sensitivity and compassion for the animals. This could have been the effect of the atmosphere created by the Buddha's teaching. Seeing the royal servants in tears, the bhikkhus also felt it necessary to inform the Buddha.

Vedics believed that animal sacrifices brought merits and this merits took them to heaven. *Ashvamedha* (horse sacrifice) was considered the king among the sacrifices. A horse used to be killed in it. Some believed that since a human being is more valuable than a horse, killing a human in *yajña* brought even more merit. Countless rituals were performed during the sacrifices. People were lead to believe that all this resulted in great benefit to the one who performed the sacrifices.

The concept of *yajñas* had dominated and overpowered Indian society. The Buddha opposed it courageously and with determination. He disabused the people of the notion of great merits earned in the *yajñas*. He didn't just voice his own views but also said that all wise sages opposed sacrifices. These sages were, in all likelihood, from the samaṇa tradition.

He noted the opinion of good sages that if one had to perform sacrificial rituals, these should be without killing and without meaningless rites. These should be joyful to people and protect animal life. A true sage would never have violence in yajña. The Buddha offered the option of non-violent yajñas to those who were attached to the concept of yajña. Such a sacrifice was beneficial. If the deities were indeed of wholesome disposition, they wouldn't approve of the violent sacrifices but would be happy with the non-violent sacrifices. It would also prove their 'godliness!'

Disapproval of Violent Sacrifices

Once a brahmin named Ujjaya came to meet the Buddha[313] and asked the Buddha if he approved of the ritual of sacrifice. The Buddha replied, "O brahmin, I don't approve of all the sacrifices. Also, it is not true that I don't approve all sacrifices."

The Buddha explained that he was not in favor of sacrifices where cows, goats, sheep, hens, pigs etc. were slaughtered. Neither liberated sages (arahatas) nor those on the path of liberation come to such sacrifices. On the other hand, I approve of sacrifices where there is no violence. Giving in charity is a good sacrifice. Wise should perform such a sacrifice. It gives great results.

In the sutta following this one, Udāyī asked him the same question and the Buddha gave the same answer. The verses differ but the meaning is not different. When the Buddha says that arahatas don't attend such sacrifices it is clear that the Samaṇa tradition opposed the violence even before the Buddha. The Buddha opposed it with greater determination, greater organization and greater strength. This did have the effect of reducing the sacrifices of Vedics.

Pushyamitra Shunga started a counter-revolution in the form of Manusmriti. He performed Horse Sacrifice to decry the Buddha's opposition to violent sacrifices. The charity taught by the Buddha was for an ethical person, an ethical cause. The charity taught by Manusmriti was for brahmins alone. Thus they were very different.

Dhamma Yajña Better Than Material Yajña

A sacrifice in which material things are sacrificed is a material sacrifice. The Numerical Discourses[314] say that the

Dhamma yajña is greater than material yajña. In other words, it is better to follow the Dhamma, (the Noble Eightfold Path) than offering meat, oil, etc. to fire.

A Brahmin Stops Violent Yajña After the Buddha's Advice

Once Uggatasarira brahmin was going to perform a great sacrifice.[315] He had brought five hundred bulls, calves, milking cows, sheep and goats to the sacrificial place. After the preparation was complete, he went to the Buddha and said, "I have heard that bringing fire for the yajña and erecting the sacrificial pillar are auspicious deeds that bring much merit."

The Buddha said that he had also heard likewise. Then the brahmin said it the second time and also the third time. Again the Buddha also said that he had heard it likewise the second and the third time. Then he said, "Master Gotama, then your and my views match completely."

Then Ven Ānanda advised the brahmin, "Don't ask such questions to the Tathāgata. Tell him, 'I wish to bring fire. I wish to erect a sacrificial pillar. Give me advice that will be for my good and happiness for a long time."

Then he requested the Buddha for advice. Then the Buddha told him, "Brahmin, a person who brings fire and erects a sacrificial pillar, even before he does so, picks up three weapons that are unwholesome, painful and that bring suffering as a consequence. These three weapons are weapons of body, speech and mind. When he thinks, 'Let me kill so many bulls for the yajña.' Thinking 'I earn merit' he earns demerit. Thinking 'this is a wholesome deed' he performs an unwholesome deed. Thinking 'I am searching a path for a good afterlife' he discovers a path that leads in the opposite direction. This is the weapon of mind. Then he speaks out, 'I should kill so many bulls in yajña.' This is the weapon of speech. Then he starts killing the bulls. This is weapon of body.

"Give up the fire of craving, aversion and ignorance; keep it away. One who is under the influence of this fire performs evil deeds with body, speech and mind and goes to miserable states.

"You should welcome three fires. The 'deserving of honor' fire, householder fire and 'deserving of offering' fire. Parents are 'deserving of honor' fire. They are the reason of our birth. Therefore, one should honor them. Wife, children and servants are householder fire. Those samaṇas and brāhmaṇas who abstain from maligning others, are endowed with forbearance and humility and are restrained—such samaṇas and brāhmaṇas are 'deserving of offering' fire.

"The fire that is built from wood needs to be lighted from time to time, needs to extinguished from time to time, and needs to be preserved from time to time."

The brahmin was satisfied with the answer. He requested to be accepted as a disciple. "I will set the animals free. Let them eat green grass. Let them drink cool water. Let them enjoy cool breeze."

Discussion

The Buddha brought about a total change of heart in Uggatasarira with his benign and touching discourse. He suggested that instead of violence, one should perform a sacrifice wherein one honors one's parents with gratitude. The man who was bent on killing animals, now started thinking of them being free and enjoying nature's bounty. His heart melted and became delicate and sensitive. His harshness turned into benevolent non-violence.

Another's Life Is as Important as One's Own

The Tathāgata was dwelling at Jetavana in Sāvatthi.[316]

King Pasenadi was in the upper floor of his palace with Queen Mallika.

He asked Mallika, "Is there anyone who is more beloved to you than yourself?"

The queen answered, “O King, to speak the truth, there is no one who is dearer to me than myself. Is there anyone who is more beloved to you than yourself?”

The king too answered, “Mallika, truly there is none who is dearer to me than myself.”

Then the king went to the Buddha and narrated the conversation.

Then the Buddha uttered an *udāna*, “Even after the mind has searched in all directions, it finds none that is more beloved to it than oneself. Similarly, to each one life is dear. Looking at oneself, one should not kill.”

Eating Meat

At the time of the Buddha and after him, critics have been distorting facts and creating confusion about the Buddha’s view on eating meat. Jīvaka Sutta[317] of the Middle Discourses is crucial to understand him on this issue.

Once he was dwelling in the mango grove of Jīvaka. One day, Jīvaka came to him and said, “Venerable sir! I have heard it being said, ‘People kill animals for Samaṇa Gotama. Even knowing that the animal is killed for his sake, Gotama eats it.’ Bhante, do these people speak the truth? Do they accuse you falsely?”

The Buddha replied that it was a lie and that these people were making false allegations. He then said, “Jīvaka, I have prohibited three kinds of meat: seen, heard and doubted. On the other hand, I have permitted three kinds of meat: unseen, unheard and undoubted.”

Then the Buddha explained his directions about alms food. “A bhikkhu dwells with loving compassion. At such a time, he is invited for a meal. The bhikkhu goes to the householder the next day. He is served food. The bhikkhu doesn’t expect to be served choice food. Whatever is served, he eats without attachment. Is such a meal flawless?”

Jīvaka said yes.

The Buddha told him that just as if the roots of a tree are cut, his craving, aversion and ignorance had been destroyed.

To further clarify his point, he added, "Jīvaka, anyone who kills an animal for the Buddha or his disciple earns five fold demerit."

The first demerit was to ask the animal to be brought.

The second demerit was to drag the animal with rope round its neck.

The third demerit was to ask the animal to be slaughtered.

The fourth demerit was the pain that the animal endured when it was killed.

The fifth demerit was serving wrong food to the Tathāgata or his disciples.

Jīvaka agreed that the bhikkhus partake flawless food, and requested to be accepted as a disciple.

Discussion

The Buddha's teaching on non-violence and meat-eating was very clear. There was no place for any doubt in it. He prohibited deliberate eating of meat. However, if a bhikkhu is offered meat in alms he was not to reject it. This flexibility was necessary because bhikkhus were expected to eat whatever was put in their alms bowl. He taught the Middle Path. This was applicable in all fields of life.

The Buddha had set three conditions about when to accept or reject meat in alms. If a bhikkhu had seen that the animal was killed for him or if he had heard any report that the animal was killed for his sake or if he doubted that the animal was killed for him; a bhikkhu should reject the meat in offered in alms.

Someone may say that rather than putting such conditions why he didn't ban all meat eating outright. The answer is clear. Most bhikkhus go from one door to door on their alms round. They are expected not to miss any house. In each house, food is prepared as per the habits, inclinations and tastes of that household. Food is not prepared for alms. If meat is cooked in a house, then part of that will go to alms. Then it is improper to say 'no'. A bhikkhu doesn't have that freedom. A bhikkhu can't avoid alms from a householder where meat is eaten and can't throw away food given in alms.

Someone may say that this is an escape route left open for meat eating. Bhikkhus were not always going on alms round. Sometimes, they received invitations to take meals in homes. Then how can such a meal, if it is meat, be acceptable?

The Buddha told about five sins regarding meat in alms food to Jīvaka. He makes it clear that it is a big demerit to kill for the Buddha or his disciples. It is clear that he prohibits householders who invite bhikkhus for meals from offering meat to them. But if a family had cooked meat for themselves or if they only had meat to offer, then he didn't want the bhikkhus to be adamant.

Meager Meals

Since we are on the topic of meat, let us see what the Buddha said about food. He gave importance to being restrained in food. He constantly advocated 'knowing the measure of one's food' that is, not overeating. The Buddha said that such a meal was beneficial for the bhikkhus. It was applicable to all but was even more important for bhikkhus. The Buddha said, "A bhikkhu who is moral, controlled, restrained in eating and mindful, doesn't fall down. He is close to nibbāna."[318]

The Buddha himself ate small meals. He also taught people to eat less. The Connected Discourses[319] contain a story about how his advice benefited King Pasenadi.

Once the Buddha was staying in Sāvatthi. King Pasenadi used to overeat. Once he came to the Buddha after his meal. He was panting because he had overeaten. Then the Buddha uttered a verse which meant: The mindful person who knows the measure of food (is restrained in food), his pain decreases. He is able to digest his food and such food helps to protect his life.

When the Buddha uttered this verse, a youth named Sudassana was standing behind King Pasenadi. The king told him, "Look Sudassana, learn this verse from the Tathāgata and every time I sit down for meals, repeat it. For this I will give you a hundred coins every day."

Sudassana started doing likewise. It helped the king to eat less. Then one day while stroking his own now healthy body, he said, "The Tathāgata has showered compassion on me for my wellbeing here and hereafter."

Discussion

Restraint in food was a characteristic of the Buddha's lifestyle. He used to eat only one meal a day. For forty-five years he followed this principle of eating less and constantly wandering to spread the Dhamma. He never used any vehicle. He walked everywhere.

Dr. Ketkar's Allegations

Some critics have made derisive comments on him out of prejudice. Dr. Ketkar says about his last meal,[320] "From Questions of Milinda, it seems that Gotama had eaten so much food that he couldn't tolerate it, he had indigestion leading to diarrhea."

The Buddha was eighty when he ate the meal about which Dr. Ketkar writes with so much malice. He had just recovered from a severe illness. His health had become fragile. His digestion was weak. Therefore, he had indigestion after Cunda's meal. This doesn't mean that he overate. Sometimes, a sick person can't digest even a spoonful. If someone then says that that person overate, we question his intelligence. The Tathāgata's body was subject to the same laws of nature—that is all.

The text that Dr. Ketkar refers to, Questions of Milinda, is in the form of questions and answers between King Milinda (Menander) and Bhikkhu Nāgasena. It is from the first century BCE. Thus it is four-five hundred years after the Buddha. But due to its importance it is included in the Tipiṭaka in the Myanmar tradition. Because Dr Ketkar is giving reference from a text from Buddhist tradition, people may believe that he is right. Therefore, we must look at the original dialogue in this text[321] and analyze it.

Contradiction Pointed Out by Milinda

King Milinda had two details about the life of the Buddha that he found difficult to reconcile with each other. He felt that one of them must be false.

The first detail is: The Elders who organized the First Synod said, "After eating the food offered by Cunda, the Buddha suffered from intense pains and he became sick. I have heard thus."

The second detail is: The meal that the Buddha ate before he became enlightened and the last meal he ate before he passed into *mahāparinibbāna* — both these meals were equally meritorious. Both the meals give the same fruit. These fruits are greater than any other alms offered to the Buddha and are praiseworthy. This is what the Buddha had told Ānanda.

Milinda thought that the information given by the Elders and the opinion expressed by the Buddha himself are contradictory. If Cunda's meal caused severe illness to the Buddha, then the first detail is wrong. If the meal made him sick, caused disease, ended his life, then how can it bring immense good fortune? This was Milinda's question. He also adds that it was rumored that the Buddha overate and as a result had bloody diarrhea. He wanted clarification to put an end to this rumor.

Disease Was Old, According to Nāgasena

Nāgasena agrees with what Milinda says about the two details. Then he says that the meal of Cunda were nourishing and praiseworthy. He adds that the deities added divine flavor to the meal as they knew that this would be his last meal. The food given by Cunda was properly cooked, tasty, nutritious, having many flavors and agreeable to stomach. He says to Milinda, "O King, the Buddha was already ailing. He had pre-existing disease. His body had become frail. His life force had become weak. Therefore, his pre-existing disease further worsened."

Similes Used by Nāgasena

To explain how this happened, he used three similes. If there is already fire and someone adds fuel to it, then the fire increases. If there is a flow of water and there is rain, the flow increases further. If the stomach is full and one eats some more, the abdomen gets bloated.

Milinda Was Satisfied

After the three similes, Nāgasena said that it was not the fault of the meal. Milinda was satisfied. They then discussed other issues of the Dhamma. Those are beyond the scope of present discussion. It suffices to say that Milinda was satisfied with Nāgasena's explanation.

Discussion

Milinda's Question and Ketkar's Allegation Are Different

What is the dilemma in front of Milinda? What Elders said and what the Buddha had opined appeared contradictory. How can a meal that caused the death of the Buddha be greatly meritorious and if it was indeed a meritorious meal than how come the Buddha died afterwards? He felt that one of the two was wrong. He expected Nāgasena to explain.

The conflict in Milinda's mind had nothing to do with the Buddha's alleged overeating. The issue of overeating is incidental but outside the purview of Milinda's dilemma. Therefore, first we will deal with Milinda's dilemma.

No Cause and Effect Relation Between the Meal and the Disease

What is Nāgasena's answer? He says that what both the Elders and the Buddha said was true. He didn't say that either one of them or both of them didn't say it. He says that the Buddha's praise for the meal was appropriate as the meal indeed was nutritious. Then were the Elders wrong. No. If you look at the similes given by Nāgasena, it is clear that there is no cause and effect relationship between the meal and the disease.

Milinda understands the Elders' statement wrongly "After eating the food offered by Cunda, the Buddha suffered from intense pains and he became sick."

There is no reason to believe that there is a cause and effect relationship between the meal and the disease. There is a temporal relation but not a causal one, according to Nāgasena. He gives a suitable answer to Milinda.

People often take temporal relation to be causal. It is possible that some of the Elders did this and thus in a way contradicted the Buddha's opinion. If that had actually happened, we would have to accept Milinda's option of rejecting the Elders' statements as wrong. But Nāgasena made it clear that the Buddha's opinion was true.

The Buddha's Body Had Already Become Frail

Nāgasena says that the Buddha's body had already become frail. He uses the word *pakatidubbala. Pakati* here means originally. It had become frail by nature due to disease. He said that the Buddha had a pre-existing disease. Was he right? Yes, he was hundred percent right!

If one looks at all the information from Mahāparinibbāna Sutta, we see that three months before his passing away, the Buddha had suffered from a life-threatening disease that had shaken Ānanda. But the Buddha survived through sheer will power for he wanted to take proper leave of the bhikkhus.

He told Ānanda while leaving Vesāli that it was the last time he was seeing Vesāli. He also told Ānanda that he was eighty, had become old and frail, had come to the end of his life's journey, and his body was like a dilapidated chariot, which had been mended at many places. It is clear that he knew that his life's end was near. This was all before the meal offered by Cunda.

The Buddha's body was frail. His life force had become weak. This resulted in aggravation in his earlier disease and resulted in his death. There was no question of Cunda's meal being the cause of his death. The Buddha himself knew this. Therefore, he had told Ānanda to make sure that no one blamed Cunda for his death.

Cunda is to be Envied

One can understand that Cunda should not be blamed but why is this meal as meritorious as the one after which the Buddha became enlightened? It is not difficult to answer this question.

The last morsel of food is no ordinary thing. In Indian society, the right to offer the last sip of water to a dying person is reserved for the true descendent, true inheritor. It carries great significance as to who offers the last sip of water to the dying person. When we take this into consideration, we understand the significance of Cunda's meal. And we also understand why the Buddha compared it to the meal after which he became enlightened. Not only is Cunda not to be blamed, he had the great fortune to give the last meal to the Buddha. Indeed, Cunda is to be envied for his great fortune!

Subject Real, Simile Imaginary

Let us now turn to Nāgasena's similes. Here we should understand that what is being described is real. It is the subject under discussion. To explain it one uses similes, which helps one to understand the subject under consideration. For example, when we say 'that warrior is like a lion', the lion is not present and not real. Similes are from a different category and don't have any direct connection to the original subject.

Eating More While Stomach Is Full Is a Simile

Nāgasena gives three similes for the same subject while answering Milinda. Let us make a chart to understand this.

Subject	Simile
Earlier state:	**Earlier state:**
Body is already frail. There is pre-existing disease	1. Fire is already lit 2. Water is already flowing 3. Stomach is already full
In addition to earlier state:	**In addition to earlier state:**
Life force has become weak	1. More fuel was added 2. More rain came down 3. Ate further
Result:	**Result:**
The disease increased further	1. Fire burns further 2. Flow of stream increases 3. Abdomen is bloated

Someone may ask why go into so much detail of these similes. Perhaps, this would have been unnecessary if Nāgasena had given only first two similes. But the third one, if not understood correctly, may create confusion in the minds of people. Therefore, it is necessary to make it clear that just as the two conditions in the first two similes were not real and didn't exist; the condition in the third simile didn't exist.

The similes are always from different categories and are used 'just as' or 'as if.' The reason for using 'just as' is because they are not real. Here the third simile of an already full stomach and an additional food is a condition that didn't exist and had nothing to do with the food eaten by the Buddha. Anyone who understands similes would understand this. In conclusion, there is no basis for Dr. Ketkar's allegations in this simile.

It is true that this simile gave an opportunity, however small and unreasonable, to malevolent people to create confusion. The first and second similes of fire and flow of water were enough. It is also possible that the third one was added later on with the intention of creating confusion!

The Meal Didn't Cause Death

Nāgasena didn't give a direct answer to the question of Milinda: "How can a meal after which the Buddha passed away be of great merit?"

But his discussion does explain it automatically. The meal of Cunda didn't give rise to any new illness. The meal indeed had several good qualities. Nāgasena says it with emphasis. It should be clear that the meal didn't cause the death of the Buddha.

Milinda Felt That It Was the Rumor-mongering by Opponents

Milinda put forth one more issue, which seems to be the basis for Dr. Ketkar's allegations about the Buddha greedy overeating. Here we must remember that it was not Milinda's doubt but he had quoted it as a rumor, whisper-campaign, mockery and false propaganda spread by opponents or other people. He felt that these rumors should be answered and should not be allowed to spread. He wanted Nāgasena to give clarification to remove any confusion.

It Is a Mere Premise

Nāgasena doesn't seem to answer this directly. One possibility is that this rumor didn't come to him. It is also not related to the main question of Milinda. Perhaps, it was added later.

But let us keep aside the issue whether it was originally present or not; and assume for the time being that it was indeed asked. Even then it doesn't stand the test of logic as it is a mere premise, not a hypothesis. This premise of the allegations of opponents is not the view of either Milinda or of Nāgasena. Naturally, it is not the view of the text, Questions of Milinda.

It Is Part of Ketkar's Manipulative Argument

Thus it is clear that though Ketkar pretends that he is making the statement on the basis of a text, it is a blatant misdirection. Ketkar bases his argument on malicious allegations. By casually mentioning the Milindapañha, he gives the impression that his allegation has basis in Buddhist tradition.

Nāgasena has made it very clear that it was the dual impact of frail body and weak life force that led to exaggeration of the pre-existing disease. The blacksmith's meal had nothing to do with it.

Then it is clear that the meal was not harmful and that the Buddha didn't eat in excess.

Blacksmith Cunda Couldn't Have Cooked Meat for the Buddha

The Buddha was invited for a meal by Cunda, the blacksmith. He offered him *sūkaramaddava*. This word is variously translated as 'pork' or 'a dish prepared from a specific plant'. Let us see what looks logical.

The blacksmith was an old disciple of the Buddha. He had heard the Buddha's sermons on several occasions. He had asked questions to the Buddha to seek clarification. He was obviously aware that the first precept taught by the Buddha was to abstain from killing. He also knew that the Buddha was against a bhikkhu eating any meat which was seen, heard or suspected of being prepared by killing an animal for the bhikkhu. He also knew about the five sins a disciple commits when he offers meat to the Buddha or his disciples. In this situation, it is not possible that a devoted disciple such as Cunda would offer meat to the Buddha towards the end of his life.

We know that *sūkaramaddava* (literally, pig-tender) is taken to mean pork by some. Even some from the Buddhist tradition do it. This is because according to local customs, weather and unavailability of vegetarian food, many of them are traditional meat eaters. Even after accepting the Dhamma, many of them couldn't change their dietary habit completely. Though they accepted other principles of the Dhamma, they find it difficult to give up meat. Naturally, they tend to search for something in the Buddha's life that would validate their meat eating. So they don't find it objectionable when *sūkaramaddava* is used to mean pork.

Actually, we can understand when some disciples in certain circumstances eat meat. However, they must take care that they don't attach to the Buddha a deed against which he fought all his life. It is wrong to make the Buddha a meat-eater to justify one's own meat-eating or condone anyone else doing it.

There Are Various Meanings of a Word

There are several relations between word and meaning. This has been shown by grammarians like Mammata, Anandavardhana in detail. Dr. Ketkar knew this well. Sometimes the same word has a literal meaning, a figurative meaning and a metaphorical meaning. Sometimes, the meaning can be not only different but also opposite to each other. Etymology differs for words and especially for conjoint words. Sometimes a conjoint word is created by sixth declension. *Pūraṇapoḷi,* a famous dish in Maharashtra means *poḷi* (bread) of *pūraṇa* (sweet stuffing). But it doesn't mean *poḷi* made of *pūraṇa*, rather it means *poḷi* in which *pūraṇa* is stuffed. *Varāhakarṇa* literally means 'ear of pig'; but is actually used for a type of arrow. *Mrigānka* (literally thigh of deer) means moon. *Mrigalochana* (deer's eyes) and *Mīnākshi* (fish eye) don't mean deer's eye or fish's eye but indicate a beautiful woman.

Someone may ask why so much preliminary information is given? It is for them who pretend not to understand.

Sūkaramaddava Is a Plant

Sūkara means pig. Apate Dictionary also gives its meaning as a type of deer. Let us keep it aside for now. But we must pay heed to Apate Dictionary saying *sūkarī* means 'a kind of moss.' *Sūkarī* is the feminine of *sūkara*. Thus *sūkara* can also mean the same. So let us concede that there is at least some possibility that *sūkara* can be a plant. T W Rhys Davids give *sūkaramaddava's*[322] meaning as 'quantity of truffles' (a king of underground vegetable). It is not without basis.

Let us now turn to *maddava*. The word used is *maddava*, not *sūkara-maṃsa* (meat of *sūkara*). *Maddava* doesn't mean meat. Therefore, it is a false interpretation to say *sūkaramaddava* means meat of pig. There are other more suitable answers.

Maddava is related to *mardava, mridu* in Sanskrit. But first, let us look at *ajamodā* (sheep-happy) and *ajamodikā*. Apate Dictionary gives its meaning as 'name of a very useful medicinal plant' (called *ovā*). It may be because people saw goats enjoying eating the plant and called it a plant giving joy to *aja* (goat). *Ajashriṅgī* (sheep-horn) doesn't mean horn of sheep. It is name of a plant. The same plant is popularly called *medhashiṅgī* (sheep-horn) in Marathi. The word *sūkaramaddava* (pig-soft) must have come about the same way—a soft plant that pigs enjoy. *Varāhakanda* (literally pig-root) is a similar word. Apate Dictionary gives its meaning as 'a kind of esculent root.' Esculent means edible. It is a root like carrot, radish, etc.

There are many such words in Indian languages. *Hastidanta* (literally, elephant tooth) means elephant tooth and it also means radish. "One ate *hastidanta*," means "one ate radish." *Hastikarṇa* (literally, elephant ear) means castor. Thus there are instances of conjoint words comprising of an animal's name and body part to denote a plant.

Kākabali doesn't mean meat of crow. It means offering to crow.
Shukādana (parrot-food) means pomegranate.
Mrigashiras (head of deer) is constellation of star.
Gokarna and *Gomukha* (cow-ear and cow-mouth) don't mean ear or mouth of cow.

In Sanskrit, *mahishī* has two main meanings: chief queen and buffalo. It can also mean "a slave woman" or "a woman of loose character". In a discussion about the chief queen if one takes *mahishī* to mean buffalo it would certainly be a mistake.

In Marathi, *kutryācī chattrī* (umbrella of dog) means mushroom.

These examples should suffice.

Sūkaramaddava means truffles. It is possible that this particular vegetable had medicinal value and Cunda prepared the dish for that very purpose. Whatever it may be, it is wrong to call *sūkaramaddava* pork.

Why Angry With the Buddha?

V. G. Apate has explained why people like Dr. Ketkar are keen to make malicious allegations against the Buddha.

He says,[323] "...Why such scrutiny of Buddhism? What does it mean when Buddhists are criticized; for example, Rāmāyaṇa says, *'Yathā hi buddhahs tathā hi chaurah.'* Why is it necessary? In my opinion there are two-three reasons for the ire of brahminical writers. First—the Buddha wanted to eradicate caste from brahminical religion and this lead to loss of brahminical dominance in society. Brahmins became angry because of this. The Buddha opposed the view that liberation was attained by following the brahminical directions and supporting only brahmins. He stated that each one is responsible for his own liberation; that there is no need for middle-men and all we need is to live a righteous life to attain liberation *(moksha)*. This also angered brahmins. On top of that the Buddha rejected the authority of brahminical scriptures and opposed violence in *yajñas*. The anger of brahmins flared further. Thus under the influence of anger their rational thought processes were lost!"

V. G. Apate further states the difference in the arguments of the Buddha and the brahminical scholars, "... but these critics used not only intelligence to refute the Buddhist thought but also trickery. I can't bring myself to say that these tricks were fair and just. To poison the mind of a third party when our own intellect fails and win an argument is not just. These critics wanted to trounce the Buddhists. Perhaps, because they thought that their intellect would be insufficient for this purpose, they started spreading myths and imaginary stories that created misconceptions about the Buddhists. This is unfortunate. …When Gotama the Buddha spread his teaching, he had to argue and debate with many contemporary scholars, but not once did he think of resorting to trickery. His entire emphasis was on rational logic. His style of debate was straightforward. There was not an iota of deception or any shadow of cunning in his speech. He is never seen being anything but generous with his opponents. If he impressed people, it was because of his rational intellect. But the conduct of brahminical critics mentioned above was different. I don't deny that there are several reasons for the decline of Buddhism; for it losing its appeal to people, for people's indifference to it and even for abhorrence. I have already mentioned those reasons earlier. But again I cannot stop myself from saying that to a large extent the decline of Buddhism was because of the unfair means adopted by its opponents."

Torturing One's Body Not Necessary

Torturing Self, Torturing Others

The Middle Length Discourses gives descriptions of people who trouble themselves and trouble others and those who do neither.

When a king performs a yajña (sacrifice), he does various things such as applying ghee and oil to his body, scratching his back with the horn of deer, sleeping on the ground, and living on milk from only one tit of cow.

He says, "I will kill so many bulls and other animals in this yajña." As a result his servants weep. Such a person is called 'Torturing Self, Torturing Others'. The Buddha implies that such people run after imaginary pleasures and fail to work for their own betterment.[324]

Dog-Vow and Cow-Vow

The Buddha didn't believe that torturing oneself gave any desirable results. This is clear from an incident narrated in the

Middle Length Discourses.[325]

Once he was dwelling in Haliddavasana in the Koliyan region. Then one day a Koliyan named Puṇṇa who had taken the vow to live like a cow (cow-vow) and Seniya who was naked and had taken a vow to live like a dog (dog-vow) came to meet him. After exchanging greetings, Puṇṇa sat to one side and Seniya too jumped like a dog and sat on another side. Puṇṇa informed the Buddha that Seniya had taken a dog-vow and only ate food put on ground. He asked the Buddha what the consequence of it would be.

The Buddha replied, "Let it be. Don't ask me."

Puṇṇa asked the second time and the third time. Then the Buddha said, "You insist on an answer. Listen then." The gist of what the Buddh said is: One who takes a dog-vow would be reborn as a dog. If one believes that by this vow, one would be born as a deity, then it is a false view. One with false view goes to nether worlds or non-human realms.

Hearing this Seniya started crying. The Buddha said that he had warned them not to ask him. Then Seniya said that he wasn't crying for his sake. He had been following the dog-vow for a long time and Puṇṇa had been following the cow-vow for a long time too. What would happen to Puṇṇa? Again the Buddha didn't answer. Seniya repeated the question and received a similar answer. Puṇṇa too cried, but agreed that he felt relieved. He requested the Buddha to give them a discourse so that they could give up their respective vows. The Buddha told them, "If one commits any physical, vocal or mental deed with evil intention, it gives bad results. If one's deeds are not unwholesome, one gets good results. This means that beings are inheritors of their actions."

Discussion

During the time of the Buddha, people used to indulge in all kinds of strange and painful rituals and vows. These friends believed that by doing all their deeds like a dog or a cow, they could become gods. Such people obviously believed in heaven and hell. The Buddha explained to them in their own jargon. He told them one's welfare lay not in these strange rituals but in virtuous conduct.

Inner Purity More Important Than Outer Cleaning

I Light the Inner Flame Rather Than Burning Wood

The Buddha's thoughts on birth (caste) and yajña are seen in Sundarika Sutta[326] of the Connected Discourses.

Once the Buddha was dwelling on the bank of Sundarika river in Kosala. At that time, a brahmin named Sundarika Bhāradvāja was performing fire sacrifice (*agnihotra*) and was making offerings to fire. After completing the fire sacrifice, he got up from his seat and looked in all four directions and thought, "Who will partake of the remainder of the offerings from the yajña?" At that time, he saw the Buddha sitting under a tree with his head covered. Seeing him, he approached him with the remainder of the offerings in left hand and a water pitcher in right hand. The Buddha sensed that someone was approaching him. He removed the cloth from his head. When the brahmin saw that he was a shaven-head, he was disappointed and turned back saying, "This is a shaven-head!".

Suddenly a thought occurred to him, "Many brahmins shave their heads. Let me ask his caste."

He approached the Buddha and asked, "What is your caste?"

The Buddha answered, "Don't ask my caste. Ask about my character. A wood can give rise to fire. A great sage can be born in low caste but be erudite and restrained due to wisdom. Such a sage is controlled, wise and lives a holy life. O performer of the yajña, request such a sage. He does fire-sacrifice at the right time. He is suitable for making an offering."

Sundarika replied, "Since I have met a sage like you, my yajña has been successful. My offering to fire has born fruit. Since I had not met you, the sacrificial remains (*havyashesh*) were eaten by someone else. Gotama, do partake this. You are indeed a brahmin."

I Don't Eat Where I Teach the Dhamma

Then the Buddha replied as he did on numerous occasions, that he didn't take food where he had taught the Dhamma. Sundarika asked, "Who should I give this to then?" The Buddha replied that he didn't see anyone other than the Buddha or his disciples who was worthy of the offering. In that situation, he asked Sundarika to throw the food at a place where there is no grass or in water where there are no creatures.

Sundarika put the offering in water. Immediately it crackled in water and flared up in fire. It was as if an iron spade lying in fire all day long was put in water. The brahmin had goose bumps on his body. He came and stood next to the Buddha.

Superficial Things Don't Give True Purity

Then the Tathāgata said, "Don't think that burning wood would result in purity. Because it is an external thing. One who thinks that he would get purified by external rituals—such purification is not called purification by the wise ones. O brahmin, instead of burning wood, I light the inner flame. This fire is constantly alive inside me. I am ever satisfied. I am an arahata. I follow the holy life.

"Conceit is your shoulder-load, anger is smoke, lying is the ash, tongue is the ladle and heart is the place of fire. A well-tamed mind is the light. O brahmin, Dhamma is a lake. Morality is the bank. It is clean and praised by the good. Wise people take bath in it. People with clean limbs cross over to other side. O brahmin, the Middle Path of truth, Dhamma, restraint and holy life is the best. Salute people who are on the right path. Such a one I call the follower of the Dhamma."

Then as would often happen with those who opposed him initially but later would come to his refuge, Sundarika too became his disciple.

Discussion

This sutta shows how the brahmins who performed fire-sacrifice abhorred the bhikkhus. They disliked the sight of a shaven headed samaṇa. Therefore, Sundarika turned around the moment he saw that the Buddha was a shaven head. Since he thought that some brahmins too shave heads, it seems that some brahmins had started becoming sanyasis and shaving their heads at that time. It is possible that Sundarika felt that if the shaven-headed bhikkhu was brahmin by birth, it was acceptable to offer him sacrificial remains. The answer given by the Buddha on being asked his caste was in keeping with his usual stand.

I Don't Take Meals Where I Have Taught

Hearing the Buddha's explanation, Sundarika changed. He was earlier unwilling to give the offering remains to a 'shavenhead' but now he requested the Buddha to accept it. The Buddha refused. It was his practice not to accept a meal where he had given a Dhamma discourse. He was often invited for meals and after meals he would certainly give an inspiring Dhamma talk. But if he happened to give a teaching for some other reason, he would not eat there.

Sant Tukaram Keeps Up the Tradition

Several saints in Indian history kept this tradition of the Buddha. Sant Tukaram's advice and practice on this issue is well-known. "Don't eat where you have done a *kirtana* (given a spiritual discourse). Don't even apply the smearing from that place to your forehead. Don't accept a garland there. Understand that you shouldn't even ask for or accept grass or grains for horse or bullock."

This matches the Buddha's practice and advice on this issue.

Attraction of Miracles—an Old Ailment of Indian Society

It is obvious that the detail about who can digest the sacrificial remains *(havyashesh)* and who cannot is added by bhikkhus to show the greatness of the Buddha and by extension that of the bhikkhus . It is distressing to see this absurd claim by those who didn't understand that the greatness of the Buddha didn't lie in miracles but in his thoughts and actions. This is an old ailment of Indian society. The real miracle was the transformation that the Buddha was bringing about in Indian society: his teaching to Sundarika that the true purification is mental purification and not the alleged one from burning wood.

Tangles Inside, Tangles Outside

Once the Tathāgata was asked what could disentangle the tangles that are both outside and inside.[327] He answered that one with morality and wisdom and one who had eradicated defilements of craving, aversion and ignorance would be able to do it.

Keeping Mind Pure is More Important Than Bathing in River

Once the Buddha was staying at Gayāsisa near Gaya.[328] It was very cold at that time. Several matted hair ascetics were bathing in river. They were giving offerings to fire. They believed that this would purify them. Seeing them the Tathāgata uttered this *udāna*, "No one is purified by water. Several take bath here. But one who has truth and the Dhamma, is truly purified. He is a true brahmin."

If Mind is Not Pure, Then What Use is Bath

Once the Buddha was dwelling at Jetavana in Sāvatthi.[329] He gave a Dhamma talk to bhikkhus. At that time, a brahmin named Sundarika Bhāradvāja was sitting next to him. He asked the Buddha, "Would you come to the Bāhukā river for bath?"

"What will the Bāhukā river do?"

"Bho Gotama, Bāhukā is well-known. People think that it is auspicious. Many people take bath in it and wash away their sins."

After listening to this the Buddha uttered some verses which meant: "An ignorant person who commits evil deeds can't become pure even if he takes bath daily in Bāhukā, Adhikakkā, Gayā, Sundarikā, Sarasvatī, Payāga and Bāhumatī. What can Sundarikā do for such a person? What can Payāga do for such a person? What can Bāhumatī do? They won't be able to help one who does evil.

"One who performs wholesome actions, for such a person any water is auspicious; he is always doing an *uposatha*. One who does pure, untainted deeds always accomplishes his vow. This is the bath that you should take, o brahmin. Help all beings. If you speak truth, abstain from killing, don't steal, have faith in good things and don't envy anyone, then what is the need to go to Gaya? Any small water pond near you is Gayā for you.

"For purification of mind, morality is important; and not taking bath twice a day."

One incident narrated in the Connected Discourses[330] throws more light on the subject.

Once the Buddha was dwelling in Sāvatthi. At that time a brahmin named Saṅgārava had become famous as *Udakasuddhika* (literally cleaner with water). He used to take bath morning and evening. Ānanda gave this information to the Buddha.

Then one day the Buddha went to him and asked him, "Do you purify yourself with water?" He said yes. When asked why, he answered, "Bho Gotama, whatever evil deeds I do in the day, I wash away by taking bath in the evening. Whatever evil deeds I do in the night, I wash away by taking bath in the morning."

On hearing that the Buddha said, "Brahmin, the Dhamma is a lake. Morality is the step to enter it. This lake is without flaws and praised by the honorable people. One who takes a bath in this lake, crosses over without getting wet."

Discussion

The Buddha emphasized purity of mind and ethical conduct over rites and rituals, external grandeur and exhibitions. He explained that it was wrong to believe that a particular river washed away a person's sins. On the other hand, for one who is pure hearted every water in the world is auspicious. He rejected not only Vedic rituals but also Buddhist rituals such as *uposatha* if the mind is not pure. On the other hand, for one with a pure mind, every day is an *uposatha* day. It is not important to observe vows on a particular day for such a person.

This doesn't mean that one shouldn't take bath or take various vows or that rivers are not auspicious but that mental purity is more important.

This teaching of the Buddha kept flowing through the words and the actions of saints who followed him through the centuries. The famous Hindi saying *'mana caṅgā to kaṭhautī meṃ gaṅgā.'* means 'If the mind is pure, one has the Ganges in one's arms.' We find a reflection of the question to Sundarika, in Tukaram's question, *"Tīrthā javunīyā kāya tuvā kele? Carma prakshālile varīvarī."* (What did you achieve by going to the holy places? You merely washed your skin superficially.)

We must also see what Swami Vivekanand said in his speech at California about the Buddha's stainless pure life.[331]

"When the Buddha was born, he was so pure that whosoever looked at his face from a distance immediately gave up the ceremonial religion and became a monk and became saved. So the gods held a meeting. They said, 'We are undone.' Because most of the gods live upon the ceremonials. These sacrifices go to the gods and these sacrifices were all gone. The gods were dying of hunger and (the reason for) it was that their power was gone. So the gods said, 'We must, anyhow, put this man down. He is too pure for our life.' And then the gods came and said: 'Sir, we come to ask you something. We want to make a great sacrifice and we mean to make a huge fire, and we have been seeking all over the world for a pure spot to light the fire on and could not find it, and now we have found it. If you will lie down, on your breast we will make the huge fire.' 'Granted,' he says, 'go on.' And the gods built the fire high upon the breast of Buddha, and they thought he was dead, and he was not. And then they went about and said, 'We are undone.' And all the gods began to strike him. No good. They could not kill him. From underneath, the voice comes, 'Why (are you) making these vain attempts?' 'Whoever looks upon you becomes purified and is saved, and nobody is going to worship us.' 'Then, your attempt is vain, because purity can never be killed.' This fable was written by his enemies, and yet throughout the fable the only blame that attaches to Buddha is that he was so great a teacher of purity."

Not Miracle—the Noble Eight Fold Path

From ancient times, certain elements in the society love miracles. Countless people have great reverence for those who show miracles. They don't get attracted to people who don't have the aura of miracles. A saying about this in India means—'There is no salute without miracles.' If people see something that they don't see in ordinary life, they are impressed. They believe that such a person has some mystical, supernatural, yogic, spiritual power. Then to solve their problems, hoping for their benefit, they become his disciples and devotees. That performer of so called miracles then gets salutations, worship, faith and devotion, wealth, prestige, luxuries and service from them.

Actually, everything in the nature is bound by the cause and effect relationship. This law can't be broken by anyone. Some people use suggestion, hypnotism, trickery, magic, deception and give an impression that they have supernatural powers. Sometimes, they have knowledge about specific qualities of specific substances which are not known to others. They use that knowledge to give an impression that they have special powers.

The Buddha explained that the Noble Eightfold Path is the real solution for the problems of humanity. Miracles can't eradicate misery. It was his important hypothesis that there is no effect without a cause. Therefore, belief in miracles can never be a part of his philosophy.

If we look at what he said about miracles from time to time, we clearly understand his views on the subject.

Feeling That It Is Day When It Is Night Is Hypnotism

If someone made claims about miracles, the Buddha wouldn't believe in them. We should look at Bhayabherava Sutta[332] in this reference.

Once the Buddha was staying in Sāvatthi. At that time, Jāṇussoṇi came to meet him. While talking to him the Buddha said, "There are some who experience day when it is night and experience night when it is day. This is their dwelling in deception, dwelling in hypnotism. I, on the other hand, experience night when it is night and experience day when it is day."

For him, experiencing day when it is night and vice versa was not an indication of any miraculous power but merely deceiving themselves. This shows how he viewed miracles. He didn't claim any such power. He also made it clear that he experiences reality as it is, just as any other person could and should.

Those involved in deception cannot bring welfare to people. They themselves are entangled in confusion and would only push others in ignorance. On the other hand, one whose nature is non-deception (non-hypnotism) spreads wisdom and works for the welfare and happiness of many.

There Is No Relation Between Miracles and the Dhamma

From his opinions expressed from time to time, it is clear that the Buddha didn't display miracles. Let us look at Pāthika Sutta[333] of the Long Discourses.

The Buddha was dwelling in Anupiyā of Malla country. Since there was still time for the alms round, he decided to go to meet a recluse of Bhaggava (Bhargava) clan. Bhaggava welcomed him and offered him a seat. Then he too sat on one side. Then he reported that a few days ago Sunakkhatta of the Licchavī clan had come to meet him and told him that he had left the Tathāgata because he didn't believe in the Tathāgata's Dhamma. Bhaggava asked the Buddha whether it was true. The Buddha said yes, that Sunakkhatta had indeed met him a few days before. While narrating the conversation with Sunakkhatta, he repeated their questions and answers.

The Buddha had asked Sunakkhatta, "Did I ever invite you and ask you to come to my Dhamma?"

"No, sir."

"Did you ever say to me, 'I will accept your Dhamma'?"

"No, sir."

"Neither did I invite you to come to my Dhamma nor did you come and tell me that you were accepting my Dhamma. Then useless fellow, what are you accepting and what are you rejecting? Isn't it your fault?"

Then Sunakkhatta had told him the reasons for his leaving the Buddha, "Sir, you didn't display any superhuman miracles to me."

Then the Buddha had asked him, "Did I ever tell you, 'Come Sunakkhatta, accept my Dhamma and I will show you miracles'?"

Again the questions and answers continued as above. Then the Buddha said to him, "Sunakkhatta, I have taught the Dhamma for the complete cessation of all suffering. Do you think that Dhamma would become complete by my performing or not performing miracles?"

Sunakkhatta said no.

Discussion

This shows the Buddha's attitude towards miracles. Sunakkhatta left the Saṅgha because the Buddha didn't perform miracles. The Buddha didn't compromise. He didn't pretend to have miraculous powers to retain his disciples. He was addressing the question of human suffering. All he was interested in was eradication of suffering. We must also note one more thing here. He never asked anyone to 'accept my Dhamma'. There was not even a request to accept his Dhamma; let alone any insistence or force or intimidation. He believed that the wish for acceptance of Dhamma must spring from within. Therefore, he never condoned violence in spread of the Dhamma. In the entire history of Buddhism too, we hardly ever see any violent coercion.

The Experience of Dhamma Is Greater Than Hearing Divine Words

We see in Mahāli Sutta of the Long Discourses that once while the Buddha was staying in Vesāli, several brahmin messengers from various regions had come there. When they learned that the Tathāgata was in the town, they set out to meet him. Otthaddha (Mahāli) Licchavī too came to meet him with several other Licchavīs. Nāgita, the then attendant of the Buddha, told them that the Buddha was meditating. They decided to wait. After some time, someone named Simha requested Nāgita again to allow them to meet the Buddha. Nāgita asked Simha to approach the Buddha himself. Simha did so and they all met the Buddha.

In their meeting, Mahāli repeated what Sunakkhatta had told him, "Mahāli, I spent about three years with the Buddha. I had hoped to hear pleasant, beautiful, entertaining divine words. But I heard no divine words." Mahāli then asked him whether Sunakkhatta didn't hear divine words because they didn't exist or because he couldn't hear them. The Buddha gave a detailed answer. He explained about various experiences in meditative absorptions *(jhānas)*. The Buddha was then asked whether the bhikkhus come to the Buddha and live the holy life for the sake of these different experiences. The Buddha explained that they lived the holy life for experiencing the greater Dhamma and the way to experience that Dhamma was the Noble Eightfold Path.

The Buddha Didn't Tell Bhikkhus to Perform Miracles

It was the Buddha's rule that he wouldn't perform miracles and wouldn't allow the bhikkhus to display miracles. This becomes clear in Kevaṭṭa Sutta[334] of the Long Discourses.

Once the Buddha was living in a mango grove named Pāvārika near Nalanda. A householder's son named Kevaṭṭa came to meet him. He told the Buddha that Nālanda was a big, rich and affluent city. People there respected the Buddha. "Therefore, the Buddha should instruct a bhikkhu to perform supernatural miracles. Due to such miracles, people in Nalanda would have even more faith in the Buddha."

The Buddha said, "Kevaṭṭa, I do not tell bhikkhus to show miracles to the white-clothed laypeople."

Kevaṭṭa continued to insist saying that he wasn't making the suggestion because he considered the Buddha lesser but because miracles would increase people's faith in the Buddha. Again the Buddha declined.

For the third time, Kevaṭṭa made the same request. Then the Buddha replied, "Kevaṭṭa, I have described three types of miracles from my own direct experience. They are the miracle of psychic power, the miracle of telepathy and the miracle of teaching."

A bhikkhu due to his psychic powers takes many forms. From one he becomes many; from many he becomes one. He manifests himself; he disappears. He goes through a wall, a fortification or a mountain without being seen by anyone as if there is empty space. He enters earth as if he is entering water and he walks on water as if he is walking on earth. He flies in the sky like a bird. He touches the sun and the moon with his hands. He keeps the brahmā realm under his control. Seeing this, one who has faith conveys his surprise to one who has no faith. Then the man without faith tells him, "O there is a charm named the Gāndhāri charm with the use of which one can perform miracles… …"

The Buddha asked Kevaṭṭa whether a person without faith would make such a claim or not. Kevaṭṭa said yes.

The Buddha said, "Seeing this fault in supernatural miracles, I avoid them, stay away from them and I dislike them."

Then the Buddha asked about whether one without faith would say similarly that a bhikkhu could do this due to a charm named Cintāmani charm, when a bhikkhu performed a miracle where he read the other person's mind. Kevaṭṭa said yes.

The Buddha then said that that was why he avoided miracles.

A bhikkhu teaches thus, "Think this way; don't think like that. Have these thoughts; don't have those thoughts. Reject this; accept that." Such teaching is the miracle of instruction. Similarly, being moral, practising meditation, etc. are miracles of instruction.

Discussion

The Buddha made it clear that he didn't tell bhikkhus to perform miracles. Miracles impress gullible people. So cunning people take advantage of this and perform miracles to impress them. The Buddha didn't want to influence and attract people in this manner.

Truth Must Pass the Test of Those Who Lack Faith

He tells Kevaṭṭa that he knew miracles and therefore rejected them. The first two kinds of miracles are different and the third kind of miracle is different. Credulous people are deceived by the first two types of miracles. Those who perform such miracles exploit these people. But one without blind faith, one who is a seeker of knowledge, is discerning and analytical doesn't fall for such miracles. Truth should stand the test of not only those with faith but also those without faith. Therefore, the first two kinds of miracles were not acceptable to the Buddha.

The third type of miracle is different. It is probably not conveyed in clear words but the meaning is clear. Rather than deceiving people, teaching people to follow the righteous path was a miracle that was acceptable and brought about desirable change in life.

The Buddha Banned Miracles

The Buddha didn't perform miracles, didn't teach how to perform miracles and had banned miracles. This is clear from an incident in Vinaya Piṭaka.[335]

Once the Buddha was staying in Kalandakanivāpa of Rājagaha. At that time, a merchant acquired an expensive piece of sandal-wood. He made a bowl out of it so that he could use the sandal wood powder and give away the bowl in charity. He then put the bowl in a basket and suspended the basket at the top of a bamboo pole. He tied it atop another long bamboo to raise its height. Then he declared, "Whoever Samaṇa or brāhmaṇa is an arahata or has miraculous powers, this bowl is gifted to him. Let him take it down." Some who had claimed supernatural powers couldn't take it down.

At that time, Venerable Mahāmoggallana and Piṇḍola Bhāradvāja had entered Rājagaha for alms. Bhāradvāja told Moggallāna to take the bowl down since he was an arahata and had supernatural powers. But Moggallāna replied, "You do it." Then Bhāradvāja rose in the sky, plucked the bowl from the top of the bamboo and circled around Rājagaha in the sky thrice. The merchant was standing with his wife and children near his house. He requested the bhikkhu to come down there. When the bhikkhu landed, he took the bowl and filled it with choice foods. Bhāradvāja then set out for the monastery. People started walking behind him, loudly discussing his miraculous feat. Hearing the commotion, the Buddha asked Ānanda about it.

Then the Buddha called Bhāradvāja and the bhikkhu Saṅgha. He asked Bhāradvāja whether what he had heard was true. Bhāradvāja said yes.

Then the Buddha condemned him, "Bhāradvāja, this was wrong, this was improper, this was unbecoming. This was not suitable for a samaṇa. This should not be done. Bhāradvāja, how could you show a miracle for wooden bowl? This was like *mātugāma* (woman) shedding her clothes for a small coin. This wouldn't make one who has no faith develop faith…"

Then he gave a Dhamma discourses and told bhikkhus, "Whoever showed miracle to laypeople will be guilty of transgression. Bhikkhus, break the pot in pieces and distribute it among bhikkhus."

Then he banned bowls made of wood, gold, silver, copper, etc. He allowed bhikkhus only iron and earthen alms bowls.

Discussion

Without going into the exact nature of Bhāradvāja's miracle, let us just understand how firmly and how strongly the Buddha opposed miracles. The words he uses to censure Bhāradvāja convey his strong view on this matter. He compared the act of

Bhāradvāja with the action of a woman of loose character. Even then he didn't show disrespect for the woman. He calls her *mātugāma* (literally one of mother's gender). He differentiates between the wrong action and the person who commits it. He felt that performing miracles was like selling morality, it was like exposing oneself in public.

The Buddha said that the expensive sandalwood bowl was insignificant. He insisted that the bhikkhus have no greed. We must also understand that when he censures the bhikkhu for displaying miracles for a minor gain, it doesn't mean that he condoned miracles for bigger gains. He had summarily banned all miracles. If a bhikkhu acquired an expensive object by performing a miracle, it had no value for the bhikkhu. The bhikkhu's only aim was to progress on the path of the Dhamma and to become enlightened. Because the sandalwood bowl, though expensive, didn't figure in this scheme, it was negligible.

The Buddha promulgated a monastic rule banning miracles. This leaves no doubt about his stand. He asked the bhikkhus to destroy the bowl. And he banned use of all bowls except iron and earthen. This shows his stringent opposition to miracles. Sant Tukaram says while rejecting miracles, *"Kapaṭa kāhī ek; nene bhulāvaya lokā; Dāu nene jaḍibuṭī, camatkāra uṭhāuṭhī."* (It is fraudulent to deceive people; (By) using charms to display miracles.)

Bhikkhus Too Rejected Miracles

Once the Buddha was dwelling in Kalandakanivāpa of Rājagaha.[336]

At that time, the Buddha and the bhikkhu-Saṅgha had acquired great prestige. Ascetics from other sects were not revered much.

A recluse named Susīma was staying in Rājagaha with a large entourage. The recluses in his retinue said to him, "Friend Susīma, become the Buddha's disciple. Learn the Dhamma from him and teach it to us. Then we will teach the Dhamma to people and we will also get reverence and prestige." He agreed and went to Ānanda, "I wish to accept the Dhamma and the Discipline of the Tathāgata." Ānanda took him to the Buddha. He received the 'going forth' and higher ordination.

At that time, many bhikkhus told the Buddha that they had achieved what they had aimed for, they had achieved their goal. Susīma heard it and went to them to ask them whether they really had said this to the Buddha. They said yes.

He asked them, "Have you acquired miraculous powers? Do you become many from one and one from many? Do you manifest yourself and disappear at will? Do you go through a wall, a fortification or a mountain without being seen by anyone as if there is empty space? Do you enter earth as if you are entering water and walk on water as if you are walking on earth? Do you fly in the sky in sitting posture like a bird? Do you touch the sun and the moon with your hands? Do you control the brahmā realm with your body?"

The bhikkhus answered 'no' to all his questions.

Then he asked them, "But then… do you hear through spotless, pure, divine ear, words that are heavenly and human; words from close and from far?"

They said no.

Then he asked them whether they could read another person's mind to see if he has greed, aversion, disenchantment, lack of hatred, etc.

Again they said no.

He asked them whether they could recollect their one, two, three… thousand… hundred thousand past lives… do you recollect who you were, what was your name, etc.

Again, the answer was no.

He asked whether he knew to which realms beings go after their death. They answered no.

Then he asked them, "Do you transcend the peaceful states and touch the formless states beyond with your body?"

They said no.

"Then how come you declare to have achieved the goal and yet you have none of the miraculous powers?"

They answered that they had become liberated through wisdom. He told them that he didn't understand what they meant by liberation through wisdom. They said that whether you understand or not, we are liberated through wisdom.

After this discussion with the bhikkhus, he went to the Buddha and gave him the report of this discussion. The Buddha said to him, "Susīma, one understands the Dhamma first and then attains nibbāna."

"Please explain in detail for I have not understood it."

"Whether or not you understand it, first one understands the Dhamma and then attains nibbāna."

Though the Buddha said this in the beginning, he went on to give a detailed exposition on the Dhamma.

Discussion

It is clear from the example of Susīma that some other sectarians were entering the Saṅgha for material benefits. Many people believe that if one gets supernatural powers then the life's aim is achieved. The bhikkhus made it clear that they hadn't attained such powers. This shows that the bhikkhus didn't believe in miracles. This was the Buddha's teaching to them. For them the important thing was to learn the Dhamma and attain nibbāna. It is most unfortunate that in spite of his clear stand against miracles, so many stories about his miracles were added later on.

Rejecting Bad Omens

While trying to remove blind beliefs in society, the Buddha had a flexible attitude in his work of social reform. In this regard, an incident in Cūḷavagga[337] in the Book of Discipline (Vinaya Piṭaka) is significant.

Once the Buddha sneezed while giving a Dhamma talk. Then the bhikkhus said loudly, "May the Tathāgata live! May the Sugata live!" This disrupted the discourse.

He asked the bhikkhus, "Is your saying 'May you live long,' when someone sneezes going to affect the person's lifespan?"

"No, bhante."

Then the Buddha laid down a rule that one should not say 'May you live long,' when someone sneezes.

At that time if a bhikkhu sneezed, the people would say, "Bhante, may you live long." In response the bhikkhu would acknowledge it by saying, "May you too live long," and thus express his goodwill. But after the incident above, the bhikkhus stopped saying it.

Then people started saying, "Why don't these samaṇas, sons of the Sākyan, say anything when we say 'May you live long, bhante,' to them?"

The bhikkhus reported it to the Buddha who said to them, "The laypeople like good wishes. Therefore, when they say 'May you live long, bhante,' I give you permission to respond with 'May you live long,' to them."

Discussion

Sneezing is considered a bad omen even in modern India. The Buddha had said more than twenty-five centuries ago that there was no relation between sneezing and any untoward event. Though he was firm about this and had made a rule about it, he didn't want the bhikkhus to hurt the sentiments of laypeople while living in the society. Rather than shocking them with dry rational thought, he tried gradual change. He knew that in the field of social reform, undue eagerness and impatience had no place. One had to be restrained and skillful.

The Buddha Rejected Astrology

The Buddha took a balanced stand about many blind beliefs. In this regard, we should study the first sutta of the Long Discourses, Brahmajāla Sutta.[338]

Laypeople used to praise the Buddha for his various qualities. This sutta gives details of such qualities. In each section there is a long list of specific blind beliefs in the society and those who used them to earn a livelihood. The Buddha made it clear that he didn't believe in any of them. Let us look at some of those blind beliefs.

At the beginning of each section, the Buddha tells the bhikkhus, "Bhikkhus, some samaṇas and brāhmaṇas eat almsfood offered with devotion by laypeople and survive through debased arts and wrong means of livelihood." Then he goes on to list the debased arts and low tricks and tells them, "Samaṇa Gotama refrains from such debased arts and wrong means of livelihood. This is the reason laypeople praise the Tathāgata."

Refraining from these blind beliefs and debased trickery is called a minor morality of the Buddha. This was not a major achievement according to the Buddha but a simple and elementary thing that should be part of the lifestyle of an ascetic.

The sutta shows the tricks that the astrologers, shamans, magicians, and sacrifice performers *(yājnikas)* used for livelihood. The list is long. Let us look at it in detail. Let us not think of this discussion as boring because it shows how the Buddha looked at them. Even modern man has not been able to get rid of many of these cobwebs in his intellect. We should know how firmly and yet easily the Buddha removed these cobwebs of intellect so that we become aware of his heritage.

Some people predict the future by looking at a body part. Some give significance to the sudden happenings in nature. Some tell meanings of dreams. Some look at bodily marks and tell fortune. Sometimes, a rat chews household items; some look at such objects and explain its significance. Some perform various sacrifices (homas, yajñas). Since we have discussed this earlier, we won't repeat it here.

Some predict the future based on specific items, farm, snake, poison, scorpion, rat, birds or their sounds. Some claim that if one chants a particular mantra, arrow won't pierce his body in a battle. Some people look at specific characteristics of precious stones, clothes, baton, weapon, sword, arrow, bow, woman, man, boy, girl, servants, elephants, horse, buffalo, cow, goat, sheep, rooster, etc.

Some predict whether or not the king would leave the palace, whether another king would visit, which king would emerge victorious. Some look at the paths of sun, moon and stars and describe the effect of their deviations from their path. Some survive by looking for *meterors*, peculiar red lights on horizons, earthquakes, thundering clouds without rains, rising and setting of the sun and the moon, and divining their meaning. Some earn their livelihood by predicting future calamities, and epidemics by palmistry, numerology, etc. Some give advice on when to get engaged, what is the auspicious time to get married, which constellations are favorable for marriage, what to do to help someone or to hurt someone, and how to change the gender of the fetus in mother's womb.

Some claim to make someone tongue-tied using mantras, some make people deaf, some claim to make people lose use of their hand, some use mirrors etc. for planchet to communicate with the dead. Some invite invisible beings through the medium of maidens to ask them questions, some entreat gods, some worship a god or the sun to achieve something special, and some use specific head movements to request gods.

Some make conditional pledges to gods and fulfill those pledges, some invite ghosts, some claim to make an impotent person potent, some try various physical actions such as putting oil in ears or putting kohl in eyes for miracles, and claim to cure incurable illnesses.

The Buddha rejected all such fraudulent means of livelihood. He insisted that one must earn an honest livelihood. It is part of the Noble Eightfold Path taught by him.

Shameful That We Still Have These Blind Beliefs

We still have many of the blind beliefs enumerated above to some extent, with some variations. Therefore, it is all the more surprising to look at the intellectual leap of the Tathāgata in his time. Not only is his advice on these matters true in principle today but the details are not far from today's reality. Should we look at it as the perspicacity of the Buddha twenty-five centuries back or the mental frailty of those of us who are born twenty-five centuries later?

Why Does the Editor of Maharashtra Dnyanakosh Get Angry?

It is painful to see the derision shown by the editor of the Maharashtra Dnyanakosh (encyclopedia). He says,[339] "We cannot call the Buddha an opponent of prejudice born of ignorance. He didn't want any knowledge based on cause. He felt that predicting eclipses, mathematics, medicine are all base arts. He used to feel proud that he stayed away from such things… We should not call him a hater of ignorance but a hater of accumulation of knowledge and one who sat with the ignorant folks and mocked the learned."

This criticism is without basis. The Buddha didn't object to predicting eclipses but only to using eclipses to exploit people by predicting the future. He didn't object to mathematical sciences but to the so-called numerology people used to commit fraud on masses. He wasn't against medicine. He had allowed bhikkhus to get treatment for their ailments. Jīvaka at the time of the Buddha and many other Buddhist experts in medicine make us proud. The Buddha objected to charlatans; those who didn't know science but pretended otherwise. Ketkar calls one who had opened learning to all the people of India, a hater of accumulation of knowledge. We need not say more about his intention. The allegation that the Tathāgata was with a gang of ignorant people stinks of a particular conceit. When it is said that the Buddha mocked the learned, it is out of the same conceit. To answer this baseless and biased allegation against the Buddha, let me quote a parable given by the Buddha himself.[340]

The Buddha said that there are four pairs that are far away from each other: earth and sky, this shore and the other shore of the ocean, the site where the sun rises and where it sets, and the *Dhamma (*nature, philosophy) of honorable people and that of dishonorable people. It is no wonder then that the Dhamma of honorable, upright persons such as the Buddha is not understood by those of opposite tendencies.

Not by Charms…

We know that the Buddha didn't believe in charms. There is a sutta in the Numerical Discourses[341] about it.

Once the Buddha told bhikkhus, "Bhikkhus, it is impossible that one who has right view would want to be purified by *kotuhalamaṅgala*." *Kotuhalamaṅgala* is superstition. Ānanda Kausalyayana translates the original Pali as, "It is impossible that a person who has right view would expect self-purification by good or bad omens." *Maṅgala* here means something that one believes gives us what we desire.

For example, thread, bead. etc. are used as charms. *Kotuhala* shows curiosity, eagerness, desire. Many follow blind faith in order to get what they want and to ward off perceived evil. People keep various lucky charms to protect themselves from any harm and to fulfill their wishes. They also feel that such lucky charms would destroy the impurities in their life and purify them.

Each substance or thing has its own characteristics that works according to these characteristics. Nothing can break the law of cause and effect operating in nature to bring about a miracle. Therefore, the Buddha advised the practice of morality and wisdom for one's welfare; and advised against the use of such charms.

Livelihood by Astrology Was Unwholesome

We see in Sūcimukhī Sutta[342] of the Connected Discourses that the Buddha's followers like Sāriputta had rejected blind faith in false knowledge that deceived people.

Once Sāriputta was living in Kalandakanivāpa in Rājagaha. After his alms round in Rājagaha he sat down to eat by the side of a wall. At that time, a wandering recluse named Sūcimukhī approached him and asked, "Samaṇa, why are you facing downward while eating?"

He answered, "Sister, I am not facing downward."

"Samaṇa, are you facing upward and eating?"

He answered, no.

Then she asked him whether he was eating facing the four quarters or between the quarters. He said no to all questions.

She said that he was saying no to all questions, how was he eating then? He answered, "Those who live by false learning; false means of divinations such as *vatthuvijjā* (*vāstuvidyā,* divinations based on buildings) and sounds of birds and animals to be facing down and eating.

"Those who indulge in stargazing; look at the constellations in the sky to predict the future are said to be facing upward and eating.

"Those who go on errands are said to eat while facing the four quarters.

"Those who live by palmistry live by facing between the quarters.

"I don't live by such false learning. I go on alms round in the Dhamma way and live by the alms received in the Dhamma way."

Discussion

Sāriputta has presented an important view here. He has differentiated between false learning where fraudulent things are done and true learning that brings real benefit in life. In *vāstuvidyā,* it is alleged that a particular place or direction is auspicious or inauspicious for construction, etc. In broader terms, it is a divining whether a particular substance or object is auspicious or not.

Even today, particular sounds of birds and animals are considered auspicious and inauspicious. These sounds are used to predict future. Sounds of crows or owls are used or a bullock is used to predict the future.

In *nakkhattavijjā*, the position of the stars and planets is used to predict the future.

In *angavijjā*, the lines on palms and forehead, and the moles on the body are used to predict the future.

Sāriputta says that these are false livelihoods. He says that he lives by the Dhamma and eats the alms food obtained the

Dhamma way. The Noble Eightfold Path makes one discerning and balanced. It is constructive and benevolent.

Why Oppose Yajñas?

The Buddha's opposition to yajñas (ritual sacrifices) wasn't just negation of a tradition but it was a foundation or a guarantee of a new, pure social structure. His view wasn't oppositional. His was a universe decorated with pure and fresh novelty.

The Buddha gave his Dhamma the foundation of morality and objective truth. He gave the social structure an ethical and learned foundation of the Dhamma. His Dhamma was not a weapon of dominance. It was a guide for a wholesome living. It was a conduct for happy living. It was a sweet combination of ethics and objective wisdom.

10

The Buddha on Women

What was the Buddha's view on women at a time when people didn't want daughters, when people thought that women should not be allowed freedom and independence? This curiosity is natural. It is also relevant today as India is facing the monster of female feticide due to the huge gender bias. Let us find out.

A Woman Can Be Greater Than a Man

The Connected Discourses[343] tell us about an incident in Sāvatthi involving King Pasenadi. He was visiting the Buddha. At that time while he was seated next to the Buddha, a messenger came and told the king that Queen Mallika had given birth to a girl. The king became gloomy on getting the news.

Seeing the king's dejection, the Buddha uttered a verse which meant: "O lord of the country, even a woman can be greater than a man—Talented, upright, she serves her mother-in-law and is faithful to her husband. She gives birth to a brave son who becomes lord of all directions."

Discussion

Anyone who cherishes equality between a girl and a boy would be thrilled by this incident. We must also put this in the context of his time as we will discuss later. At a time when women were believed to be of inferior intellect, the Buddha uses the adjective *medhavi,* which means talented and intelligent. This means that he recognized the innate potential in women.

Those who look at this from a modern perspective and those who are not aware of reality may object to the Buddha's praise. They may say that rather than praising her for her individuality, the Buddha praised her in relation to her mother-in-law, husband and son.

But let us not jump to conclusions. We need not say just how tragic and heartrending is the problem of female feticide in India. In this situation, we can only imagine how difficult and delicate is the work of creating equality in this aspect. Only if we understand the statement of the Buddha in the context of his time can we realize how revolutionary it was. Just as the Buddha expected women to be virtuous, he had put the same yardstick for morality for men. Except for those women who decide against motherhood, motherhood brings a fulfillment of womanhood for most women. These women should not be looked down upon by irrational insistence on equality.

Dhamma is Important, Not Gender

The Buddha said[344] that whether one is a man or a woman, one who followed the Dhamma would attain nibbāna. He thus acknowledged the equal right and capacity of women in the all-important sphere of liberation.

Seven Types of Wives

In a sutta in the Graded Discourses,[345] we find a description of the various types of wives found in society.

Once the Buddha went to Anāthapiṇḍika's house and sat on a seat. There was a loud disturbance in the house. The Buddha asked the reason. Anāthapiṇḍika answered, "Bhante, my daughter-in-law Sujātā doesn't respect her mother-in-law, her father-in-law or her husband. She doesn't even respect the Tathāgata…"

On hearing this, the Buddha called Sujātā. She came and sat to one side. Then he said to her, "Sujātā, there are seven types of wives. Which seven? Like an assassin, like a thief, like a master, like a mother, like a sister, like a friend and like a slave. Which one are you?" She replied that she didn't understand what he had said and requested him to elaborate.

The Buddha explained, "A woman who has an evil mind and malice in her heart ignores her husband and is attracted to other men. She is eager to kill the husband she has purchased with money (dowry). She is a wife like an assassin.

"A woman who hides some of the money that her husband earns with his effort, through business, agriculture or artisanship is a wife like a thief.

"A woman who is lazy, greedy, gluttonous, harsh, abusive, nagging, whose speech deflates her husband and makes him lose enthusiasm is a wife like a master.

"A woman who always cares for her husband and protects his wealth, as a mother always cares for her son, is a wife like a mother.

"A woman who admires and honors her husband like an elder or a younger sister, and is shy and obedient is a wife like a sister.

"A woman who is happy to see her husband just as a lover is thrilled to see her beloved after a long gap, who is virtuous, faithful and well-behaved, is a wife like a friend.

"A woman who doesn't become afraid even when her husband threatens her, calmly endures her husband's conduct and doesn't become angry but is obedient is a wife like a slave.

"Of these, the women who are like an assassin, like a thief or like a master go to the nether world after death. Wives who are like a mother, a sister, a friend and a slave are virtuous and tolerant. They go to higher realms after death.

"These are the seven types of wives. Which one are you, Sujātā?"

Sujātā replied, "From today, I am a wife like a slave."

Discussion

The Buddha Made Her Aware of Her Responsibility

It is clear from this sutta that the Buddha used to give guidance to householders about their lives. People from the same family can have different temperaments and different upbringing. A woman who comes to stay with her husband's family may come from a different background and this can lead to friction and strain. When such friction is removed skillfully and prudently, there is peace in the family. Sujātā had come from a very wealthy family and had difficulty adjusting at her in-laws (in spite of her in-laws too being very affluent). She needed guidance from an elderly person. She was not by nature cruel or insolent but behaved improperly due to youthful disobedience and immaturity. The Buddha wisely made her understand her behavior and her responsibility.

Sequence of Wives

The description is about the types of wives we see in society. Though it implies desirable behavior of wives, it doesn't make a direct comment on it. They are divided in two groups. First group is how wives should not be. The sequence in the first group looks proper. The worst is a wife like an assassin. In the second group the logic doesn't look faultless. The sequence between wife like a mother and like a sister could have been reversed. The sequence of wife like a friend and wife like a slave may certainly irk a modern mind. A friendly wife should have come after the servile wife; that is, a friendly wife should be more desirable than the servile wife.

To put a servile wife at the end and thus as the most desirable seems to be something that was added after the Buddha. It is also possible that the sequence was put in this way to avoid a total shock to a society that had such total male dominance. A saving grace, so to speak, is that though the implication is that a servile wife is the best, it is not said that a wife should be like a slave. There is no explicit statement that a slave wife is the best.

We can also look at the issue of order of these wives from a different angle. Service was important in the Buddha's Dhamma. The service rendered out of pressure of slavery and the service that is spontaneous, joyful, voluntary are different. We must state that service like a slave is undesirable. In modern times, the dominant sentiment is that a wife is a friend. It was probably an exception to have such sentiment in those days. If Sujātā declared that she would be like a slave, it was probably because of her young age and shyness in front of elders especially after the discourse by such an eminent person. One wouldn't expect in that context for a young woman to say I would be a wife like a friend.

A Nagging Dissatisfaction

It is no doubt that the Buddha gave suitable advice to Sujātā and was able to resolve the conflict in Anāthapiṇḍika's family. Even then putting a wife like a slave above a wife like a friend leaves one dissatisfied. However, as we will see later from Kosambi's analysis on the issue of Gotamī, it is not likely that the Buddha gave the order or the sequence of wives as we have it in the Tipiṭaka now.

Solution to the Dissatisfaction

A quotation from the Connected Discourses[346] describes a joyous and wholesome relation between husband and wife. To the question as to "Who is the greatest friend?" the Buddha answers "A wife is the greatest friend." When we see this answer, it becomes clear beyond doubt that the Buddha looked upon the wife as a friend of the husband and not as his slave.

The Context of His Discourse

Often the Buddha would change the tone of his discourse depending on the situation. When he wanted to restore the slave-woman's daughter Vāsabhakhattiyā to her position as queen, he talked about the importance of the father's family. It was not that he supported male dominance but this argument to Pasenadi was made for her sake. The reasoning was effective in restoring the slave-daughter from the position of a slave to the position of queen. We should look at the context for his advice. It was done for the sake of a woman who had been wronged.

Ban on Entry of Women in Saṅgha

The Buddha Refused Gotamī Admission to Saṅgha

It is well known that the Buddha gave entry to women in the Saṅgha. The circumstances under which he took this decision are described in Cūḷavagga[347] of the Book of Discipline. The same subject is also dealt with in the Numerical Discourses.[348] The gist of the description in the Book of Discipline is given here.

Once the Buddha was dwelling in Nigrodha's Park in Kapilavatthu. At that time Mahāpajāpati Gotamī approached him and requested, "Bhante, the Tathāgata has taught the Dhamma and the Discipline. It would be good if women could go forth into homelessness and ordain."

The Buddha denied the permission. He remained firm about this when Gotamī made the request for the second and third time telling her that she should not expect going forth and ordination in the Saṅgha. This made Gotamī sad and she started weeping. She saluted him in tears and left.

Gotamī Expressed Her Sorrow to Bhikkhu Ānanda

After this incident, the Buddha left Kapilavatthu and reached Vesāli in his wanderings. He stayed there in Kūṭāgārasālā. After he left Kapilavatthu, Gotamī cut off her hair, wore saffron robes and walked to Vesāli in the company of many Sākyan women. When they reached Kūṭāgārasālā, their legs were swollen, they had dirt on their bodies. They stood sad and tearful outside the gate of Kūṭāgārasālā.

Seeing them, Ānanda asked them why they were standing there. They told him that they were sad because the Buddha had refused entry to women in the Saṅgha. Ānanda promised them that he would intervene on their behalf and asked them to wait. He then requested the Buddha thrice to give admission women in Saṅgha. Thrice, the Buddha refused.

Ānanda Changed His Argument

When Ānanda realized that the Buddha was firm in his view, he decided to try in a different way. He said to the Buddha, "Bhante, do women have the capacity to become stream-enterer after going forth into homelessness and getting ordained in the Tathāgata's Dhamma and Discipline? Do they have the capacity to become once-returner and non-returner? Can they become arahatas?"

The Buddha answered 'yes' to all these questions of Ānanda. Then Ānanda reminded him that Gotamī was the Buddha's aunt. She had looked after him and nursed him after his mother had died. She had suckled him. Thus, he owed a great debt of gratitude to her. Again Ānanda requested the Buddha that if the women were capable of achieving all the high goals of the Dhamma, then they might please be given admission in Saṅgha.

The Buddha Puts Strict Conditions

After Ānanda's request the Buddha said to him, "Ānanda, if Mahāpajāpati Gotamī is willing to accept eight conditions, they can get ordination."

He put the first condition, "Even if a bhikkhuṇi has ordained a hundred years ago and a bhikkhu who has ordained on that very day arrives, she should salute him, get up to greet him with folded hands, give him proper respect. She should welcome and accept this rule; honor it, respect it, follow it and not transgress it all his life." After enumerating all the eight rules, the Buddha repeated that the bhikkhuṇis should not transgress these rules.

The Other Conditions

A bhikkhuṇi should not spend rains retreat where there are no bhikkhus.

Every fortnight a bhikkhuṇi should ask questions and seek discourse from the bhikkhu-Saṅgha.

At the end of the rains retreat, a bhikkhuṇi must atone for offences of three types: by what has been seen, by what has been heard and by what is suspected in a Saṅgha comprising of both bhikkhus and bhikkhuṇis.

A novice should train under six members of both orders for two years before seeking ordination.

A bhikkhuṇi should not abuse or criticize a bhikkhu.

A bhikkhuṇi should not admonish bhikkhus but bhikkhus may admonish and teach bhikkhuṇis.

Gotamī Accepts the Conditions

Then Ānanda went to Gotamī and told her the conditions for ordination. She replied, "Bhante, suppose there is a young girl or boy who likes to look attractive and has washed his or her hair. Such a girl or a boy gets a garland of lotus or jasmine, she or he accepts it with both hands and puts it on the greatest part of body, the head. I too accept these rules with equal joy. I will not transgress these rules throughout my life."

Then Ānanda went to the Tathāgata and informed him.

The Buddha Expresses Displeasure

Hearing Ānanda's report didn't make the Buddha happy. He said to Ānanda that if women had not been ordained, the Dhamma would have endured for a thousand years, but now it would endure only for five hundred years.

He gave some examples to support his statement. Just as a family with several women and very few men is easily destroyed by thieves and robbers, the Dhamma doesn't endure long when women are given admission to the Saṅgha. Just as a good crop of paddy is destroyed by a white diseaseor a good crop of sugarcane is destroyed by a red disease, the Dhamma too won't endure long.

Then he said to Ānanda, "Just as a man builds a dam to stop water from overflowing; I have made these eight rules to restrain bhikkhuṇis."

The Dhamma Discourse to Gotamī

Then Gotamī came to him. She asked the Buddha how she should behave with the Sākyan women who had gone forth. The Buddha gave a Dhamma discourse. After she left, he called the bhikkhus and told them, "Bhikkhus, I allow bhikkhus to give ordination to bhikkhuṇis."

After some time, other bhikkhuṇis told Gotamī. "You are not ordained. We, on other hand, have received ordination. the Tathāgata has laid down a rule allowing bhikkhus to ordain bhikkhuṇis."

Gotamī reported this to Ānanda. And Ānanda informed the Buddha. Then the Buddha said, "Ānanda, Mahāpajāpati Gotamī received higher ordination the moment she accepted the eight rules."

One day Gotamī went to Ānanda and requested him to seek the Buddha's permission for bhikkhus and bhikkhuṇis to salute each other according to seniority. Ānanda conveyed this to the Buddha. He rejected the request. This would be improper, there was no scope for such a thing, he said. He questioned Ānanda that even those belonging to other sects didn't allow men to salute the women, how could the Buddha do it. Then he told bhikkhus, "Bhikkhus whoever salutes women, gets up to greet them with folded hands and honors them would be transgressing the discipline."

Later Gotamī went to the Buddha. She asked him what should be done about the guidelines for bhikkhuṇis that were the same as bhikkhus. He told her that bhikkhuṇis should practice them the same way that the bhikkhus do.

Once Gotamī went to him and asked for a sermon on the Dhamma, saying that she would follow the Dhamma diligently.

He told her to remember that those deeds that lead to craving, acquisition, accumulation, desire, discontent, excessive socializinginactivity and distress are not the Dhamma, are not the Discipline, are not the teaching of the Buddha. Then he said that those deeds that are devoid of craving etc. are the Dhamma, are the Discipline and are the teaching of the Buddha.

Discussion

The admission of Gotamī in the Saṅgha is a major turning point in the cultural and social history of India. This small incident gave rise to several guiding principles. Even for the Buddha himself this was an extraordinary event.

On one hand there were the principles of justice and equality; and on the other hand he knew the harsh realities of practical life. He had to do a delicate balancing act that would test his skill and conscience.

Untimely Death of Māyādevi

Māyādevi had died seven days after giving birth to Siddhārtha. It was as if the lifetime of mother-son relation was expressed in seven days. She didn't live to see her son reaching the pinnacle of humanity. Even so, carrying this son in her womb and looking after him for a week after birth must have been a fulfilling motherhood for her.

Gotamī's Two Services to Society

Gotamī had the joy of seeing the supreme attainment of Siddhārtha that was denied to Māyādevi. She nursed Siddhārtha without the slightest negativity. Ānanda's narration tells us how deep her affection was. She breastfed Siddhārtha herself. In spite of being a queen, she didn't arrange for a servant to breastfeed him. Though Siddhārtha went on to attain enlightenment though his own efforts, Gotamī was responsible for raising him from the age of one week until he became independent. The saying in some parts of India 'let the mother die but let her sister live' might have its origin in this great example. Gotamī's life was an excellent example of this saying. Her motherly compassion gave rise to the Buddha's compassion for the whole world.

In addition to this first great service of Gotamī to humanity, she rendered a greater service by opening the door of the Saṅgha for women through her persistence. We know how far-sighted this decision was. It becomes even clearer when we see that about two thousand and five hundred years after the Buddha, when Savitribai Phule tried to open a school for girls in India, cow dung and stones were thrown at her.

Gotamī's Earnest Wish to Go Forth

Gotamī saw that her son was a Buddha who was guiding humanity towards liberation from all suffering. Now the pain of his going forth had disappeared. She understood his decision of leaving home. She didn't want to live in darkness when her son was giving light to the world and became consumed with the wish to bask in that light. When the Buddha reached Kapilavatthu during his wanderings, she realized that this was an apt opportunity for her. The Buddha had created a bhikkhu Saṅgha. Only men were admitted in it. She requested the Buddha to give admission to women in Saṅgha. This was not a request just for her. She knew that the Buddha had gone beyond mundane relations and her request was not personal. She didn't address him as 'son' but as 'bhante.' The Buddha didn't accept Gotamī's request in spite of her repeating it thrice.

Gotamī Was Determined to Go Forth

The Buddha had taken several difficult decisions in his life to achieve his goals. Gotamī had not given him birth but had suckled him. Their relation was that of mother and son. We can say that the milk of Gotamī flowed in his veins and contributed to his courage to take difficult decisions. It means that Gotamī too was not weak and was not likely to give up her pursuit when faced with an obstacle. When the Buddha refused her admission, she did become sad and she wept. Though she didn't argue with the Buddha, she had made up her mind to gain ordination as we see from her later actions.

As if Gotamī Went Forth on Her Own

After refusing Gotamī's request, the Buddha went to Vesāli. Gotamī decided she would leave home to live a life of a bhikkhuṇi, whether or not the Buddha gave her the going forth. Her determination can be seen from the fact that she shaved her head.

Siddhārtha Gotama's giving up the kingdom and going forth was an extraordinary event but after all he was a man. For a woman to shave her head and walk out of home at that time must have been very unusual. It must have been among the rare instances in human history when a queen took such a step.

After shaving her head, she wore saffron clothes and went to Vesāli accompanied by other Sākyan women. The Buddha had not yet admitted Gotamī in the Saṅgha and therefore she didn't have to follow the rules of Saṅgha. She could have gone in a chariot or a palanquin. She didn't. She walked from Kapilavatthu to Vesāli with the same determination with which she shaved her head and wore saffron robes.

One can imagine how difficult this journey must have been for a woman who had lived in royal luxury all her life. When she and the other women reached Vesāli, their feet were swollen and they were covered with dust. Her actions showed her ardent desire to go forth. She also displayed the necessary resolve, perseverance and faith to become a bhikkhuṇi. Seeing her condition, Ānanda requested the Buddha three times to ordain her. Again the Buddha firmly refused.

The Tathāgata Accepts Women's Rights

Ānanda was deeply moved by Gotamī's condition. He was in favor of Gotamī's admission to Saṅgha. Even though the Buddha refused his request, he skillfully overcame it. He had spent a long time in the company of the Buddha. He must have known the Buddha's views on the rights and the abilities of women. So he changed his argument and asked whether women had the right and the capacity to liberate themselves. The Buddha immediately accepted that right. This meant that they shouldn't be stopped from getting liberated. Ānanda didn't immediately push for Gotamī's cause. He reminded the Buddha all that she had done for the Buddha. Thus Ānanda moistened with emotions the logic of women's right.

The Tathāgata's Historic Decision

Though Ānanda added emotion to his appeal, it had been seen several times that the Buddha didn't give in to mere emotional appeals. Gotamī's tears had failed to change his mind. Still, Ānanda's argument was valid. It couldn't be rejected outright. The Buddha had great determination but he was not adamant. He had the flexibility of mind to accept a valid viewpoint. He was not a guru with dictatorial tendencies. He had the generous heart to consider a reasonable argument of someone younger to him. He couldn't reconcile the rights of women on one hand and his refusal to grant them the way to get their rights. He decided to change his decision. He showed through his own conduct that principles are more important than egotistical attachment to one's own decisions.

The Buddha's Practical Considerations Behind the Stringent Rules

The Buddha had earlier refused women admission to the Saṅgha. It was not out of gender bias or the tendency of a male dominated society that demeaned women. He was aware of the practical difficulties of ordaining women.

If men and women started living together, the natural attraction between them would hinder their meditation. Just how great is this attraction can be seen from the very first sutta of the Numerical Discourses. He had discussed this with bhikkhus once while living in Jetavana at Sāvatthi. There is no greater attraction for a man than the attraction to a woman's form, sound, smell, taste and touch. The same is true for a woman. The self-control and restraint that he taught would have been much more difficult with both men and women together. This was not the fault of women. It was just natural attraction that affected both men and women.

Even though he was aware of the practical difficulties, when it came to principles he gave up his earlier refusal.

The conditions that he put to women for admission to the Saṅgha are certainly not only unfair but also humiliating. It conveys inequality. It is especially painful to see the rule whereby a most senior bhikkhuṇi has to salute a newly ordained bhikkhu. These conditions that make the women secondary and lower are questionable.

Could These Really Be the Tathāgata's Words?

Let us remember one thing here. There is reason to doubt whether the language and the content that is conveyed to us has come from the Buddha himself. After his *mahāparinibbāna*, several allegations were made against Ānanda. One of these was about admission of women in the Saṅgha.[349]

This means that there was a dominant thinking in the Saṅgha that women should not have been admitted to the Saṅgha. Actually, if the bhikkhus were unhappy about this, they should have approached the Buddha in his own lifetime rather than accusing Ānanda of wrongdoing. The decision was not taken by Ānanda. It was the Buddha's decision. The Buddha was open to discussion and amendments. But it seems that the bhikkhus were unable to convince him otherwise. It is possible that these bhikkhus kept quiet during the Buddha's lifetime and when he was no more they raised the issue again. They couldn't fault the Buddha as they had supreme faith in him. Therefore, Ānanda was made the scapegoat. If they showed that the Buddha was against giving admission to women in the Saṅgha, it would be easier to blame Ānanda entirely for it.

We must therefore consider the possibility that these conditions were put in the Buddha' mouth later.

Dharmanand Kosambi Feels That the Conditions Came Later

Dharmanand Kosambi's analysis in his text[350] is noteworthy. The Buddha would lay down rules when he felt that there were mistakes or transgressions. He wouldn't lay down rules *before* the transgressions. Kosambi feels that it was not in keeping with the Buddha's usual practice to lay down rules beforehand.

Kosambi writes about these conditions, "… It must be said that these eight rules were added later on because they are at odd with the practice of how the Buddha laid down rules." He also writes, "But this was not adapted in case of Mahāpajāpati Gotamī. It seems strange that these eight rules were laid down even before any transgressions had occurred in the bhikkhuṇi Saṅgha.

Therefore, it seems that the bhikkhus made these rules later and added them in the Vinaya (Book of Discipline) and the Numerical Discourses in order to keep the control and power over the Saṅgha in their hand.

"Sutta Piṭaka (the Discourses) is older than the Vinaya Piṭaka. But some of the suttas are clearly later additions. This sutta too seems to be a later addition. It is likely that this sutta was written about a century or two before Common Era when the Mahhāyhāna sect was spreading rapidly. In this sutta, *saddhamma* means Theravhāda. The prophecy (in retrospect—this parenthesis is the translator's) of the author of this sutta was possibly that because of the formation of bhikkhuṇi Saṅgha, it would last five hundred years and afterwards Mahhāyhāna would spread everywhere. This prophecy itself suggests that this sutta was written five hundred years after the Buddha's *parinibbāna*."

I too am inclined to accept the conclusion of Kosambi. The Tathāgata himself had clarified his method of formulating rules when talking to Bhaddālī,[351] "Bhaddālī, as long as some faults don't crop up in the Saṅgha, I don't lay down rules of conduct for the disciples. Bhaddālī, when such faults crop up, then I lay down rules to remove such faults."

Even if We Assume for the Sake of Argument...

There is no possibility that the Buddha put these conditions and that he made any prediction about the relationship of women to the longevity of the Dhamma and the Discipline. But let us assume for the sake of argument that he did put these conditions and did make that prediction. Still, we can't blame him. Why? Let us see.

He didn't put these conditions spontaneously or easily. He himself said that these were like a dam. Today in the era of co-education, boys and girls study together in schools, colleges and universities. We cannot look at the society at the time of the Buddha from today's perspective.

This is not to justify the alleged unjust inequality of these eight conditions. We must understand the difference between those who denied all rights to women to create a societal structure of slavery and the great man who was trying to give women their rights but was doing so with circumspection considering the ground reality.

To criticize him for this is not only an error in evaluating him but also ingratitude. We should also remember that by doing so we hurt ourselves and we also empower those who try to break any movement of equality and independence. The Buddha's time was a time when society was totally dominated by men. Without those eight conditions, there would have been a big upheaval in the society. This would have caused the contraction of women's independence rather than its expansion.

It is also possible that it would have taken time for the bhikkhus to come to terms with this new situation. This would have weakened the bhikkhu Saṅgha. Therefore, we should understand that those who wish to create equality must be patient.

Let us take the example from a time after the Buddha. In most parts of India, religion and law were followed as per the commentary *Mitāksharā* on *Yājñavalkyasmriti*. Bengal was an exception. There *Dayābhāga* by *Jimutavāhana* was followed, who had given a widow the right over her husband's property. He had taken a positive step towards the women's right but it turned out to be a disaster. The society was so male dominated and unwilling that it strengthened the heinous atrocity of 'sati' where women burn themselves (or are forced to burn) on the funeral pyre of their husbands.

In Spite of the Conditions, Door to Independence Opened

We see that in spite of the conditions, women got admission to the Saṅgha and this event lead to positive results. Countless bhikkhuṇis did exemplary work in the field of learning. We will see these later in the chapter.

Gotamī was a strong woman but, if we were to believe the story as it comes to us, she accepted these conditions as if she were accepting a garland. She knew that this was the opening of the door for a long journey ahead. She also showed the courage to ask the Buddha to change the rule about saluting a bhikkhu. She wanted a junior bhikkhu to salute a senior bhikkhuṇi. She thus wanted to change a rule laid down recently. The Buddha refused.

Again we must remember that we are assuming here that he indeed put these eight conditions. Even if Gotamī couldn't change the rule she did sow the seed of equality of bhikkhu and bhikkhuṇi. This wouldn't have happened had she not been admitted to the Saṅgha.

The Prediction About the Future of the Dhamma

It was not an easy decision for the Buddha. It was only after Ānanda took a principled stand that he conceded. But he was aware of the practical difficulties this would create. The Saṅgha would be facing those very defilements that he was cautioning it against. It was probably not meant to be a prediction but a warning.

The Buddha had made it clear that he didn't believe that one could predict the future. It was more like predicting a likely outcome. The examples of the diseases affecting crops were probably meant to warn the bhikkhus about their precepts. Since it was not likely that the Buddha behaved in this manner, this is *sthūṇānikhanananyāya,* literally an exercise in making a pole in the ground firm by shaking it.

If we were to take just one example, we could look at his declaration while rotating the Wheel of the Dhamma that this Wheel of the Dhamma could not be turned back. Then how would he say that it would last only five hundred years?

Bhikkhuṇis and Lay Women Disciples Are the Saṅgha's Glory

Once he said that a bhikkhuṇi with clear views, humble, learned, knowledgeable, who knows the Dhamma and follows the Dhamma brings glory to the Saṅgha.[352] He also said that a laywoman who has these qualities increases the glory of the Saṅgha. Not only bhikkhuṇis but also many laywomen were endowed with these qualities.

Confidence of Bhikkhuṇis

In the Connected Discourses we find an example of how the bhikkhuṇis became confident due to the Buddha's teaching.[353]

A bhikkhuṇi named Uppalavaṇṇā was once standing under a sāla tree. Then Māra tried to frighten her, "Hey bhikkhuṇi, you are standing alone under this sāla tree that has blossomed. No other woman can compare with you when it comes to beauty. Hey you foolish woman, aren't you afraid of immoral men?"

Uppalavaṇṇā realized that Māra was trying to frighten her. She replied, "Even if a hundred such men were to come here, I wouldn't be afraid, I wouldn't tremble. Even if I am alone, Māra, I am not afraid of you."

We also find a description in the Connected Discourses[354] of Bhikkhuṇi Sukkā giving a Dhamma discourse in a big assembly and of her discourse being like ambrosia. This shows that at least some bhikkhuṇis had developed the capacity to expound on the finer aspects and subtle points of the Dhamma in big assemblies.

Once during her wanderings, Bhikkhuṇi Khemā reached a place between Sāketa and Sāvatthi. At that time, Pasenadi had also stopped there during his journey from Sāketa to Sāvatthi. He asked his attendant whether there was any samaṇa or a brāhmaṇa worth visiting there. The attendant made enquiries and didn't find anyone worthy. He did however hear about Khemā.

He told the king, "Khemā is wise, she has clear understanding, she is knowledgeable and a great orator. Such is her fame. His Majesty should call upon her." Accordingly the king went to her and received the teaching about things not fit for speculation. Later when he heard the same discourse from the Buddha he was impressed with the erudition of the bhikkhuṇi.[355]

Bhikkhuṇi Kajaṅgalikā Teaches Laymen

Once the Tathāgata was dwelling in the bamboo grove of Kajaṅgala.[356]

One day many lay disciples went to Bhikkhuṇi Kajaṅgalikā. They sat to one side after saluting her and expressed their desire to understand in detail some of the brief discourses by the Buddha.

The bhikkhuṇi told them that she had not heard these brief discourses by the Buddha or had not heard them being repeated by any bhikkhu. However, she would explain to them as she understood them. She gave a detailed explanation and ended her discourse with a humble suggestion, "I have told you as I understand these issues. Please go to the Tathāgata himself and seek clarification and follow what he says."

They agreed and left after saluting her and circumambulating her. Then they went to the Buddha and narrated what happened. He said, "Well said, well said, householders! Bhikkhuṇi Kajaṅgalikā is erudite and has great wisdom. If you had come to me, I would have explained it the same way. Therefore, follow what she has said."

Discussion

It is clear that bhikkhuṇis had cultivated qualities and intellectual grasp that allowed them to explain in detail what the Buddha had said in brief. Kajaṅgalikā herself had not heard discourses from the Buddha or from bhikkhus but had given her advice based on her own independent thinking. This shows her advancement in the Dhamma. The Buddha said that her description was totally correct. He praised her erudition and her wisdom. He asked the men to follow her advice.

It shows the good results of the doors of intellectual autonomy and achievement being thrown open to women. It also shows that the Buddha respected the independent thinking of bhikkhuṇis.

It is also noteworthy that the laymen saluted her when they came to her. They asked her to explain the Dhamma to her. Before leaving, they again saluted her and circumambulated her, which was a mark of reverence. In this sequence of events, one is pleased to see the atmosphere of equality engendered by the Buddha's teaching.

Many Bhikkhuṇis in Sri Lanka

The Pali text Dīpavaṃsa gives a list of bhikkhuṇis in India and in Sri Lanka. It lists bhikkhuṇis who had mastered the Discipline and were Guides: Paṭācāra, Dhammadinnā, Sobhita, Isidāsikā, Visākā, Soṇā, Subalā, Saṅghadāsi, Nandā, Dhammapāla, etc.

It also lists bhikkhuṇis that had gone to Sri Lanka from India and had studied the Tipiṭaka at Anurādhapura: Saṅghamittā, Uttarā, Hemā, Masaragallā, Aggimittā, Dāsikā, Pheggu, Pabbatā, Mattā, Mallā, Dhammadāsī, etc.

Saddhammanandī, Somā, Giriddhi, Dāsikā, Dhammā and Dhammapālā were learned in the Discipline. Sobhanā and Dhammatāpasā followed austere practices. Naramittā had knowledge of the Discipline. Sātā, Kālī and Uttarā were skilled in the doctrine of elders. Uttarā had studied the Tipiṭaka in Anurādhapura along with twenty thousand bhikkhuṇis.

The daughter of King Kākavaṇṇa was expert in the Dhamma. Girikālī, the daughter of a priest, was known for her erudition. Dāsī, Kālī and Subbapāpikā were daughters of a gambler. They became such experts in the Dhamma that none could find any fault in their teaching. Bhikkhuṇi Rohanā is said to have studied the Discipline with twenty thousand bhikkhuṇis in Anuradhapura.

Such was the learning of Mahādevi, Padmā and Hemāshā that King Tissa revered them. They were experts in the Discipline. Mahāsoṇā, Dattā, Sivalī, Rūpasobhinī, Appamattā, Nāgā, Nāgamittā, Dhammaguttā, Dāsikā, Samuddā, Sapattā, Channā, Upālī, Revatā, Mālā, Khemā, Tissā, Mahārūhā were other famous bhikkhuṇis. Bhikkhuṇis Samuddā, Nāvādevī and Sivalī were princesses before they joined the Saṅgha. Nāgapalī, Nāgamitta and Bhikkhunipāla were experts in the Discipline. Culanāgā, Dattā, Soṇā were much praised by honorable men in society. Gāmikaputti, Mahātissā, Sumanā and Māhākālī had gone forth from prestigious families.

Even after conceding that some information in Dīpavaṃsa could be exaggerated, one can still say with certainty that several bhikkhuṇis had done exceptional work in the field of the Dhamma.

Honored Ambapālī's Invitation When Invited By Influencial Licchavīs

Towards the end of his life, in the course of his wandering, the Buddha reached Vesāli. He stopped at the mango grove owned by a courtesan named Ambapālī.[357]

When Ambapālī came to know about it, she went to meet the Buddha in a magnificent chariot. She went in chariot as far as the road was suitable and then she walked to meet the Buddha. She saluted him and sat to one side. He gave a Dhamma discourse which she appreciated and invited him, "Bhante, please come for a meal along with the bhikkhu Saṅgha." He showed his consent by remaining silent. Then Ambapālī got up, saluted him and left.

The Licchavīs, the ruling clan of Vesāli, also learned about the Buddha's visit. They too got into resplendent chariots and left the city. Some wore blue clothes and jewelry. Their chariots too were blue. Some wore yellow clothes and yellow jewelry and had yellow chariots. Similarly, those with red clothes and white clothes also had matching jewelry and chariots.

They were going to the Buddha when Ambapālī came in the opposite direction. Rather than taking her chariot to one side and allowing them to pass as was expected because of their social status, she didn't yield. The yoke, axle and wheel of her chariot rubbed against that of the chariots of the young Licchavīs.

They were surprised and asked her, "Why are you behaving thus?" She replied, "O noble princes, tomorrow I have invited the Buddha to my home for a meal."

Then they said to her, "Ambapālī, we will give you a hundred thousand if you give up your claim and allow us to invite the Buddha to our homes." She replied, "Noble princes, even if you give to me the entire Vesāli and all other lands that you possess, I will not give up this meal."

The Licchavīs were disappointed and exclaimed, "Ambapālī has defeated us, Ambapālī has defeated us."

Then the Licchavīs went to the Buddha. When the Buddha saw them from afar, he said to bhikkhus, "Bhikkhus, those who have not seen the gods of the thirty-three realms should see these Licchavīs. Bhikkhus they are as resplendent as the gods."

The Licchavīs got down from the chariots and walked to where the Buddha was seated. They saluted him and sat to one side. The Buddha enthused and delighted them with a sermon of Dhamma. Then they invited the Buddha for a meal the next day. When the Buddha told them that he had already accepted the invitation from Ambapālī, they became agitated and again exclaimed, "Ambapālī had defeated us!" Then they saluted the Buddha and left.

The next day, Ambapālī prepared a meal in her garden and sent a message to the Buddha that the meal was ready. He came with bhikkhus for the meal. After his meal, Ambapālī offered the garden to the Saṅgha headed by the Buddha. He then gave her a Dhamma discourse. He also taught Dhamma to the bhikkhus who were with him. He gave a detailed explanation of morality, concentration and wisdom. Later, Ambapālī became a bhikkhuṇi.

The Buddha Turned a Courtesan into a Sanyasin: The Opponents Turned a Sanyasin into a Courtesan

Effort to Malign the Buddha

The Buddha guided society in the direction of equity and justice. As a result, people from other sects often used to conspire against him. In the book edited by P. V. Bapat '2500 Years of Buddhism' C. V. Joshi wrote,[358] *"Years rolled by. The Master and his disciples travelled all over the country combating old superstitions, the old values based on birth, and animal sacrifice, denouncing the spirit of revenge and praising morality, the threefold path of purity and rational thought. The Saṅgha continued to increase in strength... much to the chagrin of the brāhmaṇas and other sectarians. They tried to traduce the Buddha with the help of a courtesan named Cincā. The poor woman suffered heavy punishment for her guilt of incriminating the Buddha. A similar fate awaited Sundarī, who claimed that the Buddha was in love with her."*

We will discuss here two such conspiracies by his opponents.

The first incident concerns a sanyasin named Ciñcā and the second involves ascetic Sundarī. Of these, the first one is found in the commentary on the Dhammapada.[359]

Once the Tathāgata was dwelling at Jetavana in Sāvatthi. People had started revering him as the reputation of his exemplary qualities spread. People of other sects lost their prestige the way a light-bug becomes insignificant once the sun rises. They became jealous and started thinking of ways to malign him in public so that people stop respecting him.

At that time Ciñcā was a young and beautiful sanyasin in Sāvatthi. The Buddha's opponents decided to use her to defame the Buddha. When she came to meet them, they didn't talk to her. She asked them why they were shunning her. They then told her about how Samaṇa Gotama's fame was spreading and they were losing the patronage of people. She told them not to worry and that she would take care of it.

Ciñcā was an expert in deception. She started going towards Jetavana (Jeta's Grove) at the time when people from Sāvatthi would return from Jetavana. She would wear a beautiful dress and carry fragrant flowers with her. When people asked her where she was headed, she would reply, "What is it to you?" Then she would go the monasteries of other sects near Jetavana and spend the night there.

In the morning, many disciples in Sāvatthi would go towards Jetavana to pay respects to the Buddha. Then she would act as if she is returning from Jetavana. If someone asked where she had stayed, she would answer, "What do you care where I spent the night?"

After a couple of weeks, she changed her answer. She started saying that she had spent the night with Samaṇa Gotama in his *Gandhakuṭī*. This created a doubt in the minds of people. After three-four months, she started tying clothes on her abdomen creating an impression that she was pregnant. She started telling people that she was carrying Samaṇa Gotama's child. After eight-nine months, she tied a piece of wood on her abdomen and covered it with cloth. Then she went to the place where the Buddha was giving a Dhamma discourse and said to him, "O Great Samaṇa, you teach many people. Your speech is sweet and splendid is the touch of your lips! I am pregnant with your child. But you have not made any provision for my confinement. You have prepared no house. You have not made any preparation or asked any of your disciples such as the Kosalan King or Anāthapiṇḍika or even Visākhā. You don't tell them that they should do whatever is necessary for Ciñcā. You know how to enjoy but don't know how to take care of your child."

On hearing her, the Buddha stopped his discourse and said, "Sister, you know and I know the truth about the matter that you have spoken about."

She responded, "Indeed, Great Samaṇa, you and I have done this willfully."

At that time the seat of Sakka, the king of gods, heated up. He came to Jetavana with four angels. They took the form of mice and chewed the strings fastening the piece of wood to Ciñcā's stomach. The cloth covering the wood blew up due to wind and the wood fell on her feet. People censured her for making a false allegation and punished her.

In the Udāna of the Minor Discourses we find the second incident.[360] The description given in Sundarī Sutta is:

Once the Buddha was dwelling at Jetavana in Sāvatthi. Ascetics of other sects were jealous of his fame. They took the help of the ascetic Sundarī to defame him. They trained her and sent her to Jetavana. Once they realized that enough people had seen her going to Jetavana, they murdered her and threw her corpse in a well.

Then they went to King Pasenadi and complained, "We don't see ascetic Sundarī anywhere." When asked by the king as to what their suspicions were, they said that she had gone to Jetavana. Then the king asked them to search Jetavana. They pretended as if they were searching and found the corpse. Then they took the corpse all over the city shouting, "See the deeds of samaṇas, the sons of Sākya. These samaṇas are shameless, immoral, evil, liars and unchaste."

People in Sāvatthi were swayed by their words. They became angry at bhikkhus and started abusing them with harsh words. Then the bhikkhus went to the Buddha and reported it. The Buddha reassured them, "This commotion will not last long. It will last a week. Not more than a week." The Buddha taught them a verse to utter when the people abused them. The first part of the verse was:

One who says that it has happened when it has not happened goes to the nether world.

One who denies an act after having committed it also goes to hell.

As the bhikkhus started uttering the verse, people's attitude towards the bhikkhus started changing. They felt that since the bhikkhus were solemnly asserting it, they must not have done the evil deed. The allegations stopped after a week. Those bhikkhus told this to the Buddha. Then the Buddha said, "Just as an elephant is wounded by arrows in battle, people too sometimes cause injury because they don't know the truth. But bhikkhus should stay calm and not allow their mind to be tainted."

There is more detail to be found in commentary.[361] The opponents had two goals in sending Sundarī to the Buddha. If Samaṇa Gotama is attracted to Sundarī, he would be defamed automatically. Even if he doesn't get attracted to her, there will be opportunity to create doubt in the minds of people and then they could use Sundarī to malign him. They hired contract killers to murder Sundarī.

The king didn't depend on the opponents of the Buddha for the truth. He asked his servants to investigate. The murderers of Sundarī were once quarreling with each other over the amount they each received from the killing. One of them said to another, "You killed her with one blow and are now drinking from that money."

One of the king's men heard this and took them to the king. They confessed to the killing in front of the king. They told him that they were hired by the opponents of the Buddha. Then the king told the opponents to go around the town confessing to their crime, "We got Sundarī murdered to defame the Buddha. He and his disciples are innocent. We are guilty of the murder."

They went around the town and confessed. The people denounced them and they received punishment for their crime. The people honored the Buddha and his bhikkhus.

Discussion

When the Buddha's opponents realized that people hold him in high esteem, they decided to use unfair means to malign him. Various means used by opponents over the next twenty-five centuries had their antecedents in the Buddha's own time.

Various incidents in the commentary such as Sakka's seat getting heated and angels taking the form of mice are myths that have been added. The only relevant thing for us is that the conspiracy of Ciñcā was uncovered and the opponents failed in their attempt.

In the end, the opponents from other traditions who used these two nuns lost prestige. One woman was murdered and the other faced punishment. The Buddha's opponents made these two young women commit evil deeds for a selfish reason. These women had left home. It means that they wanted to dedicate their life for a higher transcendental goal. But wrong company and misdirection lead to their downfall.

On one hand, a courtesan like Ambapālī became a nun due to the Buddha's teaching. She left the allurement of wealth and sensual pleasures to uplift herself. On the other hand, the opponents of the Buddha caused the ruin of two women who were originally inclined towards a lofty goal. What a big difference!

Somā Bhikkhuṇi

The Connected Discourses[362] gives an excellent example of how the Buddha's discourses helped women to leave behind feelings of inferiority and gain the confidence to give a fitting answer to all critics.

Once Somā, after her alms round and meal, sat under a tree in the Blind Grove for a day's meditation. At that time Māra tried to terrorize her, "It is difficult for others to attain the heights that only sages can reach. For a woman whose intellect is limited to two fingers, it is not possible."

She recognized him to be the evil Māra and replied, "How can womanhood be an obstruction when the mind is balanced, wisdom is present and there is proper insight (*vipassanā*) in the Dhamma? Your words will affect only those who have this feeling of being a man or a woman or someone else."

Discussion

These utterances of Somā should be treasured as a momentous proclamation in the history of Indian civilization for independence and human rights that go beyond mundane differences such as gender etc. Māra who was trying to denigrate her as a woman represented the mentality of the male dominated social system. This system believed that woman didn't have the intellectual capacity to fulfill important responsibilities or to attain higher goals.

Māra said that their intellect is limited to two fingers. Women often check whether the rice is cooked properly by pressing rice grains between two fingers. The phrase common in India 'two finger intellect' refers to this practice. Māra tried to demean and discourage Somā by suggesting that women should do housework such as cooking and should not try to acquire higher knowledge, which was beyond their capacity.

Somā was no pushover. She didn't stray from her path due to the attack. She had wisdom. If one has the qualities to attain the goal, womanhood is not a hindrance. Gender ceases to be a hindrance when one realizes that one is a free and independent person who has the right to uplift oneself. Weaklings who put limits of gender etc. on themselves get distracted from their aim. Somā's determination indicated that those who transcend these constraints and listen to the inner voice of freedom are not affected by threats.

The Buddha didn't merely preach about the lofty heights women can attain in the field of intellect, learning, creativity, courage, confidence and self-expression. He ensured that countless women from India and abroad fulfill that dream.

Women Could Breathe Freedom

At a time when stringent restrictions were put on women in India, the Buddha provided opportunities to them for realizing their potential.

At a time when the birth of a girl was considered painful, he gave inspiration to the society to welcome the birth of a girl. He gave a vision to the society that a wife is a true friend of her husband.

He prepared women to challenge those who thought that women's intellect was restricted to the fingers that checked whether rice is cooked or not. Women started to face intellectual challenges fearlessly and started analyzing problems with their own free reason. It is important to note that these were not exceptions. It is a pleasant surprise to see that the Therīgāthā[363] (verses of senior bhikkhuṇis) records utterances of seventy-three bhikkhuṇis.

Saṅghamittā, Asoka's daughter, dedicated her life for the spread of Dhamma. This was a historic work. She took to Sri Lanka the sapling of the Bodhi tree under which the Buddha attained enlightenment. It is still preserved there. In India, that inspiring tree could not be preserved.

When we see all these facts, we can certainly say that due to the Buddha's Dhamma, women could breathe easy and free, they could blossom and prosper.

11

Bhikkhus, Wander for the Welfare and Happiness of Many

Siddhārtha Gotama attained Bodhi after many experiments. The principles that he discovered in this process make up the Dhamma. The medium that he used to take the Dhamma to the masses is the Saṅgha. Let us see how it was created and what was its nature.

The creation of the Saṅgha was a historic visionary work. Giving a proper structure and presentation of the Dhamma was as important as attaining Bodhi. Equally important was the creation of a disciplined Saṅgha that took the Dhamma to countless people. The usefulness of the Saṅgha was unparalleled at a time when communication was not as easy as it is today. Even a perfectly enlightened one couldn't be in two places at the same time to teach the Dhamma. But when the same enlightened one taught the Dhamma to another and made him capable of teaching the Dhamma, it could spread far and wide. This was the thought behind the formation of the Saṅgha—to reach people in their towns, in their houses and most importantly in their minds. If he had not done this, the Dhamma would not have spread so much in and outside of India. Perhaps, after the Buddha it would have disappeared not only from India but from the entire world.

Creating the Bhikkhu Saṅgha

The Tathāgata spent about seven weeks in deep contemplation in and around Uruvelā. Once he was sitting under the Rājāyatana tree. At that time, two traders from Ukkala (Orissa) Tapussa and Bhallika came there.[364] They were brothers according to the Commentary.[365] The legend is that their family deity had told them to offer honey-cake and butter milk to the Buddha so that they benefit for long from the meritorious deed. All it means is that they followed the tradition in their society and offered the food to the Tathāgata who thought, "I can't accept the food in my hands. What should I do?"

At that time the guardian dieties of four directions brought a stone bowl for him. The Commentary says that initially they offered him a bowl made of sapphire, which he declined to accept.

But this seems to be a legend created to glorify the Buddha. Probably he took a curved stone that could be used as a bowl and accepted food in it. The two traders then took refuge in the Buddha and the Dhamma; requested him to accept them as his disciples. Thus, they were the first disciples to take refuge in the two gems. It seems that the Buddha didn't give them any sermon.

We should understand this incident properly. Though the Buddha had attained enlightenment under the Bodhi tree, this is the first instance where he is seen accepting food from anyone after his enlightenment. In that sense, this is when the Buddha truly became a 'Buddhist monk.' In Buddhist tradition this is called *piṇḍapāta* (alms food). Thus, buttermilk and honey-cake were the first alms food and the stone bowl was the first bowl.

The two traders took refuge in two gems because Saṅgha did not yet exist. One person doesn't make a Saṅgha. At that moment, the Buddha and the Dhamma existed but not Saṅgha. Even after they became his disciples, they didn't form a Saṅgha because they were not bhikkhus. The Saṅgha was not yet created.

Later once the Saṅgha was created, triple refuge became a formality to become a disciple. If someone uttered refuge in triple gem and the Buddha or one of the bhikkhus agreed, the person would become a disciple. A lay disciple would not leave his house or his work. He or she wouldn't leave home. Therefore, there was no need for a formal 'going forth' and higher ordination.

After this incidence, some time later, the Buddha went to Deer Park. This was his first personal wandering *(cārikā)*. There he taught the Dhamma to his former associates. Of them, Koṇḍañña was the first to comprehend the Dhamma. He received the going forth and higher ordination first. When he received the higher ordination, the Saṅgha was created. Afterwards, Vappa and Bhaddiya and finally, Mahānāma and Assaji received ordination. Then there were six members in the Saṅgha including the Buddha.

Though the texts say that the ordination happened in this sequence, it is not necessarily so. There is no mention in the Book of Discipline (Vinaya Piṭaka) that these five were brahmins. But later it became an accepted statement that they were brahmins. We have noted earlier the doubts raised by Dharmanand Kosambi about this. Whatever it may be, it is clear that the Saṅgha was created in the Deer Park at what is today Sarnath near Varanasi.

The Saṅgha Grows

Later Yasa (Yash), son of a businessman in Varanasi, got ordained and became a bhikkhu. His four friends and after that fifty more friends got ordained and became bhikkhus. The Saṅgha now had sixty-one bhikkhus. The Saṅgha started growing.

Lay Disciple

Soon after, Yasa's father became a disciple. Since now the Saṅgha had been created, he became the first person to utter *tisaraṇa* (trisharaṇa, triple refuge). We can say that one who follows the Buddha, Dhamma and Saṅgha is an *upāsaka* (Buddhist disciple). In that sense, *Sāmaṇeras* (novices who have left home but haven't yet received higher ordination) and bhikkhus are also upāsakas. Even so, *upāsaka* is used for a male disciple who has taken refuge in the Dhamma. For women the word is *upāsika*.

Upāsaka means one 'sits close by.' Here, physical proximity is not important. Closeness to the teaching and the discipline is important.

No one was ever forced to become a disciple. It was totally voluntary. One became a disciple out of one's free will. Only when a person requested on his own was he to be accepted as a disciple.

Tisaraṇa

To become a disciple, *tisaraṇa* is important. The nature of this *tisaraṇa* is:

Buddhaṃ Saraṇaṃ Gacchāmi,
Dhammaṃ Saraṇaṃ Gacchāmi,
Saṅghaṃ Saraṇaṃ Gacchāmi.
Dutiyampi Buddhaṃ Saraṇaṃ Gacchāmi,
Dhammaṃ Saraṇaṃ Gacchāmi,
Saṅghaṃ Saraṇaṃ Gacchāmi
Tatiyampi Buddhaṃ Saraṇaṃ Gacchāmi,
Dhammaṃ Saraṇaṃ Gacchāmi,
Saṅghaṃ Saraṇaṃ Gacchāmi

Dutiyaṃ means for the second time. *Tatiyaṃ* means for the third time. These are given as *Saraṇattaya* (three refuges) at the very beginning of Khuddaka Pāṭha[366] which is the first book of the Minor Discourses. *Saraṇa* originally meant home, support, refuge, protection. A person takes refuge where he feels safe, secure; finds benefit and succor. People who took refuge in the Dhamma felt this way. But this didn't happen merely because they took refuge in the Buddha, Dhamma and Saṅgha. Though refuge inclined the person towards effort, the results came only after efforts.

Five Precepts

After *tisaraṇa* (triple refuge) a disciple would take a vow to follow five precepts. These five precepts or rules are called *sikkhapadas* (points of training). These are given immediately after *Saraṇattaya* of Khuddaka Pāṭha. A total of ten rules are listed of which the first five are for lay followers.

These are:

Pāṇātipātā veramaṇī-sikkhāpadaṃ samādiyāmi.
Adinnādānā veramaṇī-sikkhāpadaṃ samādiyāmi.
Abrahmacariyā veramaṇī-sikkhāpadaṃ samādiyāmi.
Musāvādā veramaṇī-sikkhāpadaṃ samādiyāmi.
Surā-meraya-majja-pamādaṭṭhānā veramaṇī-sikkhāpadaṃ samādiyāmi

In the third precept, for lay disciples, *kāmesu micchācārā veramaṇī* (abstaining from sexual misconduct) replaces *abrahmacariyā veramaṇī* (observing celibacy). These five precepts are known as *pañchasīla* (literally five moral precepts).

The word *veramaṇī* in every precept means 'to stay away,' 'to abstain,' 'to refrain from.' *Sikkhā* means training and *sikkhāpada* is a compound word that means rule of conduct. It indicates that these rules are steps of training.

Samādiyami means 'I accept.' *Pāṇa* means life. *Atipāta* means destruction, killing. *Pāṇātipāta* is the singular version of the fifth declension and it means 'from destroying life,' or 'from killing a living being.'

Dinna means something that is given. *Adinna* means something that has not been given. *Ādāna* means to take. *Adinnādāna* means 'taking what is not given,' that is, stealing. *Kāmesu micchācārā* means sexual misconduct. *Musā* is false and *vāda* is speech. *Surā, meraya, majja* are various alcoholic beverages. *Pamādaṭṭhāna* is place of or cause of heedlessness. Intoxicants lead to recklessness.

No Ritual to Become a Disciple

Walpola Rahula has said that there is no clear and particular rite or ritual or process to become a disciple. He writes,[367] "If one desires to become a Buddhist, there is no initiation ceremony (or baptism) which one has to undergo. (But to become a bhikkhu, a member of the Saṅgha, one has to undergo a long process of disciplinary training and education.) If one understands the Buddha's teaching, and if one is convinced that his teaching is the right path and if one tries to follow it, then one is a Buddhist. But according to the unbroken age-old tradition in Buddhist countries, one is considered a Buddhist if one takes the Buddha, the Dhamma (the Teaching) and the Saṅgha (the Order of Monks) —generally called 'the Triple Gem'—as one's refuges, and undertakes to observe the Five Precepts (*pañchasīla*)...

"There are no external rites or ceremonies that a Buddhist has to perform. Buddhism is a way of life, and what is essential is following the Noble Eightfold Path."

There are several instances in the Tipiṭaka where at the end of the discussion with the Buddha, the person requests to be accepted as a disciple. But we do not see any initiation rite being prescribed by the Buddha or the bhikkhus.

Dr Ambedkar Brought These Words from Sri Lanka

Dr Babasaheb Ambedkar had the arduous responsibility of educating his followers about the Buddha Dhamma. He had started working towards this goal long before he formally accepted Buddhism along with his followers. In his preface dated 24/2/1956 to his book *Bauddha Pujapāṭha* (literally Buddhist Worship and Chants), he says,[368] "I am constantly asked about any literature about ceremony and chants of Buddhist tradition. My illness has not allowed me to fulfill this request till date. Add to this complete loss of any Buddhist ceremony and chants, even more than Buddhist philosophy, in our country. Therefore, it is very difficult to get ceremonial processes and chants related to them. These are available only in the Buddhist countries.

"I had gone to Ceylon (sic) in 1950 and had made it a point to collect such verses. Then I made my friend Mr. Gunatilake sing them and recorded them. On returning here, I added some more verses to it with the help of some Buddhist monks."

Cārikā – Wanderings

Exhortation to the Saṅgha to Wander

Once the Saṅgha had expanded to this extent, the Buddha took up a new subject. He started by saying that he was free of all divine as well as human bondage and exhorted them to do the same; and added,[369]

"Go forth, bhikkhus, for the welfare of many, for the happiness of many, out of compassion for people and for the good, welfare and happiness of gods and men. Let no two go in the same direction. Bhikkhus, teach the Dhamma that is benevolent in the beginning, benevolent in the middle and benevolent in the end. Expound both the spirit and the letter of the holy life that is complete and stainless. There are people with but little dust in their eyes, who will be harmed if they don't hear the Dhamma but will benefit if they do hear it. I too am going to Senānī in Uruvelā to teach the Dhamma."

After that at the right time, they set out on their wanderings *(cārikā)*. The Buddha had asked the bhikkhus to keep wandering except during the period of rains retreat. We find in Compounded Discourses[370], "…Who is superior among those who keep wandering? … The Saṅgha is superior among those who keep wandering." This shows how important this wandering for the spread of the Dhamma was for the Buddha.

It seems that this was probably one of the earliest, if not the first, non-political wandering of a group for the spread of a specific thought, a specific teaching in the history of the world. It is possible that such wandering was common in the *Samaṇa* tradition prior to the Buddha. But this seems to be the first influential and distinct *cārikā* (wandering). The Buddha had walked to the Deer Park in Varanasi from Uruvelā after enlightenment. But there was no Saṅgha at that time and hence it couldn't be called the wandering of the Saṅgha. It was the first wandering undertaken with the aim of spread of the Dhamma and in that sense it was the first personal wandering.

He told the sixty bhikkhus that he had become free from all attachments and that they too had become free from all bondage. This means that regarding morality and wisdom, those sixty had become so developed as to be close to the Buddha. When the Buddha reached those heights, he did so on his own. It was his own effort. There was no help from anyone else. The case of these sixty bhikkhus was different. They had the Buddha to guide them. They had to walk themselves on the path but the Buddha taught the Four Noble Truths, Noble Eightfold Path, etc. This ready guidance made it easy for them to get liberated quickly.

Not for Personal Liberation But for the Welfare of Many

It should be noted that the Buddha told them that the aim of their wandering was for the benefit of many, for the happiness of many. He didn't tell them that it was for their meditation or for their liberation or to experience nibbāna. The bhikkhus had to do these things as part of their discipline, part of their training. But this was not the aim of the wandering.

This makes it clear that he didn't create a Saṅgha that was only interested in personal liberation and was oblivious of their social responsibilities. He told them to go in different directions so that they could reach out to each individual who was suffering and help him or her. The Dhamma that they were supposed to teach was beneficial in all angles and at all stages for the people. The bhikkhus set out to remove suffering in society. They were to teach in a way that was simple and understandable using proper language. The aim was not to dazzle people with their scholarship or to show the world how learned they were. The Dhamma was to be taught in a way that would help people to put it in practice. The personal development of the bhikkhus was certainly going to help people. But his aim was to remove suffering from as many people as possible.

For the Welfare of Many, For the Happiness of Many

The Buddha told the bhikkhus to wander for the benefit of many, for the happiness of many *(bahujana hitāya, bahujana sukhāya)*. He himself walked all over the north India and Nepal for four decades to teach the Dhamma. His sole goal was to help as many people as possible. He didn't use the word *bahujana* the way it is used today to mean a particular and major section of society. By *bahujana* he meant many, as many as possible, maximum.

Prof Jagannath Upadhyaya says,[371] "Entire Vedic (hedonist) culture had one motto—for the welfare of cow and brahmin… the Buddha on the other hand gave a clarion call of 'for the benefit of many, for the happiness of many'. The Buddha said, not for the benefit of cow and brahmins but for the benefit of many, for the happiness of many."

Disorganized Wandering Harmful

The Buddha had advised bhikkhus that wandering for the Dhamma should be balanced, systematic and measured. If it is long and disorganized, the bhikkhu is harmed in five ways:[372] He can't hear new things; he can't clarify things heard earlier; hearing one sided stories leads to loss of prudence; one may get afflicted by a big illness and one doesn't get friends.

He exhorted them to go forth and wander. He also cautioned them to be organized. He also cautioned them not to stay in one place too long as one then might develop a desire to acquire things. It may also lead to envy and other negative feelings among people. This advice is given in the same chapter of the Graded Discourses. Balanced conduct is the essence of the Buddha's advice.

Go Only One in One Direction

While sending out the bhikkhus, the Buddha instructed 'Let not two go in the same direction.' This must have taken the sixty bhikkhus to sixty different places. If they had gone in pairs, they would have reached thirty places. If they had gone in a group of three, would have reached only twenty places. The Buddha's advice meant that more people received the Dhamma. There was no opportunity to give responsibility to others and relax. This also meant that each one of them had to be vigilant and alert. This also meant that each one of them was capable of teaching and spreading the Dhamma independently.

You Have to Take Wisdom to People

He was aware that the teaching had to be taken to ignorant people. He said, "It is possible that there are some people who have minor faults but their mental aptitude is suitable for the Dhamma. If the Dhamma doesn't reach them, they won't be freed from their misery; they won't be free from bondage."

It was the duty of the bhikkhus to ensure that the progress of such people wasn't hindered; to give them a helping hand, to show them the path, to take the teaching to them.

Just as he asked the bhikkhus, he too set out wandering for the spread of Dhamma.

A Bhikkhu Who Spreads the Dhamma Must Be Tolerant

The Buddha must have given detailed instructions to the bhikkhus who set out on wandering—about how to face adversity, how to face censure, how to face opposition. We don't get details of it in the description of this event in the Book of Discipline. We do however get a sense of it from his advice to *Puṇṇa* as seen in Middle Length Discourses.[373] He wanted the messengers of the Dhamma to be extremely tolerant. This had a deep impact on many bhikkhus as we see from this example.

Once he was dwelling in Jetavana of Sāvatthi. One evening, Puṇṇa came to him, sat to one side after saluting him and asked him to give a short discourse. The Buddha told him that craving is the reason of misery and destruction of craving leads to cessation of suffering. He said at the end of his short discourse, "Puṇṇa, where are you going to go after listening to this short talk?"

Puṇṇa said that he was going to go to Sunāparānta, which is the region of present-day Thane (site of the famous Nalasopara stupa and the glorious Kanheri caves) and part of south Gujarat.

The Buddha cautioned him, "Puṇṇa, the people of Sunāparānta are fierce and harsh. If they insult and ridicule you, what will you do?"

"I will think, 'These people are civilized, in that they don't hit me with their hands.'"

"But if they hit you with their hands?"

"...I will think, 'These Sunāparānta people are civilized. They don't hit me with a lump of earth.'..."

"But if they hit you with a lump...?"

"...I will think, 'These Sunāparānta people are civilized. They don't hit me with a stick.'..."

"But if they hit you with a stick...?"

"...they don't hit me with a knife.'..."

"But if they hit you with a knife...?"

"…they don't take my life with a sharp knife.'..."

"But if they take your life with a sharp knife...?"

"If they take my life with a sharp knife, I will think, 'There are people who—perturbed, humbled, and disgusted by the body and by life—have sought for an assassin, but here I have met my assassin without any effort.' That is what I will think."

"Well said, Puṇṇa, well said. Endowed with such peace and restraint, you are fit to live in Sunāparānta."

Then Puṇṇa took the Tathāgata's leave and went to Sunāparānta. There in the first year itself, he taught the Dhamma to five hundred men and five hundred women lay disciples. He realized the three knowledges and then attained final passing away *(*parinibbāna*)*.

Then a large number of bhikkhus went to the Tathāgata and gave him the news of Puṇṇa's passing away and asked his future. Tathāgata said, "Bhikkhus, Puṇṇa was wise. He lived in accordance with the Dhamma and … he attained parinibbāna."

Discussion

Tathāgata didn't want anyone to be forced to follow his teaching. He was a proponent of freedom of thought. He wanted people to use their discretion to decide and practice the teaching for their own benefit. He knew that there would be opposition to the teaching, opposition to the spread of the teaching and even abuse of those who spread the teaching. He wanted his disciples to face the ill treatment calmly, to take the message of the Dhamma to the hearts of people. We see from his life that he was courteous even to those who insulted him, criticized him, spread false and malicious rumors about him.

Therefore, in the long history of the spread of Buddhism there are several instances of enduring persecution but few where there is coercion or torture. We can say that the Tathāgata tested Puṇṇa. He tested whether Puṇṇa had enough resolve and enough forbearance. Puṇṇa passed the test. Some may feel that it is not possible to put in actual practice what Puṇṇa said he would. Some may feel that it was an exaggeration. But we do see examples in human history where people have forgiven their assassins. Even if we feel that there is an exaggeration, we must understand that it was for didactic purpose—to impress upon the Dhamma messenger the need for tolerance. This tolerance is needed not only in the field of spread of Dhamma but also in all fields of life.

Such tolerance is not bowing down to injustice. Those who have compassion and complete confidence in their philosophy can remain firm in their view and yet forgive those who attack them with the understanding that the attacker is ignorant. They know that the solution lies in removing the ignorance. Such people are able to win the hearts of the opponents and change them. Therefore, Puṇṇa was successful in taking the Dhamma to Sunāparānta. That is why Tathāgata praised him suitably after his parinibbāna. His life was fruitful.

When Tathāgata sent the first sixty bhikkhus he must have taught them similar forbearance. This is the secret behind how the bhikkhus could spread the Dhamma to countless people without any weapon and without any threat or enticement.

Like an Elephant Enduring Arrows

The Buddha had put in practice what he preached about tolerance. He calmly endured all attacks on him. Indeed, he had once expressed his vow about tolerance,[374] "Just as an elephant endures arrows in the battlefield, I will endure abuse."

Your Abuses Stay With You!

An episode in his life tells us clearly how he had conquered anger and how he dealt with the abusive language. There are four suttas in the Connected Discourses that are relevant here namely Dhanañjānī Sutta, Akkosa Sutta, Asundarika Sutta and Bilaṅgika Sutta.[375] The gist of these suttas is:

Once the Master was dwelling in Kalandakanivāpa of Rājagaha. At that time, the wife of a brahmin from Bhāradvāja clan had developed faith in the Buddha, Dhamma and Saṅgha. Once while serving food to her husband she thrice uttered, "Salutations to the Buddha, the enlightened one, the liberated one," etc.

Her husband became upset and censured her, "You low caste! How dare you praise that shaven-head in front of me? I will tell you all the faults in your teacher."

She replied, "I don't see anyone in the world including the heavens who will be able to find fault with that great man. You should go and visit him. You will know for yourself."

Thus angry and upset her husband went to the Buddha and sat down to one side after the usual greetings. Then he asked the Buddha, "O Gotama, after destroying what does one sleep peacefully? After destroying what does one become free from all lamentation? What would you like to destroy?"

The Buddha replied, "O brahmin, having destroyed anger a person sleeps peacefully. One who destroys anger doesn't come to grief. O brahmin, noble people praise destruction of anger which may feel sweet in the beginning but is poisonous."

After listening to the reply, Bhāradvāja thanked him and said, "It is just as though you set right what had been turned upside down, revealed what was hidden, showed the way to one who was lost, or held up a lamp in the dark for those with eyesight to see. You have made Dhamma clear to me in many ways."

He went to refuge in the triple gem—the Buddha, Dhamma and Saṅgha.

The news reached another brahmin from Bhāradvāja clan. He became angry and lost his composure. He went to the Buddha and started abusing him in harsh and uncivilized language. The Connected Discourses gives his name as Akkosaka Bhāradvāja, literally 'Abusive Bhāradvāja'.

Then the Buddha asked him whether he ever received any friends or relations at his house.

"Yes, sometimes", he answered.

"Do you sometimes prepare food for them?"

"Yes, I do."

"If they do not partake the food offered by you, who do the eatables belong to?"

"They stay with me. They remain mine."

"Your abuses too are like the food. I am not using abusive language; I am not angry. I don't quarrel. You are using abusive language. You are angry. You are quarreling. I reject what you offer. It is yours and stays with you," the Buddha replied.

The Buddha then talked to him at length. This is the gist:

If one reacts to abuses with abuses, anger with anger and quarrel with quarrel; it is said that they are feeding each other, using each other's items. I don't feed you like this. I don't use your items. It stays with you.

Bhāradvāja replied that the Buddha was known as Arahata Samaṇa Gotama in the king's assembly. How would he have any anger?

Then the Buddha explained to him the importance of not getting angry. One who doesn't get angry at someone who is angry wins a difficult victory. Those who don't understand the Dhamma call such a person ignorant.

Ultimately, Bhāradvāja took refuge in the Buddha, Dhamma and Saṅgha. Later on he became an arahata.

Yet another event from the Buddha's life is recorded in the next sutta. When Asundarika, a brahmin from the Bhāradvāja clan, heard that someone from his clan had ordained under the Buddha, he became very angry. He went to the Buddha and started hurling abuses at him. The Buddha remained silent. Then Asundarika said, "You lost, Samaṇa. You lost."

Then the Buddha replied, "One who is ignorant feels that he has won when he uses harsh language. On the other hand, forbearance of a wise man is his victory."

The description afterwards is the similar to the other suttas.

In the next sutta, we find the following details: When he came to know that a man from his clan had joined the bhikkhu Saṅgha, Bilaṅgika of the Bhāradvāja clan became angry and upset. He came to the Buddha. After routine pleasantries he stood to one side. The Buddha recognized what was ailing him and said, "If a man, while wind is blowing from another man toward him, throws dust at the other man, the dust comes back to him. Similarly, if someone criticizes another one who is innocent, faultless and pure, the criticism returns to that ignorant man."

Matricheta says,[376] (Ven. S. Dhammika's translation of the original)

You conquered revilers with patience,
the malicious with blessings,
slanderers with truth and
the cruel with kindness.

Going Forth and Ordination

Many people were attracted to the Dhamma after sixty bhikkhus joined the Buddha in his mission. Many started following the Dhamma while remaining householders. But there were some who wanted to leave home and join the Saṅgha. Bhikkhus had the responsibility of bringing them to the Buddha for going forth *(pabbajjā)* and ordination *(upasampadā)*. This was not convenient for bhikkhus and also for those who wish to be ordained. This was becoming a problem in the distant regions. Therefore, the Buddha authorized the bhikkhus to independently give the going forth and ordination.

Pabbajjā literally means going forth. It means that one leaves home and adopts the homeless life. It means breaking the shackles of householder life and entering the Saṅgha as a novice *(Sāmaṇera)* who is an apprentice in the Saṅgha.

Upasampadā literally means to attain, to acquire, or to achieve. It indicates monkhood beyond the stage of novice: to be a full member of the Saṅgha. Just one bhikkhu can give *pabbajjā* (going forth) to someone. However, for ordination one needs five, ten, etc. bhikkhus.

The Book of Discipline[377] (Vinaya Piṭaka) describes going forth and ordination thus:

The man who wants to be ordained should remove moustache and beard. He should shave his head and wear saffron robes. Then he should put the upper cloth on one shoulder and pay respect to the bhikkhus. He should sit down on haunches and say thrice with folded hands, *"Buddhaṃ saraṇaṃ gacchāmi; Dhammaṃ saraṇaṃ gacchāmi; saṅghaṃ saraṇaṃ gacchāmi."*

No Admission For Those Who Shirk Responsibilities

Once while the Buddha was teaching the Dhamma to bhikkhus, a cowherd named Nanda was also listening to him. He was fascinated by the teaching and asked the Buddha to give him *pabbajjā* and *upasampadā*.[378]

The Buddha replied, "Nanda, return the cows to their owner and come back."

He said, "Sir, the cows will go back to the right place due to attraction of the calves."

The Buddha again insisted that he go back and return the cows. This time, Nanda returned the cows to the owner and came back. Then he requested the Buddha saying that he had returned the cows. He received going forth and ordination. Later he became an arahata.

Discussion

Nanda had taken on the responsibility of looking after other people's cows. It would have been irresponsible if he had not returned the cows to the owner. Even if as he had said, the cows had gone back due to the pull of their calves, it would have been improper for him to leave them alone. It was fitting that the Buddha insisted that the journey to a lofty goal didn't begin with irresponsibility.

Shaving Head

It seems that shaving head was an old and established practice in samaṇa tradition. The Buddha gave it proper form. In later period, shaven head and saffron robes became important external symbols of the bhikkhus. Even today, bhikkhus of all Buddhist traditions and all countries shave their heads and wear robes. A shaven headed bhikkhu was often referred to as *muṇḍa* or *muṇḍaka.* Shaving head still has a significant place in Indian culture.

Muṇḍaka Upanisada Originally from Samaṇa Tradition

We see rebellion against Vedic traditions in *Muṇḍaka Upanisada*. Lal Mani Joshi says,[379] "The *Muṇḍaka Upanishada* means 'the Upanishad of the shaven-headed monks'; it is obviously a post-Buddhist text deeply influenced by the outlook of munis and bhikshus. The vedic brāhmaṇas in the age of the Buddha used to address Him as a *Samaṇaka* and *Muṇḍaka*." I have discussed this Upanishada in detail in my book 'Baḷivaṃsha'.

Discussion

Lal Mani Joshi has made a factual statement about Indian philosophy and history of Indian social structure. *Muṇḍaka Upanishada* relegated Vedas and yajñas to a minor position. Therefore, one should not become confused when one hears that this Upanishada was an integral part of non-Vedic Samaṇa tradition. Vedics turned it into an Upanishad. Indians need not therefore reject it. Doing so will be tantamount to rejecting our own heritage. What is required is a discerning mind to remove the Vedic layers that it has acquired later.

Muṇḍa and *muṇḍaka* were used for Samaṇas. These were used in derogatory sense by Vedics. Addition of 'ka' suffix further denotes the derogatory sense. There were also people who respected Samaṇas and used the word with respect. Shaving head without leaving a lock of hair at the top of the head (without *sikhā* or *shikhā*) was originally a samaṇa tradition. *Muṇḍa* too is not a Sanskrit word originally.

K. P. Kulkarni says in his dictionary of etymology, "*Muṇḍa* is Sanskritized later. Original word is Prakrit." Words commonly used in Marathi such as *muṇḍi, muṇḍake* etc are related to shaving of Samaṇa tradition. At one time, a shaven head of a bhikkhu was an object of respect. Therefore, over time, even a head that is not shaved was later referred to as *muṇḍa* and *muṇḍaka*. Over time, words such as *muṇḍāse* which is a headgear worn in a particular manner or *muṇḍāvalyā,* these words were derived from *muṇḍa*. Today there is no feeling of disrespect when a common man uses the word *muṇḍi* or *muṇḍake*. They simply mean head.

There is need for further research about various Marathi figures of speech such as '*muṇḍya muragālaṇe*' (twisting head), '*muṇḍake chāṭaṇe*' (cutting of head), '*muṇḍake uḍavane*' (beheading) etc. It is well known that during the time of Pushyamitra Shunga, Buddhist monks were systematically and deliberately beheaded by royal decree. '*Muṇḍyā muragālaṇe*' (twisting head) even today refers to as killing innocent people.

Shaving Head When a Close Relation Dies

The practice of shaving one's head, moustache and beard is common even today. Sometimes, if someone shaves his head due to modern fashion, he is ridiculed, "Has your father died?"

This practice of shaving head when a close relation dies is connected to the shaving of head in Buddhist tradition. The origin may be either complementary or contradictory. Buddhism was widespread in India, and shaven headed bhikkhus were revered by masses. People had faith that bhikkhus had abandoned attachments to worldly life. When someone close dies, one develops a sense of detachment. One loses all interest in material things. It is as if the family becomes like a bhikkhu. It is possible that the practice of shaving head began to symbolize that mental state.

It is also possible that Vedics started this practice with an entirely different meaning. The implication may be that to become a bhikkhu and a death in the family was similar. It is also possible that Vedic priests took advantage of the popularity of shaving and gave it a new twist. Though shaving head had no relation to Vedic tradition, they gave it a Vedic colour for their livelihood.

Today, the business of priests is called *bhikshuki* though the word has no relation to *bhikshā*. How did it come about? When Buddhism declined in India, those from priestly background who had became bhikkhus became priests again. But they kept the word *bhikshā* alive. There is need for further research in this. When Vedics shaved their head they would shave the entire head except *sikhā* (*shikhā,* a lock of hair left unshaven at the top of the head). Bharatiya Saskriti Kosh[380] says that in Vedic sanyasa, the entire head is shaved except six hairs.

Bodako God in Goa

Prof D. D. Kosambi has said about *"Boḍako deva"* (literally shaved headed god) in Goa,[381] *"Buddhism certainly had its period in Goa, particularly northern portions, as shown by a fine image of Buddha discovered at Colvalle by Fr. Heras of the St. Xavier's*

College, Bombay: at Pernem, in the New Conquests, relics of a Buddhist shrine of some sort are still worshipped in the open under the name of 'Boḍako deva', ... "

It is obvious that the Buddha is referred to as *boḍako deva* because he had shaven head. It is also important to find the etymology of *boḍaka,* a common word in Marathi used for an uncovered head. As said earlier '*ka'* suffix was often used in derogatory sense: *samaṇaka*, *muṇḍaka,* etc. It is possible that *boḍaka* has its origin in *buddhaka* or *bauddhaka*. Perhaps *boḍaka* meant shaven head. Now it has come to mean without headgear. The superstition that an uncovered head is inauspicious or that for an auspicious ceremony one should have one's head covered might have come after decline of Buddhism in India and its consequent denigration.

Robes (*Cīvara*)

Robes Don't Make One a Bhikkhu

In going forth and ordination, in addition to shaven head, one has to wear saffron robes. These are called *cīvara*. It has three parts: an inner robe, from the waist to the knee; an upper robe, around the torso and shoulders and an extra robe that can be used as an outer garment in cold season, folded to make a seat or even as a bedding.

Though the robes were an essential symbol of bhikkhuhood, the Buddha said again and again that just taking robes didn't make one a bhikkhu. The qualities of morality etc. made one a true bhikkhu. Let us look at Saṅghāṭikaṇṇa Sutta[382] of Itivuttaka.

The Buddha said to the bhikkhus, "Bhikkhus, a bhikkhu might be following me, holding the end of my outer robe. He may follow my footsteps literally. But if he has greed in his mind, if he is inclined towards sensual pleasures, if his mind is defiled, if his intentions and thoughts are unwholesome…he has no control over his senses. Such a bhikkhu is far away from me. I am far away from such a bhikkhu. Why? That bhikkhu doesn't see the Dhamma and doesn't understand the Dhamma. Since he doesn't see the Dhamma, he doesn't see me.

"On the other hand, a bhikkhu may be dwelling hundreds of miles away from me. But he has no greed in his mind. He is not inclined towards sensual pleasures. His mind is pure. His intentions and thoughts are wholesome… he is restrained. Such a bhikkhu is close to me and I am close to such a bhikkhu. Why? Because this bhikkhu sees the Dhamma, understands the Dhamma. One who sees the Dhamma sees me."

Then he uttered verses meaning, "Even if he is following me physically, and he has greed in his mind, he is harmful. He walks behind a balanced person while himself being imbalanced. He walks behind one who has attained nibbāna while he has not attained nibbāna. He walks behind a person who has destroyed craving while he is full of craving. Therefore, he is far away from me. On the other hand, one who has comprehended the Dhamma properly, a wise man—he is like a clear lake on a windless day. He is stable with a stable person. He is without craving and walks behind a person who has no craving. He has attained nibbāna and walks behind a person who has attained nibbāna."

Robes as a Basic Need Only

The Buddha described how carefully a bhikkhu uses robes,[383] "He uses only essential robes to protect himself from cold and sun. He uses robes to protect from mosquitos, wind, sun, and serpents and for decency."

Bhikkhu

A man who is ordained is called a bhikkhu and a woman a bhikkhuṇi. Though bhikkhu was later connected to begging, the word doesn't mean begging. Bhikkhus don't beg. They go on alms round. They stand silently in front of the door of householders. They take whatever is given voluntarily. The Buddhist Dictionary[384] says, "…but bhikkhus do not beg. They silently stand at the door for alms. They live on what is spontaneously given by the supporters." A bhikkhu is not a priest. Since there is no God in Buddhism, there is no priest that mediates between the God and people.

The Buddha himself has often expressed his thoughts about who is a bhikkhu. We find his utterances in Udāna,[385] "One who has no cunning, no ego, no greed, no attachment, no covetousness and no anger, such a person is a true brāhmaṇa, a true samaṇa, a true bhikkhu." A bhikkhu transcends the division of race and caste. A bhikkhu was respected by all those who followed the Buddha's teaching. In this context, the sentence in the Connected Discourses,[386] "Khattiyas salute casteless samaṇas" is significant.

Immoral Bhikkhus Are Not Mine: Moral Ones Are Mine

When the Buddha taught bhikkhus, he expected them to lead a virtuous life. He expected their conduct to be exemplary. Not all bhikkhus fulfilled his expectations. Whenever bhikkhus behaved in less than honorable manner, the Buddha expressed his displeasure. We find this in Kuha Sutta[387] of Itivuttaka. *Kuha* means a liar or a deceiver.

The Buddha said about such *kuha* bhikkhus, "Those bhikkhus—who deceive others, are harsh, indulge in frivolous talk, have a temper, are rude and are not balanced—are not my bhikkhus. Such bhikkhus have alienated themselves from the Dhamma and the Discipline. They cannot get established, grow and develop in the Dhamma and the Discipline.

"Those bhikkhus—who don't deceive others, are not harsh, don't indulge in frivolous talk, are compassionate, polite and balanced—are my bhikkhus. Such bhikkhus have not gone away from the Dhamma and the Discipline." The Buddha had made similar comment at another place.[388]

In one of his discourses,[389] he says, "If thieves become strong, kings become weak. Then it is not easy for them to come and go in the city. They also find it difficult to go to border areas. People too find it difficult to travel. Similarly, if immoral bhikkhus increase, virtuous ones become weak. They dwell in the Saṅgha in silence (unable to voice their opinions) or they go away to distant regions. This hurts the welfare and happiness of many. It hurts the welfare and happiness of gods and men."

Appearance Does Not Make One Dhammic

Just as there are people in the world who sincerely and devotedly follow the Dhamma, there are also people who copy the appearance of the true followers of the Dhamma. Several verses in Dhammapada give differences between the two. One such verse is:[390]

Just because one is making hurried judgments,
one doesn't become a Dhammic person.
A wise man looks at both benefits and disadvantages
before making a decision.
...
One who is restrained, follows the Dhamma,
guides others with compassion
and protects the Dhamma—
such a wise man is called Dhammic.
...
Just because one speaks much,
one doesn't become Bearer of Dhamma.
One listens to a few words of the Dhamma
and follows them through his actions;
is heedless in the practice of the Dhamma—
he is true Bearer of Dhamma.

Not Years but Morality

Once Sāriputta went to meet recluses of other traditions in Sāvatthi. The recluses said that one who has completed twelve years of holy life is called a praiseworthy (*niddasa*) bhikkhu. Sāriputta did not agree or disagree with them. He went to the

Buddha and asked him whether in the Dhamma and the Discipline, one can call a bhikkhu praiseworthy simply by counting the years he has been a bhikkhu.

The Buddha replied that mere years didn't count. He described seven qualities of a praise-worthy bhikkhu. "One who is virtuous, follows the Dhamma consistently, eradicates craving, meditates, strives, is aware and has insight at present and also aspires to do so in future is called praiseworthy."[391]

The very next sutta describes how Ānanda also had a similar experience in Kosambi. The Buddha said that *niddasa* was not dependent on years in the Saṅgha. To Ānanda, the Buddha described the essential qualities of a praiseworthy bhikkhu as faith, shame in wrong doing, fear of wrong doing, erudition, willingness to make effort, awareness and wisdom.

Don't Accept Alms from a Layperson Who Disrespects You

There are three suttas[392] in the Numerical Discourses that give guidance about the relationship between bhikkhus and laypeople.

Patta-nikujjana Sutta is the first one of these suttas. *Patta-nikujjana* means turning (the alms bowl) upside down. It is well-known that the Buddha and his bhikkhus would go on alms round from one house to the next without missing any house. There was one exception. The Buddha had said that the Saṅgha could decide to turn the bowl upside down while passing in front of a householder if he were to wish harm to bhikkhus, to cause harm to bhikkhus, to drive bhikkhus out of his residence, to abuse them, to cause schism among bhikkhus and to malign the Buddha, Dhamma and Saṅgha.

The next sutta is Appasāda-pavedanīya Sutta. The Buddha knew that just as a layperson could be immoral, a bhikkhu could also indulge in wrong conduct. Therefore, he had also advised laypeople about it. If a bhikkhu were guilty of the above mentioned things, layperson also had the right to show their displeasure (by refusing to give alms to that bhikkhu).

Paṭisaraṇiya Sutta describes the penalty that Saṅgha could give to a bhikkhu who brought harm to laypeople that would be revoked if the bhikkhu's conduct improved later on.

Discussion

Laypeople used to feel happy and proud that virtuous bhikkhu accepted alms from them. They were severely affected if bhikkhus turned their bowls upside down in front of their house. Today we see a similar phenomenon among laypeople giving food to *vārakarīs* in *diṇḍī* (pilgrims in processions who travel on foot to the holy city of Pandharpur in Maharashtra—one of the biggest pilgrimages in the world). It is clear from this that alms round is not begging out of greed. It is not avoidance of work and is not excessive servility.

The Buddha has also thought about the other side of this issue. This is very important and protects laypeople from exploitation. Just as he wanted the laypeople to be respectful towards virtuous bhikkhus, he also wanted bhikkhus to be respectful towards upright laypeople. The relationship between bhikkhus and laypeople ought to be mutually respectful and beneficial.

Advice to Bhikkhus About Unity

Unity and concord among the bhikkhus was very important for the Buddha. Once when he met Anuruddha, he asked him,[393] "... Anuruddha, do you bhikkhus live in concord, without dispute, blending like milk and water, having love for each other?" If bhikkhus started quarreling with each other, criticizing each other, then they would not be able to guide society properly and would not be able to set an example.

Alms Round

The food that is given to the bhikkhus and is accepted by them for sustenance is called *piṇḍapāta* (alms). Though this is not discussed in going forth and ordination *(pabbajjā* and *upasampadā)* it is important to understand *piṇḍapāta* to know more about the life of bhikkhus.

Piṇḍa means ball; here it means ball of food or food. *Pāta* means to put (in bowl). This means giving food, serving food, offering food. In India, when we offer food to show our respect and gratitude for our ancestors it is also called *piṇḍa*. This is a common practice in India that probably has relation to *piṇḍapāta* of bhikkhus. This word signifies offering from one who gives and is not about one to whom food is offered. *Piṇḍapāta* is a donation of food. The food is offered and the bhikkhu accepts it. But he doesn't beg for it. He stands silently in front of the house. He does *not* say, "Give me alms."

Depiction of *piṇḍapāta* in popular media is often wrong. The Tipiṭaka is full of innumerable references to bhikkhus going for *piṇḍapāta* (alms round). The word occurs hundreds of times in the Tipiṭaka. The noun *Bhikkhā* or related verbs (begging) occur only a couple of dozen times. This too occurs either when others have used this noun or verb to ask questions or is a later addition. Thus, bhikkhu has nothing to do with *bhikkhā or bhikshā*.

Alms Round is Not Begging

The Buddha used to go on alms round *(piṇḍapāta)*. Bhikkhus too used to go on alms round. If we look upon the alms round as begging, we would not understand the revolutionary impact of the alms round on our society. Today the word *bhikshā* (bhikkhā) has become derogatory and related words have become symbolic of servility, helplessness and avoidance of work. The Buddha had make it clear that begging for food doesn't make one a bhikkhu. (In Pali one who begs for food is called a *bhikkhaka*, not a bhikkhu.)

In Bhikkhaka Sutta[394] of the Connected Discourses, there is an incident in which a brahmin *bhikkhaka (bhikshuka)* comes to the Buddha and asked, "O Gotama, you are a *bhikkhaka*. I too am a *bhikkhaka*. Then what is the difference between the two of us?"

The Buddha replied, "One doesn't become a bhikkhu merely because one lives on food offered by others… a bhikkhu is one who puts aside wrong concepts of merit and demerit (*pāpa* and *puñña*); and follows the holy life with wisdom."

The brahmin became a follower of the Buddha.

Objection on the Issue of Alms

Savarkar has raised serious objection to the Buddha and the Saṅgha on the issue of alms.[395] It is important that we look at his criticism.

In his play *Sanyasta Khaḍga*, there is a character named Kshārā, the wife of brahmin Shākambhaṭa. While describing how the womenfolk of Magadha despise the Buddha, she says, "When the Buddha came to their town, he took into his beggars' order, the children of devoted householders who gave him alms and thus destroyed their houses... Even women from that town started singing in derision. I heard one woman singing... O what is this, indeed this is how it is... this is my teacher; he makes a beggar out of the very person who offers him food... even his boon is a curse..."

In this play there is repeated allegation against the bhikkhus that they join the Saṅgha to get free food. Kāṇā bhikkhu, a character in his play, says that one of the advantages of entering the Saṅgha is that one gets to eat to heart's content.

Piṇḍapāta Helped in Creating Equality

Savarkar alleges that homes of the very people who fed the Buddha were destroyed because of the Buddha. Actually, the Buddha himself has clearly stated the difference between a beggar and a bhikkhu. Begging is not a quality of a bhikkhu. To be a true bhikkhu, one must possess morality, concentration and wisdom. The Buddha had clarified this numerous times. He never used deception or material allurements or force to make anyone a bhikkhu. He had made a rule that one can't become a bhikkhu without the permission of his mother and father. The allegation that he destroyed homes is a blatant lie.

He allowed the entry of lower castes and outcastes in his Saṅgha. Not only did he not destroy their homes but he raised them (who were earlier treated inhumanly) to an equal status with others and guided them to lofty heights. Those who can't tolerate this equality make false allegations against the Buddha. Sunīta who was a scavenger became the equal of khattiyas and brahmins in the Saṅgha. The Sākyans paid respect to the very Upāli who was earlier their servant. Upāli became the chief of Discipline and acquired authority to clarify the disciplinary rules. We must not ignore the social and cultural significance of this.

A Barber and His Razor

Bhikkhus who were from lower castes had an equal position in the Saṅgha. The Tathāgata was emphatic about this. Sometimes, novices or bhikkhus would continue to carry some of the symbols and equipment of their earlier trade after entering the Saṅgha. The Tathāgata didn't want them to carry any such symbols whether they came from a lower caste or a higher caste.[396]

Once the Buddha was travelling from Kusinārā to Atumā. At that time in Atumā, there was a man who was formerly a barber and had ordained in old age. He had two sons. Both were good natured, bright and skilled barbers. When he came to know that the Buddha was coming to his town, he sent his two sons to all houses with their razors and bowls (for water while shaving). He told them to work and in exchange get salt, oil, rice, etc. so that they could prepare delicious rice pudding for the Buddha. Seeing these handsome boys, even those who didn't want to get a shave, got a shave and a hair-cut from them and gave them ample rice, etc. That old man (the father) then prepared rice pudding for the Buddha and offered it to the Buddha who had already come to know what the old man had done to get the food supplies.

Still, so that others could also know, he asked the old man, "How did you prepare the pudding?"

When he answered truthfully, the Buddha reprimanded him. "Useless fellow, you didn't do the right thing. This was improper. This was not suitable for a samaṇa. One should not do such a thing. Useless fellow, how can you do this when you have gone forth?"

Then he laid down a rule, "Bhikkhus, those who come from barber caste should not carry razor etc. One who does so would be committing an offense."

Discussion

The old man who had worked as a barber for most of his life could not give up his old habit after entering the Saṅgha. He had faith in the Buddha and he sent his sons out of devotion. However, the Buddha was clear that once you enter the Saṅgha there was to be no baggage of caste with the bhikkhu. He wanted a harmonious atmosphere of equality in the Saṅgha. He took care to remove all that was symbolic of discrimination and inequality. One must leave behind both inferiority complex and superiority complex while entering the Saṅgha. If a bhikkhu was attached to old habits, the Buddha would admonish him. One has to be firm and stern in removing all traces of discrimination if one wants to usher in equality.

They Don't Eat Free Food of the Nation

The Tathāgata said that a bhikkhu who has loving compassion in heart doesn't eat free food of the nation.[397]

Once he said to the bhikkhus, "Bhikkhus, one who has goodwill and compassion in the heart for just a moment is not doing an empty meditation; he is following my teaching and not eating free food. What then to talk about one who develops and multiplies loving compassion?"

He said the same thing about one who cultivates loving compassion and one who is established in it. For those who are troubled by minor conflicts that bring misery to oneself and others, the value of goodwill is great. To offer food to those who give this invaluable goodwill is a great joy indeed. Those who are afflicted with a sense of superiority can't understand this. Superficially it may seem that standing in front of a house for alms lacks self-reliance, self-respect and honor. However, when a prince does this and stands in front of the house a common man it becomes a revolutionary thing. One must look at it in a balanced manner.

Savarkar Does Not Talk About Begging Alms in Vedic Tradition

It is important to note here that Savarkar doesn't talk about *bhikshuki* (living on alms) in the Vedic tradition in his play. But he keeps denigrating the Buddha on this issue. He makes a criminal out of the Buddha. This is an utterly biased view of Savarkar. In the *Manusmriti* in the three stages of life (Brahmacharya, Vānaprastha and Sanyāsa) twice born (especially brahmins) are supposed to live on alms. Let us look at the rules laid down in the *Manusmriti* here.

The Manusmriti says that after the thread ceremony *(upanayana)* the boy should circumambulate the fire and beg for alms. Without *upanayana,* one doesn't become twice born and as long as one is not twice born one is still a *shūdra* (low caste) even if one is born to brahmin parents. Thus *upanayana* is essential and mandatory.

And the *Manusmriti* says, one who has undergone *upanayana* has to beg for alms. Even one who is learning under a teacher has to beg for alms. The *Manusmriti* says that a *brahmachāri* should beg for alms, inform the teacher after collecting the alms and only then eat the alms food. This means that one lives on alms food until the end of one's learning.

The *Manusmriti* has also ruled that one in *Vānaprastha* (stage after the householder's life) should also beg for alms. The text says,[398] "He should bring alms food from brahmins or other householders or twice-born living in the forest."

Similarly, for one in *Sanyāsa* stage, it stays, "He should leave fire and home; and beg for alms for food; should enter town only for begging alms but not otherwise."

The Difference Between Alms in the Buddhist Tradition and in the Manusmriti

The issue doesn't end with the fact that the brahminical tradition also had alms round. There is a big difference in the Buddha's *piṇḍapāta* and *bhikshā* for *Manusmriti's brahmachāri*. The Buddha and his bhikkhus used to accept alms food from all the castes.[399] We have already seen that the bhikkhus would follow *sapadāna* system whereby they would not miss any house on alms round. We find in Vasala Sutta of Suttanipāta that the Buddha went thus for *sapadāna* alms round in Sāvatthi. The Commentary on this sutta says,[400] "*Sapadāna* is *anugaha* meaning every next house, without missing any house. The Buddha, to give opportunity to all people and to satisfy all, went beyond all caste discrimination and went on alms round in this manner."

People from all castes used to become bhikkhus. Their caste didn't affect their clothes as a bhikkhu. There was no way to know the caste of one who has shaven his head and one who took saffron robes. Lower castes and outcastes also become equal to khattiyas and brahmins in the Saṅgha. They could accept alms food from any householder.

The *brahmachāri* of the *Manusmriti* was different. First, *sudda* (lower caste) didn't have the right of *upanayana* and hence didn't have the right for alms. Even the *baṭus* (who had undergone *upanayana*) of the three remaining castes were not equal. Different skin used for seat, thread and stick are indicated for the three castes that are allowed *upanayana*. This made it easy to know the caste of the *brahmachāri* who had come for alms. Rather, this differences were kept so that the superiority or inferiority of their caste would be known. The discrimination doesn't stop here.

The address that the *brahmachāri* uses for the laywoman who is giving alms must be placed at a different place in the sentence according to the *Manusmriti*. A brahmin has to say- *bhavati bhikshām dehi*. A khattiya says- *bhikshām bhavati dehi*. One from the trader caste says- *bhikshām dehi bhavati*. Bhikkhus didn't ask for or beg for *piṇḍapāta*. They would stand silently for some time and move on.

In summary, the Buddha did accept the path of *piṇḍapāta*. But it was one that brought all the people to one level. It brought equality. It brought morality. The *Manusmriti's* rules, on the other hand, were meant to discriminate, to bring inequality and to cause disharmony. The rules of the *Manusmriti* were part of the counter-revolution that aimed at destroying the ethical revolution of the Buddha. *Manusmriti's* rule about alms was a distressing part of that counter-revolution. It was an attempt to nullify the great movement of the Buddha. When we see the rules laid down by the *Manusmriti*, it is clear that the Vedic tradition didn't reject begging for alms. It is not possible that Savarkar was not aware that until recent times, students from a particular caste survived by *mādhukari* or eating at different households on different week-days and who went to leave a mark on various fields due to their achievements. Would he call these students 'beggars'?

Actually, it was the narrow-minded meanness of the Vedic tradition to restrict alms to a particular caste. The Buddha's tradition did not have this flaw. Even then Savarkar pokes fun at him. This is certainly not just. Would the Vedics call *brāhmaṇa-bhoja* and *brāhmaṇa-dakshiṇā* (feeding the brahmins and giving gifts to brahmins) as begging? Would they call the alms given to brahmins as begged food? Isn't this offering considered an integral and greatly fruitful part of religious duty in Vedic tradition? This doesn't mean that we must restart the *piṇḍapāta* tradition in India again. Every concept and practice has its time and place.

It would be ingratitude of the highest order to reject that the *piṇḍapāta* tradition of the Buddha, nay of all the samaṇas, helped to build a better society.

Food Only For Sustenance

One needs food for sustaining life. The Buddha knew from his own experience that not taking food or taking inadequate food was not proper. He advised middle path in the matter of food just as he advocated it in other issues. In a sutta in the Middle Discourses,[401] while teaching the bhikkhus how to destroy defiling impulses, the Buddha said, "A bhikkhu reflects in the right way while partaking alms food. He doesn't eat food for the sake of physical beauty, play, lust or appearance. He eats only as much as is needed for sustenance of body, for maintaining physical health and for practising the Dhamma. He eats so that old feelings *(vedanā)* cease and new feelings don't arise. He eats for sustaining life and dwelling in the Dhamma."

Bhikkhus Would Teach After Alms

Bhikkhus would teach where they received alms. The Buddha said in Nāga Sutta of the Connected Discourses,[402] "... Senior bhikkhus go to villages or towns for alms. They teach the Dhamma there and through their teaching make the laypeople happy."

The bhikkhus were contented with the alms they were offered. If the bhikkhus teach the society the Noble Eightfold Path and through it the society becomes more harmonious, becomes more constructive, crime goes down, quarrels decrease, people become stress-free and productivity increases, then the society would happily provide food for such a great service. Such a society would not look upon such bhikkhus as shirking work or as lazy beggars. We must look at these things in their proper context, situation, needs and work accomplished.

Discipline of Bhikkhus on Alms Round

The Tathāgata has given guidelines about how bhikkhus should behave on alms round. Let us look at one incident from the Middle Discourses[403] as an example.

Once when the Tathāgata was at Kalandakanivāpa of Rājagaha, Sāriputta came to meet him. He praised Sāriputta on his dwelling in meditation of emptiness *(suññata-vihāra)* and said that other bhikkhus should also follow his example.

At that time, he advised bhikkhus, "A bhikkhu should check whether he has any attraction, craving, hatred, ignorance or disgust for any form that he sees with his eyes when he enters a town for alms round *(piṇḍapāta)*, when he walks in the town for alms round and when he leaves the town after the alms round. If he finds that he has defilements in mind, then he should try to rid himself of those sinful, unwholesome defilements. On the other hand, if he finds that he has no defilements in mind, then he should dwell in wholesome *dhammas* day and night. The same applies to other sense doors."

He repeatedly told bhikkhus to be restrained while on alms round.

This shows us how the Tathāgata inspired bhikkhus to attain higher stages in self-development.

Society Should Take Responsibility For Those Who Serve Society

Siddhārtha Gotama had enough wealth to last him all his life. Still, he chose to live on alms food. There was certain social principle behind this choice. Those who strive for the welfare of society should not waste their time, effort, power and intellect for their own livelihood but use the same for contemplation and guidance for society's benefit. He therefore felt that such a person should be supported by the society. The laypeople at that time used to take up this responsibility willingly and happily. Rather, they considered it not as a burden but as an opportunity to do good, to perform meritorious deed. Such an opportunity was an honor for them. To be denied that opportunity was a humiliation for them.

The caste-based society put the burden of inequality and exploitation on the common masses so that a handful few could live in heedless luxury. On the other hand, the Buddha set in motion the flow of equality and humanity; and all he expected from the society in return was one daily meal for the bhikkhus. One can see the obvious contrast between the exploitative social structure and the Buddha's tradition both from the point of view of intentions and actual conduct.

Pilgrimage of the Vārakarīs

It is not out of place here to compare the pilgrimage of *Vārakarīs* who walk to sacred places such as Pandharpur, Alandi, Dehu, etc. As we have seen in the beginning of the book, the *Bhāgavat* tradition of the *Vārakarīs* has received inheritance from the Buddha. This can be seen in several things. In the Buddhist tradition, the bhikkhus would walk under the leadership of the Tathāgata or Sāriputta or some other elder. They would walk on foot. People would provide food and shelter for bhikkhus.

The pilgrimage of the *Vārakarīs* is similar. The food that is offered to the *Vārakarīs* is never looked upon as begging. On the other hand, lay people of Maharashtra feel happy and honored to get the opportunity to offer food to the *Vārakarīs*. I had seen this in my own home from the joy that my mother and father derived from serving food to the *Vārakarīs*. It is also very important to note here that when food is offered to the *Vārakarīs* no one asks or thinks about their caste.

In modern times, except for a few countries such as Sri Lanka, Myanmar etc, the tradition of alms round *(piṇḍapāta)* is almost lost. But during the Buddha's time and for a long time after that the tradition of going on alms round *(piṇḍapāta)* was respected, not detested. People looked upon it as a means of upliftment of society. We can see how deep the faith was when we look at the pilgrimage of the *Vārakarīs* today. This pilgrimage does not have the symbols of shaven head and saffron robes but its inner core resembles that of the alms round of the Buddha.

If we see Dr. R. C. Dhere's opinion or opinions of others that he has quoted, in which he says that Viṭṭhala of Paṇḍharī is a form of Buddha, then the resemblance becomes clearer.

Still, even at the time of the Buddha, there were those who detested bhikkhus going on alms round.

Piṇḍapāta is the Lowest of Livelihood

Though it is clear that *piṇḍapāta* is not begging for food, it is still not a self-reliant way of feeding oneself. The Buddha discussed this in Jīvika Sutta[404] of Itivuttaka.

Once the Buddha said to the bhikkhus, "Bhikkhus, this alms round is the lowest among all the livelihoods. People say with loathing 'You are going around for food with bowl in hand.' When people from good families turn to this livelihood, they do so for a reason, with a purpose. They don't do so to escape punishment of the king or to protect themselves from thieves. They don't do so to avoid paying their debts or for some such reason or because they have no other livelihood. Afflicted with birth, old age, disease, death, grief, lamentation, sorrow, sadness, distress, agitation of mind, suffering; they wish to eradicate all suffering and this thought makes them take up this livelihood of alms round.

"Bhikkhus, it is possible that a clansman who has gone forth with this purpose develops greed in mind, gets attracted to sensual pleasures, defilements arise in his mind, his thoughts become polluted. He loses concentration of mind. He loses awareness and alertness. He becomes dissatisfied. His mind becomes distracted. He loses restraint of senses. Bhikkhus, just as a log of wood that is burnt at both ends and is darkened in the middle when it is taken out of a funeral pyre cannot be used again in the town for fuel and cannot go back to forest as tree, such a bhikkhu is deprived of both sensual pleasures of a householder's life and higher attainments of a samaṇa life."

Then to further clarify the meaning he said, "Those who take on robes, indulge in sinful actions and foolish conduct—such sinners suffer due to their sinful actions. One who is immoral and ignorantly eats the king's alms, it is as if he eats a red hot ball of iron."

Discussion

There are four important things that the Buddha has said about alms round in this sutta.

1. It is an inferior way of livelihood.
2. Clansmen don't adopt it for selfish gain or to escape responsibilities.
3. They follow it to eradicate suffering of the people.
4. A bhikkhu who doesn't follow morality after accepting this path is neither a bhikkhu nor a householder (gets benefits of none); therefore, one who follows this path must live a moral life.

It need not be said separately that the path of alms round is neither self-reliant nor self-respecting. It involves facing refusals and rejection. It involves humiliation and censure. The Buddha knew this. Even then why did he give up the prestige of royal luxuries to follow this path? He didn't do it to avoid punishment or to avoid debt or for such selfish gain. Other bhikkhus also didn't do it for such reasons.

They all did it for a lofty objective. They did it after dissolving their ego, making themselves humble and to teach people the way out of suffering. Of course, not all who start the journey with idealism and high aims continue to be steadfast till the end. Some stray from their path and become a victim of defilements.

The Buddha Attacked Caste System Through Alms Round

Let us look at yet another aspect of alms round *(piṇḍapāta)*. The Buddha was born in a clan that was thought of as being a very high lineage. Several other bhikkhus such as Ānanda were also born in that clan. Several bhikkhus had come from wealthy and prestigious families. The Tipiṭaka has several details about this.

In a society poisoned by caste system, a high caste prince stood for alms at the door of a low caste person and respectfully accepted food offered by a person who was humiliated by the system. We can imagine how this must have brought so much joy and self-respect to the one who offered food and how it must have shaken the caste hierarchy that discriminated between people. Those who speak derisively about alms round of the Buddha are in fact angry about his attack on the caste system and artificial greatness of a few. We cannot understand the *piṇḍapāta* in its entirety without first knowing the background of the caste system.

There is one more significant aspect to this. Mankind has created discrimination through various ways. It has divided human beings as high and low. Throughout the history of India, Vedic tradition made discriminatory rules about food and water that were not just arrogant but also cruel. The Buddha created a big upheaval through *piṇḍapāta* and brought all people to one level.

In a society where if a person from low caste were to be given water or food it was done from a distance, where they were given left-overs with disdain; in the same society the Buddha respectfully accepted food from people from lower castes. But many Indians closed their eyes to the light that this great man brought to us. They engulfed themselves in darkness for centuries. Those very people, who would have received gifts from him had he not gone forth, refused him food and even water at times. He not only gave up royal comforts but also put up with all the humiliation and remained steadfast in his service to society.

The Buddha Doesn't Get Alms Food

We see in Piṇḍa Sutta[405] of the Connected Discourses that there were times when the Buddha didn't get any alms.

Once he was dwelling in a brahmin town of Pañchasālā in Magadha. One day when the young girls were supposed to exchange gifts, the Buddha went for alms round. At that time, Māra had influenced the people of the town not to give alms to the Buddha.

The Buddha went to the town with an empty bowl and came back with the same empty bowl. Then evil Māra went to the Buddha and asked, "Samaṇa, did you get alms?"

The Buddha replied, "You had made arrangements that I shouldn't receive alms."

Māra said, "O bhante, in that case the Tathāgata should go to the town for the second time for alms. I will make sure that you get alms food."

The Buddha replied, "Māra has done great wrong by this treachery… I have nothing (no alms food) but I live contented. I will partake joy and shine like the gods."

Then Māra became sad and disappeared thinking, "The Tathāgata knows me, the Sugata knows me."

Discussion

To avoid blaming a human being, Māra is blamed here. However, Māra is not some being living outside the human mind. It was a convenient imaginary figure that represented the defilements in the human mind. Therefore, all this means is that on that day the people of the town didn't give alms to the Buddha. It is well known how the great saint Dnyāneshwar and his siblings faced a similar situation in later period.

The Buddha's utterances in the end show the stability of his mind. He has not received food. Still, he is not angry or disgusted or upset. He doesn't blame anyone in the town. Blaming Māra is blaming the defilements. Rather than blaming a person as a criminal, the criminal tendencies in the person are blamed. He was as contented without alms food as he was with alms food. He knew that food was necessary for sustenance. However, when he declares himself as partaking joy, he proclaims that love and affection is the greatest food for humans.

To Prevent the Buddha From Drinking Water…

In a sutta[406] in Udāna, we see that some brahmins hated the Buddha so much that not only did they not want him to get alms but they also tried to prevent him from getting water.

Once the Buddha was dwelling in Malla. Along with a big retinue of bhikkhus, he reached a brahmin town named Thūṇa.

When the brahmins in the town came to know about it they filled the well in the village with grass and sawdust so that 'those shaven head samaṇas shouldn't get water to drink.'

When the Buddha reached the town, he sat under a tree near the well and asked Ānanda to bring water from the well. Then Ānanda informed him what the brahmins had done to the well. Again the Buddha asked him to bring water and again Ānanda gave the same answer. But when the Buddha asked him the third time to bring water, Ānanda went to the well and found that the grass had vanished and clean water was overflowing. Ānanda was surprised. He filled the water pot, brought it to the Buddha and requested him to drink it. Then the Buddha uttered spontaneously, "If there is water everywhere, what is the need for the well *(udapāna)*? If craving is destroyed from the root, what else is there to search?"

Discussion

When the Tathāgata asked thrice, Ānanda went to the well and found that the well was overflowing with clean water. If the spring in the well was powerful it was possible that the grass would be swept away and clean water would come up. But this would be trying to find a rational explanation for the phenomenon.

However, if one looks at the utterance at the end, it indicates something else. The Buddha didn't drink the water brought by Ānanda. It seems that he was not talking about ordinary water. He was talking about the fundamental issue of suffering. His utterance suggested that one who had eradicated suffering need not worry about minor inconveniences.

If one looks at this incident in the context of the vast history of India, it indicates a social reality. The brahmins had stopped access to their knowledge, authority, etc. that is, stopped access to the well and blocked the access to water for thirsty people. But these people when they got the water that eradicated all suffering, they had scant need for the earlier water. It is clear from a verse in Bhagvad Gitā[407] that this meaning is not far fetched. "Just as when there is water everywhere there is hardly any need for well water *(udapāna)*, similarly one who has attained the high brahmā knowledge has hardly any need for the Vedas."

When there is plenty of water available everywhere, one need not depend on a small well. Similarly, one who has attained superior wisdom does not have to depend on any of the four Vedas.

This verse is among the few verses in Bhagvad Gitā that preserve the original thoughts of Krishna. This verse has not only echoed the essence but also the parable and has used the same key word *udapāna*. It says that the four Vedas are mere *udapāna* when compared to true wisdom.

Bhikkhus Scorned

Once Mahākaccāna was staying in a hut in Makkarakata forest in Avanti.[408] At that time, many brahmin disciples of Lohicca brahmin came outside the Mahākaccāna's hut. They started making noise and saying that the shaven headed samaṇas were inferior, dark, etc. and that the laypeople revered them without any reason.

Hearing the commotion, Mahākaccāna came out and said, "Boys, don't make noise. Let me teach you the Dhamma."

Then the boys became calm. Mahākaccāna told them how the brahmins of the past were restrained and how brahmins of the present day recite Vedas, were conceited due to arrogance of caste and behave rudely. He explained to them how matted hair was of no use and that loving all beings was the true way to attain Brahmā. The boys became angry listening to this. They went to Lohicca and reported, "Do you know? Samaṇa Mahākaccāna is criticizing the Vedas." On hearing this, Lohicca went to Mahākaccāna. However, he was satisfied after discussion with Mahākaccāna.

Like the Buddha, his disciples too would respond to insults with restraint. They would softly and skillfully convey the importance of moral conduct.

Why Look at the Shaven Head?

We see in Ghaṭikāra Sutta[409] of the Middle Discourses how the brahmins looked down upon the shaven headed bhikkhus.

Ghaṭikāra was a young potter. He was a follower of Kassapa Buddha. A young brahmin named Jotipāla was his friend. Once Ghaṭikāra asked his friend to go with him to meet the Buddha. Jotipāla said, "What is going to be achieved by looking at the shaven headed *samaṇaka*?"

Later, when both were returning after a bath, Ghaṭikāra again tugged at Jotipāla cloth and requested him again to go with him to meet the Buddha. Again Jotipāla refused.

Then Ghaṭikāra put his hand on Jotipāla's hair and made the same request. Jotipāla thought that since Ghaṭikāra, in spite of being from a low caste was touching his hair after bath, it must be something extraordinary and agreed to go to Kassapa Buddha. Later Jotipāla went forth and got ordained. Even then his earlier comment on shaven head *samaṇaka* and his surprise at a person from a lower caste touching his hair, show his mentality.

Samaṇa Gotama Inauspicious According to Māgaṇḍiya

In Māgaṇḍiya Sutta[410] of the Middle Discourses we find the following story.

Once the Tathāgata was living in Kammāsadamma town of Kuru. He was offered a mat made of grass in the fire house of a brahmin from Bhāradvāja clan.

One day when the Tathāgata had gone on alms round, the recluse Māgaṇḍiya happened upon the fire house during his wanderings. He saw the mat and said to Bhāradvāja brahmin, "For whom is this mat spread? It is suitable for use by a samaṇa."

Bhāradvāja praised the Tathāgata and said that it was for the Tathāgata.

Māgaṇḍiya responded, "Bhāradvāja, what a painful thing that I had to look at the bedding of the inauspicious Gotama."

Brahmin Bhāradvāja requested him not to speak thus.

But he persisted, "Bhāradvāja, I would say to Gotama's face that he is inauspicious. Why? Because our scriptures say so."

Bhāradvāja asked him whether he had any objection if he told this to the Tathāgata.

Māgaṇḍiya replied, "No objection. Feel free to repeat this conversation to Gotama!"

Later this recluse met the Tathāgata and changed his view. But his earlier statements show how some people were angry at and disgusted with the Tathāgata. It is also clear that some brahmins revered him.

Order of Disciples (Sāvaka-Saṅgha)

There are several descriptions of the Tathāgata's Sāvaka-Saṅgha in the Tipiṭaka.

For example, in the Middle Discourses,[411] the Saṅgha of disciples is described as *supaṭipanna, ujupaṭipanna, ñāyapaṭipanna* and *sāmicipaṭipanna*. It means *practicing the right way*, *walking on the straight path*, *being on the just path* and *being on the proper path*. The Tathāgata had given a discipline to the Saṅgha. He had given them a goal. He had told them how to walk towards the goal in proper manner. Therefore, his disciples were worthy of these epithets.

The Dhamma is for Liberation; Not for Increasing Number of Disciples

Though the strength of the Saṅgha needed to increase for the spread of the Dhamma, the Buddha was not in favor of increasing number of disciples by any and all means. This can be seen from the following incidence.[412]

Once a recluse named Nyagrodha severely criticized the Buddha. When the Buddha met him, he was won over by the discussion with the Buddha. Then he felt remorse about his earlier utterances. The issues narrated by the Buddha show his magnanimity.

The Buddha said, "Nyagrodha, any upright, artless, straightforward and intelligent man may come to me. I will teach him the Discipline and the Dhamma. If he does as I teach, he will achieve the goal for which clansmen go forth, experience the ultimate reality for himself within seven years. Why seven years, he will do so in six years… five years… four years… one year… he will attain the goal within a week.

"Nyagrodha, do not think that Samaṇa Gotama is saying this because he wants to gather disciples. Let your teachers remain your teachers.

"Do not think that Samaṇa Gotama is saying this to distract you from your path. You may continue with your current aims.

"I teach the Dhamma to remove distressing unwholesome things… so that the listener may attain perfection of wisdom; so that he may know, experience and attain true wisdom."

Discussion

There are several so-called Gurus or teachers who bind a disciple, even turn them into slaves. The Buddha was not that kind of teacher. He wanted those who follow the Dhamma to be independent and self-sufficient. He didn't want the Saṅgha to be a crowd of those who have shut their eyes. He wanted to teach them to set them free; not to bind them. Acharya Goenka's following statement echoes the Buddha's sentiments. "The only conversion involved in Vipassana is from misery to happiness, from bondage to liberation."

Self-Discipline; Not Enforced Discipline

The Buddha's discipline involved compassionate explanation. He wouldn't control bhikkhus like a dictator or by humiliating them. We see this in the Kakacūpama Sutta in the Middle Discourses.[413]

Once while the Buddha was living at Jetavana, Bhikkhu Moliya Phagguna used to spend a lot of time in the company of bhikkhuṇis. If anyone criticized the bhikkhuṇis in front of him, he would complain to the Saṅgha. Bhikkhuṇis too would get angry if anyone criticized him. Once a bhikkhu told the Buddha about this. On hearing about it, the Buddha sent for Moliya Phagguna and asked him, "Do you like to spend a lot of time with bhikkhuṇis?"

Phagguna said yes.

Then the Buddha told him that it is not proper for a man who had gone forth from a good family with faith to spend so much time in the company of bhikkhuṇis. Then he gave him a detailed Dhamma discourse. While telling him that he didn't want to discipline him through punishment, the Buddha gave an example.

"Suppose there is a chariot at cross road to which horses are yoked. There is an alert and skillful charioteer with a whip and able to control the horses. Then he takes the rein in left hand and whip in right hand. Then he makes the horses take the chariot in whatever direction he wishes to take them. Just as the skilled charioteer doesn't wish to use the whip, I too don't wish to discipline bhikkhus through punishment. I just remind them, make them aware. Therefore, bhikkhus, abandon unwholesome deeds. Apply yourself to wholesome deeds. If you do this, you will get established and grow in the Dhamma and the Discipline."

Discussion

The Buddha didn't want to use force to control bhikkhus. He wanted the bhikkhus to use self-discipline and look after their own welfare. A skilled charioteer has a whip in his hand, but he hardly needs to use it. He doesn't beat up the horses to control them. He trains the horses such that they do the right thing. The Buddha was using this method. We have already seen how well he had organized the bhikkhu Saṅgha in the Dhammacetiya Sutta[414] of the Middle Discourses.

Division Leads to Downfall: Unity Brings Welfare

A principal aim behind the formation of the Saṅgha was spread of the Dhamma. The Buddha constantly urged the Saṅgha to be unified in order to be successful in this aim. This is not applicable only to the Saṅgha but to every family and every society. It was relevant in his time and is relevant today. There are two suttas[415] in Itivuttaka that are significant in this regard. One is about division in Saṅgha and the other about unity.

"There is one thing that, when it arises, causes harm to many, suffering to many and loss to many. This one thing is schism in the Saṅgha. When there is schism in the Saṅgha, there are quarrels. There are threats. There is backbiting. Relations get strained. When this happens those who don't have faith in the Dhamma, don't generate faith and those who have faith lose it.

"One who causes split in the Saṅgha; who looks after narrow self interest; who gets pleasure from causing schism; who causes harm; who goes to lower realms is against the Dhamma. He destroys welfare and goes to nether worlds after causing split in the Saṅgha."

The sutta about unity says, "Unity in the Saṅgha brings welfare to many. If there is unity, there is no quarrel. Then those who don't have faith in the Dhamma develop faith and those who have faith develop more confidence. Unity in the Saṅgha gives joy. One who likes harmony, promotes unity is a noble person who doesn't destroy welfare. Unity of the Saṅgha brings happiness."

Discussion

There is a history of successes and failures of countless generations in the past and enough light for hundreds of future generation to walk in the right direction in this advice of the Buddha. This advice is invaluable. The society, where people's minds are troubled by minor issues, cannot walk in one direction. It cannot build a consensus. It cannot act at the right time.

People rather than complementing each other obstruct each other. Rather than nurturing each other and helping each other grow, they malign each other, bring each other down and terrorize each other. Such a society doesn't grow and doesn't become mature.

People in such a society remain weak and immature. Such a society is afflicted by quarrels, envy and jealousy. It gets enslaved by others.

On the other hand, in a unified society every individual's genius and creativity flourishes. Every person's dormant capacity gets opportunity. Such a society dreams big and noble dreams. In such societies those who have sorrow benefit from harmony. Those who are already joyful get further incentive to be happier and more successful.

He Who Serves the Sick Serves Me

Another refreshing aspect of the Buddha's Dhamma was service. Man cannot live alone. People living together in society need each other. No one can be completely self-sufficient. Therefore, helping each other and serving each other is a strong link that joins people together. Such links build society. The Buddha gave advice about how to build unity in the Saṅgha. Serving the sick is an important aspect of such unity. We find this in Gilānavatthu Kathā of the Book of Discipline.[416]

Once a bhikkhu had dysentery and was lying in his own excreta. At that time, the Buddha went to him with Ānanda.

He asked the bhikkhu, "Isn't there anyone to take care of you?"

The bhikkhu said no.

The Buddha asked, "Why no one is taking care of you?"

The bhikkhu replied, "Bhante, I didn't serve other bhikkhus so others don't take care of me."

Then the Buddha sent Ānanda to bring water and they bathed and cleaned the bhikkhu. Then they lifted him and put him on a bed.

Then the Buddha called all bhikkhus together and asked them about the sick bhikkhu. The other bhikkhus told him that because the sick bhikkhu had never served anyone when he was healthy, others were not inclined to take care of him.

Then the Buddha advised them, "Bhikkhus, there is no mother or father to look after you. You must take care of each other. If you don't serve each other, who will serve you? Bhikkhus, one who wishes to serve me, should serve the sick. If your teacher or preceptor or disciple or colleague becomes sick, then his disciples or others should serve him or the Saṅgha should serve him. If one doesn't serve the sick it will be transgression of the discipline."

Discussion

The advice given by the Buddha here is not only for bhikkhus. It is applicable to every person in the society. Though the example given here is that of a sick person, in the figurative sense it has a much broader meaning. True service and compassion for all mean that society should lend a helping hand to those who are weak, disadvantaged and needy. The society, community or family that adopts service as a joyous duty, stays together with love and affection. Their unity springs from within and is unbreakable.

Often people jump with alacrity for an opportunity to serve an important person. However, they disregard the common needy people. This is not following the Buddha, not practice of the Dhamma and not protection of the Saṅgha. A true follower of the Buddha, Dhamma and Saṅgha serves those who are poor and disadvantaged.

Therefore, the Buddha asked the Saṅgha to serve the sick. And he made it an offense not to serve the sick bhikkhu. "Rather than vying with each other to serve me, serve the sick" was the message he wanted to convey.

The Saṅgha Makes the Dhamma Complete

No matter how great a person, if there is not a community of people who follow and spread his message, that person's work remains incomplete. The Buddha ensured that this didn't happen by creating the Saṅgha and complementing it with lay followers. We find the Buddha talking about this.[417]

Once the recluse Mahāvaccha asked the Buddha, "Other than you, is there at least one bhikkhu who has in this very life eradicated all defilements and who is liberated?"

The Buddha replied, "Not just one, not just one hundred or five hundred, there are a large number of bhikkhus who are liberated."

Then he asked the same question about bhikkhuṇis and received the same reply.

Then he asked about laymen followers and laywomen followers. The Buddha gave the same answer.

Then the recluse said that if only the Buddha had become liberated, the Dhamma would have been incomplete; if only the Buddha and the bhikkhus... if only the Buddha, the bhikkhus and the bhikkhuṇis... if only the Buddha, the bhikkhus, the bhikkhuṇis and laymen followers had been liberated still the Dhamma would have been incomplete. Finally, he said that the Buddha, bhikkhus, bhikkhuṇis, laymen and laywomen followers all together make the Dhamma complete in all aspect.

There is a similar dialogue between Ānanda and recluse Sandaka in the Sandaka Sutta[418] of the Middle Discourses. When Sandaka asked Ānanda how many teachers there were in the Discipline and the Dhamma, Ānanda answered that there were more than five hundred of them.

The Saṅgha is as Important as the Buddha and the Dhamma

The Tathāgata gave as much importance to the Saṅgha as he gave to the Buddha and the Dhamma. Otherwise, he would not have put forth the concept of the triple refuge so strongly. Had he not created the Saṅgha, at the time of his *mahāparinibbāna*, the Buddha and the Dhamma would have immediately become weak. The Saṅgha spread the light of the Buddha and the Dhamma all over the world.

I regret that I have not been able to discuss here the various rules in the Book of Discipline (Vinaya Piṭaka) that bound the Saṅgha together. But all those who work to reform the society towards a more equal and just society would benefit from the Vinaya rules after they are adapted to our time. This would help the modern reformers in their personal life and also make the reformist movement more successful.

True Meaning of Saṅghaṃ Saraṇaṃ Gacchāmi

The Saṅgha created by the Buddha was the biggest, most disciplined, most efficient, and most mindful non-military organization that worked towards its aim. Even if we look at the history of the world, the Saṅgha was the first such organization in the known history of the world. The Buddha's message spread far and wide, within and outside of India, because he created the Saṅgha.

From the fifth century BCE to about twelfth century, the Dhamma held sway over a major section of the Indian society. There were ups and downs in this period too. But overall Indian society cherished and nurtured the Dhamma. A historian feels that at one time there were more followers of the Buddha than any other religion.[419] "Gautam, the Buddha (Pali Gotama), the founder of the Buddhist faith, which at one time numbered in all probability more adherents than any other form of religious belief, was born…" Even today hundreds of millions of people in various countries all over the world follow the light of the Dhamma. This is possible because of the Saṅgha. The Saṅgha became the vehicle of the Dhamma. If instead of triple refuge there had been just double refuge, the Dhamma would not have spread. When we understand this immense capacity and strength of the Saṅgha, we get further perspective on *Saṅghaṃ Saraṇaṃ Gacchāmi.*

People in the society that don't follow the principle of refuge in the Saṅgha, even though they suffer from common troubles, can't come together to overcome suffering. Such a society is confused, divided and trusts enemies more than the friends. They make it easy for the enemies to conquer them. A society that understands the importance of refuge in the Saṅgha, behave politely with each other, understand each other, respect each other and help each other in times of need.

Siddhārtha Gotama saw that people fight with each other and suffer as a consequence; that their situation was like fish in inadequate water. When he left home and his loved ones, it was as if he set out to fight a great war against suffering. When he discovered the Dhamma and won that war, he created the Saṅgha.

Let the Indian society at least now welcome the principle of the Saṅgha and live according to that principle! This will ensure that we benefit from that great man's efforts and visionary compassion!

12

Gratitude for Past Traditions

Great men arise time and again to give a novel and benevolent turn to the flow of social life. The chemistry of their personalities has two important components.

They have keen comprehension of social realities, rare talent for new creation, and a refreshing mix of qualities required for welfare of human society. Their creative genius helps in their revolutionary work.

On the other hand, it is equally true that no great man arises all of a sudden like a comet. In whichever society he is born, he gets a certain inheritance from that society. He gets a background. That society has reached a certain stage already. In this situation, the great man who arises in the flow of time through his unparalleled vision ushers a new era by starting from the stage where the society has already reached. He uses his own talent to inspire the inner strength of the society.

When we say that he gets a certain background, it doesn't take away any credit from his great work. When we show gratitude for an earlier tradition, it doesn't deny the truth of the novel revolutionary creation of that person.

The same thing happened with the Tathāgata. He discovered the Dhamma and taught the Noble Eightfold Path. But humility and gratitude made him give (perhaps more than was due) credit to the earlier tradition.

Discovering a New Path

The Buddha told his five former companions that when he attained Bodhi, he discovered principles that he had not heard about before. This means that he had discovered something new.

Once Ānanda was living in Kalandakanivāpa of Rājagaha. Not much time had passed since the passing away of the Buddha. One day, before alms round, Ānanda went to the farm of Gopakamoggallāna brahmin, who welcomed him and asked, "Is there anyone among the bhikkhus who is endowed with all the qualities of the Buddha?"

Ānanda said no and replied,[420] "O brahmin, the Tathāgata was the discoverer of a new path. He knew and showed the path that had not been known by anyone before him. He taught what none had taught before him. He was knower of the path, expert of the path and adept in the path. All those who come after him follow in his footsteps."

This means that according to Ānanda the path shown by the Buddha was discovered anew by him.

Sāriputta too once made a similar statement.[421]

The Tathāgata was once talking to bhikkhus who had gathered for *pavāraṇā* (at the end of the rains retreat) at Pubbārāma in Sāvatthi. At that time, Sāriputta said about the Tathāgata, "Bhante, the Tathāgata is discoverer of a new path. He knows that which was not known earlier. He teaches what was not taught earlier. He is knower of the path, understands the path and is adept in the path. Bhante, the disciples walk on that path."

The Buddha himself told bhikkhus the same thing.[422]

Once while he was living in Sāvatthi, he said to the bhikkhus, "Bhikkhus, the Tathāgata, Arahata, Sammā Sambuddha is called so because he has become liberated through disenchantment, cessation and non-attachment about form, sensation, etc."

He added that the bhikkhus too can become liberated thus. When the bhikkhus asked him the difference between the

Sammā Sambuddha and a bhikkhu liberated through wisdom, he explained the difference. He said that the Sammā Sambuddha was the discoverer of a new path and his disciples walk on that path.

I Have No Teacher

We have seen the Buddha's meeting, after his enlightenment, with Upaka Ājīvaka, on the way to Varanasi with the aim of rotating the wheel of the Dhamma.

Upaka asked him, "Who is your teacher? Whose Dhamma do you like?"

The Buddha answered, "I have no teacher."[423]

This answer was neither impudent nor arrogant. He was being truthful. He did have gratitude for Āḷāra Kālāma and Udaka Rāmaputta but he had not acquired the knowledge of the Dhamma under any teacher's guidance. He had experimented himself. He had used his own intellect and wisdom to discover a new effective solution for the suffering of humanity. It was entirely his own effort.

It is important for cultural history that the Buddha himself had made such statements. In the times since the Buddha, several great people were born in India. But often the credit for their work was not given to them. It was given to someone else, at times to a fictional teacher. Therefore, it is good that the Buddha stated in no uncertain terms that he had no teacher.

I Retell the Path of the Past Sammā Sambuddhas

We also find in the Tipiṭaka that he told bhikkhus that the path he was showing to them was the same one that the Buddhas of the past had walked upon.[424]

He gave the following example to clarify his statement.

"Suppose a man is walking in the forest. While wandering he sees a path that had been used by people in the past. He keeps walking on that path and reaches the capital city. It is a delightful city full of buildings, gardens, lakes, etc. that was once occupied by people. Then that man goes to the king or his minister and requests them to occupy the city again. Soon the city becomes populated, prosperous and affluent. O bhikkhus, similarly I discovered an ancient path followed by the Buddhas of the past. The Noble Eightfold Path is that path."

On the face of it, there is a discrepancy in these two statements. He wanted to present the path that he had discovered to the people. But he also wanted to avoid any appearance of arrogance or impudence. He followed the civilized manner of acknowledging the help that he has received from the past tradition and humbly showing gratitude for it.

Let us look at the tradition that he had inherited.

Kapilavatthu (Kapilavastu) was Suddhodana's capital. It is obvious that Suddhodana received the inheritance of the samaṇa tradition of Kapila. Siddhārtha too must have received it. The act of Siddhārtha sitting for meditation in childhood means that he had seen meditating samaṇas or heard about them. He had met a samaṇa before he left home. After leaving home he went to the monasteries of two samaṇas: Āḷāra Kālāma and Udaka Rāmaputta. They must have had some influence on Siddhārtha. Therefore, he remembered them on attaining Bodhi. Whenever the Buddha talked about these two samaṇas, he did so with respect.

Shiva and Buddha: Creators of the Same Cultural Stream

We can trace the origin of the samaṇa tradition in the Indus civilization. Indian society reveres both Shiva and the Buddha. Both are great combined heritage of Indian society. We can see this from various aspects of Indian history.

Many scholars believe that the meditating man found in Indus civilization is Shiva. Dr. R. N. Dandekar quotes Aiyappan A. in his book *Harappan Bibliography,* "…the figure in yogic posture on Mohenjo-Daro seal is either Siva or Agni—it is near to Siva than to Agni…"

If we look at a non-Vedicized original form of Shiva we can say that he is the original man of the samaṇa tradition. The yogic meditation that came from Shiva is found in non-Vedic Sāṅkhya and Yoga schools of philosophy. The Buddha had this inheritance. The Buddha gave immense importance to meditation as is clear from his life and his teachings.

In the book *2500 Years of Buddhism* edited by P. V. Bapat[426] we find this about Kanishka in the chapter by Prof Bharat Singh Upadhyaya, *Some Great Buddhists After Asoka*, "...Though an ardent Buddhist himself, Kanishka respected all other forms of faith, as is shown by his coins, which bear images of gods worshipped by the Greeks, Persians and Indians. Thus, besides Sakaymo Bodo (Sākyamuni Buddha), there is Oesho (Siva), the fire god Athsho (Persian: Atash), the Greek sun god Helios, and several others. This liberal attitude in matters of religious worship was shown equally by another Buddhist ruler, Harsha. He came nearly six centuries after Kaniska and showed equal reverence to Siva, the cult of the Sun and certain other forms of religious faith." That the great king Harsha too revered both Shiva and the Buddha further brings forth the connection between them.

Shiva is a beloved and revered ancestor of the *bahujana* society. (Here *bahujana* means non-upper caste section that forms the overwhelming majority of the Indian society. This was not the sense in which the Buddha used the word when he said *bahujana hitāya*. The Buddha meant for the welfare of many—not for the welfare of a particular section of society. His *bahujana* did include this majority underprivileged section. Though the use of this word can be confusing when used for this section of society, there is no good English substitute for it.) Shiva was successfully adopted by the Vedic tradition to dominate the *bahujanas*.

The Buddha tried to remove inequality and injustice from the Vedic tradition. It was not possible to oppose and refute the Buddha's teaching easily because it was based on a strong ethical foundation. Therefore, many indirect efforts were made. One such effort was to put Shiva, who was very popular with the *bahujanas*, in opposition to the Buddha. This created confusion in the mind of the masses. They removed the Buddha to establish Shiva.

Inspiration from Indus Civilization

Indus civilization is an ancient civilization of India. It is pre-Vedic. In Indus civilization the pipal tree (*ficus religiosa*) had a special place. Pipal is called *ashvattha* in Sanskrit and *assattha* in Pali.

Bharatiya Sanskriti Kosh has the following to say about *ashvattha*,[427] "It seems that in the pre-Vedic Indus civilization, *ashvattha* was a symbol of creation. In one of the coins (*mudrā*) found there, we see a goddess standing between two branches of *ashvattha*. In another coin, there is a sampling of Pipal and two goddesses have embraced it to protect it. Mahishamuṇḍa (literally one with head of a buffalo) was a great goddess of Indus people and she lived on *ashvattha*. It seems that Mahishamuṇḍa is the creator goddess in Indus civilization. It could be the predecessor of Vedic Prajāpati. The main symbol of Indus civilization is shaped like V. It is made of two branches of *ashvattha* rising from root."

The same encyclopedia says about Pipal,[428] "In Indus civilization, Pipal leaf indicated increase in prosperity and happiness." It is clear that the Pipal tree has great significance in Indian society from the time of Indus civilization. We can say that when Siddhārtha Gotama sat under this tree, he drew inspiration and energy from the same tradition.

The Word Ashvattha Has Origin in Vernacular

The importance of Pipal in the culture of the *bahujanas* is clear from the Pali word *assattha*. In Sanskrit is called *ashvattha*. This can be split as *ashva + ttha*, which means a place where horses are tied. It is also split as *a+shva+ttha*, which means 'that which won't be there tomorrow.' This split is done to indicate that the universal Pipal tree is ephemeral, impermanent.

Both the splits and the meanings look far-fetched. It is certain that the word has come to Sanskrit from Pali. T. W. Rhys Davids say while discussing this word,[429] "Vedic *ashvattha*… standing place for horses, which etymologically is problematic; it is likely that the Sanskrit word is borrowed from a local dialect." The words used for this tree also seem to have connection with the *bahujanas*.

Swapan Kumar Biswas has said that in India many clans use this tree's name as family name or individual name.[430] In Maharashtra, Pimpale is one of the family names.

Dr. R. N. Dandekar

Some quotes from Dr. R. N. Dandekar's work that show a relation between Pipal and Indus civilization are relevant here:

S. R. Goel says, "...Indus Valley Civilizatoin was pre-Vedic and non-Vedic; some of the most important elements of the religious life, of later-day India go back to Indus Civilization: Shiva, Mother-Goddess, pippal tree, bull..."

E. Abegg says,[432] "...in the pipal-worship of Buddhistic art is to be seen a remnant of Indus Valley tree-worship."

Duplicity of Vedics about Pipal

Vedic tradition has taken a duplicitous stand on Pipal. On one hand, there is an effort to incorporate it into Vedic culture by honoring it as a tree of the brahmins. In the same note on *ashvattha* quoted above from Bharatiya Sanskriti Kosh, a verse is given that means, "*Ashvattha* belongs to brāhmaṇa varṇa and it is the king of all trees. Worship of *ashvattha* is equivalent to worship of all." Later Ashvattha was made into a form of Vishnu. The same Kosh tells us that the tree undergoes thread ceremony *(upanayana)* and that it is married to Tulsi in a ceremonial ritual. Mahabharat[433] on the other hand says that the *ashvattha* is the tree of khattiyas and the fig tree (*udumbar, audumbar, umbar*) is the tree of brahmins.

On the other hand, we also see immense aversion for Pipal. Bharatiya Sanskriti Kosh says about Pipal, "It is believed that *muñjyā* from ghost realm lives on Pipal." It is surprising that on one hand, the tree is considered auspicious and on the other hand it is connected to ghost realm. If a brahmin child dies before its *upanayana* it is said to become a ghost and live in the Pipal tree. This ghost is called a *muñjyā*. This means that the Pipal is related to non-performance of *muñja* (*upanayana,* thread ceremony). This is an important ceremony in Vedic tradition. Without this ceremony a child doesn't become a *dvija* (a brahmin). Even if a child is born to brahmin parents, if it doesn't undergo *upanayana,* it is considered a *sudda* (low caste) according to scriptures. Thus connecting the Pipal to *muñjyā* is suggestive of the Pipal being non-Vedic.

The Pipal is Sacred for Buddhists

The Pipal is famous as Bodhi tree because the Tathāgata attained Bodhi under this tree. The Pipal leaf is heart-shaped. When it is connected to the compassionate heart of the Buddha, it becomes a meaningful symbol. Naturally, the tree is sacred for the followers of the Buddha. In India, it is usually not cut down. In Sri Lanka, it is revered. In cities, wherever there is Bodhi tree, it is worshipped in some way or the other. This is indirectly worship of enlightenment. This tree symbolizes Bodhi.

In many places in Sri Lanka, we find earthen pots next to the trunks of the Bodhi trees. To show respect, people use these pots to bring water from nearby ponds and offer water to the tree. They circumambulate the tree three times and at the end of each round, offer water. This is symbolic of triple refuge in the three gems of the Buddha, Dhamma and Saṅgha. Though this is supposed to be the principle behind it, in practice it has become a blind ritual.

Ter (in Osmanabad district) in Maharashtra, which was a famous Buddhist centre, has an abundance of Bodhi trees. The village, it seems, is still unknowingly preserving the Buddhist tradition.

We know that Emperor Asoka sent a sapling of the original Bodhi tree to his friend King Devanām Piya Tissa in Sri Lanka with his daughter Saṅghamittā. The tree still survives in Anurādhapura. Now some of the branches have been supported by iron scaffolding.

Mahāvaṃsa writes in great detail the importance of Bodhi tree in the life of Asoka and Tissa. When Tissa's sister in law wished to go forth but couldn't get *pabbajjā* because the bhikkhus couldn't give it, Mahinda suggested to Tissa to invite Saṅghamittā and to request her to bring a sapling of Bodhi tree with her.

Tissa conferred with his ministers and decided to send one of his ministers Arishṭa, who also happened to be his nephew, to Asoka. Arishṭa put a condition that on returning from India, he should be allowed to go forth (to become a bhikkhu). When Tissa agreed, Arishṭa went to Pāṭaliputra (present day Patna) in India and conveyed the message of Tissa and Mahinda to Asoka and Saṅghamittā. Asoka consulted with the Bhikkh Saṅgha. Moggaliputta Tissa agreed. Then the king decided to send a Bodhi sapling.

To implement his decision, the king went to the Bodhi tree with a big army and the Bhikkhu Saṅgha. There he donated his kingdom and worshipped the Bodhi tree. (It seems that donating the kingdom meant offering all cash reserves in the treasury in charity. It could also be symbolic of royal patronage.).

Asoka declared, "I am offering my kingdom to worship the Bodhi tree." Then he ceremoniously worshipped the tree with flowers etc. Then after taking a branch of the tree, he again worshipped the tree by offering his kingdom. Then he took the branch to the capital. Then he arranged for Saṅghamittā's journey. On reaching the sea shore, he again worshipped the tree by offering his kingdom. When Saṅghamittā with some other bhikkhuṇis and Arishṭa boarded the ship, the king said to them, "I have thrice offered my kingdom in worship of the Bodhi tree. King Tissa should also do the same." When the branch reached Sri Lanka, Tissa did likewise. The tree was planted in Mahā Meghavana. The tree has stood there for more than two millennia. This has been narrated in Mahāvaṃsa.[434]

It is said that King Shashāṅka destroyed the Bodhi tree. Prof. D. D. Kosambi says about Shashāṅka, who was Harsha Vardhan's enemy,[435] "His enemy Narendragupta-Shashāṅka from Bengal raided Magadha, cut down the Bodhi tree at Gaya, and wrecked Buddhist foundations wherever he could."

Banyan Bark on Pipal Trunk

In Marathi there is a saying which can be literally translated as "putting a banyan bark on a pipal trunk". It means giving a false façade to hide true nature of things. It is difficult to say how the saying originated. But it may be related to the cultural history of India where at one time the Buddha's teaching had enriched the minds of majority of the people. Vedic tradition either pushed aside the Buddha's teaching or incorporated it but gave it a different appearance. We have seen the importance of Pipal in the Buddhist tradition. The platform around Pipal tree was and is a major centre of social discourse in many villages. If we consider that the bark of banyan is a Vedic symbol, we may get a pointer as to how the saying about applying the bark of banyan tree to hide the pipal tree might have come about.

King Bali and Buddha

Kapilamuni was a great sage of the Indus Civilization. He was one of the two sons of Pralhāda. The second son was Virocana. The famous Balirājā (King Bali) is the son of Virocana. Because he was the son of Virocana, he is called Vairocana or Vairocani. Among the five Buddhas of the Buddhist tradition, the middle one is Vairocani Buddha. The Buddhist Monastery at Tabo in Spiti valley of Himachal Pradesh is famous as the Ajanta of Himalayas. In the assembly hall of the main cetiya, there are four statues of Vairocana Buddha. These statues are facing the four directions with their backs to each other. I have written elsewhere how Balirājā is called a Buddha in the Mahābhārata.

Cetiya in Shatapatha Brāhmaṇa

Prof. D. D. Kosambi writes,[436] "The satapatha Brāhmaṇa 13.8.1.5 and 13.9.2.1 refers to round funerary barrows of the Asuras, which should mean pre-Aryan structures not later than the 7th Century BC."

Of the two references given above from *Shatapatha Brāhmaṇa*, the first one occurs in the discussion on *pitrimedhanirūpaṇa*. The gist of it is: gods and *asuras* were fighting at various places. The gods drove *asuras* out of their territories. They were thus defeated. Since then gods started making funerary mounds with four corners; and asuras as well as easterners started making round funerary mounds... To the east and south is the door of ancestors. The host sends the dead to ancestral realm through this door.

Asuras used to make round memorials of their ancestors. It is clear that the round part of the Buddhist stupas is the next step of asuras's round memorials. Shatapatha Brāhmaṇa has added people of the East to asuras. When we note that the *samaṇa (shramaṇa)* traditions of Buddhists and Jains thrived in eastern UP, Bihar and part of Bengal, we can see that the stupas have come from the asura culture, from Indus Civilization.

Past Buddhas

As we have seen in the Introduction to this book, the Buddha tells his father Suddhodana that his lineage is the Buddha lineage.

Mahāpadāna Sutta[438] of the Dīgha Nikāya names six past Buddhas: Vipassī, Sikhī, Vessabhu, Kakucchanda, Kanakamunī and Kassapa. One Buddhist tradition believes that there were twenty-four Buddhas before Gotama and that Gotama was the twenty-fifth Buddha. It is difficult to say more about these Buddhas but it is clear that the Tathāgata had inherited a rich samaṇa tradition.

Lal Mani Joshi says,[439] "Although an inscription of the third century BC celebrates a stupa of Kanakamunī Buddha, and although a few of the immediate predecessors of Sākyamuni seem to have been historical teachers of the *shramaṇa* thought, it is very difficult at the present state of our knowledge, to write a satisfactory account of the former Buddhas of the Buddhist tradition. It is certain, however, that Shakyamuni continued the ancient religious tradition of non-Aryan and non-Vedic *munis* and *shramaṇas*."

Pacceka Buddhas of the Past

Once the Tathāgata was living on the Isigili (mountain that swallows rishis) mountain near Rājagaha.[440] At that time, he told bhikkhus that the mountains had different names in the past. Isigili too had a different name. In the past, five hundred *Pacceka* Buddhas (Silent Buddhas) used to live there. They were seen entering the mountain but then they would disappear. People said, "The mountain swallows sages." Thus it was called Isigili, which literally means (a mountain that) swallows rishis.

The Buddha told them the names of the Silent Buddhas. Some of these names are given in the Middle Discourses. Some of the names at the beginning of that list are Ariṭṭha, Upariṭṭha, Tagarasikhī, Yasassī and those at the end are Jeta, Jayanta, Padma, Kāṇha (Krishṇa).

Though we need not take the names given in the Middle Discourses as historical, we also can't reject them as totally imaginary. Whatever it may be, it is clear that some sages were meditating in Isigili and since the Tathāgata called them Buddhas, they were from the samaṇa tradition. Though people could see these samaṇas going towards the mountain, they could not see them afterwards as the samaṇas meditated in seclusion. They were so detached from the outside world that it was as if the mountain had swallowed them. The Tathāgata exhorts bhikkhus to salute these Buddhas who had left all craving behind and had attained nibbāna. This makes it clear that the Tathāgata had received an inheritance from the samaṇa tradition and he was respectful of the tradition.

There is yet another place where past Buddhas have been referred to.[441] While the Tathāgata was living in Jeta's Grove, the bhikkhus expressed surprise about how much the Tathāgata knew about the past Buddhas. It is clear that the Tathāgata came from the Samaṇa tradition.

Twenty-Four Buddhas of the Past

Buddhavaṃsa,[442] a text from Tipiṭaka, gives biographies of twenty-four Buddhas that came before Gotama the Buddha. Their names are: Dīpaṅkara, Koṇḍañña, Maṅgala, Suman, Revata, Sobhita, Anomadassi, Paduma, Nārada, Padumuttara, Sumedha, Sujātā, Piyadassī, Atthadassī, Dhammadassī, Siddhārtha, Tissa, Phussa, Vipassī, Sikhī, Vessabhu, Kakusandha, Koṇāgamana and Kassapa. Siddhārtha Gotama is the twenty-fifth and Metteyya (Maitreya) is the next Buddha.

The historicity of the twenty-four Buddhas is not as doubtless as that of Gotama the Buddha. It is possible that some of these really were historical persons and were known as saintly beings. Since Emperor Asoka renovated the stupa of Koṇāgamana (Kanakamuni), it is possible that he was a historical person.

It is likely that some of these were historical saints who were accepted by the Buddhist tradition as the past Buddhas. It is clear however that none of these left a clear and lasting imprint on human history. All that we learn from this is that Gotama the Buddha had received an intellectual inheritance from the samaṇa tradition. He built on it with his superlative philosophical genius and gave humanity his own special gift in the form of the Dhamma. Indeed, the Dhamma was the ripe fruit of his creative wisdom.

The Jātaka Tales

The Jātaka tales are considered an important aspect of the Buddhist tradition. It comes from *jāta* meaning "having born." It is believed that the present Siddhārtha Gotama took many births in the form of Bodhisatta in the past. The Jātakas are supposed to be descriptions of these past births.

Any further detailed discussion of the Jātaka tales is beyond the scope of this book. Still, we need to note a few things here. The Jātaka takes are not actual historical events. They do however indicate that the Buddha had an inheritance of some important personages from the past. Some of them are useful as tales with a moral. Some show a continuous refreshing cultural flow while some of them are undesirable and even unacceptable. I would have liked to discuss the tales about Sibī, Mahājanaka, etc. But I would restrict myself to Dasaratha Jātaka here.

Rāma, the son of Dasaratha, was a Bodhisatta

Dasaratha Jātaka says that Rāma was a Bodhisatta.[443]

Let me first give the original story of the Dasaratha Jātaka and then the information given in the Commentary.

Bharata gives Rāma the news of King Dasaratha's death. At that time, thinking that Lakkhaṇa (Laxman) and Sitā won't be able to contain their grief, Rāma asks them to get into lake and then tells them the news. Rāma didn't display any grief.

Bharata asked him, "Where did you get the strength to not grieve and lament on such an occasion? Why are you not upset and miserable on hearing the news about our father's death?"

Rāma answers Bharata in ten *gāthās* (verses). These verses mean:

1. Even after grieving if one is not able to save one for whom one grieves, then is it proper that a wise man should distress himself?
2. Whether young or old, ignorant or wise, rich or poor, everyone dies.
3. Just as ripe fruit on the tree is ever at risk of falling, a being who is born is ever at risk of dying.
4. Of the numerous beings that we see in the morning, we don't see some in the evening; and of those seen in the evening, many are not seen next morning.
5. If lamenting is going to be of any benefit, surely a wise one should lament. But lamenting, distressing oneself merely makes one thin and pale. And it doesn't bring the dead back to life. Therefore, grief is useless.
6. When a house is one fire, water is used to douse the fire. A wise and learned person dispels grief just as wind blows away cotton.
7. A being is born alone. A being dies alone. Animals meet by accident. Therefore, an intelligent, learned, wise man who knows the Dhamma and has seen the world here and yonder doesn't allow even big catastrophes to afflict his mind and heart.
8. I, who know my duty, will give in charity; will enjoy (my possessions); and will help my brethren and others too.

At the end of the Dasaratha Jātaka, Rāma is called *kambugrīva* (one having a beautiful neck) and *mahābāhu* (one with great arms).

The Commentary[444] gives a detailed description of the Dasaratha Jātaka.

Once the Tathāgata was living in Jeta's Grove. At that time a family was grieving because their father had died. Then the Buddha told them the story of Dasaratha and Rāma.

In the past in Varanasi, there lived a king named Dasaratha. He was a virtuous and just king. Rāma was the son of his chief consort. After she died, Dasaratha made another queen the chief queen. She bore him a son named Bharata. After her son was born, the king granted her a wish due to the joy of the birth of the son. She accepted it but didn't ask for anything immediately.

After seven-eight years she asked the king to give the kingdom to Bharata. Then the king admonished her that he couldn't do so while there were two elder sons. She was afraid but kept making the same demand. The king worried that she may plot against the elder two sons. He called them and told them that if they stayed on in the capital city, their life was at risk. He advised them to leave the city and go to the forest or to some other kingdom and to return after his death to claim the kingdom.

Then Rāma, Lakkhaṇa (Laxman) and Sitā went to Himalaya. Later, after nine years, Dasaratha couldn't bear the separation from his sons and died of grief. After his funeral, the queen demanded the kingdom for her son Bharata. The ministers refused to do so saying that the rightful heir was living in the forest. Then Bharata said that he would go and bring back Rāma. He went and gave him the news of Dasaratha's passing away. But Rāma didn't grieve. Rāma gave the news to Lakkhaṇa and Sītā. It was after this that the above mentioned dialogue between Rāma and Bharata occurred.

The council of minister expressed satisfaction on hearing what Rāma had to say about grief. Bharata urged Rāma to accept the kingdom. But Rāma said that his father had told him to accept the kingdom after twelve years and he wouldn't go against his father's wishes. Rāma said that he would return after three years.

Bharata asked him, "Who will rule for three years?"

Rāma replied, "*You* will rule."

Bharata refused.

Then Rāma said that until his return his sandals would rule. He handed over his sandals to Bharata and he ruled thus for three years. Rāma returned after three years and accepted the crown. He ruled righteously.

At the end of the Commentary, the Tathāgata gave the following explanation, "At that time Suddhodana was Dasaratha. Mahāmāyādevi was Rāma's mother. Rāhula's mother was Sitā. Ānanda was Bharata. Sāriputta was Lakkhaṇa. The Buddha's retinue was the council of ministers. And I was Rāma."

Discussion

We cannot say that this Jātaka is entirely historical but there are seeds of history in it. These seeds became manifest in various aspects of Indian culture in future; sometimes desirable and sometimes in undesirable forms.

Dasaratha Jātaka is a part of the Buddhist literature. Here Rāma's biography is given in brief. The Commentary has expanded it. Dasaratha Jātaka doesn't make a tight narration but overall it can be said that the personality of Rāma portrayed here is restrained, discerning and balanced.

The other biography of Rāma we have is from Vālmikī Rāmāyaṇa. Some scholars believe that the root of this story is in Dasaratha Jātaka. Bharatiya Sanskriti Kosh[445] says,

It is clear that some stories about Rāma were prevalent before Vālmikī. We find proof of this in the Buddhist Tipiṭaka. We can say that these stories about Rāma are the source for the story of Rāma. There is a verse in Harivaṃsha to that effect:

Gāthām apy atra gāyanti ye purāṇavido janāḥ
Rāme nibaddhatattvārthā māhātmyaṃ tasya dhīmataḥ
(Harivaṃsha *41.149)*

Meaning: Those verses are also sung where the principles of Rāma are included and the greatness of that wise man is depicted.

It is clear that all these verses are pre-Vālmikī.

According to the Commentary, the Buddha says that he was the Rāma depicted in the Dasaratha Jātaka. We cannot say that the Commentary is a true account of history. But it does show that there is some intellectual connection between Rāma and the Buddha. Both the Buddha and Rāma were from Okkāka clan (Ikshvāku, Sun Dynasty).

In this situation, we are faced with a complicated scenario. What should be our stand about Rāma? In my opinion it is not a question of whether or not we accept Rāma but rather in what form do we accept Rāma. If the Dasaratha Jātaka is the source of Rāma's story and if the Buddhist tradition believes in unity between Rāma and the Buddha and if the Rāma was vedicized later; then we could reject the Vedicized Rāma but we can and should certainly accept the original form of Rāma. It is not just because that form is connected to the Buddha but because he is a balanced personality.

Republics and Saṅgha

While creating and developing the Saṅgha, the Buddha followed many systems from the republics of those times. To respect the opinions of others, to try to build consensus, to decide things by majority opinion, to take into consideration opinion of someone who has not been able to attend the meeting due to illness, etc. were some of the guidelines of the functioning of the republics. He organized these principles further as we can see in the Book of Discipline.

Enriched the Tradition

The Buddha took elements from the Samaṇa tradition and added some new elements. The tradition had its origin in the Indus Civilization. It was not that the tradition had everything and the Buddha was a mere link in it. His contribution made the tradition glorious and gave future generations a bright and bountiful inheritance.

Every generation has to adopt some elements from the existing tradition and add other benevolent elements. Our generation is no exception.

Reject Only Undesirable Elements; Don't be a Parasite

While we inherit a long tradition, we have to live in the present. What should we do? On one hand, we should accept and preserve whatever is constructive, ethical and inspiring in our tradition. We should also take care not to continue whatever is undesirable, harmful and against progress. In other words, accept the modern, lively and fresh values.

On the other hand, while accepting modern fresh values, we should not reject outright and in totality whatever has come down in our tradition. If we reject our entire inheritance, we will be foreigners, we will be strangers, we will even become parasites and orphans. We must strike a balance so that we continue our journey on a path that leads to greater and better things. This is real flow of culture.

The society that rejects the long established lofty principles and goals, pushes them away for minor and temporary benefits, is sure to decline.

Neither Darkness of Tradition Nor Viruses of Novelty

Every generation is faced with choices. The skill of not dissociating from past tradition and yet accepting the change of modernity is not an easy one. We must ensure that while we preserve our tradition, we don't become blind by the darkness in it. And while we accept the new, we must ensure that we don't give entry to destructive new viruses. This is a delicate and difficult task but if it is done then our society will remain vibrant and fresh.

The Buddha gave the tradition due respect and was grateful to it. He added his creative energies in strengthening the flow and keeping it fresh. We should also be careful if we want our society to endure, remain fresh and prosper.

This is an important message from the life of the Tathāgata.

13

Whether Known or Unknown The Buddha Dwells in Our Heart

The impact of the Buddha's teaching and his personality on Indian culture is deep, lasting and indelible. Even the Vedics who considered him a sworn enemy couldn't avoid his influence. Whether due to conviction or as part of a strategy or combination of the two, they changed radically due to the Buddha. Even Adi Shankaracharya who was a staunch opponent of the Buddha was criticized by his own people as a Hidden Buddha (*pracchanna bauddha*). In such a condition, it is not possible that any non-Vedic tradition remained totally untouched by the Buddha. Let us look at the impact through these twenty-five centuries.

While doing so, I don't have any particular sect or group or community in mind. I have tried to look at and understand as many viewpoints as I could. While doing so, I have overlooked their limitations, errors, differences of opinions or criticisms leveled by them against each other. I have tried to look at their contributions. This is not a comprehensive overview. This may not be a balanced and measured evaluation of their work. I humbly wish to make a few indicative notes to understand the depth and breadth of the Buddha's influence.

Dhamma Councils

No one person was appointed as the Buddha's heir. He had said that the Dhamma would be your guide. Naturally, it was necessary to give a stable and organized form to the Dhamma in his absence. Therefore, a few days after his passing away a meeting of five hundred arahatas was called at Rājagaha. The Sutta Piṭaka (Discourses) and the Vinaya Piṭaka (Book of Discipline) were ratified here. This was the first synod or the First Dhamma Council in the history of Buddhism.[446]

About a hundred years after the passing away of the Buddha, the Second Dhamma Council was held at Vesāli (Vaishali).[447] It was organized when differences arose between Vajjī bhikkhus and Venerable Yasa, etc.

The Third Dhamma Council was held during the reign of Emperor Asoka as we have noted in the Introduction.

One opinion holds that the Fourth Council was held about 100 CE under the aegis of Emperor Kanishka.

The Theravada tradition considers the Council organized by King Vaṭṭagāmaṇī in Sri Lanka to be the Fourth Council. This was held under the guidance of Mahāthera Rakkhita.

However, some believe that the first Council in Sri Lanka was held at Anurādhapura during the reign of King Tissa (247 to 207 BCE) under the guidance of Elder Ariṭṭha, the first Sri Lankan disciple of Mahinda. They consider the Council held during Vaṭṭagāmaṇī's reign to be the second council. Some believe that a third Council in Sri Lanka was held at Ratnapura in 1865.

The Fifth Council was held at Mandalay in Myanmar in 1871, which continued for five months. In addition to reciting the Tipiṭaka, it was also carved onto marble slabs. Two thousand and four hundred bhikkhus took part in this council. The Sixth Council was held in Myanmar in 1954 under the guidance of Bhadanta Revata. An authentic edition of the Tipiṭaka along with commentaries and sub-commentaries was printed in Myanmar script during this council.

Emperor Asoka

Countless people, traditions, and institutes have preserved and spread the Dhamma in the last two and a half thousand years. In all these efforts, the most prominent contribution is that of Asoka. He organized the Third Council and helped in re-establishing the original form of the Dhamma and the Saṅgha. As a follower of the Dhamma and as a righteous king who ruled according to the Dhamma, his work is unparalleled at least in the history of India. He was a just and compassionate ruler.

He sent Dhamma messengers not only throughout India but also abroad to countries such as Sri Lanka, Myanmar, Turkey, Greece, etc. This work is unforgettable in the history of Buddhism. If he had not done so, perhaps when the Dhamma vanished from India, it would have vanished from the entire world. The very idea is frightening!

He sent his son Mahinda and daughter Saṅghamittā to Sri Lanka for the spread of Dhamma. These siblings never returned to India. They couldn't meet their parents or see their motherland again. They became one with the Sri Lankan society in their effort to spread the Dhamma and finally became one with the land there. It is because of their efforts that the Tipiṭaka and its commentaries that were lost to India was preserved in Sri Lanka and is now available to India and the world.

Prof. Shanti Rakshit Shastri writes about how vast the literature is that was preserved in Sri Lanka,[448] "The literature of that great sage and its commentaries is thrice that of the entire Mahābhārata." This literature had originated in India but was lost here. P. V. Bapat and Nalinaksh Dutta write,[449] "... It is indeed ironical that not a single Buddhist work, with the exception of Mañjushri Mūlakalpa, has been found within the borders of India.

"The Buddhist literature that we study today has come to us from monasteries outside India, in Ceylon (sic), Burma, Siam (sic), Nepal, and translations from Tibet, China and Mongolia. An idea of the vastness of the literature can be formed from the works mentioned in Chinese and Tibetan catalogues. A remarkable addition to our knowledge of Buddhist literature has been made by the discoveries of manuscripts in Central Asia and Gilgit as well as the manuscripts photographed in Tibet by Rahul Sankrityayan and collected by Prof. T. Tucci. The original Sanskrit manuscripts found in Central Asia, Gilgit and Tibet, belonging mostly to the fifth or sixth century AD or to an earlier period were preserved in Central Asia and Gilgit in stone chambers built under the stupas or monasteries and in temples in Tibet."

Mañjushri Mūlakalpa is a later day text that is not included in the Tipiṭaka, commentaries or subcommentaries. If Emperor Asoka had not sent his children and several other messengers, at times across the seas, to other countries, we would not have recovered even a single letter of this vast literature. It is possible that because Asoka sent the Dhamma across the seas, the Vedics tried to ostracize those who crossed the sea.

Even at the beginning of the twentieth century, the situation of Buddhist literature in India has been described by Swapankumar Biswas,[450] "In 1908 it was decided to teach Pali in Calcutta University. There was only one book in the curriculum 'Dhammapada Aṭṭhakathā.' Even this book was not available in India and had to be imported from Sri Lanka."

One thing should be noted here. We cannot say that the Dhamma was totally lost from the India subcontinent when we see that in areas adjacent to Tibet such as Ladakh, Sikkim, Lahaul-spiti valley, etc in India, the Tibetan Buddhist tradition has been preserved continuously for long. Even then overall, we can say that the Dhamma was lost from India at least externally. In the country that boasted of Nalandā with its ten thousand students and fifteen hundred teachers, it is painful that all the Dhamma literature was lost.

Tipiṭaka in Writing for the First Time

The history of Buddhism, the Tipiṭaka was set down in writing for the first time in Sri Lanka. In 43 BCE, Vaṭṭagāmaṇī lost his kingdom after he was defeated in war. War and terrible famine claimed many, many deaths. The bhikkhus who had memorized the Tipiṭaka also started dying. Therefore, it was felt that the Tipiṭaka should be written down for posterity. In 29 BCE, Vaṭṭagāmaṇī reclaimed the kingdom and ruled till 17 BCE. Mahāvaṃsa[451] says, "The gifted bhikkhus of the past had memorized and preserved the Tipiṭaka and the commentaries in the past. But seeing that those bhikkhus were dying, it was decided to write down Tipiṭaka to preserve the Dhamma for long."

This first writing of Tipiṭaka was done at Aluvihara (Āloka Vihāra) in Sri Lanka.

Vālmikī Rāmāyaṇa on the Tathāgata

When we talk of Sri Lanka, the attention of Indians naturally turns to the descriptions of Sri Lanka in Vālmikī Rāmāyaṇa. We have already seen that in the Buddhist tradition, Rāma of Dasaratha Jātaka was a Bodhisatta. We find some glimpses of that tradition even in today's Rāmāyaṇa.

Saluting the Cetiya

When Bharata went to Rāma to bring him back, Rāma gave him detailed advice about political administration. At that time, he also asked Bharata several questions about his conduct. One question[452] is about cetiyas. He asks, "Do you salute all the cetiyas such as Siddhārtha cetiya etc?"

Discussion

We get to peep through a pin-hole here into our history. The adjective Siddhārtha for cetiyas is significant. It is clear that these were Buddhist cetiyas. It indicates that revering cetiyas was a duty of the king. When this part of Rāmāyaṇa was written, cetiyas must have existed and some segments of society were respectful towards them. Of course, such remnants are an exception in today's Rāmāyaṇa. The overall direction of the extant Rāmāyaṇa is to do away with such descriptions. We will see below how Rāmāyaṇa is opposed to cetiyas.

Destruction of Cetiyas

In the Sundarakāṇḍa[453] of Rāmāyaṇa, we see the description of Hanumana wrecking havoc in Lanka. We see how a cetiya was destroyed.

"After killing the servants, Hanumana thought, 'I have destroyed the garden but I have not destroyed the cetiya. Let me today destroy the cetiya.' Thinking thus with great enthusiasm he jumped atop the cetiya that was tall like the peak of Meru mountain. After he damaged the cetiya, he started shining in all his glory. Then he flexed his muscles and slapped himself on his arms and thighs (as a show of strength). This created such a huge deafening sound that birds fell down to the ground and the watchman of the cetiya fell unconscious. Then Hanuman roared loudly to terrify the monsters. Hundreds of other protectors of the cetiya came and surrounded Hanuman. Then he snatched the golden pillar of the cetiya and twirled it with such force that it burst in fire and the cetiya was burned down."

Discussion

This is a description of how Hanuman destroyed cetiya. This accomplished many things. Rāmāyaṇa was created at the time of Pushyamitra Shunga or afterwards. During that period, cetiyas were being destroyed and Hanuman's description is a literary sample of that destruction. At the same time, the writers took care to put the responsibility of the destruction on Hanuman who was a leader of the masses.

Criticism of Buddha

Those who wanted to destroy cetiyas wrote many things against the Buddha. When Rāma went to forest, Bharata went to him to bring him back. Rāma refused to return and urged Bharata to return. At that time, a brahmin minister named Jābāli criticized Rāma's decision.[454] He suggested to Rāma that no one belonged to anyone and therefore there was no need for Rāma to obey his father Dasaratha's order. He also said that ancestral offerings were useless. When someone ate dinner here and someone else felt satiated there, it was useless to carry food on journey—just make an offering here. He also said that yajñas were useless. He praised direct evidence and requested Rāma to accept the kingdom.

In response to Jābāli, Rāma made several arguments and refuted Jābāli's logic. Rāma said that he would not stray from the path of truth. He censured Jābāli for his *nāstika* (*natthika*, literally non-believer) statements,[455] "Honorable men say that truth, Dharma, effort, compassion towards all beings, pleasant speech, and worship of brahmins, gods and guests is the way to heaven… I decry the deed of my father whereby he appointed a fool like you to the royal court."

Rāma further added,[456] "The Buddha is like a thief. Understand the Tathāgata as a *nāstika* (non-believer). Therefore, a king who wants to serve his subjects should not become partial to a non-believer."

Then Jābāli told Rāma that he was not a *nāstika* but had made those statements to bring Rāma back.[457] Vashisṭha (Vāseṭṭha) seconded Jābāli's statement and said that indeed Jābāli had spoken thus to dissuade Rāma from going to the forest.[458]

Discussion

Here the petty attack on the Buddha is made without any relevance to the context. It seems that in this narration superfluous additions have been repeated. The effort is to make Jābāli put forth arguments on behalf of Cārvāka and the Buddha; and then to put words in Rāma's mouth that refute them. The *nāstikas* that Jābāli refers to when giving examples of ancestral offering etc. are Cārvākas.

Jābāli also says, "Whoever remains entangled in himself—thinking this is my mother, this is my father—is insane. Because one had no relation to anyone else."

Actually this thought is not from Cārvāka philosophy and is totally against the Buddha's teaching. The Buddha had often emphasized service of mother and father. He had talked about not having attachment but he never talked about not having gratitude and compassion for *all* beings. Certain statements from Dasaratha Jātaka and Jābāli's dialogues are similar but Jābāli's statements are not representative of the Buddha's teaching.

Rāma decries *nāstikas* (non-believers). At the same time he says that worshipping brahmins takes one to heaven. Though these seem to come from Rāma, it is clear who the real author of such statements is.

There was no reason to criticize the Buddha here. It is clear that someone has added this episode to Rāmāyaṇa to give vent to his malice. We can even understand when the Buddha is called a non-believer because he had rejected the Vedic tradition and therefore for Vedics he could be a non-believer. But to call him a thief is a low blow indicative of a deranged mind. Such words don't stigmatize the Buddha's character. How could the same Rāma, who asked Bharata whether he saluted the Siddhārtha cetiya, also call the Buddha a thief! In reality, Rāma and the Buddha are not opposite to each other. They are complementary. It was because the Rāmāyaṇa underwent Vedic influence that the impression was created that these two great men were opponents.

Aṅgulimāla and Maharshi Vālmikī

Aṅgulimāla was a notorious robber in Pasenadi's kingdom.[459] He was called Aṅgulimāla (literally, garland finger) because he would cut a finger from whoever murdered and added it to the garland around his neck. The story of Valyā (later Vālmikī) is similar. In Valyā's story, he puts a stone in a pot after each murder.

People, even in groups of 20, 30, 40 and 50 dared not use the road through the area where Aṅgulimāla lived. People abandoned village after village, town after town due to his terror. But one day the Buddha set out alone in that direction. Herdsmen, farmers, travellers saw him going in that direction and advised him, "Samaṇa, don't go in that direction." They told him the story of Aṅgulimāla.

Even after that the Buddha calmly went in that direction. Aṅgulimāla was surprised when he saw the Buddha. He felt insulted because even large groups dared not venture on that path and this samaṇa had come there alone. He decided to kill him. He took his sword and shield as well as his bow and arrow and ran after the Buddha. Then he paused and called out, "Samaṇa, stop. Samaṇa, halt." The Buddha replied, "I have stopped, Aṅgulimāla. You too stop." Aṅgulimāla asked, "How can you say that you have stopped when you are walking and ask me to stop when I have already stopped. Samaṇa, tell me how?"

The Buddha replied, "Aṅgulimāla I abstain from killing all beings. Therefore, I have stopped. And you are unrestrained in killing other beings. Therefore, you have not stopped."

This answer had a deep impact on Aṅgulimāla. He threw away his weapons. He touched the Buddha's feet and asked for the going forth. The compassionate Buddha said, "Come bhikkhu." Those two words were Aṅgulimāla's going forth.

Then the Buddha started walking towards Sāvatthi. Aṅgulimāla followed him. Together they reached Jeta's Grove.

At that time a big crowd had gathered outside King Pasenadi's palace. People were complaining about Aṅgulimāla. Then Pasenadi set out with cavalry of five hundred to capture Aṅgulimāla. Before going the forest, Pasenadi went to greet the Buddha. Seeing the cavalry, the Buddha asked him whether King Bimbisāra of Magadha, the Licchavīs from Vesāli or someone else had attacked him. Pasenadi said that that was not the case and narrated the story of Aṅgulimāla.

After listening to Pasenadi's report, the Buddha said, "O king, what will you do if you see Aṅgulimāla has shaved his head, taken saffron robes, has gone forth, abstains from killing and lying, eats one meal a day, follows the holy life, is moral and follows the Dhamma?"

Pasenadi replied, "I will salute him, stand and welcome him, offer him a seat, and present him with robes, alms and medicine. I will protect him." Then he added, "But bhante, how can that immoral evil man have such morality and restraint?"

At that time Aṅgulimāla was sitting next to the Buddha. The Buddha pointed at Aṅgulimāla and said, "King, this is Aṅgulimāla!"

On hearing this Pasenadi was frightened but the Buddha reassured him, "Don't be afraid. You have nothing to fear from him."

Then Pasenadi regained his composure and offered robes etc. to Aṅgulimāla who said that he already had what he needed. Then Pasenadi said to the Buddha, "Surprise it is, wonderful it is. The Buddha subdues those that are not subdued. He calms down the agitated. He gives nibbāna to those who have not attained it. Bhante, one who we couldn't subdue with punishment and weapons, you have subdued without punishment and weapons."

Later in the company of the Buddha, Aṅgulimāla became an arahata. Once Aṅgulimāla went to Sāvatthi on alms round. Then some people threw lumps of soil at him. Some hit him with stick. Some threw stones at him. He was wounded and blood flowed from his wounds. His bowl broke. His upper cloth was torn. He went to the Buddha in that state.

The Buddha said that he had experienced the effect of the karmas in this very life, karmas that otherwise would have caused him to suffer in hell for hundreds of thousands of years.

Then Aṅgulimāla spontaneously uttered several verses. The first one was:

Having been heedless earlier
One who becomes heedful;
Like the moon that comes out of clouds,
He lights up the world.

Discussion

The whole story of Aṅgulimāla is extremely dramatic. It has a special place in Indian cultural history. It is a practical demonstration by the Buddha that through change of heart and change in thinking, one can change a man. The Buddha didn't want to destroy the cruel but wanted to reform them and bring them on the right path. K. Shri Dhamananda says,[460] "The Buddha did not appear in this world to destroy wicked people but to show them the correct path."

We see how Aṅgulimāla changed from a highwayman to an arahata. His life gives an inspiration of how one who has fallen into evil ways can come out of that state and change himself to live a clean and upright life.

When Aṅgulimāla became a follower of the Buddha, he bore all the injuries and insults with great fortitude without reacting. He could have been killed but he didn't oppose the people. The same people who were afraid to go anywhere near him were now attacking him. But he bore it all without blaming people and with the understanding that it was the result of his own past deeds. He calmly put up with all the attacks. This is how a person changes. This episode gives a glimpse into the meditation that Aṅgulimāla must have done under the guidance of the Buddha. His utterances tell us how he restrained himself.

Matriceta (Mātṛceṭa) says,[461]

The rough became soft,
The thrifty became generous;
The cruel became compassionate,
Such is your skillful teaching.

Nanda became restr(ained,
Mānastabdha became humble;
Aṅgulimāla became tolerant,
Who will not be amazed!

(Nanda was constantly distracted by sensual thoughts. Mānastabdha—literally, stiff with pride—was so proud that he wouldn't respect his own parents. Both changed after the Buddha's guidance.)

The path followed by Aṅgulimāla in bearing the injuries inflicted on him by people is the path that leads to total transformation. Aṅgulimāla's story is historical. It is an inspiration to all of us. We all know about how Siddhārtha became a Buddha but Aṅgulimāla's story, whereby a fallen person was transformed by the Dhamma, is no less inspiring. From it we learn to rouse the conscience within and to courageously take responsibility for our views, decisions and actions rather than blaming others.

The transformation of Valyā to Vālmikī is similar.

Ten Strengths of the Tathāgata

The Tathāgata was said to endowed with ten strengths. One of the chapters in Nidāna Saṃyutta of the Connected Discourses[462] is called 'Ten Strengths.' The first two suttas of this chapter are also called 'Ten Strengths' Sutta. This is significant in reference to several happenings in the history of India.

Both these suttas don't give details about the ten strengths. It is found in the Commentary[463] and the Subcommentary[464] of the suttas. The Commentary says that *kāyabala* (strength of body) and *ñāṇabala* (strength of intellect) are two types of strengths. After describing the Tathāgata's *kāyabala*, the Commentary says that it is not due to his *kāyabala* that he is called *dasabala*. *Kāyabala* is superficial and of lower variety. Even animals such as lions possess it. This strength doesn't help one to understand suffering, to remove the cause of suffering and to attain the goal. strength of intellect *(ñāṇabala)* manifests in ten different ways that give stability and support:

1. Knowledge of cause and non-cause.
2. Knowledge of karmas of past, future and present with cause.
3. Knowledge of the universal benevolent path.
4. Knowledge of various aspects or components of the world.
5. Knowledge of what goes on in the mind of others.
6. Knowledge of all that which comes in the field of senses of animals.
7. Knowledge of defilements, purity and upliftment in reference to meditation, liberation, concentration *(samādhi)* and attainments.
8. Knowledge of past existences.
9. Knowledge of arising and passing away of animals.
10. Knowledge of eradication of defiling impulses.[465]

What About Rāvaṇa?

Rāmāyaṇa says that Rāvaṇa had ten heads. In real life, it is not possible for a person to have ten heads. This means that the

Ten-Headed Rāvaṇa is a myth, not a historical person. There is no question of condoning Rāvaṇa's abduction of Sītā. It cannot be said that he did so because Lakkhaṇa (Laxmana) cut off his sister's nose. There can't be an ethical justification for abducting a woman for her brother-in-law's offense. This Rāvaṇa is definitely a villain.

There is another Rāvaṇa that can be acceptable to us. We find this Rāvaṇa in the Mahāyāna Sanskrit text 'Laṅkāvatarasūtra,'[466] a Rāvaṇa who is Sri Lanka's king and who accepts the teaching of the Buddha. This Rāvaṇa too is not a historical person but a myth. According to this text, once the Buddha was dwelling on a peak in Sri Lanka. At that time, he emerged from the house of Nāgarāja. He thought about teaching the Dhamma to Rāvaṇa who too heard that the Buddha had emerged from the house of Nāgarāja. He requests the Buddha to teach the Dhamma to him and the people of Sri Lanka. The Buddha did so. For the writer, Rāvaṇa may be symbolic of the Buddhists of Sri Lanka.

Anger at Emperor Asoka

Those who were angry with the Buddha were also angry with Emperor Asoka. Pushyamitra Shunga killed Asoka's descendent, performed the Horse Sacrifice *(ashvamedha yajña)*, created Manusmriti and also started changing the nature of various epics such as Rāmāyaṇa and Mahābhārata. During this period, Emperor Asoka too was maligned.

Asoka-Ārāma and Asoka-Vanikā

Rāmāyaṇa describes how Rāvaṇa kidnapped Sītā and kept her at Asoka-Vanikā. In Araṇyakāṇḍa[467] we see him ordering, "Take Maithili (Sītā) to Asoka-vanikā." Then the same text tells us that Sītā was taken to Asoka-vanikā.[468] Vana means forest or grove. Vanikā is a small forest or woods. Teak, Deodar forests are common but we don't hear of Asoka forests. But Asoka-vanikā indicates a forest of Asoka trees. How could this be?

One way to understand this is that in Sanskrit, *ārāma* is also used for garden. It is well known that during the life of the Buddha, Bimbisāra, Anāthapiṇḍika, Āmrapali, etc. had donated gardens to the Buddha as we can see from the names Bamboo Grove *(veḷuvana)*, Jeta's Grove (Jetavana), and Mango Grove *(ambavana)*. In these gardens *(vanas, ārāmas)* cetiyas and *vihāras* (monasteries) were built.

It is well known that today's Bihar had many *vihāras* built for samaṇas. Bihar comes from *vihāra*. In Hindi *v* often become *b*. Since many of the *vihāras* (monasteries) were built in ārāmas, the word *ārāma* also came to signify Buddhist monasteries.

Among the countless *vihāras* that were built at various times, Asoka- *ārāma* (Ashokārāma) is famous. Mahāvaṃsa[469] describes that since there were 84 thousand parts in the Dhamma taught by the Buddha, Asoka built through local kings 84 thousand monasteries. He took up the construction of Asoka *ārāma*. *Ārāma* and *vana* are used interchangeably as we have seen earlier. Thus Asoka *ārāma* and Asoka *vana* are related. Even granting that the number 84 thousand is an exaggeration, we can safely assume that Asoka built many monasteries.

The relation of Asoka and Sri Lanka is famous and historical. He helped establish the Dhamma in Sri Lanka. The island of Sri Lanka became a Dhamma island. It is also the island that preserved the Tipitaka and the commentarial Pali literature when it was lost in India. Thus for Vedics, the island of Sri Lanka was an Asoka-*vana* connected to the Buddha Dhamma. Therefore, each such *vihāra* was inauspicious for Vedics. Showing Sītā's detention or imprisonment in Asoka-*vana* could be symbolic of imprisonment of our culture by Asoka.

Why is Rāvaṇa's Son Named Meghanāda?

Rāvaṇa's son is named Meghanāda.[470] The Bodhi sampling that Asoka sent with Saṅghamittā to Sri Lanka was planted in Meghavana according to Mahāvaṃsa,[471] "Thus the king of trees, Maha Bodhi tree kept showering upon the people of Sri Lanka welfare and glory. It stood in the beautiful Meghavana of Sri Lanka for long." Tissa had given this Meghavana to Mahinda in donation.[472]

Just as *dasabala* and *dasamukha* are similar, Meghavana and Meghanāda are similar. Meghanāda is the son of Rāvaṇa. Mahinda is a son of Asoka. Thus Asoka or Asoka and his descendents are looked upon as Rāvaṇa. There is absolutely no evidence to show that Rāvaṇa was a historical king in Sri Lanka. It is also possible that Tissa was looked upon as Rāvaṇa. We have already seen the descriptions in Purāṇas that due to the deceptive teaching of the Buddha, demons became Buddhists.

The Tathāgata, the King of the Dhamma

Rotating the wheel of the Dhamma is similar to the Wheel Turning Monarch. Therefore, the Tathāgata was called Dhammarājā, the King of the Dhamma. We find that in Connected Discourses[473] it is said, "Dhammarājā lives in Jetavana."

In Anāthapiṇḍikovāda Sutta of the Middle Length Discourses[474] too, the Buddha is called Dhammarājā. When Sela brahmin asked him,[475] "You could have been a Wheel Turning Monarch, the king of kings. Then why did you become a samaṇa?" the Buddha replied, "I am Dhammarājā. I rotate the wheel of the Dhamma that cannot be turned back." He also added that Sāriputta was the General of the Dhamma.

In Mahābhārata, Yudhisṭhira was referred to as Dhammarājā. Many noble qualities of Yudhisṭhira and his epithet Dhammarājā are significant. We have seen the description in the Numerical Discourses how the Buddha would walk on a mountain of dirt without touching the dirt. We also know the description in Mahābhārata how the wheels of the chariot of Yudhisṭhira would not touch the ground. We should also remember that a large part of Mahābhārata was expanded during the time of Manusmriti (second century BCE).

Bhagavad Gitā

In the book edited by P. V. Bapat the following opinion is given regarding Bhagavad Gitā.[476] "This author believes that the Gitā came into existence after the Buddha because we find Buddha's teachings in the Gitā."

Kashinath Upadhyay says about the Gitā,[477] "It would not, therefore, be impossible from the chronological point of view to consider the Bhagavadagitā as having been composed under the impact of the newly developed thought of Buddhism…

… These similarities of expressions and ideas are sufficient indication to the fact that the B.G. has assimilated all those Buddhistic elements which could be conveniently fitted into its scheme. But in other matters, like atheism and renunciation etc. it sharply reacts against the Buddhist approach."

Prof. D. D. Kosambi says about the Gitā,[478] "… Gitā very skillfully puts in the mouth of the incarnation of Vishnu most of the gist of Buddhism…"

King Milinda

Emperor Asoka has sent his messengers to Greece. From that time, the Dhamma was known in Greece. In the cultural history of India, the Indo-Greek King Milinda has a special place. His original name was Menander. He ruled in the north-west part of India of that time. Due to the influence of the Buddha, his kingdom was a welfare state. He had become a devoted Buddhist. The Pali text Milinda Pañha (Questions of Milinda) which contains his questions about the Dhamma to Nāgasena and his answers is famous. In the Myanmar tradition, it is included in the Tipiṭaka. Many scholars put Milinda in the first century BCE. They believe that the present day Sialkot in Pakistan was King Milinda's capital. He had built a monastery named Milinda Vihāra and donated it to Nāgasena. He handed over his kingdom to his son and became a bhikkhu towards the end of his life. His coins have the wheel of Dhamma on them.

Kanishka

Kanishka from Indo-Scythian dynasty was an important king in the Buddhist history. He ruled from 101 to 78 BCE. He had organized the Fourth Dhamma Council. It was probably held at Jalandhar in Punjab or Kashmir. Vasumitra presided over the council. Ashvaghosha was his deputy. The statues of the Buddha started being made during this time and Sanskrit started being used in Buddhism. Kanishka built many *vihāras* and cetiyas. The Kanishka-stūpa that he built was four hundred feet tall. Kanishka was tolerant of other faiths. His capital was the present day Peshawar in Pakistan. Ashvaghosha, the great Buddhist poet, belonged to the royal court of Kanishka. 'Buddhacarita' and 'Saundarananda' are two of his famous epic poems.

Nāgārjuna

Such is the importance of Nāgārjuna in Buddhism that the Buddhists in China, Japan and Tibet often consider him as the second Buddha. He is considered a philosopher of the highest order because of his brilliant intellect and skillful reasoning. His major contribution is the concept of *śunyatā* (emptiness). He is also celebrated as the founder of Mahāyāna or the father of Mahāyāna. Some scholars believe that though he was perhaps the earliest and the greatest organizer of the Mahāyāna tradition, he was not the founder of that school. His most important text is *Mādhyamikashāstra*. It is also called *Mūlamādhyamikakārikā*. He has several other texts to his credit though scholars disagree about whether all of them were authored by him or not.

Medicine in Buddhist Tradition

Vedic tradition considered the practice of medicine to be a lowly profession. Ashvinīkumāra of Rigveda was a famous physician but he still didn't have the right of *somapāna* (right to drink *soma*). In the Varṇa system, he was considered a *shudra (sudda)*. Though in Theravāda, bhikkhus were forbidden all livelihoods including that of a physician, medicine was a highly respected tradition in Buddhism due to value it put on service. We have already seen that the Buddha had declared that whosoever served a sick person, serves the Buddha.

The Buddha was called Peerless Physician, Peerless Surgeon (*sallakatto anuttaro*) in Mahāvagga of Sutta Nipāta. The Buddha is often referred to as Great Physician (*Mahābhisaka, Mahābhishaka)*. He is called a Great Physician in Questions of King Milinda. This indicates the respect shown by the Buddhist tradition to medical profession.

In non-Vedic tradition of Indus Civilization, Ayurveda was studied. Jīvaka is a famous physician in the Buddhist tradition. When we look at the state of health sciences in those times, it is clear that there was no alternative to Ayurveda.

The followers of the Buddha wandered far and wide for the welfare for many, for the happiness of many. Caraka Samhitā is famous in Ayurveda. *Caraka* means one who does *Cārikā*. We cannot look at all the opinions expressed about Acharya Caraka. Let us just look at a couple of them.

Rudra, an author who wrote commentary on *Bruhajjātaka* of *Varāhamihira* writes about Caraka,[479] "He was a very learned physician. To serve the people, he had become a bhikkhu and would wander from town to town to teach medicine and to treat the people. It is possible that because he was a bhikkhu who travelled *(cārikā)* a lot he was called *caraka*." The same author says[480] that Caraka was an expert in yoga and medicine; and was a heretic *(pākhaṇḍi)*. It is well known that the Buddhists were called *pākhaṇḍi*.

Many scholars believe that like Ashvaghosha, Caraka too was connected to King Kanishka. He might even have been the royal physician. In the introduction of the third edition of Caraka Samhitā, Acharya Yadav Sharma writes,[481] "As long as we don't find any other famous Caraka in the Vedic or Buddhist literature, this must have been the famous royal physician of Kanishka we find in Buddhist literature… I feel that there should not be any objection to this view."

We need to write separately about this. The least we can assume with certainty is that the Buddhist bhikkhus used to treat people during their wanderings. This was part of their service to the people.

Vāgbhaṭa

Several Buddhist teachers (*āchāryas, acariyas)* continued the tradition of study of Ayurveda after Acharya Caraka. Vāgbhaṭa is one such teacher. The elder Vāgbhaṭa was the author of *Ashṭāṅgasaṅgraha* while his grandson also named Vāgbhaṭa wrote *Ashṭāṅgahridayam*. There is an opinion that both these texts were written by the same person. *Ashṭāṅga (aṭṭhaṅgika,* eight-fold) in the title of both these texts suggests the relation to Noble Eightfold Path of the Buddha.

At the outset of the Ashṭāṅgahridayam,[482] "I salute that Great Physician (the Buddha) in the world who totally destroyed all the defilements that arise out of craving which afflicts all human beings and which creates agitation, heedlessness and distress in their mind."

Dr. Ganesh Krishna Garde has written a footnote about the Buddha, "In keeping with the rule in the *maṅgalācaraṇa* (auspicious opening verses), there should be blessing, salutations or reference, in this verse the author has expressed salutations and has also indicated the subject. The verses indicate that the salutations are to the Buddha. Not only that, if we look at the *maṅgalācaraṇa* of the elder Vāgbhaṭa, we will see that the adjectives in both the verses are similar and the elder Vāgbhaṭa clearly says *'Buddhāya Tasmai Namah,'* then it becomes clear that the Great Physician who destroyed defilements of craving etc. is the Buddha."

Garde on Vāgbhaṭa

It is relevant to quote here that Garde[483] stated in his introduction of the translation that Vāgbhaṭa was a Buddhist.

"It must have become clear to readers that Vāgbhaṭa was a Buddhist. Many old people still doubt this. Some even go to the extent of make a futile attempt to prove that he was a brahmin. The evidence is ample to show that he was a Buddhist.

"1. Vāgbhaṭa says in the *maṅgalācaraṇa* of Ashṭāṅgasaṅgraha, 'I salute the Buddha who subdued the terrible serpent of mind through the strength of wisdom.' This sentence leaves no doubt whatsoever that Vāgbhaṭa was a Buddhist. Many claim that the word Buddha should be taken to mean one with knowledge and hence God. But if we take that meaning then the sentence structure doesn't fit. Because if the God has no mind, then how can God have a mind with defilements such as craving and hatred. If someone says that the subduing of the defiled mind indicates others, then the immediate next sentence becomes problematic. Therefore, 'Buddha' in the first sentence doubtlessly refers to the Buddha. The Buddhists say that one who through his own pure conduct and wisdom has freed himself from all karmas is called a Buddha or a Jina. Therefore, here the word 'Buddha' refers not to God but to Jina.

"2. In both the texts, while preparing an important formulation of medicine the verses that are given for recitation are Buddhist verses, not Vedic. They have words such as *tathāgata, arhata, samyak sambuddha, jina*, etc. These verses are found twice in the eighth chapter, in the 27th chapter, in second chapter of *cikitsāsthāna* and at couple of other places.

The first gods mentioned are Avalokiteshvara and Tārā, who are Buddhist gods, followed by Vedic gods. In the chapter on leprosy, we find a suggestion to worship Jina, Jinasuta and Tārā. Jinasuta is Avalokiteshvara or a Bodhisatta. Tārā is a goddess that occurs in no other tradition except the Buddhists. There is a verse in *Padmāvatipūjāstotra* of the Jains which means: O Goddess Bharati Jagadambe, you are given a name Tārā in Buddhism… Similarly, in *Kathāsaritsāgara* there is a description of Takshasilā with a comment that all the people in the city are Buddhists and are affluent due to the blessing of goddess Tārā.

This also shows that Buddhism had spead widely in ancient Sindh (Indus Valley) which was the birthplace of Vāgbhaṭa. Takshashilā is from Sindh. Even some Jains due to attachment to their own tradition have criticized Tārā at times, then how could brahmins ask for worship of Tārā? In the *Jvaracikitsā* (literally fever therapy) of *Ashṭāṅgasangraham* the two goddesses mentioned, Shabarī and Aparājitā, are both Buddhist deities. The text has certain other Buddhist recitations such as *Tathāgatoshṇīsha* (armor of Buddha) and *Māyurī Vidyā*.

There is a significant additional information that Garde gives here,[484] "Buddhist scholars had written several important texts on all branches of science. For example, Kāshikāvrittī on grammar by Jayāditya and Vāman (both Buddhists from 7th century), Amarasinha's famous dictionary of linguistics (6th century), Siddhasena Suri on astrology and texts by Satyāchārya (6th century) and two famous texts by Vāgbhaṭa on medicine (4th century).

Atrideva Gupta on Vāgbhaṭa

Garde says that the *maṅgalācaraṇa* of *Ashṭāṅgasangraham* has *"Buddhāya tasmai namah."* But opponents of the Buddha have made changes in the *maṅgalācaraṇa* of this text. Some editions have simply removed it!

In the text edited by Kaviraj Atridev Gupta, which also has Hindi commentary, we find this verse "*Buddhāya tasmai namah.*"[485] The meaning of the complete verse is: "In the burrow of the body, we find a terrible serpent in the form of mind. Craving is its length. Wrong thoughts are its head. Immense hatred is its hood. Greed and anger are its poison. Doubt is its teeth. Craving is its big eyes and ignorance is its mouth. We salute the Buddha who has subdued this serpent with the strength of his wisdom."

Gupta says about Vāgbhaṭa,[486] "It is as clear as the sun that Vāgbhaṭa was a Buddhist. The efforts to prove him a brahmin or a Vedic are more due to prejudice than a reasonable argument. Some people believe that other than brahmins or Vedics, others cannot do good work. But this is not true. Other castes and people from non-Vedic traditions have made significant contributions to medicine, philosophy and other fields. Their contributions to the field of knowledge are a priceless heritage of our country. Therefore, if Vāgbhaṭa has given us a great text in spite of not being a brahmin or a Vedic, there is no harm!

"If we look at the heart of this text, we find more Buddhist thought in these texts than Vedic thoughts. ... In *"namo bhagavate bhaisajyagurave,"* etc. *arhata* is saluted... There is much evidence to prove that the author of this text is Buddhist: Dhāriṇī, Tārā, Avalokiteshvara, four types of deaths of Saugatas, ten deeds of the Buddhists. Not only that, we find Ashvaghosha's Dīpa quoted exactly by Vāgbhaṭa. Ashvaghosha was a Buddhist... It is mere stubbornness to try to prove Vagbhat as a brahmin or Vedic. The brahmins don't want that the creator of such a splendid text should be outside of their tradition. If any other tradition gets credit for these texts, then their prestige and fame would suffer. But there are magnanimous and honest scholars such as Yadavji Trikamji Acharya, Paradkarji, and Rudradevdasji who clearly declare him to be a Buddhist based on truthful evidence.

"There is one more thing, in spite of being a Buddhist, Vāgbhaṭa keeps a tolerant attitude towards all other religions."

He says in a footnote,[487] "My commentary on *Ashṭāṅgahridayam* has been published by Chaukhamba Sanskrit series. In its preface, the editor has expressed some views. I don't support those. This book's editing and publication was done without my knowledge by the publisher. By editing, I mean reading of final proofs. He has said in his letter 885/50 of 6/10/1950 in response to Dr. Satyapala's letter of 3/10/1950, 'By editing I mean checking the final proof.'"

If even a proof-reader is interfering with the author's favorable views on the Buddha, we can imagine how difficult it is to find objective writing in this field.

Buddhist Universities in Ancient India

The Buddha removed the restrictions on access to knowledge, and later, several Buddhist universities had started to take learning to *all* the seekers. Takshashilā existed even before the time of the Buddha. Jīvaka, the physician who treated the Buddha, had studied at Takshashilā. Some scholars believe that Takshashilā was the oldest university in the world. It is somewhere close to Islamabad in modern Pakistan.

From the 5th century CE to the 12th century CE, Nalandā did stupendous work in the field of learning. This university had the patronage of the Pāla kings. There were hostels for both teachers and students. The library was nine stories high. Students from Korea, Japan, China, Tibet, Indonesia, Persia, Turkey, etc. came to study here. S. Dutta says,[488] "We can guess how big this university was from Huan Tseng's description that there were ten thousand students and a thousand and five hundred teachers there." It was an architectural masterpiece.

King Dharmapāla (reign from 783 to 820 CE) had established Vikramashilā in Bihar. This university was functioning till about the 12th century. Dharmapala had also established a Buddhist monastery in Odāntapuri. This was granted the status of a university. Huen Tseng had visited Valabhī in Saurashtra in 7th century CE. The ruler there was a follower of the Buddha. Rāmapāla (1084 to 1130 CE) of the Pāla dynasty had established a Buddhist university named Jagaddala near his capital.

Chinese Travellers

The Chinese travellers who came to India have a special place in the history of Buddhism. The hardships they endured fills us with gratitude. Their travelogues are a precious treasure of Indian history. S. Dutta says in the book edited by P. V. Bapat,[489] "It was therefore felt by the Buddhist monks of China of that era that they must turn to the homeland of Buddhism in order to reform and purify Chinese Buddhism—to collect original scriptures and learn the proper rites and ceremonies. This, apart from the spiritual benefit of pilgrimage, was the motive that started a stream of intrepid Chinese scholar-monks on the long trek to India, thousands of miles over deserts and mountains. According to the findings of a modern Chinese historian, as many as 162, out of the number of Chinese pilgrims who went out to India during the 5th, 6th, 7th and 8th centuries, can be traced from Chinese sources of information. 1. The 'records' (Ki in Chinese) of only three of them have been explored and translated by Sinologists— those of Fa-Hien, Yuan Chwang (Huen-Tseng, parenthesis added by translator) and I-tsing, covering the periods 405-411 A.D, 629-646 A.D. and 671-695 A.D. respectively."

K. A. Nilakanta Shastri writes in the same book,[490] "Fa-hien spent six years in travelling from Ch'ang-an to central India; he stayed there for six years, and it took him three more years to reach Ch'ing-chou. The countries he passed through amounted to rather fewer than thirty. From the sandy desert westwards all the way to India, the dignified deportment of the priesthood and the good influence of the faith were beyond all expression in detail. As, however, the ecclesiastics at home had had no means of hearing about these things, Fa-hien had given no thought to his own unimportant life, but came home across the seas, encountering still more difficulties and dangers. ... he wrote down on bamboo tablets and silk an account of what he had been through, desiring that the gentle reader should share this information."

Huen Tseng (Yuan Chwang) is the most famous of the Chinese travellers. He travelled for a long period all over India. He took about 600 texts from India to China; and translated them into Chinese with the help of his associates.

I-Tsing was another famous Chinese traveller. Nilakanta Shashtri says about him,[491] "He was away for 25 years (671 to 695 A.D.) and travelled through more than thirty countries. After his return to China in 695 A.D., he translated 56 works out of about 400 he had brought back with him, between the years 700 and 712 A.D. He died in 713 A.D. in his seventy-ninth year."

These Chinese travellers translated so many texts into Chinese and thus preserved them and we could get them back. This shows us what a great debt of gratitude we owe to them.

Emperor Harsha Vardhana

Harsha Vardhana was a memorable personality. To him fell the responsibility of the crown after his elder brother Rājyavardhana was assassinated by King Shashānka. He took on this responsibility and discharged it so selflessly that he didn't even put the prefix of king (mahārāja) to his name. He used to call himself Shīlāditya. Both his elder brother Rājyavardhana and his sister Rājyashrī were devoted Buddhists. Harsha himself was an ardent follower of the Buddha's teaching. He also respected his past tradition and worshipped Shiva and the sun.

Huen Tseng visited India during his reign. Harsha welcomed and honored him. Harsha used to give up all his material possessions at the confluence of Ganges and Yamuna rivers every five years. Huen Tseng was present for the sixth such charity. On the first day of the event, the Buddha was worshipped. After giving away all his wealth in charity, he accepted an old cloth from his sister as gift and worshipped the Buddha in all ten directions. He built many stupas and supported Nalandā university. Buddhism flourished during his reign.

Harsha wrote a play named Nāgānanda. He wrote this play to emphasize the importance of non-violence that the Buddha had promoted. The hero in the play was Jīmūtavāhana. The core theme of the play was that he sacrifices his life to protect a nāga named Shaṅkhachūḍa, and as a result, the people of the nāga lineage from eagle. This act was worthy of a Bodhisatta. Even the eagle was impressed and at the end tells Shaṅkhachūḍa, "I have done great wrong. I have killed a Bodhisatta." Actually, later it is found that Jīmūtavāhana has survived.

Before the play begins there are two verses that salute the Buddha. This shows that Harsha revered the Buddha. "Māra's women asked the Buddha with mock anger, 'Which woman are you thinking about while pretending to meditate? Open your eyes and look at us. We are struck by Cupid's arrow. You are our savior but you don't even look at us. Your reputation of being compassionate seems to be false. Which other man could be more cruel than you?'

"May the Jina (Buddha) who has sat down to meditate protect you. Cupid has picked up his bow. Soldiers of Māra are beating their war drums. The eyes of the divine beauties have become fickle with frowns, tremulousness and smiles. The sages have bowed their head. Sakka is excited with surprise and anticipation. At a time such as these let the king of sages, who is meditating and is steadfast on the path of liberation, protect you."

Though in the *part after the curtains come down* the Buddha is not explicitly named, it is full of his teaching. The last verse says, "Let all the worlds be happy. Let all beings delight in the welfare of others. Let all flaws disappear and let all beings be happy."

Asaṅga, Vasubandhu, Dignāga and Dharmakīrti

In the fourth century, the brothers Asaṅga and Vasubandhu were famous as Buddhist philosophers. Dignāga in the fifth century and Dharmakīrti in the seventh century were great philosophers.

Acharya Padmasambhava

Acharya Padmasambhava is revered in the Tibetan Buddhist tradition. Buddhists of Sikkim and Bhutan also revere him. He considered the founder of the "Nigma" sect in Tibet. Other sects too respect him. He was invited to Tibet by King Dechen in 810 CE as per the advice of Acharya Shāntarakshita. He was born at Uḍḍiyana. But the exact location of this place is not known. Various scholars place it at Orissa, Himachal Pradesh, Rajasthan and Swat valley of Pakistan. Many Tibetan Buddhists look upon him as the second Buddha. The Central Institute of Buddhist Studies at Leh has published the Hindi translation of his biography.

Acharya Dīpaṅkara Shrijñāna

After Acharya Padmasambhava, Acharya Dīpaṅkara is the most respected teacher among the Tibetan Buddhists. He translated many Sanskrit texts into Tibetan. Tibetans call him Atish. He was born in 982 CE. His parents were closely associated with Vikramashilā University. He spent a large part of his life on Sumatra island. He stayed in Tibet for 13 years. He passed away in 1054 CE.

Vast Influence of the Tathāgata's Teaching

A note in the Marathi Encyclopedia[492] says, "He rejected caste as the criteria for being high and low in society and insisted only our deeds make us so. This became accepted even by brahmins as we see in the Mahābhārata (Shāntiparva chapter 254; Udyoga 43.27.29) and Bhāgavata (1.8.52; 7.11.35 and 9.2.23). Later this thought spread through Rāmānanda, Chaitanya Mahā Prabhu, Kabir, Siddha Sect, Nātha Sect, Ekanātha, Tukārāma, Lingāyata and Mahānubhāva literature and reached the Vārakarī Sect."

Buddhists and Mahānubhāva Sect

Mahatma Chakradhara founded the Mahānubhāva Sect. Certain characteristics of this sect connect it with Buddhism: rejection of *varṇa* (caste) system, empowering women, promoting Prakrit, etc.

In the Tipiṭaka, many great sages including the Buddha are referred to as Mahānubhāva. In the Mahāvagga[493] of Book of Discipline we find that a matted hair ascetic refers to the Buddha as Mahāsamaṇa Mahānubhāva. In the Acchariya-Abbhuta[494] Sutta of the Middle Discourses, bhikkhus express their surprise and admiration at the *mahānubhāvatā* quality of the Buddha. In Isigili Sutta[495] of the Middile Discourses, the Buddha tells about five hundred Silent Buddhas and advises the bhikkhus to salute these and other *mahānubhāvas*.

The Tathāgata and Basaveshvara

Kumar Swami writes in his book Buddha and Basava,[496] "Buddha and Basava both fought against caste, idolatry, sacrificial rites, untouchability and the inhuman treatment of women. Both preached their religion through the medium of the common man, one in Pali and the other in Kannada. Both emphasized mercy as the heart of religion. Both gave freedom of thought, expression and action to the masses by liberating them from the shackles of superstition and ignorance. Both gave full rights in social and religious matters to women. Both founded fraternities open alike to the young and old, to the touchable and untouchable, to the rich and poor, to the male and female, to the wise and ignorant."

Influence on Namdev and Tukaram

It is well-known that earlier Marathi used to be referred to as Prakrit. Naturally, those saints who wrote in Marathi had the influence of the Samaṇa traditions that used Prakrit. The influence of Buddhist thought on Namdev and Tukaram is huge. This is clear from the contents of their *gāthās* (verses). Even the word *gāthā* is indicative of that connection.

Samaṇa tradition and Gāthās

Gāthā is that which is sung. One can also say that poetry is *gāthā*. In Indian history, verses that are called as *gāthās* have special significance. *Gāthās* are found in poetry of the samaṇa tradition, in the Vedic tradition and in Prakrit. The works of both Namdev and Tukaram are called *gāthās*. The word is also found in the Parsi scripture Avesta.

More important than the source of *gāthās* here is the way they are looked at. They are important in samaṇa traditions but are considered unimportant, and at times are even looked down upon, in the Vedic tradition.

Gāthās in Samaṇa Tradition

In the Tipiṭaka, the verses of the Buddha are called *gāthās*. Theragāthā is the collection of verses of the prominent bhikkhus at the time of the Buddha and Therīgāthā that of prominent bhikkhuṇis. Monier Williams describes *gāthā* in his Sanskrit English dictionary as "the metrical part of a Sutra." In their dictionary, T. W. Rhys Davids and William Stede say about *gāthā*, "As a style of composition, it is one of the nine Angas or divisions of the Canon. (see *navanga satthu sasana*)."

The sermons of the Buddha are divided into nine parts: *sutta, geyya, veyyākaraṇa, gāthā, udāna, itivuttaka, jātaka, abbhutadhamma* and *vedalla.* Thus *gāthā* is an important part of the Tipiṭaka, the collection of the discourses of the Buddha.

Gāthā is connected to non-Vedic tradition of India. Hāla's famous work in Prakrit is *Gāthāsaptashati.* It shows a close connection between *gāthās* and Prakrit language. V. S. Apate in his dictionary gives the meaning of *gāthā* as 'a Prakrita dialect.' He says a *gāthākāra* (composer of *gāthās*) is 'a writer of Prakrita verses'.

Gāthās are not just part of Prakrit languages but is also important as a medium of expression for the masses.

How Vedics Look at Gāthās

The Vedics showed their antipathy towards the samaṇas by denigrating *gāthās*. In Bharatiya Sanskrit Kosh edited by Mahadev Shastri Joshi, the note on *gāthā*[497] says, "Aitareya Brāhmaṇa says that *richā* is divine while *gāthā* is human. (7.18) ...Atharva Veda includes *gāthā* and *nārāshansī* along with *Purāṇas*... (Atharva 15.6.12)...*yad brāhmaṇah shamalamasit; sā gāthā narashansyabhavat.* (Taittiriya 1.3.2.6). Brahmā is mantra. Its dirt is *nārāshansī gāthā*... The language of *gāthās* found in Vedic literature is different from the language of mantras. Their grammar too is different from Vedic grammar. *Gāthās* are more lucid than Vedic mantras. *Gāthās* are put together with *Itihāsa, Purāṇas* and *Nārāshansī*. In Vedic tradition, *Itihāsa* and *Purāṇas* are not considered as auspicious as Vedic mantras.

Later *gāthās* were not just considered insignificant but also were looked down upon with disgust as we can see in Taittiriya brāhmaṇa. This shows the aversion of the Vedics towards the samaṇas who used *gāthās* to express their heartfelt emotions.

Monier Williams says about *gāthā* in his dictionary, 'a verse, stanza (especially one which is neither Ṛic, nor Sāman, nor yajus, a verse not belonging to the Vedas, but to the epic poetry of legends or Ākhyānas, such as the Śunaþśepa-Ākhyāna or the Suparṇ).'

V. S. Apate says about *gāthā* in his dictionary, "A religious verse, but not belonging to any one of the Vedas."

The *Abhaṅgas* of Namdev and Tukaram are called *gāthā*.

Tukaram

We have seen at several places in this book how the Bhāgavat Sect and especially Tukaram were influenced by the Buddha. Tukaram encouraged Bahiṇābāi to translate the book *Vajrasūcī* by Ashvaghosha (which opposed the caste system) into Marathi. Bahiṇābāi expressed the sentiment that (it is as if) in our times the Buddha himself has entered the body of Tukaram.

Tukaram used to meditate on Bhandara mountain near Dehu. His wife would bring food for him there. Sometimes, she would get upset when troubled by the thorns on the road but still she wouldn't miss bringing his food. He used to meditate in a Buddhist cave. Prof D. D. Kosambi writes about it,[498] "The next hill, Bhandara, (where Tukaram also meditated) has a good microlith site, with Buddhist caves and a stupa, which have passed without notice by The Gazetteer and by archaeologists. …From Bhandara with its stupa and Buddhist caves favored by Tukaram…" In recent times, more books are being written showing the connection between Kabir, Tukaram, etc. to the Buddha. Some of these texts are *Buddha Tatvagyani Kabir*[499] in Hindi, *Marathi Sant Sahityavar Bauddha Dharmacha Prabhav*,"[500] and *Sant Tukaramavar Bauddha Dharmacha Prabhav*.[501]

In Dharmanand Kosambi's biography, we find evidence about the inheritance of the Buddha that Tukaram received. The biographer writes that Kosambi was influenced by Tukaram in his childhood and adds,[502] "Buddhism inspired Indians to serve the society. The echo of the Buddhist teaching that one should serve others even at the cost of one's own comforts is found in the literature of Marathi saints. P. M. Lad says, 'Even before coming in contact with the Buddha's teaching, Dharamanand got connected with the Buddha through Tukaram.'"

Dr. Dhere

Dr. R. C. Dhere has written in detail about the Buddha's influence in Maharashtra in his book *Shrī Viṭṭhala: Ek Mahāsamanvaya.*[503] He writes, "In Marathi literature, it has been repeatedly expressed that Viṭṭhala is Buddha. The same thing is expressed through paintings and sculpture in Maharashtra. When *panchāngas* (religious calender) started getting printed in Maharashtra, nine planets or ten incarnations were printed on the cover page. In the ten incarnations, on the ninth position a picture of Viṭṭhala (alone or with Rukhmini) used to be printed, and so as to leave no doubt in our mind, the picture would be labeled Buddha or *Bauddha*."

He says that he has such panchanga in his collection. He adds. "In a recent publication named *Shri Rāma Sahasranāma* along with Garuda and Hanumana, pictures of Viṭṭhala-Rukhmiṇī are printed and are labeled *Bauddha*. There are two sculptures that I know where in the ten incarnations instead of Buddha, Viṭṭhala is used. One is at Tasgaon in Sangli district in the Ganesha temple built by Vinchurkars and the other in the campus of the Mahalaxmi temple in Kolhapur."

Dr. Dhere writes about the influence of Buddhism in Maharashtra,[504] "For about 1000 to 1500 years immediately before Dnyandev and Namdev, Maharashtra was full of the followers of the Buddha. There is no mountain in Maharashtra where we don't find the cave temples carved by the Buddhists. In these hundreds of caves, the sound of *Buddhaṃ Saraṇaṃ Gacchāmi* by bhikkhus was constant. The echo of that great *mahā-mantra* of non-violence and compassion spread through the entire land of

Maharashtra. We see the proof in the inscriptions of these caves which state that all including royalty, farmers and artisans were eager to serve the virtuous bhikkhus. The bhikkhu was an object of respect. As a result of that respect, the names Bhikoba and Bhikubai had become widely prevalent in rural Maharashtra…

"We cannot deny that the river Indrayani through which the great flood of universal compassion that Dnyandev and Tukaram spread throughout Maharashtra had its origin in the area where countless bhikkhus had lived—bhikkhus who were inspired by the compassionate Buddha…

"When Tukaram connects to the entire humanity by saying 'Recognize he who empathizes with the downtrodden as the true saint; he truly is a god' he does so due with the support of that tradition! Therefore, I have no hesitation in saying that the Buddha lived in Maharashtra for one to one and a half thousand years. And while disappearing in the twelfth-thirteenth centuries, the Buddha overturned in this land the container of the compassion from his heart. And then the saints mixed many currents of their devotion in it to keep it flowing strongly. At least in Maharashtra, Buddhism that had declined through the corruptions of Tantra lost all those taints and re-appeared in the form of Bhāgavata Dharma."

Mahatma Phule and Buddhism

Mahatma Phule is called the Father of Indian Social Revolution. He was among the first who drew attention to the Buddha's teaching in modern times. He praised Buddhism in his book *Gulāmagirī* (Slavery) that was published in 1873. It is clear from M. S. More's narration[505] that there was no Buddhist text available in Marathi at that time, "Before 1910 CE, only three noteworthy texts on the Buddha were published in Marathi. The first was Vasudev Laxman Athavale's 52 page booklet *Bauddha Dharmacha Sansthapak Sākyamuni Gautama Yanche Charitra* published in 1883. The second was Govind Narayan Kane's 100 page text *Shri Jagadguru Gautama Buddha Charitra Athava Mahabhinishkraman* published in 1894. The third was

Krishnarao Arjun Keluskar's 158 page text *Gautam Buddhache Charitra* published in 1898."

Long before the publication of these three texts Mahatma Phule wrote in his book *Gulamagiri* (Slavery),[506] "...the Buddhist had rejected and defeated all scriptures including the Vedas."

He added that the Vedics had destroyed most of the Buddhist books and wrote, "Only *Amarakosha* was preserved for their own use."

Amarakosha is a famous Sanskrit dictionary by Amarasinh who was a Buddhist. This detail is not known to many even today when information is freely available. It is then surprising that Mahatma Phule knew this. Amarakosha is among the earliest dictionaries in Sanskrit and there are more than fifty commentaries on it. The Marathi Encyclopedia writes about it,[507] "... it is the work of Amarasinh...it is generally believed that he was a Buddhist. It is said that in the movement against Buddhism in India, all the Buddhist texts were destroyed except Amarakosha."

Mahatma Phule wrote in his book about farmers,[508] "...Later on four neutral pious learned people who didn't like the deception of brahmins established Buddhism and started rapidly liberating ignorant *sudda* farmers from the bondage of brahmins. Then the clever Shankaracharya tried for long to engage the upright Buddhists in debate and to push them out of India. But this didn't affect the goodness of Buddhism one bit and that religion kept on prospering day by day."

One of Phule's *akhaṅḍas* is,[509]
"The Buddha corrected the wrong;
Earned fame all over the world.
The brahmins were distressed;
Cried openly, beating their chests."

Sayajirao Gaikwad

The respect that Baroda's King Sayajirao had for the Buddha is seen indirectly through his policies for the welfare of the people and directly through observations by Dharmanand Kosambi.[510]

Once Sayajirao had organized a five lecture series by Dharmanand Kosambi on Buddhism. He was very serious about these. Therefore, he remained present for all of them. The biographer notes an incidence from P. M. Lad's book *Akashaganga* (page 21, 22). Before the lecture series, a delegation of people from an area had requested that alcohol shops should be closed down in that area. But Sayajirao had rejected the demand because it would cause a loss to the exchequer. In his lecture, Kosambi mentioned that Emperor Asoka had banned alcohol. Afterwards, Sayajirao too banned sale of alcohol in that area.

It is relevant here to write about some other noteworthy work by Sayajirao. Prof Rajwade from the Pali department of Baroda College published the Marathi translation of the Long Discourses (Dīgha Nikāya) in 1918. In the preface he wrote,[511] "About three years back His Majesty King Sayajirao ordered me to translate Pali texts into Marathi. Accordingly, I took up the translation of the Long Discourses… His Majesty… has great respect for and inclination towards the teachings of the Buddha."

The second part of this translation was published in 1932 after Rajwade's death. C. V. Joshi wrote the preface,[512] "There are several deep prejudices in Maharashtra about the Buddha and his teaching. Some self-proclaimed researchers and Dnyankoshkar have increased this prejudice to a large extent. But it is hoped that the publication of the Pali texts will help in dispelling that prejudice."

Guruvarya Keluskar

Krishnarao Arjun Keluskar's book *Gautam Buddhache Charitra* was published in 1898. There were only two small Marathi books available on the subject before this. Even outside Maharashtra, in India very little was written about the Buddha. In the same period, we see that many texts were being written in the West on the Buddha as is clear from Paul Carus's preface to his *Gospel of the Buddha* published in 1894. He wrote,[513] "This booklet needs no preface for those who are familiar with the sacred books of Buddhism, which have been made accessible to the Western world by the indefatigable zeal and industry of scholars like Beal, Bigandet, Bühler, Burnouf, Childers, Alexander Csoma, Rhys Davids, Dutoit, Eitel, Fausböll, Foucaux, Francke, Edmund Hardy, Spence Hardy, Hodgson, Charles R. Lanman, F. Max Müller, Karl Eugen Neumann, Oldenberg, Pischel, Schiefner, Senart, Seidenstücker, Bhikkhu Nyānatiloka, D.M. Strong, Henry Clarke Warren, Wassiljew, Weber, Windisch, Winternitz &c.".

This long list of names makes it clear how when we in India knew very little about the Buddha, the West was immensely curious about him. Given the apathy in India, Keluskar's book is very important. This book led to a big revolution in India as we can see here in the preface by Dr. Ambedkar to his The Buddha and His Dhamma.[514]

"The year I passed the English Fourth Standard Examination, my community people wanted to celebrate the occasion … I was the first boy in my community to reach this stage… (the organizers) went to my father to ask for his permission. My father flatly refused… Those who wanted to celebrate the event were greatly disappointed. They, however, did not give way. They went to Dada Keluskar, a personal friend of my father, and asked him to intervene. He agreed. After a little argumentation, my father yielded, and the meeting was held. Dada Keluskar presided. He was a literary person of his time. At the end of his address he gave me as a gift a copy of his book on the life of the Buddha, which he had written for the Baroda Sayajirao Oriental Series. I read the book with great interest, and was greatly impressed and moved by it….

"This is how I turned to the Buddha, with the help of the book given to me by Dada Keluskar. It was not with an empty mind that I went to the Buddha at that early age. I had a background, and in reading the Buddhist Lore I could always compare and contrast. This is the origin of my interest in the Buddha and His Dhamma."

Keluskar writes at the end of his biography of the Buddha,[515] "It is natural that we feel proud that the World Teacher to whom the world is indebted due to his great intellect and the power of his ethical character. We must develop earnest desire to know about this life. By succumbing to such a desire, I have narrated this biography to the best of my ability to the people of Maharashtra. I hope that they will read it carefully and get to know more about this great man."

Maharshi V. R. Shinde

Maharshi Shinde had studied the Buddha's teaching. He said,[516] "If we are to make paintings and sculpture about religion, we have to consider both aesthetics and ethics (principles)… If we select subjects related to the Buddha's selfless service, Guru Nanak's reforms, Kabir's love for truth and Tukaram's devotion, etc. and if artists such as Ravi Verma were to then use their creative genius, it would go a long way in adding to the beauty and auspiciousness of temples."

Maharshi Shinde used to have regular gatherings at his house. In a letter dated 16 June 1926 for such gatherings he has quoted a *gāthā* from the Dhammapada (21.3). In one such gathering he said,[517] "On April 1, 1928 in the gathering led by Annasaheb, he elaborated on the Sukhavagga of the Dhammapada… He discussed the Buddha's Wheel of Dhamma. He said, 'When would we be really happy? If we can keep our peace even when we see enmity, cruelty, suffering and disappointments around us, then we can be happy in this world. How easily we say that saints such as the Buddha and Tukaram were pessimistic but if we look at things objectively we would know that these saints were *ānandavādī* (promoting happiness) and optimistic; and we are irritable and pessimistic as we are entangled in our selfish world."

Dr. Babasaheb Ambedkar

In the history of Buddhism, Dr. Ambedkar is a bright star along with the great names such as Asoka, Milinda, Kanishka, Nāgārjuna, Harsha Vardhana and Padmasambhava. This book is not the place for enumerating his great contributions to several fields. But we must note here that his work in the field of the Dhamma is as incomparable and memorable as his other contributions. His revolutionary embrace of the Dhamma in 1956 and bringing the Buddha back to Indian society is so famous that we need not dwell more on it here. But we must express our gratitude to him for his work. We must also take note of a few steps he took on the path of the Dhamma.

He brought back to life some important symbols of the Buddha in Indian society. He was proud of his work. At the Third World Buddhist Conference held at Yangon in December 1954, "… Ambedkar declared… As maker of the Constitution he had already achieved several things to that end. He described the provision for study of Pali in the Constitution, the inscription of a Buddhistic aphorism on the frontage of the imposing Rashtrapati Bhavan in New Delhi and the acceptance of Ashoka Chakra by Bharat as her symbol, as his personal achievements. The government of India had declared Buddha Jayanti a holiday mainly through his efforts. He had effected this wonderful change, he proudly stated, without any opposition; so lucid and effective was his exposition in Parliament."[518]

His scholarly classic The Buddha and His Dhamma is a work that guides an era. If he had lived for just five more years, it would have been immensely beneficial for Indian society and Buddha Dhamma.

The Dalai Lama

The fourteenth Dalai Lama is a personality whose conduct and thoughts mirror those of the Buddha clearly and prominently. He is a gentle, balanced, reasonable, wise and calm person. Tom Lowenstein writes about him,[519] "… the Dalai Lama, in this life and teachings, … exemplifies the bodhisattva's vow…

"… the fourteenth Dalai Lama is perhaps the first and only Buddhist master to achieve international celebrity. Instantly recognizable from innumerable media images, the Dalai Lama projects a happiness and modesty which make him one of the best loved 20th century public figures. Exiled head of a devastated nation, His Holiness is honoured for his lifelong devotion to this people and for a compassion that transcends his own tragic status."

Acharya Satya Narayan Goenka

In modern times, Acharya Goenka (1924-2013) has spread Vipassanā throughout the world. Vipassanā which was lost in most parts of the world, was brought to India and spread to the entire world by him. He came to India in 1969. He took the Buddha's teachings to the people here. We must be grateful to him for his work of explaining further to the Buddhists the teachings of the Buddha and for creating a positive feeling for the Buddha and his teaching among the non-Buddhists. There are more than a thousand assistant teachers of Vipassanā. In India, most states have Vipassanā centres. Vipassanā centres have also been established the world over in several countries including Nepal, Sri Lanka, Myanmar, Cambodia, Indonesia, Japan, Mongolia, Taiwan, Thailand, Australia, New Zealand, many European countries and Latin American countries, USA and Canada.

Outside of India

The Buddha's teaching had flourished in several countries including Sri Lanka, Myanmar, Cambodia, Thailand, Tibet, China, Korea, Java, Sumatra, Afghanistan, Pakistan, Turkey etc. Many of these countries still have that influence. Much literature is available about the nature of Buddhism in these countries. Therefore, we need not go in more detail about it in this book. The same is true about Buddhist art and culture of these countries. We must make the mention of Anāgārika Dhamma Pāla for his work in Sri Lanka and India.

Buddha Dhamma in the West

The literature about the Buddha reached Europe around the middle of the nineteenth century. Eugene Burnoff (1801-1852) recognized the importance of Buddhism. Max Muller published translations of Buddhist texts. The Pali Text Society, which was established mainly due to the initiative of T. W. and Carolyn Rhys Davids, published the Pali Tipiṭaka. In 1879, Sir Edwin Arnold published The Light of Asia which was based on Lalitavistāra, a biographical account of the Buddha. In 1924, the English Buddhist Society was established. After 1960-70, there was an increased curiosity and attraction for Buddhism in Europe. Many Tibetan bhikkhus left Tibet after the Communist Revolution. They went to the West. Many people there came in contact with the Buddhism as a result. In 1967, Sangharakshita established "Friends of the Western Buddhist Order". This has spread to India as well. It is called Trailokya Bauddha Mahasangha Sahayaka Gan in India.

Tarkatīrtha Laxman Shastri Joshi

Tarkatīrtha Joshi wrote about the Buddha,[520] "Gautama the Buddha established the first universal religion in the world. A universal religion is one that has the potential to transcend the boundaries of race, caste and nation; and has the inspiration to give the humanity a message of peace and truth. Gautama Buddha brushed aside some of the fundamental questions of religions. He ignored the questions such as God and its nature, life after death, origin of the universe, etc. He gave priority to the issue of suffering in the world... He opposed the Vedic religion's yajñas (ritual sacrifices), caste system and permanence of soul. He taught that moral conduct is more important than rituals and that is the true way of liberation. He explained the futility of rites, rituals, vows, fasts, pilgrimages etc. and taught that eradication of craving was the true path for liberation. The gist of his teaching is that the true fulfillment of human life lies in virtues such as non-violence, truth etc...."

The Buddha's Teaching Lives in Our Heart

From the discussion above about India, it is clear that the Buddha's teaching never completely vanished from India. Sometimes, a dry river bed may suggest that the flow of water has ceased. But when we remove some sand from the surface we find a flow of water beneath. It looks as if the river of the Buddha's teaching had dried in India, but this is just a superficial appearance, just a temporary phenomenon. Even those who frowned upon the Buddha's teaching were carrying his message in their blood! They didn't know that the Buddha continued to live in their heart! They didn't know it, so they didn't give credit to him for his teachings. Even then their heart couldn't lie. Sooner or later, they would recognize their own heart and then they would speak words full of the sweet music of the Buddha's teaching.

14

Farewell

We have discussed the Buddha through this book. Now it is time to bid farewell. The company of the Buddha has filled me with joy. The cup of joy is overflowing. I have a sense of fulfillment that will accompany me all my life. Still there is also a regret at having to depart. I get a sense of what Ānanda must have felt at the time of the Buddha's *mahāparinibbāna*. This is not a shortcoming of the Buddha's teaching. It is my own limitation.

The farewell is twofold: farewell to the Buddha and to the readers. As the Buddha explained to Ānanda, all associations are temporary. I too must accept that. I would like to mention one thing here. Several influences brought me closer to the Buddha. These influences and inspirations have been very helpful. But the inner pull that I felt towards the Buddha was entirely my own. It was neither a reaction to something nor an imitation. Let us briefly discuss a few important issues at this farewell.

The Enemy is Strong When We Are Careless

I remember a discourse by the Buddha where he gave the following advice to bhikkhus at Kūṭāgārasālā in Vesāli.[521]

"Presently the Licchavīs use a wooden block as a pillow. They remain heedful and work enthusiastically and tirelessly to achieve their goals. Therefore, King Ajātasattu of Magadha doesn't find an opening to attack them. But in coming time, the Licchavīs will become delicate. They will sleep on soft beds. They will lie in bed for a long time, long after sunrise. Then Ajātasattu will find an opening.

"Presently the bhikkhus too are like the Licchavīs. But if they become careless, if they become addicted to comforts, then Māra will find an opening to attack them. Therefore, you must live a simple and frugal life. You must be heedful."

Discussion

There is no need to take this discourse literally and use a wood block as a pillow. Let them who wish to. The important point here is the figurative meaning. Those who become addicted to luxuries and forget their duties and goals start declining and slide towards their own defeat. This was the warning that the Buddha gave.

This is what happened to Indus Civilization. It couldn't repel the attack of Vedics.

Then the same thing happened after the Buddha and Asoka. Then came the Manusmriti.

Now if we too become lazy, careless and merely enjoy the fruit of the efforts of past generations and forget our duties, we will face a similar fate.

The Licchavīs didn't heed the Buddha's advice. Ajātasattu then attacked and defeated them. The enemy is always looking for an opening. This enemy can be external or it could be our own inner weakness, our own defilements. We must be careful.

If We Have Only One Eye

All those who follow the Buddha and dream of an India that follows the Dhamma must read about an incidence from the life of the Buddha.[522] It gives us guidance about how to spread the Buddha's teaching to more and more people.

Once the Buddha was living in Jetavana in Sāvatthi. At that time a bhikkhu named Bhaddālī had transgressed a rule of discipline. He then confessed his mistake to the Buddha. He asked the Buddha why the Saṅgha launches a serious enquiry about one bhikkhu's misconduct but doesn't do so for another. The Buddha said that the Saṅgha takes a soft approach towards a bhikkhu who admits his transgression but follows a tough approach towards one who doesn't admit his mistakes.

The Buddha explained, "When a bhikkhu works with faith and devotion for the Dhamma, other bhikkhus feel that if they are too strict with him, he may lose his faith and devotion for the Dhamma."

Then the Buddha gave an example, "When a person has just one eye, his family, friends and relatives take care not to harm that eye. Similarly, bhikkhus feel that a bhikkhu who (lacks in conduct and) has only faith and devotion should be nurtured. They avoid any harsh action may hurt his faith and devotion."

Discussion

This example explains the care and precautions we must take when we take the Dhamma to the world. It tells us how we must be balanced, reasonable and magnanimous. If a man has opened his eyes to the path but his steps are still tentative, rather than putting him down, we should take note of the fact that his eyes are open. We must be compassionate towards him. If we do this, his steps will become firm and he will walk further on the path of Dhamma. But if we don't do this, if we attack him or are insensitive to him, if we point out only his faults, if we humiliate him or blame him, he won't take further steps on the path. Not only that, his eyes that were open to the truth of the Buddha would again turn elsewhere.

Therefore, if someone has developed faith towards the Buddha, we must protect that faith with utmost care. The Buddha didn't want his Dhamma to be forced down the throat of others.

His example of the one eyed man guides us about out conduct. If a one eyed man loses his eye, he loses all vision. Therefore, any sensible person is careful with that eye.

Similarly, if someone has developed faith in the Buddha then we must carefully look for ways to nurture that faith, to help the faith blossom into proper understanding and suitable action. Whatever shortcoming one wants to point out, one must do so with utmost care and skillful communication.

Don't Ask One Who Ploughs...

If we start blaming one who ploughs his field that he doesn't sow; and if we blame one who is sowing that he doesn't harvest his field, we will not be able to take the Dhamma to all the people of India. Don't criticize him for that which he has not done. Give credit for what he has achieved. Otherwise, we will alienate people.

The Buddha has profoundly explained the value of gratitude in life. Once while teaching about the field of an honorable man and the field of dishonorable man, he said,[523] "...Bhikkhus, a dishonorable man is ungrateful. Unwise men praise ingratitude. Ingratitude is the field of the dishonorable...bhikkhus, an honorable man is grateful *(kataññu, katavedi)* ... Gratitude is the field of upright people. Wise people praise gratitude."

He emphasized gratitude again and again in his discourses to bhikkhus and laypeople. *Kataññu* is grateful. *Katavedi* means who is aware of the good deeds done to him; help rendered to him by others. The Buddha would be kind even to those who were harsh and ungrateful to him. It is no wonder then that he was very grateful to those who had helped him in any way. Matricheta says,[524]

You help those who are unkind to you
more than most people help those
who are kind to them.

Actually, the problem is not with the land; the problem is with the mind. That is why someone has said,[525] *"Bārishe-rehmat hui, lekin jamin kābil nā thī."* (It rained compassion, but the land was not fertile.)

This is what the Buddha meant when he talked about the field of dishonorable men.

I feel that we Indians have been ungrateful enough. Now that light is being shed again on our history, we must be grateful to the Buddha. We must also be grateful to all those who, to the best of their ability, tried to put into practice and spread his teaching. We should not have reservations about them. We should remove our bias and go beyond our differences to acknowledge their contributions.

How Are We Going to Judge Ourselves

Sometimes individuals, institutes and movements that work to spread the Dhamma are criticized by others who also follow the Dhamma. There is nothing wrong in judging and evaluating the work of others. But at times critics focus only on the negative aspect of the work and launch a destructive attack on them. There is no need to state whether such attacks are helpful in spreading the Dhamma. It is clear that if one truly loves the Dhamma, one would not do such a thing.

How can we expect anyone—an individual, an institute or a movement—to be hundred percent perfect and totally flawless? Such complete perfection would indicate achievement of Buddhahood! What is going to be our position on such issues? When we attack others for their shortcomings, we may be merely saying that they are short of the Buddhahood and by extension may even suggest that we have no flaws and are hence have attained the ultimate state.

We know that we are on the path to the Buddhahood. We are not there yet. Are our words and actions going to suggest that we have reached the end of the journey? If indeed that is the case then there is no place for arrogance in that state. There will be an effort to guide but there will be equal concern not to insult others. And if we admit that we are still journeying on the path, then we won't look down upon others. Someone may be a few steps ahead or behind. That is all. And if we start attacking them then we start journeying in the reverse direction!

We must pose such questions and express such doubts to ourselves and try to answer and clarify them honestly to ourselves.

Let Us Admit Everyone's Freedom

Those who follow the Buddha's teaching may or may not formally call themselves Buddhists. On the other hand, there could be some people who call themselves Buddhists but don't follow the Buddha's teaching. Let us agree that each one of us has the freedom to decide who among those are closer to us. This is the Buddha's way. I also agree that others may feel differently about it.

The Buddha's Way of Changing the Hearts of the Audience

Those who wish to take the Buddha's teaching to more and more people should adopt the Buddha's way of teaching. They will find useful guidance in Upāli Sutta[526] in the Middle Discourses.

There were several philosophers in India contemporary to the Buddha. Once Dīgha Tapassi, a disciple of Nigaṇṭṭha Nāṭaputta, returned after a discussion with the Buddha. While he was narrating the discussion to Nigaṇṭṭha, a lay disciple named Upāli (not to be confused with bhikkhu Upāli) was present there. Upāli expressed desire to debate with the Buddha saying that he would totally destroy the Buddha in debate. He said that just as a strong man would pull a sheep with long fleece, he would pull and throw the Buddha around in debate. He gave many such examples. At that time, Dīgha Tapassi warned his teacher not to allow Upāli to go to the Buddha saying that the Buddha knew a trick that changed one's opinion. Even then Upāli went to the Buddha. While talking to the Buddha, he had a change of heart. He became a follower of the Buddha.

When he returned and reported what happened to his original teacher, his teacher said to him, "You who were boasting 'I would do this, I would do that' have been tricked and enticed by Samaṇa Gotama."

Then Upāli said, "Sir, this is indeed an auspicious trick. It is good for one's welfare. Sir, let my community be tricked and enticed by Gotama. It will bring happiness and welfare for long."

He added that he wished all khattiyas, brahmins, merchants, low castes, gods, Māras, brahmas along with all samaṇas and brāhmaṇas as well as all gods and humans change by this trick and enticement. Let them all be happy.

Discussion

Even today, some people are afraid that they will be enticed by the Buddha's skill. This keeps them from getting close to the Buddha. At such times at least those, who have understood how benevolent the Buddha's teaching is, should take responsibility to dispel their fear. Once they see the Dhamma for themselves, they will know how truthful, straightforward and benevolent it is. This is easily possible even if we keep just a fraction of the confidence that Upāli had.

Advice to Donate to Other Sectarians...

Upāli who had come to debate with the Buddha was convinced about the Dhamma and requested the Buddha to accept him as a devoted disciple.[527] At that time, the Buddha advised him, "Householder, you should think carefully before you act. For people like you (who are prominent in society) it is proper that you act carefully...Your house has been like a wellspring for Nigaṇṭṭhas. Therefore, don't stop giving alms to them." The Buddha had given the same advice to General Siha who had also left the Nigaṇṭṭhas to follow the Buddha.[528]

Many times, people take important decisions impulsively, under the sway of emotions. Once the flood of emotion passes, they regret their decision. Therefore, the Buddha asked Upāli and General Siha to consider carefully. He had also shown magnanimity in asking them not to stop the alms for Nigaṇṭṭhas. This generosity, tolerance and civilized behavior was the core of his Dhamma.

Tarkatīrtha Laxman Shastri says,[529] "Buddha Dhamma brought this tolerance to the eastern religions. Credit goes to Buddha Dhamma for this."

It is because of this tolerance that there is no stubbornness or the slightest extremist streak in the conduct and thoughts of the Buddha. His teaching had no place for any insistence that others must accept his views. Therefore, any effort to force his Dhamma on the others would defeat that very Dhamma.

We must be careful and alert that this doesn't happen. Water that is given at the roots of the plant goes through the roots, through the stem, through the branches to the peduncle of the bud, permeates the bud without anyone noticing it and makes the bud blossom into flower. The teaching of the Dhamma should also be like this. It must touch the heart of others. It must liberate their heart and let the fragrance spread. It is a grave mistake to think that we can convince them about the Dhamma by hurting them.

Ask Yourself

Whom should we ask whether we are walking on the path of the Dhamma? We must look inside and ask ourselves. We all have at least a little of the Buddha's wisdom and balance. Use that to judge yourself. If that voice of wisdom gives a favorable verdict, then we need not worry too much about what others say. If the inner verdict is not favorable then the favorable words of others shouldn't make us proud.

Don't Encroach on Others' Freedom

The tendency to encroach on the freedom of others often brings misery to oneself and others. Some like to dominate others.

This gives them perverse joy. They feel it is a victory when they make decisions for others. This tendency has many shades; from giving mental pain to others to such extreme intolerance for dissent that one destroys the very existence of others.

There is a vast difference between a tiger killing a deer and a man killing a man. For a tiger it is a fight for his own survival. The tiger has not reached a stage in the evolutionary ladder where it can change its diet and still survive. Man is different. He has several options. He has acquired knowledge about how to live a better life. He understands the disastrous effects of violence. He has the necessary capacity for introspection and efficiency to avoid violence. Therefore, we must behave in an appropriate manner. We must avoid not only physical violence but also verbal and mental violence.

While respecting the lives of others and giving them space, we must also have affectionate and cordial relations with them. We may need advice, help and guidance and also need to give advice, help and guidance. If we feel that something new would help others, let the desire to change spring from within their hearts. Don't force those changes on them. We need to have discretion in this—for example, how much should parents force on their children by way of health practices and education. We should take care that we don't become dictators but that our actions always spring from compassion.

Be a Bridge

The two shores of a river are far away from each other. If there is a strong bridge that straddles the two shores, people on the two sides come in contact with each other, connect with each other, communicate with each other. They establish relationships. But if there is no bridge, they remain separated.

The bridge connects the communities on the two side of the river. It connects their hearts and connects their minds. It creates harmony among them. How do people on either side of the bridge view it? If they view it with a sense of ownership and claim exclusive use of it, then there is conflict. Then the bridge doesn't do its work of connecting people. We thus put boundaries around ourselves. We hinder our own growth. We restrict our own world. Therefore, we should not try to establish an ownership over the bridge. We should let it connect people.

Let it connect the people on the two shores. Let it bring them together. Soon they will mix with each other like milk and water. Let there be many bridges. Let us not abandon the earlier bridges. Let them preserve them and use our constructive energies to create new bridges.

Let the Mirror be Large and Unbroken

If every follower of the Buddha insisted that he will paint a picture of the Buddha exactly as he wants, we won't get the totality of his personality. When a mirror breaks, the pieces often show broken and incomplete images. It is true that it is very difficult to have a mental mirror that will show the entire personality of the Buddha. However, we must try to make the image as complete as possible, as close to the original as possible. If the broken pieces of the mirror get scattered, the image too gets scattered. Therefore, we should try to avoid breaking the mirror. Even if it happens, we can keep the pieces together so that we can get as complete and uninterrupted an image as possible.

The Pain of Dependence

While keeping harmonious relation with other Buddhists (indeed with non-Buddhists too), we must take care not to lose our independence. The Buddha repeatedly emphasized the importance of freedom and independence. He advised not to depend on others for learning and to experience the truth for oneself. An incident from his life[530]—

Once he was living in monastery of Migāramātā Visākhā in Sāvatthi. At that time, Visākhā had some work at the royal court of King Pasenadi. However, the king was not giving decisions in favor of Visākhā. Once Visākhā went to the Buddha early in the morning. He asked her the reason for coming so early. She told him that the king was obstructing her business. After hearing her plight, the Buddha uttered a verse that meant:

"Whatever is dependent on others is suffering. Whatever is independent is happiness. If we are dependent then we are disappointed even in small things. Then things that we wish for don't happen."

Discussion

The Buddha has clarified the difference between freedom and lack of it. We see it even in the mundane world. Visākhā's example clarifies it further. The Commentary gives us more detail: Visākhā had some business. Her merchandize was taxed at a higher than usual rate. She tried to get it reversed in royal court. But she wasn't getting justice.

In *Manusmriti* too we find a similar quote describing how freedom is happiness and dependence on others is misery: *Sarvaṃ paravashaṃ dukkhaṃ sarvamātmavashaṃ sukhaṃ.*[531] This is often used to praise and glorify *Manusmriti*. Those who do so often forget completely that the whole tone and tenor of *Manusmriti* is against this quote. *Manusmriti* snatches freedom of the majority of people. The reason for this contradiction is clear. This is not an original verse of *Manusmriti*. It is originally from the Udāna where it is in keeping with the teaching of the Buddha. *Manusmriti* was composed about four hundred years after the Buddha.

The Buddha is not talking merely about freedom in the material sphere. His statement about freedom is equally relevant in the intellectual and psychological field. We must maintain our intellectual freedom. We must ensure that our intellect is free. This is essential for us to live as human beings. We must heed this message of the Buddha from the Udāna. His Dhamma makes one free. It doesn't liberate us from one prison to imprison us in another one—not at all.

The Core of the Buddha's Compassion

The Buddha was also called the Compassionate One. The essence of his compassion is seen in a verse in Metta Sutta in the Suttanipāta.[532] "Just as a mother protects her only child with all her life, let us have infinite selfless love for all beings."

This is very difficult. But the Buddha has lived that life and set us an example to follow. Let us at least move a little in that direction. This much is easy. Whatever small distance we move, we will fulfill our life as a human. We will become blessed! We will come closer to our own Buddhahood!

The Fragrance of Virtuous People

In the Numerical Discourses, we find a comparison between the fragrance of a flower and the fragrance of a noble person.[533]

Once Ānanda said to the Buddha, "Bhante, the smell of flowers and *sapsand* roots only goes in the direction of the wind. Is there any smell that goes both in the direction of the wind and against the direction of the wind?"

The Buddha said yes. He then gave a detailed explanation.

"A man or a woman living in a village or a town takes triple refuge; abstains from killing, stealing, lying, sexual misconduct and alcoholic beverages; lives a moral and wholesome life and lives at home without harboring any ill-will in mind….The good name of such a person travels in all directions through samaṇas, brāhmaṇas and gods….Ānanda, this is the fragrance that travels both in the direction of wind and also against the direction of the wind."

The Buddha added, "The smell of flowers doesn't travel in the direction opposite to wind. Neither sandalwood nor jasmine. The fragrance of the virtuous noble beings travels in all directions."

The fragrance of the Buddha's life and work spread like this in all directions over a long distance and continues to fill the atmosphere hundreds of years later.

Don't be Heedless

What was his last advice for us? He didn't simply make a dry, neutral statement that all compound things are impermanent before breathing his last. He uttered a short exhortation just before his last breath. That exhortation was not meant only for bhikkhus present there but also for countless generations after him.

We have no time to waste, to be heedless. We must strive with awareness, with alertness, with wisdom, without procrastination and without making excuses. We must take the last words of the Buddha to our heart: *appamādena sampādetha.*

We must live that exhortation: in our thoughts, in our speech and in our actions. It was said about his speech that all the people in the world could hear his speech and that people of all ages can hear his speech. If we keep aside the poetic exaggeration in this statement and just understand the figurative meaning, we will see that it does apply to his last advice. This advice is timeless. It is for all people from all places. It is as if he is saying to us at this very moment, *"Attain your goal without being heedless."*

Let the Buddha Arise Again!

When Mūlagandha Kuṭī Vihāra was established in Sarnath, Rabindranath Tagore had composed a Bengali poem titled "*buddhadevera prati*". He says in his poem:

Bhārata-aṅganatale āji tava nava āgamanī;
Ameya premera vārtā shatakaṇṭha uṭhuaka nihsvani

Bring to our country once again the fortunate name.
It made the land of your birth sacred to lands far and wide!
Let your great awakening under the Bodhi-tree be fulfilled,
Blowing away the veil of ignorance. Let at the end of a
dark night,
Your memory blossom again afresh in India!

The emotions that Rabindranath expressed are also our emotions. The Buddha won't come back to us in his body. But his thoughts can come back afresh. Let his teaching take root and blossom again in India. Let us all take a vow to do our utmost for it!

Let us be a Buddha-flower

Lastly, I would say to myself:

If you can't be the sun, be a sunflower;
Incline your head; let the sun light up your life!
If you can't be the Buddha, be a Buddha-flower;
Open your heart; let his inspiration guide you!!

Appendix – Tipiṭaka

Sutta Piṭaka ***Vinaya Piṭaka*** ***Abhidhamma Piṭaka***

1. Dīgha Nikāya 2. Majjhima Nikāya 3. Saṃyutta Nikāya
4. Aṅguttara Nikāya 5. Khuddaka Nikāya

1. Khuddakapāṭha 2. Dhammapada 3. Udāna 4. Itivuttaka
5. Suttanipāta 6. Vimānavatthu 7. Petavatthu 8. Theragāthā
9. Therīgāthā 10. Apadāna 11. Buddhavaṃsa 12. Cariyāpiṭaka
13. Jātaka 14. Niddesa 15. Paṭisambhidāmagga

Note:

According to the tradition in Myanmar (Burma), three additional books are included in the Tipiṭaka:

Nettipakaraṇa, Peṭakopadesa and *Milindapañha.*

For example,\535\ *"According to the tradition of Myanmar (Burma), these three books are considered to be an integral part of the Tipiṭaka because of their importance*

Please check English meanings
Sutta - discourse
Piṭaka - basket, box, scriptures
Vinaya - discipline, code of conduct for bhikkhus
Abhidhamma - higher Dhamma, supreme Dhamma
Dīgha - long
Nikāya - collection, compilation
Majjhima - middle-length
Saṃyutta - connected, mixed, compounded
Aṅguttara - graded, gradual, numerical
Khuddaka – small, minor

Notes

Chapter 1

1. *Marathi Vyutpattikosha* - the term *'bhagavā,'* with annexure third edition, Shubhada Saraswat Prakashan, Pune 5, reprinted - 1996
2. *Bouddha Manishā* - Compilation of Prof. Jagannath Upadhyaya's essays, Part 2 (Hindi), Ed. Prof. Ramshankar Tripathi, Pub. - Kendriya Bouddha Vidya Sansthan, Choglamsar, Leh (Ladakh), 2001, pg. 512-513
3. Dr. Babasaheb Ambedkar; author Dhananjay Keer; Publisher: Popular Prakashan, Mumbai 35, second edition 1977, pg. 408-409
4. Pali-English Dictionary; Ed. T. W. Rhys Davids, William Stede; Publisher: Motilal Banarsidass Publishers Private Limited, Delhi; First published: London 1921-1925, Indian Reprint - 2003, pg. 296
5. JA, *Avidūrenidānakathā,* VRI Vol. 70, pg. 61
6. JA, *Avidūrenidānakathā,* VRI Vol. 70, pg. 66
7. *Bhagavān Buddha: Jivan aur Darshan*; Hindi trans. - Shripad Joshi; Pub. on behalf of Sahitya Akademi, Lokbharatī Prakashan, 15 A, Mahatma Gandhi Marg, Allahabad 1; Edition 1987, pg. 1
8. What the Buddha Taught, Walpola Rahula, First Pub. - The Gordon Fraser Gallery Ltd., London and Bedford, 1959, First paperback edition 1978, pg. 1
9. Discerning the Buddha, Lal Mani Joshi, Pub. - Munshiram Manoharlal Publishers Pvt. Ltd., Post Box 5715, 54 Rani Jhansi Road, New Delhi 110 055, First Published - 1983, pg. 168
10. *Piṭṭhi me āgilāyati; tamahaṃ āyamissāmi.* AN, *Dasakanipāta, Yamakavagga, sutta* 8 - *Dutiyanaḷakapāna Sutta*, VRI Vol. 40, para 68, pg. 104, Hindi Part 4, pg. 187
11. AN, *Tikanipāta, Kusināravagga, sutta* 4 - *Bharaṇḍukālāma Sutta*, VRI Vol. 35, para 127, pg. 312, Marathi Part 1, pg. 303

12. *Iṅgha me tvaṃ, Ānanda, antarena yamakasālānaṃ uttarasīsakaṃ mañcakaṃ paññapehi, kilantosmi, Ānanda, nipajjissāmi.* DN, *Mahāparinibbāna Sutta, beginning part of Pancamabhāṇavāra,* VRI Vol. 2, para 198, pg. 104, Hindi pg. 140
13. *Tena kho pana samayena bhagavā gilānāvuṭṭhito hoti aciravuṭṭhito gelaññā.* AN, *Tikanipāta, Ānandavagga, sutta* 3 - *Mahānānasakka Sutta,* VRI Vol. 35, para 74, pg. 249, Marathi Part 1, pg. 240-241
14. *Sāvatthinidānaṃ. Tena kho pana samayena bhagavā vātehābādhiko hoti;* SN, *Brahmaṇasaṃyutta, Upāsakavagga, sutta* 3 - *Devahita Sutta,* VRI Vol. 23, para 199, pg. 203-205, Hindi pg. 140
15. SN, *Bojjhaṅgasaṃyutta, Gilānavagga, sutta* 6 – *Tatiya Gilāna Sutta*, VRI Vol. 27, para 197, pg. 99, Hindi pg. 657
16. SN, *Devatāsaṃyutta, Satullapakāyikavagga, sutta* 8 - *Sakalika Sutta*, VRI Vol. 23, para 38, pg. 31, Hindi pg. 27
17. *Sutta* 16, VRI Vol. 2, para 163 onwards, pg. 77 onwards, Hindi pg. 129 onwards
18. *Sannyasta Khaḍga, Samagra Savarkar Vāṅgmaya,* Vol. 7, pg. 539-640, *Kavya-Nāṭaka* section, Pub. Shankar Ramchandra Date on behalf of Maharashtra Prantik Hindu Sabha Samagra Savarkar Vanmaya Prakashak Samiti, Tilak Smarak Mandir, Tilak Road, Pune 2; First ed. 1965, pg. 555
19. SN, *Indriyasaṃyutta, Jarāvagga, sutta* 1 - *Jarādhamma Sutta,* VRI Vol. 28, para 511, pg. 292-293, Hindi pg. 722
20. *Ahaṃ kho panānanda, etarahi jiṇṇo vuddho mahallako addhagato vayo-anuppatto. Āsītiko me vayo vattati. Seyyathāpi, Ānanda, jajjarasakataṃ veṭhamissakena yāpeti, evameva kho, Ānanda, veṭhamissakena maññe Tathāgatassa kāyo yāpeti.* DN, *Mahāparinibbāna Sutta,* final para in *Duitīyabhāṇavāra*, VRI Vol. 2, para 165, pg. 78, Hindi pg. 130
21. *'Siddhārtha uṭṭhāhi etasmā pallaṅkā, nāyaṃ tuyhaṃ pāpuṇāti, mayhaṃ eva pāpuṇāti'ti āha. ...Atha māro mahāpurisaṃ āha 'Siddhārtha, tuyhaṃ dānassa dinnabhāve ko sakkhī'ti. Mahāpuriso 'tuyhaṃ tāva dānassa dinnabhāve sacetana sakkhino, mayhaṃ pana imassamiṃ ṭhāne sacetano koci sakkhī nāma natthi, tiṭṭhatu tāva te avasesattabhāvesu dinnadānaṃ, vessantarattabhāve pana ṭhatva mayhaṃ sattasatakamahādānassa dinnabhāve ayaṃ acetanāpi ghanamahāpathavī sakkhī'ti cīvaragabbhantarto dakkhiṇahatthaṃ abhinīharitvā 'vessantarattabhāve ṭhatvā mayhaṃ sattasatakamahādānassa dinnabhāve tvaṃ sakkhī na sakkhī'ti mahāpathaviabhimukhaṃ hatthaṃ pasāresi. Mahāpathavī 'ahaṃ te tadā sakkhī'ti viravasatena viravasahassena viravasatasahassena mārabalaṃ avattharamānā viya unnadi.* JA, *Avidūrenidānakathā,* VRI Vol. 70, pg. 82-83

22. SN, *Mārasaṃyutta, tritīyavagga, sutta* 1 - *Sambahula Sutta,* VRI Vol. 23, para 157, pg. 139-140, Hindi pg. 101
23. Pub. Kaushalya Prakashan, N-11, C-3/24/3, HUDCO, Aurangabad; fourth ed. 28 January 2002, pg. 135
24. Pub. Justice R. R. Bhole for the People's Education Society. Anand Bhavan, Dadabhai Naoroji Road, Mumbai 400 023, second ed. 1974, pg. 2
25. *Tassa mayhaṃ, rājakumāra, etadahosi, 'abhijānāmi kho panāhaṃ pitu sakkassa kammante sītāya jambucchāyāya nissinno vivicceva kāmehi vivicca akusalehi dhammehi savitakkaṃ savicāraṃ vivekajaṃ pītisukhaṃ paṭhaṃ jhānaṃ upasampajja viharitā; siyā no kho eso maggo bodhāyā'ti.* MN, *Majjhimapaṇṇāsapāḷī, Rājavagga, sutta* 5 - *Bodhirājakumāra Sutta,* VRI Vol. 13, para 335, pg. 297
26. MN, *Mūlapaṇṇāsapāḷī, Māhāyamakavagga, sutta* 6 - *Mahāsaccaka Sutta,* VRI Vol. 12, para 381, pg. 315
27. JA, *Avidūrenidānakathā,* VRI Vol. 70, pg. 67-68
28. *Lalitavistāra* - ed. and Hindi trans. - Shantibhikshu Shastri, Pub. Uttar Pradesh Hindi Sansthan, Mahatma Gandhi Marg, Lucknow, 1992, *sloka* 324, pg. 266
29. Sanchi, Pub. Archaeological Survey of India, Government of India, 2003, pg. 48
30. Ajanta, Ed. Debala Mitra, Pub. Archaeological Survey of India, Government of India, Twelfth ed. 2003, pg. 53
31. *Brāhmaṇasaṃyutta, Upāsakavagga, sutta* 1, VRI Vol. 23, para 197, pg. 201-202, Hindi pg. 138-139
32. Ibid. *Bhagavān Buddha,* pg. 144
33. *Koṭiyaṃ niviṭṭhagehato paṭṭhāya sapadānaṃ piṇḍāya cari. ... ayaṃ, mahārāja, rājavaṃso nāma tava vaṃso, amhākaṃ pana dīpaṅkaro koṇḍañño... ...kassapoti ayaṃ buddhavaṃso nāma.* JA, *Santikenidānakathā,* VRI Vol. 70, pg. 95-99
34. SN, *Dutiyavagga, sutta* 5 - *Rāmaṇeyyaka Sutta,* VRI Vol. 23, para 261, pg. 269, Hindi pg. 183
35. *Agni Purāṇa,* 16. 1-4
36. *Bhāgavat Purāṇa,* 1.3; 1.3.24; 10.40.22
37. *Narasiṃha Purāṇa, Adhyāya* 36; 36.9; 53.67-68
38. *Harivansha,* 41.164
39. *Shri Vitthala: Ek Mahasamanvaya,* Pub. D. D. Kulkarni, Shrividya Prakashan, 250, Shaniwar Peth, Ashthabhuja Road, Pune 411 030, first ed. 1984, pg. 232-233
40. The Complete Works of Swami Vivekanand, Mayawati Memorial Ed. Vol. III, Pub. Advaita Ashram, Mayawati, Almora, Himalayas, Ninth ed. September 1964, pg. 528

41. *Buddha: Bhartiya Itihāsātīla Lokashāhī, Svātantrya va Samatecā Agnishrota;* Author Sharad Patil; Pub. Satish Pahurkar, Savitribai Phule Prakashan, Kala Maruti Chowk, Yeola; 25 December 1999, pg. 3
42. Osho on Buddha, Author / Pub. Swami Dhyan Sandesh (Adv. Sandesh Bhalekar), 746 Vaishali Nagar, Nagpur 440 017, first ed. 14th October 1998, pg. 16, 25
43. Ibid. *Bouddha Manishā,* pg. 12
44. The Satapancasatka of Matrceta; Sanskrit text, Tibetan trans. and commentary and Chinese translation; ed. D. R. Shackleton Bailey; with an introduction, English trans. and notes; Pub. The Syndics of the Cambridge University Press; 1951, *sloka* 112
45. *Opammasaṃyutta, sutta* 7, VRI Vol. 24, para 229, pg. 243, Hindi pg. 308
46. *Pahīnalābhasakkārā titthiyā lābhakāraṇā;*
sayaṃ kāsāyamādāya vasiṃsu saha bhikkhuhi. Mahāvaṃsa 5.229
Yathasakaṃ ca te vādaṃ 'buddhavado'ti dīpayuṃ;
yathāsakaṃ ca kiriyaṃ akariṃsu yathāruci. Mahāvaṃsa 5.230
'Kiṃvādī sugato, bhante!' iti pucchi mahīpati;
te sassatādikaṃ diṭṭhiṃ vyākariṃsu yathāsakaṃ. Mahāvaṃsa 5.269
Te micchādiṭṭhike sabbe rājā uppabbajāpayi;
sabbe saṭṭhisahassāni āsuṃ uppabbajāpitā. Mahāvaṃsa 5.270
Mahāvaṃsa, para 5, Pub. Bouddha Aakaar Granthmala, Mahatma Gandhi Kashi Vidyapeeth, Varanasi 2, first ed. 1996
47. *Abhāsitaṃ alapitaṃ tathāgatena bhāsitaṃ lapitaṃ tathāgatenāti dīpenti... bhāsitaṃ lapitaṃ tathāgatena abhāsitaṃ alapitaṃ tathāgatenāti dīpenti... anāciṇṇaṃ tathāgatena āciṇṇaṃ tathāgatenāti dīpenti... āciṇṇaṃ tathāgatena anāciṇṇaṃ tathāgatenāti dīpenti... apaññattaṃ tathāgatena paññattaṃ tathāgatenāti dīpenti... paññattaṃ tathāgatena apaññattaṃ tathāgatenāti dīpenti te, bhikkhave, bhikkhū bahujanaahitāya paṭipannā bahujanaasukhāya, bahuno janassa anatthāya ahitāya dukkhāya devamanussānaṃ. Bahuñca te, bhikkhave, bhikkhū apuññaṃ pasavanti, te cimaṃ saddhammaṃ antaradhāpentī"ti. Ekakanipāta, Dutiyapamādādivagga,* VRI Vol. 35, para 132-139, pg. 25, Marathi Part 1, pg. 25
48. *Idha, bhikkhave, bhikkhu evaṃ vadeyya – 'sammukhā metaṃ, āvuso, bhagavato sutaṃ sammukhā paṭiggahitaṃ – ayaṃ dhammo, ayaṃ vinayo, idaṃ satthusāsana'nti. Tassa, bhikkhave, bhikkhuno bhāsitaṃ neva abhinanditabbaṃ nappaṭikkositabbaṃ. Anabhinanditvā appaṭikkositvā tāni padabyañjanāni sādhukaṃ uggahetvā sutte otāretabbāni, vinaye sandassetabbāni. Tāni ce sutte otāriyamānāni vinaye sandassiyamānāni na ceva sutte otaranti na vinaye sandissanti, niṭṭhamettha gantabbaṃ – 'addhā, idaṃ na ceva*

tassa bhagavato vacanaṃ arahato sammāsambuddhassa; imassa ca bhikkhuno duggahita'nti. Iti hetaṃ, bhikkhave, chaḍḍeyyātha. AN, *Catukkanipāta, Sañcetaniyavagga, sutta* 10 - *Mahāpadesa Sutta,* VRI Vol. 36, para 180, pg. 194

49. *Dveme, bhikkhave, tathāgataṃ abbhācikkhanti. Katame dve? Yo ca neyyatthaṃ suttantaṃ nītattho suttantoti dīpeti, yo ca nītatthaṃ suttantaṃ neyyattho suttantoti dīpeti. Ime kho, bhikkhave, dve tathāgataṃ abbhācikkhantī"ti. Dukanipātapāḷi, Bālavagga,* VRI Vol. 35, para 25, pg. 76
50. Ibid. *Bhagavān Buddha,* pg. 20, 24, 24
51. Vin, Hindi trans. *Bhūmikā*, pg. 7
52. *Buddhacaryyā,* Pub. Bhartiya Bouddha Samiti, Lucknow, third ed. 1995, *Bhūmikā,* pg. 6
53. Sākya Or Buddhist Origins, by Mrs Rhys Davids, Pub. Oriental Books Reprint Corporation, 54 Rani Jhansi Road, New Delhi 110 055; first Indian ed. 1978, originally Pub. 1928, pg. 3

Chapter 2

54. *Sutta* 14, VRI Vol. 2, para 53, pg. 22, Hindi pg. 103
55. Ibid. *Bhagavān Buddha,* pg. 104-105
56. MN, *Majjhimapaṇṇāsapāḷī, Rājavagga, sutta* 5 - *Bodhirājakumāra Sutta,* VRI Vol. 13, para 324-346, pg. 287-307, Hindi pg. 347-355
57. *Aṭṭhakavagga, sutta* 15, VRI Vol. 48, v. 941-944, pg. 219-220; *Phandamānaṃ pajaṃ disvā, macche appodake yathā; aññamaññehi byāruddhe, disvā maṃ bhayamāvisi.* (v. 942)
58. Ibid. *Bhagavān Buddha,* pg. 105
59. MN, *Mūlapaṇṇāsapāḷī, Mahāyamakavagga, sutta* 6 - *Mahāsaccaka Sutta,* VRI Vol. 12, para 371, pg. 306, Hindi pg. 148
60. VRI Vol. 48, v. 407-408, pg. 143
61. MN, *Mūlapaṇṇāsapāḷī, Opammavagga, sutta* 6 - *Pāsarāsi Sutta,* VRI Vol. 12, para 272-287, pg. 219-235, Hindi pg. 103-111
62. Ibid. *Bhagavān Buddha,* pg. 107
63. Ibid. *Bhagavān Buddha,* pg. 105-106
64. *Bodhisattva,* Hindi trans. and ed. Kasturmal Bantiya and Jamnalal Jain, Pub. Kendriya Uccha Tibeti Shiksha Sansthan, Sarnath, Varanasi, first ed. 2001, pg. 38, 39, 41
65. Ibid. *Bodhisattva,* Preface pg. 14
66. SN, *Mārasaṃyutta, vagga* 3, *sutta* 5 - *Māradhītu Sutta,* VRI Vol. 23, para 161, pg. 146-150, Hindi pg. 106
67. *Bhagavān Buddha aur Unka Dharma,* Hindi trans. by Bhadant Anand Kausalyayan of Dr. Babasaheb Ambedkar's The Buddha and His Dhamma, Pub. Buddhabhumi Prakashan, Nagpur, 1997, *Namra Nivedana*, pg. 14

68. *Pañcakanipāta, vagga* 20 - *Brahmaṇavagga, sutta* 6 - *Mahāsupina Sutta,* VRI Vol. 37, para 196, pg. 220-222, Hindi Part 2, pg. 425-427
69. Ibid. *Bhagavān Buddha aur Unka Dharma, Namra Nivedana*, pg. 14
70. Ibid. *Bhagavān Buddha,* pg. 98
71. Ibid. *Bhagavān Buddha,* pg. 110
72. JA, *Avidūrenidānakathā,* VRI Vol. 70, pg. 70
73. What Buddhists Believe, reprinted and donated by The Corporate Body of the Buddha Educational Foundation, Taiwan, fifth ed. 1993, pg. 9
74. MN, *Mūlapaṇṇāsapāḷī, Sīhanādavagga, sutta* 2, VRI Vol. 12, para 146-162, pg. 99-117, Hindi pg. 45-53
75. *Rathakāravagga, sutta* 5 - *Sacetana Sutta,* VRI Vol. 35, para 15, pg. 134-136
76. SN, *Nidānasaṃyutta, Āhāravagga, sutta* 1 - VRI Vol. 24, para 11, pg. 12-13, Hindi pg. 198
77. SN, *Dutiyavagga, sutta* 1 - *Pāsāṇa Sutta,* VRI Vol. 23, para 147, pg. 130, Hindi pg. 95
78. *Yakkhasaṃyutta, sutta* 3, VRI Vol. 23, para 237, pg. 239-240, Hindi pg. 164-165
79. JA, *Avidūrenidānakathā,* VRI Vol. 70, pg. 77-79
80. JA, *Avidūrenidānakathā,* VRI Vol. 70, pg. 80
81. Ibid. pg. 10
82. *Vippassanāni kho te, āvuso, indriyāni, parisuddho, chavivaṇṇo, pariyodāto.* Vin, *Mahāvagga, Mahākhandaka,* VRI Vol. 89, para 11, pg. 11, Hindi pg. 79
83. *Devatāsaṃyutta, Sattivagga, sutta* 6 - *Pajjota Sutta,* VRI Vol. 23, para 26, pg. 17-18, Hindi pg. 16
84. *Catukkanipāta, vagga* 15 - *Ābhāvagga, sutta* 1 - *Ābhā Sutta* and next four suttas, VRI Vol. 36, para 141-145, pg. 160-161, Hindi Part 2, pg. 135
85. *Avyāpāritasādhustvaṃ tvam akāraṇavatsalaḥ; asanstutasakashca tvam anavaskritabāndhavaḥ.* Ibid. *sloka* 11
86. *Akritvā-īshyrāṃ vishishṭeshu hīnān anavamatya ca; agatvā sadrishaiḥ spardhāṃ tvaṃ loke shreshṭhatāṃ gataḥ.* Ibid. *sloka* 27
87. Original Sanskrit Ed. CE 1974, present ed. with Hindi trans. 1988, Pub. Kendriya Bouddha Vidya Sansthan, Choglamsar, Leh-Ladakh, sarg. 2, *sloka* 2

Chapter 3

88. *Uparipaṇṇāsapāḷī, Anupadavagga, sutta* 2 - *Chabbisodhana Sutta,* VRI Vol. 14, para 98, pg. 78, Hindi pg. 471
89. *Yā kācimā duggatiyo, asmiṃ loke paramhi ca; avijjāmūlikā sabbā, icchālobhasamussayā. Dukanipāta, sutta* 3, VRI Vol. 48, para 40, pg. 26

90. AN, *Ekakanipāta, Kalyāṇamittādivagga,* VRI Vol. 35, para 76-80, pg. 18, Marathi Part 1, pg. 19
91. *Tikanipāta, Puggalavagga, Samiddha Sutta,* VRI Vol. 35, para 21, pg. 141-143, Marathi Part 1, pg. 143-145
92. *Etha tumhe, kālāmā, mā anussavena, mā paramparāya, mā itikirāya, mā piṭakasampadānena, mā takkahetu, mā nayahetu, mā ākāraparivitakkena , mā diṭṭhinijjhānakkhantiyā, mā bhabbarūpatāya, mā samaṇo no garūti. Yadā tumhe, kālāmā, attanāva jāneyyātha – 'ime dhammā akusalā, ime dhammā sāvajjā, ime dhammā viññugarahitā, ime dhammā samattā samādinnā ahitāya dukkhāya saṃvattantī'ti, atha tumhe, kālāmā, pajaheyyātha. Tikanipāta, Mahāvagga, sutta* 5, VRI Vol. 35, para 66, pg. 216-222, Marathi Part 1, pg. 209-214
93. Ibid. What the Buddha Taught, pg. 2
94. AN, Hindi trans. Part 2, Pub. Mahabodhi Sabha, Kolkata, 1963
95. *Bhagavā etadavoca – "vīmaṃsakena, bhikkhave, bhikkhunā parassa cetopariyāyaṃ ajānantena tathāgate samannesanā kātabbā 'sammāsambuddho vā no vā' iti viññāṇāyā"ti. Mūlapaṇṇāsapāḷī, Cūḷayamakavagga, sutta* 7, VRI Vol. 12, para 487-490, pg. 399-402, Hindi pg. 191-192
96. AN, *Chakkanipāta, Mahāvagga, sutta* 6 - *Hatthisāriputta Sutta,* VRI Vol. 38, para 60, pg. 100-105, Hindi Part 3, pg. 93-94
97. *Majjhimapaṇṇāsapāḷī, Brāhmaṇavagga, sutta* 10, VRI Vol. 13, para 473-474, pg. 433-445, Hindi pg. 424-426
98. *Buddhacarita* 9.73-74
99. *Mālavikāgnimitra* 1.2
100. MN, *Majjhimapaṇṇāsapāḷī, Brāhmaṇavagga, sutta* 5 - *Caṅki Sutta,* VRI Vol. 13, para 422-435, pg. 383-394, Hindi pg. 395-402
101. *Maharashtriya Dnyānakosha, Prastāvanākhaṇḍa,* section 4, *Buddhottara Jaga*, Pub. Shridar Venkatesh Ketkar on behalf of Maharashtriya Nyanakosh Mandal Ltd., Nagpur, 841, Sadashiv Peth, Pune, 1923, pg. 153-154
102. *Sutta* 13, VRI Vol. 1, para 518-559, pg. 214-227, Hindi pg. 86-92
103. Ibid. *Buddhottara Jaga*, pg. 154
104. DN, VRI Vol. 1, para 1-6, pg. 1-3, Hindi pg. 1-2
105. *Ahitāvahite śatrou tvaṃ hitāvihitaḥ suhṛd; doṣānveṣaṇanityepi guṇānveṣaṇatatparaḥ. Yato nimantraṇaṃ tebhūt saviṣaṃ sahutāśanaṃ*; *tatrābhūd abhisaṃyānaṃ sadayaṃ sāmritaṃ ca te.* Ibid. sloka *120-121*
106. *Sutta* 28, VRI Vol. 3, para 141-163, pg. 73-86, Hindi pg. 246-251
107. *Mahāvagga, sutta* 4 - Sarabha Sutta, VRI Vol. 35, para 65, pg. 123-216, Marathi Part 1, pg. 206-209
108. AN, *Catukkanipāta, Mahāvagga, sutta* 5 - *Vappa Sutta*, VRI Vol. 35, para 195, pg. 227, Hindi, pg. 189

109. DN, *Sutta* 16, VRI Vol. 2, para 212-215, pg. 112-115, Hindi pg. 144-146
110. *Ākaṅkhamāno, Ānanda, saṅgho mamaccayena khuddānukhuddakāni sikkhhāpadāni samūhaneyyā'ti.* VRI Vol. 90, para 441-444, pg. 456-458
111. Marathi trans. Dr. A. H. Salunkhe, Pub. Maharashtra Rajya Sahitya ani Sanskriti Mandal, Mumbai, first ed. 1988

Chapter 4

112. *Yo kho, Vakkhali, dhammaṃ passati so maṃ passati; yo maṃ passati so dhammaṃ passati. Khandasaṃyutta, vagga* 9 - Theravagga, *sutta* 5, VRI Vol. 25, para 87, pg. 108-110, Hindi pg. 373-374
113. *Tassa mayhaṃ, bhikkhave, etadahosi, 'yaṃnūnāhaṃ yvāyaṃ dhammo mayā abhisambuddho tameva dhammaṃ sakkatvā garuṃ katvā upanissāya vihareyya'nti. Catukkanipāta, vagga 3 - Uruvelāvagga, sutta 1 - PaṭhamaUruvelā Sutta,* VRI Vol. 36, para 24-26, Hindi Part 2, pg. 20-22
114. *Paṭisotagāmiṃ nipuṇaṃ, gambhīraṃ duddasaṃ aṇuṃ; rāgarattā na dakkhanti, tamokhandhena āvuṭā'ti.* Vin, *Mahāvagga, Khanda* 1 - *Mahākhandaka, Brahmayācanākathā, Ajapālakathā,* VRI Vol. 89, para 7-9, pg.5-10, Hindi pg. 77-78
115. *Sutta* 12, VRI Vol. 1, para 501-517, pg. 205-213, Hindi pg. 82-85
116. It, *Catukkanipāta, sutta* 10 - *Nadisota Sutta,* VRI Vol. 48, para 109, pg. 80-81
117. *Saḷāyatanavaggapāḷī, Gāmaṇisaṃyutta, sutta* 7, VRI Vol. 26, para 359, pg. 301-303, Hindi pg. 583-584
118. *Viduṣāṃ prītijananaṃ madhyānāṃ buddhivardhanam; timiraghnaṃ ca mandānāṃ sārvajanyam idaṃ vacaḥ. Mātṛceṭakṛta Ibid. sloka 78*
119. *Ete kho, bhikkhave, ubho ante anupagamma, majjhimā paṭipadā tathāgatena abhisambuddhā, cakkhukaraṇī ñāṇakaraṇī upasamāya abhiññāya sambodhāya nibbānāya saṃvattati.* Vin, *Mahāvagga, Khaanda* 1 - *Mahākhandaka, Pañcavaggiyakathā, Ajapālakathā,* VRI Vol. 89, para 13, pg.13, Hindi pg. 80-81
120. *Tikanipāta, vagga* 3, *Puggalavagga, sutta* 1 - Samiddha Sutta, VRI Vol. 35, para 21, pg. 141-143, Marathi Part 1, pg. 143-145
121. *Catukkanipāta, vagga* 24 - *Kammavagga, sutta* 3, VRI Vol. 36, para 234, pg. 267-268, Hindi Part 2, pg. 221-227
122. *Dukanipātapāḷi, vagga* 4 - *Samcittavagga,* VRI Vol. 35, para 35, pg. 78-79, Marathi Part 1, pg. 79
123. DN, *Sutta* 22, VRI Vol. 2, para 402, pg. 233-235, Hindi pg. 197-198
124. DN, *Sutta* 18, VRI Vol. 2, para 289-290, pg. 159-160, Hindi pg. 165

125. SN, *Maggasaṃyutta, Avijjāvagga, sutta* 6 - *Paṭhama - Anyatarabhikkhu Sutta,* VRI Vol. 27, para 6, pg. 7-8, Hindi Part 3, pg. 622
126. SN, *Maggasaṃyutta, Paṭipattivagga, sutta* 5 - *Paṭhama-sāmañña Sutta,* VRI Vol. 27, para 35, pg. 23, Hindi Part 3, pg. 631
127. Ibid. What Buddhist Believe, pg. 80
128. KN, *Khuddakapāṭhapāḷī, sutta* 5, VRI Vol. 47, pg. 4-5
129. SN, *Maggasaṃyutta, Avijjāvagga, sutta* 4 - *Jāṇussoṇibrāhmaṇa Sutta*, VRI Vol. 27, para 4, pg. 4-6, Hindi, pg. 620-621
130. *Iti imasmiṃ sati idaṃ hoti, imassuppādā idaṃ uppajjati.... Iti imasmiṃ asati idaṃ na hoti, imassa nirodhā idaṃ nirujjhati. Udānapāḷī, Bodhivagga,* first three verses, VRI Vol. 47, para 1-3, pg. 69-71
131. DN, *sutta* 15 - *Mahānidāna Sutta,* VRI Vol. 2, para 95, pg. 43, Hindi pg. 110
132. Ibid. *Bhagavān Buddha,* pg. 126-127
133. Ibid. *Bhagavān Buddha,* pg. 270
134. Ibid. *Bhagavān Buddha, Āmukha*, pg. 13
135. *Kyā Buddha Dukkhavādī The?* Pub. VRI, Dhamma Giri, Igatpuri, Dist. Nashik, 422 403, third ed. 2001, pg. 16
136. MN, *Mūlapaṇṇāsapāḷī, Mūlapariyāyavagga, sutta* 4 - *Bhayabherava Sutta,* VRI Vol. 12, para 55, pg. 29, Hindi pg. 16
137. MN, *Mūlapaṇṇāsapāḷī, Mūlapariyāyavagga, sutta* 6 - *Ākaṅkheyya Sutta,* VRI Vol. 12, para 66, pg. 42, Hindi pg. 22
138. MN, *Mūlapaṇṇāsapāḷī, Mūlapariyāyavagga, sutta* 8 - *Sallekha Sutta,* VRI Vol. 12, para 81-82, pg. 51-53, Hindi pg. 28
139. Ibid. *Kyā Buddha Dukkhavādī The?* pg. 46-47
140. To Have Or To Be? An Abacus Book, Reprint 1999, pg. 165-166
141. Ibid. pg. 17
142. SN, *Bhikkhusaṃyutta, sutta* 7 - *Visākha Sutta,* VRI Vol. 24, para 241, pg. 253-254, Hindi pg. 314
143. *Dukanipāta, vagga* 13 - *Dānavagga,* VRI Vol. 35, para 142-143, pg. 110, Marathi Part 1, pg. 108
144. Dp, *vagga* 24 - *Taṇhāvagga,* VRI Vol. 47, v. 354, pg. 57
145. *Sutta* 27, VRI Vol. 3, para 111-118, pg. 59-62, Hindi pg. 240-241
146. *Desito, ānanda, mayā dhammo anantaraṃ abāhiraṃ karitvā. Natthānanda, tathāgatassa dhammesu ācariyamuṭṭhi. Yassa nūna, ānanda, evamassa – 'ahaṃ bhikkhusaṅghaṃ pariharissāmī'ti vā 'mamuddesiko bhikkhusaṅgho'ti vā, so nūna, ānanda, bhikkhusaṅghaṃ ārabbha kiñcideva udāhareyya. Tathāgatassa kho, ānanda, na evaṃ hoti – 'ahaṃ bhikkhusaṅghaṃ pariharissāmī'ti vā 'mamuddesiko bhikkhusaṅgho'ti vā.* DN, *sutta* 16, *Mahāparinibbāna Sutta*, VRI Vol. 2, para 165, pg. 78, Hindi pg. 130

147. *Abhijānāmi kho panāhaṃ, aggivessana, anekasatāya parisāya dhammaṃ desetā. Apissu maṃ ekameko evaṃ maññati – 'mamevārabbha samaṇo gotamo dhammaṃ desetī'ti.* MN, *Mūlapaṇṇāsapāḷī, Māhāyamakavagga, sutta* 6 - *Mahāsaccaka Sutta,* VRI Vol. 12, para 387, pg. 317, Hindi pg. 149
148. AN, *Catukkanipāta, vagga* 14 - *Puggalavagga, sutta* 9 - *Dhammakathika Sutta,* VRI Vol. 36, para 139, pg. 158, Hindi Part 2, pg. 134
149. SN, *Kassapasaṃyutta, sutta* 3 - *Candūpama Sutta,* VRI Vol. 24, para 146, pg. 177-178, Hindi pg. 277-278
150. MN, *Majjhimapaṇṇāsapāḷī, Parivrājakavagga, sutta* 7 - *Mahāsakuludāyi Sutta,* VRI Vol. 13, para 240, pg. 206-207, Hindi pg. 309
151. MN, *sutta* 39, *Majjhimapaṇṇāsapāḷī, Rājavagga, sutta* 9 - *Dhammacetiya Sutta,* VRI Vol. 13, para 370, pg. 331, Hindi pg. 368-369
152. DN, *sutta* 33, VRI Vol. 3, para 302, pg. 168, Hindi pg. 282
153. AN, *Navakanipāta, vagga* 1 - *Sambodhivagga, sutta* 4 - *Nandaka Sutta,* VRI Vol. 39, para 4, pg. 180-181, Hindi Part 4, pg. 9-10
154. AN, *Pancakanipāta, vagga* 21 - *Kimilavagga, sutta* 2 - *Dhammassavana Sutta,* VRI Vol. 37, para 202, pg. 227-228, Hindi Part 2, pg. 431
155. AN, *Catukkanipāta, vagga* 16, *Indriyavagga, sutta* 10 - *Sugatavinaya Sutta,* VRI Vol. 36, para 160, pg. 169-171, Hindi Part 2, pg. 141
156. AN, *Pancakanipāta, vagga* 21 - *Kimilavagga, sutta* 1, VRI Vol. 37, para 201, pg. 227, Hindi Part 2, pg. 430-431
157. *...na tāva jātarūpassa antaradhānaṃ hoti yāva na jātarūpappatirūpakaṃ loke uppajjati. Yato ca kho, kassapa, jātarūpappatirūpakaṃ loke uppajjati, atha jātarūpassa antaradhānaṃ hoti. Evameva kho, kassapa, na tāva saddhammassa antaradhānaṃ hoti yāva na saddhammappatirūpakaṃ loke uppajjati. Yato ca kho, kassapa, saddhammappatirūpakaṃ loke uppajjati, atha saddhammassa antaradhānaṃ hoti.*
Na kho, kassapa, pathavīdhātu saddhammaṃ antaradhāpeti, na āpodhātu saddhammaṃ antaradhāpeti, na tejodhātu saddhammaṃ antaradhāpeti, na vāyodhātu saddhammaṃ antaradhāpeti; atha kho idheva te uppajjanti moghapurisā ye imaṃ saddhammaṃ antaradhāpenti. Seyyathāpi, kassapa, nāvā ādikeneva opilavati; na kho, kassapa, evaṃ saddhammassa antaradhānaṃ hoti.
Kassapasaṃyutta, sutta 13 - *Saddhammappatirūpaka Sutta*, VRI Vol. 24, para 156, pg. 203-204, Hindi Part 1, pg. 285-286
158. VRI Vol. 30, pg. 179

159. *Dhammadāyādā me, bhikkhave, bhavatha, mā āmisadāyādā.* MN, *Mūlapaṇṇāsapāḷī, Mūlapariyāyavagga, sutta* 3 - *Dhammadāyāda Sutta,* VRI Vol. 12, para 29-30, pg. 17-18, Hindi pg. 10-11
160. Ibid. *Sannyasta Khaḍga,* pg. 585
161. DN, *Pāthikavagga, sutta* 3 - *Cakkavatti Sutta,* VRI Vol. 3, para 80, pg. 42, Hindi pg. 233
162. MN, *Uparipaṇṇāsapāḷī, Devadahavagga, sutta* 8 - *Gopakamoggallāna Sutta,* VRI Vol. 14, para 79-82, pg. 56-60, Hindi pg. 457-461
163. *Saḷāyatanavaggapāḷī, vagga* 19 - *Āsīvisavagga, sutta* 1 - *Āsīvisopama Sutta,* VRI Vol. 26, para 238, pg. 176-179, Hindi pg. 522-523
164. MN, *vagga* 4 - *Māhāyamakavagga, sutta* 8 - *Mahāmaṇhāsaṅkhaya Sutta,* VRI Vol. 12, para 401, pg. 330-331, Hindi pg. 156
165. MN, *Mūlapaṇṇāsapāḷī, vagga* 3 - *Opammavagga, sutta* 2 - *Alagaddūpama Sutta,* VRI Vol. 12, para 240, pg. 188-189, Hindi pg. 87-88
166. MN, *Mūlapaṇṇāsapāḷī, Opammavagga, sutta* 4, VRI Vol. 12, para 252-260, pg. 201-208, Hindi pg. 95-98
167. *Tumhehi kiccamātappaṃ, akkhātāro tathāgātā.* v. 276, *vagga* 20 - *Maggavagga,* VRI Vol. 47, pg. 48
168. SN, *Khandhasaṃyutta, vagga* 5 - *Attadīpavagga,* VRI Vol. 25, para 43, pg. 39-41, Hindi pg. 341
169. SN, *Sāgāthāvaggapāḷī, Kosalasaṃyutta, vagga* 1, *sutta* 5, VRI Vol. 23, para 116, pg. 89-90, Hindi pg. 70
170. *Saḷāyatanavaggapāḷī, saṃyutta* 8 - *Gāmaṇisaṃyutta, sutta* 6 - *Asibandhakaputta Sutta,* VRI Vol. 26, para 358, pg. 299-301, Hindi pg. 582-583
171. DN, *sutta* 29, *Pāthikavagga, sutta* 6 - *Pāsādika Sutta,* VRI Vol. 3, para 186, pg. 99, Hindi pg. 257
172. *Jīranti ve rājarathā sucittā, atho sarīrampi jaraṃ upeti. Satañca dhammo na jaraṃ upeti...* SN, *Sāgāthāvaggapāḷī, Kosalasaṃyutta, vagga* 1, *sutta* 3 - *Jarāmaraṇa Sutta*, VRI Vol. 23, para 114, pg. 87, Hindi pg. 69

Chapter 5

173. MN, *Mūlapaṇṇāsapāḷī, Opammavagga, sutta* 30 - *Cūlasāropama Sutta,* VRI Vol. 12, para 312, pg. 261, Hindi pg. 125
174. KN, *Udānapāḷī, vagga* 6 - *Jātyandhavagga, sutta* 4 - *Paṭhama Nānātithīrya Sutta,* VRI Vol. 47, para 54, pg. 145-148
175. MN, *Mūlapaṇṇāsapāḷī, Opammavagga, sutta* 2 - *Alagaddupama Sutta,* VRI Vol. 12, para 242-243, pg. 189-191, Hindi pg. 88-90

176. MN, *Uparipaṇṇāsapāḷī, Saḷāyatanavagga, sutta* 5 - *Cūḷarāhulovāda Sutta,* VRI Vol. 14, para 416-419, pg. 334-336, Hindi pg. 597-598
177. SN, *Bhikkhunīsaṃyutta, sutta* 10 - *Vajirā Sutta,* VRI Vol. 23, para 171, pg. 160-161, Hindi pg. 113
178. *Ekakanipāta, Aṭṭhānapāḷī, vagga* 1, VRI Vol. 35, para 270, pg. 38, Marathi Part 1, pg. 38
179. AN, *Catukkanipāta, Rohitassavagga, sutta* 9 - *Vipallāsa Sutta,* VRI Vol. 36, para 49, pg. 59-60, Hindi pg. 53-54
180. *Mūlapaṇṇāsapāḷī, Cūḷyamakavagga, sutta* 9 - *Brahmanimantanika Sutta*, VRI Vol. 12, para 501-513, pg. 409-424, Hindi pg. 196-199
181. AN, *Chakkanipāta, Sītivagga, sutta* 9 - *Dutiya-abhabbaṭṭhāna Sutta,* VRI Vol. 38, para 93, pg. 139, Hindi Part 3, pg. 128
182. AN, *Dasakanipāta, Sacittavagga, sutta* 10 - *Girimānanda Sutta,* VRI Vol. 40, para 60, pg. 91, Hindi Part 4, pg. 173
183. DN, *sutta* 9 - *Poṭṭhapāda Sutta,* VRI Vol. 1, para 425-427, pg. 170-173, Hindi pg. 72-73
184. SN, *Saḷāyatanasaṃyutta, vagga* 9 - *Channavagga, sutta* 2, *Suññataloka Sutta,* VRI Vol. 26, para 85, pg. 60, Hindi pg. 495
185. SN, *Nidānavaggapāḷī, Nidānasaṃyutta, vagga* 7 - *Mahāvagga, sutta* 1 - *Assutavā Sutta,* VRI Vol. 24, para 61, pg. 83-85, Hindi pg. 233
186. *Bouddha Darshan,* author - Rahul Sankrityayan, Pub. Kitab Mahal, 15, Tharnhill Road, Allahabad, first ed. 1943, seventh reprint 1989, pg. 35-37
187. Ibid. *Bouddha Manishā,* pg. 483
188. *Evaṃ vutte, ahaṃ, mahānāma, te nigaṇṭhe etadavocaṃ – 'kiṃ pana tumhe, āvuso nigaṇṭhā, jānātha – ahuvamheva mayaṃ pubbe na nāhuvamhā'ti?* MN, *Mūlapaṇṇāsapāḷī, Sīhanādavagga, sutta* 4, *Cūḷadukkhakkhandha Sutta,* VRI Vol. 12, para 180, pg. 130, Hindi pg. 60
189. *Tena kho pana samayena sātissa nāma bhikkhuno kevaṭṭaputtassa evarūpaṃ pāpakaṃ diṭṭhigataṃ uppannaṃ hoti – "tathāhaṃ bhagavatā dhammaṃ desitaṃ ājānāmi yathā tadevidaṃ viññāṇaṃ sandhāvati saṃsarati anañña"nti.*
Kassa nu kho nāma tvaṃ, moghapurisa, mayā evaṃ dhammaṃ desitaṃ ājānāsi? Nanu mayā, moghapurisa, anekapariyāyena paṭiccasamuppannaṃ viññāṇaṃ vuttaṃ, aññatra paccayā natthi viññāṇassa sambhavoti? Atha ca pana tvaṃ, moghapurisa, attanā duggahitena amhe ceva abbhācikkhasi, attānañca khaṇasi, bahuñca apuññaṃ pasavasi. Tañhi te, moghapurisa, bhavissati dīgharattaṃ ahitāya dukkhāyā'ti. ... MN, *Mūlapaṇṇāsapāḷi, Mahāyamakavagga,* VRI Vol. 12, para 396-414, pg. 325-342, Hindi pg. 153-162
190. SN, *Saḷāyatanavaggapāḷī, saṃyutta* 10, *Abyākatasaṃyutta, sutta* 9, *Kutūhalasāla Sutta* VRI Vol. 26, para 418, pg. 363-365, Hindi pg. 613-614

191. MN, *Mūlapaṇṇāsapāḷī, Yakkhasaṃyutta, sutta* 1, VRI Vol. 23, para 235, pg. 238, Hindi pg. 164
192. AN, *Tikanipāta, Rathakāravagga, sutta* 8, VRI Vol. 35, para 18, pg. 137, Marathi Part 1, pg. 139
193. MN, *Majjhimapaṇṇāsapāḷī, Bhikkhuvagga, sutta* 3 - *Cūḷamāluṅkya Sutta,* VRI Vol. 13, para 122-128, pg. 97-102, Hindi pg. 253-255
194. *Sanskriti ke Char Adyaya,* Pub. Lokbharati Prakashan, 15 A, Mahatma Gandhi Marg, Allahabad 1, reprint 1993, pg. 176
195. Ibid. pg. 177, 179
196. *Kassapasaṃyutta, sutta* 12, VRI Vol. 24, para 155, pg. 202-203, Hindi pg. 285
197. SN, *Nidānavaggapāḷī, Nidānasaṃyutta, Āhāravagga, sutta* 5 - *Kaccānagotta Sutta,* VRI Vol. 24, para 15, pg. 17-18, Hindi pg. 200-201
198. *Abyākatasaṃyutta, sutta* 10, VRI Vol. 26, para 419, pg. 365-366, Hindi pg. 614
199. Ibid. pg. 63
200. *Pṛṣṭenāpi kvacin noktaṃ upetyāpi kathā kṛtā; tarṣayitvā paratroktaṃ kālāśayavidā tvayā. Bahūni bahurūpāṇi vacānsi caritāni ca; vineyāśayabhedena tatra tatra gatāni te.* Ibid. *sloka* 127, 130
201. AN, *Catukkanipāta, Rohitassavagga, sutta* 2 - *Praśravyākaraṇa Sutta,* VRI Vol. 36, para 42, pg. 52-53, Hindi Part 2 pg. 46
202. AN, *Catukkanipāta, Puggalavagga, sutta* 2 – *Paṭibhāna Sutta,* VRI Vol. 36, para 132, pg. 154, Hindi Part 2, pg. 132
203. MN, *Majjhimapaṇṇāsapāḷī, Paribrājakavagga, sutta* 2 - *Aggivaccha Sutta,* VRI Vol. 13, para 187-192, pg. 160-166, Hindi pg. 284-286
204. AN, *Sattakanipātapāḷī, Abyākatavagga, sutta* 1 - *Abyākata Sutta,* VRI Vol. 38, para 54, pg. 211-212, Hindi Part 3, pg. 88-89
205. DN, *sutta* 9 - *Poṭṭhapāda Sutta,* VRI Vol. 1, para 420, pg. 166-167, Hindi pg. 71
206. *Tikanipātapāḷī, Mahāvagga, sutta* 1 - *Titthāyatanādi Sutta,* VRI Vol. 35, para 62, pg. 202-206, Marathi Part 1, pg. 196-200
207. *Swami Vivekanand Grantavali - Sancayan;* lecture given in Detroit, USA, Pub. Swami Vyomarupanand, President, Ramkrishna Mutt, Dhantoli, Nagpur 440 012, 27 May 1988, pg. 242-244
208. SN, *Khandhavaggapāḷī, Khandhasaṃyutta, sutta* 3 - *Anicca Sutta,* VRI Vol. 25, para 45, pg. 41-42, Hindi pg. 342
209. SN, *Saḷāyatanavaggapāḷī, Saḷāyatanasaṃyutta, sutta* 7 - *Udāyī Sutta,* VRI Vol. 26, para 234, pg. 170-172, Hindi pg. 519-520
210. *Yo kho, āvuso, rāgakkhayo dosakkhayo mohakkhayo-idaṃ vucchati nibbāna'nti. Jambukhādakasaṃyutta, sutta* 1 - *Nibbānapañhā Sutta,* VRI Vol. 26, para 314, pg. 246, Hindi pg. 559

211. SN, *Sāmanḍakasaṃyutta, sutta* 1 - *Sāmanḍaka Sutta,* VRI Vol. 26, para 330, pg. 255, Hindi pg. 563
212. *Bouddha Sanskriti,* first ed. 1952, reprint Pub. Kaushalya Prakashan, N 11, C 3 / 24 / 3, HUDCO, Aurangabad 431 003,pg. 24
213. AN, *Dasakanipāta, Upālivagga, sutta* 5 - *Uttiya Sutta,* VRI Vol. 40, para 95, pg. 164-166, Hindi Part 4, pg. 240-242
214. SN, *Khandhavaggapāḷī, Khandhasaṃyutta, Pupphavagga, sutta* 2 - *Puppha Sutta,* VRI Vol. 25, para 94, pg. 125-126, Hindi pg. 381

Chapter 6

215. *sutta* 29, VRI Vol. 3, para 178-181, pg. 95-96, Hindi pg. 255-256
216. *Dukanipāta, Adhikaraṇavagga,* VRI Vol. 35, para 20-21, pg. 75, Marathi Part 1 Bālavagga, pg. 15
217. *Sahassampi ce vācā, anatthapadasaṃhitā;*
ekaṃ atthapadaṃ seyyo, yaṃ sutvā upasammati. Vagga 8 - *Sahassavagga,* VRI Vol. 47, v. 100, pg. 26
218. We know that archaeological excavation often lead to finds that have remained unknown for thousands of years such as rich culture of Mohanjodaro and Harappa. Often we find that in the life of an individual or family or society remains of hundreds or thousands of years' old culture unknown to us. My wife's name was Sirama (Shirama). Until last generation, we find this name of women especially in rural area. I was curious about the etymology of this word. A Marathi word that is close to this one is Shrimanti (affluence). I used to feel that Sirama must be a form of this word. But I used to feel the etymology somewhat far-fetched, even artificial. Recently, I read that they have found a statue of a Buddhist deity named Sirima in Barhut in Rajasthana near a Buddhist stupa. I also saw the photograph of that statue. Now that statue is in Indian Museum of Kolkata. I realized that Sirama didn't originate from Shrimanti but from Sirima. This means that at one time, in our society Sirima was a prestigious deity and that impression continued unknowingly for hundreds of years in the flow of the culture in our society. If wewant to know ourselves we must thus dig deep inside our cultural heritage. Reference for Sirima deity. –The Way of the Buddha, Pub. By The Director, Publications Division, Ministry of Information and Broadcasting, Government of India, Old Secretariat, Delhi-8; on the occasion of the 2500th Anniversary of the Mahaparinirvana of Buddha. Photograph of the statue pg. 139, description pg 309.
219. AN, *Catukkanipāta, vagga* 15 - *Ābhāvavagga, sutta* 8-9, VRI Vol. 36, para 148-149, pg. 162, Hindi Part 2, pg. 136

220. *Uparipaṇṇāsapāḷī, Devadahavagga, sutta* 3, VRI Vol. 14, para 34-40, pg. 25-29, Hindi pg. 440-442
221. AN, *Bālavagga, sutta* 5, VRI Vol. 35, para 5, pg. 126, Marathi Part 1, pg. 127-128
222. AN, *Ekakanipāta, Aṭṭhānapāḷī, vagga* 2, VRI Vol. 35, para 285-286, pg. 40, Marathi Part 1, pg. 39-40
223. AN, *Tikanipāta,vagga* 3, *Puggalavagga, sutta* 8 - *Gūthabhāṇī Sutta*, VRI Vol. 35, para 28, pg. 150-151, Marathi Part 1, pg. 151-152
224. MN, *Mūlapaṇṇāsapāḷī, Sīhanādavagga, sutta* 8, VRI Vol. 12, para 199-205, pg. 155-162, Hindi pg. 71-74
225. *Yathāvādī, bhikkhave, tathāgato tathākārī, yathākārī tathāvādī, iti yathāvādī tathākārī yathākārī tathāvādī, tasmā tathāgatoti vucchati. Catukkanipāta, sutta* 13 - *Loka Sutta,* VRI Vol. 48, para 112, pg. 85-86
226. Vin, *Cūḷavagga, khandha* 5 - *Khuddakavatthukkhandhaka,* VRI Vol. 90, para 285, pg. 260, Hindi pg. 445
227. Ibid. *Bouddha Manishā,* pg. 516
228. *Smritisthala;* ed. V. N. Deshpande, Pub. Venus Prakashan, 'Tapashcarya,' 381 Ka, Shaniwar Peth, Pune 411 030, sixth ed. January 1995, pg. 21
229. Dr. Komal Singh Solanki has quoted this from *Santavani Sangraha,* Part 1, pg. 63, in his book - *Nathapantha aur Nirguṇa Santakāvya,* Vinod Pustak Mandir, Agra, first ed. 1966, pg. 37
230. KN, Sn, *Cūḷavagga, sutta* 4 - *Maṅgala Sutta,* VRI Vol. 48, v. 264, pg. 123

Chapter 7

231. *Cattārome, byagghapajja, dhammā kulaputtassa diṭṭhadhammahitāya saṃvattanti diṭṭhadhammasukhāya. Katame cattāro? Uṭṭhānasampadā, ārakkhasampadā, kalyāṇamittatā, samajīvitā.* AN, *Aṭṭhakādinipātapāḷī, vagga* 6 - *Gotamīvagga,* sutta 4 - *Dīghajāṇu Sutta*, VRI Vol. 39, para 54, pg. 109-113, Hindi pg. 350-351
232. *Cattārimāni, gahapati, sukhāni adhigamanīyāni gihinā kāmabhoginā kālena kālaṃ samayena samayaṃ upādāya. Katamāni cattāri? Atthisukhaṃ, bhogasukhaṃ, ānaṇyasukhaṃ, anavajjasukhaṃ.* AN, *Catukkanipātapāḷī, vagga* 7 - *Pattakammavagga, sutta* 2 - *Ānaṇya Sutta,* VRI Vol. 36, para 62, pg. 80-81, Hindi Part 2, pg. 70-71
233. *Dāliddiyaṃ, bhikkhave, dukkhaṃ lokasmiṃ kāmabhogino'ti. Chakkanipāta, vagga* 5 - *Dhammikavagga, sutta* 3, VRI Vol. 38, para 45, pg. 65-68, Hindi Part 3, pg. 59-62
234. Ibid. *Sannyasta Khaḍga,* pg. 566

235. *Aṭṭhakanipāta, vagga* 4 - *Dānavagga, sutta* 4, VRI Vol. 39, para 34, pg. 70-71, Hindi Part 3, pg. 314-315
236. *Tikanipāta, vagga* 9 - *Samaṇavagga, sutta* 3 - *Khetta Sutta,* VRI Vol. 35, para 84, pg. 261, Marathi Part 1, pg. 252
237. *Tikanipāta, vagga* 10 - *Loṇakapallavagga, sutta* 2, VRI Vol. 35, para 94, pg. 274-275, Marathi Part 1, pg. 264-266
238. *Tikanipāta, vagga* 2 - *Rathakāravagga, Pāpaṇika* Suttas 9 and 10, VRI Vol. 35, para 19-20, pg. 138-139, Marathi Part 1, pg. 139-142
239. *Sutta* 31, *Pāthikavagga, sutta* 8, para 242-274, pg. 136-146, Hindi pg. 271-276
240. AN, *Catukkanipāta, vagga* 7, *Pattakammavagga, sutta* 3 - *Brahmā Sutta,* VRI Vol. 36, para 63, pg. 81-82, Hindi Part 2, pg. 71-72
241. AN, *Catukkanipāta, vagga* 6, *Puṇyābhisandavagga, sutta* 3 - *Paṭhamasaṃvāsa Sutta,* VRI Vol. 36, para 53, pg. 66-68, Hindi Part 2, pg. 58-62
242. AN, *Ekakanipāta, vagga* 8, *Kalyāṇamittādivagga,* VRI Vol. 35, para 71, pg. 17, Marathi Part 1, pg. 18
243. AN, *Aṭṭhakanipāta, vagga* 1 - *Mettāvagga, sutta* 1 - *Mettā Sutta,* VRI Vol. 39, para 1, pg. 1-2, Hindi Part 3, pg. 250-251
244. SN, *Devatāsaṃyutta, vagga* 6, *Jarāvagga, sutta* 3 - *Mitta Sutta,* VRI Vol. 23, para 53, pg. 42, Hindi pg. 37
245. *Opammasaṃyutta, sutta* 4 - *Okkhā Sutta*, VRI Vol. 24, para 226, pg. 241, Hindi pg. 307
246. SN, *Maggasaṃyutta, vagga* 1 - *Avijjāvagga, sutta* 2 - *Upaḍḍha Sutta,* VRI Vol. 27, para 2, pg. 2, Hindi Part 3, pg. 619-620
250. MN, *Majjhimapaṇṇāsapāḷī, vagga* 5 - *Brāhmaṇavagga, sutta* 9 - *Subha Sutta,* VRI Vol. 13, para 462-472, pg. 421-432, Hindi pg. 417-423
251. SN, *saṃyutta* 11 - *Sotāpattisaṃyutta, vagga* 6 - *Sappaññavagga, sutta* 4 - *Gilāna Sutta,* VRI Vol. 28, para 1050, pg. 471, Hindi pg. 799-800
252. Ibid. *Sanskriti ke Char Adyaya,* pg. 181
253. SN, *saṃyutta* 11 - *Sakkasaṃayutta, vagga* 2, *sutta* 8, VRI Vol. 23, para 264, pg. 270-271, Hindi pg. 184-185
254. AN, *vagga* 3 - *Vājjisattakavagga, sutta* 1 - *Sārandada Sutta,* VRI Vol. 38, para 21, pg. 168-169, Hindi Part 3, pg. 148
255. Ibid. *Bhagavān Buddha,* pg. 48
256. DN, VRI Vol. 5, para 131-135, pg. 95-101, Hindi pg. 117-120, footnotes
257. AN, *Sattakanipātapāḷī, vagga* 7 - *Mahāvagga, sutta* 3 - *Nagaropama Sutta,* VRI Vol. 38, para 67, pg.241-246, Hindi Part 3, pg. 218-222
258. *Bhante, udakakalaho"ti āhaṃsu. "Udakaṃ kiṃ agghati, mahārājā"ti? "Appagghaṃ, bhante"ti. "Khattiyā kiṃ agghanti*

mahārājā"ti? "Khattiyā nāma anagghā, bhante"ti. "Ayuttaṃ tumhākaṃ appamattataṃ udakaṃ nissāya anagghe khattiye nāsetu"nti. DpA, *vagga* 15 - *Sukhavagga,* VRI Vol. 51, para 196-199, pg. 147-148

259. DpA, *vagga* 4 - *Pupphavagga,* v. 47, VRI Vol. 50, pg. 191-204
260. Ibid. *Sannyasta Khaḍga,* pg. 567-568, 568, 569, 570, 603, 615, 583
261. Ibid. *Sannyasta Khaḍga,* pg. 568
262. Ibid. *Sannyasta Khaḍga,* pg. 620-621
263. *Agnipurāṇa,* 49.8
264. *Dr. Babasaheb Ambedkaranchi Bhashane Khand 1 (Buddhadhammavishayaka Bhashane),* ed. Dr. Prakash Kharat, Pub. Usha Wagh, Sugava Prakashan, 562, Sadashiv Peth, Chitrashala Building, Pune 411 030, first ed. 4 October 2003, pg. 82
265. *Shakyon aur Koliyon ke Ganatantra ka Nash Kyon Hua?* Pub. VRI, Dhamma Giri, Igatpuri, Dist. Nashik, 422 403, second ed. February 2004, pg. 10, 16-17, 17
266. *Seyyathāpi, bhikkhave, yā kāci mahānadiyo, seyyathidaṃ – gaṅgā, yamunā, aciravatī, sarabhū, mahī, tā mahāsamuddaṃ pattā jahanti purimāni nāmagottāni, mahāsamuddo tveva saṅkhaṃ gacchanti; evameva kho, bhikkhave, cattārome vaṇṇā – khattiyā, brāhmaṇā, vessā, suddā. Te tathāgatappavedite dhammavinaye agārasmā anagāriyaṃ pabbajitvā jahanti purimāni nāmagottāni, samaṇā Sākyaputtiyā tveva saṅkhaṃ gacchanti. Pātimokkhaṭṭhapanakkhandhaka,* VRI Vol. 90, para 385, pg. 396, Hindi pg. 511
267. *Kammaṃ vijjā ca dhammo ca, sīlaṃ jīvitamuttamaṃ; Etena maccā sujjhanti, na gottena dhanena vā.* MN, *Uparipaṇṇāsapāḷī, Saḷāyatanavagga, sutta* 1, VRI Vol. 14, para 388, pg. 314, Hindi pg. 586
268. AN, *Tikanipāta, Brāhmaṇavagga, sutta* 7, VRI Vol. 35, para 58, pg. 187-190, Marathi Part 1, pg. 185-186
269. SN, *Kosalasaṃyutta, sutta* 4, VRI Vol. 23, para 135, pg. 117-119, Hindi pg. 85-m86
270. *Samamabrāhmaṇe dānaṃ dviguṇaṃ brāhmaṇabruve; Prādhīte śatasāhastramanantaṃ vedapārage. Manusmṛti* 7.85
271. AN, *Dasakanipāta, vagga* 17 - *Jaṇussoṇivagga, sutta* 10 - *Cunda Sutta*, VRI Vol. 40, para 68, pg. 104, Hindi Part 4, pg. 187
272. '*Kiṃ pana, brāhmaṇa, sabbo loko brāhmaṇānaṃ etadabbhanujānāti – 'imā catasso pāricariyā paññapentū'ti. ... Nāhaṃ, brāhmaṇa, 'uccākulīnatā seyyaṃso'ti vadāmi, na panāhaṃ, brāhmaṇa, 'uccākulīnatā pāpiyaṃso'ti vadāmi.* MN, *Majjhimapaṇṇāsapāḷī, Brāhmaṇavagga, sutta* 6, VRI Vol. 13, para 436-444, pg. 395-401, Hindi pg. 403-406

273. *sutta* 4, VRI Vol. 1, para 300-322, pg. 97-111, Hindi pg. 44-47
274. *sutta* 3, VRI Vol. 1, para 254-299, pg. 76-96, Hindi pg. 34-43
275. MN, *Mūlapaṇṇāsapāḷī, Opammavagga, sutta* 6, VRI Vol. 12, para 272-273, pg. 219-220, Hindi pg. 103-104
276. MN, *Majjhimapaṇṇāsapāḷī, Bhikkhuvagga, sutta* 9 - *Goliyāni Sutta,* VRI Vol. 13, para 173, pg. 143, Hindi pg. 276
277. Sn, *Pārāyanavagga, Vatthugāthā,* VRI Vol. 48, para 982-1037, pg. 225-230
278. *Tasmād brāhmaṇah śkatriyayam adhastād upāste. Brihadāraṇyaka Upaniṣad* 1.4.11
279. Ibid. *Buddhottara Jaga,* pg. 154
280. ...*Pahūtavittūpakaraṇo, rājā hoti patāpavā. "Iddhimā yasavā hoti, jambumaṇḍassa issaro; Ko sutvā nappasīdeyya, api kaṇhābhijātiyo.* AN, *Sattakanipātapāḷī, Abyākatavagga, sutta* 9, VRI Vol. 38, para 62, pg. 227-228, Hindi Part 3, pg. 205
281. Ibid. *Sannyasta Khaḍga,* pg. 584
282. AN, *Catukkanipāta, vagga* 19 - *Brāhmaṇavagga, sutta* 7, VRI Vol. 36, para 187, pg. 207-209, Hindi pg. 172
283. MN, *Majjhimapaṇṇāsapāḷī, Brāhmaṇavagga, sutta* 3, VRI Vol. 13, para 401-411, pg. 362-371, Hindi pg. 389-393
284. MN, *Majjhimapaṇṇāsapāḷī, Rājavagga, sutta* 4, VRI Vol. 13, para 317-323, pg. 280-286, Hindi pg. 343-346
285. *Uragavagga, sutta* 7, VRI Vol. 48, v. 116-142, pg. 103-106
286. *vagga* 26, VRI Vol. 47, v. 383-423, pg. 61-65
287. Ibid. pg. 509
288. Vin, *Mahāvagga, Khanda* 1 - *Mahākhandaka, Bodhikathā, Ajapālakathā,* VRI Vol. 89, para 3-4, pg.2-3, Hindi pg. 76
289. Bodhivagga, *sutta* 4, VRI Vol. 47, para 4, pg. 72
290. SN, *saṃyutta* 7 - *Brahmaṇasaṃyutta, Arahantavagga, sutta* 8 - *Aggika Sutta,* VRI Vol. 23, para 194, pg. 193-195, Hindi pg. 133-134
291. MN, *Majjhimapaṇṇāsapāḷī, Brāhmaṇavagga, sutta* 8, VRI Vol. 13, para 454-461, pg. 413-420, Hindi pg. 412-416
292. *Ime hi nāma Sākyakumārā agārasmā anagāriyaṃ pabbajissanti. Kimaṅga panāha"nti. ... Atha kho bhagavā upāliṃ kappakaṃ paṭhamaṃ pabbājesi, pacchā te Sākyakumāre.* Vin, *Cūḷavagga,* - *Saṅghabhedakakkhandhaka,* VRI Vol. 90, para 331, pg. 318-319, Hindi pg. 478-479
293. *Atha kho āyasmā mahākassapo saṅghaṃ ñāpesi – 'Suṇātu me, āvuso, saṅgho. Yadi saṅghassa pattakallaṃ, ahaṃ ānandaṃ dhammaṃ puccheyya'nti.* Vin, *Cūḷavagga, Pañcasatikakkhandhaka,* VRI Vol. 90, para 439, pg. 454, Hindi pg. 542
294. Pali text that was created some time between CE 352 to CE 450. My copy. Ed. and Pub. Dr. Parmanand Singh, member-secretary,

Bouddha Aakaar Granthmala, Mahatma Gandhi Kashi Vidyapeeth, Varanasi 2, first ed. 1996; *sloka* 4.7, 11, 13, 34-45; 5.29, 36, 44
Parinibbutamhi sambuddhe upālithero mahāgaṇī;
vinayaṃ tāva vācesi tiṃsavassaṃ anūnakaṃ. 4.41

295. Ibid. *Mahāvaṃsa,* para 3, *sloka* 30-33
Upālitheraṃ vinaye sesadhamme asesake;
Ānandattheramakaruṃ sabbe therā dhurandhare. 3.30

296. *Etadaggaṃ, bhikkhave...vinayadharānaṃ yadidaṃ upāli.* AN, *Ekakanipāta, Etadaggavagga,* VRI Vol. 35, para 228, pg. 34, Marathi Part 1, pg. 34

297. Ibid. *Mahāvaṃsa,* 5.105, 106

298. *Dvādasakanipāta, Sunītattheragāthā,* VRI Vol. 56, v. 620-631, pg. 245-246
Tato disvāna maṃ satthā, devasaṅghapurakkhataṃ; sitaṃ pātukaritvāna,.... v. 630

299. *na jaccādīti adhippāyo. Na hi jātikulapadesagottasampatti-ādayo ariyabhāvassa kāraṇaṃ, adhisīlasikkhādayo eva pana kāraṇaṃ.* Vip Vol 62, Para 631, pg. 193

300. *Sattakanipāta, Sopākattheragāthā,* VRI Vol. 56, v. 480-486, pg. 229-230
Lābhā aṅgānaṃ magadhānaṃ, yesāyaṃ paribhuñjati; cīvaraṃ piṇḍapātañca, paccayaṃ sayanāsanaṃ; paccuṭṭhānañca sāmīciṃ, tesaṃ lābhā"ti cābravi. v. 484

301. VRI Vol. 62, pg. 117-120; *Hīnajacco, vayasā taruṇataro'ti vā acintetvā dassanāya maṃ upasaṅkama.* pg. 120

302. SN, *Devatāsaṃyutta, Chetvāvagga, sutta* 11 - *Araṇa Sutta,* VRI Vol. 23, para 81, pg. 52-53, Hindi pg. 47

303. Ibid. *Buddhottara Jaga,* pg. 154

304. AN, *Catukkanipāta, vagga* 3 - *Uruvelāvagga, sutta* 2 - *Dutiya Uruvelā Sutta,* VRI Vol. 36, para 22, pg. 26-28, Hindi Part 2, pg. 22-23

305. *Manusmṛti* 2.154-156

306. *Kumarilabhatta's Tantravartika 1.3.7*

307. *Bhagavān Buddha ani Jativyavastha,* Pub. Anagarika Lokamitra, for Triratna Granthamala, Pune, 1981, original Pub. 1969, Marathi trans. Chandrabodhi, pg. 53

308. Ibid. Complete Works… pg. 461

309. *Uparipaṇṇāsapāḷī, Anupadavagga, sutta* 3 - *Satpuruṣa Sutta,* VRI Vol. 14, para 105-108, pg. 85-93, Hindi pg. 473-476

310. Uragavagga, *sutta* 6, VRI Vol. 48, v. 91-115, pg. 100-102

Chapter 9

310. *Cūḷavagga, sutta* 7 - *Brāhmaṇadhammika Sutta,* VRI Vol. 48, v. 298-299, pg. 128-129

311. SN, *Sāgāthāvaggapāḷī, Kosalasaṃyutta, vagga* 1, *sutta* 9 - *Yagña Sutta*, VRI Vol. 23, para 120, pg. 92-93, Hindi pg. 72
312. AN, *Catukkanipāta, Cakravagga, sutta* 9 - *Ujjaya Sutta,* VRI Vol. 36, para 39, pg. 47-48, Hindi pg. 43-44
313. AN, *Dukanipāta, Dānavagga,* VRI Vol. 35, para 142-143, pg. 110, Marathi Part 1, pg. 108
315. *Esāhaṃ, bho gotama, pañca usabhasatāni muñcāmi jīvitaṃ demi, ... Haritāni ceva tiṇāni khādantu, sītāni ca pānīyāni pivantu, sīto ca nesaṃ vāto upavāyata'nti. Sattakanipāta, Mahāyaññavagga, sutta* 4 - *Dutiya-aggi Sutta,* VRI Vol. 38, para 47, pg. 191-195, Hindi pg. 167-171
316. *Sabbā disā anuparigamma cetasā, Nevajjhagā piyataramattanā kvaci; Evaṃ piyo puthu attā paresaṃ, Tasmā na hiṃse paramattakāmo'ti. Udānapāḷī, vagga* 5 - *Soṇavagga, sutta* 1 - *Piyatara Sutta,* VRI Vol. 47, para 41, pg. 122-123
317. MN, *Majjhimapaṇṇāsapāḷī, Gahapativagga, sutta* 5, VRI Vol. 13, para 51-55, pg. 35-38, Hindi pg. 222-223
318. *Kathañca , bhikkhave, bhikkhu bhojane mattaññū hoti? Idha, bhikkhave, bhikkhu paṭisaṅkhā yoniso āhāraṃ āhāreti – 'neva davāya na madāya na maṇḍanāya na vibhūsanāya; yāvadeva imassa kāyassa ṭhitiyā yāpanāya vihiṃsūparatiyā brahmacariyānuggahāya. Iti purāṇañca vedanaṃ paṭihaṅkhāmi, navañca vedanaṃ na uppādessāmi, yātrā ca me bhavissati,* ... AN, *Catukkanipāta, Cakkavagga, sutta* 7 - *Aparihāniya Sutta,* VRI Vol. 36, para 37, pg. 45, Hindi Part 2, pg. 40
319. *Kosalasaṃyutta, vagga* 2, *sutta* 3 - *Doṇapāka Sutta*, VRI Vol. 23, para 124, pg. 99-100, Hindi pg. 76
320. Ibid. *Buddhottara Jaga,* pg. 149
321. KN, *Milindapañhapāḷī, Meṇḍakapañha, vagga* 3 - *Panāmitavagga, Piṇḍapāta Mahapphalapañha,* VRI Vol. 81, para 6, pg. 180-182
322. Ibid. *Kośa,* pg. 721
323. *Bouddha Dharmaca Sadyant Itihas - Bouddha Parva,* first ed. 1994, present ed. - Pub. Kaushalya Prakashan, N-11, C-3 / 24 / 3, HUDCO, Aurangabad 431 003, June 2002, pg. 211, 166-167
324. MN, *Majjhimapaṇṇāsapāḷī, Gahapativagga, sutta* 1 - *Kandaraka Sutta,* VRI Vol. 13, para 9, pg. 6, Hindi pg. 209
325. MN, *Majjhimapaṇṇāsapāḷī, Gahapativagga, sutta* 7 - *Kukkuravatika Sutta,* VRI Vol. 13, para 78-82, pg. 57-61, Hindi pg. 233-235
326. SN, *saṃyutta* 7 - *Brahmaṇasaṃyutta, sutta* 9, VRI Vol. 23, para 195, pg. 195-198, Hindi pg. 134
327. SN, *Sāgāthāvaggapāḷī, Devatāsaṃyutta, vagga* 3 - *Sativagga, sutta* 3 - *Jaṭā Sutta,* VRI Vol. 23, v. 23, pg. 15-16, Hindi pg. 14
328. KN, *Udānapāḷī, Bodhivagga, sutta* 9 - *Jaṭila Sutta,* VRI Vol. 47, para 9, pg. 75-76

329. MN, *Mūlapaṇṇāsapāḷī, Mūlapariyāyavagga, sutta* 7 - *Vattha Sutta,* VRI Vol. 12, para 79-80, pg. 49-50, Hindi pg. 26-27
330. SN, *Brahmaṇasaṃyutta, Upāsakavagga, sutta* 11 - *Saṅgārava Sutta,* VRI Vol. 23, para 207, pg.212-213, Hindi pg. 146
331. Ibid. Complete Works, pg. 524-525
332. MN, *Mūlapaṇṇāsapāḷī, Mūlapariyāyavagga, sutta* 4, VRI Vol. 12, para 50, pg. 27, Hindi pg. 14-15
333. DN, *sutta* 24, VRI Vol. 3, para 1-6, pg. 1-4, Hindi pg. 215-216
334. *sutta* 11, VRI Vol. 1, para 418-500, pg. 195-204, Hindi pg. 78
335. Vin, *Cūḷavagga, khandha* 5 - *Khuddakavatthukkhandhaka,* VRI Vol. 90, para 252, pg. 228-230, Hindi pg. 422-423
336. SN, *Nidānavaggapāḷī, Nidānasaṃyutta, vagga* 7 - *Mahāvagga, sutta* 10 - *Susīma Sutta,* VRI Vol. 24, para 70, pg. 105-112, Hindi pg. 242-243
337. Vin, *Cūḷavagga, khandha* 5, VRI Vol. 90, para 288, pg. 261, Hindi pg. 446
338. DN, *sutta* 1, VRI Vol. 1, para 1-149, pg. 1-41, Hindi pg. 1-16
339. Ibid. *Buddhottara Jaga*, pg. 154
340. AN, *Catukkanipāta, vagga* 5 - *Rohitassavagga, sutta* 7 - *Suvidūra Sutta,* VRI Vol. 36, para 47, pg. 57-58, Hindi Part 2, pg. 51
341. AN, *Chakkanipāta, vagga* 9 - *Sītivagga, sutta* 9 - *Dutīya-abhabbaṭṭhāṇa Sutta,* VRI Vol. 38, para 93, pg. 139, Hindi Part 3, pg. 128
342. SN, *Khandhavaggapāḷī, saṃyutta* 7 - *Sāriputtasaṃyutta, sutta* 10, VRI Vol. 25, para 341, pg. 235-237, Hindi pg. 432

Chapter 10

343. *Itthīpi hi ekacciyā, seyyā posa janādhipa; medhāvinī sīlavatī....* SN, *Kosalasaṃyutta, sutta* 6, VRI Vol. 23, para 127, pg. 103-104, Hindi pg. 71
344. *Yassa etādisaṃ yānaṃ, itthiyā purisassa vā; sa ve etena yānena, nibbānasseva santike'ti.* SN, *Devatāsaṃyutta, Ādittavagga*, *sutta* 6 - *Accharā Sutta*, VRI Vol. 23, para 46, pg. 37, Hindi pg. 32
345. AN, *Sattakanipātapāḷī, Abyākatavagga, sutta* 10 - *Bhariyā Sutta,* VRI Vol. 38, para 63, pg. 229-231, Hindi Part 3, pg. 205-209
346. *...Kiṃsūdha paramo sakhā? ... Bhariyā ca paramo sakhā.* SN, *Devatāsaṃyutta, Jarāvagga*, *sutta* 4 - *Vatthu Sutta*, VRI Vol. 23, para 54, pg. 43, Hindi pg. 38
347. *... Bhabbo, ānanda, mātugāmo tathāgatappavedite dhammavinaye agārasmā anagāriyaṃ pabbajitvā sotāpattiphalampi sakadāgāmiphalampi anāgāmiphalampi arahattaphalampi sacchikātu'nti.* Vin, *Cūḷavagga, Bhikkhunikkhandhaka, Paṭhamabhāṇavāra,* VRI Vol. 90, para 402-406, pg. 415-423, Hindi pg. 519-523

348. *Aṭṭhakanipāta, Gotamīvagga, sutta* 1 - *Gotamī Sutta*, VRI Vol. 39, para 51, pg. 103-108, Hindi Part 3, pg. 344-350
349. Vin, *Cūḷavagga, Pañcasatikakkhandhaka, kathā 2 - Khuddānukhuddaka-sikkhāpadakathā,* VRI Vol. 90, para 443, pg. 458, Hindi pg. 545
350. Ibid. *Bhagavān Buddha: Jivan aur Darshan*, pg. 153-154
351. MN, *Majjhimapaṇṇāsapāḷī, Bhikkhuvagga, sutta* 5 - *Bhaddāli Sutta,* VRI Vol. 13, para 145, pg.117, Hindi pg. 262
352. *Bhikkhunī, bhikkhave, viyattā vinītā visāradā bahussutā dhammadharā dhammānudhammappaṭipannā saṅghaṃ sobheti. ... Upāsikā, bhikkhave, viyattā vinītā visāradā bahussutā dhammadharā dhammānudhammappaṭipannā saṅghaṃ sobheti.* AN, *Catukkanipātapāḷī, Bhaṇḍagāmavagga, sutta* 7 - *Sobhana Sutta,* VRI Vol. 36, para 7, pg. 9, Hindi Part 2, pg. 8
353. *Sataṃ sahassānipi dhuttakānaṃ, Idhāgatā tādisakā bhaveyyuṃ; Lomaṃ na iñjāmi na santasāmi, Na māra bhāyāmi tamekikāpi.* SN, *Bhikkhunīsaṃyutta, sutta* 5 - *Uppalavaṇṇā Sutta,* VRI Vol. 23, para 166, pg. 155-156, Hindi pg. 110
354. *Yakkhasaṃyutta, sutta* 9 - *Paṭhamasukkā Sutta,* VRI Vol. 23, para 243, pg. 246, Hindi pg. 169
355. *Paṇḍitā viyattā medhāvinī bahussutā cittakathā kalyāṇapaṭibhānā'ti.* SN, *Abyākatasaṃyutta, sutta* 1 - *Khemā Sutta*, VRI Vol. 26, para 410, pg. 345, Hindi pg. 606-607
356. AN, *Dasakanipāta, Mahāvagga, sutta* 8 - *Dutiyamahāpañhā Sutta,* VRI Vol. 40, para 28, pg. 46-49, Hindi Part 4, pg. 130-133
357. DN, *sutta* 16, *Mahāparinibbāna Sutta*, VRI Vol. 2, para 161-162, pg. 75-77, Hindi pg. 127-129
358. Ibid. ed. Bapat, pg. 22
359. Dp, v. 176 A, *vagga* 13 - *Lokavagga,* VRI Vol. 51, *Ciñcamāṇavikāvatthu,* pg. 102-104
360. KN, *Udānapāḷī, Meghiyavagga, sutta* 8 - *Sundarī Sutta,* VRI Vol. 47, para 38, pg. 117-120
361. A, VRI Vol. 52, para 38, pg. 207-216
362. *Yaṃ taṃ isīhi pattabbaṃ, ṭhānaṃ durabhisambhavaṃ; na taṃ dvaṅgulapaññāya, sakkā pappotumitthiyā'ti. ... Itthibhāvo kiṃ kayirā, cittamhi susamāhite; ñāṇamhi vattamānamhi, sammā dhammaṃ vipassato.* SN, *Bhikkhunīsaṃyutta, sutta* 2 - *Somā Sutta,* VRI Vol. 23, para 163, pg. 152-153, Hindi pg. 108-109
363. KN, *Therīgāthā,* VRI Vol. 56, pg. 303-354

Chapter 11

364. Vin, *Mahāvagga, Mahākhandhaka, Rājāyatanakathā,* VRI Vol. 89, para 6, pg. 4, Hindi pg. 77

365. Vin, *Mahāvagga, Mahākhandhaka,* VRI Vol. 94, para 6, pg. 231
366. VRI Vol. 47, para 1, pg. 1-2
367. Ibid. What the Buddha Taught, pg. 80-81
368. Dr. Babasaheb Ambedkar's Writings and Speeches, Vol. 16, Pub. Education Department, Government of Maharastra, 1998, pg. 727
369. *Caratha, bhikkhave, cārikaṃ bahujanahitāya bahujanasukhāya lokānukampāya atthāya hitāya sukhāya devamanussānaṃ. Mā ekena dve agamittha. Desetha, bhikkhave, dhammaṃ ādikalyāṇaṃ majjhekalyāṇaṃ pariyosānakalyāṇaṃ sātthaṃ sabyañjanaṃ kevalaparipuṇṇaṃ parisuddhaṃ brahmacariyaṃ pakāsetha. Santi sattā apparajakkhajātikā , assavanatā dhammassa parihāyanti, bhavissanti dhammassa aññātāro. Ahampi, bhikkhave, yena uruvelā Senānīgamo tenupasaṅkamissāmi dhammadesanāyā'ti. Mahāvagga, Mahākhandhaka,* VRI Vol. 89, para 32, pg. 25, Hindi pg. 87
370. SN, *Devatāsaṃyutta, Chetvāvagga, sutta* 4 - *Vuṭṭhi Sutta,* VRI Vol. 23, para 74, pg. 49
371. Ibid. *Buddha Manishā,* pg. 196
372. AN, *Pañcakanipāta, Dīghacārikavagga, sutta* 1 - *Paṭhamadīghacārika Sutta,* VRI Vol. 37, para 221, pg. 237, Hindi Part 2, pg. 437
373. MN, *Uparipaṇṇāsapāḷī, Saḷāyatanavagga, sutta* 3 - *Puṇṇovāda Sutta,* VRI Vol. 14, para 395-397, pg. 320-323, Hindi pg. 590-591
374. Dp, v. 320, *vagga* 23 - *Nāgavagga,* VRI Vol. 47, pg. 53
375. SN, *Brahmaṇasaṃyutta, Arahantavagga, sutta* 1-4, VRI Vol. 23, para 187-190, pg. 187-191, Hindi pg. 129-131
376. *Akroṣṭāro jitāḥkśāntyā drugdhāḥ svastyayanena ca; satyena cāpavaktārarstvayā maitryā jighānsavaḥ. Ibid. sloka 122*
377. *Mahāvagga, khandha* 1 - *Mahākhadhaka, Pabbajjūpasampadākathā,* VRI Vol. 89, para 34, pg. 26, Hindi pg. 88
378. SN, *Saḷāyatanasaṃyutta, vagga* 19 - *Āsīvisavagga, sutta 4 - Paṭhamadārukhandhopama Sutta*, VRI Vol. 26, para 241, pg.183, Hindi pg. 525-526
379. Ibid. pg. 52
380. Ibid. *Sanskṛtikośa, Khandha* - 9, *'Sanyāsa'* reference
381. Myth and Reality, Pub. Popular Prakashan, Mumbai, first impression, May 1962, pg.167
382. *Tikanipāta, Pañcamavagga, sutta* 3, VRI Vol. 48, para 92, pg. 65-66
383. MN, *Mūlapaṇṇāsapāḷī, Mūlapariyāyavagga, sutta* 2 - *Sabbāsava Sutta,* VRI Vol. 12, para 23, pg. 13, Hindi pg. 8
384. Buddhist Dictionary, Ed. Nyanatiloka, Pub. Buddhist Publication Society, Kandy, Sri Lanka, Reprint 2004, pg. 40
385. *Udānapāḷī, Nandavagga, sutta* 6 - *Pilindavaccha Sutta,* VRI Vol. 47, para 26, pg. 100

386. *Devatāsaṃyutta, Chetvāvagga, sutta* 11 - *Araṇa Sutta*, VRI Vol. 23, para 81, pg. 52-53
387. *Catukkanipāta, sutta* 9, VRI Vol. 48, para 108, pg. 79-80
388. AN, *Catukkanipāta, Uruvelāvagga, sutta* 6 - *Kuha Sutta*, VRI Vol. 36, para 26, pg. 31, Hindi Part 2, pg. 27
389. AN, *Dukanipāta, Samacittavagga*, VRI Vol. 35, para 40, pg. 84, Marathi Part 1, pg. 84
390. Dp, *vagga* 19 - *Dhammaṭṭhavagga,* VRI Vol. 47, para 45-46, v. 256, 257, 259
391. AN, *Sattakanipātapāḷī, Devatāvagga, sutta* 11 - *Paṭhamaniddasa Sutta,* VRI Vol. 38, para 42, pg. 186-187, Hindi Part 3, pg. 163-165
392. *Aṭṭhakanipāta, Sativagga, sutta* 7-9, VRI Vol. 39, para 87-89, pg.164-165, Hindi Part 3, pg. 398-399
393. *Kacci pana vo, anuruddhā, samaggā sammodamānā avivadamānā khīrodakībhūtā aññamaññaṃ piyacakkhūhi sampassantā viharathā"ti?* MN, *Mūlapaṇṇāsapāḷī, Māhāyamakavagga, sutta* 1 - *Cūḷagosiṅga Sutta,* VRI Vol. 12, para 326, pg. 270, Hindi pg. 128
394. *Na tena bhikkhako hoti, yāvatā bhikkhate pare. Brāhmaṇasaṃyutta, Upāsakavagga, sutta* 10, VRI Vol. 23, para 206, pg. 212
395. Ibid. *Sanyasta Khaḍga,* pg. 555, 583
396. *Mahāvagga, Bhesajjakkhandhaka, Vuḍḍhappabbajitavatthu,* VRI Vol. 89, para 303, pg. 325-326, Hindi pg. 253-254
397. AN, *Ekakanipāta, Accharāsaṅghātavagga,* VRI Vol. 35, para 53-55, pg. 13, Marathi Part 1, pg. 14-15
398. *Manusmṛti,* 6.27, 43
399. *Atha kho bhagavā sāvatthiyaṃ sapadānaṃ piṇḍāya caramāno....* SN, *Uravagavagga, sutta* 7, *Vasala Sutta,* VRI Vol. 48, pg. 103
400. *Sapadānanti anugharaṃ. Bhagavā hi sabbajanānuggahatthāya āhārasantuṭṭhiyā ca uccanīcakulaṃ avokkamma piṇḍāya carati. Tena vuttaṃ "sapadānaṃ piṇḍāya caramāno"ti.* SnA, *Uragavagga, Aggikabhāradvājasuttavaṇṇanā,* VRI Vol. 55, pg. 139
401. *Mūlapaṇṇāsapāḷī, Mūlapariyāyavagga, sutta* 2 - *Sabbāsava Sutta,* VRI Vol. 12, para 23, pg. 13-14, Hindi pg. 8
402. *Opammasaṃyutta, sutta* 9, VRI Vol. 24, para 231, pg. 244-245, Hindi pg. 309
403. *Uparipaṇṇāsapāḷī, Saḷāyatanavagga, sutta* 9 - *Piṇḍapātaparisuddhi Sutta,* VRI Vol. 14, para 438, pg. 356, Hindi pg. 607
404. KN, It, *Tikanipāta, Pañcamavagga, sutta* 2 - *Jīvika Sutta,* VRI Vol. 48, para 91, pg. 64-65
405. *Mārasaṃyutaṃ, vagga* 2, *sutta* 8, VRI Vol. 23, para 154, pg. 135-136, Hindi pg. 95
406. *Udapānaṃ tiṇassa ca bhusassa ca yāva mukhato pūresuṃ - 'mā te muṇḍakā samaṇakā pānīyaṃ apaṃsū'ti. Cūḷavagga, sutta* 9 - *Udapāna Sutta,* VRI Vol. 47, para 69, pg. 161-162

407. *Yāvānartha udapāne sarvataḥ samplutodake; tāvān sarveṣu vedeṣu brāhmaṇasya vijānataḥ. Bhagavadgita sloka* 2.46
408. SN, *Saḷāyatanasaṃyutta, vagga* 13 - *Gahapativagga, sutta* 9, *Lohicca Sutta,* VRI Vol. 26, para 132, pg. 123-126, Hindi pg. 499-500
409. MN, *Majjhimapaṇṇāsapāḷī, Rājavagga, sutta* 1, VRI Vol. 13, para 283-284, pg. 248-249, Hindi pg. 328-329
410. MN, *Majjhimapaṇṇāsapāḷī, Paribbajakavagga, sutta* 5, VRI Vol. 13, para 207, pg. 180, Hindi pg. 295-296
411. MN, *Mūlapaṇṇāsapāḷī, Mūlapariyāyavagga, sutta* 7 - *Vattha Sutta,* VRI Vol. 12, para 74, pg. 48, Hindi pg. 26
412. *Siyā kho pana te, nigrodha, evamassa – 'antevāsikamyatā no samaṇo gotamo evamāhā'ti. Na kho panetaṃ, nigrodha, evaṃ daṭṭhabbaṃ. Yo eva vo ācariyo, so eva vo ācariyo hotu.* DN, *sutta* 25 - *Udumbarika Sutta*, VRI Vol. 3, para 78, pg. 40, Hindi pg. 232
413. MN, *Majjhimapaṇṇāsapāḷī, Opammavagga, sutta* 1, VRI Vol. 12, para 222-223, pg. 174-182, Hindi pg. 80-84
414. *Tassa mayhaṃ, bhante, etadahosi – 'acchariyaṃ vata, bho, abbhutaṃ vata, bho! Adaṇḍena vata kira, bho, asatthena evaṃ suvinītā parisā bhavissatī'ti.* MN, *Majjhimapaṇṇāsapāḷī, Rājavagga, sutta* 9, VRI Vol. 13, para 364-374, pg. 328-333, Hindi pg. 367-370
415. *Ekakanipāta, sutta* 8 - *Saṅghabheda Sutta*, *sutta* 9 - *Saṅghasāmaggī Sutta*, VRI Vol. 48, para 18-19, pg. 10
416. *Yo, bhikkhave, maṃ upaṭṭhaheyya so gilānaṃ upaṭṭheyya. Mahāvagga, Cīvaraskandhaka,* VRI Vol. 89, *kathā* 224, para 365, pg. 393-395, Hindi pg. 290-291
417. MN, *Paribbājakavagga, sutta* 3 - *Mahāvaccha Sutta,* VRI Vol. 13, para 194-195, pg. 167-169, Hindi pg. 287-289
418. *Paribbājakavagga, sutta* 6, VRI Vol. 13, para 236, pg. 203, Hindi pg. 306
419. Encyclopaedia of Religion and Ethics, Ed. James Hastings, Vol. II, Pub. T & T. Clark, Edinburgh, New York: Charles Scribner's Sons, Latest Impression - 1967, Buddha, Life of the, pg. 881
420. MN, *Uparipaṇṇāsapāḷī, Devadahavagga, sutta* 8 - *Gopakamoggallāna Sutta,* VRI Vol. 14, para 79, pg. 56, Hindi pg. 457
421. *Bhagavā hi, bhante, anuppannassa maggassa uppādetā, asañjātassa maggassa sañjanetā, anakkhātassa maggassa akkhātā, maggaññū maggavidū maggakovido. Maggānugā ca, bhante, etarahi sāvakā viharanti pacchā samannāgatā.* SN, *Sāgāthāvaggapāḷī, saṃyutta* 8 - *Vaṅgīsasaṃyutta, sutta* 7 - *Pavāraṇā Sutta*, VRI Vol. 23, para 215, pg. 221-222, Hindi pg. 152
422. SN, *Khandhavaggapāḷī, Khandhasaṃyutta, vagga* 6 - *Upayavagga, sutta* 6 - *Sammāsambuddha Sutta,* VRI Vol. 25, para 58, pg. 60-61, Hindi pg. 351

423. *Ne me ācariyo atthi.* Vin, *Mahāvagga, Mahākhandhaka, Pañcabaggīyakathā*, VRI Vol. 89, para 11, pg. 11, Hindi pg. 79
424. SN, *Nidānasaṃyutta, Mahāvagga, sutta* 5 - *Nagara Sutta,* VRI Vol. 24, para 65, pg. 93, Hindi pg. 237-238
425. Pub. Bhandarkar Oriental Research Institute, 1987, pg. 353
426. *Bauddha Dharma Ke 2500 Varṣa,* Ed. Prof. P. V. Bapat, Pub. Director, Publication Division, Ministry of Information and Broadcasting, Government of India, Patiala House, New Delhi 110 001, second ed. May 1997, pg. 170-171, 172
427. Ed. Mahadevshastri Joshi, Pub. Bhartiya Sanskritikosh Mandal, Pune 411 002, first ed. 1962, Vol. 1
428. Ibid. Kosh, first ed. 1968, Vol. 5
429. *'Assattha,'* pg. 90
430. *Bauddha Dharma: Mohanjodaro Harappa Nagaron ka Dharma,* author Swapankumar Biswas, Hindi trans. Satyaprakash, Pub. Orion Books, Mrs. Shikha Biswas, 24, Alipore Estate, 8 / 6 / 1, Alipore Road, Kolkata 700 027, first ed. (English) 17 March 1999; first ed. (Hindi) 26 January 2002, pg. 127
431. Ibid. pg. 364
432. Ibid. pg. 353
433. *Ṛtusnātā ca sāśvtthaṃ tvaṃ ca vṛkśamudumbaram; pariṣvajethāḥ kalyāṇi tata iṣṭamavāpsyathaḥ. Anuśāsanaparva* 4.27
434. Ibid. Mahāvaṃsa 18.35-36, 59-60, 66; 19.8-9, 13, 41, 85
435. Ibid. pg. 29
436. Ibid. pg. 140
437. *Śatapatha Brāhmaṇa* 13.8.5
438. *sutta* 14, VRI Vol. 2, para 1-94, pg. 1-42, Hindi pg. 95-109
439. Ibid. pg. 47
440. MN, *Uparipaṇṇāsapāḷī, Anupadavagga, sutta* 6 - *Isigili Sutta,* VRI Vol. 14, para 133-135, pg. 114-117, Hindi pg. 485-487
441. MN, *Uparipaṇṇāsapāḷī, Suññatavagga, sutta* 3 - *Acchariya-abbhuta Sutta,* VRI Vol. 14, para 198, pg. 161, Hindi pg. 511
442. KN, *Buddhavaṃsapāḷī,* VRI Vol. 58
443. Jā. 461, *Ekādasakanipāta* Ja. 7 - *Dasaratha Jātaka,* v. 84-96, VRI Vol. 68, pg. 184-185
444. *Tadā dasarathamahārājā suddhodanamahārājā ahosi, mātā mahāmāyādevī, sītā rāhulamātā, bharato ānando, lakkhaṇo sāriputto, parisā buddhaparisā, rāmapaṇḍito pana ahameva ahosinti.* story *461,* JA, VRI Vol. 73, pg. 112-119.
445. Bhartiya Sanskritikosh Mandal, ed. Mahadevshastri Joshi, Vol. 8, first ed. 31 August 1974, 'Rāmāyaṇa' pg. 171-172

Chapter 13

446. Vin, *Cūḷavagga, Pañcasatikakkhandhaka, Saṅgītinidāna,* VRI Vol. 90, para 437-445, pg. 452-462, Hindi pg. 541-547
447. Vin, *Cūḷavagga, Sattasatikakkhandhaka,* VRI Vol. 90, para 446-457, pg. 463-479, Hindi pg. 548-557
448. Ibid. *Buddhavijayakāvyam,* 1.16
449. Ibid. ed. Bapat, pg. 113
450. Ibid. pg. 45
451. *Piṭakattayapāliṃ ca tassā aṭṭhakathaṃ pi ca; mukhapāṭhena ānesuṃ pubbe bhikkhū mahāmatī. Hāniṃ disvāna sattānaṃ tadā bhikkhū samāgatā; ciraṭṭitatthaṃ dhammassa potthakesu likhāpayuṃ.* Ibid. *Mahāvaṃsa,* 33.100, 101
452. *Kaccid gurūśca vṛddhāśca tāpasān devatātithīn; caityānśca sarvān siddhārthān brāhmaṇānśca namasyasi. Śrimadvālmīkīyarāyaṇam; Ayodhyākāṇḍa* - 100.61; the book used by me, Pub. Gitā Press, Gorakhpur, 2020 Vaikramābde, second ed.
453. Vālmiki Rāmāyaṇa, *Sundarakaṇḍa, adhyāya* 43; *tataḥsa kiṅkarān hatvā hanūmān dhyānamāsthitaḥ; vanaṃ bhagnaṃ mayā caityaprāsādo na vināśitaḥ.* 43.1 *Tasmāt prāsādamadaiyavamiṃ vidhvansayāmyaham; iti sañcintya hanūmān manasā darśayan balam.* 43.2 *Caityaprāsādamutplutya meru śṛaṅgamivotratam; āruroha hariśreṣṭho hanūmān mārutātmajaḥ.* 43.3
454. Vālmiki Rāmāyaṇa, *Ayodhyakāṇḍa, ādhyāya* 108
455. *Ayodhyakāṇḍa, ādhyāya* 109.31, 33
456. *Yathā hi coraḥ sa tathā hi buddhastathāgataṃ nāstikamatra viddhi; tasmāddhi yaḥ śakyatamaḥ prajānāṃ sa nāsthike nābhimukho budhaḥsyāt.*
Ayodhyakāṇḍa, 109.34
457. *Ayodhyakāṇḍa, ādhyāya* 109.38-39
458. *Ayodhyakāṇḍa, ādhyāya* 110.1-2
459. MN, *Majjhimapaṇṇāsapāḷī, Rājavagga, sutta* 6 - *Āṅgulimāla Sutta,* VRI Vol. 13, para 347-352, pg. 308-315, Hindi pg. 356-360
460. Ibid. What Buddhists Believe, pg. 16
461. *Yat sauratyaṃ gatāstīkṣṇāḥ kadaryāśca vadānyatām; krūrāḥ peśalatāṃ yātāstat tavopāyakauśalam. Indriyopaśamo nande mānastabdhe ca sannatih; kṣamitvaṃ cāngulimāle kaṃ na vismayam ānayet.* Ibid. *sloka* 124-125
462. SN, *Nidānavaggapāḷī, Nidānasaṃyutta, Dasabalavagga, sutta* 1-2 - *Dasabala Sutta, Dutiyadasabala Sutta,* VRI Vol. 24, para 21-22, pg. 26-27, Hindi pg. 207
463. AN, VRI Vol. 30, para 21-22, pg. 39-46
464. SN, Nidāna*vagga* Ṭīkā, VRI Vol. 33, para 21-22, pg. 46-54

465. MN, *Mūlapaṇṇāsapāḷī, Sīhanādavagga, sutta* 2 - *Mahāsīhanāda Sutta,* VRI Vol. 12, para 148, pg. 101-103, Hindi pg. 45-46
466. *Saddharmalaṅkāvatārasutram* - Bauddhasanskṛtagranthāvali 3, ed. Dr. P. L. Vaidya, Pub. Mithila Vidyapeeth, Darbhanga, 1963, pg. 1-2
467. *Araṇyakāṇḍa* 56.30
468. *Araṇyakāṇḍa* 56.32
469. Ibid. *Mahāvaṃsa* 5.78-80, 29.36
470. *Uttarakāṇḍa,* 28.2
471. Ibid. *Mahāvaṃsa* 19.41, 19.85
472. Ibid. *Mahāvaṃsa* 15.8, 15-17
473. *Sāgāthāvaggapāḷī, Devatāsaṃyutta, Ādittavagga, sutta* 8 - *Jetavana Sutta*, VRI Vol. 23, para 48, pg. 38, Hindi pg. 33
474. MN, *Uparipaṇṇāsapāḷī, Saḷāyatanavagga, sutta* 1, VRI Vol. 14, para 388, pg. 314, Hindi pg. 586
475. *Rājāhamasmim selāti, dhammarājā anuttaro; dhammena cakkaṃ vattemi, cakkaṃ appaṭivattiyaṃ. Majjhimapaṇṇāsapāḷī, Brāhmaṇavagga, sutta* 2 - *Sela Sutta*, VRI Vol. 13, para 399, pg. 359, Hindi pg. 386
476. Ibid. Ed. Bapat, pg. 254-255
477. Early Buddhism and the Bhagavadgita, Pub. Motilal Banarsidas, first ed. 1971, Delhi, Reprint 1983, Delhi, pg. 58-59, 131
478. *Prachin Bharatiya Sanskriti va Sabhyata,* The Culture and Civilization of Ancient India in Historical Outline, Diamond Publications, Pune 411 030, Marathi first ed. 2006, pg. 279
479. Carakasanhita, Acharya Yadav Sharma, fourth ed., Pub. Munshiram Manoharlal Publishers Pvt. Ltd., New Delhi 55, 1981, Upodghāt, pg. 7
480. Ibid. Carakasanhita, *Upodghāta*, pg. 7, footnote
481. Ibid. Carakasanhita, *Upodghāta*, pg. 10
482. *Sārtha Vāgbhaṭa* - *Vāgbhaṭakṛta Aṣṭāṅgahṛdaya va tyāce bhāṣāntara,* trans. Dr. Ganesh Krishna Garde, Pub. Anmol Prakashan, 683, Budhwar Peth, Pune 2, first ed. 1891, present ed. 1999
483. Ibid. *Sārtha Vāgbhaṭa,* Dr. Gadre, *Upodghāta*, pg. 28-29
484. Ibid. *Sārtha Vāgbhaṭa,* Dr. Gadre, *Upodghāta*, pg. 27
485. *Tṛṣṇādīrghamasadvikalpaśirasaṃ pradveṣañcatphaṇaṃ kāmakrodhaviṣaṃ vitarkadaśanaṃ rāgapracaṇḍekṣaṇam; mohāsyaṃ svaśarīrakoṭaraśayaṃ cittoragaṃ dāruṇaṃ prajñāmantrabalena yah śamitavānbuddhāya tasmai namah.* 1.1. *Śrīmadvāgbhaṭṭaviracitah Aṣṭāngasangrahah, prathamo bhāgo*, Hindi commentator: Kaviraj Atridev Gupt, *Vidyālankār bhiṣargatna,* Superintendent, Ayurvedic Pharmacy, Kashi Hindu Vishwavidyalaya, Varanasi, Pub. Krishnadas Ayurveda Series 31, Krishnadas Academy, Varanasi, 1993, pg.12-13

486. Ibid. *Aṣṭāṅgasaṅgraha,* Atridev Gupta's Preface, pg. 12-13
487. Ibid. *Aṣṭāṅgasaṅgraha,* Atridev Gupta's Preface, pg. 12, footnote
488. Ibid. Ed. Bapat, pg. 156
489. Ibid. Ed. Bapat, pg. 155
490. Ibid. Ed. Bapat, pg. 219
491. Ibid. Ed. Bapat, pg. 226-227
492. Marathi Vishvakosh, ed. Tarktirtha Laxmanshastri Joshi, Pub. Maharashtra Rajya Marathi Vishwakosh Nirmiti Mandal, Mumbai, 1983, 'Buddha,' pg. 646
493. *Mahākhandhaka, Uruvelāpāṭihāriyakathā,* VRI Vol. 89, para 40, pg. 31, Hindi pg. 90
494. MN, *Uparipaṇṇāsapāḷī, Acchariya-abbhuta Sutta, vagga* 3 - *Suññatavagga, sutta* 3, VRI Vol. 14, para 198, pg. 161, Hindi pg. 511
495. MN, *Uparipaṇṇāsapāḷī, vagga* 2 - *Anupadavagga, sutta* 6 - *Isigili Sutta,*, VRI Vol. 14, para 135, pg. 117, Hindi pg. 487
496. Pub. V. R. Koppal, Navakalyanamath Bhuspeti, Dharwar, 1957, pg. 10
497. Vol. 2, first ed. 1964, pg. 779-781
498. Ibid. Myth and Reality, pg. 97, 126
499. Author Baban Lavhatre, Pub. Rahul Kala Kendra, 6/22, Rambaug Colony, Nagpur 440 003, second ed. 6 December 1999
500. Author Dr. Bhau Lokhande, Pub. Ashok Prakashan, Ajani, Prabuddha Nagar, Nagpur 3, first ed. 1979
501. Author Mahadev Vithji Labhane, Pub. Sugava Prakashan, 562, Sadashiv Peth, Pune 30, first ed. June 2006
502. *Dharmanand - Acharya Dharmanand Kosambi yance Atmacaritra ani caritra,* ed. and author - J. S. Sukhtankar, Pub. Chitnis, Kalavibhag, The Goa Hindu Association, Gomantdham, 358, Dr. Bhadkamkar Road, Mumbai 400 007, 27 November, 1976, pg. 246-247, Sukhatankar notes that P. M. Lad's quoted sentence is from his book 'Akashaganga' (pg. 17).
503. Ibid. *Shri Viṭṭhala,* pg. 230-231
504. Ibid. *Shri Viṭṭhala,* pg. 233-235
505. *Maharashtratil Buddhadhammaca itihas,* Pub. Anagarika Lokamitra, for Triratna Granthamala, 2B, Parnkuti Housing Society, Yeravda, Pune 411 006, 1981, pg. 93-94
506. *Mahatma Phule Samagra Vāṅmay,* ed. Y. D. Phadke, Pub. Secretary, Maharashtra Rajya Sahitya ani Sanskriti Mandal, Navin Prakashan Bhavan, Mumbai 400 032, corrected fourth ed. 14 April 1999, pg. 166
507. Vol. 1, ed. Tarktirtha Laxmanshastri Joshi, Pub. Maharashtra Rajya Sahitya Sanskriti Mandal, Mumbai, 1976, 'amarkosh,' pg. 360
508. Ibid. *Samagra Vāṅmay,* pg. 265-266
509. Ibid. *Samagra Vāṅmay,* pg. 571

510. Ibid. Dharmanand, pg. 286. Sukhathankar has noted that the details by P M Lad are in the footnotes of his book 'Akashaganga' (pg. 21-22).
511. Reprint of second ed. October 2005, Pub. Dr. Ashok Gaikwad, Kaushalya Prakashan, N-11, C - 3/24/3, HUDCO, Aurangabad 431 003, for 'International Centre for Buddhist Studies'
512. Second ed. 2003, Pub. International Centre for Buddhist Studies
513. *Buddha Gāthā,* original author Paul Carus, Hindi trans. Publication Division, Ministry of Information and Broadcasting, Government of India, Patiala House, New Delhi 110 001, reprint, 2000
514. From the website of Columbia University. UNPUBLISHED PREFACE; April 6, 1956. [Text provided by Eleanor Zelliot, as prepared by Vasant Moon]
515. *Gautam Buddhache caritra,* original ed. 1898, new ed. Pub. Gajendra Vitthal Raghuvanshi, Raghuvanshi Prakashan, 242 B, Shukrawar Peth, Pune 2, pg. 200
516. *Maharshi Vitthal Ramji Shinde - Jivan va Karya,* author Dr. G. M. Pawar, Pub. Prakash Vishwasrao, Lokvanmaya Griha, Bhupesh Gupta Bhavan, 85, Sayani Road, Prabhadevi, Mumbai 400 025, first ed. May 2004, pg. 93
517. Ibid. Dr. Pawar, pg. 403-405
518. Dr Ambedkar: Life and Mission, Dhananjay Keer, Page 481-2
519. The Vision of the Buddha, first Pub. USA, 1996, the ed. used by me, Pub. Duncan Baird Publishers for One Spirit, 1997, pg. 167
520. Tarktirtha Laxmanshastri Joshi Lekha-sangraha, Vol. 1, Pub. Shrividya Prakashan, 250 Shaniwar Peth, Pune 30, first ed. 1982, pg. 177-178

Chapter 14

521. SN, *saṃyutta* 9 - *Opammasaṃyutta, sutta* 8 - *Kaliṅgara Sutta,* VRI Vol. 24, para 230, pg. 243-244, Hindi pg. 308
522. MN, *Majjhimapaṇṇāsapāḷī, Bhikkhuvagga, sutta* 5 - *Bhaddālī Sutta,* VRI Vol. 13, para 134-147, pg. 109-119, Hindi pg. 259-263, *Seyyathāpi, bhaddāli, purisassa ekaṃ cakkhuṃ, tassa mittāmaccā ñātisālohitā taṃ ekaṃ cakkhuṃ rakkheyyuṃ – 'mā yampissa taṃ ekaṃ cakkhuṃ tamhāpi parihāyī'ti; evameva kho, bhaddāli, idhekacco bhikkhu saddhāmattakena vahati pemamattakena. Tatra, bhaddāli, bhikkhūnaṃ evaṃ hoti – 'ayaṃ kho, āvuso, bhikkhu saddhāmattakena vahati pemamattakena. Sace mayaṃ imaṃ bhikkhuṃ pasayha pasayha kāraṇaṃ karissāma – mā yampissa taṃ saddhāmattakaṃ pemamattakaṃ tamhāpi parihāyī'ti.* VRI Vol. 13, para 144, pg. 116

523. *Asappuriso, bhikkhave, akataññu hoti akatavedī.* AN, *Dukanipāta, Samacittavagga,* VRI Vol. 35, para 33, pg. 78, Marathi Part 1, pg. 78
524. *Nopakārapare pyevam upakāraparo janaḥ;*
apakārapare pi tvam upakāraparo yathā. Ibid. *sloka* 119
525. This line has been quoted by Uruvala Dhammaratana Thera on the basis of 'Mahabodhi Journal' (1960, pg. 177) in his above mentioned book, pg. 41-42
526. *Bhaddikā, bhante, āvaṭṭanī māyā; kalyāṇī, bhante, āvaṭṭanī māyā;*
piyā me, bhante, ñātisālohitā imāya āvaṭṭaniyā āvaṭṭeyyuṃ;
piyānampi me assa ñātisālohitānaṃ dīgharattaṃ hitāya sukhāya.
MN, *Majjhimapaṇṇāsapāḷī, Gahapativagga, sutta* 6 - *Upāli Sutta,* VRI Vol. 13, para 74, pg. 52, Hindi pg. 230-231
527. MN, *Majjhimapaṇṇāsapāḷī, Gahapativagga, sutta* 6 - *Upāli Sutta,* VRI Vol. 13, para 66-68, pg. 48-49, Hindi pg. 228
528. AN, *Aṭṭhakanipāta, Mahāvagga, sutta* 2 - *Sīha Sutta,* VRI Vol. 39, para 12, pg. 25-32, Hindi Part 3, pg. 277
529. Ibid. Tarktirtha Laxmanshastri Joshi Lekha-sangraha, pg. 178
530. *Sabbaṃ paravasaṃ dukkhaṃ, sabbaṃ issariyaṃ sukhaṃ. Udānapāḷī, Mucalindavagga, sutta* 9 - *Visākhā Sutta,* VRI Vol. 47, para 19, pg. 88-89
531. *Sarva paravaśaṃ duḥkhaṃ sarvamātmavaśaṃ sukham. Manusmṛti* 4.160
532. *Mātā yathā niyaṃ puttamāyusā ekaputtamanurakkhe;*
evampi sabbabhūtesu, mānasaṃ bhāvaye aparimāṇaṃ.
Uragavagga, sutta 8, VRI Vol. 48, v. 149, pg. 107
533. *Na pupphagandho paṭivātameti, na candanaṃ tagaramallikā vā;*
satañca gandho paṭivātameti, sabbā disā sappuriso pavāyati. AN, *Tikanipāta, vagga 8 - Ānandavagga, sutta* 9 - *Gandhajāta Sutta,* VRI Vol. 35, para 80, pg. 256-257, Marathi Part 1, pg. 240-241
534. *Buddha Kavyanjali,* ed. Dr. Shriprasad, Pub. Kendriya Ucca Tibbati Shiksha Sansthan, Sarnath, Varanasi, first ed. 1996, pg. 50

Chapter 15

535. DN, VRI Vol. 1, Introduction, pg. 12